After a lifetime spent between Ghana and Britain (and quite a few other places), Lesley Lokko finally put her long years of architectural training to good use and designed her own home in Ghana. As soon as it was finished, she turned straight round and went to live in Hackney.

Bitter Chocolate is Lesley's third novel and she's hard at work on her fourth. Her previous two novels, *Sundowners* and *Saffron Skies*, are both available from Orion. If you'd like to find out more about Lesley (or to see pictures of her house), visit www.lesleylokko.com. She really does answer her emails.

Bitter
Chocolate

Lesley Lokko

An Orion Paperback

First published in Great Britain in 2008
by Orion
This paperback edition published in 2008
by Orion Books Ltd,
Orion House, 5 Upper Saint Martin's Lane,
London WC2H 9EA

An Hachette Livre UK company

3 5 7 9 10 8 6 4

A CIP catalogue record for this book is
available from the British Library.

ISBN 978-0-7528-7927-7

Typeset by Deltatype Ltd, Birkenhead, Merseyside

Printed and bound in Great Britain by Clays Ltd, St Ives plc

The Orion Publishing Group's policy is to use papers that
are natural, renewable and recyclable products and
made from wood grown in sustainable forests. The logging
and manufacturing processes are expected to conform to
the environmental regulations of the country of origin.

www.orionbooks.co.uk

In memory of my mother

After a rather long hiatus, it's finally here! In no particular order but with equal gratitude, I would like to thank Christine Green, Kirsty Crawford, Genevieve Pegg, Kate Mills, Barbara Slavin and Lisa Milton. It was written in five different places on three different continents and each place, in some way, has shaped its outcome. In Scotland, I would like to thank Alastair and Susan Cowan of Eastside Farm and Jason Lockyer of Len Cottage, Peebles for two wonderful writing spots. In South Africa, Iain Low, Paula White, Jo and Joy Noero, Sonja Petrus-Spamer, Tina Muwanga, Andreas Werner; Ruth and Kofi Kwakwa, Dianne Regisford-Guèye, Moky Makura, Adrian Hallam, Janet Solomon and Kofi Amegashi were all wonderful in helping me settle in. In England, I would like to thank Ceri and Christine for the very generous loan of a quiet and peaceful house in Exeter and Lindsay Herford in Oxford for her lovely Magdalen Road flat. In Ghana, I owe a particular debt of gratitude to Rinette of the Ivy Café in Accra who allowed me to use her café as an office when the electricity and internet services went down! Several books were invaluable in providing background information, not least of which were West African Weaving by Venice Lamb (Duckworth: 1975); Print in Fashion by Marnie Fogg (Batsford: 2006) and Bonjour Blanc: A Journey Through Haiti by Ian Thompson (Vintage: 2004). I would also like to thank Yemi Osunkoya of Kosibah Creations for the inspiring conversation that sparked it all off. Ilona KanKam-Boadu, Vanda Felder, Marisa Battini, Salim Baroudi, Randa Gajar, Elkin Pianim, Gigi Dupuy-McCalla and Rebecca Clouston were all fantastically generous in giving their time, advice and opinions during the (very) numerous re-writes; and finally, heartfelt thanks to my 'crew' in Accra – I am, as always, very grateful.

PART ONE

Prologue

'You're sure you don't want me to come with you?' he asked, his eyes searching her face.

She shook her head. 'No, I'd rather go alone.'

'You'll be fine,' he said softly, pulling her towards him. 'You'll know exactly what to do when you see him.'

She sank into the calm solidity of his body. For a moment, she couldn't speak. In less than an hour, thirteen years of wondering would come to an end. She looked down at her hands and began twisting the slim gold band of her wedding ring slowly around. 'Wh ... what if he doesn't want to speak to me?' she asked after a moment.

'He will. Trust me.'

She drew in a deep breath, steadying herself. And then let it out slowly. 'I'd better go,' she said, slowly disengaging herself. 'I'll call you later. When ... when ...'

'Just call when you're ready.' Bending his head the kiss was fierce, almost bruising. 'It's going to be fine,' he said firmly. 'You'll see.' She nodded and walked to the door. He was watching her, the same calm, careful gaze he'd always had, right from the start. She gave him a quick, unhappy smile and opened the door.

Outside it was a chilly November day and the cold, northerly winds were already sweeping in from the lake. She belted her coat and pulled the collar up, tucking her cloudy mass of hair in and trapping its warmth. She walked along Willow to Fremont, her mind racing ahead of her. What would she say? What *could* she say? How would she explain? She couldn't quite believe she'd found him. After a year of false starts and false, painfully dashed hopes, she'd finally found him. She'd spoken to his parents, Howard and Geraldine, over the phone, twice. Once after the first, tentative letter, thanking them for their understanding and the second time, a few weeks ago, to tell them of her intentions to visit him. On both occasions they'd been cautious but kind. No, they'd never told him, they assured her. Oh, they'd thought about it often enough, but somehow the timing had never been right. They'd talked about it again a few months ago. And then, of course, she'd written to them. Out of the blue.

She walked up Fremont. The oak trees that lined the sidewalk were in the last few days of foliage; the ground underfoot was damp and sticky with their fallen red and gold leaves. She looked up at the houses; it was clear that the Ellisons were very well-off. A tall, elegantly imposing red-brick with magnificent views across the park towards Lake Shore Drive. Yes, they were more than comfortable – after all, how else would they have been able to afford him?

A gust of wind suddenly blew down the street, sending leaves flying. She walked past a tiny basketball court in the open space between two buildings. A group of young men were playing. She stopped for a second to watch.

'Yo! Darrell! Go for it, man!' She stopped suddenly. A young man jumped higher than the others, the grey sweatshirt he was wearing yawned suddenly, baring his stomach. He paused, suspended in the air for a fraction of a second before aiming for the hoop. A shout went up as he landed, half a dozen hands going up in the air to slap his own. *Perfect. Cool, man. Nice shot.* He swivelled as he took up his place at the edge of the court, his eyes meeting hers for a second. He gave her a quick, easy grin. A couple of the other players whistled at her as they took up position at the centre of the court. 'Yo, baby!' one of them shouted. The others laughed. Teenagers. A mixed bunch, all dressed in the standard urban uniform – baggy pants and hooded sweatshirts. Practically indistinguishable from one another. Except for one. She felt something inside her turn. She felt the blood rise in her cheeks and her heart begin to accelerate. She would have known him anywhere. Anywhere in the world.

I

Port-au-Prince, Haiti 1985

On a hot, sultry afternoon in May when the breeze had stopped
and the air was oppressively still, Améline, the *reste-avec* in the
St Lazâre household, pushed open the door to the parlour,
dragging her bucket and floor polishers behind her. It was
three o'clock and the heat was still intense. Madame St Lazâre
was taking her customary afternoon siesta and the house was
silent. Nothing moved, not even the hands of the grandfather
clock in the corner that had stopped when Madame's husband,
whom Améline had never seen, died. Or so Madame said. Five
minutes past three on a Sunday afternoon. Améline wasn't sure
she believed her.

She closed the door behind her carefully. It was the only
time she was allowed in the parlour. Cléones, the ancient maid
and cook, could no longer bend down and the task of polishing
the wooden floorboards had naturally fallen to Améline. She
put down her bucket and picked up the dusters, working her
way quickly across the surfaces of the dark, heavy furniture that
Madame favoured and which showed up every speck of dust,
ghostly white, like the talcum powder Améline occasionally
sprinkled over her skin on Sundays when she and Cléones
went to church. She lifted the brass candlesticks, long empty
of candles, noticing that they too needed polishing, and set
them down carefully again, making a mental note to tackle
them before Madame's eagle eyes noticed and she earned herself a rebuke. She ran her cloth gently over the two porcelain
figurines that Laure, Madame's sixteen-year old granddaughter,

had told her came from a shop in Paris, in France. First the painted heads, then the smooth, stiff folds of their skirts, and finally the bases. And that was when she saw it, lying face up, on the green cloth. A pale blue airmail letter. She stared at it, her eyes widening. She hesitated for a second, then picked it up, her heart beginning to beat faster. She looked around her then quickly slipped it into the front pocket of her apron. Madame wouldn't come downstairs again until five o'clock, when the sun had finally gone down. Laure would be in her favourite position: three branches above the ground in the jacaranda tree outside her bedroom window; she had to get it to her. Fast. Before Madame woke up.

She gave the cushions a quick beating, straightened the covers on the sofa and hurriedly swept the floor. She would wax and polish it later; right now there were more pressing issues to attend to. She quickly ran the duster along the top of the door and closed it, hurriedly stowing her bucket and mop in the cupboard next to the kitchen door. Then she bolted through the house before Cléones came through to inspect her work.

She darted out of the back door and ran into the garden, the letter creasing against her thighs as she ran. There would be hell to pay when Madame discovered the letter was gone but they'd cross that bridge later. They would have to make up some excuse as to how the letter had found its way into Laure's hands – never mind that it was *addressed* to her. *Laure St Lazâre*. In Belle St Lazâre's handwriting. Belle St Lazâre. Laure's mother, who lived in Chicago. She ran towards the jacaranda tree, waving it in front of her. 'Lulu! Lulu! Look! Look what I found!'

Améline's whispered shout floated up through the leaves and brought Laure St Lazâre's day-dream to an abrupt halt. She sighed. Such a *pleasant* dream, involving, as they usually did, . her immediate departure from Haiti, suitcase in hand, walking across the tarmac to the enormous plane that would take her to Chicago and her mother and away from the stifling atmosphere of her grandmother's house and the sticky afternoon heat that made her hair frizz and put a permanent shine on her nose. She peered down through the branches.

'What is it?' Améline was holding something up to her, waving it urgently. She looked more closely. It was a letter. Her heart started to beat faster. A letter? From Belle? She hardly dared look.

'I found it,' Améline whispered, thrusting the letter above her head. 'Just now. When I was cleaning the parlour. Here, take it. Quick! Before Cléones sees it.' She climbed nimbly on to the lowest branch and held it out. Laure reached down and grabbed it, her heart thudding. An airmail letter, of the pale blue sort that could only mean one thing. A letter from Belle. From *Maman*. She held it gingerly in her hands as though she couldn't quite believe it.

She looked down again but Améline was already gone, her slight, wiry figure weaving through the garden until she disappeared from view. She looked at the letter again. Yes, it was her mother's childish, looping scrawl; a Chicago postmark. She peered at the date: *3rd March, 1985*. It had taken over two months to reach her. She stared at it again, then slid a trembling finger under the flap.

2

London, UK 1985

Melanie Miller looked at the clock on the mantelpiece. Ten past nine. She blinked, fighting back the tears of disappointment, avoiding her mother's anxious gaze. The two of them sat in uneasy silence on the plush, velvet couches in the living room, neither, it seemed, willing to speak.

'He's probably been held up at the airport or something,

darling,' Stella Miller said eventually, unable to keep the edge of annoyance from her own voice.

'But it's my *birthday*,' Melanie said in a tight, angry voice. 'He *can't* have forgotten!'

'He hasn't, darling. I'm *sure* he hasn't. I'm sure he'll be here any minute.'

'You've been saying that since seven and he's *still* not here!'

'I know, darling. He'll be here any minute.'

'Why d'you keep on saying that?' Melanie's voice rose. She stood up abruptly.

'Oh, darling ...' Her mother scrambled to her feet. Her shoulders sagged helplessly. 'He'll make it up to you, I promise.'

'Did you remind him?' Melanie could feel a single tear begin its journey down her face. She blinked furiously. She hated crying in front of her mother.

'Yes,' her mother lied quickly. 'I spoke to him this afternoon ... they were leaving for the airport. He was ... he was going out to get a present for you and ...'

'Oh, *please*,' Melanie groaned. 'I'm *eighteen*, Mum, I'm not a child. You don't have to lie to me!'

'I'm not lying, darling,' her mother stammered, her cheeks immediately betraying her. 'Where ... where are you going?'

'Out.' Melanie started walking towards the door.

'Out?' her mother called after her, her voice rising in alarm. 'Out where?'

'What do you care?' Melanie shot back as she disappeared up the stairs. She slammed her bedroom door shut and gave vent to the hot, angry tears that had been forming behind her eyes all evening.

'Oh, bloody *hell*, Mike,' Stella muttered angrily, reaching for a cigarette. Poor, poor Melanie. She'd been looking forward to her eighteenth birthday dinner for weeks. Mike's PA had booked a table at Le Caprice; Melanie had bought herself a new outfit ... it was supposed to have been a celebration, the last before her exams. She felt like crying herself. She'd reminded him, not once, but *three* times since the beginning of the week – and, would you believe it, he'd *still* forgotten. And she'd gone to such an effort – lots of lovely presents, including the beautiful silver and diamond necklace from Tiffany's that he'd told her to buy. 'Hang the fucking expense,' he'd instructed her happily on the phone from Düsseldorf or Munich or wherever the hell it was they were playing. 'She's my baby girl – only the best.' It had been on the tip of her tongue to say 'she doesn't want the best, just make sure you're there'. But of course she hadn't. And of course he wasn't.

'I'm going round to Polly's,' Melanie's voice interrupted her suddenly. She stood in the doorway, a tight, unhappy scowl on her tear-stained face.

'All right, darling.' Stella looked at her and then looked away. Melanie's hurt was almost too painful to bear. 'Shall I drive you over?' she asked gently.

'No, I'll walk. I've been indoors all day.' Melanie shoved her hands in the pocket of her coat. 'See you,' she muttered.

Stella watched helplessly as she left the room, her shoulders hunched against the disappointment that was burning inside her. Bloody *hell*, Mike, she repeated to herself. Damn you. *Damn you.*

3

Laure was trembling but she certainly wasn't about to let her grandmother see it. She straightened her back, thrust her chin out just that little bit further and met her grandmother's rigid, frosty stare. There was absolute silence in the room. Upstairs, on the landing, a clock chimed faintly. It was two o'clock in the afternoon, the hottest part of the day.

'Where did you get this?' Grandmère said finally through gritted teeth. Laure swallowed.

'It was lying on the table. In the hallway.'

'Who gave it to you? That idiot?'

Laure felt a quick, immediate stirring of anger. She hated the way her grandmother spoke about Améline. Améline might only be the *reste-avec* but she was more like a sister to her, someone who cared far more about her than Grandmère ever did. 'She isn't an idiot,' she said indignantly. 'It's not her fault. It's *my* letter. It's addressed to *me*.'

'No, it is *not* your letter. Your mother should know better. She's always filling your head with nonsense. You don't understand anything, Laure.'

Laure's fists tightened surreptitiously. 'No, I don't. I don't understand anything because no one *tells* me anything.' Her heart was thudding. 'She wants me to come … look, she said so.' Laure held out the letter. Grandmère took no more notice of it than she did of the fly that buzzed drowsily around the room.

'You're too young to understand.'

'I'm *sixteen*! I'm not a child.'

'You're a child until I say otherwise,' Grandmère said imperiously, waving her hand at Laure in dismissal. 'Now, take that damned letter and burn it. Your mother doesn't know what she's talking about. Bring you to America indeed! Oh, I could *slap* that girl!'

'Maybe that's why …' Laure burst out suddenly. 'Maybe she …'

'Laure!' her grandmother barked at her angrily. 'Enough! Go to your room. I don't want to see you again for the rest of the day. How *dare* you! Go on, get out. *Out!*' Grandmère rose to her full height and glared menacingly at her. Laure took one look at her angry, contorted face and fled up the stairs, two at a time. She burst into her room and flung herself across the bed. The overhead fan creaked noisily, drowning her sobs. In her hand she clutched the precious letter, the thin airmail paper already damp with sweat. A shiver ran up her spine. Her mother had written. She *hadn't* forgotten her, after all. She wanted her to come. She was in Chicago, a huge city in the middle of the

United States and she wanted her, Laure, to come. She'd been waiting all her life to hear those words.

She didn't go down for supper that evening. She could hear Améline and Cléones bustling around, setting the table as they did every evening – polished silver, the gleaming chinaware, the crystal glasses that Grandmère insisted on using even when it was only the two of them. Laure hated the sight of the carefully laid table; everything seemed perfect but when you looked a little closer, the signs of decay were there. The linen tablecloth was threadbare and all the plates were chipped. The crystal glasses had been washed and polished too many times and bore a thousand tiny scratches ... even the mahogany sideboard was peeling in the humidity and there was no one left to repair it. The Swiss joiner who had always looked after Grandmère's possessions had long since fled the country. The vast, creaking house in which they all lived – Grandmère, Laure and Améline, along with Cléones and 'Ti Jean, whom Grandmère had dragged out of the burning ruins of Madère, the St Lazâre's ancestral country home – was a little like Haiti itself ... doomed, despairing and yet beautiful still. She smoothed out the sheets for the umpteenth time, her fingers lingering over her own name. *Laure St Lazâre*. At times, for reasons she couldn't quite explain, it felt more like a curse.

4

Améline looked at Laure's unhappy face and felt like crying herself. She couldn't bear it when Laure was sad. She racked her brains for something to say that would cheer her up. But what? Even she could see the situation was hopeless. Even though she herself had never been to a single party in her entire life, she knew exactly how Laure felt. According to Laure, at her school they'd been talking about nothing but Josette Demarchelier's upcoming sixteenth birthday party for months. At first Madame had simply refused to even countenance a request to *attend* the party, never mind fork out the money for a new dress, shoes and a little handbag of the kind she'd seen Laure's snobbish best friend, Régine de Menières, carrying into her room. White, with little pink roses and gold buttons. Améline had never seen anything quite as delicately pretty before. She'd stared at the bag and matching shoes until Régine had caught her out and ordered her to bring her a glass of orange juice from the kitchen downstairs. 'She gives me the creeps,' Améline had heard Régine whisper as she left the room. She also heard Laure's tart reply. 'She's like my older sister so don't you dare be rude to her.' She'd grinned to herself all the way down the stairs. Even though she wasn't Laure's older sister – and certainly no one other than Laure herself ever treated her as such – it felt so nice to be thought of that way. But no, she reminded herself sternly, she wasn't Laure St Lazâre's sister, she was the *reste-avec*. A 'stay with', as they were known in Haiti, dispatched by her family when she was three or four years old – no one was quite sure of Améline's age – to be a companion to the newly born Laure St Lazâre, who lived with her mother and grandmother in the enormous plantation house on the horizon, just beyond the church. Améline couldn't remember how or when she'd arrived. They said she'd come on the back of a donkey but Améline had no memory of it. She couldn't really remember anything about her life before she arrived at Madère. She'd been told her parents had both died a few months after her arrival, though no one said why or how. They also said she had siblings, most of whom had been taken in by neighbours or distant relatives who lived in or near Jacmel, which was where they said she was from. But she'd never heard a word from any of them. She wasn't even sure how many brothers and sisters she had. Not that she really cared. Lulu was all the family Améline needed. Although she was a few years older than Laure, with her thin, scrawny frame set against Laure's tall, voluptuously curvy body, it was Améline who actually looked the younger of the two.

★

And now this. Josette's party. She looked at Laure's face and felt her own mouth tug downwards in sympathy. After months of pleading, Grandmère had finally capitulated and allowed her to go – but she'd flat out refused to give her the means to buy anything to wear.

'Régine's aunt bought her a dress from Miami,' Laure said glumly after a while. 'It's white. *And* she's got matching shoes.'

'She'll still look like a horse,' Améline said loyally, if inaccurately. True, Régine didn't have Laure's high cheekbones and almond-shaped eyes but in a culture obsessed with skin tone, Régine was the right shade of light, creamy brown and Laure wasn't. Plain and simple. That was a fact. Laure was nearly as dark as Améline – a smooth, bitter chocolate. In Haiti, at least, unpardonable. Belle, Laure's beautiful, wayward mother, had given birth to a child the colour of burnt molasses. Améline knew it was just another of the reasons Madame couldn't bring herself to forgive her daughter. It was bad enough that Belle St Lazâre had found herself pregnant at the age of fifteen – but the fact that she'd done 'it' with a coal-black stable hand and produced a daughter the colour of burnt toffee ... well, the tongues in Pétionville where they lived, high in the hills above the slums of Port-au-Prince, were *still* wagging. Sixteen years later and mostly in barely disguised glee. Yes, it was true the girl was beautiful, they had to admit it, but ... so *dark*? *Such* a shame. Generations of careful breeding gone to waste.

Laure didn't give a damn about the ladies who lived in the villas around them, but Améline knew that school was different. Especially now that Laure was sixteen. It was the year of parties and boys and secret notes, giggled over hotly between friends. Laure was only just beginning to find out that perhaps it did matter after all. She liked a boy in the class above her but it was beginning to dawn on her that *he* didn't like *her* – for the same reasons Madame had cut her own daughter out of her life. *Dark* was not a good description for someone of Laure's social standing. Why, the St Lazâres were practically white. Lightest of the light. Generations of light-skinned, fair-haired and blue-eyed Créole women. Until Belle had gone and thrown it all away.

'I know,' Améline began suddenly, an idea only just beginning to form. 'Remember that time we went into the attic? We found those old clothes in the trunk? At the back? Come on, let's see if there's anything there. Let's go and look before Madame gets up.'

It was hot and dark in the attic. The windows were all firmly closed. The heat of the house rose slowly up the stairs and through the wooden floorboards. Améline tugged at one of the tiny windows until it gave way, releasing some of the trapped warmth inside the long, narrow room. They looked around nervously. Laure shivered suddenly, despite the heat. The attic was the room to which her mother had been exiled; all evidence of Belle St Lazâre bundled up and shoved into the trunks that stood at one end. She stood looking at the trunks for a moment, suddenly hesitant. She had very little memory of her mother. She was two when Belle ran away and Grandmère had taken pains to ensure there was nothing left to remind anyone of the woman they'd once fêted as the most beautiful in all of Port-au-Prince. Not a single photograph. It was almost as if she had never been. But Laure did have one thing – the only item that had survived the cull. A tiny, slightly out-of-focus photograph in a mottled silver frame that Améline had found one day, lying behind a dresser in the parlour. She'd quickly slipped it into her apron pocket, just as she'd done with the letter, and given it to her. Together they'd pored over the image, Laure unconsciously tracing her own features as they stared at it – her mother's face composed in a way Laure had never seen before – her shiny, glossy red lips parted, but not in a smile. *Belle. Maman. My mother.* She'd tried to compare the picture of the young, haughtily beautiful girl to the mothers she knew – Régine's mother, or Sabine's. No. Belle was nothing like that. Even though Régine's mother was pretty and Sabine's mother had nice clothes, Belle's look was different. Belle ... pouted. Sexy. Laure was twelve at the time and only just beginning to understand about such things. It made her uncomfortable to look at the picture; she put it away from her, disturbed by the image of something she was only just beginning to discover in herself. But she wanted to know more. She begged Améline to tell her. Did she have Belle's eyes? Her mouth? Once, when she'd been at Régine's house, Régine's mother told her about a ball they'd all gone to as teenagers and how Papa Doc had eyes only for Belle ... Grandmère had bundled them both in the back of the car and sent them straight home, such was her fear. Belle was only thirteen at the time but already she'd begun to attract men. Was it true? Had Améline seen her that night? What was she wearing?

Améline did her best to fill in the gaps but even she could hardly remember the details. Belle had hardly ever spoken to her except to send her to pick up a dress Cléones had ironed or fetch her a glass of cold water from the fridge. Améline had always been afraid of Belle, afraid of her temper and her wild, uncontrollable outbursts. She was like a rare, trapped butterfly in that house full of rules and strictures. Even though she was too young to understand it fully, she wasn't at all surprised when Belle ran away.

Améline walked over to one of the trunks they hadn't opened before and hauled it across the floor to the light. Clouds of ghostly dust followed her; it had been over a year since anyone had been up there. She prised the lid open, there was a loud creak as it lifted and suddenly the air was filled with the scent of stale perfume, cigarette smoke ... Belle's scent. The two of them stood there in silence, breathing deeply.

'Look,' Améline whispered, kneeling down and pulling out something silvery. She stood up, holding it against her. It was a long, slinky dress, made up of thousands of tiny, shimmering sequins, like fish scales catching the light. Laure stared at it. On Améline's thin, wiry frame, with no breasts or hips to speak of, the dress would hang hopelessly slack. Laure could only imagine what it had looked like on Belle: she'd overheard Madame Dupuy once, whispering to Grandmère, 'Dear God, she's got Belle's breasts, as well' ... and a shiver ran lightly up

17

her spine. In that way, then, if in no other, she and Belle were alike. There was a faint singing in her head as they bent down to pull things out of the trunk.

There was a small jewellery box on top of the pile; they opened it and an untidy collection of necklaces and rings spilled out. Both girls gasped. 'Look at these,' Améline murmured, holding up a pearl necklace with an ornate gold and turquoise clasp. 'And these ...' she slipped a large, glittering ring onto her finger. 'Is it a diamond?'

'No, silly,' Laure laughed suddenly. 'It's glass ... and this blue one ... it's topaz, I think,' she said, squinting at it. It was nothing if not gaudy. She turned back to the fabrics in the trunk.

'How about this one?' Améline pulled a gauzy, black scrap of material with tiny, spaghetti-like straps. It was practically transparent. 'Look, you could wear it with these!' She plucked a pair of gold shoes with ridiculously large bows at the toes. Laure shook her head. Améline's dress-sense was hazy at the best of times. 'Or what about this?' Améline shook a small, white lace dress with puffed sleeves. She yanked a thick, black belt out of the trunk. 'With this ... and *this* ... look!' She pointed to a black shawl. 'You could put it round your ...' she looked a bit nonplussed for a second, then brightened, 'round your head. Like this!' She held one end of the shawl and draped it over her head, mantilla-style.

Laure shook her head. 'You look like M. Habib's wife,' she giggled. M. Habib was the Syrian shopkeeper who sold vegetables and fruits halfway down the hill. 'It's a *shawl*, you idiot. Not a headscarf. And anyway, you can't wear a headscarf with an evening gown.'

'Why not?'

'Because.'

'Well, *I* think it'll look nice,' Améline said, a touch defiantly. She put her hand into the trunk, rummaging around and then suddenly froze. 'Lu ... Lulu ...' she said, her voice strained.

Laure looked up. 'What?'

'There's something in here ... oh my God ... Lulu, it's got my hand!'

'What're you talking about?' Laure quickly scuttled over to where Améline knelt, her hand stuck in the trunk, an expression of pure terror on her face. Laure felt something cold clutch at her insides. 'What is it? What's got your hand ... show me!'

'I *can't* ... it's stuck,' Améline wailed.

'Hold on!' Laure grabbed Améline's forearm and yanked it out of the trunk. There was a second's stunned silence as both girls contemplated the grinning fox head – and then Laure burst into peals of laughter.

'What? What is it?' Améline almost shrieked.

'Shh!' Laure cautioned, taking hold of the head. 'Grandmère'll hear us. It's a stole, Am, that's all ...'

'A *what*?'

'A stole. Something you put round your neck. Here, don't move ... it's the ring ... it's got stuck on its teeth,' she whispered, still giggling. Carefully, she prised the dead animal's jaw open and Améline's hand slid free. She pulled the ring off Améline's finger and quickly threw it back inside the trunk. 'Your *face*,' Laure spluttered. 'If you'd only seen your face ...'

'Jesus Christ! Why would anyone want to carry a dead animal round their neck?' Améline demanded, her whole body still shaking with fright.

'I expect it was the fashion,' Laure said, wiping her eyes.

'Crazy!' Améline said indignantly. 'In this heat?'

'I know,' Laure sighed. 'I wish I could remember more ... you know, Maman and Grandmère and Madame de Menières ... can you imagine? All dressed up, like in the movies ...'

'Madame de Menières? That sausage? She'd never fit into any of these,' Améline said scornfully. She disliked Régine and her mother equally.

Laure chuckled. It was true. She turned and lightly touched the fabrics that were lying in piles all around them. Silks, satins, linens, lace ... fabrics she'd never seen before. She ran her hands over the stiff chiffon of a long, black evening gown; the thick, furry velvet of a knee-length, pencil skirt. Even in the dim half-light of the attic, she could see there were colours and textures for which she had no names. Turquoise, teal, sand, bronze ... there were ribbed fabrics, fabrics with ruffles, pleats, folds, tucks ... Belle belonged to another era in Haiti – a time of wealth and cocktail parties and men in black dinner jackets, Cuban cigars in their hands. Now there was none of that left. She thought of the functional, plain dresses that Grandmère wore, day in, day out, and of the neatly ironed pile of faded T-shirts and sensible cotton skirts that were practically all she was allowed to wear. She looked at Améline and her heart contracted. Améline had even less than she did; three or four old, grubby T-shirts and a single, pale green skirt that Laure dimly remembered as hers. Had Améline ever owned anything that hadn't been Laure's first?

'That one,' she said suddenly, getting to her feet. 'That'll do.' She picked up the sequinned dress that Améline had picked out first.

Améline stared at her in delight. 'Oh, Laure ... it's so beautiful ...' she breathed. 'It'll look ...'

'Let's go,' Laure said abruptly, closing the trunk with the heel of her foot. 'I don't want to look any more.' She poured the dress into Améline's arms. 'We can alter it later. I ... I don't feel well,' she said, afraid she would suddenly burst into tears. She turned and almost ran down the narrow spiral stairs, leaving a bewildered Améline in the middle of the dusty space with the dress made of diamonds flashing angrily in her hands.

Three days later, on the afternoon of Josette's party, Laure tucked her hair behind her ears, smoothed down the dress that Améline had altered by chopping it off at the knee and giving it wider straps from the leftover fabric, and followed Améline nervously down the stairs. She tapped on the drawing room door. It was just after four. The sun was finally beginning its lethargic drop over the mountains that continued above the Pétionville hills, and the shadows were lengthening on the ground. Inside, just as she did every afternoon without fail, Grandmère was playing solitaire in the drawing room that she kept locked throughout the day. Laure hated the smell of the room – a mixture of camphor and cognac and the musty smell of the upright chairs that were rarely, if ever, used.

'*Oui*.' Grandmère's imperious voice rang out. Laure pushed open the door, followed closely by Améline, still grinning.

'What is *she* grinning about?' Grandmère said without looking up. Laure knew without turning round that Améline would have quickly wiped the smile off her face. It puzzled and angered her the way Grandmère loved to torment poor Améline. She simply couldn't stand the sight of her.

'Nothing, Madame,' Améline replied, quick as a flash.

'Tsch.' A little sound of exasperation, a sucking together of the teeth. It was Grandmère's only concession to Créole, a language she detested. French, she insisted a dozen times a day, was the only language she would tolerate in her home. Créole was for the ignorant, the great, impoverished, illiterate masses – all of whom were black, like *you-know-who*, she would sometimes add – who lived at the bottom of the hill and who, in her carefully considered opinion, were ruining the country. Simply *ruining* it. *Oh, she could remember the days when* … Laure would invariably start thinking about something else when Grandmère began reminiscing about the past. For one thing it never included Belle and for another, it always ended the same way. 'With your complexion, my dear, finding a suitable husband will be difficult. Well, we live in hope.' Lately it had been getting more difficult to refrain from telling Grandmère that she never, ever wanted to get married anyway. Who would want to? As far as Laure could tell two things happened when you got married. One, you ended up like Grandmère, a bitter and sharp-tongued old woman whose husband had probably decided upon death as the only way out, or two, you wound up like Belle, running away. Neither appealed, frankly. What did it matter how dark she was?

She heard the door close behind her as Améline slipped away. She swallowed. Grandmère was looking at her closely.

'Where did you get that dress?' she asked, her voice deceptively mild.

'I … I found it. It was …' She swallowed again. She was

21

sweating under the arms. 'In the attic.' She met Grandmère's stare defiantly.

'The attic?' Grandmère echoed.

'Yes. In one of the trunks. Améline helped make it fit.'

'I see.' There was a carefully held silence in which Laure was almost too afraid to breathe. Then Grandmère looked down at her green baize-covered card table and slowly dealt herself another hand. '*Bon*. 'Ti Jean will come for you at eleven. Make sure you're ready to go when he arrives. I don't want him kept waiting.'

Laure blinked. That was it? She stared aghast at her grandmother's bent head. Was she imagining it ... was that ...? No, it couldn't be. Slowly she watched as a single tear dropped from the powdered, wrinkled edge of Grandmère's chin and landed – *plotch!* – on the table. She turned and fled.

5

'Here ...' Someone handed her a tumbler. 'It's from America. *American* Coke.'

Laure took a gulp. She couldn't tell the difference. Trust Josette's father to import even the Coke. 'It's lovely,' she said, hoping she sounded sincere.

'Yes, it's *much* nicer,' the young man said, grinning with self-importance.

Laure looked more closely at him. She recognised him vaguely as Jean-Pierre someone-or-other; she couldn't remember his last name. He was a couple of classes above her. He looked down at her as if about to say something and then a loud cheer from the other side of the patio made both of them turn. Philippe and Anton Delacroix had just arrived – all eyes were drawn to them as they sauntered into the room. They stood in the doorway, shoulder to shoulder, accepting the praise and adoring looks from everyone around them. It was their due, after all. Barely a year apart, they were from one of the richest and longest-standing families in Haiti. Philippe was tall and lithe, his skin the colour of sand. Greenish-blue eyes, a straight, narrow nose ... and lips that seemed to split his face in half when he smiled – which wasn't often. It made the rare occasions when he did smile that bit more special. He'd never spoken to Laure St Lazâre in her entire life but she'd been around Régine when Philippe stopped and deigned to speak to her in the schoolyard. Just looking at him look at Régine brought out a sudden longing in Laure that made her squirm. No one ever smiled at her like *that*.

Laure's new companion vanished suddenly, wanting to be part of the crowd surrounding the gorgeous brothers. She took another sip of the *American* Coke and watched as Anton, the shorter of the two, detached himself from the crowd and wandered towards the swimming pool. Heads were turning ... Laure swallowed ... he was walking towards *her*. She blinked in confusion – was that ...? No. It couldn't be ... could it? Was he smiling – at her? Her eyes widened in surprise, her stomach lurching in that ridiculous way. Anton was close to her now; *agonisingly* slowly, he turned up the wattage of his smile. Laure responded. And then he stopped. And wrinkled his nose. And turned away, slowly and oh so *deliberately*. She felt the tears burn at the back of her throat. Quicker than she could blink she'd been acknowledged and *dismissed*.

She tried to move behind one of the pillars before any of the others saw but she wasn't quite quick enough. Francine Lescoufleurs had seen her and whispered something to the school bitch, Marie-Jo Masimon. *What did he do? What happened? Oh, how awful!* Laure's fingers were shaking as she put down her glass and pushed past a group of giggling girls. And then, suddenly, and without warning, her mother spoke to her, loud and clear. *What's the matter with you, girl? Who the hell is Anton Delacroix? You're a St Lazâre, for heaven's sake. Go into the bathroom, wash your face, put on a bit of the lip gloss you and Améline bought the other day and walk out with your head high. You're every bit as good as anyone here – better, even. Don't you know who your grandfather was? He wouldn't have slunk away like a scared dog. Besides, when you come to Chicago it'll all be different. You'll have any boy you want, I promise you. Just you wait and see.*

She saw, out of the corner of her eye, Régine's surprised glance as she straightened up and turned to face Marie-Jo and Francine. Without saying a word, she pushed past them and walked into the bathroom. A few minutes later she emerged, lips shining, hair brushed back and yes, her head held high. Just as Belle instructed. She sought out the young man who'd offered her a drink and asked him to dance. He was only too happy to oblige.

6

The three adults stared uncomprehendingly at Melanie. Melanie stared at the floor, counting the cracks in the wooden boards.

'I don't know what to say, Melanie,' Mrs Vickers, the head-mistress, said finally. 'I mean, I just don't understand it. What were you *thinking*?'

'It's just so *unlike* her,' her mother burst out, seeing that nothing further from Melanie seemed likely. Her father said nothing. He looked bored. 'What're we supposed to do now?' her mother turned a beseeching face towards the headmistress.

Mrs Vickers looked at the two of them. 'Perhaps I could have a word with the two of you? Alone? Melanie, if you don't mind …?' Mrs Vickers said gently. Melanie shrugged. What*ever*. She stood up, ignoring the look of desperation on her mother's face, and walked towards the door. Her father was rummaging in his pockets for a cigarette. She closed the door but not before her mother's plaintive voice struck up again.

'She's never behaved like this before,' she could hear her saying as she walked away from Mrs Vickers' office. She pushed open the heavy front door and closed it quickly behind her. She didn't want to hear any more. She walked down the corridor, away from the administration block towards the gardens. She was vaguely aware of a couple of junior girls looking curiously at her – word had gone round the school pretty quickly: Melanie Miller had walked out of her A-level English exam a few minutes after it had started – but they were too shy or in awe of her to speak. She ignored them and pushed open the French doors leading to the courtyard. It was cool outside, despite it being early summer. She pulled her cardigan around her shoulders and headed for the little bench in front of the rose bushes. She sat down, glad of the fresh air and relieved to be out of the stuffy little office with the three adults looking at her, wondering if she had gone quite mad. Two adults, she quickly corrected herself. Her father hadn't really looked at her at all. Not even the threat of her failing her English A-level had managed to rouse his interest. He'd just looked at her the way he always did – lip curled sardonically; one arm hanging languidly over the back of the chair, a bemused, ever so slightly bored expression on his face. She knew how much he hated a domestic crisis. In fact, it was only just beginning to dawn on her how much he hated the whole concept of 'home'.

'Melanie?' She could hear Diana, Mrs Vickers' assistant, looking for her. She sighed and stood up. 'Melanie? Oh, there you are ... Mrs Vickers is looking for you. I think your parents have gone ... can she have a word?'

Henrietta Vickers didn't pretend *not* to be studying the sullen young woman in front of her. She'd known Melanie Miller ever since the girl had arrived at Weldon, almost six years earlier. She took after her father, that was certain. Glossy, dark brown hair, pale, clear complexion and those startlingly blue eyes. She even had something of his manner – languid, elegant, bored – but sharp and funny, too, when she wanted to be. Nothing like the mother who seemed prone to hysterics. She sighed. Another beautiful, rich, troubled young woman. It was a familiar story, sadly. The exclusive girls' school she ran had more than its fair share of the daughters of celebrities and royalty ... and they didn't come much more famous than Mike Miller. He'd been a bona fide rock star when *she'd* been growing up and he showed no signs of slowing down. In fact, the older he got, the more attractive he became. He'd been the archetypal bad boy in his youth and although he had to be in his late fifties, maybe even early sixties, he'd lost none of his self-deprecating charm or his looks. He was always in the papers and the celebrity magazines, usually with a starlet younger than his daughter perched precariously on an arm or a knee. Henrietta Vickers had lost count of his wives ... was he on his fifth or sixth? Melanie lived with her mother, who'd been his second wife, if she remembered correctly, and *her* third husband, a famous Swiss architect. The poor girl had been shuttled from home to home, growing up all over the place until her mother had finally come to her senses and brought the girl to Weldon. It was perfectly obvious to Henrietta Vickers that Melanie was crying out for attention – anyone's attention, she guessed – and that she'd figured out if coming top of the class wasn't going to do it, she'd just have to try for bottom. It was such a shame. The girl was bright, *really* bright.

'Is everything all right? At home I mean, Melanie, my dear?' she enquired gently. There was a second's hesitation, enough to tell her that the young woman in front of her was obviously struggling to compose herself. The blue eyes were clouded over, and there was a tremulous quiver about her bottom lip but, as so often seemed to be the case with the young girls she saw, she'd learned how to mask the pain. After a moment's hesitation, Melanie shrugged, affecting a bored insouciance that, Henrietta Vickers supposed, fooled many.

'Yeah.'

'Are you sure? Is there anything you'd like to talk about? Not about the exam, I mean ... but anything else?'

'No.'

Henrietta sighed. She had seen it before; the turning inwards, shunning all attempts to reach out and help; the closing of the face and the film of hurt that came over the eyes ... yes, she was in a great deal of pain. But Melanie wasn't a child; short of offering her the usual counselling, which she somehow doubted the girl would take, there was really nothing she – or anyone else at Weldon's, for that matter – could do. Oh, it wasn't the end of the world. She'd fail her exams, but – so what? It didn't mean it was the end of her life. She could always come back the following year – there were several girls to whom something similar had happened. Though none quite so drastic as walking out exactly two minutes after the exam had started ... she had never seen *that* before.

'You do realise, Melanie, that you can come back at any time you please. We're always here for you. I know this probably isn't the way you wanted to leave ...'

'I'm not coming back.' The finality in the girl's voice was absolute. Henrietta paused.

'You may feel that way now, Melanie ... but believe me, you don't really want to throw away your life just because—'

'It's my life, Mrs Vickers. I'll do what I like with it,' Melanie interrupted her. Not rudely, as such, but with the same air of finality. Henrietta stopped. For once, she was at a loss for words. She could find nothing to say, nothing that would bring some measure of relief to Melanie or, for that matter, to herself. She could only watch in pained silence as the girl got up from the chair opposite her and walked, unhurriedly, mind, out of the room. She continued to stare at the blank, closed face of the door for a long time after she'd left.

7

That evening, sitting at the dinner table with her mother and Norbert Kreizer, her stepfather, Melanie remained silent as her mother recounted – with the requisite drama, of course – the story of what Melanie had done. As she spoke, Norbert glanced at Melanie and quickly looked away again, as he usually did. If it were possible, Norbert was even less interested in her than her father. He was forever reminding her mother that Melanie wasn't *his* child. Not that it would have made much difference. Norbert Kreizer paid very little attention to anything that wasn't glass and steel. Melanie had no idea what he saw in her mother, or vice versa, for that matter. They'd been married for four years, during which time Norbert Kreizer had steadily grown more and more famous, exactly the sort of situation her mother had sworn she would never fall into again, although to which, it had to be said, she seemed hopelessly drawn. Stella was just the sort of bright, dizzy blonde divorcée who got invited to all sorts of things, including a rather pompous dinner party for a TV producer who had commissioned an unknown, rather pompous Swiss architect to design his new offices ... several months later, she and the pompous architect were married in a stark, monochromatic wedding in a stark, monochromatic town outside Basel with sixty guests and thirty photographers obviously hoping Mike Miller would show up. He didn't. Twelve-year-old Melanie was a bridesmaid and exceptionally pretty, so they photographed her instead. Melanie was quite used to seeing her father on the cover of *Hello!* magazine and her stepfather on the front page of *The Times* – in the same day. The important thing about both of them, however, at least from Melanie's perspective, was that neither seemed to register her presence.

At the end of supper, she slid, unnoticed, from the table.

A couple of months later, she sat perched on the edge of the window sill, hidden by the branches of the leafy oak tree now in full bloom, and slowly smoked one cigarette after another. It was three o'clock on a Saturday afternoon. Almost eight weeks since she'd upset everyone by flunking her A-levels *and ruining her life*, or so they all said. She snorted. Utter rubbish. She couldn't understand what the fuss was all about. Her one act of defiance had failed to capture her father's attention ... she might as well not have bothered. In fact, nothing had changed.

Her mother still fussed and clucked around her, her stepfather seemed to have difficulty remembering who she was; Polly, her best friend, thought she was mad and her father seemed to have forgotten why he'd been called away from his European tour to spend half an hour in Mrs Vickers' study in the first place. The morning after they'd been called in to 'discuss Melanie', he'd phoned from Milan, unusually for him, and told her to cheer up, not to fret. He'd promised to take her to LA for a month as soon as they'd finished playing Europe. She'd spent the next fortnight in a fever of anticipation, broken only by long, expensive shopping trips to Harrods and Selfridges where she'd bought everything she thought she would need for a month in the sun ... and then, as usual, nothing happened. He forgot. He'd come back from Europe, taken her to dinner and seemed to have forgotten he'd ever mentioned it. She'd tried to bring the subject up, but aside from a vague promise that he'd call her later to discuss it, he dismissed the idea just the way he dismissed everything else about her. A quick smile in her direction, a pat on the behind ... and then she disappeared from his mind.

She swung her legs round from the sill, stubbed out her cigarette and pulled the window shut. She looked at her watch. Twenty past three. There was no one in the house. Her mother was out shopping, the housekeeper had left for the weekend and God only knew where her stepfather was. He'd been nominated for some stupid architecture prize and the phones had been ringing off the wall. You'd have thought he'd won the bloody Nobel prize, Melanie thought to herself morosely. She ran over her options – go round to Polly's, but she'd been there the day before, *and* the day before that. Boring. Cinema? Bike ride? Nothing appealed. She walked into the bathroom and looked at herself in the mirror. Her hair looked a little lank. She turned on the shower and quickly stripped off her clothes. A shower would wake her up, make her feel better. She might even be able to think of something to do.

★

Ten minutes later, she sat in front of her dressing table, a towel tucked under her arms and began to tease the tangles out of her long, dark hair. The towel slipped but the house was quiet so she left it bunched loosely around her waist. It was summer; a cool breeze wafted through the windows, pulled through her bedroom by the open door on to the landing. She hummed to herself as she brushed her hair. She pulled the long wet strands over her shoulder and smoothed them down her naked breasts, pouting in the mirror the way the models in the fashion magazines that littered the house did. She was mouthing the words to a song, holding her hairbrush in both hands, when she suddenly became aware she was no longer alone. She glanced behind her in the mirror and froze. Her stepfather was standing in the doorway, on his way to the enormous master bedroom at the end of the corridor. Melanie swallowed. He stood there for a moment longer, an unfathomable expression in his normally reserved, aloof eyes. Then he dragged his eyes away from her, turned on his heel and vanished. Seconds later, she heard the bedroom door slam shut. She was aware of a stinging heat in her cheeks that swept down the entire length of her body. She slowly pulled the towel up around her breasts and, with trembling fingers, pulled her hair into a knot. Nothing happened. Nothing *had* happened. He'd come upon her by mistake; nothing more embarrassing than being caught mouthing the words to some silly song. But she was sharply aware of a pleasurable, tightly curled knot in the pit of her stomach. *He'd been unable to take his eyes off her.* Norbert Kreizer, the forty-something world-famous architect, her mother's husband ... he'd been unable to look away. She had *made* him look at her; he who barely registered her presence. And the most remarkable thing of all? She hadn't said a word.

8

'Hey, baby … you … yes, *you* …' The voice belonged to a soldier standing on the steps outside Gaspard's General Store on Rue L'Ouverture. He stood with one arm raised casually above his head, forehead touching one of the pillars, a sweating can of beer held against his cheek. Laure pretended not to notice him. She sauntered past, her hips swaying just a fraction as they drew level. 'Hey … you.' He smiled at her. 'Come over here, baby. C'mon. I won't bite you.' He pointed at her, not at Régine.

Next to her, Laure heard Régine stiffen. 'Laure, don't talk to him!' she hissed. She tugged at Laure's sleeve. 'Let's *go*. He's American. They're from the base at Jacmel.'

The soldier lowered his arm and jumped off the step, coming towards them. 'C'mere, sugar. I ain't gonna *eat* you!' he laughed. 'I promise.' His French was good but his accent was atrocious.

Laure met his gaze. 'Hi,' she said coolly, feeling Régine's scandalised stare on her face.

'Laure!' Régine whined. 'I thought you wanted to go *swimming?*'

'I do,' Laure said slowly, her eyes still on the soldier. 'You go ahead. I'll catch up with you.'

'Oh my *God*, Laure …' Régine moaned. 'We'll get into so much trouble if anyone sees us.'

'You go. I'll be there in a minute. No one will see me.'

'I don't *understand* you,' Régine hissed. 'You almost got grounded after Josette's party. If your grandmother catches you …'

'Jesus, Régine, will you shut up?' Laure nudged her. 'She *won't* catch me. Now, will you just *go*? I'll be there in a minute.'

'Well, don't say I didn't warn you,' Régine said haughtily as she turned and walked quickly away. Laure looked after her, amused. For all Régine's popularity she was such a little scaredy-cat. She turned to look at the soldier standing in front of her. He was tall and well built in the way only Americans could ever be – all shiny, polished skin and bulging muscles gleaming with sweat. He was the smooth, buttery-brown colour of milk chocolate; with short, black, cropped hair ... and the smile, of course – rows of flawless, white teeth. American teeth.

'So, baby ... you gon' tell me your name?' he asked, his voice all silky and soft.

'Laure,' she replied, feeling her stomach jump and the hair on the back of her neck start to rise. 'What's yours?'

'Delroy. Delroy Weaver, ma'am.' Laure could hear the smile in his voice. She looked at him, her stomach tensing in anticipation of something she couldn't quite name.

'You're American?' she asked, squinting up at him.

'Yes, ma'am.' He looked her up and down and then pushed himself off the step. Without saying a word, they fell into step beside one another. Laure didn't think about where they might be headed; it was enough to walk next to him. She felt daring in a way she hadn't ever before. They walked up the street towards the park at the top of the hill.

'So ... where were you off to, Laure?' Delroy asked. His sleeve brushed loosely against hers as they walked, sending little shudders of pleasure running up her arm.

'Oh, just to the pool. We were about to go swimming.'

'You live around here?'

She flushed at the almost-hidden surprise in his voice. She knew exactly what he was saying – *my, aren't you a little dark-skinned to be living in these parts?* 'Yes, with my grandmother. The house on the corner.'

'Well, can I come visit you sometime?' he asked, his pace slowing. She stopped and turned to face him. Dark, flashing black eyes ... like hers.

'I don't think so. My grandmother wouldn't like it,' Laure said reluctantly.

'She have to know?' It was a statement, not a question.

She looked at him. 'Well, I guess ... no, I suppose not. I

mean, how … well, what …' she broke off, confused. Delroy was laughing at her.

'Can't you say you're goin' someplace else? With your friend? The one who didn't like me?'

'I guess so …' Laure hesitated.

'How 'bout tomorrow night? I get off at eight.'

'Nine,' Laure said, suddenly decisive. Her heart was thumping. It would be the first time she'd ever sneaked out of the house. By nine, Grandmère would be safely upstairs. She could slip out of the house unnoticed.

'*No problem.*' He said it in English.

Laure suppressed a giggle. She could hardly speak a word of English, despite almost four years of it in school. But everyone knew what *no problem* meant. All the soldiers said it. She looked quickly at him. 'OK. Well, I guess … I'll see you tomorrow, then …' Laure said, a little uncertainly. He was smiling down at her. She liked very much the way his eyes folded at the corners when he smiled.

'Sure thing, baby. See you, Laure.' He winked at her and sauntered off, whistling as he went.

'Are you *crazy*?' Régine hissed at her as she slid into the pool, half an hour later.

'Crazy? No, I don't think so,' Laure said, the water immediately cooling her burning cheeks.

'He's a *Marine*, Laure … my mother says they're *disgusting* … they go to 'Ti Marie's, you know.' Régine looked meaningfully at her. 'Ti Marie's was an infamous brothel at the bottom of the hill, down there in the city.

'So what? Maybe *he* doesn't go there. They're not all the same, you know.'

'Oh, Laure … of *course* he does. You can tell.'

'How?'

'I don't know … you just can.'

'You mean *you* can. God, Régine, you're such a snob.'

'I am not!' Régine said indignantly. Laure shook her head and submerged her burning face under water. She was annoyed.

33

Every time Régine kissed a boy or got a note in class, or made eyes at someone, *she* had to listen to her – for hours on end. This was the first time Laure had *ever* had anything to talk about ... and Régine just couldn't stand it. Fine. If that was how she wanted it ... Laure couldn't have cared less. She had other things to think about. The following evening, for one.

Laure looked at herself anxiously in front of the mirror. She had no idea where he might take her and she had no idea what to wear. She'd tried on half a dozen skirts – too childish, somehow – and then each of her three pairs of jeans in quick succession. She'd finally settled on the tightest pair – the ones Régine said made her walk like a bad, *bad* girl – and a plain white T-shirt. She left her hair loose, for once, although she knew she would pay for it the following day when she couldn't get a comb through it. As a last-minute afterthought, she fastened a necklace around her neck. It made her look marginally less like a schoolgirl.

She waited, breathlessly, until she heard Grandmère's door close at eight on the dot. She could hear the faint sound of the radio being switched on, and the familiar creak of the floorboards as Grandmère walked to the high, wrought-iron bed in the middle of the room. By eight-thirty the house was silent. She waited a further fifteen minutes then opened the jalousie window in her room as quietly as she could. She lifted a leg over the sill and climbed out. The narrow balcony outside served as a stepping stone on to the jacaranda tree – from there it was a quick slide down the enormous trunk and a soft landing on the grass. She brushed the bark and dust from her jeans, tucked her hair behind her ear and slipped through the hedge at one side of the house.

The street was silent and almost pitch-black – the street lights in Pétionville had long since ceased to function. She looked up and down the deserted road. There was no one about. She stood at the side of the road, waiting, her stomach churning nervously. She'd never done anything like this before. She peered at her watch – it was almost nine. Wasn't he coming?

34

Perhaps he'd changed his mind? She stood hopping uncertainly from foot to foot, wondering where he was, wondering if she'd got the time wrong, or the day perhaps, wondering if the jeans and T-shirt she'd chosen might not be the right sort of thing to wear on a ... a date? Was it a date? Yes. He'd asked her out, hadn't he? That made it a date. Her first ever. *You look fine*, Belle's voice popped into her head suddenly. *I like your top*. Laure smiled to herself in the darkness.

'Hey.' A voice broke somewhere to her left. She almost jumped out of her skin. He was standing a few feet away from her; she caught a glimpse of his teeth in the dark. He was smiling.

'You scared me!' she whispered. 'I ... I didn't notice ... I didn't see you coming.'

'You know why?' he asked softly, moving closer to her. Laure shook her head. 'Soldiers. Never see us coming,' he said and touched her elbow. She shivered, despite the heat.

'What ... where shall we go?' she asked, suddenly gripped by a desire to get away from the house as quickly as possible.

'You ever been to the Napoli?' Delroy asked. Laure gaped at him. Café Napoli was in the centre of town – not only was it a good fifteen miles away, it was also Port-au-Prince's most infamous bar. He laughed at her expression. 'Come on. The jeep's parked on the next road. I figured you'd want to keep things a little hidden.' Unable to do anything else and with her heart in her mouth, she followed him.

The blue neon sign above the entrance to the Café Napoli was missing two letters; the 'N' and the 'o'. Café-ap-li. Laure gazed up at it as she and Delroy walked towards it. The windows were plastered with advertisements for Prestige beer and the wall was peeling paint. Delroy pushed open the door – it was crammed and foggy inside, smoke spiralling lazily upwards towards bare bulbs. The tiny bar area was packed. People turned to look at her as Delroy threaded his way towards the bar, holding her by the wrist and propelling her through the throng of paunchy, middle-aged men and vacant, glassy-eyed girls glued to their sides. The music was loud and thumping. At the bar, she followed Delroy's lead and scrambled up on to the stool next to him.

'What do you want to drink?' he asked her, shouting above the din. Laure looked helplessly at the row of bottles above the bartender's head. *Beer. Whisky. Rum.* She shook her head in bewilderment. *Anything*, she mouthed at him. She had no idea what to ask for. Apart from the odd glass of wine at mealtimes she'd never really had anything alcoholic to drink before. She watched as Delroy ordered two glasses of rum and argued for a couple of ice cubes. The bartender looked at her rather strangely as he pushed their glasses along the bar.

'You wan' any Coke with that?' he asked, staring at her. Laure shook her head, too excited to speak. Delroy's hand was on her knee – she could feel the heat of his palm through her jeans. She risked a cautious glance to her left and right. Régine would *die* when she heard what she'd been up to. All around her, sweating and shiny-faced from the music, the dancing, the noise, were men and women, the likes of whom she'd never really seen before. Sure, on the rare occasions she'd been to the city with Grandmère, occasionally to the market at Champs de Mar and sometimes on the occasional school trip outside of the protected, upper-class enclave of Pétionville, she'd encountered what Grandmère disparagingly called 'the people' – the dark-skinned, rambunctious, noisy men and women who were, she supposed, her fellow countrymen – but she'd always shied away from any *real* contact. A whispered '*merci*', as a stall owner pressed an extra banana in her hand, perhaps, when she was little. Once, when she'd desperately needed the toilet while out shopping in the marketplace with Cléones, she'd been taken round the back of the stalls to someone's toilet – a hole in the ground, really – and it had taken all of her reserves of good manners to remember to thank the woman and *not* hold her hand to her nose. *Les gens du peuple* were dirty, primitive and violent – that was what Grandmère said and until now, sitting on a barstool surrounded by them, Laure had never had any reason to doubt her.

But the woman standing a couple of feet away didn't look dirty – or primitive, or violent. Laure stared at her – long, braided hair woven into elaborate curls and swirls; huge hoop earrings that flashed every time she bent her head to whisper into the ear of her companion, a man almost half her size who could do little except stare at the magnificent breasts spilling out of her tight, shiny dress and into his face. Her lips were glossy and red, painted to match her nails – or the other way around. Her skin was so black it was almost blue. At that moment, she was the most beautiful, exotic creature Laure had ever seen. And people thought *she* was dark?

As the rum burned its way down her throat, chased by the chilled sweetness of a tiny, rapidly melting ice cube, Laure gazed about her in lazy, sensual pleasure. Delroy's hand was now on her waist, his voice was a warm, erotic buzz in her ear. The reverberations of the music, the swirling smoke coils, the low, intimate din of murmured conversation made her almost drowsy. Delroy pulled her chair closer; she leaned against the solid wall of muscles that was his chest and watched him push her empty glass across the bar – *another one, my man*. With the next mouthful, Laure felt the last jagged crystals of insecurity and uncertainty melt away. Down here, in Port-au-Prince, with the jostling, laughing crowd around her, she felt strangely at home.

It was almost two in the morning when Delroy gathered the little pile of black chips and flung down his last card. A happy roar went up around the table. They'd been playing cards for almost two hours ... she, Delroy and a clutch of Marines from the base at Fort Islet. She was perched on the arm of his chair; his arm was tight around her waist in some kind of claim as they played. He grabbed his beer, swallowed it and turned to her, pulling her closer.

'So, where to now, ma'am?' he asked, grinning at her. He'd won some money, she noticed. A man was busy exchanging the pile of chips for a bundle of notes at the far end of the table. She pressed her head into the sweat and heat of his shoulder, seeking some sort of assurance to a question she didn't yet know how to ask. They had danced together, earlier – she'd felt the taut hunger of his body against her. All she wanted was for the night not to end. There was school tomorrow ... a cold shock ran through her as she remembered the world outside the nightclub to which *she* belonged, most firmly. *This* – the noise and the smoke and laughter and the feel of Delroy's arm around her waist – this was a dream. Any second now she would wake up and the glorious image in front of her would disappear.

'Home?' she said shyly, half-hoping he would suggest some-where else.

'Can't go to mine,' he whispered in her ear as he accepted his winnings and stuffed them into his jacket pocket. 'I'm at the base. And I guess we can't go to yours ...?' Laure shook her head, every nerve in her body alive with the thrill of what he was suggesting, offering. 'How about we spend a little of this?' he suggested, patting the pocket where he'd stuffed his winnings. Laure pulled back from him hesitantly. She was more than a little tipsy ... and the enormity of his suggestion registered only dimly. He wanted ... her. His hand slid underneath the flowered shirt, trailing a delicate path across her back. She was melting, floating, slowly dissolving. Yes, she nodded dreamily, turning to face him and receiving his warm, hungry lips with hers. Out of the corner of her eye she noticed one or two of the Marines looking at them – jealously, she understood, with a tiny, fierce stab of pleasure. They were jealous – of him. He had *her*, half-sitting across his lap, his hands buried somewhere under her shirt, his tongue seeking hers. 'Come on, baby,' he murmured, gently pushing her off his lap. 'Let's get out of here.'

It was hot in the little room to which he'd brought her. Hot and dark – a secret place. She listened to him and the slow, steady sound of his voice as he prepared her in a way she'd only ever heard about, read about. First the rum – warm, sweet – in a glass that they shared, turnabout. Fingers on skin, sliding up and down, touching parts of her that sent shivers down her spine. She heard herself; the deep, throaty laugh that he said he *loved* but that everyone else said was just like Belle's. Delroy said it was the most exciting thing he'd heard. 'You have the sexiest laugh, baby ... you know that?' Hands moving up and down her spine, sliding her T-shirt up and over her head – he flung it, almost angrily, to one side. Then her jeans ... slowly, taking care to unzip them properly before sliding them down her legs. She heard his sharp intake of breath as she lay across the bed in the room he'd taken for the night, just for her – and then there was the wonderfully heavy, insistent weight of his body sliding up and down hers, his face blotting out the light. He felt her with his hands first, stroking her, mumbling things in English she couldn't understand, and then, at last, the sharp stab that hovered somewhere between pain and pleasure ... she gasped. He seemed to lose control, his face tightening in what seemed to her to be agony as he pushed himself against her, again and again ... a terrible, breathless beating against something she had no idea she possessed and then his groan of release and the dead, heavy weight of him against her trembling body, suddenly gone slack. He said nothing for a few minutes as he slowly came back to her, his hand stirring every now and then against her hot, damp skin.

'You are just the best,' he mumbled at last, turning his face into the warm, sticky skin of her neck. *The best*. The warm glow that had started between her legs rose slowly to her face. It was the first time anyone had ever said that about her. Ever.

9

It started as a game. A silly, harmless game. She would never have *done* anything – of course not. He was her mother's husband; at least thirty years older. She'd never really liked him, never even really talked to him. He was strange to her, and not just because he was foreign, but for the first time, she began to look at him properly. He was good-looking, in a rather cold sort of way. Tall, with a broad, powerful build; the sort of man who commanded attention, accustomed to the gaze of others. He had dark hair, greying at the temples and steely grey eyes which seemed to see through everything and everyone, including her. In the four years since her mother had brought him triumphantly to their house, she could practically count on one hand the number of times they'd spoken beyond the mundane exchanges that living together in the same house required. As he'd steadily grown more famous, he'd grown even more remote. He was often away and on the occasions when he was with them, he seemed to have little to say to either of them. At least when her father was around, things were lively, if short-lived. Norbert Kreizer, on the other hand, was the absolute antithesis of fun. Melanie wasn't sure she'd ever seen him smile.

But now, after the little incident in front of the mirror, he avoided her almost completely. If he had to talk to her, he did so with a tightly controlled expression and brought the conversation to a halt as quickly as he could, as if she were something odious, or unpleasant. At first it hurt. Then it began to annoy her. She started to bait him, asking him the odd direct question or two at the dinner table whenever the three of them were present, staring at him, making it impossible for him to ignore her. Her mother was pleasantly surprised. It was such a relief, she overheard her telling a friend one afternoon. She was *so* pleased they finally seemed to be getting on. It made the atmosphere at home much, much easier. She knew they'd get along *eventually*. Melanie turned away guiltily. How could she tell her mother she didn't dislike him any *less* – she was just playing a silly game. She just wanted to see how far she could push him, or if she could push him at all. He certainly didn't seem keen to be pushed into anything – on the contrary, he seemed keen to avoid her at all costs. She found it exciting in way she'd never imagined possible.

★

And then there came a day when things got horribly out of hand. It started off innocently enough. A Saturday, like many others that summer – boring beyond words. She and Polly had gone to Parson's Green to play tennis. Polly's mother dropped her off afterwards and as she ran quickly up the path to the front door, she noticed that Norbert's black Saab was parked in the driveway – and that her mother's silver Mercedes was not. She vaguely remembered her mother saying something about going to have her hair 'done' – a process that usually took most of the day.

She slid her key in the lock with a mounting sense of excitement at the thought of being alone with him. The house was quiet. She put her racket in its place in the downstairs cupboard and quickly looked into the sitting room. He wasn't there. She went downstairs into the enormous black and white kitchen – no, not there either. She fished a bottle of water out of the fridge, ignoring her mother's pained grimace in her mind's eye as she lifted it to her lips, and wandered back upstairs. As she walked down the landing, she could hear voices coming from the upstairs sitting room at the end of the hallway. She walked towards it; yes, she could hear Norbert's voice. She pushed open the door a crack and peered round. He was sitting in front of the enormous television, watching something ... she frowned. He was watching himself on TV! Some sort of interview ... she remembered hearing him tell her mother about it. It was very odd, seeing his face on the screen and the back of his head in front of her. She pushed open the door silently.

She was almost behind him when she spoke. 'Oh, hul*lo*,' she said, feigning surprise. 'Didn't think anyone was in.' He jumped as if he'd been shot. Melanie smiled to herself. She plopped herself down on the couch beside him. Close, but not too close. She didn't want him to run away.

'Oh. It's you.' He couldn't possibly have sounded less thrilled to see her. Melanie hesitated for a second, then stretched her legs out on the table in front of her. She was still wearing her short white tennis skirt and was acutely aware of the taut skin of her thighs and calves showing tanned and smooth against the cream-coloured whorls of the patterned couch.

'What're you watching?' she asked, in a voice into which she poured as much enthusiasm as she could summon. 'That's you, isn't it?' she went on, before he had a chance to answer. She could feel the sofa shift beneath her. 'Gosh, it must be exciting, being on television. I was on TV once, you know ... but the silly woman really only wanted to talk about my dad. He's really famous, a bit like you, I suppose, only ...'

'Melanie. What do you want?' he interrupted her abruptly. His voice was cold.

She made her blue eyes as wide as possible. 'Me? Nothing ... I just heard the TV and ...'

'Stop playing games,' he said, so quietly she thought at first she might have misheard him. 'You know exactly what I mean.' He stared at her, his expression unreadable. He suddenly seemed very grown-up and very, very distant.

Melanie began to feel uncomfortable. 'I ... I don't know what you're talking about,' she stammered, the heat rising in her face. She glanced at him uncertainly. This wasn't quite what she'd planned.

'Of course you do.' He was looking at her in a way she didn't recognise. His face was full of ... anger? She shifted uncomfortably. 'You shouldn't do this,' he said, his accent suddenly becoming more pronounced. 'Really you shouldn't do this. You don't know what you're doing.'

She lifted one leg off the table; there was a sudden movement and the sharp, hissed intake of his breath and then he touched her. She had no idea how it happened. She was aware of the lemony scent of his aftershave and then the bristly feel of his cheek as it grazed hers. The sound of the television receded to a single point; all concentration caught up in the few moments of complete silence before she felt his hand on her knee. His touch was sure, deft, nothing at all like the tentative, fumbling gropings of the boyfriends she'd had before. She closed her eyes against the fierce wave of longing that raced through her as soon as his hand touched her bare skin. He cleared his throat and the pressure on her knee grew. He seemed to be trying to say something but there was confusion in the cold grey eyes behind the lenses she could see through her own lashes and when she carefully moved her cheek so that her mouth was resting just under his, she felt something in his body give way as his hand slid further up her thigh and his mouth finally, sweetly, touched hers. She drew in her breath sharply as the most suffocating joy took hold of her. She began to kiss him back, her arms going up around his neck without her even realising it. He was leaning heavily against her, and it seemed to her that he could never be heavy enough; she gripped the starched white collar of his shirt and drew his head closer, wriggling herself into his arms. She didn't hear the front door open, nor the sound of heels as someone walked down the corridor towards them; she was held in the tense, uncontrollable excitement of having finally broken something in him. The fact that he was her stepfather didn't even cross her mind – he had never been anything other than a shadowy, aloof presence in her life; before that moment he had been every man she'd ever met – disinterested, disengaged, dismissive. And yet ... it had taken so little to change that. His hand danced lightly across the thin cotton fabric of her panties. She thought she might die of pleasure.

And then it came. 'Oh *God*! Oh my *God*!' The scream from the doorway shattered the silence. It all happened so fast. Norbert shoved her away from him so viciously she hit her head against the armrest. There was a second's awful, shocked silence and then her mother began screaming again. 'You *bastard*! You fucking *bastard*! How could you!'

'*Nein*, Stella ... it's not like that ... *nein*. I wasn't ... she ...' She heard Norbert's voice, felt the sofa give as he struggled upright. Melanie closed her eyes.

'You little *bitch*!' He spat the words out at her. 'You fucking little bitch!' And then she heard the living room door slam shut. She listened to his footsteps chasing down the corridor and her mother's angry screams as she raced up the stairs, Norbert in heavy pursuit. She pressed her hands against her ears, only partially blocking out the sound of the shouting and the steady, monotonous drone of her stepfather's voice coming to her from the screen a few feet away.

'And do you have a favourite city?' The interviewer's saccharine voice faded away.

'Well, too many to name ... Venice, of course, and New York. Such energy. I really love America. Everything in America is so fresh. So young. So new.'

10

Améline had almost finished shelling the tiny, black-eyed peas when Cléones marched out through the kitchen door, slamming it loudly behind her, and dumped an armful of laundry on the ground. Améline looked up.

'What is it?'

'That ... that *girl*!' Cléones spat out, practically stamping her foot in rage.

'Who? Laure?'

'Who *else*?'

'What's the matter? What's she done?'

'Fourteen T-shirts ... *fourteen*? In one day? Who can wear fourteen T-shirts in *one day*? She tries one on, then she drops it in the laundry basket; then she tries another one on ... who the hell does she think she is?'

'Shall I wash them?' Améline asked, sighing. What was wrong with Laure? Ever since Josette's party, she'd changed. She'd become more secretive, somehow, less willing to share things ... she'd even caught her talking to herself one day – it was all very strange.

'No, she can wash them herself! That's it. I'm going to tell Madame.'

'Oh, no ... no, look, I'll do them. I don't mind ... I'll tell Laure she's not to do it again. Here, give them to me.'

'Hmph. What is it with you two? You're always sticking up for her. Anyone would think ...' Cléones stopped, as usual. Améline sighed. It was the pattern of their conversations around the subject of Laure St Lazâre. For as long as she could remember, Améline had felt there was more to the story than Cléones – or anyone else for that matter – was willing to divulge. There was always something held back, a detail omitted, an unfinished sentence hanging in the air … something that would complete the picture of how and why they all had come to live in the rambling house on Rue Trouillat, almost at the top of the hill. Améline could barely remember Madère, which was where they'd lived before coming to Pétionville. But she could remember a time when the house had more servants, more flowers in the garden and *two* cars, not just the old, throaty Jaguar that Madame still drove every Sunday afternoon. It seemed a very long time ago.

'Anyone would think what?' Améline asked hesitantly.

'Nothing, you silly girl. Here, if you want to ruin your hands, *you* wash them!' She scooped up the pile of clothes and deposited them at Améline's feet. Améline half smiled to herself – ruin her hands? They were already ruined, like the rest of her. Cléones turned on her broad, flat heels and stomped back into the kitchen.

A few hours later, the washed and ironed T-shirts in her arms, she tapped on Laure's bedroom door. There was no answer. She knocked again, louder. There was still no answer. Very cautiously, she pushed open the door. The room was empty. She frowned. It was three o'clock on a Saturday afternoon and she definitely hadn't heard anyone leave the house and she knew she wasn't sitting up in the jacaranda tree … where was she? She laid the pile of T-shirts on the edge of the bed and closed the door. Wherever she was, she'd better be back before Madame got home.

A month later, for the third time in a week, Améline watched Laure slip past the window and push her way through the hedge. She heard the quiet cough as the soldier started his jeep and inched it forward to the corner of Rue Lamarre. Seconds later, she heard the door slam shut and then the vehicle roared off into the night. They were gone. God only knew where.

She carried the candle away from the window and set it carefully down beside her bed. It was nine-thirty, perhaps ten o'clock in the evening. Améline had no watch but she'd gone to her room at the rear of the house at eight-thirty, after clearing the dinner table and doing the dishes, and she'd been lying down reading by candlelight for at least an hour before she heard the soft thud as Laure landed on the ground outside her window. She bit her lip – should she say something? Could she? It wouldn't be long before Madame found out ... it had been going on for a month and now it was only a matter of time. She dreaded to think what would happen if Madame happened to look outside the window one night just as Laure was shimmying down the tree. Améline crossed herself involuntarily. Madame's temper was ferocious. She'd never actually seen her hit Laure, but Améline had been on the receiving end of her slap more times than she cared to remember – and these days, it was getting worse, not better.

She sat down on the edge of her bed. Perhaps she should say something to Cléones ... she always knew what to do in that household where nothing was as it seemed. No ... Cléones would only report Laure to Madame. She was always going on about how much like Belle Laure was turning out to be – and it was no compliment. Cléones reserved a special brand of disapproving sarcasm whenever Belle St Lazâre's name was mentioned. It was bad enough that the girl was so dark in complexion; her character was equally dark, as Cléones was fond of saying. *Like mother, like daughter. The fruit never falls far from the tree.* And so on. Améline couldn't understand it. As far as she was concerned, Laure was the prettiest girl she'd ever seen. She longed to have thick, wild, curly hair like Laure's. She wasn't skinny, like Améline was, with knock-knees and a gap between her front teeth; no, Laure was tall and curvy and, she pronounced the word with some difficulty, voluptuous. Laure had shown it to her in the dictionary and they'd both agreed that yes, that's what Laure was. So what if she were a shade or two darker than Madame? Améline had heard it said that Madame had been a beauty in her day, as well. Privately, Améline couldn't see how. Madame looked like a tired, old horse, especially when she smiled. Thankfully, that didn't happen often. Her skin was light and papery, criss-crossed by a thousand tiny lines of anger, disappointment … and grief, Cléones whispered to her one day. Cléones knew almost everything that had happened to the St Lazâre family. Almost everything. Améline knew there were certain things that no one ever talked about but, as Cléones always said, it was better that way.

She blew out the candle and quickly undressed in the dark. Her room had no curtains and there was no telling who might be looking through the hedge. Although the houses in this part of Pétionville were large, elegant villas with wooden jalousied windows to keep out the light and huge, lush gardens and hedges high enough to keep out the prying eyes of neighbours, among the servants in the area there was no such discretion. Améline knew of at least two maids in the streets surrounding them who'd supplemented their income nicely by keeping an unnaturally close eye on the comings and goings of others – and were paid to keep quiet.

She pulled back the thin sheet covering her bed and slid in. It was stiflingly hot. Like everyone else she couldn't wait for the rains to begin. Down there on the flats by the sea, the city would be awash with mud. In Pétionville, up in the hills, in contrast, it would be lovely and fresh. That was why *les blancs*, the whites, and then the mulattos, had chosen it.

She closed her eyes, wondering how to warn Laure to be very, very careful.

Laure was in a quandary. Delroy Weaver was quite possibly the most exciting thing that had ever happened to her and *there was no one she could tell*. She certainly couldn't talk to Régine about him. She longed to be able to tell someone about the time they drove to the beach at Gonaïves with the top down and the way it took her hours to get the tangles out of her hair before Grandmère saw her ... but who? And how? Just thinking about Delroy and the things they did together brought the heat to her face and sent shivers down her spine. She felt as though she'd been split in two; one half of her went to school every day and sat demurely next to Régine and Martine, listening with one ear while the teachers droned on and on. The other half of her was elsewhere; with Delroy. In the little room at the pension he took her to every other night. *That* Laure danced half the night away in bars down there in the city and lay perfectly still beside a chocolate-coloured man who brought dripping ice cubes to the narrow bed and trailed them up and down her bare skin. *That* Laure had done things to Delroy that Régine and most of the girls in her class had probably only ever heard about – and even then only in whispered rumours. She wanted desperately to tell someone, to bring the two parts of her life – and herself – together; but whom? She'd tried, once, to hint at her secret after-hours life to Régine, but Régine had just looked at her as though she were mad.

'What clubs? What're you talking about?' she asked, staring at her.

'Oh ... you know ... in the city.'

'You went to the *city*? Are you crazy, Laure?'

'Why do you always say that? What's wrong with the city?'

'It's full of ... of ... *people*!' Régine finally managed to spit out.

'Of course it's full of people. It's the city.'

'Yes, but not people like us.'

Laure rolled her eyes in exasperation. Régine could be so narrow-minded at times. No, make that *all* the time. She looked around her at the slowly emptying classroom in frustration. She'd known most of the people in it all of her life – and she was sick and tired of them. They were so snobbish and small-minded. Hardly anyone ever ventured outside the little gilded enclave of Pétionville and when they did, they brought back reports of a place so alien as to be foreign to them – and yet it was their home. Cité Soleil and Jalouzi – places that she was sure few of them would ever have heard of – were just as much a part of Haiti as the villas of Pétionville and the ice-cream parlour at the Oloffson where they liked to spend their afternoons. No, trying to explain to Régine what that other part of her life was now like would be impossible. Not to mention foolish. She and Régine had been friends since playschool, although Régine was the popular one, always surrounded by a clutch of pretty, light-skinned girls who looked down their noses at Laure. Laure didn't mind. She had Améline and besides, Grandmère didn't let her go out half as much as the other girls. She liked being on her own, perched above the house in the jacaranda tree, reading or daydreaming. Régine's other friends didn't bother her in the least. Régine thrived on being popular, sought after; she needed it. Laure didn't.

But in the past year, the balance between them had subtly begun to change. As the girls turned fifteen, then sixteen, Laure's beauty – despite her dark skin – began to emerge; in her, Belle's prettiness took on another, deeper hue. Régine was destined to be petite and pretty but Laure was tall and striking, with the easy, languorous grace of a ballet dancer – not that she'd stuck at her ballet lessons for long. She played basketball with the boys; was one of the fastest girls on the track and took home the swimming prize, year after year. There were many boys – and girls – that summer who began to gravitate towards Laure and her deep, throaty laugh. Régine noticed and was not pleased. Laure didn't seem to care. The little jealousies that gripped Régine from time to time seemed irrelevant to her; life, she had begun saying, was too short. It seemed to annoy

Régine even further. Too short for what? *That*, Laure's flashing dark eyes seemed to say, *is something I can't tell you.*

'What's it like in America?' Laure asked Delroy late one night as they lay half covered by the thin cotton sheet.

'It depends. Depends where you mean.' Delroy leaned across her and reached for his cigarettes. In the flickering neon light from across the street, he seemed more beautiful to her than she could ever describe.

'Well, what's Chicago like?' she asked curiously.

'Oh, Chicago's beautiful. Real nice. Lots of black folk.'

'Black ... what, like you? But you're not really black, you know,' Laure said automatically. He was mulatto-coloured. Not black.

'Baby, where I'm from, if you got even a *touch* of black, you black. I can never figure it out – y'all are just too damned hung up on the colour of a person's skin. If you ain't white, you're black. That's all there is to it.'

'Is that what it's like in America?'

'You betcha.'

'I want to go to America.'

'*I wanna live in America*,' Delroy sang softly in her ear, in English. '*I wanna be an American*.' He smiled. 'You ain't never seen it?'

'What?' Laure couldn't follow the words.

'*West Side Story*. It's a film. You ain't never seen it?'

'Not yet,' Laure said softly, determinedly. 'Soon. I'm going to go and live with my mother, you know.'

'What you talkin' about?'

'My mother lives in Chicago.'

'Oh, yeah? Lake Shore Drive. Grant Park. Navy Pier. You'd love it. Yeah, it's a beautiful city.'

'What's Lake Shore Drive?' Laure asked, pronouncing the words with some difficulty.

'It's a long, beautiful street right by the lake. Lots of sky-scrapers, real nice apartment buildings. Where does your mom live?'

'I ... I don't remember,' Laure said quickly. 'I don't remember the name of the road.'

'Prob'ly South Side. There's a lot of Haitian folk down there. Say, we should meet up when you get to the States. You'll be older then,' he turned his body towards her, 'and a whole lot more experienced.' His voice dropped an octave. Laure felt the familiar surge of cool, sweet delight wash over her. She turned her face to meet his.

'Aren't I experienced enough now?' she whispered the words, as if afraid someone would hear her.

'Oh, no. Baby, there's a whole lot more I could show you ...' His hand began its lazy trail down her cheek, slipping into the fold of her neck, stroking her lightly.

'Show me.' Laure could scarcely believe her own boldness. She felt him hesitate for a second, then felt his hands go up into the tangled mass of her hair. He held her head between his hands and then brought her face lower. And lower still. He chuckled, a rich, deep sound against her ears.

'Quick learner, ain't you?'

12

What was to be done about Melanie? Her mother couldn't bear the sight of her. Immediately afterwards, her stepfather disappeared, claiming he had to supervise the opening of his new Hong Kong office. Melanie spent five of the most uncomfortable days of her entire life inside the house, too scared to leave her bedroom. Aside from one, awful meeting on the landing when she'd tried to talk to her mother but had been pushed aside, Stella grinding the words out, 'Don't talk to me. Don't you *dare* talk to me,' there had been no communication between them. None whatsoever. There had been long telephone conversations between her mother and father; at night,

Melanie could hear Stella sobbing into the receiver whenever she opened her bedroom door. She pressed the palms of her hands flat against her head and tried not to think about what she'd done. But what *had* she done? Nothing had happened. Not really. And it was he who had turned to her, not the other way round. She was sure of it. *He* was the one who should be punished with Stella's anguished, reproachful face. There was something else in her face, too – fear. Melanie couldn't quite understand it – what did her mother have to be afraid of? Polly rang a few times; what was the matter with her? She'd missed Sebastian Whyte's eighteenth birthday party – they'd been looking forward to it for months. What was wrong? Melanie couldn't bring herself to answer. She sat in her room, staring at the walls, biting her nails. She couldn't bear the currents of anger and tension flowing through the house. She longed to get out, to escape ... but to where?

On the fifth day, when she wasn't sure she could stand it any longer, her father's Bentley pulled up outside the house. Her mother was out. Melanie rushed from her bedroom, her heart pounding. She wasn't sure what sort of reception she would find – what had her mother told him? He stood at the bottom of the stairs, looking impatient. Melanie stopped.

'Come on then, popsicle,' he said, using his nickname for her and looking up at her through his cigarette smoke. 'Let's go to dinner. Find something a bit more feminine than those awful jeans, will you? You know I can't stand women in jeans.' He winked at her. She felt relief flow through her, warm and comforting, like alcohol. He wasn't angry with her. Tears began to smart behind her eyes. She turned and ran back upstairs. It took her five minutes to dress, brush her hair and present herself for inspection. 'Yeah, that'll do,' Mike drawled, looking her over. 'Come on. Car's waiting.'

Over dinner at his favourite London restaurant, having successfully dodged the odd persistent photographer or two, Mike put down his wine glass and looked at her. 'Maybe it'd be best to go away for a bit, Mel,' he said, almost sadly. Melanie's eyes filled with tears. 'No, no, it's not like that – no one's sending you away. You haven't done anything wrong – at least I don't think you have. Your mum's just a bit strung out over this one … can't say I blame her. What the fuck was he *thinking*? You're still a bloody teenager!' Melanie said nothing. It was a *tad* hypocritical of her father to be cross with Norbert – after all, his current girlfriend was hardly older than she was! He caught her eye and grimaced. 'Yeah, all right. I know, I know … I'm a fine one to talk. Oh, dear, I don't suppose I've been a particularly good role model, have I?' he said, not sounding in the least bit contrite. He lifted his glass of wine. 'I suppose I should've been around a bit more, shouldn't I?'

Melanie was quiet for a moment. It was most unlike her father to admit to a mistake, however obliquely. She looked at him, suddenly emboldened. 'Dad … can I ask you something?' she said hesitantly.

'What?'

'Wh … why did you marry Mum? In the first place, I mean. You've never really got along.'

Mike studied his glass for a second, unusually quiet. Then he sighed. 'If you really want to know …' he said, putting it down again. 'Smashing legs. She had great legs. Still does, actually. And then … well, then you came along.'

'But you hated being at home, didn't you? After I was born. Mum said you weren't even there for my first birthday party.'

'Yeah, well … you were a pretty baby, and all that …' Mike said, smiling slightly. 'But then you started crying and peeing all over the place … dunno, I s'pose I just wanted a bit of peace and quiet. And whatever else you've been, popsicle, you've never been quiet.'

'Well, I can see where I get it from,' Melanie said tartly.

Mike grinned. 'Look, Mel … I'm not going to pretend it's been all roses,' he said, draining his glass, summoning the waiter and patting her hand all at the same time, 'but come on. I've never pretended to be anything I'm not, have I? I never said I was going to be much of a dad. And I'm not. But that's just the way I am. You'll just have to deal with it – *not* by flirting with your poor mum's husbands, though. Poor Stella – she's had enough disappointment to deal with.'

'Well, where'm I supposed to go?' Melanie asked petulantly, not liking the turn in the conversation. It was about *her*, for once, not her mother.

Mike said nothing for a minute, frowning. Then he raised his eyebrows, as if in surprise. Something had occurred to him. 'How about LA?' he said, brightening. 'You could stay with Tina … how about that? You'd like that, wouldn't you?'

Melanie nodded, her eyes widening. Tina Rose was her father's American booker. Melanie had known Tina for most of her teenage years. She was forty-four (or –five or –six, depending on how she felt and who she was talking to). She'd been instrumental in the band's success in the US in the early days for which she'd earned herself a nice little fortune and Mike's enduring trust. She handled all their live tours and promotion and Melanie thought she was the coolest person she'd ever met. For all Melanie's self-assured aloofness, she was in awe of Tina Rose. Somehow the twenty-odd year age gap between them didn't seem to matter – Tina was like the mother Melanie had always longed for. Cool, hip, smart. Not a hysterical bone in her body. 'Oh, *could* I, Dad? I won't be a nuisance, I promise. I'll be ever so …'

'OK, OK. I get the picture. You want to go. I'll ring Tina tomorrow. Might be the best thing all round. Hang out with her for a couple of months, just till you sort out what you want to do. I don't suppose you're much interested in college, are you? Nah, didn't think so. *I* wasn't either.'

Melanie said nothing. She wasn't sure what she was interested in. All she knew was that she wanted to get as far away as possible from all the things she seemed to have done wrong.

Three days later, she flew out of London. First class with over one hundred kilos of luggage. If she was going to leave, she told herself grimly, she might as well do it in style. Her Louis Vuitton suitcases were stuffed to the brim with new clothes – cotton print dresses; long, floaty skirts; tiny white denim shorts;

half a dozen Day-Glo Frankie Goes to Hollywood T-shirts; ten pairs of identical jeans with holes in different places, some of which she'd made herself with a pair of scissors and Polly's strategic eye – *gosh, isn't that hole a bit too close to your bum?* – and dozens of those gorgeous sequinned boob-tubes they'd seen in Chelsea Girl just before she left. She and Polly had spent a short afternoon and a small fortune in Peter Robinson at Oxford Circus, staggering out with arms full of bags. 'Dad said I could get anything I wanted,' Melanie said as they struggled into a taxi.

'You're so lucky,' Polly said enviously, scattering bags left, right and centre as she clambered in. Melanie said nothing. She didn't *feel* lucky. She felt like shit.

Tina picked her up at LAX in a white convertible sports car which could only take a quarter of her luggage. No matter. A stretch limo was quickly commandeered to take the rest and they drove through the Valley to Encino, the wind wildly whipping their hair about their faces. Tina pulled smartly into the driveway of a pretty pale yellow bungalow with a white painted fence and pink spray roses creeping along the walls. Melanie gaped at it. It couldn't have been more different from Chelsea. Nestled in the foot of the hills, Encino was one of those quintessentially American suburbs – rich, pretty, silent. It was very different from Tina's previous home, a huge loft-like space in the centre of Manhattan. 'Oh, I *love* it here,' Tina said as she screeched to a halt in front of the garage and blew the horn. 'I got *so* sick of New York. Too much goin' on, know what I mean?' Melanie didn't, but she nodded enthusiastically all the same.

She blinked, startled. An exceptionally good-looking young man clad only in denim cut-off shorts had suddenly appeared in front of them. She'd never seen quite so many muscles on display before. He gave them both a friendly wave. 'Who's that?'

'Oh, that's Tim, the pool man,' Tina said arily. 'He does *every*one's pools around here.' She pressed the remote and the garage doors slid open silently. 'He's very good. Plus he's cute. It helps.'

Melanie could only nod. 'Cute' wasn't quite the word she would have chosen to describe the six-foot bronzed Adonis with dark brown hair, green eyes and the sort of stomach she'd only ever seen on television. He was also only the hundredth person of absolute physical perfection she'd seen since her arrival – and she'd only been in LA for a couple of hours. Even Tina had undergone a radical LA-inspired transformation since Melanie had last seen her. She'd had her nose 'done', her breasts 'shaped' and stomach 'tightened.' She worked out 'every fucking morning', she explained to the astonished Melanie who'd never even seen the inside of a gym. Her hair was coloured and cut every month; her nails were manicured; her make-up was discreet. She topped up her tan every morning before going to the office. 'This is LA!' she said, tossing a perfect white smile over her shoulder to Tim as he hauled Melanie's suitcases into the hallway. 'Gotta keep up, haven't you?'

'Er, yes …' Melanie said, bewildered.

'You'll be in here,' Tina said, leading Melanie down the corridor. She pushed open the door to a pretty, spacious room which overlooked the garden and the shimmering turquoise pool. 'You can keep an eye on Tim,' she giggled as Tim staggered into the room.

'Damn,' he said, grinning as he lowered a couple of suitcases onto the floor. 'What you got *in* those bags, anyway?'

'Oh, just a few …'

'She's a *celebrity*, Tim.' Tina laughed. 'Mike Miller's little girl. You know how they travel!'

'Oh, I'm not a celebrity … no, I …' Melanie interrupted hurriedly.

'You English?' Tim asked suddenly, looking down at her. Melanie nodded shyly. He was almost too good-looking to be real. 'That's cool. I *love* the English.'

'Like you know any,' Tina laughed, rolling her eyes. 'Come on, let's leave little Ms English to freshen up. Take a shower, take a nap … whatever you want. Feel at home. I've got a couple of errands to run and then we can have a couple of drinks in the garden before dinner. Get us in the mood. I've booked a table at Spago's. I met Jack Nicholson there last night. Ooh, and Harrison Ford the other week! He is *so* totally Indiana Jones – *super* cool.'

'Sounds like you ladies are gonna have a fun evening,' Tim said, giving Melanie a slow wink that sent her stomach immediately into knots. 'You sure you don't want some company?'

'We *got* company,' Tina laughed again, pushing him out of the room. 'Each other. Now, get out of here. Leave the girl in peace.' She closed the door behind her, still chuckling. Tina was always laughing. That was why she'd come.

13

Améline's knees were knocking so badly she was sure Père Estimé, the elderly family priest, could hear them. Although, technically speaking, he wasn't really a priest. He'd been thrown out of the Catholic Church over twenty years ago – God alone knew why – but he kept his stiff, starched white collar and air of avuncular concern, and people still called him Père, regardless of what had happened in the past. There were even rumours among the servants that he was a *Macoute*, a member of Duvalier's dreaded secret police. Améline had no idea if it were true, not that she cared. It was terrifying enough sitting next to him, keeping a wary eye on his hands. His wandering hands. She'd heard about those, too. She sat as far away from him as possible, her own hands trapped firmly underneath her thighs. Madame was in the front parlour with Madame de Menières and a group of her friends and she was alone in the back room with him.

'So, *ma p'tite* ...' Père Estimé murmured. 'You haven't seen your little friend?' Améline shook her head in petrified silence. She knew exactly who he was talking about. 'You're not alike, you know … very different. *Très différent*,' he mused, almost to himself. He stroked the tip of his moustache with one dark, liver-spotted hand. '*Bon.*' He reached across and brought his hand to rest on her shaking knee. The pressure inside her threatened to boil over. 'If you do happen to see her, tell her … won't you? That I asked after her? It's been a while since I've seen her and these days, one can't be too careful. There's no telling what sort of company she might fall into. Why, perhaps she's fallen already?' He slid his hand further up Améline's thigh. Fortunately, the sound of Madame's voice brought his explorations to an abrupt halt. Améline could have fainted with relief.

'Père Estimé,' Madame called out to him. 'Do come through. You are so kind to spend time on these foolish young girls but come, enough. Madame de Menières was just saying …'

Père Estimé got up, breathing heavily and patted Améline on the head. She steeled herself not to shrink from his touch, and fled the room.

Back inside the safety of her own room, she pushed shut the door and leaned against it, willing herself to breathe normally. In a few seconds, she would be called to take the trays that Cléones and Pricienne, the part-time cook, had prepared. Her mind was racing. Had he seen Laure somewhere? Had someone reported her? Haiti was full of secrets; whispering informants were simply part of the culture. Someone, somewhere, must have said something. But what?

'Améline!' She heard Cléones shout for her. She secured her springy hair in as tidy a knot as she could and with shaking hands opened her door. 'Come on! Hurry up. Take this tray through. Wait … take the teapot, you imbecile!'

Père Estimé sat in the upholstered chair at one end of the room. He beamed at her as she walked forwards, carefully setting the tray down. It was only when she straightened up that she realised he'd been looking straight down her dress. Flustered, she turned, holding the teapot, and knocked against

58

the table. Cups rolled in their saucers, teaspoons rattled and to make matters worse, she spilled some of the scalding tea on the carpet.

'*Quelle idiote!*' Madame hissed at her as she hurriedly put down the teapot and backed towards the door. 'Honestly. You just can't get the staff these days. It must be in their blood … this one, she's been with us since birth … and still. Look.'

'*Oui*,' Madame de Menières murmured, looking Améline up and down with thinly disguised disdain. 'Idiots, every last one.'

'Oh, come now, ladies,' she heard Père Estimé say, his voice laced with thick, treacly charm. 'A little Christian charity, surely?'

Améline almost vomited.

Later that evening, when Madame had retired to bed, Améline slipped into the house and ran lightly up the stairs to Laure's room. She tapped as quietly as she could on the door. Laure wouldn't take kindly to being disturbed in the middle of her preparations for going out. Améline had heard the water trickling down the drainpipe as Laure showered.

'What is it?' Laure opened the door a crack.

'I need to talk to you,' Améline whispered. 'It's urgent.'

Laure frowned, then opened the door. Améline slipped in silently. 'What about?' Laure asked, picking up her hairbrush. Améline stared at her. She'd never seen Laure with make-up on. Her hair was released from its usual grips and rubber bands and hung in clouds of curls around her face. Her lips were shiny and there was something sparkly above her eyes. She looked like a picture in a magazine. Beautiful. Frightening.

'It's Père Estimé,' Améline began haltingly. She struggled with the words. 'He was here this afternoon … and he asked about you. He said …' She swallowed. 'He said something about you not being there … and asked where you were. And it sounded like … well, as if he knew … or he'd seen you somewhere …' Her voice trailed off.

'Fucking goat,' Laure said scornfully. She put down her

hairbrush. 'Just tell him to go to hell,' she said, turning her back to Améline. 'And to mind his own business.'

'Oh, Lulu … I can't say that. He might … he might tell … you know, he might say something.'

'Like I care?' There was anger in Laure's voice. Then, to Améline's surprise, she fished in her pocket for something and brought out a packet of cigarettes. Améline stared at them in disbelief. When had Laure started smoking?

'Lulu … I'm just worried …'

'Don't be.' Laure lit a cigarette and blew the smoke out quickly – too quickly. She had only just started smoking, Améline saw. 'I can take care of myself,' she said with a confidence that Améline had never seen before. 'Look, I've got to get ready.' She stubbed out the cigarette and walked towards her bathroom. 'You haven't said anything, have you? To anyone?'

'Me? Of course not!' Améline was indignant. 'I'd never say anything. I'd do anything to protect you …'

'Oh, stop being so melodramatic. Nothing's going to happen to me. I'm just having a little fun, that's all. I'll bring you back something,' Laure added, turning to smile at her. 'I promise.'

Améline could only stare at her. Laure disappeared into the bathroom. Améline had no option but to leave. Her heart was heavy as she walked silently down the stairs. She desperately hoped Laure was right.

A few days passed and nothing happened. Améline began to breathe more easily. Since Père Estimé's last visit, she'd kept well out of his way. Oh, she'd heard the stories, mostly through Cléones, about what he got up to with the servant girls in the houses around them but he wouldn't dare to come near *her*, would he? She was the *reste-avec*, not a servant. True, Madame didn't seem to think there was much distinction but she'd always thought *she* was safe. She shuddered. She hoped she was right. He was repulsive.

She heard Cléones yelling for her. She hurried through to the kitchen. 'Madame has guests again,' Cléones said, banging the cups angrily onto a tray and thrusting it at her. 'Quick! Take these through to her. Hurry, girl.' Améline took the tray and walked down the corridor. This time, Père Estimé was seated behind her as she bent down to pour the tea. When she straightened up and turned, she could see his hooded eyes sweeping over her entire body. She felt faint with disgust. 'Bring some more hot water,' Madame barked at her. 'You know Madame Dupuy doesn't like her tea strong.' Améline scuttled out of the room.

She had just finished setting the hot water on the tray and was about to open the kitchen door when she heard footsteps in the corridor outside. The door opened and Père Estimé stood in the doorway, a coldly lascivious smile on his face. 'Allow me to help, *ma p'tite*,' he said, holding the door open for her. There was barely enough room to squeeze between his protruding stomach and the door, Améline saw, her mouth suddenly dry. Whichever way she did it, she would have to squeeze some part of her body against his. She swallowed. '*Viens*. Madame is waiting,' he murmured, lowering his gaze to her chest, as flat as it was.

Suddenly, the back door opened and Cléones stepped in. She looked up as she entered, and caught Améline's frightened eye. Something passed between them, much to Améline's surprise. Cléones was a servant. Under normal circumstances she shouldn't even have been bold enough to look Père Estimé directly in the face. He was a priest, albeit a fallen one, on a social par with her employer, Madame St Lazâre. Améline looked on in amazement as Cléones folded her arms, eyed Père Estimé calmly and then told her to put the tray down and to wait outside. Améline hesitated.

'Go on, girl,' Cléones repeated softly. 'I'll take it. You won't be serving tea any longer. Not while I'm in this house.' She lifted her chin. Père Estimé made a short sound of annoyance and moved away from the door. Cléones and Améline watched it swing once, twice, in silence, before it settled back in its place. Cléones moved towards the counter and picked up the tray. 'He won't bother you again,' she said quietly, nodding at her. And with that, she pushed open the door and disappeared. Améline blinked slowly. Cléones? She'd protected her?

14

'They're great, aren't they?' Tina shouted to her above the sound of the music. Melanie nodded slowly. Actually, they weren't *that* great – she'd heard bands that were much, much better – but Tina seemed to like them ... and Tina had good taste, didn't she? 'Fucking *awe*some!' Tina shouted, lifting her hands above her head and clapping enthusiastically with the rest of the crowd. Sometimes it was hard to believe Tina was over forty. Melanie looked around her. They were in Shakey's on Sunset, *the* venue in LA for hot new acts. It was so dark inside she could hardly see anything; instead she concentrated on the drink in her hand and the sound of Tina's voice somewhere next to her left ear. She sighed. She'd been in LA for almost a month and, though she would never, ever say so, especially not to Tina, she was just a little ... well, bored, to tell the truth. Tina was at work or at the gym most of the day, leaving Melanie to float around in the turquoise pool or flop in front of the giant TV screen in the living room with a bowl of microwaved popcorn which seemed to be the only food in the house. Tina did not cook. Or eat. Period. Melanie couldn't drive and taking public transport to go anywhere in LA was absolutely out of the question. Tim, the gorgeous pool man, only came once a week and, after a couple of afternoons spent lying in the water watching the muscles rippling in his back as he cleaned the pool, she'd realised there wasn't a whole lot they could talk about. His conversation skills were pretty limited. 'Oh, yeah?' 'Really?' 'Cool.' And that was about it. No matter *what* she said, his responses were always the same. After a month, she was longing to talk to someone. *Any*one. Even her mother. Especially her mother. But Mike had warned her not to try. 'She'll come round,' he'd said to her the last time they'd spoken. 'Give her a bit of space.' Well, she was fed up giving everyone space. She wanted someone to talk to. Now.

The band on stage screamed into their microphones one last time, whirled around a couple of times and the lead singer did the obligatory splits. The crowd yelled their approval, the music reached a crescendo and ... that was it. The lights went down on stage, went up at the back of the hall and the concert was over.

'Melanie? Over here! Come on,' Tina shouted to her over the voices around them. 'Let's go backstage.' Melanie swallowed the rest of her drink in one gulp and followed Tina through the crowd. It was one of the perks of Tina's job – she got to meet everyone, and therefore Melanie did. Melanie wasn't sure she really wanted to meet the band but twenty minutes later, sitting in a small booth at Judy Juke's, the diner across the road from Shakey's where everyone who was anyone in the rock world went, she soon changed her mind. Rudy, the lead singer with Lone Star, the band she'd just heard, was a quiet, intense young man who had a way of looking at her that made her blush to the roots. He was taut, lean, dark ... beneath the thin skin of his temple a pulse throbbed faintly, persistently. Melanie sat next to him, her pulse quickening. Suddenly LA seemed a lot more interesting.

15

Laure sat on the edge of the bath and closed her eyes in anguish. How could it have happened? Delroy was careful – overly careful. There was simply no way a teenage girl in Haiti could hope to get her hands on any form of birth control so he'd told her to leave it all to him. And so she had. As much as she hated the messy little *capots* he seemed to have in unlimited supply there just didn't seem to be any other choice. And it seemed to work. Until now. She turned and retched into the toilet bowl for the second time. The truth of the matter was that the nausea in her stomach was nothing compared to the fear that now flowed through her veins. At the thought of Grand-mère's face when she found out … she threw up again … and again.

Half an hour later, she crept into the kitchen, the taste of bile still fresh in her throat, and opened the fridge door. She needed something – orange juice, lemon juice, anything – to clear the taste from her mouth. She had just finished pouring herself a glass when the back door swung open and Cléones walked in. Laure looked up. Cléones looked at her and, in that instant, the knowledge of what had happened to her passed silently between them. Cléones knew. Of course she knew. There was very little that escaped Cléones' eyes. Her hand shook as she lifted the glass to her mouth.

'Piece of bread. Dry.' Cléones' tone was matter-of-fact.

Laure was silent. She could hear Améline coming through into the kitchen from the yard. Seconds later, the bile rose in her again and she barely managed to make it to the sink before doubling over and retching.

'What's the matter with her?' she heard Améline ask as she came into the kitchen. Cléones said nothing. 'Are you all right?' she asked, coming over to the sink. Laure could only nod. Then a fresh wave of nausea flowed over her and she retched again. 'Lulu!' Améline sounded alarmed. 'What's wrong? Did you eat something bad?' Cléones made a small sound of exasperation. Améline looked up. 'What's the matter with her?' she repeated.

Laure straightened up, wiping her mouth with the back of her hand. 'I'm fine,' she said, in a voice that indicated she was anything but. 'I'm fine.'

'Don't know how anyone can call being in your condition "fine",' Cléones snorted, pulling the singing kettle off the stove.

Améline stared at her, then at Laure. 'What're you talking about? What condition?' she whispered.

Laure closed her eyes. There was a long, drawn-out silence in which she could hear her heartbeat, a steady, powerful thump, and the ticking of the clock in the hallway. She could feel Améline's eyes on her but no one said a thing. Then Cléones picked up the kettle, poured the hot water into the waiting teapot and stomped out of the room.

Laure cleared her throat. The sound was loud in the empty kitchen. Then she turned and fled.

In the ghostly neon light flickering through the shutters, Delroy looked at her, his expression unreadable. Laure sat on the stiff wooden chair in the room they'd been coming to at the Hotel d'Amour for the past few months and stared at her feet. His reaction wasn't quite what she'd expected. They sat in uneasy silence for a few minutes.

'I could ...'

'Don't you know ...?' They both spoke at once. Delroy lit a cigarette. Laure cleared her throat.

'I could ... we could keep the ... baby,' Laure said hesitantly. 'I mean, I know we never talked about ... about that, but Améline could come and live with us and ...'

'What are you talking about?' Delroy's cigarette almost fell out of his mouth. 'Are you crazy?'

'No ... I just ... I thought ...'

'Girl, my wife will go ape-shit over this ...'

'Your *wife*?' It was Laure's turn to look incredulous. 'You have a wife?'

''Course I have a wife. What kind of a question is that?'

'But ... you ...' Laure stared at him, aware of the fierce and sudden burning behind her eyes. Of *course* he had a wife. The man sitting opposite her on the bed drawing smoke up into his lungs was not the same man she knew. With those three little words – *I'm pregnant* – everything had changed. Including him. She sat stiffly upright, her whole body held rigid against the pain and fear – yes, fear – that was slowly seeping through her veins. He had a wife. There would be no happy ever after. He looked as though he couldn't wait to get away.

'Don't you know somebody?' he asked her, stubbing out his cigarette. 'Somebody who can help you?'

'Help me?' Laure repeated woodenly.

'Yeah. Get rid of it. You ain't planning on keepin' it, are you?'

'I ... I don't know ...'

'Girl, have you lost your mind? Shit, you so scared of your grandmother. How the hell are you gonna tell her?'

Laure sat very still. She drew a deep breath, feeling the last remnants of hope slip away. Her lips tightened, almost imperceptibly. *Come to me.* She heard her mother's voice suddenly, loud in her ear. *I'll take care of you.* She lifted her eyes and looked at Delroy. 'Don't worry. I'll figure something out.' Then she got up very carefully, picked up her little handbag and walked out of the room.

Améline hovered outside Laure's door, unsure whether to go in. She heard the grandfather clock chime downstairs. It was almost six. Madame would be on her way back from the club and she still hadn't finished preparing supper. She chewed her lip, still hesitating. Finally, she tapped on the door. 'Lulu, it's me ... I've got something. Can I come in?' She heard Laure's faint answer and pushed open the door. She was sitting on the bed, her arms wrapped protectively around her stomach. 'Cléones said to give this to you,' Améline said, sitting gingerly beside her. 'Quinine,' she held out a small glass vial. 'And peacock flower.' She put down a glass of water on the bedside table.

'Wh ... where did ... what is it?' Laure asked, her voice hoarse. She looked at the little glass bottles. The first was a milky, watery liquid; the second was a dark, thick paste. She shuddered.

'She said it works,' Améline said quietly. 'She said you'll have some pains first, but then the blood will come. Take the quinine first,' she said, remembering what Cléones had told her. 'It's a little bitter but it's quick. When the bleeding starts, take

66

the other one. I'll come up later.' She put an arm round Laure and hugged her tight. Laure leaned against her for a moment, dizzy with fear. She grabbed hold of Améline's hand. Améline hugged her again and got up. 'I'd better go,' she said. 'Madame will be here any minute. Shall I bring you something to eat? If you don't want to come downstairs?' Laure shook her head weakly. Food was the last thing on her mind. 'I'll be back later,' Améline said, reaching for the door. 'I'll bring you some juice.' Laure couldn't bring herself to answer. She stared at the bottles Améline had left behind.

The quinine *was* bitter. She gagged and forced herself to swallow every last drop. The inside of her mouth felt raw, then a rush of saliva flooded in, triggered by the sharp, unpleasant taste. She waited for a few seconds then took a sip of water. What was supposed to happen next? She lay back against the pillows, feeling a little short of breath. Her mind was whirling. Her mother had spoken to her, told her to come. At the time, watching Delroy shrink from her, it had seemed the only way out. But once she was back in her room, it seemed an almost impossible feat. How would she go? She had – she'd checked as soon as she got to her room – less than a hundred dollars in her little savings book. She would need a plane ticket, a visa, some money … she didn't even know where Belle lived or her telephone number. There was no way of contacting Belle unless she asked Grandmère, and at the thought of it her stomach contracted painfully. She looked at her watch. Fifteen minutes had passed – perhaps it was working already? Relief began to flow through her in place of the cold, liquid fear that she'd slowly grown used to. She closed her eyes and prayed that whatever was supposed to happen, it wouldn't hurt. She had never been able to stand pain.

But nothing happened. Améline crept up the stairs after supper with a plate of cold chicken and rice, neither of which Laure could face. She had been in and out of bed every thirty minutes … not a drop of blood. The thick, semi-hardened paste of peacock flowers lay, untouched, on the saucer beside her. She sat up, waiting for the by-now familiar wave of nausea to hit. Améline would be up any minute … she felt a sharp stab of fear. What would she suggest next?

Laure looked from Améline to Cléones and slowly shook her head. No. There was *no* way she was going to visit a *hougoun*, a priest-doctor of the Haitian *vaudoun* religion that Grandmère so despised. No priest. No voodoo. No *way*. Cléones looked at her, shaking her head. '*Li nwa tan kou bombon siwo*,' she said, looking straight at Laure. *It'll be dark as sugarcane syrup cake.* Laure stared at her incredulously. Did Cléones think it was because she was afraid the baby would come out dark that she wanted to get rid of it?

'I don't *care* what colour the child is,' she said, stung by Cléones' words. 'I don't want it, d'you hear? I don't *want* it.'

'You're a St Lazâre,' Cléones said disparagingly. 'Of course you care.'

'What are you talking about?' Laure stared at her.

'St Lazâres,' Cléones said calmly. 'They *always* care about the colour. That's why …' She stopped suddenly.

'That's why *what*? Laure said, her pulse quickening. 'I don't understand. What are you talking about?'

'Maybe you should just give her another dose of quinine,' Améline said hurriedly, trying to change the subject. Cléones had that wild, dangerous look in her eyes that usually preceded an attack on the St Lazâre family. Améline was sure it was the last thing Laure needed to hear at a time like this.

Laure ignored her. She looked at Cléones. 'You'd better tell me exactly what you mean,' she said quietly. 'If you've got something to tell me, do it now.' There was a tense silence. Then Cléones started moving around the kitchen, slamming down pans and closing cupboard doors with a bang. Finally, she stopped and turned to Laure. Her face bore a strange, almost twisted smile.

'You ask your grandmother where she comes from,' she said finally. 'Ask her who she married – and ask her who *she* is.' She pointed to Améline. 'Ask your grandmother 'bout Casales. See what she tells you. And *then* you come back and see me about

68

the *hougoun*.' She kicked one of the cabinet doors shut, threw down her dish-towel and marched out of the kitchen. Améline stared after her for a second, then, without saying a word to Laure, disappeared after her.

Laure sat for a few moments in the kitchen, her thoughts whirling around in her head. What was Cléones talking about? What did she mean about Grandmère? Who or what was Casales? And what was that about Améline? She buried her hands in her thick cloud of hair. It was all too much. She was in trouble and, as far as she could see, there was only one solution. The thought of it made her ill with fear.

There was complete silence in the room. Laure sat on the edge of the upholstered chair, holding on to the sides as if she might fall off.

'How far?' Grandmère spat the words out after what seemed like an eternity.

Laure could not meet her eyes. 'Two months,' she whispered.

'*Two* months?' Grandmère swallowed. 'And the father?'

Laure shook her head. She couldn't – or wouldn't – say.

Grandmère said nothing. Minutes went by. Finally, she spoke. '*Bon.* You had better go away. To Chicago. To Belle. It's what you always wanted, *n'est ce pas?*' Then she got up stiffly from her chair and walked out of the room.

PART TWO

16

Chicago, USA 1985

It was like stepping off the edge of a cliff or falling through a crack in the road, tumbling out of one world and suddenly finding herself, lost and abandoned, in another. First the long, silent drive to the airport, heartsick at the sight of Améline's stricken face in the doorway and the tightening of Grandmère's lips as they walked slowly towards the car. She'd dreamed about leaving Haiti for almost as long as she could remember but she'd never thought about leaving *this* way. In disgrace. In the weeks leading up to her departure, the accusations were flung silently at her, despite Grandmère's attempts to cover everything up. *Just like her mother. Well, what do you expect? The apple never falls far from the tree.* Madame de Menières took one look at her and guessed correctly. 'Off to America, hmm, Laure? To see your *maman*? Well, it's for the best, I suppose. Can't be helped.'

And then there was the terrifying flight from Port-au-Prince to Miami. She looked out the window as the plane began to thunder down the runway and almost vomited in fear. She'd never been in an aeroplane before; much less been at a busy international airport. At Miami airport she was shunted from one terminal to the next, her heart in her mouth as she struggled to make sense of what was being said to her. The English spoken in America was a million miles away from the quiet, sedate British voices she'd half-heartedly paid attention to in school. Here they swallowed their words, spoke through their noses and always, always ... those terrifyingly dazzling smiles. She saw Delroy in everyone she met.

A few hours later she boarded another flight that took her north, to Chicago. Belle was not at the airport to meet her. She had the address; in her halting, schoolgirl English, she found a taxi driver who seemed to know where 76 N. Keeler might be. If anything, the drive from the airport through the wintry, powdery streets of the biggest city she'd ever seen in her life was even more terrifying that the flight. Chicago appeared to be nothing more than shiny tongues of concrete carrying more cars than she'd known existed. She leaned back in the seat and tried not to think. Four months ago, she'd been a carefree teenager shimmying up and down the thick, gnarled branch of the jacaranda tree outside her bedroom, rushing off to meet Delroy without a thought or care in the world. School, Régine, Saturday afternoons at the club pool ... three meals a day on the table and there was always Améline to talk to. At the thought of her, Laure's throat tightened painfully. What was Améline doing now? In the week before Laure's departure, Améline had cried every day, almost without stopping. Laure couldn't cry. Ever since Grandmère had spoken to Belle on the phone – *imagine, she'd known all along how to contact her!* – she'd been unable to think about leaving Améline. She'd barely given a thought to leaving school, even if it did mean leaving Régine and Martine, and she certainly wasn't going to miss Grandmère. But Améline ... she had talked to Améline every day of her life; they were like sisters ... they *were* sisters. Laure hadn't spent a single night of her life away from home or away from Améline; not once, not ever. It was inconceivable to her that where she was going, Améline wouldn't be able to follow. Her heart felt as though it were slowly being squeezed to death. She tried instead to concentrate fiercely on what lay ahead.

After what seemed like hours, the cab finally pulled up to a building just after six. The driver turned his head to look at her. 'This it, lady?' he asked her. Laure looked at him blankly. 'This the place you lookin' for?' he repeated.

She shook her head. 'No understand,' she said hesitantly.

'Shit. Here, gimme that.' He held out his hand for the

paper Laure had been hanging on to for dear life ever since the plane left Port-au-Prince. She handed it over. He glanced at it. 'Yeah, seventy-six North Keeler. This is it.' He shoved the paper back through the glass opening. Laure looked up at the façade from the safety of the back seat. She had never, in all her life, seen anything as ugly. The building was huge, an enormous, dirty, blank-looking fortress – she gazed up at the broken windows, graffiti-plastered walls and stunted bare trees in a yard surrounded by chicken-wire and gulped. This couldn't be it. There had to be some mistake. This couldn't be Belle's home, could it?

'Keeler Avenue?' she asked the driver. He nodded impatiently.

'Yeah, this here's seventy-six North Keeler, lady. Why'nt you go on up and see if whoever's expecting you is home? Go on, girl. This here's it.' He got out of the cab and walked round to her door. He held it open for her. 'Go on now,' he said, a little less gruffly as he noticed her protruding stomach. 'Look, I'll wait for you, make sure they're home. This here ain't no neighbourhood for you to be hangin' around in.' Laure shook her head helplessly. She hadn't understood a word. She took a deep breath and pulled herself out of the cab. She shivered in the cold air. It was colder than anywhere she'd ever been. She pulled the cardigan she'd taken from the trunks in the attic around her shoulders and walked up the steps.

A kid on a broken tricycle appeared out of nowhere and began weaving a pattern around her as she stood uncertainly in front of the gate.

'Yo!' he shouted at her, noticing her gaze. 'Who you lookin' at?' Laure stared at him. So aggressive for someone his size! She lifted and shrugged her shoulders. She couldn't understand a word of what he said either. 'Yo!' the child shouted at her again. Across the road, the cab driver was watching her with a weary air. She swallowed and pushed open the wire gate.

There was a row of names and buzzers to her left. The front door to the building – she saw now that it was an apartment complex – was a thick, solid steel door with multiple locks and bolts and a wire screen covering a tiny porthole. She peered in. She couldn't see a thing; it was completely dark inside. She turned and looked at the buzzers. *Lewis. Gonzalez. Marimba. Taylor. St Lazâre.* She stopped. *B. St Lazâre.* She lifted a finger, crossed herself quickly, then pressed the buzzer. A few seconds passed. Nothing happened. She turned to look at the cab driver, now sitting inside, smoking and reading a paper. She turned back. And pressed the bell again, harder. This time there was a loud, angry answering buzz from the steel door. She pushed at the door quickly, and suddenly, she was in.

It took a few seconds for her eyes to adjust to the dim and gloom – and for her nose to adjust to the smell. Urine, spilt beer, cigarette smoke. She almost gagged. She looked left and right down the corridor, straining to see. 1A, 1B, 1C. The silvery numbers glinted back at her. She looked down at the paper. There was no apartment number, just the street number. She bit her lip. She had forgotten to look on the row of buzzers. She was just about to turn and push open the heavy door again when a door opened at the far end of the corridor. A woman stood in the doorway, framed by the light.

'Laure? *C'est toi?*' Laure looked down the hallway, her heart thumping, the sound of her own breathing loud in her ears. It was Belle.

'*Oui,*' she called back softly. She had almost lost her voice.

'*Viens.*' Come. She gripped her bag and began to walk towards her. She stared at the woman standing in the doorway. Tall, like herself, strong-looking, maybe a little heavier around the middle than she'd imagined. Fair skin, the colour of milky coffee; straightened hair, light brown, falling over her face in loose curls ... and the face. She'd carried the image of the poised, carefully composed face of the nineteen-year-old Belle in her head since the day Améline had found the photograph – it bore no relation to the thirty-something-year-old woman who stood in front of her, smoking calmly; a tiny, almost un-noticeable trembling in her fingers as she lifted the cigarette to her mouth again and again, the only sign that there was anything even remotely emotional about their reunion. Was it

76

even a reunion? She had no memory of her mother; nothing ... not a single thing. She was two when Belle left, leaving behind a trunk in the attic full of perfumed, smoky clothes and her baby daughter, promising to return. She never did. And now here she was.

'*Viens*,' Belle said again, holding open the front door. She looked briefly at Laure's stomach as she squeezed herself past. The door closed behind them. 'Come on in,' she said, leading the way down the narrow corridor. 'Sitting room's in here.'

Laure looked around her, her nose wrinkling involuntarily in disgust. The house in Pétionville might no longer be quite as elegant, perhaps, as it once had been but at least it was clean. Between Cléones, 'Ti Jean and Améline, there wasn't a square centimetre of the entire place that wasn't polished and shining. *This* – she looked nervously around the room again – this was *dirty*. No, filthy. Squalid. Her eye fell on the carpet. Mottled with stains, covered in fluff and bits of dirt, worn thin in places ... the walls were stained – coffee and the remnants of food that had been flung against the walls. She swallowed again, feeling the bile rise in her throat. *This* was what Belle had asked her to come to? She saw again the pale blue envelope, reread the lines, '*Ma chère Laure ... come to me. I am your mother, now and always, no matter what they say.*' It wasn't true. If it were, how could she have brought her to this? It came to her suddenly, flooding her mouth, alongside the bile she'd been fighting to keep down. Grandmère was right. Belle didn't *really* want her. Belle wasn't even capable of looking after herself. Oh God, what had she let herself in for?

A couple of hours later, after an uncomfortable and inedible dinner in front of the television during which Belle talked almost incessantly about herself, Laure found herself in the narrow little room which Belle said was now hers. She sat down gingerly on the unmade bed, too stunned to even think clearly. From a source of understanding she wasn't even aware she had, it came to her that Belle didn't like having her pregnant, teenage daughter around. Just as it had been before, Laure supposed. She hadn't wanted her then and she didn't want her now. Simple as that. Perhaps the sight of Laure's burgeoning stomach was too strong a reminder of who she'd been, once – of what she, Belle, had done? Perhaps Belle simply wanted to forget; just as Laure did now. Like mother, like daughter. History playing the same song, over and over again. Madame de Menières was right. *The apple had fallen at the foot of the tree.*

Laure buried her head in the thin, hard pillow in the room that smelled of dirt, booze and cigarettes and tried to forget about everything she'd known before she came here. It was the only way she could manage, she told herself. Forget it all. Everything. But she couldn't forget Améline, no matter how hard she tried, nor the growing reminder inside her of what she and Delroy had done.

17

Port-au-Prince, Haiti 1985

The day Laure left was, without doubt, the worst day of Améline's entire life. She thought her heart would simply split in half. She'd begun crying a full week before Laure was due to leave; she was come upon in the hallway or out in the backyard, face ugly and swollen with tears, weeping as if there were no end to the tears her body could produce. But the day Laure left was worse. Even Cléones was moved to shed a tear or two in the hour before Père Estimé and Grandmère drove Laure to the airport.

After the black car had slipped below the horizon and Améline was left on the sidewalk, ignoring the pursed lips and sideways glances of the neighbours and their servants, she walked into her little room, pulled back the covers and slid into bed. She ignored Cléones' increasingly strident demands that she get out of bed – 'now! Girl, will you get up!' – and give her a hand with supper preparations. When Madame returned from the airport and was told that Améline refused to get up, even she pushed open the door and enquired in a stiff, controlled voice if there was anything genuinely wrong with her. Améline couldn't answer. She turned her face to the wall and – she couldn't believe she'd had the guts to do it – ignored her.

'What on earth is the matter with you, girl? Are you sick?' Madame asked impatiently. There was only silence from the lump in the bed.

'Answer Madame, you wretch!' Cléones spat at her in Creole. Améline said nothing. She didn't even move.

'But whatever is the matter with her?' she heard Madame ask, as both she and Cléones were forced to retreat.

'She's just acting,' Cléones said brusquely. 'Making such a fuss over ... you know who.'

'Yes, well, if we *all* gave in to our feelings ...' Madame's voice trailed off as she walked back inside the house. Améline bit hard on her finger to stop the swell of rage that was threatening to choke her. *Feelings?* The old cow had none! Who was she to talk about feelings? She closed her eyes and tried to imagine what Laure was doing at that very moment. She couldn't. Améline had never left Port-au-Prince, never sat in an aeroplane, never seen the sea. Laure had tried to show her where she was going in the big atlas that Grandmère kept in the parlour but 'America' meant very little to her – she'd seen pictures of big cities on television; it was almost impossible to understand that that was where Laure would be, now. She could hear Cléones banging pots and pans angrily in the kitchen; she turned her face to the wall and wept.

Améline went about her household chores, fractionally reduced in number now that she was no longer required to look after Laure, or her things. But she still cleaned Laure's room every day, carefully dusting the few possessions that had been left there as though she might return at any moment. There was a little glass ballerina figure that Régine's mother had given her after the two girls started ballet together, before Madame had put an end to the classes. Too expensive, she'd said. Améline touched the figurine lightly, lovingly. It was so pretty. There was a round, heavy paperweight ... 'New York City', it read. A miniature landscape of impossibly tall buildings in a transparent, faintly blue liquid: when you turned it upside down, tiny white flakes filled the object. Snow, Laure had told her. Neither of them had ever seen snow before. Delroy had given it to her, Laure had told her. Améline wondered why Laure had left it behind. Two tortoiseshell hair clips, an empty pink silk wallet ... there wasn't much.

Sometimes she left a flower in the little silver vase that had stood on Laure's dressing table for as long as she could remember. Not knowing what else to do, she prayed for Laure. She clasped her hands together, fervently asking God to watch over Laure now that she no longer could. She missed her more than she could put into words.

In that strange, empty frame of mind dominated by thoughts of Laure, it occurred to her suddenly one morning a week or so after Laure had gone that she too might leave. Why not? What would the future hold for her? She could see quite clearly what was being mapped out for her. Cléones was getting on; she was no longer able to do much more than cook. 'Ti Jean could barely look after the garden; he couldn't bend down, he told a pursed-lipped Madame one morning. Perhaps Améline ought to start weeding the vegetable patch? Améline heard them discussing the already long list of her duties – now that Laure was gone, they seemed to think she had nothing to do all day. Améline listened to them with a sinking heart. She knew what usually happened to the servants in the big houses around them. Now that she was no longer really a *reste-avec*, the person for whom she'd been a childhood companion having left the house, the same would surely happen to her. What would happen when Cléones wasn't around to protect her, not just from Père Estimé, but from anyone else who managed to worm his way into the St Lazâre household? Madame would probably be only too glad to get rid of her, the way things were going. And even if *that* didn't happen, what else was there? A lifetime spent cleaning, cooking, carrying ... working herself into the positions left over by Cléones and 'Ti Jean. She wouldn't be the first *reste-avec* to graduate downwards from companion to cook, but Améline wanted more. Something else. A different kind of life. She couldn't do what Laure had done – leaving Haiti was about as likely as going to the moon – but there were other options, weren't there? She'd heard about jobs in some of the hotels that dotted the hills around them. Maids, concierges, waitresses ... she'd do anything to get out of the house that reeked of sadness and was still full of the sounds of Laure's voice. Anything to get away from *that*.

That Sunday, ten days after Laure's departure and propelled along as if by some unseen force, Améline walked the three and a half miles to the Hotel Palme d'Or, on the neighbouring hill, and presented herself at reception. She'd heard from the cook at the de Menière's that the manager at the Palme d'Or was looking for extra staff for Christmas, which was just over a month away. It had taken her barely five minutes to decide. She'd pulled off her apron, combed her hair back and scraped it into a small bun. A neatly pressed white shirt that she'd found in Laure's cupboard – something that she'd left behind – Laure's old school skirt which fell just before her knees. She'd looked at herself quickly in the mirror in the hallway before Madame descended for breakfast. She looked decent enough, didn't she? Clean, neat, tidy ... what else was a maid supposed to look like?

'*Oui?*' The frosty, very light-skinned mulatta at the reception desk looked her up and down imperiously.

'I ... I heard ... someone told me ... about a job here,' Améline began, butterflies whirling around in her stomach. She couldn't quite believe what she was doing. She'd worked at Madame St Lazâre's all her life; she could imagine no other. And yet here she was, having walked three and a half miles to get here, applying for a job that would take her away from everything she'd ever known. But with Laure gone, what was the point of staying?

'Ah. *Gaspard*!' The woman turned and shouted through to the back office. 'Someone's looking for you.' She motioned Améline through with a red-tipped fingernail and a bored expression on her face. 'Ask him. *I* don't handle the staff.' I bet you don't, Améline thought to herself as she walked around the counter.

'*Oui*?' Gaspard, a pasty-faced Frenchman, looked distinctly unimpressed.

'I was ... I heard that you might be looking for staff,' Améline began nervously. 'For Christmas ... maybe longer? My friend ...'

'What can you do?' The man's tone was brusque.

'I can cook,' Améline said hesitantly.

'No. I don't need a cook. I'm looking for chambermaids. You know what that is?'

'Of course I know what a chambermaid is,' she said, a little more sharply than she ought. She forced herself to meet his gaze.

Gaspard looked at her properly for the first time. 'My ... aren't we the little feisty one,' he said archly. 'What's your name?'

'Améline, sir.'

'Améline? Just Améline?'

'Just Améline,' she said quietly. He looked at her appraisingly.

'How old are you?'

'Twenty-one,' Améline hazarded a guess.

'Well ... when d'you want to start?'

'Tomorrow?' Améline asked, unable to keep the excitement from her voice.

'Tomorrow? Well, yes, I suppose so ... why not? We have two shifts a day. One starts at six a.m. and ends at four p.m., and the other's from four p.m. to midnight. Thirty rooms, four suites and the restaurant area. All to be spotless by the time your

82

shift ends. You'll get lunch if you work the daytime shift and dinner if you work at night. Six days a week, mind ... pay's not much, I have to tell you, but if you're in need of accommodation, we can work something out. That suit you?'

'Oh, *yes*. Th ... thank you. Thank you *so much*.' Améline was suddenly close to tears.

'Well, let's see how you get on before you start thanking me. It's hard work, you know, *ma p'tite*.'

'I know. I'm a hard worker, *m ... m'sieur*.' She didn't know what to call him.

'Call me Gaspard. I'm the duty manager. That's Rosalie on reception. There's two other chambermaids ... you'll meet them tomorrow and the rest of the restaurant crew. We're not the biggest in Port-au-Prince but we aim to be the best.'

Améline nodded, too overcome with gratitude to speak. She didn't care how hard she had to work. Anything – *anything* – would be better than staying where she was.

She practically ran all the way back to the house. She finished her chores, ignoring the look of suppressed outrage on Cléones' face – where had she been? Améline refused to say. She picked up her dusters and brooms and exited the kitchen before Cléones could ask too much. For the rest of the day she kept well out of her way. As she moved about the rooms, just as she had before, it was hard to believe she'd somehow found the courage to run three and a half miles to seek another kind of life. It was impossible to think that the following day, she'd be gone.

It was only later that night, lying in the inky blackness of her own room, that it really hit her. She was leaving. It had taken her all of fifteen minutes to stuff her worldly possessions into an old bag of Laure's, which she'd carefully placed beside the door. She lay in the dark, open-eyed, almost until dawn.

Cléones was in the kitchen, preparing vegetables for Madame's lunch. Améline pushed open the kitchen door, her bag in hand. Cléones turned and looked at her, blinking slowly.

'I'm ... I'm leaving, Cléones,' she said hesitantly. Cléones had never shown her the slightest bit of affection, but still ... they'd lived and worked together for as long as Améline could remember. She'd never forgotten how Cléones had protected her when she'd expected it least.

'You too?' Cléones' hands continued their peeling and cutting.

'Yes.' Améline felt the sting of tears behind her eyes.

'*Dieu pran swen.*' *God be with you.* Cléones looked at her briefly and then turned her back. That was it.

Améline let the swing door fall shut and turned away. 'Ti Jean wasn't around ... there was no one else to tell. Don't you *dare* start feeling sorry for yourself, she muttered as she opened the back gate. It was almost midday. Fortunately, the sky was overcast and the breeze was cool. She picked up her bag and let the gate swing shut behind her. For the last time.

18

Los Angeles, USA 1985

Things weren't always what they seemed. That, after nearly two months in her new home, was what Melanie had learned about LA. And about life, too. Take Tina, for example – when she was 'on', she was great fun, good company, interested in Melanie and interesting to talk to. Well, perhaps that was stretching it a little ... Tina really only understood one world; the music world and, after two months, Melanie was just the teeniest bit bored with it. But when she was 'down', as she put it, she was almost a different person entirely. Melanie was never sure exactly what type of person to expect each morning when Tina emerged from her room. It was beginning to get on Melanie's nerves. It was like living with two or three different people, none of whom bore any relation to each other. If she didn't know better, she'd say Tina was on drugs. But she wasn't. Was she? And Rudy? Well, what could she say about Rudy? She liked him *a lot*, which, for Melanie, was rather unusual. She was used to being the one whom others sought, especially boys. Part of it, she'd always known, was the fact that she was Mike Miller's daughter ... everyone wanted a piece of Mike and if Melanie was the closest thing available, so be it. *What's your dad really like? Is he as wild as they say? Are you?* The constant refrain had been so much a part of her teenage years that she wasn't sure quite what she'd do if she met someone for whom it was unimportant. Someone who didn't care who her father was. Like Rudy. He didn't seem the slightest bit interested in Mike. *Cool*, was what he'd said when someone told him. And then nothing further. Melanie could have wept with relief. It meant he really liked her, didn't it?

But ... did he? He was maddeningly non-committal. And unpredictable. And inconsistent. He would ring her up at nine a.m., ask in that lazy, laconic voice of his if she wanted to have breakfast ... and then not show up until well after lunch. Something always 'cropped up'. He would ask if she wanted to meet him at Ed Debevedic's on Beverly Boulevard or at Shakey's on Sunset or any of the bars they usually hung out at ... she'd get there, all breathless with anticipation and he'd be there with thirty other people and would barely speak to her all night. He'd kissed her a few times, the sort of kiss she'd always dreamed about – long, slow, warm – but that was it. Sometimes he would put a proprietary hand on her knee, stroking the skin just above her kneecap making her weak with an unspecified, all-over desire, and then he would stop. Turn away. Do something else. She just didn't get it. Bewildered, she would withdraw into herself for a while and then he'd ring up at midnight and spend the next two hours on the phone. No, she didn't get it at all. 'It's LA, honey,' was all Tina would say, maddeningly, whenever Melanie tried to bring the subject up. 'Gotta play the game.' What game? What were the rules? She just didn't get it.

She was drying her hair one evening, having resigned herself sulkily to a Friday night on her own. Rudy had promised to ring her that afternoon, and of course he hadn't. She'd spent most of it staring at the silent phone in her room, willing him to call. He didn't. Tina was at work or at the gym. The house was silent; the maid who came in three times a week had left the place spotless and the polished floorboards squeaked under her bare feet. She twisted her still-damp hair into a knot and wandered into the kitchen, wondering how on earth to go about making dinner. Two months of living with Tina sadly hadn't improved her culinary skills and without a car or friends to go to dinner with, she was beginning to wish she'd paid more attention in her home economics classes. She pulled open the enormous fridge door and stared inside. Champagne, beer, white wine … a piece of yellowed cheese wrapped in cling-film, a bag of lettuce … what on earth could she make with *that*? As she stood there rubbing the bare sole of her foot against her leg, the phone rang. She padded out to the hallway and picked it up. It would be for Tina, of course. It always was.

But for once it wasn't. It was Rudy. Did she want to go to a party? Melanie almost wept with relief.

'I'll pick you up in twenty,' he said and abruptly put down the phone. Melanie almost broke her neck rushing back to the bathroom.

Fifteen minutes later, she was ready. She'd borrowed a silver lamé halter-neck top from Tina's vast wardrobe and slithered herself into a pair of skinny black jeans, somehow managing to zip them up by lying on the bed and forcing herself not to breathe. She looked at herself anxiously in the mirror. Lots of hairspray, a pair of high-heeled patent black stilettos and tons of mascara. She'd begun to copy Tina's make-up – dark, heavily made-up eyes, carefully shaped eyebrows and not much else. She applied a little lip-gloss and stared at herself in the mirror. She certainly didn't look eighteen. She looked … grown up. *Sophisticated*. How could Rudy fail to be impressed? She heard a car pull up into the driveway. He was early! She grabbed her bag and ran to the living room. It wasn't Rudy – it was Tina.

'Wow!' said Tina, opening the front door. 'You look *amazing*, honey. Good enough to eat. Are you going to this party too? *Everyone's* going ... it's gonna be fun. Rudy pickin' you up?'

Melanie nodded, relieved that Tina would also be there. At least she'd have someone to talk to if Rudy sloped off. 'I just want him to notice me,' she murmured, the words slipping out of their own accord. She could feel her cheeks beginning to burn.

'He will, he does ... believe me. He's just playing it cool,' Tina said, smiling at her. 'That's the way it is here. No one wants to chase. Everyone wants to *be* chased. It's like some weird law of the jungle.'

'But why? Why can't he just ... *like* me?' Melanie knew she was sounding plaintive but she couldn't help herself. Three months of 'playing it cool' was killing her.

'He does, he does, baby. Look, stop worrying about Rudy. Just go out and have a good time. You look *amazing*, the men are going to go nuts for you. Just enjoy it!' Tina gave her a firm push towards the door. 'If *I* had your body ...' she said, grinning at her. 'Fuck ... and you don't even have to work at it. *Some* people ...!'

Tina hadn't been exaggerating. *Every*one was indeed standing in line outside the sleek grey concrete and steel box with six giant pink palm trees – fake, of course. Like almost everything else in LA. Powerful floodlights threw streams of light into the sky overhead and even from a block away, they could hear the music. Rudy tossed his keys to the valet and walked quickly across the road, Melanie tripping as fast as she could behind him. The bouncers recognised him, of course, and they were waved through the doors. It was intensely gratifying to see the looks of pure envy thrown her way as Melanie followed him in. There were girls a thousand – no, a *million* – times better-looking than she was, hopping from one high-heeled foot to the other while she just waltzed straight through. Inside, everything was glass and steel – an ultra-modern, ultra-slick interior of the sort that Norbert would probably swoon over. She felt an uncomfortable twinge at the thought of him. It had been nearly three months since she'd spoken to her mother.

'Rudy! Over here, man!' Someone shouted across the crowded floor to them, thankfully interrupting her line of thought. She gazed around her as she followed Rudy. The restaurant tables had been removed and the huge cavernous space was filled with the sound of people drinking, chatting and posing for photographs. As usual, there were more beautiful people per square inch than anywhere else in the world. Even the waiters looked as though they'd stepped out of the pages of a glossy magazine. The man who'd shouted at them wove through the crowd, leading them to a private room at the back of the restaurant – the inner circle of friends of the owner. 'Come on in,' he said, opening the door for them. 'Party's in *here*!' There were perhaps ten or fifteen people sitting in low, leather chairs around the room; Rudy seemed to know them all. 'C'mon, take a seat, man. You too, baby.' Melanie sat down gingerly. She looked around her nervously. Everyone looked incredibly glamorous and ... grown up. She felt like a schoolgirl. The women eyed her up and down, sizing her up in an instant. The men took their time. She could feel her cheeks beginning to burn.

'This is Melanie. From England.' Rudy lazily introduced her to the rest of the table.

A woman held out a red-tipped hand. 'Hello, *Melanie-from-England*. I'm Julie.'

'Mike Miller's daughter,' Rudy added unnecessarily. 'She's with me. So be nice to her. OK?' Everyone laughed.

'Really? Mike Miller's your dad?' Someone else spoke. Melanie nodded reluctantly. 'Cool. That's pretty cool. You sure don't *look* like him.'

'Thank God.' Someone spoke from across the room, laughter in his voice. Melanie looked up. Dark hair pulled back in a ponytail, a tanned, square face, carefully shaved goatee; startlingly blue eyes ... she swallowed. The man looked at her, his gaze direct and frank. She felt the heat rise in her cheeks.

'Oh, *Steve*,' a woman standing next to him said, slapping him playfully on the wrist. 'Didn't you hear what Rudy said? Be *nice* to her.'

'I'm just saying,' the man called Steve said mildly, walking round to where Melanie was sitting. 'Decent enough singer, maybe, but would you want his face on your daughter?' He looked down at Melanie. 'You must take after your mum.' Melanie could only nod dumbly.

'Steve's from England, too,' someone else piped up.

'Steve di Marco,' he said, extending a hand. Melanie took it, hoping he wouldn't notice her shaking fingers. He had rather unnerved her. 'A Londoner, I take it. Whereabouts?'

'Um, Chelsea,' Melanie mumbled, suddenly lost for words.

'A Ranger, no less. Well, well …' Steve looked at her, the corners of his mouth lifting slightly.

'OK, OK. So now we all know each other,' Rudy broke in, sounding faintly irritated. 'Can we get something to drink?' He held up an empty glass. Steve nodded at the two waiters who were hovering discreetly in the corner.

'What can I get you, sir?' One of them came forward, smiling brightly.

'Southern Comfort. On the rocks.'

'Why d'you drink such awful whisky?' Melanie whispered, shaking her head at him.

'What's wrong with it?' Rudy's voice was unnaturally loud. 'What the fuck should I drink?'

Melanie immediately blushed. She hadn't meant to provoke *that* sort of response. 'I only meant … there's lots of other whiskies that are … nice,' she stammered.

'If I want a *nice* drink, I'll have an orange juice. This is *whisky*. There's a difference.' Rudy's voice was positively nasty. Melanie looked at him, confused.

'She's right,' Steve di Marco spoke up suddenly. 'Let me get you something else.' He got up from his chair and walked to a small cupboard at the back of the room. He came back to the table, bearing a half-empty bottle of Glenlivet. Melanie smiled at him, ridiculously grateful. 'This is the good stuff. This is what *I* drink. Here, have a glass. You'll see what she's talking about.'

Rudy shrugged, not bothering to hide his annoyance. Melanie looked quickly at both of them in turn – what was going on? Steve di Marco lifted the bottle and looked straight at her. 'Want some?'

'Er, yes, please.' She was hopelessly out of her depth. She was the youngest person in the room – by at least ten years, she reckoned. Rudy's hand had come to rest possessively on her thigh and she dimly understood she'd embarrassed him. But she hadn't meant to – she'd commented on his choice of whisky simply to have something to say. She took the glass Steve di Marco offered gratefully. Glenlivet was her father's favourite drink. She knew that much. At least.

For the rest of the evening she was subdued, preferring to stay on safer ground by contributing as little as possible to the chatter going on around her – not that she understood much of it anyway. They all talked about people she'd never heard of, and probably never would. Suddenly, she felt terribly homesick. She longed for the safety and familiarity of her room in the house on King's Road and for the sound of Polly's voice. She missed her mother. It felt like ages before the group finally got up and, amidst much noise and laughter, moved out into the main restaurant space. Rudy had gone from gripping her thigh to pretending not to know her. Tina hadn't shown up and no one paid her much attention; Steve di Marco was swallowed up immediately in the crowd of adoring, impossibly gorgeous people who packed his new restaurant. She stood awkwardly to one side, nursing her third glass of Glenlivet and wishing desperately she were somewhere else. A few people smiled at her as they rushed past, obviously on the lookout for someone more beautiful, more famous, more worthwhile than she. She was on the verge of pushing her way through the crowd to find Tina and beg her leave when she felt someone's presence beside her. She turned.

'All on your lonesome?' It was Steve di Marco. Melanie jumped.

'I ... I was just going ...' she stammered, the heat in her rising again at the sound of his voice.

'Going? Going where? Not home, I hope? Party's only just started.' His voice was quiet and seemed to carry with it an invitation she couldn't quite read.

'Oh ... I ... I'm a bit tired,' she said lamely, cursing the butterflies that were whirling around inside her stomach. 'I ... we were out late last night and ...'

'Come on. There'll be dancing later on. You look like a girl who likes to dance.' His voice was close to her ear; so close she could almost feel it. Her stomach lurched again. She liked the way he described her.

'Well ... OK. It's just ... I don't really know anyone here ...' she said hesitantly. 'I'm a bit ...'

'Overwhelmed?' he asked with surprising insight. Melanie looked quickly at him. His expression gave nothing away. She nodded slowly, relieved. For someone as successful and obviously popular as Steve di Marco, he was surprisingly easy to talk to. He gave a tight smile. 'I felt like that, when I first got here. I'm from Balham. South London. You've probably never even been there, have you?' Melanie shook her head. 'Working class, we were. My dad owned an ice-cream van. I always wanted to come here, come to Hollywood ... live in the sun. My parents are Italian, you know. Sun's in my blood.'

'Yes, your name. It's quite ... er, *Italian*,' Melanie said, not knowing what else to say.

He laughed. 'Yeah, well. Stefano di Marco. Doesn't get much more Italian than that, now, does it? Been here nearly fifteen years. Got here when I was eighteen. Not much younger than you, I reckon. How old are you, anyway?'

'Twenty-one,' Melanie said automatically.

'Old enough, then.'

'What for?' Melanie asked, suddenly flirtatious. Steve looked at her, his expression unreadable. There was a second's hesitation; he seemed about to say something but then a tall, statuesque blonde suddenly appeared, shrieking her delight at seeing him, and pulled him away. Melanie had the sensation of having been offered something tantalisingly unspecific and then having it quickly snatched away. She stared at the back of his head, now a few feet in front of her. She took in the details; the thick curl of his ponytail; the broad shoulders hidden beneath an expensive-looking blue shirt; sleeves rolled at the elbow; the silver flash of a watch. He was tall and carried himself well; he had the tight, coiled stance of someone who was perpetually alert. Quick, watchful ... almost predatory, but in an erotic, sensual way. No wonder the butterflies in her stomach refused to die down. Melanie had never met anyone quite like him. He was – she did the maths – thirty-three. She was eighteen. He was fifteen years older than her. Old enough to be ... well, her father, almost. Or Norbert. Except he was nothing like her father or Norbert. He was like no one else. She suddenly longed to talk to him again. He was the closest thing to normal she'd met since she'd arrived. But he was gone. Swallowed up by someone else.

19

For the first few days after her arrival, Laure was careful not to say anything about the state of the apartment or, more worry-ingly, the state of Belle. What did her mother do? She didn't seem to work – at least not at a conventional job. She left the apartment every evening, picked up by a man she introduced to Laure as 'Uncle Frank'. He was a sullen-faced, taciturn man with a frighteningly ugly scar down one side of his face. He hardly said a word but his eyes were watchful. Laure shrank from him. Belle stayed out most of the night, sometimes re-turning to the apartment in the early hours of the morning.

Laure tried not to think about what she was doing or where she'd been. Sometimes she heard voices in the living room; more than one man, sometimes two or three; but Belle never said what she did or who her visitors were and Laure kept her mouth firmly shut.

But after a week or so of keeping quiet and trying to be as unobtrusive as possible, she'd had enough. She stopped worrying about offending Belle and tried instead to concentrate on turning the hovel in which Belle seemed quite content to live into something fractionally more homely. It wasn't easy. She'd never washed a dish or a plate in her life – she had no idea what to use for what task. Not that Belle had anything even remotely resembling cleaning products. But at the end of her first week, faced with yet another slice of stale pizza for breakfast, she realised she had to do something. She couldn't go on eating the disgusting leftovers that Belle left out on the kitchen table and she couldn't face opening the fridge without cleaning it, however inexperienced she was as a cleaner. She decided to go and look for a supermarket to buy some cleaning products. Surely there was a supermarket nearby? And how difficult could cleaning really be?

She made her way to Pulaski Avenue, the main street running through Garfield Park. Mostly by following the sound of traffic. It was, without question, the widest street she had ever seen and there were more cars speeding up and down it than along the highway that linked Pétionville to Port-au-Prince. She stood by the side of the road, too nervous to even attempt a crossing. Someone shouted something to her – she had no idea what; she did her best to ignore him. There were barbers' shops; nail salons; stores that sold wigs and hair products; a tattoo parlour – she shrank from the window in fright; something called a 'funeral home' and, from where she stood, she counted at least four petrol stations. There was nothing that remotely looked like a supermarket or even a small convenience store. She thought of Pétionville – even along Rue Rigaud there were half a dozen small shops selling everything from fresh vegetables to wine. Here, apart from the hairdressers' and beauty salons, there was nothing. Didn't people in America shop? Didn't they cook? Or did they all live, like Belle seemed to do, on takeaway pizzas and unidentifiable pieces of meat floating around in a bright orange sauce – 'sweet 'n' sour', Belle had called it. It was disgusting.

She walked down Pulaski towards the freeway and found herself on a wide bridge. Down below were even more cars, travelling even faster. Swoosh, whish, swoosh … she leaned against the railings and watched them rush towards her and then immediately disappear. On the other side of the bridge was yet another petrol station and – she peered at it – what appeared to be a small shop. '7-Eleven', she read. And, underneath, in neon lights, something called 'g-r-o-c-e-r-i-e-s'. *Groceries*. Maybe that meant food? She walked quickly towards it.

There was a terrible *gong*! as she walked in through the door which made her almost jump out of her skin. The man behind the counter laughed and said something. She shook her head. *No understand*. It was indeed a small supermarket – she looked around her, relieved. There was bread and milk and stuff in cans … she walked quickly down the aisle. Cleaning products … she stopped. The labels were all in English but she thought she recognised washing-up liquid and there was even a packet of the same blue and white check cloths that Améline used. She swallowed. She felt a sudden, desperate wave of longing for Améline's cheerful, pointed face. Her fingers gripped the bottle of bright green liquid that she supposed was for washing dishes and the bottles in front of her wavered dangerously. She steeled herself. This was not the place to cry. She moved along the aisle. 'B-l-e-a-c-h'. A bright pink bottle with a blue cap. She opened it and took a strong whiff. Ah … *javel*. The smell of it nearly made her retch. She still vomited occasionally in the mornings; all it took was a particular smell or taste and she would find herself running to the toilet. The toilet. Belle's entire bathroom – she would need more than *javel* for that. She scanned the products … didn't Améline use something blue for cleaning the toilets? She picked up a blue bottle. 'Mrs Wright's Liquid Blueing. Makes Whites Whiter!' She had no idea what it meant but it certainly looked blue. She took two bottles. The entire bathroom needed cleaning.

Half an hour later, she had what she thought was enough to at least make a start. She understood nothing of the friendly patter of the sales assistant; she just nodded every time he seemed to address her. She carefully counted out the money – $18.69 and picked up the two bags he'd packed for her. At least she knew how to say thank you. He smiled at her as she walked out. Two bags full of assorted cleaning products, a packet of eggs and a loaf of bread. She knew how to boil an egg – sort of.

Cleaning a house, she soon discovered however, was no joke. To begin with, none of the products she'd bought seemed to make a dent in the overall mess. The soft blue and white check cloths she'd been so relieved to see simply weren't up to the task of removing several years' worth of grease on most of the kitchen surfaces, not to mention the walls and the floor. Mrs Wright's Liquid Blueing did little other than turn everything it came into contact with blue – was it a dye? It even stained the floor blue. She looked at it dubiously. At least before the dirt and stains had blended in with the original flooring which was a brown linoleum – now it was brown and blue, like Régine's Dalmation puppy. The sink looked as dirty as ever and as for the stove top … she swallowed. Nothing would shift the dirt. Nothing. Not even a whole bottle of *javel* left for several hours. Plus the whole house was beginning to stink of it – it didn't smell clean, unfortunately, it just smelled. It made her throw up, twice.

Belle didn't even notice. She came home later that evening, threw her coat on the ground and opened up another one of those awful paper cartons full of Chinese food. Laure had never eaten Chinese food in her life. It looked lurid and horribly unidentifiable. She fried herself another egg and made herself some toast. She was exhausted. She who had never washed a dish in her life … now all she did was wash. And wipe. And sweep. Was this what Améline did all day long? At the thought of Améline her throat thickened and filled with tears. She'd

95

written to Améline and Régine almost every day since she arrived but had heard nothing back. She'd gone from speaking to Belle in her head to speaking to Améline. Was this the way it would be for her, for ever? Perpetually addressing someone she never saw?

One particularly bad morning, after her customary trip to the bathroom – *would this morning sickness never end?* – she walked into the living room and nearly wept. Belle had come in well after five in the morning and had slept in the living room, or so it seemed. And not on her own, either. Bottles of beer, empty cigarette cartons, empty plastic bottles of soda and three fresh cigarette burns on the new cover Laure had bought for the sofa the week before out of her precious, dwindling stash of US dollars. She stared at the mess and the wreckage of the living room she'd cleaned only the previous afternoon and something inside her finally snapped. She sank down on to the dirty couch, beyond caring that it was covered in ash. She put her face in her hands. She was almost five months pregnant. She had no money, no qualifications, no prospects ... on paper, at least, there was precious little to go on. She lived with a mother who was incapable of mothering her and she herself was about to become a mother to a child she didn't want. The film of tears covering her eyes broke; her throat thickened painfully. Why had it all gone so wrong? What had she done to deserve *this*? She stared at the silent flickering TV screen which Belle had forgotten, as usual, to turn off. Happy, smiling faces on a perpetual game show, babbling away in a language she could barely understand. She felt like a prisoner, afraid to leave the house for fear of being misunderstood. The few times she'd been to the corner shop to buy milk or bread she'd almost been reduced to tears at her inability to understand what was being said, unable to buy even the simplest things for herself. She'd brought a big dictionary with her but she just couldn't make sense of the way things were strung together and her accent seemed impenetrable to those around her. *Meelk. Meelk.* She'd almost walked out of the 7-Eleven in tears.

She watched the figures on the screen turn to each other, all shining eyes and grinning faces as they racked up another set of prizes, and another. Winning, it seemed, was everything. Americans loved winners. Well, that pretty much ruled her out, she thought to herself as a fresh wave of tears slid down her face.

Suddenly, there was a knock at the front door. She lifted her head, wiping furiously at her cheeks. Who could it be at – she peered at the clock on the wall – ten o'clock in the morning? She wiped her cheeks again and got to her feet. The person knocked again, harder this time. She went to the door, her heart beating a little faster with nerves.

'Yes?' she called out, unwilling to open the door. She'd seen the sorts of people who hung around the street during the day.

'Mailman,' someone answered through the door. 'Letter for Miss Laure St Lazâre.' He pronounced her name with some difficulty. 'She home? She's gotta sign for it.'

Laure couldn't understand anything other than the sound of her own name. She swung the latch, pulled back the bolt and opened the door a crack. There was a man in a grey-blue uniform, holding something out. She stared at it. A letter! An airmail letter. 'Yes ... for me?' she asked, opening the door a little wider.

'You Miss St Lazâre?'

'Yes. *Moi. C'est moi.*'

'OK, miss. Could you sign here?' He pushed a clipboard and pen through the door. Laure signed her name and took the letter, her heart thudding.

'Tha ... thank you,' she stammered and had just enough time to see his answering smile before she closed the door. She stared at the letter. Laure St Lazâre. In Améline's neat, precise handwriting. She almost tore the letter trying to open it.

She read it five times, from start to finish. Five precious, bittersweet times. Every word, every sentence. When she was finished, she put her head in her hands and wept. In shame. While she'd been sitting on the couch in Belle's hovel of an apartment, Améline had simply got on with things. She'd left home. She'd walked all the way to a hotel on the other side of Pétionville, applied for a job – and got it. She was now a chambermaid in the Hotel Palme d'Or. She had her own room, her own uniform and a salary every month. Laure stared at the letter over and over again. *Ma chère Lulu*.

She heard a sound. It was Belle. Laure stuffed the letter in her pocket and wiped her cheeks. As she got up and walked into the kitchen to begin preparing lunch for them both, she made herself a solemn vow. No more tears. She'd wiped her face for the very last time. Améline's letter had shamed her. If Améline, with nothing to her name, had done it ... why the hell couldn't she?

20

Four thousand miles away, Améline was getting ready for work. She tied the stiff white apron strings around her waist, made sure her hair was tidy and closed the door to her little room behind her. It was six-thirty in the morning; the air was still cool and she had a long, hard day ahead of her. Gaspard hadn't been joking; it was hard work. Thirty rooms, four suites and a restaurant area that ran the entire front of the building, including the verandah where most of the guests liked to sit. But Améline would have worked three times as hard if she'd had to. She was *free*. She savoured the word, savoured the feeling of waking up in the morning knowing that *she* was in charge of what she did during the day. She alone. There was no one to tell her what to do, other than those whose *job* it was to direct her. At the end of every day, they all went their separate ways to do whatever they pleased. The hotel staff weren't a bad bunch – even Rosalie, when it came down to it, wasn't half as snobbish as she seemed. They were all working for a living, *that* was what made it special. No one was there because they'd had the misfortune to be born there; no, they were all there out of choice.

She was a hard worker; after a fortnight on the job, Gaspard asked her if she wouldn't like a little more responsibility – she would be in charge of the linen cupboard, ordering new sheets, making sure everything came back from the laundry, keeping it stocked with soap powder and the like. For a small increase in salary, naturally, and three meals a day instead of two. Améline readily accepted. She didn't care how long or hard she worked. Sometimes she even worked *both* shifts, starting at dawn and finishing at midnight. She would crawl, exhausted, but satisfied, into the bed. Home. She'd never understood just how sweet the feeling of having *earned* the right to eat or sleep might be. The room was bare and it bore the marks of a number of her predecessors but Améline didn't care. It was *hers*. She'd earned it.

There were other things she noticed, too. In many ways, the Palme d'Or was like the rest of Haiti: little by little, crack by crack, it was disintegrating. Not quickly – just a long, slow slide into something no one could quite put their finger on. She could tell that the Palme d'Or attracted fewer and fewer tourists. The linen, just as it had been at Madame's, was threadbare; there had been no new deliveries in the past year. The embroidered motif – a palm tree – had long since disintegrated on most of the sheets and pillowcases and no amount of washing could get rid of the marks where the threads had once been. The towels were wearing thin; the bathrobes in the four suites had disappeared and it was getting harder and harder to stock the rooms with the little toiletries that gave the Palme d'Or the right to call itself a four-star hotel. Gaspard kept a precious stash of miniature shampoo and conditioner bottles in a large safe at the back of his office; Améline was now the only other employee, other than Rosalie, entrusted with its key.

One morning, a few weeks before Christmas, she was in the dining room dusting the tables when someone spoke, as if to her.

'Am I in any danger of being served round here?' Améline looked up in surprise. The voice belonged to a middle-aged tourist sitting alone on the verandah. She put down the duster and hurried over.

'I'm sorry, sir – the waitress must have just gone out ...' She looked round. Marcelle was nowhere to be seen. 'Can ... can I get you anything, sir?'

'Well, breakfast would be a good start. What's on the menu?'

Améline paused. It was a well-known trick at the Palme d'Or. Marcelle or Ynez, the Dominican waitress, would rattle off a list of specials, patiently take the customer's order and then simply bring out whatever the cook had managed to produce. Usually fried eggs on toast. Sometimes, and then only rarely, a croissant or two. 'I think it's fried eggs, sir,' Améline said nervously.

'Ah. As before. The daily special. Oh, well ... fried eggs it is, then. Could I trouble you for some coffee? Or is that another department?' Améline looked blank. The tourist gave a short, humourless laugh. 'Don't mind me. I've been trying to get into the Palais National for almost a month. It's always some other department. No, eggs, coffee and toast, please. If you don't mind.'

'No, sir ... I'll ... I'll let the kitchen know.' Améline hurried away.

Twenty minutes later, a bored-looking Ynez put down a plate of fried eggs, two slices of toast and a small pot of coffee in front of him. The tourist ate everything without comment and left a small tip. As he got up to go, he nodded in Améline's direction. 'Wasn't bad. Considering.' Considering what? Améline couldn't follow the red-faced man with his white panama hat and long khaki trousers. He looked like ... she frowned. She wasn't sure *what* he looked like, except that he looked like ... a tourist. He read her expression. 'Considering it's the same as yesterday. And the day before. And most probably the day before that.' He tipped his hat at her and disappeared down the stairs. Améline stared after him. Most odd. She wondered where he was from. His French was good; but she didn't think he was French. American? She had no idea. She picked up the duster and went back to work.

The following morning he was at the same table. This time a bored-looking Marcelle took his order. Again he tipped his hat at Améline who was wheeling one of the laundry trolleys out of the dining room. She gave him a hurried, confused smile ... what did he want with her?

On the third morning, having gone through the whole order-taking, hat-tipping exercise for the third time, Améline felt emboldened enough to stop by his table and ask if he wouldn't perhaps like a croissant or something ... she could have a word with the cook, perhaps?

'Oh, gracious, no ... fried eggs are fine. Very kind of you to ask, by the way.'

'You're ... er, welcome ...' Améline stammered. She had no idea how to talk to guests. Her job at the hotel was very much a behind-the-scenes affair; she made sure things ran smoothly so that she *wouldn't* have to talk to them. She excused herself quickly and practically ran down to the laundry room.

The following morning he wasn't there. Améline wasn't sure whether to be relieved or ... or what? Perhaps he'd gone home for Christmas? She continued counting sheets. At lunchtime, somewhat to her surprise, she found herself flicking quickly through the register as she chatted to Rosalie. *Iain Blake. Room 26. Anglais.* She saw his name on the second page. So he was English? She'd never met an Englishman before.

'Saw you chatting to him the other day,' Rosalie said, paring her nails.

Améline blushed immediately. She knew exactly whom Rosalie meant. 'Me? Oh, no ... well, just to ... he wanted something ... I just ...'

'It's OK. You're allowed to talk to the guests, you know. Actually, Gaspard rather encourages it.' She lowered her voice. 'Some of the guests are quite lonely. It's a good way to make a little bit on the side.'

Améline stared at her. 'Wh ... what are you talking about?'

'Oh, come on ... don't sound so shocked. You mean to tell me you don't know what goes on around here?'

'No ... I don't. It's none of my business.'

'Fine.' Rosalie adopted her usual bored expression. She went back to filing her nails. 'Forget I said anything. I just thought you'd be interested in making a little on the side. Like the rest of us.'

'Well, I'm not,' Améline said primly.

'Fine. Forget it.'

After that, things were a little frosty between them. Suddenly Améline saw all sorts of things about the Palme d'Or she'd never fully understood. Or wanted to, perhaps. She understood now why Marcelle and Ynez disappeared for such long breaks in the middle of the day; she saw that Rosalie sometimes left the hotel in the company of a guest who'd recently checked in. Gaspard turned a blind eye to the goings-on under his roof. Perhaps, as Rosalie hinted, he even encouraged it? Even Améline could see it was good for business. Times were definitely getting harder. Up there in Pétionville, in the cooler air and the lush gardens, among the cerise and purple bougainvillea bushes and the waving graceful palms, it was easy to forget what was happening further down the hill. In the slums of Marché de Fer and Feuilles de Carrefour a powder keg of tension and resentment was slowly kindling. Word sometimes reached the hotel via a stunned guest – the Tonton Macoutes had arrived at a bar and beaten everyone up, including the guest who had only just managed to escape. Within minutes, usually, he had packed his things and was gone. From Haiti and from the fever brewing under the lid. Améline listened to the stories but somehow couldn't connect the simmering build-up *down there* to the decaying splendour *up here*. It was as if Haiti was actually *two* countries, running side by side along a parallel track. But every once in a while, as the conversation with Rosalie showed, they collided. Améline closed her eyes and ears. She had enough to worry about on her own.

A week before Christmas, a familiar face showed up among the palm fronds and paintings in the dining room. Iain Blake was back. He greeted her with an old-fashioned, almost grave formality that brought the heat to Améline's cheeks. She was conscious of Rosalie's eyes on her – mocking her, she thought – as she answered his questions, secretly hoping Ynez was taking care – in every sense of the word – of another guest. It would give her an excuse to linger a little longer, listening to the melodious sound of his voice, asking her a little about Port-au-Prince and the places she knew. She wasn't used to talking in this way. The last person with whom she'd had anything even approaching a normal conversation was Laure. She blinked rapidly. Her eyes had filled unexpectedly with tears. She almost ran from the table.

The following morning, she saw him sitting on the balcony overlooking the hillside. He was writing in the small black notebook she'd seen him carry everywhere he went. She paused. And then walked to his table.

'Good morning, sir,' she said, hoping that her voice at least sounded steady.

'Ah. Our very own *Girl with a Pearl Earring.*' He smiled at her. Améline looked at him blankly. 'Vermeer. Dutch painter. He painted a young servant girl. With a pearl earring, much like yours.' Améline's hand went up to the two earrings Laure had given her. Régine had given them to Laure on her sixteenth birthday but, typically Laure, she'd wrapped them and given them to Améline instead. Améline had never taken them out. She touched her earlobes, ridiculously pleased. She suddenly longed to hear more about Vermeer and the servant girl.

21

Iain Blake, forty-seven years old, recovering alcoholic and washed-up-writer-attempting-a-comeback, put down his coffee cup and watched the young chambermaid wind her way through the tables. He was intrigued by her. Améline. She didn't have a surname, she'd told him. She'd just started at the splendidly faded Palme d'Or. He chuckled whenever he thought about the name. The golden palm – there was nothing golden, or even palm-like, about the place. An old, much-faded colonial plantation home, it had obviously seen better days. There was a faint air of desperation about the place – much like the country itself. Like a grand old dowager, the hotel still put its best foot forward; the old man playing the piano every evening in the bar downstairs, for example, and the ever-dwindling supply of some truly excellent wines. But then the toilets often blocked and there was a power cut every other evening. The waitresses were pretty and quite often on the take, as well. That one at reception – she'd indicated once or twice that there was a lot more he could expect than having his towels changed every other day ... he just had to say the word. He groaned. That was the last thing he needed. But Améline ... now, that was different. There was something about her. *Oh, Iain*, he could practically hear his ex-wife saying in exasperation. *There's always something about them. Each and every bloody one.* But it was true. She wasn't beautiful, as such, not like the girl on reception. At least, not at first. But the more you looked at her, and talked to her, the more attractive she became. Small, pointed little face, curious lively eyes, nice mouth, especially when she smiled. Good teeth, as the islanders often had – a lovely row of pearly whites. He prodded his own teeth with his tongue – he was paying for years of neglect. There was always something wrong. His mind drifted back to Améline. Smashing little figure, too. Bit on the small side. *Oh, Iain*, Viv's voice reprimanded him sharply. He groaned again. No, a girl was the last thing he needed. He was on assignment to write about Haiti, in Ballard's words, 'an insane tropical sitcom', and his editor back in London was already cabling him to say he was anxious to see a draft, a few pages, a sketch of an idea ... just an idea ... *anything* that would assure him he was working, not drinking, and that HarmondButterworth's faith in him had not been misplaced.

Problem was, he'd been in the tropical sitcom for all of four months and he *still* hadn't really put pen to paper. It was partly the heat. It sucked everything out of you, including the will to work. For the first few weeks, he'd been content just to observe. He'd taken a *tap-tap* into town every morning. Into town. A euphemism, if he'd ever heard one. Port-au-Prince wasn't a town. It was a sprawling, chaotic mess. Beggars on every street corner, Macoutes driving around in open-top jeeps, sending chickens, hawkers and pedestrians scuttling for cover every time they appeared; roadside kiosks selling everything under the sun except, of course, anything you'd be tempted to buy ... he'd even tried to get into the National Palace but that had disintegrated into a farce. He'd been pushed around from department to department; from the press office of the City Government to the protocol officer of the Ministry of Information (another misnomer); from the secretary to the Minister of Foreign Affairs to the assistant to the Chief of Defence Staff ... the list was endless. In the end, he had to accept defeat. He wasn't going to be allowed in. Full stop. End of story.

Except, of course, it wasn't. He had a book to write. After three months in Haiti, a country which ought to have inspired in him not just the desire to write, but the desire to write *the* book that would rescue his failing career, restore Peter's touching faith in him and persuade HarmondButterworth, his hapless publishers, to issue another, all-important cheque ... nothing had happened. Nothing. He'd moved from the terrible Oloffson Hotel (where Greene had written *The Comedians* – Iain couldn't quite picture it ... perhaps it had been better in his day?) at the bottom of the hill to the positively gracious Palme d'Or at the top, hoping that the change of air and scenery would inspire

him, but the most inspiring thing he'd seen, somewhat predictably, he had to admit, was the bloody chambermaid. Now, how
pathetic was that? Except, he thought to himself as he watched
her walk away, perhaps it wasn't quite as silly as it seemed.
Peter had asked him in exasperation when he thought he'd be
able to produce something – anything – and he'd replied that
he was having difficulty getting into Haiti: he still felt like an
outsider. It was closed to him and he couldn't quite find his
way in. Now, however, without meaning to, a little slip of a
chambermaid had piqued his interest and for the first time, he
began to think he might actually have found a way. Not to get
into her – no pun intended – but to get into Haiti *through* her.
Not, he mused, that the former wasn't an option … He closed
his notebook with a decisive snap. Don't go there. Please. Not
again. Not ever again.

22

It was December in Chicago and the weather was changing,
becoming colder by the week. There were days when the wind
blew in off the lake and Laure shivered in her flimsy cardigans
and cotton skirts. She could feel herself sinking lower than she'd
ever imagined possible. Mornings were the worst. She began
to fear falling asleep for it meant that she woke early, when
the light was still grey and her future stretched thick and dark
in front of her, almost smothering her with its bleakness. She
couldn't stop worrying about what would happen after May,
when the baby was due. She sat in front of the television all day,
trapped inside a silent bubble of sounds she couldn't decipher,
stunned by the mess she seemed to have made of her life. It was
almost impossible to believe that in four months her world had
been turned upside down – and it was all her own fault. She
couldn't believe how stupid she'd been. What in the world had

possessed her to walk off with Delroy that day? Why hadn't she just done as Régine did, and ignored him? Was it true what everyone said? That she was just like Belle? Just looking at the broken, hopeless woman Belle had become was punishment enough – it wasn't possible that she'd wind up like her, was it? She shuddered just thinking about it. Once or twice, when she was sitting on the saggy purple couch staring blankly at the TV screen, she'd noticed Belle getting ready to go out – she would bring her plastic make-up bag to the table squashed in the corner of the room and start to apply her 'face', as she called it, a cigarette in one hand, mascara wand in the other. At those moments Laure could just glimpse the beauty that everyone had talked about suddenly emerge from beneath the powdered face – a quick, flirtatious tilt of her head, the smoky, grey-green eyes turned towards her, legs narrowed elegantly at the ankle and knee ... the beauty that Belle had carelessly thrown away. She turned back to the television, the figures obscured by the thin veil of tears. Surely that wasn't what was coming to her?

One night, a few days after the most miserable Christmas Laure could remember, when the temperature outside had dropped below freezing and she lay in bed, struggling to keep warm, she heard the front door slam and the sound of a man's angry voice in the hallway. She heard Belle stumble towards her own room, slamming the door shut. There was silence for a few seconds, and then suddenly the sound of the door splintering as it was kicked in. She sat up in bed, her heart pounding. Belle's voice pleading ... then the sound of something hitting the wall. She sat there, too afraid to get out of bed, but afraid, too, for Belle. The man's voice continued for a few more minutes – Laure didn't understand the words but she understood their meaning. 'Fucking whore. You ain't nothin' but a cheap, nasty whore.' She closed her eyes. *Whore.* She understood immediately what it meant. Belle was a whore. Then she heard the apartment door being yanked violently open and the sharp, metallic blast as he slammed it shut. There was a stunned silence in his wake. Laure slid out of bed, pulled a dressing gown over her high, hard stomach and opened the door. She could hear Belle sobbing in her room. She went in to find Belle on the ground, half-lying, half-sitting against the unmade bed. The room stank of alcohol, cigarettes, cheap perfume. Laure's nose wrinkled as she bent down awkwardly beside her mother.

'*Maman*, are you OK?' she asked. It was dark inside the room. She didn't want to put on the light, afraid of what she might see. Belle's sobs were ugly, harsh sounds in the sudden quiet after the man's departure. '*Maman?*' she asked again. Belle gave what sounded like a groan and flinched as Laure put out a hand and touched her face. Her hand came away sticky. Laure swallowed nervously. 'Can I put on the light?' she asked, her hand already groping for the switch beside the bed. The room was suddenly flooded and Belle's head jerked instinctively away. Laure looked at her and gasped. 'Oh, *Maman*,' she whispered. Belle had been beaten, badly. One of her eyes was almost closed, the other was swollen and puffy and there was an ugly welt on one cheek – the imprint of a buckle could be seen quite clearly against the grainy, tear-streaked skin. Her mouth was bleeding; he had obviously slapped her – and hard.

'Don't ...' Belle started to speak, wincing.

'It's OK. Shh. Here, let me wipe ...' Laure struggled to pull her upright. 'I'll get a cloth.' There was no reply from Belle. Her face had fallen forwards, on to her chest. She was still very drunk. Laure left her, ran to the bathroom and found a washcloth. She ran it under the hot tap for a few moments then came back into the room. Kneeling down beside Belle, she gently and carefully washed as much of the blood and dirt away as she could. 'Come, *Maman* ... try to stand. Come on,' she coaxed, trying to lift her. Belle was too heavy, especially for her now. She put her hands under Belle's armpits and tried to get her to stand. 'OK ... put your foot there ... that's it ... and the other one.' Weeping and mumbling incoherently, Belle was finally persuaded to stand. She stood passively, tears rolling down her cheeks, as Laure undressed her and helped her into bed. Laure pulled up the covers and sat on the end of the bed, watching her until the deepening, hoarse breaths told her

Belle was falling asleep. She bundled up the dirty clothes and put them outside in the hallway, turning only once to put out the light.

Back in her own room, she climbed into bed. *Never*, she whispered to herself as she shut her eyes and tried to control her breathing. *Never. I will never wind up like that.* She repeated it to herself over and over again. Whatever happened to her – and she touched her stomach with the heel of her hand – she would *never* wind up like Belle.

That night, everything changed. Seeing Belle at her lowest had offered her a frightening glimpse into a future she was determined would never be hers. She had to get out. First of all, she had to learn English. The baby was due in early May – that meant she had four months to get to grips with the strange and difficult language. Without it, her future would be over before it had even begun.

Armed with only a dictionary, she did the only thing she knew how to do – she sat in front of the television, day and night, and forced herself to learn. She'd had the rudiments of English in school – sitting in front of the television with a pen and paper in hand was a little like being back at school. She steeled herself against the nostalgia that swept over her whenever she thought about the life she'd left behind and instead concentrated ferociously on the task ahead. Whenever the pain of loneliness and despair threatened to overwhelm her, she thought of Améline. Plucky little Améline. She'd done what no one expected her to do – she'd left and was making a life for herself. Just as Laure had to now.

She switched on the television now and stared at the screen. The news had just come on. Frowning with concentration she managed to glean that something terrible had happened somewhere in the world ... Lebanon. Beirut. Ah, Liban. She watched as a young man was interviewed by the obviously shocked reporters. She couldn't quite make out what he was saying but she was struck by the look of intense fury on his face. He seemed oblivious to the protocols of television reporting, gesticulating angrily towards the camps that even the cameramen appeared reluctant to enter. She switched it off, frustrated by her inability to grasp what was going on.

23

'Hi. Is Steve in?' A month and a half after it had begun, it still gave Melanie the biggest thrill to walk up to the bouncers in front of the Pink Palm Lounge and ask for Steve.

'Go on up, Melanie.' That was the other big thrill. They all knew her name. She gave Mikey, the huge Irish ex-boxer, a quick smile and walked in. The place was packed, as it always was. Whatever else Steve di Marco had done in the fifteen years he'd been in LA, this, his latest venture, was without a doubt his most successful. A fortnight was a very long time in the life of a new restaurant in LA, he'd told her, and for six weeks running, he'd been overbooked each and every day – breakfast, lunch and dinner. It was a simple formula – a hip, modern interior of raw-but-polished materials softened by white leather seats, fake lurid pink palm trees, and good, simple all-American food. Oh, and great music, too. At the weekends, some of LA's top DJs came to spin for the blend of hip diners and cool, cool customers. The atmosphere was casual and yet utterly chic. Steve had a couple of hundred supermodels and young actresses on speed dial and their presence ensured the trendy, young actors, movers and shakers in town came, and *their* presence ensured that The Beautiful People came ... It seemed to go on in a never-ending spiral of gorgeous, smiling, successful people. And now she was one of them. Melanie. Steve di Marco's beautiful, young girlfriend. No one even *mentioned* her father. There were days when she couldn't quite believe it had happened to her. After that first night at the opening of the Pink Palm Lounge, when he'd taken her up on to the roof to look at the lights of Beverly Hills and had kissed her, his mouth tasting of Glenlivet, Melanie was smitten. Absolutely, unequivocally smitten. Rudy had simply ceased to exist. Steve di Marco was the real thing. A real man. *Her* man.

Steve was on the phone when she entered his office. A huge, white room on the first floor, it contained an enormous glass desk, two white swivel chairs and a sideboard – and little else. Melanie sometimes wondered how he managed to run his restaurant from one impossibly tidy desk which held little other than a white telephone. She'd never seen him in the kitchen, or out on the restaurant floor, all he did was bark instructions into his phone. He had an incredible array of staff – there were drivers, gofers, PAs, 'fixers', people who 'got him things'. 'Get me' was one of Steve's favourite phrases. *Get me Spike on the line. Get me a coffee. Get somebody to take care of it. Get me the hell out of here.* All the while, hovering like butterflies around him, there seemed to be an army of people who were ready to do just that. She waved her fingers at him, reluctant to interrupt his call.

'Hi. Gimme a minute, will you?' Steve hardly broke his conversation as she entered. Whoever he was on the phone to was almost silent; it was Steve who did all the talking. Something about a delivery that had gone to the wrong address. 'Fucking sort it out, will you? I don't need to hear anything else. Just sort it out, mate.' He put the phone down without saying goodbye and beckoned her over. 'C'mere.' He patted the glass table top beside him. Melanie hesitated. He didn't mean for her to sit on it, surely? 'It's perfectly safe, sweetheart,' he said, reading her mind. 'It won't break. *I* sit on it and I probably weigh twice as much as you.'

'OK.' Melanie felt a little self-conscious as she hitched up her dress and perched on the edge. He put one hand on her bare thigh and picked up his phone again with the other. Someone had obviously pissed him off. The muscle in his cheek twitched impatiently as he listened to whatever the person on the other end of the line had to say. Throughout the conversation,

Melanie was conscious only of his face. She could have studied it for ever, she thought, her eyes following its planes and angles, the thick lower lashes that fringed his eyes, the shadow of stubble across the cheekbones and the neat, precisely clipped edges to the triangular beard around his chin. There were one or two flecks of grey among the dark brown bristles. Melanie couldn't have said why but seeing them sent the most delicious waves of pleasure through her. Steve di Marco was nothing like anyone she'd ever known. Brash, confident, quick as all hell and impatient to a fault. Nothing slipped his attention; absolutely nothing. He could spot a new colour of lipstick or a new perfume from across the room, give orders down the phone *and* count a stack of dollars as thick as a brick … all at the same time. What the hell did he see in her, she asked herself a dozen times a day. Tina wasn't much help. 'He likes pretty young girls,' she said, whenever Melanie asked her. 'You're young. You're pretty. He digs you. Don't complicate it.'

'But d'you think he *likes* me? *Really* likes me?' Melanie asked her, only every other minute.

'Honey, how should I know? Ask him.'

'But you said … remember? I had to learn to play the game. Play it cool.'

'So play it cool. Stop sweating it. If he doesn't like you, he'll tell you.'

'But it makes me feel so … helpless.'

'You *are* helpless. They all are.'

'They? H … how many has …?'

'Play it cool, Mel. Play it cool.'

How?

'Tie a fucking snake around it and send it straight over.' Steve's voice was cold. Melanie stiffened, tearing her eyes away from his face. What was he talking about? She eyed him nervously. He was still talking in that quiet, scary way. 'How the fuck should I know?' he growled down the phone. 'Do I look like a fucking zoo-keeper? Just get a snake. Any snake.' He put the phone down and looked at her, his face expressionless.

Melanie wrinkled her nose at him. 'A *snake*?' she said, pull-ing a face. 'Why d'you want a snake? Are you serious?'

'Babe, I'm *always* serious.' Steve slid a hand further up her thigh. Melanie felt as though she might melt.

'But what ... what are you going to do with a ... a snake?'

'Never you mind.' Steve's hand continued its circular caress. 'Now, have you decided where you want to go tonight?'

'No ... not really. I thought ... well, we could always just stay in, couldn't we?' Melanie held her breath. *Staying in*, a silly, childish euphemism for making love – it was all she could think about when she was near him. Just the touch of his hand on her bare skin was enough to make her weak at the knees.

'Can't, sweetheart. You know I've got to be seen around town.'

Melanie sighed. That was something else she couldn't quite follow about Steve di Marco. She was used to those around her *not* wanting to be seen; her earliest memories seemed to involve running *away* from the paparazzi, not running towards them. Scum of the earth, her father called them. Especially after they'd caught him in a compromising position. Melanie was so used to the flash of cameras and of being recognised, especially in London, that she barely registered their presence. Steve, on the other hand, didn't seem to care whether photographers saw him or not; they were not the audience he sought. But Melanie couldn't quite work out who his audience might be. People, he said airily. The right sort of people. It was important for the restaurant. She couldn't work out why. 'I don't know. How about Pinafarina's? You know, the one by the Beverly Centre.'

'Good idea. Check out the competition.' He pushed his chair back and stood up. 'Nice dress,' he said, touching the hem of her skirt. 'Nice legs.' Melanie thought her heart would burst. She slid off the glass table and followed him obediently out of the room.

It was after three in the morning when Steve's driver pulled up in front of his house in the Hollywood Hills. Melanie was almost asleep, her head lolling in the space between Steve's shoulder and neck. He was on the phone, of course, talking quietly to someone who seemed to do little other than say 'yes' every other minute. His skin carried with it the faint aroma of expensive aftershave and the starch of his laundered shirt. His fingers brushed Melanie's bare shoulder every once in a while, sending a sweet ache racing towards her groin. She was a little drunk – she'd stopped counting after her third cocktail but Steve always saw to it that she didn't go overboard. He couldn't stand drunk girls, he'd told her on their second date. He couldn't stand people without self-control. 'Come on, Mel,' he said as the car stopped. 'Proper lightweight, you are. Come on. Here we go.' He slid an arm round her waist and helped her out of the car. 'Come back in about an hour,' he said to the driver. 'And then take her home.'

'Can't I stay …?' Melanie said sleepily. That was the other funny thing about Steve. He never let her stay the night, no matter how late they got back. He couldn't sleep with anyone else in his bed.

'Make that an hour and a half.' He took Melanie's hand and pulled her close to him. He didn't bother to reply.

He undid the zipper at the back of her dress almost without her noticing. The fabric slid away and she was semi-naked in front of him. There was an odd scent in the air – he was smoking a joint, she realised. He handed it to her. She took a cautious pull. She'd smoked before, in school, of course, but hadn't really liked it. It gave her a headache and not much else. But now, with Steve sitting on the white leather couch in front of her, his tightly controlled expression relaxing just a fraction as she took first one puff, then another … this was different. He took the joint away from her and set it carefully aside. She continued to stand in front of him, swaying slightly, a delicious warmth stealing through her in anticipation of what was to follow.

'Come.' He beckoned her forward. She sank to her knees, her heart beating faster as he slowly unbuckled his belt and slid his fingers under her chin. Control. More than anything, Steve liked being in control. It came as a surprise to Melanie to realise just how much *she* liked it. Especially when, as now, he came close to losing it altogether. She lay back on the white sheepskin rug and closed her eyes as he pushed apart her legs and slid the length of his hard, heavy body on top of her. It didn't occur to her to wonder why *he* was always the one to lose his head, and not her. She was so intoxicated with the power she seemed to have over him that the little fact of her own pleasure simply disappeared. It wasn't about her; it was about him. About what *she* could do to him. She didn't seem to expect anything for herself. Neither did he.

24

To her surprise, it only took a couple of weeks of sitting in front of the television for things to slowly start to make sense. One morning, a few weeks into the new year, she was surprised to find that the noise emanating from the screen had suddenly broken apart and reformed itself in a series of distinct words and sentences she could suddenly grasp. She understood fragments of what was being said. Not everything – not nearly enough – but it was a start. Excited, she walked the three blocks to the 7-Eleven without dread settling in the pit of her stomach, eager to practise her new-found fluency.

'Hi, Lori, how you doin'?' Duane, the huge, sleepy-eyed sales clerk called out to her when she walked in every other day to practise her conversation skills. He couldn't quite get his tongue around *Laure*.

'Good, thank you. And how are you?' It made him smile, he said, just listening to her accent. She had a lovely voice. A real lovely voice. 'Do you have any fresh … *fruits*?' This last pronounced in French. *Frew-ee*.

'*Frooots. Frooots*, honey. Not *frew-ee*.' Duane grinned at her.

'Though I kinda like the way *you* say it. Yeah, we got some. Whatcha want? Got some bananas, some grapes … oh, there's a couple oranges, too.'

'All. Thank you, Duane,' Laure said carefully, handing over the money. She clutched the paper bag full of all the fresh fruits 7-Eleven had to offer.

'Don' mention it, honey. You have a nice day, Lori.'

'Thank you, Duane. Bye-bye.'

The first time she felt the baby move inside her she stopped dead in her tracks, walking back to the apartment from the supermarket, overcome with the dread that swept through her. It turned. The baby turned and shifted inside her and it was all she could do to move on without screaming out loud for help. She hurried back to the apartment, praying that Belle would either be asleep or out. She wasn't sure she could face anyone at that moment. She opened the front door and walked in quietly. Belle's door was closed. She slipped into her own room and sat down on the bed, pressing her hand to the side of her high, hard stomach. It. The baby – *her* baby. Her baby was alive inside her. She lay back against the pillows, breathing hard. Delroy. She fought it but his name still produced the same sweet, giddy rush in her that hearing his car horn outside her window the first time had; the same breathless, burning anticipation. Things hadn't turned out quite the way she'd expected, but what *had* she expected, anyway? She'd known, hadn't she, all the while she was doing it – slipping out at night, climbing into his jeep, drinking rum and letting the ice cubes melt in her mouth before kissing him, tasting him – it couldn't last. She would be found out. It would come to an end. The schizophrenic double life she'd been living those last few months couldn't continue. She'd known that, somehow, hadn't she? She touched her stomach again. What would the baby look like? A boy or a girl? Like her? Like him? She tried to picture a creature made of the two of them; her dark, chocolate colour and his lighter, creamier *café au lait*. Brown eyes, like his; her dark, thick hair. She lay in the dark for a very long time, imagining, imagining.

25

An odd routine had developed between Améline and Iain – she would stop by his table in the mornings and at lunchtime, chat about this or that. She never sat down with him. In the evenings, after dinner had been cleared away, she would lean against the balcony railings and talk to him, sometimes long into the night. He was very good at listening and Améline, who had long since grown out of the habit of talking, was slowly persuaded to tell him things about herself that she'd almost forgotten herself. He'd asked her about her family, where she came from and was puzzled by her reply.

'What d'you mean, a *reste-avec*?' he said, having never heard the term before. 'A "stay-with"? What's that?'

'It's like ... someone who stays in the house. From a poorer family.'

'But where *is* your family? D'you mean you were just taken away? What happened to them?'

'I ... I don't know,' Améline admitted, for the first time seeing the rather harsh nature of her condition. 'I think ... well, they told me my parents had died. But I don't remember them. I don't even know their names.'

'Are you serious? What's your last name? This sounds bloody barbaric,' Iain said, reaching for another drink.

'I ... I don't know. I ... I don't have a last name.'

Iain stared at her in disbelief. 'What d'you call yourself?' he asked. 'Just Améline?'

'Yes.'

'Good God. It's like the Middle Ages. And this woman, the one you call "madame" ...? Who is she?'

'Madame St Lazâre? She ... she brought me here, to Pétionville. To be a companion.'

'To whom?'

Améline had to swallow before replying. 'To her granddaughter, Laure. She ... she's like my sister, Laure. I ... I miss her.'

'But where is she?'

Améline looked at her hands. 'In America,' she said quietly. 'She ... she had to leave. One day, when I go to America, I'm going to go and find her.' Iain said nothing. But she could feel his eyes on her for a long time afterwards. It was the first time she'd ever been ashamed of her humble beginnings. She didn't even have a surname. The fact had never troubled her before.

The following Sunday, when she was off duty, he asked her if she would like to accompany him into town. He took her to the National Palace at the end of the Champs de Mars and pointed out the statue of Dessalines. She knew who Dessalines was, much to his surprise. She might have been a chambermaid but she was surprisingly well educated. She'd shared lessons with the daughter of the family she'd been taken in by, she told him. He'd often wondered about her pleasant, precise French – another of the *many* advantages of being a *reste-avec* to the St Lazâres, she told him, laughing unexpectedly. She had a surprising sense of humour, too, he saw.

He wasn't the only one to show her things. She took him into the sprawling slum market nearby and slipped into a completely different person, haggling in Créole with the shopkeepers, triumphantly reducing the price of things by a *gourde* or two. He hadn't the heart to tell her it didn't really make a difference. Compared to where he came from, everything in Haiti was dirt cheap.

He bought her a falafel sandwich in the Rue Corbe and pointed out the Arabic names on the shopfronts. He certainly wasn't courting her – in the three months she'd known him, he had never once so much as hinted at anything other than the rather unusual friendship he offered.

By the end of January there were almost no guests left at the hotel. Just Iain, and a couple of UN officers. The owner of the Palme d'Or, a florid-faced Belgian named Pierre Dalry whom Améline had never seen before, started coming in, eating alone on the terrace where Iain often sat. One afternoon, a couple of missionaries came in. They sat a few feet away from him, staring disapprovingly at the bottles of beer that were slowly mounting on his table, like oversized birthday candles. Dalry burped loudly to show he didn't give a damn. Gaspard and Rosalie hovered nervously behind the reception. The air was tense. The country seemed to be holding its breath; though no one seemed sure why. There was talk of riots in the streets of the city below them; in Gonaïves, someone said, the whole town was ablaze. The slum-dwellers of Raboteau had risen up in protest against the regime and the protests were spreading.

At night Améline could hear the sirens howling as patrol cars and jeeps tore along the highway that separated Pétionville from Port-au-Prince; even the neighbourhood dogs joined in the fracas, howling for hours at a moon long disappeared from the sky. She wondered how Madame and Cléones were. She'd been back only once, on a Sunday afternoon, to visit, but Cléones had made it clear she wasn't to come again. Now that she was gone, they didn't want to be reminded of her. Améline didn't understand it. What she did understand, however, was that she was completely on her own. She was afraid it was only a matter of time before the hotel finally shut its doors … and then what? Ynez had left, Rosalie muttered that every day would be her last – everything was sinking. And soon Iain too would be gone.

'Wh … when d'you think you'll be … going?' she asked him one Sunday evening at the end of January, aware of a faint but uncomfortable pressure behind her eyes. Surely she wasn't going to cry?

'Quite soon, I imagine. Situation's not getting any better, is it? My editor thinks I ought to leave before anything really drastic happens.' He was watching her carefully.

Améline nodded slowly. Well, that was just the way it was. He was a rich, white tourist, really, wasn't he? Why would he stay? Haiti was continuing its slow, tortured descent into – what? Madness? Tension in the city was running at an all-time high; there were fresh rumours each day that Baby Doc and his wife were gone, that they'd fled the country, or committed suicide, or had been beaten by their own Tonton Macoutes, or that they'd been poisoned or worse … none of it was yet true. She tried not to think about what would happen to them or to his wife, the exquisitely beautiful Michèle Bennett, if the uprisings succeeded. She concentrated instead on her job. But now, even her job was no longer the same. She still followed a routine, to be sure, but now she was conscious of changing sheets for visitors who no longer came, and ordering laundry supplies in a country that had run out of soap. Iain was one of the last foreigners there – and now he too was leaving. The staff were doing their best to pretend it would all blow over, that the next season would be better, that things were looking brighter. There was something almost comical about their efforts to keep things up. Dalry was now to be found almost every afternoon, slowly drinking himself to death on the verandah of what had once been a fine establishment. Every now and then he would look up and see Améline or one of the other girls passing by, tray in hand, and raise a glass in mock salute – though at whom or what Améline could never tell.

'Would you like to go to dinner tomorrow?' Iain asked her a week later, looking at her closely. 'It's your day off, isn't it?'

'Dinner? With *you*?' Améline blurted the words out before she could stop them. She was embarrassed to see his face turn pink.

'Yes, well … might not be *quite* up to your usual standard but I just thought … since I might be gone soon,' he said quickly, trying to make a joke of it. Améline's face was on fire.

'No, no … I … just didn't expect … you know, it's not …'

'Just for dinner,' he said gently. 'Somewhere else other than here, I meant. We've been chatting over the same table out on the balcony for three months. I just thought it might be nice to go somewhere else. To say goodbye properly.'

A wave of disappointment flooded through her. He really was leaving. The only friend she had. She looked at him and forced herself to smile. 'That would be nice. I … I don't know anywhere else,' she said hesitantly. 'I've never been to … a restaurant.'

'Then I'll see if we can find somewhere nice,' Iain said, smiling at her. 'If there's anywhere left open. I'll ask Gaspard to order a taxi. Eight o'clock, shall we say?'

'Yes. That would be fine,' she said gravely. She looked quickly around her. 'I … I'd better get back to work,' she stammered. 'Before anyone sees me.'

'Of course,' Iain smiled at her. Or at her pretence. 'Shall I meet you at the front of the hotel? Say, quarter to eight?'

'Yes.' And then she fled.

Somehow, Iain had found a functioning restaurant a few miles away, further up in the hills. For Améline, dressed in a slightly too big borrowed skirt and top that Rosalie had been kind enough to lend her, the evening had a magical air that blocked out completely the sound of sporadic gunfire coming from the valley below. They talked of his book and the excitement it seemed to have produced in his long-suffering editor. He pulled a typewritten page out of his jacket and smoothed it on the table between them. She couldn't read the English. 'For Améline,' he translated for her. 'This is her book too, and is for her.' Améline stared at him. She couldn't understand what on earth would have inspired him to write such a thing.

'It's true,' Iain said, smiling at her. 'I learned most of what I wrote about by talking to you. Seeing Haiti through your eyes, not mine.'

'Oh.' Améline looked at her hands. What was there to see? Haiti was dying. They all knew it. As if on cue, another burst of machine-gun fire stuttered into the black night sky.

'You'll be all right, Améline, won't you?' His voice was suddenly urgent.

'Yes, of course.' Améline hastened to assure him.

'What will you do? Where will you go if … if things get worse?'

Améline shrugged. She had no idea. 'Maybe things will get

better,' she said, suddenly playful. And then there was a sound like nothing she'd ever heard before. A deafening 'whump', a single moment when everything around them slowed and then the sky exploded in an orgasm of light. The rat-tat-tat of gunfire and slow, steady whoosh of something else, unidentifiable, that made the windows vibrate and the salt-and-pepper shakers roll off the table and crash to the floor. Everyone froze – outside the dogs were howling and the lights flickered. Suddenly the restaurant was plunged in darkness; yet another power cut. Someone was shouting in the grounds outside, 'Baby Doc is gone! They're gone!' Inside, no one moved.

Iain suddenly pushed back his chair. 'I think,' he said slowly, putting down his napkin, 'that we'd better get out of here.'

'Where ... where to?' Améline could barely speak.

'We'd better make for the British Embassy. I rather have a feeling that that was artillery fire.'

'I ... but ... I ... I'd better go back to the hotel,' Améline stammered. What was the point of her going to the British Embassy?

'You,' Iain said, reaching across the table and grabbing her hand, 'are coming with me.'

The terrified taxi driver could only be persuaded – and then only with the remainder of the money that Iain had brought with him – to take them halfway. They ran the rest. There were helicopters whirring overhead as Iain followed the road the driver had indicated, stopping every now and then, flattening themselves against a wall or a fence as an armoured vehicle or a minibus loaded with screaming, gun-toting men drove past. They were both beyond fear. Améline hadn't stopped to think about *her* fate if she were caught with a white man twice her age, running towards the centre of town where the embassy compound lay. She simply clung on to Iain's arm and ran when and where he directed her. It seemed hours before they reached the walled and guarded compound, with Iain shouting at the armed soldiers to let them through immediately. There was a moment's confusion, Améline couldn't follow the fast and furious exchange, and then someone came out who obviously recognised Iain and the next thing she knew, the heavy gates were being swung open and the two of them were almost dragged in. She stood in the spotlight, her whole body shaking with fright, as Iain seemed to be arguing with the man who'd let them in. It was perhaps fortunate she couldn't understand a word. The man in a white shirt with a badly knotted tie kept pointing at her and shaking his head. She closed her eyes. She could imagine the rest.

Iain thought his heart would burst, not only from the adrenalin and fear that had driven the two of them down the hillside to reach the embassy, but from anger. It was so bloody typical – fucking little bureaucrats. Simpson, the odious little fuck who was the First Secretary and whom he'd seen on more than one occasion in the arms of a couple of the whores who frequented the bars near the Palais National, was doing his best to earn a punch in the face. 'Who,' he kept enquiring frostily, 'is *that*?' Pointing to Améline with all the sarcasm, racism and distaste he could muster in one little word – *that*.

'That' – and then under his breath, 'you pompous little prick' – 'is my wife.'

'Your *wife*?'

'Yes. My wife.' Oh, how he longed to punch him. Although he'd almost equally surprised himself when the words slipped out. But what else was he to do? He couldn't leave her up there, abandon her to whatever fate might be waiting, could he?

'I see. And have you any identification on you? That might ... er, *prove*, as it were, her, er, *status*.'

'Jesus *Christ*, Simpson. We were having *dinner* when the whole show blew up. My bloody passport is in the hotel safe. Where you lot instructed us to keep them. We *ran* down the fucking hill. Couldn't even get a taxi to bring us here. What the fuck d'you expect me to do? Go back *and get my marriage certificate*?' he roared. Eton. Oxford. It worked. Simpson backed down immediately.

'Er, no. It's just … the thing is … we'll have to get you out via the Americans … they're the only ones with helicopters. Take you out to Miami, sir.'

'And?' Iain glared at him.

'They'd normally ask … you know. For papers.'

'There's a war going on, Simpson. In case you hadn't noticed.'

'Yes, sir. Right. I'll … er, I'll sort it out. There's a couple of other … er, wives, sir … in the same boat. If you'd just like to come through …' There was another deafening volley of gunfire. All three of them ducked instinctively. 'Inside, sir! And you, miss! Mrs Blake, I mean. This way! Hurry, please!'

26

By the end of January, Laure could understand almost everything that was said on the TV. She no longer squinted with the effort of concentration, translating every single word. She'd even begun to dream in English. As the mound of her belly grew, so did her confidence. She began to think about what would happen after the birth, in May; she was desperate to leave Belle's apartment but first she had to find a job – and no matter how she tried, she couldn't imagine how she would ever find one with a baby strapped to her side. Perhaps, when the baby was three or four months old, she could find something part-time? Something where she could bring it along? She racked her brains to think about what that sort of job might be … and gave up. She simply had no idea what to do.

One bitterly cold evening in early February, she finished cooking and took her plate of rice and beans into the living room. She settled herself awkwardly on the sofa and switched on the television. It was almost six o'clock, although it had been dark for a couple of hours. It was freezing outside; Duane had told her earlier that day that it would snow soon. There would be news on shortly. She was just about to take a mouthful of food when an image of Port-au-Prince flashed across the screen. Her pulse quickened immediately. She put down her plate and turned the volume up. 'There's been trouble in the Caribbean island of Haiti,' the newscaster began, smiling inappropriately as though it were good news, not bad. 'Crowds hostile to the deposed president and his wife ...' Laure stared at the screen. 'The US has sent in a battalion of Marines ...' She put down her fork, fear rising in her stomach. It had been almost a fort-night since Améline's last letter. Please God, let her be safe. As the images flickered, so familiar to her, her heart sank. She eyed the telephone sitting on the counter beside the kitchen. She hadn't spoken to Grandmère since she'd arrived. She'd dialled the number once or twice, when the loneliness at the beginning had been too much to bear, but at the last minute, remember-ing the look of anger and disgust on Grandmère's face as they drove her to the airport, she'd lost her nerve. She looked back at the screen. It was obvious the reporter had no idea where he was. 'Down in the valley, in Pétionville,' he shouted above the noise of a whirring helicopter. Idiot, she thought to herself. Everyone knew Pétionville was *up* in the hills. She looked at the phone again. Belle would *kill* her if she made an international call. She bit her lip, trying to summon up the courage to ring home. Finally she picked up the receiver and with a shaking hand, dialled the number of 3, Rue Rigaud. The phone rang once, twice ... on the third ring, someone picked it up. '*Oui?*' Grandmère's imperious voice rang out, sounding exactly as it always had done. Laure waited for a few seconds and then put the phone down, her heart thumping. She simply didn't have the nerve to speak to her. But at least she knew she was alive. It would take a lot more than a few helicopters and a bunch of Marines to disrupt Grandmère's life. She'd proved that long ago. She turned anxiously back to the TV screen.

27

Améline looked around her, almost fearfully. She half expected something – someone, a policeman, a Macoute – to jump out of the wardrobe and ... and ... well, do what, exactly? She took a deep breath. Iain had gone out to make arrangements for their onward journey to London. The past two days had been the most frightening of her life; not just because of the violence that had erupted in Port-au-Prince, but because everything that had happened to her had happened for the very first time. It was the first time she'd been in an aeroplane; the first time she'd left Haiti; the first time she'd been addressed as 'Mrs', even though she knew it wasn't true. She'd asked him, as soon as they arrived in Miami, if they could go to Chicago and look for Laure. He'd laughed gently. Chicago was 6,000 miles away, he told her. Further even than Haiti. He'd found a map of the United States and pointed it out to her. It was the first time she'd ever seen Chicago on a map. She'd looked at him, disappointment clouding her face. It was the only thing she'd clung to during that frightening helicopter ride as they rose over the burning city. Lulu. She would see Lulu again. We'll look for her some other time, he'd said, patting her hand lightly.

And now he wanted to take her to London. He wanted to help her. Get her on her feet. She had no idea what he meant, or what to think.

There was another tap at the door. Améline almost jumped out of her skin.

'*Oui*?' she ventured after a while. Then, more loudly, 'Yes?' The door opened slowly.

'Housekeeping. I forgot to bring you a set of towels earlier.' The young Spanish-looking maid smiled at her as she entered the room. Améline stared back at her blankly. She hadn't under-stood a word. The girl pointed to the towels. 'Towels?'

'Tow-els.'

'Yes. ¿Dominicana?'

'Non, Haitienne.' Améline understood enough Spanish to know what she was asking.

'Ah. ¿No hables español?'

'Non. Français.'

'Ah. No lo hablo. ¿Aquí?' She smiled cheerfully and pointed to the bathroom. Améline nodded hesitantly. The girl laid the fluffy towels on the racks provided and, still smiling, left the room. Améline was once again alone. And *freezing*. She was colder in the air-conditioned room than she'd ever been in her life. Yet another first. She got up and went into the bathroom. She pulled one of the fluffy towels off the rail and sat on the bed, wrapping it around her shoulders. It felt wonderfully soft and warm; she leaned back against the pillows that were bigger and softer than any she'd ever seen or touched. The journey, the incomprehensible language, the constant smiles and the sudden leap into a completely unknown and unknowable future – it was exhausting, as well as frightening. She did the only thing she could think of – she went to sleep.

Iain came in half an hour later. He peered into the dim interior, seeing only the shape of the girl for whom he'd abandoned his customary caution to the winds, huddled in one corner of the bed as though afraid to take up any more space than was strictly necessary, and nearly wept. He entered the room, shutting the door quietly behind him and found her cuddled up with a towel over her shoulders. What on earth have I done? he asked himself, as he carefully pulled up the covers over her sleeping form. He'd got Améline out of Haiti almost without thinking. He was in a hotel room somewhere in the centre of Miami without a fucking clue what to do next. He ran a hand over his face. Whatever else might transpire, one thing was clear – he was responsible for her now. But then what? Take her back to Malvern? He somehow couldn't picture Améline in the cottage on Elgar Lane. What would Viv say?

He eased his feet out of his shoes and padded across the room in his socks. First things first – he desperately needed a shower. He turned on the faucet and stood under the blast of cool water. My poor, poor Améline. What next?

Améline woke as soon as she heard the water being turned on. She lay in bed for a few minutes, wondering what she ought to do. She had only the clothes she'd arrived in; Rosalie's borrowed skirt and shirt, the same sandals she'd been wearing for over a year. The water stopped abruptly and she heard the sound of the shower door being opened. Her heart began to race. She quickly got out of bed, smoothed down her skirt and her hair and was standing by the window when the bathroom door finally opened and Iain emerged.

'Améline.' He stood in front of her in the ridiculously large dressing gown the hotel provided. His expression was kind, warm. She had no idea what to do or say.

'Look, why don't I get dressed? You must be hungry ... shall we go somewhere for dinner? Pick up where we left off?'

'Thank ... yes, please.' Améline was starving. She'd been too scared to eat on the flight. Besides, she couldn't understand a word of what was said to her – how was she supposed to say anything back? She sat down at the desk at the window as Iain disappeared into the bathroom again and emerged a few minutes later, looking remarkably clean, even in the clothes he'd been wearing for the past twenty-four hours. She looked down at her feet; she had nothing else to wear ... would it be all right? She wrung her hands nervously. What would people think?

'You look absolutely fine,' Iain said, reading her thoughts. 'But we'll go shopping tomorrow, get ourselves kitted out. Don't want to spend another twenty-four hours in these,' he gave a short, mirthless laugh. Améline looked away. She had nothing – not a single *gourde* to her name. She was in such unfamiliar territory – what was she supposed to say? 'Come on, love. It's been a while since I was last in Miami but I think they still serve good steaks on Ocean Boulevard. After you ...' he held open the door for her. She caught a whiff of soap and the faint scent of the hotel shampoo as she passed. He smelled clean and solid, and somehow reassuring. She blinked back her tears. Now was not the time to cry.

The following morning, when she woke up, Iain was gone. She lay in the enormous bed which he had courteously offered to her after they'd come back from the restaurant, saying he would be perfectly fine on the couch. Time enough to cross those bridges, he'd murmured. Améline didn't know what to say. There was a note stuck to the dressing room mirror. She slipped out of bed and picked it up. 'Make sure you spend it all!' There was a small pile of money on the table. She picked up the wad, staring at it in disbelief. Two hundred dollars. She calculated rapidly – it was more money than she had ever seen in her life. Spend it all? Was he insane? She fingered one of the notes gingerly. Twenty dollars. The slim green banknote with the face of some dead American president looking sternly back at her. She swallowed. She didn't even know where to go. Yet, despite her hesitation, there was something wonderfully warm and pleasurable beginning to sweep through her – the slow, almost unrecognisable burn of excitement. She'd never been shopping for clothes – or anything else other than food – in her life. She'd accompanied Laure once or twice to the shops in Port-au-Prince when they'd still been open, and Laure always made sure she bought something for Améline but the thought of walking into a shop and choosing what *she* wanted . . . it made her almost dizzy with pleasure. But where would she go? Come on, Améline . . . *think*! She spoke a few words of Spanish . . . enough to ask one of the maids for help, perhaps? She jumped up from the bed. Iain had been gone over an hour and all she'd done was sit on the edge of the bed, staring at the pile of money. She was being weak and silly. It was time to get moving.

Half an hour later, showered, her hair pulled back neatly off her face, she was ready. She thrust her feet into her battered sandals, pushed the pile of banknotes into her bra and opened the door. There was no one in the silent, sanitised corridor. She closed it, making sure she had the key in her hand, and walked to the elevator. They were on the fourteenth floor, overlooking some sort of harbour. She had no idea of the topography of Miami – all she knew was that it was hot, very bright and, most impressive of all, very clean and very shiny. Just like the TV shows that she and Laure used to watch.

The elevator whooshed her silently down to the ground floor. As the doors opened on to the marble polished floor and the uniformed bellhops pushing huge cases about, she had a blinding moment of panic. She felt so out of place! Everyone around her was dressed beautifully, with clean, bright clothes and the unmistakable air of confidence that money bought. She steeled herself to move forward. Head down, she walked across the floor. Her palms were sweating and her heart was racing. Everyone was staring at her, she was sure. She walked up to the front desk and looked quickly around. Everyone seemed so busy, so self-assured ... so *perfect*.

'Hi, can I help you?' The smiling blonde girl at the counter looked at her.

'*Es ... español, por favor?*' Améline almost whispered.

'*Si ... puedo ayudarle?*' There wasn't even a moment's hesitation. Within five minutes, the receptionist had given Améline a map of the city and a list of shops in the Galleria, the nearest mall and organised a cab with a Martiniquean driver named Joey to take her there – *and* bring her back. As easy as that. Somewhat dazedly, Améline walked out of the hotel. Seconds later, she was in the back of a cab speeding down the road.

The mall was bigger and more terrifying than any place she'd ever been. So many people: they streamed in through the mall's many entrances, bags carried purposefully over their shoulders, heads held high; children running ahead of the parents ... everyone animated by the excitement of what lay ahead. When she walked into the main entrance, she gasped. The glass atrium stretched upwards, almost to the sky. Thousands of pricks of pin-point light showered down on to the gleaming marble floor; in the centre was a magnificent fountain throwing up jets of coloured water which cascaded down a rock wall; there was music all around and the smell of perfume wafted through the air. There were little metal kiosks dotted around the enormous ground floor, selling huge, puffy whirls of pink; tiny bread rolls smelling of cinnamon and a hundred other spices she couldn't identify; hotdogs with mustard and ketchup oozing out as kids took giant-sized bites ... her legs almost gave way beneath her. She'd never seen anything like it. *Oh, Iain ... why couldn't he have come with her?* She was too scared to enter this earthly paradise – she felt dizzy with fear.

It took her a good twenty minutes to pull herself together. Oddly, it was Madame who came to the rescue. How would *she* behave? Améline wondered. Madame was the only person of stature Améline had ever met – all she had to do was imagine what *she* would do, and then do it. Madame would *never* shuffle along, head down, hands twitching nervously at her sides as Améline was – was she *kidding?* Madame's head would be held high, her posture ramrod straight, nose slightly in the air – *look down on me if you dare!*

She took a deep breath, picked herself up and walked straight into the nearest shop. It was an enormous department store, full of little cosmetics counters and women holding out bottles of perfume that they sprayed every time you wandered near. She couldn't read any of the signs but it wasn't long before she found herself in the department selling underwear. She walked dazedly along between the racks selling the most beautiful bras and panties and other, less identifiable garments that she'd never seen before. She put out a finger and gingerly touched a pale pink and green lace bra with tiny flowers along the seams – it looked good enough to eat, never mind wear. Who would ever wear anything quite so delicate and *small?* Not her.

She left the racks of lingerie and wandered around until she found the kind of clothing more suited to someone of her standing. Plain white underwear – yet still whiter and softer than anything she'd ever worn. T-shirts; a pair of blue jeans, just like Lulu's; two pairs of sensible shoes – *real* shoes, closed, front and back. She couldn't believe just how far two hundred dollars could go. At the end of an hour, with more apparel than she could carry, she still had $125.95 left.

As she staggered towards the exit, she caught sight of a solitary little black dress, hanging by itself. She stopped and stared at it. It was beautiful – a simple, knee-length dress but what had caught her eye was the bodice of tiny, black sequins, just like the dress she and Lulu had altered that day. She let her bags drop to the ground. How much was it? She gingerly turned over the price tag. One hundred and ninety-nine dollars! She snatched her hand away as though it might bite. She gazed at it longingly for a few seconds longer and was just about to pick up her bags again when a salesgirl descended on her, smiling and babbling away. Améline shook her head.

'You should try it on, ma'am,' the girl said, her mouth stretching into an even wider smile. Améline shook her head in incomprehension. Her heart was beating fast – the way these Americans talked and smiled. It was terrifying!

'*Non, non . . . trop cher,*' Améline stammered, struggling to get away. '*Cher, cher . . .*' she said, rubbing her thumb and finger together in the universal sign for money. Universally understood, it seemed, by everyone except Americans.

'Could I interest you in a bag or some shoes to go with it, ma'am? It's black, which is such a great colour . . . everything goes with . . . what? Ma'am? Are you all right?'

There were tears of frustration in Améline's eyes. She shook her head. Then, to the salesgirl's horror, she reached into her bra and took out her money. She thrust her remaining hundred-odd dollars into the girl's hand. She pointed to the price tag and shook her head.

'But it's on *sale*,' the girl said, still recovering from the sight of money emerging from Améline's chest. She pointed to the enormous red '50% OFF!' tag hanging off the bodice. 'It's on *sale* – for ninety-nine dollars. You have enough . . . would you like it?'

Five minutes later, her head still spinning, she left the shop with the beautiful, precious dress wrapped in tissue paper and nestled in a box all of its own. She was almost too excited to think. Joey was waiting for her just where he'd dropped her off. As soon as he saw her, he jumped out of the car to help her, chuckling. She'd gone into the store looking all lost and confused, he said to her – now look at her. She couldn't even carry everything she'd bought. Welcome to America!

He was still chuckling when he dropped her off at the front door. She handed him her last twenty dollar bill, fishing it out from her bra. He shook his head, but she insisted. 'Please,' she said, thrusting the money into his hands. 'Thank you for taking me ... and waiting. I would never have gone if you hadn't taken me.'

'Man, that's real kind of you, miss. You ever need something ... you give me a call, you hear?'

'I will.'

'And,' he added in a stage whisper, just before she closed the door, 'I'd get a ... uh, purse, if I was you. Over here, they don't like it too much if you carry your money there.' He tapped his chest and winked knowingly. Améline's face felt as though it were on fire. She smiled her thanks and picked up her bags. A bellhop jumped forward and took some of the heavy ones. She ignored the surprised glances of the people around her and walked straight to the elevator. She hoped Iain wasn't yet back – she wanted to take a shower, throw off her old clothes and wear something – *anything* – new.

She opened the door to the room, her heart beating fast. He wasn't there! She tipped the bellhop with her last couple of dollars and dragged all the bags inside the room. She glanced at the bedside clock. It was almost five o'clock. She hadn't eaten a thing all day – she'd been too nervous.

It took her half an hour to neatly fold and put away her new things. She looked proudly at the wardrobe when she was done. Now *her* things outnumbered Iain's few shirts and trousers hanging to one side. She stood staring at her purchases for a few more minutes then turned to go into the bathroom. She stripped quickly and stuffed the decades-old T-shirt, skirt and hateful sandals in the waste-paper basket. Goodbye to all *that*. She stepped under the torrent of hot water and washed every last trace of Haiti out of her hair and from her body. Then she wrapped herself in the giant bathrobe and walked to the bed. She stepped into a pair of snow-white panties and fastened the new bra with trembling fingers. She caught sight of herself in the dressing room mirror and blinked. She looked ... *good. Clean. Pretty.* If it wasn't for her hair, springing up around her head like the innards of an old mattress – she scraped it hurriedly into a bun at the nape of her neck. The new black dress fitted perfectly, clinging to her skin like a glove. Tight and shimmering across the breasts and hips, opening out just a little at the knees so she could walk. She looked at her watch again. It was six o'clock. It was almost dinner time. Her stomach rumbled again. She wriggled her way to the bathroom and began to put on some of the make-up she'd bought. She couldn't quite remember the sequence of all the little bottles and boxes she'd bought. Did that funny brown liquid go on first? What about the powder? And what was the difference between the red powder and the brown powder? She lifted a brush and began to apply what she thought ought to go where.

Iain opened the door and saw Améline lying fast asleep on the bed, a black dress rucked up around her thighs, a pair of sensible flat shoes strapped rather incongruously on her feet. The bedside lamp was on, casting a soft warm glow over her sleeping body. She looked completely different. The dress was beautiful, tight across the hips, slit at the sides and showed off her pretty breasts. He swallowed. She looked so peaceful and innocent, lying there like that. He caught sight of her face. 'What the ...?' he murmured to himself, peering at her closely. What on earth had she done to her face?

Suddenly, she woke with a start. 'Ugh,' she moaned, as if she didn't quite understand where she was. She struggled upright. Iain was still standing over her, peering at her face. 'Améline ... what on earth are you wearing? What have you done to your face?'

'This?' She put up a hand self-consciously. Iain felt his heart contract. 'I ... I thought ... the girl at the shop ... she gave me …' the words came tumbling out of her mouth. He switched on the overhead light.

'Who on earth …' he began, bending down so that his face was level with hers. She burst into tears. 'Oh, Améline … no, no … don't cry, love … no, don't. You look lovely, honestly, really pretty,' he stammered.

Améline only wailed even more. 'I don't …' she sobbed, pulling the dress over her knees. 'I didn't know what to do with all the … the …'

'Shh … pet, don't … please don't cry. Please. We'll go out to dinner, just like I said … come on, old girl …'

'Old? I'm not *old* …'

'Of course not, it's just an English saying. Bad translation. No, you look lovely. We might have to take a little bit of this stuff off …' he said, pointing to her cheek. 'You've got a teeny bit too much of the red on your cheeks, that's all. Come on, let's get you up.' He held out a hand. Améline took it gingerly. 'What d'you fancy eating? Seafood? Italian?'

'Anything,' Améline said, her chest still heaving.

'What did you have for lunch?'

'No … nothing …'

'Why ever not?'

'I didn't know … I didn't know what to ask for … and I can't use the telephone.' Fresh tears were threatening. Iain stared at her. He was appalled at his own thoughtlessness.

'Oh, Améline … look, I won't leave you alone any more. Next time I have to go out, you come with me. We'd better start teaching you a bit of English, my girl. Can't take you back home with me and there's you not understanding a word of it.' He looked at her, wondering if she'd understood what he was proposing. He was going to take this poor girl back to London with him. And he was – he swallowed – he was going to marry her. What else was he planning to do? It was – at least to some extent – the code he'd tried to live by; what he'd been taught. Help those who need it. Améline had helped him in a way she wasn't even aware of; now it was his turn.

He was conscious as he went into the bathroom to help her

wash her face of how it would appear to everyone else. Viv's voice came into his head again. *Oh, Iain* – in that exaggerated, exasperated way of hers. *What on earth are you doing?* And Améline? The sight of her vulnerable, painted face and body as she lay waiting in a hotel room for him had almost brought on a heart attack – of sympathy, yes, and pity – his heart ached for her. But, and this was the all-important question, pity was hardly the basis for marriage, was it?

'Here you go,' he murmured, handing her a flannel. She rubbed her face the way a child might, squeezing her eyes against the intrusion of soap and hot water. He watched her, quite overcome. Well, lust hadn't turned out to be such a winner, either, he thought, thinking again of Viv. And it wasn't as though he didn't fancy Améline. God, as much as it appalled him, seeing her slim, brown legs and the smooth dark skin of her breasts as they spilled out of the sequinned bodice of her dress had brought on an erection the likes of which he could hardly remember. Careful, Blake, he schooled himself. She's little more than a child. She wasn't – she was in her early twenties he guessed – but there was something so naïve and innocent about her. Jesus, what was he getting into? What was he getting *her* into?

Améline put down her fork and knife and stared at him. 'Marry you?' she repeated, not sure if she'd heard right.

'Yes. Marry me.' His eyes were fixed on hers.

'But ... you don't ... you don't know me ...' Améline said, her mind in turmoil. Was this the reason ...?

'Améline, you're an extraordinary person. I ... I want to help you,' he said lamely. He seemed unsure of what to say.

'You *have* helped me,' she insisted. 'I don't know how I can ever repay you ...' She looked around the restaurant where he'd brought her. She stared at her plate; at the untouched lobster and scalloped potatoes and vegetables whose names she'd pronounced for the very first time that evening. Two days ago she'd been eating boiled collard greens – it had been months since she'd eaten meat.

'Marry me,' he repeated, with more urgency this time. His food too lay untouched.

Améline swallowed. Was this what it was all about? Was that the reason he'd brought her out of Haiti? To marry her? She swallowed again. The proposal was about as far from her imagination as anything could be. When she and Laure had talked dreamily about boyfriends and love and weddings, she'd never really connected the fantasies of a church and a white dress and all the things that seemed to accompany the idea of a marriage with *her*. Laure, yes, of course – and there had been many, many conversations about Laure's chances of finding the right person seeing as she'd turned out so dark – but none of the conversations had ever really involved her, Améline ... not seriously, at least. The best she could have hoped for would have been someone who worked in one of the neighbouring households; perhaps not a gardener or a night watchman, nothing as low as *that* ... but still, Améline had always, always understood that the fantasy of the white dress and the special day would never – *could* never – belong to her. And now – here she was, sitting in a restaurant the likes of which she'd never even dreamed of *serving* in, opposite a man old enough to be her father and a *white* man at that, dressed in clothes he'd bought her in a country he'd brought her to. She could feel the thick tightening of her throat and the tears that would surely follow.

'Améline ... oh, dear ... is it as awful a proposition as that?' Iain looked at her with such dismay that she reached across the table and touched his hand, the first time she'd touched him of her own accord.

'No, no ... it's not that ... of course not. I'm just ... I don't know what to say ...'

'Say "yes". Please say "yes".' His face was still tense.

She opened her mouth. Everything around her slowed to a halt. The sounds of the restaurant receded, everything pushed back before the enormity of the question he'd just asked her. Madame, Laure, Cléones ... and yes, Père Estimé, too, though she tried hard not to think about him. Everything flashed before her eyes, swirling like the kaleidoscope Laure had shown her once, narrowing to this one single point. *Yes or no.* Behind her lay Haiti and the accumulated unhappiness of twenty-four years. Ahead of her lay ... what? A chance at something else? She didn't love Iain Blake; how could she? He wasn't hers to love – he belonged to a different world and one which, under normal circumstances, would never cross paths with her own. But the circumstances weren't normal, wasn't that the point? Haiti had erupted, exploded – everything was suddenly changed, including her. She couldn't go back. Iain Blake held the key to whatever future she had. *A single answer. Yes or no.* She drew a deep breath. 'Yes.'

There was a brief pause in which nothing moved, neither spoke. Then Iain passed a hand over his face. 'Thank God for that, old girl,' he said, lifting his wine glass with a shaky hand. 'Thank God for that.'

28

On February 7, 1986, accompanied by his wife and a clutch of faithful followers, Baby Doc Duvalier fled Haiti on board an American aeroplane. For days Laure remained glued to the television. The army had taken over; it wasn't clear who was to succeed Duvalier. Overcoming her fear, she'd rung home only to find the lines had been cut. She couldn't even get through to the de Menières. No letters came; there was no further news. Just silence. Belle was no help; she was unmoved by the crisis rapidly unfolding in the country, shrugging her shoulders whenever Laure tried to bring the subject up and turning away. 'Fools', she called them, though Laure wasn't sure who she meant. 'They deserve it,' Belle remarked acidly, lighting a cigarette and glancing disinterestedly at the screen. 'Every last one of them. Rotten to the core.'

'But what about Grandmère?' Laure asked timidly. 'And Améline?'

Belle shrugged again. 'Especially *her*.' It was clear whom she meant. Laure held her tongue. Here too were things that seemed better left unsaid. She kept quiet and scoured the papers with a sinking sense of unease. Still nothing came. No word from anyone.

One morning, almost three months after the overthrow of Baby Doc and with a month or so to go until the birth, Laure woke to the sound of someone tapping at her door. She struggled upright, peering at her watch. It was light outside but the curtains in her room were drawn.

'Laure? You awake?' It was Belle. She sounded uncharacteristically friendly.

'Yes ... I'm awake.'

'Can I come in?' Laure looked at the door, puzzled. Belle never asked for permission to enter her room. Half the time she seemed to forget Laure was in it.

'Sure.' Belle came in trailing a cloud of perfume and the belt of her tattered silk dressing gown. Her hair was sticking up on end as though she'd just woken up. She held an unlit cigarette in one hand and immediately plonked herself on the edge of Laure's bed.

'Honey,' she began excitedly. 'I've been thinking.' Laure looked at her nervously – what on earth had brought this warmth on?

'About what?' she asked tentatively.

''Bout the baby. *Cherie*, I know you don't want this child. I haven't asked you, but I'm not blind.' Laure was quiet. Belle hadn't shown the slightest interest in the child ... why now? 'I've been talking to Marie,' she went on. Laure nodded cautiously. Marie Nithèse was a friend of Belle's, a Haitian woman who lived on the north side of the city, where most of the Haitian community in Chicago lived. She was a nurse and sometimes brought things over for Belle from the hospital when things with one or other of Belle's 'friends' got a little out of hand. 'The thing is,' Belle continued, lighting her cigarette, waving the smoke in Laure's face, 'Marie says there's a whole lot of couples she knows just *dying* for a child.' She looked at Laure. 'Adoption, *ma p'tite*. You could have someone adopt the baby.'

Laure swallowed. Her hands went instinctively, protectively, around her stomach.

'And,' Belle went on carefully, 'the beauty of it is they're willing to pay. Big bucks. You could do it privately. She knows this one couple ... a black couple. She's a lawyer or something ... he's some big-shot businessman. They've been trying for ages, honey ... she told them about you.'

Laure opened her mouth and tried to speak but nothing came out. For sale. Of course. Belle wanted her to sell her child. No wonder she'd come stumbling into her room at eight in the morning, half-asleep.

'I have to ask you this, honey,' Belle said, laying an arm on Laure. 'The baby's father ... is he ... well, was he ... you know, *dark*? Was he dark?'

Laure almost threw up. 'I ... don't ... I can't ... I have to go to the bathroom,' she said, the words tumbling out of her mouth. She stumbled out of bed, ignoring Belle's hand and practically ran into the bathroom. *Her mother wanted to sell her child!* She leaned against the sink, weak with nausea.

'Look,' Belle's voice sounded from the doorway. Laure turned around. She was standing there, smoking and coolly regarding her daughter. 'You're young, honey ... you have your whole life in front of you. They're offering ten thousand dollars for a baby, Laure! Ten thousand dollars! *Imagine!* And what's more – if the baby's dark, *really* black, we could probably get more. Mr Ellison? He's as black as the ace of spades!' Belle's high, tinkling laughter echoed around the tiny bathroom. Laure sat on the toilet seat, unable to look up at her. 'Think about it, honey,' Belle advised, turning to go. 'But don't take too long, will you, *chérie*? They're *real* keen for this to happen.'

Laure sat there for a long time after the door had closed, struggling with her thoughts. Give the baby up? She couldn't put her finger on the moment when she'd stopped thinking about it as the most terrible thing that had ever happened to her and started to get used to its presence inside her. She'd grown used to its sudden kicks and the queer, turning motion as it moved and settled; she'd even begun murmuring to it as she passed her hand over the smooth, tight skin. In a month or so, she would meet the tiny person she carried – and now Belle was asking her to consider giving it away. No, selling it. The thought of it made her feel sick. And yet what could she possibly provide for it? She looked around the tiny room. As hard as she tried, it was impossible to imagine bringing a child back to this. The apartment stank of stale cigarettes and unwashed dishes, no matter how hard she tried to keep things clean. Belle's constant shouting, the whirr and buzz of helicopters overhead, the occasional sound of gunshots further down the alley. If it were a boy what would he become? One of the young 'runners' who hung about on the street corners, alerting the older, harder drug dealers to an approaching cop car? Or a girl … what would her choices be? To wind up like Belle or the under-age prostitutes who plied their trade under the neon gloom of the street lights? She shuddered. It was the hardest thing she had ever had to think about. It wasn't a choice. You couldn't call it that.

29

She never saw it. It was taken from her at 6.03 a.m., June 4, 1986, after almost six hours of agonising labour. She knew it was a boy; that he was healthy – 6lbs 4oz – with ten fingers and ten toes … and that was it. The midwife who attended her told her it was better that way. All the nurses knew the pretty young girl in room seven had chosen to give the child up for immediate adoption and were well schooled in the procedures.

'It's better you don't even hold him, honey,' she said as they cleaned her up. 'It makes it harder.' Laure couldn't speak. She stared at the nurse, her whole being flooded with an emptiness that she couldn't express. To be without him, suddenly, with a snap of the fingers ... it was harder than she'd dared imagine.

'What ... colour ... is he?' she asked, after a moment. The midwife looked at her, confused.

'Colour? What d'you mean, honey? He's black. Like you,' she laughed.

'No, I mean ... is he dark? Light?'

'Oh, they all come out light, honey. He'll darken after a few days, you'll see.' Then she stopped. 'Well, I guess you won't be seein' him. But anyway, he's fine. Gonna be a cute little boy. That's all you need to know, darlin'.' Then she was gone. Laure lay back against the starched sheets and turned her face to the wall. *Forget about this. Forget about him. You did the right thing for him.* She whispered the words to herself. She knew she had no alternative. If she thought about it, she would die. She put the heel of her hand on her trembling, jelly-like stomach and prayed for the strength to forget.

Belle was waiting for her when they discharged her the following day. She was in agony. Her breasts were heavy and aching and her legs wobbled when she walked. Her emotions ran amok – one minute there was relief, the next minute tears would roll down her face, unsummoned and unstoppable.

'You OK?' was all Belle said as she put Laure's bag into the trunk of Uncle Frank's shiny green car. He was behind the wheel; he barely glanced at her as she got in. Laure turned to look out of the window. Cook County Hospital. She knew enough about Chicago to know that that was where the poor went; blacks, Hispanics, those on welfare and Medic-Aid. Although, she remembered, she wasn't exactly poor. Ten thousand dollars. That was what the couple from Lincoln Park had paid for him. Laure had met them the week before the birth; the wife had insisted on meeting her and Belle in person. Laure sat across from them in almost total silence as Belle prattled on and on. She couldn't quite believe what she was doing – *selling her child?* – but, God help her, she couldn't even summon the strength to protest. *It isn't like that. I'm giving him a better life.* She repeated the words to herself over and over again. She felt the wife's eyes on her, there was something in her expression – disgust? – Laure couldn't tell. She didn't want to know. She listened to Belle organising the details of the payment – a deposit of five hundred dollars which they gave to Laure in cash; the balance would be paid after the baby was born. Healthy. That was the condition. They didn't want damaged goods.

Well, she'd delivered her side of the bargain. A perfect baby boy. She wiped the tears from her cheeks and huddled down further in the car. She wanted to die.

An hour later, she was looking at Belle, not sure if she could believe what she was hearing, her legs threatening to buckle under her.

'The thing is,' Belle said, lifting a cigarette to her lips with shaking fingers, 'I was *gonna* put the money in the bank … I just don't know what happened … it was here, right *here* and I swear I don't know who's taken it …'

'Get out,' Laure said suddenly, in English. She felt her legs give way and she sat down heavily on the bed. 'Please. Get out.' She looked down at her clenched hands. Something had finally snapped inside her. Belle looked at her uncertainly and then hurried out of the room. Laure's breasts were aching, almost as much as her heart. The ducts would dry up of their own accord, the midwife had told her – just as soon as her body realised there was no child to feed. *No child to feed.* She held herself very, very still, biting down on her tongue to stop herself from crying out loud. She ignored the pain and the sudden, warm rush of blood in her mouth. In a minute or two, if she held herself very still, the wave of black desolation would sweep over her and then it would be gone. She sat there motionless, waiting.

A little later, she brushed back the tears with the edge of her sleeve and blew out her cheeks. She picked up her purse, put a nightdress, a toothbrush and a change of clothing for the next morning into a small holdall and stood for a second at the window, drawing deep breaths. Enough. She'd had enough. Belle had stolen the money the Ellisons had paid. She had the five hundred dollars they'd given her before the birth and some change ... that was all. But it was enough. It had to be; she had no other choice. She had her passport; a couple of books and her letters from Améline. She looked at the bedside table. There, still in its frame, was the photograph Améline had given her of Belle. She slipped it out of its frame and slowly, deliberately, ripped it in half. Then in half again.

She switched off the light and stepped into the hallway. She could hear Belle and Frank arguing, probably over her money. She'd been in America less than six months; she'd given birth to a child and she'd sold him. Nothing anyone did to her could be worse than that. She walked away from Belle without saying goodbye. Just as Belle had done to her.

30

It took her over a month to find a job. Five weeks of pounding the hot, dusty pavements, her breasts still aching, her stomach quivering, day after day, walking into offices, shops, supermarkets ... anywhere, anything. Each time, it was the same conversation, over and over again: 'What's your social security number? You don't have one? Oh, you're not legal? I'm sorry, I just can't.' It finally dawned on her that she would have to go about it differently. Not through the front door, but through the back. Applying for regular jobs – as a secretary, a receptionist, a supermarket checkout girl – just wasn't going to work. Never mind that she couldn't type. She would have to look elsewhere, in the places that those without papers or the legal right to work would look. She wasn't stupid – six months of sitting in front of the television had taught her more than just how to speak passable English. She'd watched the news; she'd seen the statistics. Chicago, she knew, was supposed to hold a million and a half illegal immigrants. People who, at one point, might have come into the country legally, on an airline, just as she had done. And, just as had happened to her, their visas had expired, were not renewed – who knew the reasons why. A million and a half people could not be sitting starving to death in this great, big city. They were out there, working, supporting themselves and families, putting food on the table. The question was where to find them – and those who employed them. Where would they be likely to work? What sort of small-scale businesses would hire such people? Think, Laure ... *think*! She sat on the bed in the dingy little motel she'd gone to after leaving Belle's, staring out of the back window at the clear blue early summer sky, racking her brains and trying not to slide into the black hole of despair that constantly threatened to overwhelm her.

It came to her, suddenly, later that night. Restaurants. Of course! Waitresses and kitchen staff. She sat upright. Girls who served behind the counter at the small beauty salons that dotted the neighbourhood. Girls who swept up at the hairdressers. All of a sudden a whole world of potential employment opened itself up to her – never mind that it was a million miles away from the schoolgirl conversations she'd had with Régine ... *what do you want to be when you grow up*? She bit down on her lower lip. The sooner she forgot about those conversations the better.

The following afternoon she struck lucky. She was hired as a waitress in a small restaurant on Milwaukee run by two rather cheerful Cuban brothers. She'd walked in, asked to see the manager and gone through her usual story – she'd arrived from the Caribbean, was awaiting her papers but in the meantime was looking for a job. Anything – she was a hard worker and not afraid of long hours ... she'd tried not to look desperate. Julio, the elder of the two, as she later found out, must have felt sorry for her. OK, he said finally, we'll give it a try. She stared at him, almost unwilling to believe her ears. He led her through to the back, introduced her to the cook and his brother, to two other waitresses and pulled an apron off the peg. One of the waitresses had quit on them the day before, he said, and left them short. 'It's your lucky day, *señorita*!' Laure took the apron with shaking fingers, tied it around her waist and followed him through to the front. Now that she'd found a job, she was petrified. She had no idea how to do it or even what to do.

Someone must have been watching over her that afternoon, however, because at the end of it, Julio handed her a twenty-dollar bill and told her to come back the next day. She walked out of the restaurant and all the way back down Washington to the motel in a daze. On impulse, she went into the supermarket where she'd come almost a month before and bought herself an ice cream. She handed over the same twenty-dollar bill to the cashier and ignored her worried glance. It was only when she got outside that she realised she was crying. No wonder the cashier had looked so perturbed.

A couple of days later, she stared at the three plates in her hand, confused. *Merde* . . . which was which? Who had asked for the chicken *burrito* and who wanted the beef? It was her third day on the job and, if anything, it was worse than the first. 'Excuse me, sir . . . chicken?' she asked, trying desperately to balance the other two plates in her other hand while lowering the chicken to him.

'No, I'm vegetarian,' the man answered, looking rather annoyed. 'And it's an *enchilada*. I ordered a vegetarian *enchilada* and my wife here has a *chimichanga*. Not,' he peered at the dish she was attempting to lower, 'a *burrito*.'

'Oh. OK, er, just wait one second, sir . . . I'll be right back,' Laure could feel the sweat breaking out down her back. It was so hot inside the tiny restaurant. Had she written down the wrong thing? All those *burritos* and *enchiladas* and *tacos* and *chimichangas* . . . she just couldn't keep up. As well as traditional Cuban fare, Irazú catered for the whole Latin American sub-continent. That meant not only did she have to master the more usual things like *burritos* and *tacos*, but all sorts of strange-sounding dishes like *carne en jocón*, beef in a tomato and pepper sauce; *chuchitos*, also known as *tamales* in Mexico; a simple dish like rice and beans had about four different names – *fríjoles con arroz, gallo pinto, asopao* in Guatemala, with the addition of pieces of chicken – *quesadillas* which seemed to be soft *tortillas* but baked with cheese … in the first few hours, her head was spinning.

She ran back downstairs, still balancing the plates on her arm. But why three? she asked herself, reaching the bottom. There were only two at the table she'd just served … oh, shit … maybe she'd gone to the wrong table. She turned around and hurried back upstairs. Sure enough, there was a table of three sitting by the window looking distinctly pissed off. She apologised, putting each plate down carefully.

'Excuse me,' someone said loudly from behind. She turned round guiltily. It was another customer, pointing to his watch. 'Lady, I ain't got all day, you know.'

'Coming, sir, coming …' Laure rushed back to the kitchen and picked up two more plates of steaming food before running up the stairs again. Now, who'd ordered these? She turned to her left – was that the vegetarian *enchilada*? Or the chicken *chimichanga*? And what about the *tostada* that the gentleman by the window had ordered? She turned left again, then right, confused. It was one turn too many. The *enchilada* plate slipped out of her hand. She let go of the *chimichanga* plate in the other hand in order to try and catch it – there was a shout, someone scraping back their chair … and the unmistakable crack of china hitting cement. A customer yelled as something hit her leg. Laure put her face in hands. Julio had to come running from behind the counter. The floor was a mess of beans, avocado slices, salsa and bits of chicken. He held her by the shoulder.

'*Mira, chica. Vé abajo,*' he said, surprisingly gentle. 'Go downstairs. Take a coupla minutes' break, OK? Go on, now.'

Laure nodded dumbly. She was too ashamed of herself to speak. She fled downstairs, avoiding the curious stares of the customers who'd just seen her make such a fool of herself. She couldn't even manage a waitressing job. She pushed open the door to the little office that Julio and Léon worked in before the restaurant opened. There was a chair in the corner. She sat down, her legs feeling like jelly, and put her head on her knees. She would be fired, of course – no question about it. Three days on the job and she'd already messed it up.

'*Chica*,' Julio said, coming into the room a few minutes later and wiping his hands on his apron. He looked at her. She stared up at him with those huge black eyes brimming with tears. He felt sorry for her. *Really* sorry. She was a nice kid.

'I'm so … sorry,' she stammered, getting up immediately. 'I thought I could do it … I'm really sorry.'

He held up a hand to stop her. 'No problem. You take your time. Today's a busy day. You go home, OK? You come back tomorrow.' He wasn't sure *why* he was giving her a second chance but there was something so tough and yet so fragile about her – shit, she was only a kid. Eighteen at the most. He shook his head. She'd get better at it. He'd give her another shot.

She stared at him. 'But … I can't do it … I'm useless. I'm no good at it. I—'

''S OK. Don' ask me why … I think you OK. I like the way you laugh – I heard you laugh that one time. But you don't laugh enough. So go home, OK? Come back tomorrow.' Julio interrupted her. Laure looked at the floor, afraid she would burst into tears. 'You know something funny, *chica*?' he asked her, turning to go back upstairs. 'You *so* bad, baby, you make *me* look good!' He laughed again, hard, and disappeared up the stairs.

31

You didn't have to be a genius to work it out. The signs were there; Melanie just hadn't read them properly. She hadn't

148

wanted to. She'd been so preoccupied with other, more important things. Like getting Steve to agree to her moving in with him that she'd barely given a thought to what he did when he wasn't at the Pink Palm Lounge. She begged, pleaded, cajoled, cried … anything to get him to break his golden rule. No one stays over. Ever. He'd obviously never met anyone quite as determined as Melanie. Three months after she'd begun her assault, he finally gave in. Melanie was over the moon. She moved into his luxurious penthouse apartment overlooking the Hollywood Hills an hour after he put down the phone. It took her a week to cart over her possessions from Tina's and another week to figure out what was really going on.

Steve di Marco was no ordinary restaurateur. In fact, Steve di Marco was *hardly* a restaurateur. Steve's real business was drugs. Blow. Snow. Cocaine. But by the time Melanie worked it out, she wasn't sure she cared. After all, her own father had famously done drugs, tons of them. Everything under the sun he'd often said, not without a touch of pride. She'd grown up with little white lines criss-crossing the smooth surface of the marble kitchen counter or the sink in the downstairs loo every time he came to visit. She knew all about the rushes and the highs and lows; the way he moved through the house like an electric storm; the pills he took afterwards to help him sleep. He had been in and out of rehab more times than Melanie remembered and, she also remembered with a sense of awe at having forgotten it in the first place, the sense of calm that had followed when Norbert Kreizer moved into the house. She remembered looking at him in the first few months of his marriage to her mother, wondering if it were possible for two men to be so utterly different. War and peace. Fire and sand. How could she have forgotten? The funny thing was, Steve di Marco was actually a little of both. He had Norbert's steely, watchful determination and Mike's wicked, almost adolescent sense of humour. No wonder she'd fallen so hard. He was everything she wanted in a man. The small fact of his rather unusual business interests wasn't a problem for her at all. In fact, she soon discovered, she rather liked it. She liked the thrill of danger and the whiff of something illicit in the air. People came and went at all hours of the night and day; important people, not the petty hustlers and small-time crooks she'd always associated with drug dealers. No, Steve di Marco was high, high up the food chain. He dealt with the big boys, serious men. Men in expensive Italian suits, with bodyguards and drivers whose guns showed under the flaps of their tailored jackets. Steve was all-powerful, all-knowing and she liked that. It made it that much more special that he'd chosen her.

She loved his house too. White, just like his office, with only a minimum of furniture, the sort of glamorous, empty-looking interior that featured prominently in magazines and films; a sparse, wonderfully clean environment in which no one seemed to live. Everything was white; walls, floors, sofas, tables, the kitchen ... absolutely everything. The enormous plate-glass windows opened out on to a terrace that overlooked a shimmering turquoise pool; in the afternoons Melanie lay out on a white sun-lounger, working on her tan. LA had finally made its mark on her. She took off her top because Steve said he didn't like tan lines.

In fact the only cloud on her horizon was her mother; and, of course, the little matter of not being able to go home. Not that she *wanted* to go home – on the contrary. But after nine months of stony silence from across the Atlantic, her mother's studied refusal to even *talk* to her was really beginning to upset her. Not enough to completely spoil her day, but enough to suddenly plunge her into sadness in a way she couldn't understand, or control.

Steve didn't seem to notice, or if he did, he made no comment, probably hoping her sudden dark moods would quickly go away. Steve wasn't 'into' sadness, he told her. He liked those around him to be 'up' and full of energy and positive good humour, all the things he said he'd come to America for. His father owned an ice cream van and had worked from dawn till dusk in the spring and summer months when ice cream was sold on the streets of Balham. He'd been handing out soft scoop cones when he had his first heart attack. Steve told her he'd come to America partly to escape a lifetime doing *that*, and partly to make enough money so that his father no longer had to. Melanie listened to his stories in awe. Her own childhood, punctuated by her father's sudden appearances and equally abrupt departures, seemed flat and empty compared to the warm, cosy picture of Italian domesticity that Steve painted. She couldn't quite imagine what it might be like to have your mother wait on the sidelines at sports day or tuck you up in bed with hot cocoa on winter nights. Stella, Melanie realised, was nothing like the kind of mother Steve seemed to have had. Stella would sooner have cut off her hair than make Melanie's dinner – and that was really saying something. She'd had waist-length, platinum blonde hair for as long as Melanie could remember and spent an inordinate amount of money and time keeping it that way. Money. It was the one thing she'd always had and Steve hadn't. When Melanie felt bold enough to contribute a story or two of her own, Steve laughed at her and called her a Jewish American Princess. 'But I'm not Jewish,' she protested. 'And I'm not American.'

'Right little princess, though,' he murmured. 'Aren't you?'

But Melanie didn't feel like a princess. She felt like someone who'd been thrown away.

32

She'd been working at Irazú for almost three months when she noticed the flyer one morning, tacked up in the window of the grocery store halfway down Milwaukee. It was hard to miss. Neon yellow, big bold type. 'Do you want to earn extra money in your free time? Are you young, attractive, with a good figure? Earn $$$ in your spare time. Call 312-466-9901. Today!' Laure eyed it suspiciously. Yes, she desperately wanted to earn more money. She liked working at Irazú but she could barely make ends meet; and she still hadn't been able to move out of the Sunshine Motel, much to her disappointment. To move, she needed a security deposit and a month's rent – how on earth was she supposed to manage that on thirty bucks a day? She looked at it again. 'Are you young?' Yes, she was young. 'Attractive?' She didn't really think about her appearance these days but she supposed she had a good figure. She knew she was thinner now than when she'd arrived – some of her clothes had to be held in with a safety pin. She looked at it yet again. 'Earn \$\$\$ in your spare time.' She turned her head and walked quickly down the street. No, there was probably a catch to it. There had to be.

'You comin' out with us tonight, Laure?' Marilí, the Guatemalan cashier called out to her as she gave the counter top one last wipe and peeled off her gloves. Laure hesitated. It was the fourth time in a fortnight that Marilí had asked her to come out. She really ought to say 'yes'. She liked Marilí – she was lively, funny and smart. She was several years older than Laure and was studying part-time at one of the local community colleges. From the little Laure had heard, she'd arrived in Chicago from Guatemala two years ago, completely alone, and in that time had managed to find an apartment, enrol in school and hold down two part-time jobs – Laure was in awe of her. Everyone liked Marilí – customers, the other waiters, Julio and Léon ... *every*one. She smiled at Laure again. 'Come on ... what you gonna do? Sit home and watch TV?'

'Well, if ... if you're sure ...'

''Course we're sure. Come on, go get your stuff.'

Laure practically ran down the stairs to the office. It was the first time in almost a year that she'd been out anywhere other than work, the grocery store and, on the very odd occasion, to the shops along Milwaukee. She'd seen almost nothing of Chicago and while her co-workers at Irazú were more than kind to her, theirs was still a strictly working relationship – when was the last time she'd sat with anyone over a coffee and just *talked*? Her fingers were trembling a little as she did up the buttons on her coat.

'Comin' with us?' Julio walked out of his office, jangling an enormous bunch of keys in his hand. He sounded surprised. Laure nodded shyly. 'Great! Always wondered how come you dash off home like that. Got a jealous boyfriend, is that it?' He smiled at her kindly. Laure had to look away. She shook her head, not trusting herself to speak.

An hour later, sitting with the four of them around a table in a tiny, packed-to-the-rafters *mèrengue* club off Milwaukee, Laure found herself tapping her feet without even realising it.

'Aiee!' Marilí laughed, pointing at her. 'You see! Look at her. You *do* like to dance. You see that, Léon?'

'I sure do,' Léon chuckled. 'This is your kind of music, isn't it?'

Laure shook her head, smiling. 'No, this is *Dominican* music ... Haitians always say *mèrengue* is Haitian but everyone knows it isn't. I like it, though.'

'You wanna dance?' Léon pushed back his chair.

'You go, girl!' Marilí shouted encouragingly. Laure had no option but to follow him on to the packed dance floor.

Within seconds, she'd forgotten why she'd ever said 'no' to coming out with them. Within minutes, she was back in the smoky clubs Delroy had taken her to down the hill, in Port-au-Prince. Léon was a good dancer; she followed his snake-like hips, moving her own in the distinctive style of Dominican *mèrengue*, like salsa, but slower, more sensuous.

'Wow!' Léon said, looking down at her. 'You're a good dancer.'

'So're you,' Laure laughed, slowly shaking off the gloom and anxiety of the past few months. Out there on the dance floor, she was just another girl losing herself in the music, a cold glass of beer waiting for her at the table where her friends were sitting. She was just like anyone else; she was, for the first time since she'd come to America, *enjoying* herself. Léon was Cuban and therefore *born* dancing, he told her proudly. 'I could go on all night!' After half an hour, sweat pouring down her back, Laure begged off. She returned, laughing, to the table and gratefully gulped down her beer. Two rum and Cokes later, she was telling a joke – although with some hesitancy. It was hard to be funny in a language that was not your own, she'd discovered. Not that Julio or Marilí seemed to notice; they were in stitches from the moment she started. It wasn't even a particularly funny joke – it was rather long and complicated, involving a Haitian nun and an American tourist, one that Régine had told her. But Julio said the funniest thing was seeing her face – he'd never seen her look so excited. She ruined the punchline by blurting it out a minute too early. No matter. It was *still* the funniest thing he'd heard all day.

They walked her home at two a.m., Julio still chuckling. 'Thank you,' Laure said, as they reached Pulaski. 'I'm staying just across the road. I … I had a great time,' she said shyly.

'Yeah, it's good to see you smile.' Julio winked. 'Come out with us again – and bring some more jokes!'

'*Buenas noches, chiquita*,' Léon called as she walked across the road. '*Hasta luego.*'

'Bye,' Laure said softly, pushing open the door. She hadn't felt this good in years. For almost an entire evening, she'd forgotten who she was, what she'd done, what she *hadn't* done. She'd forgotten everything. Once in a while, it felt good to forget.

A week later, the flyer on Milwaukee was still there. She stopped, looked around her and quickly fished a pen from her bag. She copied the number as quickly as she could and hurried off. It didn't really say what the job was that could bring in '$$$' in her spare time but it had to be something to do with modelling – 'Are you young, attractive?' She didn't feel either, to be honest, but the thought of earning extra money was too tempting to resist. She felt in her bag for the paper on which she'd scribbled the number. She rang the next morning but there was only an answering machine asking her to leave her name, number and the time of her call … she hung up.

She tried the number again the following morning, and again the morning after that and it was only on her fourth attempt, just as she was about to hang up, that a man answered. Her heart beating faster, she quickly explained that she'd seen the flyer in the grocery store on Milwaukee and was calling to find out a little more: what did the job entail?

'How tall are you?' the man asked. Laure's heart jumped. It *was* a modelling-type job.

'Er, five foot eight,' she replied, quickly converting the metric.

'How heavy?'

'Er, I don't know … maybe fifty-five kilos?'

'Say what?'

'Sorry … I don't know in pounds … not very much,' she said hurriedly. Americans weren't too keen on metric.

'How much is "not very much"?'

'Hundred … a hundred twenty-five, maybe?' she guessed, trying to work it out.

'Okay. Race?'

'Er, black. No, Afro-American,' she corrected herself quickly.

'Great. When can you come into the studios?'

'Monday?' Laure asked hopefully. It was her only day off.

'Sure. Be there at … say, eleven o'clock?'

'That's fine. You … er, in your ad, you mentioned … I was just wondering … how much are you paying an hour?' It came out hesitantly. She still found it difficult to talk about money. Where she was from, people from good homes just didn't.

'Depends on you, honey. Some girls make five hundred bucks a day, maybe even more. Depends what you wanna do. Here, lemme give you the address and we'll see you Monday. We can talk about what you might be interested in doing then.' He gave her an address in Humboldt Park, about a half-hour bus ride from her apartment. She took the details, thanked him and hung up. Five hundred dollars *a day*? She almost passed out. She felt a tiny shiver of anticipation run through her; it had been so long since she'd felt excited about anything.

The night before the appointment, after she got back to the motel from work, she took a long, hot shower and washed her hair, enjoying for the first time in ages the thick, silky weight of it against her shoulders and back. It had grown so long. She usually wore it pulled back off her face in a long, twisted chignon. She braided it, sitting cross-legged on her narrow bed, squeezing out the last drops of water before winding the braids up and tying them together on the top of her head. In the morning, she knew, her hair would be thick, glossy and wavy, not frizzy, and would help her look her best. It was almost two in the morning before she finally slid into bed, laying her head gently on the pillow. She had to be careful not to move too much or too frequently – an hour or two in the wrong position and she'd wind up with a thick, wiry cobra sticking above her head.

In the morning, she looked at herself anxiously in the mirror above the sink. Her hair hung round her face in shiny, gently waving coils; she'd bought some lipstick and blusher at the supermarket earlier that week and she applied it cautiously, blotting her lips together the way Régine had taught her to do, and stood back. There were butterflies in her stomach. She hadn't felt *those* in a while. She checked herself one last time, picked up her coat and bag and walked downstairs. If she got the job, she whispered to herself as she walked across the lobby, she would find herself somewhere decent to live – it would be the first thing she did. The Sunshine Motel couldn't possibly have been more inappropriately named. There was nothing remotely sunny about it. But it was the first motel she'd come to after running away from Belle's that terrible morning and at least it was familiar. And cheap. But she longed for the day when she could finally leave.

It took her almost forty-five minutes to find the address. She took the bus down Milwaukee to Armitage, then another along Armitage to Kedzie. It was one block after Kedzie – Spaulding. That was it. 4546 North Spaulding. She looked around her as she walked down the street. The houses resembled those in Garfield Park, only here the lawns outside the little houses were cut and the streets were clean. Two-storey, compact houses of brick and painted wood; a porch out front and a little post-box mounted on the gate with an American flag ... it was all rather uniform. She wondered what a photographer's studio would be doing in among the suburban-looking homes. 4546 North Spaulding was a house. She looked up at the façade. There was nothing about it to suggest any kind of business went on inside. It crossed her mind for a brief second that perhaps the place wasn't as clean-sounding and professional as she'd thought ... but the thought of five hundred dollars a day spurred her on. She could find an apartment! Her head spinning, she pushed open the little gate and walked up the steps. The front door opened before she reached it; a tall, heavy-set man was standing in the doorway, arms folded across his chest as he watched her walk up the path.

'Hi,' Laure said, a little uncertainly. He looked rather menacing. 'I ... rang on Thursday ... about the ad.'

'Who'd you speak to?' he growled.

'I'm sorry, I forgot to get his name ... it was a man, I think he was ...'

'It's cool, Jim. I remember her. Let her in.' A voice called from the hallway. The man named Jim stepped aside and Laure walked in.

It was dim inside. She was in an entrance hall with closed doors leading off all round, on all sides. A heavy-looking wooden staircase wound its way up to the floor above. The walls were dark and wood-panelled. The whole place had a dark, sombre, rather dilapidated air. Laure swallowed nervously. The fresh, early autumn air outside seemed a million miles away. Someone cleared his throat. She turned. The young man who had just spoken – and presumably the same man she'd talked to over the phone – was standing to one side of the hallway. He was dressed in a dark suit, a light blue shirt and tie; on his little finger a diamond glittered as he lifted up his hand in greeting.

'Hi, you must be Laure, right?' Laure nodded. He made no move towards her. She stood where she was as his eyes travelled up and down the length of her, slowly, appraisingly. He nodded. 'Come this way, please,' he said finally. With a nervous glance backwards at Jim, Laure followed him into one of the rooms. It was an office, dominated by a large, somewhat battered wooden desk. Laure quickly took the seat he indicated.

'My name is Aaron,' he said in a clipped, accented voice, settling into the swivel chair on the opposite side of the desk. 'Nice to meet you.' He extended a hand across the table. Laure shook it, her mind whirling. She couldn't tell where he was from. A door opened just behind him and another man walked out, a camera slung around his neck. Laure breathed a sigh of relief. Ah, the photographer. She'd begun to have doubts about the whole thing. He also looked at her appraisingly, then turned to Aaron and said something in a guttural-sounding language unfamiliar to her. She watched as the two of them discussed her, stopping every now and again to look at her. 'Laure, will you stand up for us? Turn around, please,' Aaron asked her suddenly. She did as she was told. 'Look at me, over your shoulder. Good ... smile for me, that's it.'

'She'll do,' the photographer said, fishing in his pocket for a cigarette. He held out the packet to Laure. She shook her head. He shrugged and lit up. Laure watched the smoky coils glide and twist towards the ceiling.

'OK, Laure.' Aaron swivelled round in the chair and addressed her. 'So ... we both think you'll do very nicely. Very nicely indeed.' Laure stared at him. 'Have you done any modelling before?' he asked silkily.

Laure shook her head again. 'N ... no,' she stammered. 'I ... I never thought about it ...'

'Well, you should. You're very beautiful. We offer many different kinds of modelling experience ... glamour, erotic, adult. It's your choice. We both think you'd do equally well in all three.' Laure swallowed. She wasn't stupid. Glamour, erotic, adult. She knew what he meant. 'Of course, adult is the best paid,' Aaron went on smoothly. 'You could earn yourself a small fortune. There are a couple of portfolios over there in the corner. Take a look, see what we offer. We'll come back in a while.' He got up from the desk and the two of them left the room.

Laure got up slowly from her seat, clutching her bag, and moved to the shabby sofa in the corner of the room. There were several photo albums stuffed haphazardly into a box. She pulled one out and opened it cautiously. A glossy-lipped, semi-clad blonde girl stared provocatively out from the picture. She had large, impossibly tanned and firm breasts and a lollipop placed suggestively against her red, juicy lips. Laure gulped. She hurriedly flicked through the cellophaned pages. There were hundreds of girls in the albums, posing in a variety of ways, from the ridiculous to the most sexually explicit. Laure closed it with a snap, her face burning. She picked up another one. This was less troubling – calendar-type photos, mostly of semi-nude girls leaning over the bonnets of luxury cars. She put it down and pulled out another. She closed it hurriedly. Ugh! The fourth album contained rather different pictures. *Almost* artistic, mostly black and white photographs of nude girls, some of them staggeringly beautiful – yes, she could do that. With the right make-up and hair ... it might even be fun having someone fuss over her face and hair like that. She put the book down and stood up. As if they'd been watching her, the door opened and Aaron and his sidekick appeared.

'So ... what do you think? Think you'd like to give it a try?' Aaron said, all unctuous smoothness. Laure nodded doubtfully.

'The fashion, and the more ... you know, artistic photographs ... how much do you pay for those?' she asked.

'Oh, no ... those are different. Dave, you idiot, I told you to take those albums out. No, those are where the models pay *us*, you see. They use the photographs for getting ... you know, different kinds of work. It helps to have as much experience as possible. Sorry, we shouldn't have left those in there.'

'Oh. So, what could I ... I mean, if I don't want to do the other kind ... you know ... without my clothes?' Laure asked, disappointed.

'You're not interested in those? Pity, it's where you make the most money and you really have the face and body for it, you know. No? You don't want to? OK, well ... the lingerie work isn't badly paid. Maybe a hundred to two hundred a day, depends on demand. You wanna try that?' Laure nodded, more firmly this time. 'So … we can start today, if you want. Dave will set up the studio, we'll take a few pictures, see what comes out. Sound OK to you? Today will just be a test day. I'll pay you a hundred bucks. Cash. OK?' Laure's mouth dropped open.

'Yes, of c … course,' she stammered, a feeling of warmth stealing through her. A hundred dollars for a couple of hours' work? Her head was spinning. She followed Aaron into a back room that smelled of damp and bleach but she was too thrilled to care. The heavy curtains were drawn and there was a tall lamp in the corner of the room giving off a yellowy, rather dim glow. He pointed to a bag of lacy garments in the corner of the room and told her to choose whatever she liked.

'Put some of this on.' He handed her a small spray bottle of colourless liquid. 'It'll make your skin shine. It's great for photographs. Just try not to get it on the clothes. I'll be back in ten.' He closed the door behind him. Laure looked around the small room. There was a mattress on the floor and next to it, a pile of blankets – fur, silk, velvet. She felt a twinge of shame as she stripped off her sweater and jeans but the garments she'd pulled out of the bag were really quite pretty and the thought of walking away from the house with a hundred dollars in her pocket … she didn't care. How else could she make that kind of money without doing what Belle did … and there was no way she would do *that*. She pulled on a lacy black bra, fastening it deftly behind her back and bending forward to let her breasts fall into place. There was a full-length mirror behind her. She turned and almost gasped. She looked every bit as glamorous and beautiful as any of the models she'd seen in the albums outside. Aaron was right. The oil made her skin glow in the dim light; it made her look darker, much more sultry. With her thick, heavy hair coiled around her neck and falling over her breasts, she looked *sexy*, she thought to herself slowly, and with some surprise. God, it had been so long. She twisted her torso sideways. The lacy black cami-knickers – the fullest pair of briefs she could find in the bag – looked good against her dark brown skin. There was a tap at the door.

'Ready?' It was Aaron.

'Yes, I'm ready,' she called out, her hands already covering her bra. How on earth was she going to lie down on the mattress and let a strange man photograph her practically nude body? she asked herself as Aaron and Dave came through the door. They both stopped when they saw her and smiled for the first time.

'Wow!' Aaron said, nodding as though impressed. She smiled shyly. It felt nice to be appreciated. He motioned her over to the couch. 'Just sit yourself down over there, Laure,' he said, as Dave began to set up his camera. 'Lie back just a little ... that's it ... against the cushions. Fantastic. OK. Dave, you ready? Here we go, Laure. Just look at the camera ... that's it. Great. These are gonna be *great*. I can feel it!'

Two hours later, she took the slim white envelope from Aaron scarcely able to believe her luck. She peeled it open as soon as she got outside. Yes, a hundred dollars in crisp, clean notes. She almost screamed. In two hours she'd earned what it took her almost a week to make, not counting tips, of course ... but *still* – a whole week of brutal running up and down stairs, balancing dishes, being screamed at by customers and flopping into bed at night, too tired even to eat. This was easy. Oh, yes ... *this* she could do. With her eyes closed.

Aaron was as good as his word. She called him back two days later, as she'd been instructed, and was told that her pictures had come out very well, just as they'd hoped. 'When can you come back?' he asked impatiently. 'This afternoon?'

'Not until next Monday,' Laure said hesitantly. 'It's my only day off.' She looked around Julio's empty office quickly. She didn't feel like telling anyone what she was about to do.

'Where d'you work?' He sounded bored.

'In ... in a restaurant. I ... I could ask my boss to swap my shift,' Laure said quickly. 'It's just that I'd have to—'

'Look, Laure, you wanna make some money or not?' Aaron interrupted her.

'Of course! I ... I'll speak to my boss and ... and I'll ...'

'You do what you have to do,' Aaron said, even more abruptly. 'But there are lots of girls who'd give anything to do what we're offering you, Laure. Remember that.'

'Of course ... w ... would tomorrow be OK?' Laure whispered, fighting a wave of panic. She would just have to call in sick.

'OK. See you tomorrow. Come early. We'll do a full day's shooting.'

'Th ... thank you,' Laure stammered as she hung up the phone. She bit her lip. She hated lying – to anyone. And Julio and Léon had been so kind to her. But two hundred dollars for a day's work! How could she turn it down? How could she possibly turn a chance like that down?

The next day she was at the house on Spalding at nine o'clock on the dot. Self-conscious in her new outfit and worried that she'd been too liberal with her make-up, she stood outside and pressed the bell with a fluttering stomach and racing pulse. Aaron answered the door and from the look her gave her, Laure was instantly reassured. She hadn't overdone it. She looked good. His eyes told her so.

He led her into the back bedroom where Dave was already at work setting up his lights and props. There were several 'outfits' lying on a small table at one end of the room. Laure looked at them nervously. Mostly white, feminine undergarments with more lace, ruffles, bows and ribbons than she'd ever seen. Surely they weren't expecting her to wear those? They were. They would be sending the results of the day's shoot over to the director of a company that manufactured oil for car engines, Aaron explained. They wanted a contrast between the heavy, dirty workmanlike aspect of the product and the fresh, almost doll-like innocence of the model – a good concept. Tried and tested. It had sold thousands of calendars and marketing brochures before she came along. Laure picked up one of the garments. It was a bodice of sorts, with a half-cup bra, a hundred tiny eyelets into which pink lace was threaded and tied into bows, a suspender belt, again full of bows and ribbons, and the most ridiculous frilly piece of sateen that Aaron showed her would go around her thigh with heart-shaped clips to hold up her stockings. She swallowed. It was all a bit cheap, though, wasn't it? Aaron and Dave were immediately reassuring. No, no, not cheap – silly, maybe, but hey, the client was the boss, right? He knew what sold. Laure nodded dubiously.

'Put the whole thing on, see how it looks,' Aaron said, signalling to Dave to leave the room. 'If you're really uncomfortable, we'll change it. But I think you'll look dynamite. Swear to God. We'll be back in a minute. And don't forget the oil, will you?' They left, shutting the door behind them.

Outside, Aaron looked at Dave and crossed his fingers. 'Shit, I hope she goes along with it,' he said, looking at the closed door. Dave nodded. 'She's the best-looking girl we've had in ages.'

'Yeah, she's a looker, all right. Best ass I've seen in a *long* time.'

'Wonder where she's from. She doesn't sound American.'

'Who cares? They're not paying her to speak.'

'Hey, hey ... you never know,' Aaron cautioned softly. 'Play our cards right ... who knows? We might get her into films yet. Be nice with her, you hear me? Break her in gently. Don't do a Deirdre on her.'

Dave shrugged. He'd been in the business too long. He'd seen the girls come in, all fresh-eyed, hopeful innocents, and he'd seen them exit a few years later, degraded beyond belief, burned out and useful for nothing. Like that stupid slut Deirdre. This one looked like a nice girl. It would be a shame if she ended up the same way. 'I'll see if she's ready,' he said, turning back to the door.

Laure turned round to face him, the heat in her cheeks almost unbearable. She held her arms over her breasts and crossed her legs awkwardly. Dave had spread the black silk cover over the mattress and it took him almost ten minutes of coaxing to get her to lie down. Bit by bit, he managed to loosen her up, calm her nerves, soothe her pride. No, she didn't look silly, was she kidding? She looked *hot*. Under a steady stream of compliments and directions, Laure finally managed to relax enough for him to start work properly. It was harder than it looked. She had to hold poses for up to five minutes while he fiddled around with lights and pulled the sheet this way or that, adjusted the strap on her bra, fluffed her hair out. It was almost hypnotic, lying there under his intense, focused gaze. He never once took his eyes off her, except to have a cigarette break halfway through the morning. After a while, Laure even began to enjoy it.

'Look at me, that's it. Push your lips out just a little, pout for me ... a little more ... more, that's it. Great. Fan*tastic*. Hold it there for a second ... a little longer. That's it.'

'Like this?' Laure asked, trying to do as he directed.

'Perfect. Great. Beautiful. You look like you've been doing this for a while.'

'Really?' Laure was suddenly pleased.

'Yeah, really. I mean it. You're like a pro. Now, just pull your breasts out a little more ... just a bit, yeah, that's it. Here, let me do it. Man, you look amazing.' Laure's face was burning – she couldn't quite believe she was lying on a silk sheet with her breasts spilling out of her bra, taking directions from a man she'd only met a couple of days before.

But when it was over and he gave her the thumbs-up, pronouncing it one of the best sessions he'd ever had, it was hard to suppress the rush of pride that swept through her. Not only could she *do* this, she was *good* at it.

After she'd wiped the oil off her body and dressed herself again, she walked into the hallway. Aaron was talking to a young girl, obviously another young hopeful. She was not pretty; a thin, sallow-faced girl with badly cut hair and loose, baggy clothing. Laure looked at her for a second and then looked away, embarrassed. He was turning her down. He left her and came over to Laure, fishing in his pocket for something. 'Here,' he said, pulling out an enormous wad of twenty-dollar bills. He counted off ten, folded the bills in half and pressed them into Laure's palm. 'You did real good today,' he said warmly. 'We're pretty sure the client'll take them. Great work – it's a really good start.' Laure was too pleased to speak. She clutched the money, glanced at the girl who was looking enviously at her and walked towards the door. Just before she closed it, she heard Aaron say, 'That's someone we hired last week. She's beautiful ... *that's* what we're looking for in the glamour stuff. If only you looked liked *her* ...' The door closed on his words. She practically ran down the path, despite her heels, unable to believe her luck. She looked at her watch. It was one o'clock. She'd been at work for four hours. Unbelievable.

It was only a matter of time before she quit her job at Irazú. It took her three weeks to pluck up the courage to tell Julio and Léon. In that time, she'd lied to them countless times about being sick in order to make the journey north to Spalding where she earned in a few hours what it took her a week to make at Irazú. Compared to running up and down the stairs for eight hours straight, it was *easy*. So why didn't she feel right about quitting?

She knocked on the office door after her shift was over, her heart in her mouth. Julio and Léon had not only hired her; they'd been good to her. They and Marilí were the only friends she had in Chicago; she couldn't bear the thought of losing their friendship, as well as their respect. But the money – it was too good a chance to pass up. She rapped on the door again.

'Yeah ... come in.' Julio was hunched over a stack of invoices. He turned and smiled at her. 'What's up, *chica*?'

His smile made her falter. 'Julio? I just wanted to ask you ... well, the thing is ... I've been offered another job, Julio,' she stammered, aware that her face was already on fire.

'Oh, yeah? Wow ... somebody else gonna take you on? No kidding ... what d'ya pay him?' Julio tried to make light of her obvious discomfort. Laure felt like bursting into tears.

'It's not waitressing ... something else. It's a bit different.'

'Well, good for you, *chica*. I never really asked you what you wanted to do. Kinda figured you weren't gonna stick around for ever. So what've you lined up? Something exciting?'

'I ... it's a modelling job.'

'Oh yeah? We gonna see you in all the magazines and stuff?' he said, a smile breaking out over his face.

Laure blushed even harder. 'Oh, no, nothing like that. It's just ... you know, little things. Catalogues, stuff like that.' There was a sudden silence.

'You know what you doin', *chica*?' Julio asked her gently. Laure nodded, her face on fire.

'Yeah, it's fine, it's OK. They're really nice guys ...' she stammered. He looked at her.

'Listen, *chica*, if it don' work out, or you need somethin' ... it don't matter *what* it is, you come to me, OK?' His voice was unexpectedly insistent. Laure nodded, too ashamed to speak. He knew what she was up to, no question about it. He held out a hand. 'You take care of yourself, Laure, – you hear me? And if you need anything ... *anything* at all ... you call us. You got that?' He shook her hand, then pulled her quickly to him, hugging her hard. She hung her head in shame. Then he disengaged himself gently and left the room. She heard his footsteps on the stairs. She'd been hearing the sound of people – usually herself – running up and down the rickety wooden staircase for nearly a year. It was almost impossible to think she would never hear it again. She put a hand up to her cheek; it was wet with tears.

But money, she soon discovered, could take the edge off most things. Even guilt. A month later, she sat on her bed and counted out her earnings. $1,876.81. An absolute *fortune*! She was ready to take the next, important step. She was ready to move out of the motel. She shoved the shoebox under her bed and pulled the sheaf of newspapers she'd bought towards her.

An hour later, she had half a dozen appointments to view places that were variously described as 'delightful', 'charming', 'beautifully appointed' and, without exception, were slightly worse than fleapits. On the eighth viewing, she actually had to hold a handkerchief to her nose as the owner, a short, balding Puerto Rican, showed her in. 'No, no ...' she shook her head. 'No, thank you. Haven't you got anything ... well, better?'

'You ain't never gonna find anything better for the kind of money you're lookin' to spend,' he told her, shaking his own head. 'This is what two hundred dollars a month gets you. Anything better's gonna cost ya at least five hundred. *At least*? Laure was silent. She thanked him and fled.

At a nearby coffee shop, she pulled out a notebook and went over the figures again. Could she afford five hundred dollars? She was making roughly a thousand five hundred dollars a month. She'd sworn to save at least a third of that, leaving her with roughly a thousand dollars to live on. If she spent five hundred on rent ... She sighed. There didn't seem to be much option. She would sooner have *died* than live in one of the fleapits she'd just seen. No, it was important to find somewhere decent, even if it meant cutting down on every other conceivable expense. She would tighten her belt, beg Aaron for more work, do practically anything it took. She had to find somewhere better to live. Somewhere she *wanted* to live.

A week later, she noticed a sign in the window of the 7-Eleven on Milwaukee. She scribbled down the number and ran to the nearest phone booth. An hour later she stood in the late afternoon sunlight, squinting up at the façade of an old building in Wicker Park. A woman drew up in a car and introduced herself as the sister of the owner. The place had just recently been refurbished, she explained, leading the way up the short flight of stairs. It was very small – just two small rooms – but really quite nice.

'Doesn't get a lot of sunlight, that's why the rent's a bit on the low side,' she said, unlocking the front door. The hallway was dark but it smelled fresh and clean, a huge contrast from the places Laure had recently seen. The apartment was on the second floor of a three-storey building and as soon as the woman opened the door, Laure knew she would take it. Small, yes, but *clean*! Freshly painted. A wooden floor. A small, built-in kitchen with a stove, refrigerator and large white cupboards.

'I'll take it.' Laure heard herself speak.

'Great! You're the first person I've showed it to. I only just put the sign up, you know.'

'I'll take it,' Laure repeated. She couldn't believe her luck. This place would be hers? 'Should I pay you now?'

Two hours later, having run back to the motel to collect her things at breakneck speed, she opened the door with trembling hands and stood in the middle of the living room, scarcely able to breathe. She looked around carefully, not wanting to miss a single thing.

A small, narrow entrance, opening out on the diagonal to an exposed brick wall on one side, and a white, painted wall on the other. There was a tiny bedroom off to one side – just enough space for a bed and a little dresser – and then back to the living area again. There wasn't really enough room for a dining table but it was just as well – she had absolutely no furniture to speak of. Not even a bed. The kitchen was tiny, like the rest of the place, but it was very clean. Freshly painted cupboards, a grey worktop with a sink and a draining board in front of the small window; cupboards beneath the sink and a large refrigerator standing next to the back door. There was just enough room for a sofa and a TV in the living room. Laure closed her eyes, unable to take it all in. She could have lived there with nothing at all. Nothing at all. She sat down on the floor, cross-legged, and laid her cheek against the wooden floorboards, her eyes still tightly shut. It was the beginning of the rest of her life.

PART THREE

33

Malvern, England 1986

If he'd thought, even absent-mindedly, in passing, *even for just one second*, that Viv's reaction to the news of his fortnight-old marriage would be, well, less than enthusiastic, Iain Blake saw that he'd been deluding himself. There was a moment's stunned silence after he'd finished breaking the news to her, then she grabbed him by the forearm hard enough for him to feel her nails digging into his veins and dragged him into the kitchen.

'Have you lost your *mind*?' she hissed at him, her eyes wide with shock and ... contempt?

'Let go,' he hissed back, jerking his arm away. He ran his fingers over its punctured surface. 'That fucking *hurt*.'

'Not anywhere near as much as you're going to hurt that poor child,' she spat out, eyes narrowing in the way he remembered only too well.

'She's not a child!'

'The hell she's not. She's a *teenager*! How could you, Iain. How *could* you?'

'She's twenty-four, Viv. She's a grown woman.' He was irritable and defensive, and he'd barely been in the house five minutes. Christ, how had he managed thirteen years with the woman?

'She doesn't speak *English*!'

'So what? Half the fucking world doesn't speak English. What's that got to do with it?'

'She's *black*!'

'Oh, for crying out loud ... Is that what's bothering you?'

'No, but I'll tell you something for free. That's *exactly* what's going to be bothering half the people around here. You *can't* leave her here! Are you mad? What the hell is she supposed to do?'

'She's going to go to school, she's going to learn English. We've talked about it, Viv ... it's the best place for her. The people around here'll get used to her ... they will, you'll see.'

'Jesus Christ, Iain. Couldn't you at least take her to London? I mean, this is *Malvern*, for Christ's sake. Most of the people round here have never seen—'

'Will you *shut* up!' Iain roared suddenly. He'd had enough. 'Just shut *up*. This is *my* decision, all right? I invited you over to meet her because, like it or not, you two are going to be neighbours. If you don't want to get involved, that's fine by me. I just thought, seeing as we're such *friends* and all that,' he glared at her, 'that you'd be on my side. But fine. If you can't handle it—'

'This has nothing to do with being able to *handle* it,' Viv cut him off abruptly. 'We *are* friends. I care about you, Iain. Honestly, I do. And it's *precisely* because I care about you that I'm worried.'

'What's there to be worried about? I love her, Viv. She's my *wife*, for God's sake.'

Viv looked at him. 'And her? Does she love you?' she asked quietly.

There was a moment's silence. Her blue eyes were on him in a way that made him squirm. She had him. Jesus Christ. It had been ten years since their divorce and she could *still* nail him with a single word. 'She will. She's ... learning to, you know ... get used to me. To things. It's a big change for her, remember?'

'Oh, Iain.' Viv put out a hand again, gently this time. He shook it off. He certainly didn't want her pity.

'I'll make us all a cup of tea, shall I?' he said, hoping his voice was steady. He turned to plug in the kettle. Her reaction had more than unnerved him – he was suddenly very worried. It was all very well talking in the abstract about what Améline would do once she got to England. Sitting in the sweltering heat of Miami, out of both their contexts, it was possible to believe anything could be achieved. Back home in Malvern, however, in the familiar cool, damp grey of the English countryside, he suddenly felt very vulnerable. Perhaps Viv was right – everyone would think he was an ageing pervert who'd picked up a young prostitute while on holiday – a mail-order bride …? His skin suddenly began to crawl with shame. Was that what it looked like? Was that, he swallowed suddenly, what he *felt*?

For all the difficulty she had in following English, Améline understood exactly what was being said in the kitchen. She was no fool. She had been married a total of six days and in that short time she'd understood the looks that passed between people whenever she and Iain were together in public. She might be naïve but she wasn't stupid. She knew what it looked like to the outside world.

She looked at the floor. There was some sort of patterned carpet that went all the way to the edge of the walls, just as it had done in the hotel in America. How did you clean it? she wondered. It wasn't like a rug that you took outside and beat, the way she'd cleaned similar-looking rugs at Madame's. And if you put a broom to it, you'd just wind up pushing the dirt from one patch to another. Not that you'd even see the dirt. With all those flowers and ribbons and circling lines you'd be hard-pressed to find a cigarette in there. She looked at the sofa opposite. It was almost falling apart. She was confused. She'd assumed Iain was rich. But this shabby little house he'd brought her to was dreadful. Almost as threadbare as Madame's. Tall, narrow rooms, barely enough space to turn round; the walls were covered in some sort of patterned paper … she almost put out a hand to touch it; she'd never seen anything like it. The house smelled too, of damp and something she couldn't quite identify – sharp and sour, as if the place hadn't been cleaned properly. She wrinkled her nose. He had a flat in London, he'd told her, but it was only a studio flat that he'd had since he was a student. He'd bought this cottage – as he called it – with the money he'd made from his earlier books. He'd shown one to her – a slim book about Cuba. She'd stared at it, unable to imagine how a little thing like that could buy a whole house.

'Améline, darling ... will you have some tea?' Iain came through, a tray in his hands. Améline jumped up, alarmed. *She* ought to be the one carrying the cups and saucers, not him. She tried to take it from him. 'No, no ... it's fine. I've got it. Just sit down, please.'

The woman he said was his ex-wife was right behind him. Améline saw the way she looked at him, rolling her eyes in exasperation, although what the hell did she have to be exasperated about? Améline met her stare coldly. She said something to Iain that Améline couldn't understand, of course – the woman apparently couldn't speak French very well.

'There you go,' Iain said, handing her a cup. Améline sat with the saucer balanced awkwardly on her knee. She was grateful for the lessons she'd received from Madame when she was still quite small on how to hold her knife and fork properly, how to drink from a cup and saucer. She even knew how to hold her little finger away from the cup, just as she'd seen Madame do all her life. She could feel the woman's eyes on her again as she drank and sank her teeth into one of the soft and rather sweet biscuits he'd brought.

'Iain say to me you go school,' the woman said, in terrible schoolgirl French.

'Oui, *madame*,' Améline replied.

'School for English? Very good speak English.'

'Oui, *madame*.' She was determined not to say anything more. Out of the corner of her eye, she could see Iain moving around nervously.

'Her name's Viv, darling,' he told Améline, laughing a little falsely. 'Not "madame".'

'Yes, yes. Vivian. Me.' The woman pointed rather ridiculously at herself.

Améline rolled her eyes. She'd discovered a latent streak of stubbornness in herself. '*Oui, madame*,' she said demurely, sipping her tea. Iain coughed. He looked distinctly uneasy.

'Right-ho.' He got up quickly from his position on the falling-down couch. He said something to the woman … *finishyourtea*. Améline liked the sound of English words. The woman drained her cup and stood up. There were a few awkward sentences between the two of them; she caught sight of the woman's backwards, pitying glance, and then she was gone.

'Well, that didn't go too badly, did it?' Iain came back into the room, rubbing his hands. Améline looked at him. Did he think her stupid as well?

'She doesn't like me. She thinks it's a mistake.'

'Oh, she'll come round. Don't you worry about her.'

'I don't think so,' Améline said firmly. 'I don't think she ever will.'

34

Laure pushed the trolley slowly around the cavernous super-market. There was so much choice. *Too* much choice. Thirty different kinds of lamps; forty different rugs; blue plates, white plates, canary yellow plates; tumblers; wine glasses; stainless steel forks and knives … She edged her way slowly up the aisles. Things she'd never even known she needed. An egg-slicer – what was wrong with a knife? A long, thin metal stick with a thermometer attached – she picked up the label – for sticking into your turkey. A little porcelain dish for corn on the cob. She shook her head. There were machines for doing everything Cléones and Améline had done in the kitchen back home – whisks, beaters, slicers, cutting machines … In America, she thought to herself, there was a machine for everything. She walked down another aisle. Clothes – racks of T-shirts for a dollar; hooded sweatshirts for five dollars; tennis shoes, piles of socks, packs of underwear … how could they *afford* to sell everything so cheaply? She wandered on, dazed. Suddenly, without noticing, she came upon the children's clothing. She stopped, aware of a tightening in her chest. She stood in front of a rack of baby jumpsuits in pinks, blues and whites; traditional colours for newborn babies. Almost without thinking, her hand went out for a light blue, fluffy cotton jumpsuit with a pale yellow teddy bear embroidered across the middle: $9.99. She held the tiny garment in her hands, steeling herself against the surge of emotion that swept over her. She folded it carefully and laid it in her basket. The tears were full and thick in her throat when she handed over her money to the cashier. It took her almost the entire journey home to swallow them.

She let herself into her apartment and put the two bags on the kitchen counter. She switched on the light and stood for a moment in the narrow hallway. Out of nowhere, it seemed, she'd managed to create a home. Just a few things: a second-hand tartan sofa; a smoky, glass-topped coffee table; a small television on a wooden TV 'console' – she loved the sound of the word – so grown up and sophisticated. The salesman had shown her half a dozen before she'd finally made her choice. It was in dark wood veneer – it didn't quite match the coffee table but she'd seen the console *after* she'd bought the table – she didn't care. The room now looked lived in, properly inhabited ... it looked like a home. Sandra, the stripper who lived upstairs and with whom she was friendly, was impressed. She told Laure she had *style*.

She carefully took one of the plastic bags and knelt down on the rug in front of the TV. She could hear Sandra moving around above. Click-clack, click-clack ... She wore the most ridiculously high-heeled fluffy slippers, even in her own house and the wooden floors meant that Laure heard her every step, every movement. She didn't mind. Now that she'd got to know her, it made her feel a little less alone. With shaking fingers, she pulled the precious jumpsuit out of the bag and laid it on the sofa, breathing deeply. The rush of pain and guilt was as unbearable as it was immediate; she could feel it rising in her throat, tearing at her. She tried to hold on to it, to push it down, as she usually did but the hammering fists of anguish overwhelmed her. She rolled off the sofa, on to the bare floor, the jumpsuit clutched to her chest and began to weep, groaning uncontrollably to the sound of Sandra's heels. The sounds that came from her were as frightening as the emotion she struggled to contain. She lay there for what seemed like hours, a steady stream of tears sliding down her cheeks as she wept for the child she'd abandoned. She hadn't even named him. It had seemed silly at the time; naming someone she would never see. Sometimes she wished they hadn't told her it was a boy. It would have made it easier to forget it had ever happened. But that was the point, wasn't it? Lying there on the floor, stuffing her fist into her mouth to stop the sounds of pain from escaping – *that* was the point, wasn't it? She *couldn't* forget it had ever happened. A baby *wasn't* just a bad memory, or a friend with whom you'd quarrelled. A baby was for *life*. Her life, as well as his. She could no more forget him than she could forget herself.

It took her half an hour to bring her breathing under control. Alongside the pain of having given him up, was the guilt. That, too, was for life. She pressed the soft material of the jumpsuit against her lips until they bled, forcing the tears to stop. She heard Sandra crossing the floor and then, seconds later, the sound of her heels coming down the stairs. Any second now she'd be tapping at the door. She screwed up her eyes, took several deep breaths and then scrambled to her feet. There it was. Sandra's brisk tap at the door. 'I'll be there in a moment,' she called out. She ran to the bathroom, splashed cold water on her face and patted it dry. Swallow it, push it down, don't think about it, she counselled herself, wondering what Sandra would make of her reddened eyes and blotchy skin. She tucked her hair behind her ears, feeling the knife edge of pain slowly slide under her ribs, where it usually stayed. That was better. That was where the pain lived, not on the floor in front of the television, there for all the world to see. She closed the bathroom door and went to the front door.

'Hey, girl.' Sandra looked at her closely. 'What's up?'

'Nothing. I was just … I just came back from the store.'

If she noticed something was amiss, thankfully she chose not to say. 'You wanna get somethin' to eat? I'm *starving*. Let's go to Flo's.'

Laure looked at her watch. She wasn't due at the house on Spalding for another few hours. 'Sure,' she said. 'Why not?'

'C'mon, get your coat. Let's go. I gotta start work in a coupla hours.'

'Me too.' Laure picked up her bag and her coat and followed Sandra down the hallway. In a funny way, she reminded Laure of Améline. There was something tough and capable about Sandra that brought Améline to mind, despite the dull ache of loss.

As they ate – a hamburger, fries and a milkshake for Sandra; a tuna sandwich for Laure – Laure watched the traffic slush past on Western and listened with half an ear to Sandra's tales of woe. She was always fighting with Richard, her boyfriend, principally over money. Sandra always wanted more. 'It costs *money* to look this good' was her favourite expression. She'd grown up just west of Garfield Park, in a predominantly Hispanic area – she could hold her own with *anyone*. Her mother still lived there, along with two brothers, and a younger half-sister whom Sandra didn't like. Hell, was how Sandra described her childhood. But she was out of it, thank God, and even though her current position as the part-time squeeze of a married man and her job as a stripper wasn't something she'd write to her mother about, hell, it made more money than waitressing … the same money that she sent over to her mother every once in a while. 'She ain't fussy where it comes from,' Sandra grinned.

'But don't you sometimes, I don't know, think that it could have been different?' Laure asked timidly, sipping her Coke.

'It *is* different,' Sandra said, draining the last of her milkshake. 'And I get down on my knees every night and thank God.' Laure was quiet. Sandra was probably right. What she was doing now was no doubt an improvement on what she'd done before, judging from the stories she told. 'C'mon, let's get out of here. I need to buy something for later tonight. Richard's coming over after my shift ends and I can only think of one way to make a man pay up ... know what I mean?' Laure shook her head. 'Oh, c'mon, don't go all innocent on me,' Sandra said, laughing as she got up. 'I bet you could teach me a thing or two!' Laure just laughed. Sandra had her all wrong. At least, she thought as she followed Sandra out of the door, she wasn't sleeping with someone just to pay the rent. She hadn't quite got *that* desperate.

When she arrived at work that afternoon, Aaron was looking worried. 'What's wrong?' she asked, as she followed him into the studio. He scratched his head and looked at her sheepishly.

'Well, thing is ... you know the stuff we did for the car shop guy? About a month ago?' Laure nodded. It had been her first job. 'He's changed his mind, he doesn't like the photos. But here's the thing. He liked *you*. A *lot*. What he's offering is a lot more money ... if you could, you know ... take it all off.'

'What?' Laure stared at him.

'Nude. It'll still be real tasteful, of course. But he's willing to pay a whole lot more to have you nude. Whaddya say? Need some time to think about it? Sure, take a few moments. I don't have anything else for you right now, that's the other thing. I feel kinda bad you coming all the way here today, but I'm sure something will come in the next couple of weeks. So you think about it and let me know, OK?' And then the next thing she heard was the sound of the door shutting behind him. Followed immediately by the cold, horrible rush of fear. *Nothing for you this week ... maybe in a couple of weeks.* She knew exactly what that meant. She shoved her fist in her mouth. Only the other day Sandra had expressed total disbelief at Laure's description of Aaron and Dave. 'Nice guys? You're kidding. You mark my words,' she'd said scornfully. 'They're gonna try to make you do other stuff. You're much too cute for the tame kinda shit you're doing.'

'I don't care what they ask me to do, I'm not doing it,' Laure

179

said defiantly. 'Besides, they're not like that. They're nice.'

'Honey, ain't nobody nice in this business. Wise up, girl.'

Well, it looked as though Sandra was right. She stood in the middle of the path for what seemed to her like hours, the thoughts going round and round in her head. She thought of Grandmère, of Améline ... what would they say if they knew where she'd ended up? Bad blood, Grandmère would say bitterly. Like mother, like daughter. Was this what had happened to Belle? She thought of the shoebox with over three thousand dollars saved; the little white lamp she'd bought the other day and the feeling of safety and security that the money brought her. Could she go back to counting every dime, to hesitating over a loaf of bread or a packet of coffee – *real* coffee? She thought of the little French bakery that she'd found on North Avenue where she went on her way back from a photo session just to have a coffee and a buttery, deliciously flaky croissant and, of course, the chance to speak her mother tongue. Could she bear to give all of that up?

Aaron chose that moment to reappear. He opened the front door and read the surrender in her eyes. He held the door open for her as she walked back in.

After the first few sessions, she came to the conclusion that it wasn't *that* different – or difficult. Sure, there were moments of real agonising embarrassment as Dave asked her to open her legs a little wider, or to cup her breast with her hand ... At those moments she felt the blush steal over her like liquid heat, producing a fiery redness to her cheeks that Dave, typically, said was even more alluring. But after she'd done it four or five times, she found herself getting used to it, to not thinking about it other than when the room was too cold, or too hot, or if the lights were too bright. Slowly but surely she got used to it. She couldn't quite say she enjoyed it, but she did enjoy the wad of cash she received at the end of her first week. She took Sandra to dinner on the proceeds – on the half that she allowed herself to spend – and over steak and lobster at the Surf 'n' Turf Grill on Broadway, she confessed to getting used to it.

'Yeah, well … you gettin' used to the cash is what it is,' Sandra said, her mouth full of lobster.

'I guess so. Sometimes … I … I'd like to think of something else to do, you know … have a career, maybe?'

'You've *got* a career, honey. Just not in the business you want. But you must be making OK money, ain't you?'

'Yeah, I suppose so. I'm saving it. Maybe I'll go to college or something.'

'I bet they love you over at the bank,' Sandra said, spearing another piece of steak.

'The bank?' Laure was puzzled. 'What bank?'

'*Your* bank. If you're putting in all your money every week, I bet they just *love* you.'

'Oh, I don't have a bank account. I … I don't have a social security number,' Laure said, shrugging.

'How come?'

'Well, I'm … I don't have a work permit.'

'What d'you need a work permit for?' Sandra looked at her, puzzled.

'I'm not American, you know.'

'I know *that*. I can hear that. But how'd you get here?'

'On an aeroplane,' Laure said, rolling her eyes. 'But I over-stayed my visa. And now I'm illegal.'

'No *shit*! Oh, man, you got *balls*, Laure,' Sandra said admiringly through a mouth full of food. Laure laughed. 'So, what d'you do with all your money?' she asked, her eyes still on Laure.

Laure giggled. 'I guess I shouldn't,' she said sheepishly, 'but I keep it in a shoebox. In my closet.'

'Baby, you are *too* wild.' Sandra grinned.

'I like counting it. It makes me feel good,' Laure said simply.

'No shit. *I'd* feel good if I managed to save any.'

'Don't you have any savings?' Laure asked, surprised. Sandra shook her head.

'Savings? On my salary? You must be jokin'. Only Asians save money, didn't you know?'

'*I* save.'

'Yeah, well ... You ain't American. Pass the ketchup, will ya?'

35

Aaron had judged her correctly. From posing nude to acting nude ... slowly, inexorably, Laure was beginning to slide. The time wasn't *quite* right, he said to Dave in an aside one morning, but he could see the beginnings of a slow, weary acceptance in her eyes. He was still paying her well – some weeks she earned almost four hundred bucks but not *too* often, he calculated. Just once in a while. Enough to whet the appetite. She was looking good – a better diet, a few days off a week, better make-up and clothes ... Yes, if he – they – played their cards right, they would have a star on their hands. They could start to market her properly. Start off with the lower end of the range, the *Men Only* magazines, then work their way up the ladder, so to speak. Who knew ... maybe even a *Playboy* or *Penthouse* spread? From there, Aaron knew, it would be easy. The jump from centrefold to adult films was small and linear. A porn star. She had a better body than anyone they'd seen in the past couple of years; full, rounded, not an inch of fat, but voluptuous in that sensual, erotic-but-nice way, not sleazy, not at all. Perfect skin – the right colour and tone that suited the camera: not too dark like some of the blue-black whores they'd had in the past couple of years and not so pale you'd have to slather make-up all over their bodies. No, Laure was the real thing and if they timed it right, they could make money. *Serious* money. It was just a question of time – and timing. Dave, the idiot, had a soft spot for her. It annoyed him. They were there to make money, not make love – if that was what he was after. But he knew Laure had grown to trust Dave and for that reason he had to tread carefully, with both of them. He had to stop rubbing his hands with glee. With the right script, the right props, the right action, this girl could be *big*. Bigger than Suzy Lords, bigger even than that silly blonde English chick who was in all the magazines ... Samantha somebody. Fox. Samantha Fox. Now, if he could make a movie with the two of *them* together ... Ebony and Ivory.

He was sweating already.

'Change my name?' Laure said, looking from Aaron to Dave in surprise. 'Why would I want to do that?'

'It's too difficult to pronounce,' Aaron said smoothly. 'For Americans.'

'But who's going to want to pronounce my name?'

'Laure, will you just trust me?' Aaron said, his voice rising in irritation. 'Haven't we done right by you? Aren't you making the kind of money you only ever dreamed of?' Laure flinched. She hated it when he got angry. 'What were you making when you came to us? Huh? Thirty bucks a day?'

'OK ... yes, you're right. I'm sorry,' Laure said quickly. 'I'm just surprised, that's all. I just didn't think ...'

'You're not supposed to do the thinking. *I'm* here to do that. Now, me and Dave discussed it, we think Lulu Saint is a good name for you. It's a cute name. Lulu. We like it.'

'Yeah,' Dave broke in eagerly. 'And it's real close. I mean, Laure ... Lulu ... it's nearly the same thing.'

Lulu. It was Améline's childhood name for her. It hit her, just below the ribs. The thought of her seeing her in this seedy, desperate place made her want to cry. She had managed – with great difficulty – to block Améline and everything she'd left behind out of her mind. It was the only way to cope. 'I ... not Lulu, please,' she whispered. 'Anything else but Lulu. Please.'

'OK, OK,' Aaron said impatiently. 'Whatever. Lori. Lisa. Whatever you like. We're offering you the biggest chance you're ever going to get, Laure. What do you care what we call you?'

'Lori's fine,' Laure whispered, not daring to lift her eyes. She didn't want him to see her tears.

'OK. Look, what we were thinking of doing,' Dave said, changing the topic, 'is a proper spread, you know ... kind of like what you'd get in *Penthouse*. You know it?' Laure shook her head. 'Get us a couple of copies, will you?' he said to Aaron. Then he turned back to her. 'It's the big league, Laure, you could be making *thousands*.' The excitement in his voice rose as he described the girls who'd gone from car oil calendars to being pin-ups and *Playboy* centrefolds. Thousands of dollars a shoot, he said, his eyes glazing over. *But I don't want to make thousands of dollars*, Laure wanted to cry. *I just want to make enough to take care of myself and to not have to worry where the next meal is coming from. I don't want to be rich – not by spreading my legs for some cheap, nasty magazine that would give my grandmother and everyone I know a heart attack if they saw.* But she didn't say that. She kept her mouth firmly closed and opened it only when Dave had spread out the magazines in front of her. And even then all she said was 'oh'.

She got home late that night. It had been a hard day. She peeled off her clothes as soon as she got in the door and almost ran into the shower. She felt as though she were covered in a film of filth, an invisible second skin of shame that, try as she might, she could not remove. She scrubbed at her skin until it was raw and angry, and then gritted her teeth as she turned the shower on full blast, full heat. She felt as though she were being boiled alive. Anything was better than the thought of what she'd done – what she was doing. *This isn't what I planned for me*, she cried to herself as the water streamed over her hair and shoulders. *This wasn't how it was supposed to be.*

But, despite her anguish, the shower did her some good. She stepped out, her skin tingling from the heat, and wrapped herself tenderly in one of the luxuriously soft towels she'd bought, what, only the other day? That was the hard part of this. It afforded her luxuries that almost – *almost*, but not quite – made it all right. She'd made five hundred dollars that day. Five hundred minus Aaron's cut. He'd promised her the same again the following day. With those pictures, he could begin auctioning her – and then the sky was the limit. *Six months*, she said to herself, rubbing her hair dry. *I'll do this for six months. I won't save half of what I make, I'll save three-quarters. Then I'm getting out of here.* She had no idea where she would go – just that she would leave. And with enough money to start again, somewhere else, away from the dirt and the filth in which she felt herself buried.

She walked into the bedroom, opened the closet to take out a nightdress then dropped to her knees and reached for her shoebox. She hadn't looked at it since she'd deposited her last three hundred dollars, just over a week ago. She would have close to four thousand now. She smiled to herself, already brightened by the thought. Her hands went to the usual spot, just behind the coat. There was nothing there. She moved to the left ... nothing ... and then back to the right. Her heart missed a beat. She leaned forward, shoving the shoes and bags out of the way. In a broad sweep, left to right. Nothing. She leaned back, her heart racing. She pulled the coat and the surrounding clothes off the hangers and stared into the empty space. There was nothing. No shoebox – nothing. She swallowed, feeling fear flood into her mouth. Her heart was hammering, she couldn't breathe properly. *Calm down. No ... you must have put it somewhere ... think, Laure. Think! When was the last time you saw it? When ... a day, two days ... when?* She was having difficulty breathing. *OK. Go upstairs ... ask Sandra if she's seen anyone coming in and out. Anyone unusual.* And then, suddenly, it hit her. Sandra. She hadn't heard the sound of Sandra's heels for what ... a few days? A week? She stuffed the ball of her fist in her mouth to stop herself from screaming out loud. Sandra ... she had a key! She had Laure's spare key! They'd given each other a spare set in case one of them got locked out. Dread was sinking into every pore. When had Sandra suggested it? A couple of days after the conversation in the restaurant – the Surf 'n' Turf – after Laure had told her that she didn't have a bank account. She almost passed out. *She'd even told her! A shoebox at the back of my closet.* She stood up, feeling dizzy. She ran into the kitchen, rummaged around in one of the drawers and found Sandra's key. Without even bothering to put on a pair of slippers, she ran upstairs and with shaking fingers, slid the key in the lock. She opened the door. And slid to the ground. The apartment was empty. Nothing ... all gone. Sandra too was gone. With her money.

36

Once. *One* film – two hours long – in which she held her breath, closed her eyes and tried to think of anything – anything at all – other than what was happening around her. Aaron was beside himself, rubbing his hands with glee. *The feel of the bark of the jacaranda tree as she slid down it; the bump of landing on the soft, sometimes spongy grass.* 'OK ... Laure? You ready? John ... get in beside her, that's right.' *The soft ticking of the grandfather clock in the parlour downstairs and the peculiar stillness of the humid air first thing in the morning when the heat has silenced even the birds.* 'Laure, will you at least *try* to look like you're enjoying this? Put your hand on his cock ... yes, *on* it. Not next to it. OK. Dave, you ready?' *Staring at the back of Améline's head after her hair had been washed and ironed straight; the smell of shampoo and burnt dampness as Cléones and Améline tried to do the same to her own.* 'Now, take it in your mouth ... Don't bite him, will you? Good ... John? Some sounds from you, please. Talk to her ... nasty, if you want. Great.' *Anything. The scent of pigeon peas simmering on the stove and the sound of Cléones cleaning the pots. Anything at all.*

She collected the money the following day. A thousand dollars in crisp, twenty dollar bills. Aaron was pleased with her. Despite a little woodenness on her part, the film looked great, he said enthusiastically. *She* looked great. He had all sorts of ideas for more. Something dark and exotic. Wasn't it voodoo they had on her island? Something kinky, maybe even a storyline.

'Hey, cheer up. It wasn't so bad, was it? We'll do it again on Friday. Take a break.' She shook her head and tried to smile. She slipped the envelope containing the money into the inside pocket of her coat and turned to go.

'So, see you Friday?' Aaron called after her as she reached the front door.

'Sure,' she said softly but didn't turn around. She pushed open the door and walked out into the cold. She would never go back.

37

There was tension in the air as Steve picked up one of the bundles of notes and slid it across the desk to Melanie. She stared at it. What was she supposed to do with it?

'Count it, will ya?' Steve said, pulling open a drawer.

The two men sitting opposite him shifted uneasily. Melanie slit open the bundle exactly the way she'd seen Steve and his flunkies do a hundred times before; insert the tip of the knife under the paper strip, a quick flick of the wrist and the bundle came easily apart. One-hundred-dollar bills. Crisp, clean-smelling. She picked the block of notes up, tapped them into a brick and began counting. Every so often, again as she'd seen them do, she pulled out a note and held it up to the light looking for the telltale tiny red threads buried in between the layers of each bank note that signalled its veracity. So far, so good. But the two men in front of Steve were still nervous. She looked at the man closest to her. She could see a trickle of sweat make its way down the back of his neck and settle in the collar of his shirt. A muscle in his back twitched occasionally as she counted. Two thousand two hundred, two thousand three hundred, two thousand four hundred ... she stopped. She held the note up – there was something wrong. The note was smoother than the others, she could feel it on her fingertips. She screwed up her eyes – no, the red threads were definitely not there.

'Steve,' she said nervously, 'this one … there's a couple more … I'm not sure …'

'Give it over,' Steve said, his voice dangerously silky.

Melanie handed over a small pile. Beads of sweat began to run down the man's neck. His hands were trembling. There was no sound in the office as Steve picked up the notes, one after the other, and held them to the light.

'Get Carlos in here,' he said to Melanie, a few minutes later. His voice was calm. 'Now.'

Melanie jumped off the desk and opened the door. Her own hands were shaking. There was something about the whole set-up that made her nervous as hell. She knew it was a big drug deal. The two men sitting opposite Steve were newcomers and as a rule, Steve didn't like dealing with people he didn't know. Someone else had vouched for them. Melanie had heard snippets of conversation over the past few months – the deal would have been one of the biggest Steve had ever done. For that reason alone, he was edgy. Melanie had never actually *seen* what happened when Steve got edgy but she could guess. Remember the snake? She'd been puzzled: why send someone a dead snake? Now she understood it was his trademark stamp of disapproval. If a deal went wrong, depending on the amount of money at stake and the severity of the double-cross, there were a number of punishments available in his repertoire. A dead rattlesnake wrapped around a bunch of roses, delivered to your doorstep or the doorstep of someone you loved, was one. Just for starters. There was something unbelievably sinister and threatening about his acts of revenge. When Tina first explained them to Melanie she'd thought she was joking. She wasn't, and neither was Steve. It partly explained his success. He was the type of man who, given other circumstances, might have become a famous artist or a film-maker … he had a decidedly creative touch. Melanie once said to Tina that she thought it was a shame he'd never had the chance to do things properly, legitimately. Tina had just laughed at her and told her to stop being so square.

Carlos and Lukas, two of Steve's 'fixers', followed Melanie into the room. Steve looked up as she came in. 'Not you, love. Wait outside for me, will you? Here, take the car keys.' He slid his keys across his desk. Melanie took one look at the terrified faces of the two men, grabbed the keys and fled.

Half an hour later, Steve opened the door of his 911 Porsche and slid into the driver's seat. Melanie turned her head to look at him. It was seven in the evening and the light was almost gone. He was breathing fast but said nothing as he started the engine. She looked at his forearms. His sleeve was faintly speckled with something – dirt?

'Dinner,' he said, not looking at her. It wasn't a question. 'There's a new place over in Studio City. Good steaks.'

'Yes, sure.' Melanie kept her voice as light and neutral as possible. She knew from experience that it would take him a little while to come round. He threaded the car around the winding roads that led over the Hollywood Hills and within half an hour they had pulled up in front of the restaurant. A valet attendant whisked the car away and Steve held Melanie's elbow lightly as they walked inside. As they were seated, she noticed that the specks of dirt on his sleeve were not dirt at all. If she were not very much mistaken, it was blood. She swallowed. She'd often wondered, almost idly, just how far Steve would go – had gone. Now she knew. She shivered, suddenly cold despite the heat.

38

Améline paused, her hands covered in flour. She cocked her head; yes, someone had just knocked at the door. Iain was in London. He wasn't due back until the following afternoon. She wondered who it was. She quickly rinsed her hands and went to the door. She could see the person's outline through the frosted, distorting glass.

'Oh.' It was Viv.

'Hello.' Viv's painted mouth opened and closed. Améline eyed her warily. She now spoke enough English to be able to communicate with people – not that she had many people to speak to. Those she did speak to – the women at the supermarket, the bus driver, the postman – were all perfectly pleasant but Améline suspected she would never know what went on behind their blank, smiling faces. Their neighbour on the one side was deaf; and the house on the other side was empty, up for sale. So there really wasn't anyone to talk to. 'I brought you some eggs,' Viv was saying briskly, as if she really didn't have time for the visit. 'And a newspaper.'

'Oh. Thank you.' Améline was puzzled. She *had* eggs. And if she wanted a newspaper … She caught sight of the paper. *Le Soir*.

'It's French,' Viv said, absurdly. 'Thought you might like to read … something.'

Améline took the eggs and the paper with a hand that shook just a little. The kindness – for that was what it was – was completely unexpected, and therefore overwhelming. 'Th … thank you,' she stammered again.

'Not at all. Well, I'd best be off. Lots to do. Spring's in the air.' Viv gave her a quick, fleeting smile. 'Gardening and all that.' She turned and disappeared down the garden path. Améline stood in the doorway, a lump in her throat. She hadn't expected *that*.

'Oh, she's not a bad sort, old Viv,' Iain said to her the following day. 'She can be awfully sweet. At times.'

'Well, it was very kind of her,' Améline said, smoothing out the pages of the newspaper that she'd read and reread twenty times. She wondered where Viv had bought it. There weren't any shops in Malvern that would sell French newspapers. At least none that she'd discovered and she'd been to every corner of the pretty little town.

'Granted. Now, what did you say you'd made for dinner?'

'Beef Wellington,' Améline said proudly. It had taken her almost the entire day, particularly as she'd been reading an English cookery book. But if there was one thing she knew how to do, it was cook – although cooking in England was a very different affair. She was used to going to the market, to testing the shape, firmness and size of vegetables and fruit before buying; to standing arguing with the butcher over the cut and quality of meat. Here, she'd discovered quickly, you disappeared into a cavernous supermarket where everything was covered in plastic and half-cooked already. There was more variety than she was used to, but the staples she'd bought every day – green, curved plantains, wrinkled sweet yams, smooth, waxy okra – none of those were available in Safeway and, what was more, no one had ever heard of them. 'Plan-tayn? What's that, dearie? D'you mean a banana? No? Oh, dear ... never 'eard of it. Sorry, love.'

She did like the way strangers spoke to each other, though. *Love. Dearie. Sweetheart.* There was always a little endearment tacked on to the end of every sentence, whether the speaker meant it or not. It softened the panic that still rose in her every time she spoke.

A routine was beginning to develop that gave her some hope. Iain left on Monday morning for London, catching the 7.05 a.m. train from Great Malvern, the station at the bottom of the hill. He sometimes came back on Tuesday afternoon, and then left again on Wednesday morning, but more often than not he stayed in London until Friday afternoon when he caught the one p.m. from Paddington and was back home by four p.m. During the week, Améline attended a private college where she studied English from nine a.m. until one p.m. and then from two p.m. until four p.m. English. English. English. Her tongue hurt from pronouncing and repeating words from morning until night.

On the evenings Iain wasn't home, she sat curled up in front of the television, practising, listening, learning. She cleaned the house from top to bottom, scrubbing furiously away at the accumulated dirt and odours until the place gleamed like a newly minted coin. She left nothing unturned. Even though it was only April and an unseasonably cold one at that, she still waded out into the garden in an old pair of rubber boots that belonged to Iain and uprooted the weeds, cleared the gutters and cut the lawn with something that resembled a cutlass ... until she'd spotted a small crowd gathered on the other side of the road, watching her, open-mouthed. What were they looking at? Someone kindly explained to her that in England they had lawnmowers to do that sort of thing ... and the grass really oughtn't to be cut just yet. 'Early summer's the time, love. Not now. It's still freezing.' Améline stammered her thanks.

Slowly, very slowly, she began to grow accustomed to her surroundings and to the shape and direction of her life. Iain was remarkably undemanding. He had a weak heart; it was one of the first things he'd told her in that offhand, half-joking way of the English that she'd come to understand signified anything but. He took a barrage of tablets every morning and, to her relief, he confessed that they somewhat suppressed 'the old appetite', as he put it. It took her a while to understand which appetite he referred to. On the few occasions that he'd asked for more than the oddly comforting cuddle, it was all over so quickly that she wondered if anything had happened at all. She wondered sometimes, lying awake at night in the large bed under the attic eaves, if she would ever be able to feel anything at all. She was very fond of Iain, and grateful to him, of course, but her feelings for him were nothing like those she and Laure had discussed in breathless whispers, years ago, in Laure's room next to the jacaranda tree. Laure had talked of shortness of breath, of dizziness, of feeling as though her heart would burst. They'd read novels together in which heroines wasted away for love and heroes waded through swamps. The lukewarm comfort that stole over her when she looked at Iain's reclining figure on the shabby sofa or listened to his shallow breathing when he'd fallen asleep seemed to have nothing to do with that world of ripped bodices and fluttering hearts. Perhaps it would come, in time? In the meantime, she cooked, cleaned, learned English and performed her wifely duties as best she could. Iain certainly seemed happy enough. He'd lost none of the old-fashioned wit and charm he'd displayed in Haiti and the evenings he was home, as they sat together in the living room watching television or chatting, he made her laugh. It was hard to remember the fear and hunger she'd left behind. Haiti receded in her memory like a bad, distasteful nightmare. Every morning when she awoke, she remembered less and less. But not of Laure. She hadn't forgotten a single thing about Laure. Her hunger to know what had happened to her grew, if anything. It would come upon her in the strangest of times. In the bath sometimes, lifting an arm to soap herself. Or walking down the hill to the bus stop. Watching an American film. What was she doing? Was she happy? Did she remember the life they'd left behind? She would close her eyes, pinch herself, slowly count her breathing ... Anything until the ache had passed and she'd controlled the urge to speak.

At the beginning of May when it seemed at last that the weather would warm up, they celebrated Iain's forty-eighth birthday with a very good bottle of wine (his choice) and an excellent casserole (hers). Améline, who wasn't used to drinking, found herself smiling more and more as she listened to Iain's account of a meeting with a rival journalist; after a while, she contributed a little story of her own. Iain laughed in genuine appreciation. There was a warm glow inside her as she stood up to collect their empty plates and take them carefully through to the kitchen. She placed everything in the warm soapy water, wiped the table and the stove and went back into the cosy living room, the kitchen in perfect order. Iain had opened another bottle; he lay on the rug in front of the television and patted it as she came through. Sit, he said, smiling at her. Sit beside me. She knelt down a little awkwardly but he pulled her close to him. She lay alongside him, unsure of what to do. He poured another glass and passed it to her. The warmth inside her belly grew and her head began to swim, lightly. Iain put out a hand and began to caress her gently. She moved closer to him, enjoying the feel of his fingers trailing across her skin. She wasn't quite sure what to expect. Tonight, after a good meal and a bottle of wine, his heart seemed to be holding up. He was clearly excited by her; soon his hands were underneath her cardigan, peeling the garment away. It didn't take long for him to dispose of most of the rest of her clothing and before she quite realised what was happening, she was practically naked.

But, despite the promising beginning, it was all over within seconds. His whole body stiffened suddenly and he clutched at one of her breasts, hard. She squirmed in pain and fright and then, with a strangled moan, he stiffened, his whole body jerking in spasms. Améline lay next to him, her heart thumping, her mind whirling. He wasn't having an attack, was he? 'Shh,' he mumbled, withdrawing his hand and bringing it up round her shoulders. He pulled her towards him. 'Shh,' he repeated, although she wasn't making a sound. 'It's all right. Still here.' He gave a hoarse, hollow laugh. Améline kept still, afraid to move. Presently, he fell asleep.

She lay in the dark beside him, troubled that something might have happened to him. If, God forbid, something *did* happen, what on earth would she do? Suddenly, as it always happened, her longing for Laure took her by surprise. She would have given anything to hear Lulu's voice once more; to pick up a brush and attempt to untangle the wild, springy mass of curls as the two of them sat on Lulu's bed, talking, talking, talking. She had never felt quite so alone.

PART FOUR

39

Laure was wary of signs but this one *looked* genuine enough. 'Cocktail waitresses wanted for after-hours jazz bar. Good rates of pay. See manager inside.' She looked up at the building, a nondescript, single-storey with an enormous, empty car park in front of it. The Blue Room. She hesitated. Well, she could always just *enquire*, couldn't she? Good rates of pay? And if it looked in any way like ... well, like *you-know-what*, she could always just turn around and walk back to the bus stop. She couldn't possibly go back to Irazú and she was terrified she would run out of money soon. It had been over a month since that last, dreadful day of the film. She shouldered her bag and walked across the parking lot.

The door to the club was actually at the side; a single, un-painted doorway with the words 'The Blue Room' painted along the wall. She tapped on the door. Nothing happened. She tapped again, louder – still nothing. She was just about to turn and walk away when a voice growled through the door, 'Yeah? Who is it?'

'Er, I just saw your sign,' she began hesitantly.

'What? Who is it? I can't hear you.'

'I saw your sign,' Laure repeated, louder this time. 'Outside. The sign for cocktail waitresses.'

'Just a sec,' the voice came through the door again, softer now. There was the sound of bolts being slid back, of a key being turned and then the door was pushed open. A tall, dark-haired man with a moustache looked out. He looked her up and down. 'You're lookin' for a job?'

'Er, yes. I saw the sign and ...'

'Ever done any waitressing before?' He wasn't *un*friendly, Laure thought to herself. A little gruff, perhaps, but certainly not sleazy.

'I'm working in a restaurant right now,' she said, after a moment's hesitation. 'I was just wondering ... Well, it says "good rates of pay" – I just wondered what you ... how much ...'

'Depends,' he said. 'Come in.' He turned to go back inside.

Laure followed him in, down a short flight of steps which opened on to a large, cavernous basement area. It reminded her a little of the Café Napoli, which Delroy had taken her to. Despite the sharp stab of pain that thinking about him produced almost automatically, she suddenly felt at home. There was a semicircular stage with a large grand piano at one end; a few dozen tables and chairs, and then, at the back, a row of more private, upholstered booths. It looked clean – even in the dark.

He led her to one of the booths and slid inside, motioning to her to take a seat alongside.

'I'm Don,' he said, lighting a cigarette. 'I'm the manager here. What's your name?'

'Laure,' she said, sliding in opposite him.

'Cute name. OK, Laure. Here's the deal. I'm looking for a couple of waitresses – we're open four nights a week, Wednesday through Saturday, from ten p.m. to four a.m. We're an after-supper kind of jazz club – good music, really good guest singers. We've had everyone from Miles to Branford in here. It's hard work but the money's good, especially the tips. I like to run a clean ship – no drugs, no drinking on the job and no goin' home with the customers, you dig?' Laure nodded quickly. 'I've got six girls workin' the floor and three behind the bar. The best gigs are selling shots – you buy a bottle from the bar, fill up your glasses and sell straight off your tray. You can make thirty bucks on each bottle and tips can sometimes go up to fifty. But,' he said, looking at her sternly, 'I only give shots to the best girls. That means girls who work hard, who build up regulars and who don't give me no trouble. We're comin' up to Christmas – it's gonna be busy. You think you can handle it?'

'Yes ... yes, I think I can,' Laure said, her eyes lighting up. She couldn't say why but she liked Don. She liked his brusque, no-nonsense manner. He reminded her a little of Julio. Minus the handlebar moustache and flared trousers, of course.

'Yeah, I think you probably can,' Don said, getting up. 'What I normally do, Laure, is take a girl on for a week, see how she does. If it looks like it's gonna work out for both of us, I'll take you on permanent. You're not an actress, are you?' he asked suddenly.

Laure was glad the room was dark. She could feel her cheeks burning. 'No,' she said, as normally as she could.

'Good. Can't tell you how many fucking actresses I get in here ... then I find them screwing men who *say* they're agents in the toilets every night.' He gave a short laugh. 'OK. When d'you wanna start? Tonight?'

'Tonight?'

'Yeah. Friday night. It's our busiest night.' Laure nodded. 'Be here at nine sharp. Bring a black skirt and a white T-shirt. I'll have one of the girls show you the ropes. Sound good to you?'

'Yes! Oh ... I ... I don't have a ... social security number,' she said slowly, thinking it was probably best to tell him now rather than later. She would hate to work hard all evening only to be told she couldn't be paid for it.

'Do I look like I'm in bed with Uncle Sam?' Don asked, chuckling. 'This is a cash business, honey. Once a week, in an envelope. *Comprende?*' Laure nodded. 'So ... See ya later,' he said and ambled towards the door.

At nine that evening, dressed in a brand-new short black skirt and T-shirt, Laure walked into the club, her stomach twisting nervously. As soon as she walked down the stairs, heard the low, rumbling tones of the musicians warming up and the deep, throaty voice of the singer, she felt calm. It was exactly like Café Napoli, only better. There were no prostitutes at the bar but the atmosphere was the same: music, smoke, laughter … everyone out to have a good time, especially the band. She could feel the tension at the nape of her neck slowly begin to loosen. She was beginning to thaw.

'Hi!' one of the other cocktail waitresses greeted her cheerfully. 'You're the new girl, right?'

Laure nodded cautiously. After all, Sandra had been friendly, too. 'Yes, it's my first night.'

'Cool. What's your name?' she called over her shoulder as she jostled to get to the bar.

'Laure.'

'Nice to meet you, Laure,' she said, holding out a hand. 'I'm Shelley.' She looked down at Laure's legs. 'Oh, boy,' she smiled, tapping out a cigarette from a packet in her hand, 'the guys are gonna love *you*,' she said. '*Great* legs.'

Laure blushed. But before she could fumble a reply, Don appeared.

'Nice legs,' he said, causing her to blush even harder. 'OK. Follow me,' he said, beckoning her. 'We got a few minutes before the crowds start comin' in. Let Shelley show you the ropes.'

Don was right, she quickly discovered. The work *was* hard. Up and down the rows of tables with a tray of drinks in your hand; the same worry of trying to remember who'd ordered what; what each drink cost; who was owed change and who'd told her to keep it. Her months at Irazú would come in handy. The customers were a lively, mixed bunch of young and old, black and white, male and female. Everyone was in a good mood, helped smoothly along by the music which was spectacular. Even she, who couldn't tell one end of a saxophone from the other, could see that the musicians were in a class of their own. Cassandra, the lead singer, was a dusky, throaty-voiced beauty with the same kind of fur stole slung casually across a bare arm that she and Améline had found in Belle's trunks. When she grabbed the microphone with both hands and poured herself into it, all five foot four inches of coffee-coloured smoothness, even the bartenders momentarily stopped shaking the drinks. A wild round of applause greeted each song until finally, smiling coyly at the crowd, winking and blowing kisses, the band retired for a break. It was the signal for the tables to start ordering. Laure ran, along with all the other girls, from the bars to the tables and back again for almost four hours straight.

At the end of the night she barely had the strength to haul herself into one of the empty booths with Don and two of the other girls who'd been taken on trial that night. To her amazement, Don told both of them to find other careers and, when they'd staggered away from the table, told her she was hired. She stared at him, open-mouthed, too surprised to speak.

'You made a coupla mistakes tonight,' he said, lighting up a cigarette, 'but I like the way you talk to the customers – real professional, real nice. That's important to me. You laugh a lot – you got a *great* laugh, anybody tell you that? You sound like her,' he said, pointing to Cassandra, who was across the floor with a customer slowly sipping a whisky and inhaling her cigarette. '*And* you've got a great ass.' Laure's cheeks were on fire again. 'Don't worry,' he said, shaking his head. 'I'm as queer as they come.'

She was given her pay packet for the night and ten dollars for the cab that was waiting outside. The other girls, whose names she could barely remember, waved at her as she stumbled outside. 'See you tomorrow!' In the back of the cab, she opened the envelope – fifty dollars, and, she pulled the ball of crumpled notes out of her purse, forty-two, forty-three ... forty-*eight* dollars in tips! If she worked hard, she could earn a hundred bucks a night. She quickly made the calculation. Four nights a week, four hundred dollars a week. *Decent* money, if not wholly legal – that was the most important thing. Within a few months she could have quite a few thousand saved. She leaned back against the sticky, fake leather seat in the cab, too exhausted to smile. All she could think about was stepping into the shower and crawling into bed.

40

Melanie finished applying her new lipstick, blotted her lips carefully and stared at her reflection in the bathroom mirror. She
didn't *look* any different. She put up a hand to touch her face.
Just over a year ago she'd been a London schoolgirl – well, OK,
a schoolgirl-who-was-also-the-daughter-of-a-rock-star – but a
schoolgirl nonetheless. Was it only a year and a half since she'd
walked out of her A-levels in a desperate bid to draw attention to herself? She could scarcely believe it. Here she was,
having drawn the attention she craved from Mike for all the
wrong reasons, living with her boyfriend in a glamorous white
cube of a house in Hollywood, surrounded by his bodyguards
and fixers and minders, a white convertible Mercedes and a
driver at her disposal, a wardrobe full of the sorts of clothes
she wouldn't even have *dreamed* of wearing back in London ...
and yet there was something missing. Something was definitely
missing. Go on, admit it, she mouthed to her reflection in the
mirror. You're lonely. There, you've said it. She looked down
at the ruby red lipstick in her hand. She lifted the gold cylinder
up to the mirror. *I'm lonely*. She carefully wrote out the words,
feeling the soft tip give way under her fingers. She inspected
the damaged tube. And then chucked it in the bin. She could
always buy another one. It might even give her something to
do.

  She sighed and turned away disconsolately from the mirror.
Her mother had finally – *finally* – come round. She'd phoned
one day, completely out of the blue, chatting away as if nothing
had happened. Melanie had been too stunned to respond. And
then, of course, she'd burst into tears as soon as she put the
phone down. Hearing Stella's chirpy, ever-so-English voice
had brought on a wave of homesickness the likes of which
she'd never experienced. Steve, of course, was unsympathetic.
Go back to London if you want, he shrugged. Melanie quickly
dried her eyes. No, of course she didn't want to go back. She

was just, well, a little homesick, that was all. He rolled his eyes. Homesick for what? What on earth did England have to offer anyone?

She picked up the new Gucci bag she'd bought to cheer herself up the other day and slid her black Wayfarer sunglasses on. She'd heard Steve's car pull up while she'd been examining her face – and fate – and she knew he wouldn't take too kindly to the sight of dried tears. She sighed. There were so many things he didn't 'take' to, especially where she was concerned. He didn't like her going out without him; he didn't like it when she showed up at the restaurant unannounced; he didn't like it when she complained about being bored or the fact that she had no friends; he didn't like it when she was homesick. In fact, she was beginning to wonder, what *did* he like? Money and power, of course. And sex. And ... her, surely? He loved her. He didn't say it very often ... in fact, she wasn't sure she'd ever heard him say it. She bit her lip nervously. No, she was being silly. Of course he loved her. Why else would he have let her move in? She checked her reflection once more and opened the bathroom door.

'If I have to ask you one more fucking time, mate,' she heard Steve bark into the phone as she descended the glass staircase. He was standing by the giant glass doors that overlooked the pool, an angry expression on his face. Melanie took one look at him and decided it might be prudent to leave the house for a while.

'I'm going to the hairdressers,' she said quickly as he looked up enquiringly. 'Won't be long.'

He covered the mouthpiece with his hand. 'Don't be. We've got dinner with the guys from New York at eight. Don't be late.'

'I won't,' Melanie promised, struggling to remember who the guys from New York were. She looked at her watch. It was just after noon. She would get Carlos to drive her to the Beverly Centre. Scott at Carlton's on the fourth floor would do her hair. Another of the advantages that knowing Steve di Marco brought. He supplied most of the stylists and hairdressers in the city with their recreational drugs and they, in turn, did whatever he asked, whenever he asked it. Including squeezing Melanie in on five minutes' notice.

An hour and a half later she was sitting under the drier, half-heartedly flicking through a magazine when someone was shown into the seat next to her. She quickly moved her hand-bag out of the way.

'Thanks,' came a perky, little-girl voice. Melanie threw her a quick glance. One of those impossibly tall, impossibly toned LA girls who made her feel like a pale, wilting English rose.

'You're welcome,' Melanie said, giving her a quick smile. Damn, the girl really *was* beautiful. Short, cropped blonde hair, the kind of flawless skin you only ever saw in magazines, and features so delicate they looked as though they'd been painted on.

'Say, aren't you Steve di Marco's girlfriend?' the girl asked suddenly, looking expectantly at her.

Melanie felt a warm glow of pleasure spread through her. 'Yes, yes ... I am. Have we met before ...?' She hesitated, then stuck out her hand.

'Kim Saunders. I've seen you around a couple of times – at the restaurant. Steve's an old friend.'

Melanie had a sudden moment of panic. It was always like this – every so often a reminder would hit her that Steve had a life and associations that she would never – could never – know anything about. Stop it, she told herself firmly, forcing herself to smile. 'Oh, the restaurant's always so busy,' she said apolo-getically. 'So many people ...'

'Yeah, he's pretty popular,' Kim laughed. She had perfect teeth, Melanie noted jealously. Everything about her was perfect. She had on a tiny white mini-skirt, a simple black T-shirt that stopped well before her navel and a flat, beautifully sculpted torso. Melanie couldn't stop staring. 'So what're you gettin' done today?' Kim asked, looking her over in turn.

'Oh, nothing much ... just a trim.'

'I like your hair. It's pretty.'

'Oh, thanks. I ... um ... I don't do much with it. I keep thinking I ought to cut it or something. It's a bit boring but ...'

'Oh no, it's not boring,' Kim said coolly, picking up a magazine as if to say the conversation was over. Melanie groaned inwardly. She cursed herself for being so gauche. Why the hell couldn't she just accept a compliment and shut up?

She sat next to Kim in silence as she waited for Scott to reappear, desperately trying to think of something to say. She couldn't remember the last time she'd spoken to another girl – she hardly ever saw Tina these days. After a few minutes, Kim put down her magazine and turned to her.

'Where d'you hang out?' she asked, taking Melanie by surprise.

'Hang out?'

'Yeah. What do you like to do?'

'Do?' Melanie echoed. 'Oh! You mean, like, every day?'

'Yeah, every day.' Was she laughing at her?

'Oh, I ... well, I don't really ... I'm not working or anything ...' Melanie stuttered. 'I ... I just ...'

'You wanna hang out?'

'Um ... yes! Wow ... where? I mean, when ...?' She was sounding over-eager but she couldn't help it. She couldn't quite believe Kim wanted to hang out with *her*.

'What're you doing tomorrow?'

'Tomorrow morning?'

'Morning? Are you crazy? Sweetheart, I don't get up before noon,' Kim laughed out loud. 'How about lunch? You wanna meet for lunch? Like, around two, maybe?'

'Yeah, that would be great!' Melanie couldn't keep the excitement from her voice.

'I'll pick you up,' Kim said, rising to her feet as her stylist came through the door, full of apologies at having kept her waiting. 'You'll be at Steve's, right?'

'Er, yes.' It crossed Melanie's mind fleetingly – how did she know where Steve lived? She pushed the thought away. Kim wanted to have lunch with her!

'Cool. See you tomorrow.' She picked up her bag and

followed the stylist out of the room. Melanie looked at her departing back in the mirror. She could scarcely believe it. She had a new friend!

She was ready by two p.m. on the dot the following afternoon; in fact, she'd been ready since noon. She'd tried on at least three different outfits before settling on a dress with a pretty lace detail at the neck. She fingered her gold chain nervously – did she look too dressy? Too childish? What would Kim be wearing? At 2.15 p.m., she heard the gates swing open. She rushed to the windows and looked down on to the driveway. Kim pulled up in a black BMW sports car, identical to Steve's white one. She hurried downstairs to welcome her. As soon as she saw her striding up the manicured path, her face fell. She immediately felt overdressed and, worse, childish. Just as she'd feared. Kim was wearing blue jeans, faded and torn in exactly the right places; a crisp white shirt with no bra; black cowboy boots and a pair of Ray-Ban sunglasses pushed up on top of her head – casual, simple and frighteningly stylish.

'Oh *my*,' Kim said, her eyes widening as she took in Melanie's outfit. She put her sunglasses back on. 'Aren't you a sight for sore eyes. Isn't that a little, like, *cheerful* this early in the day?' she asked, pointing at Melanie's matching yellow bag and shoes.

'Well, it's lunchtime,' Melanie protested, embarrassed.

'Forget *lunch*,' Kim said, grinning. 'We need to go *shopping*. Let's go to Rodeo. You been there yet?' Melanie shook her head. 'Come on, I'll drive. We're gonna have some *fun*!' She led Melanie out to the black convertible. It was all too chic for words.

They drove down the twisting canyon towards Beverly Hills, the wind whipping Melanie's long hair around her face, snatching away her words. She suddenly felt a surge of excitement. She'd grown so used to the daily cycle of home, pool, television, going out with Steve and his cronies that she'd forgotten how much fun it was to hang out with a girlfriend, go shopping or for a coffee … and Kim Saunders was a *lot* of fun.

They hit Rodeo Drive just after three. Kim marched her straight into Victoria's Secret, her favourite underwear store with strict instructions to buy everything she was told to and not to argue. They emerged almost an hour later with more underwear than anyone would ever know what to do with. Kim wasn't shy about modelling what she'd picked out for Melanie, either. The assistants were almost besides themselves. Melanie could only sit on the plush, upholstered chair and gape as Kim paraded out in the most gorgeous assortment of minuscule bras and panties she'd ever seen. Melanie wasn't exactly prudish but it took some nerve to wriggle in and out of the little lace scraps that the salesgirls kept producing. And finally, when Melanie was persuaded to try a few things on herself, Kim looked her up and down with a critical, knowing eye and said that the next stop had better be the beauty salon because, in her words, 'You need to get rid of some of *that*,' she giggled, pointing. Melanie looked down at herself, mortified. 'You never heard of a bikini wax?' Kim asked incredulously. Melanie shook her head. 'It's not *sooo* painful. C'mon ... there's a salon upstairs where I sometimes go. Let's see if they can fit you in.'

Half an hour later, feeling as though someone had cauterised the entire lower half of her torso, Kim pronounced her fit for society. 'Don't they do it in England?' she asked, almost kindly. Melanie shook her head. 'How the hell do you go to the beach?' she asked, wrinkling her nose.

'Um ... Well, there isn't much of a beach in London, actually,' Melanie said, her school regulation Speedo springing rather shamefully to mind. Clearly, Kim's idea of swimming bore little relation to hers.

'That's too bad,' Kim said, sounding as though she meant it. 'Anyhow, it's all done now. And the best thing is, you only have to do it, like, every two weeks. It's not like you have to do it every *day*.'

'Two weeks?' Melanie croaked. Two *months* would've been too soon.

'Yeah. But you have to keep it up,' Kim said sternly. 'It looks *gross* if you don't.'

Kim, Melanie decided rather glumly, was obviously made of sterner stuff. She followed her meekly down the escalators and into another round of shops. Despite the pain, she couldn't help feeling that her life was about to change. Again.

41

The week before Christmas, Chicago was caught in the grip of a massive snowstorm – huge clouds of it drifted in off the lake, blowing down the alleyways and piling up at the sides of the roads. The salt trucks worked through the night, their yellow lights blinking eerily up and down as they cleared the main roads in preparation for the next working day. Every night at four-thirty a.m., Laure sat in the back of a cab speeding along Lake Shore Drive towards Wicker Park, marvelling at the powdery ice that fell over everything, muffling all sound. The city was silent, almost suffocated by the thick, cold blanket. Lake Shore Drive. Navy Pier. Grant Park. Was it really only a year and a half since Delroy Weaver had traced the outline of the city on her bare stomach, telling her how much she would like it? She propped her face on her chin and looked out of the cab window. Thinking about Delroy no longer produced the same giddy rush of pain the way it had in the beginning. She'd grown up. Too many things had happened, too many disappointments and setbacks and times when things just hadn't worked out the way she'd planned. But she'd managed, hadn't she? She'd hadn't just given up, sitting around on her ass all day long the way Belle did, waiting for some man to come in and give shape to the day. She'd gone out and found a way to pay her rent, put food on the table ... keep it together. Yes, there were things she wished she'd done differently – or not done at all – but she was taking care of herself, wasn't she? She was *managing*. That was the important bit. Before you could succeed at anything, you had to manage first. And that was exactly what she was doing.

The club was packed the following night. Despite the snow, customers were coming through the doors in droves. With only four days to go until Christmas, everyone was in a good mood. Laure ran up and down the stairs, balancing her tray above her head, wriggling her way through the crowd.

'Laure! Table six ... you forgot the brandy!' The bartender shouted across the heads clustered at the bar.

'*Shit!* Thanks!' Laure shouted back. She stopped in her tracks, turned carefully around and walked back, balancing her tray in front of her. She reached across for the bottle he held out to her.

'Hey, sweetheart!' A large, very merry man blocked her path. 'How you doin'?'

'I'm doing fine, sir ...' Laure nodded, trying to get past. She kept a wary distance from the customers who, after several drinks and an hour of Cassandra's erotically mournful voice, were all too ready to stop and talk – more if they could get away with it. She paid them no attention, which the other girls saw, and liked. She could tell that they were relieved they didn't have to worry about their tips being pinched or finding their best customers had suddenly switched their affections.

'Say, I been watchin' you, girl,' the man carried on drunkenly. 'You know something? You're one *helluva* waitress, you know that?' he leered at her, putting a hand out to touch her shoulder. She ducked and quickly moved round him and tried to wriggle her way through the crowd. She was almost past him when she felt a hand on her ass.

'No, honey ... really. You are one *helluva* waitress and this is one *helluvan* ass,' he said, slapping it. His tongue was practically in her ear. She froze.

'Sir,' Laure began carefully, mindful of the fact that she was carrying six glasses, a bottle of brandy and a bottle of wine. 'Take your hands off me.'

'Whassa matter, honey, you don' like what I'm doin' to ya?' His hand moved lower. Laure snapped. Still holding onto her tray she turned round as carefully as she could and brought her knee up swiftly. There was a gasp and the man's cigar fell out of his open mouth. A space had suddenly cleared itself around her, there was a murmur as people moved away and the man's hands went protectively to his prick. '*You* ...' he breathed in fury as his cigar bounced off his trousers and fell to the ground. 'You little *bitch*,' the man roared above the noise of the music. Laure looked quickly around, spotted a table and set her tray down. Someone gasped as the man raised his hand as if to strike her but before he could do anything, Laure grabbed his forearm and shoved it right back against his chest.

'You *touch* me again, asshole, and I swear I'll crack this fuck-ing bottle over your head,' she hissed, her voice trembling with rage.

'Hey, hey ... What's going on?' She could hear Don's voice. He pushed his way through the crowd surrounding Laure. 'Hey ... what's the matter, honey?' he asked Laure. He turned to the man who was standing looking at Laure with a mixture of rage and disbelief. 'What did you do to her?'

'He was feelin' her up,' someone shouted out, 'and she fuck-ing *gave* it to him, man!'

'You OK?' Don turned back to Laure. She nodded, too angry to speak. 'OK. Get him outta here,' Don shouted to Miguel who was coming up the stairs. 'Go on, sir, nice and easy, now ... We don't want no trouble. Just leave.'

'Cocksuckin' *bitch*,' Laure could hear him yelling as Miguel and one of the other bouncers escorted him down the stairs. 'All I fuckin' *did* was ...' His voice was lost as they opened the club doors and unceremoniously threw him out.

'You sure you're OK?' Don asked again, as the crowd closed around them again. Laure nodded tightly. All she could remember was feeling his hands move down her buttocks and then the blinding, red anger that swept through her. She would have cracked his skull open if he'd tried anything further. Don was looking at her, concerned. 'Take a minute, Laure,' he said softly, taking her tray away. 'Go wash your face. I'll get some-one else to serve these.' She nodded and walked quickly to the bathroom. Ten minutes later, her breathing under control, she was back on the floor.

'You were pretty impressive back there.' The man she was serving suddenly spoke up. Laure looked up. 'Sorry,' he said quickly. 'I didn't mean to—'

'Will that be all, sir?' Laure asked politely. She didn't feel up to making small talk. Not tonight.

'Yes, thanks. Keep the change,' he said as she started fishing for change.

'No, you've given me sixty dollars ... the drinks come to $41.50,' Laure said automatically.

'No, really. Keep it. You certainly earned it tonight.' Laure looked at him warily. 'What an asshole that guy was. Is it always like this?'

'No, not usually ... it's Christmas, I guess,' Laure said, giving a half-smile. The man's tone was friendly, at least. She looked at him quickly. A college student, probably from the very expensive, very private University of Chicago several blocks away. They occasionally came into the Blue Room though they rarely stayed very long, and rarely came back. It wasn't quite their scene.

'Season of goodwill and all that?' His voice had a smile in it. She wondered where he was from – he didn't sound American.

Laure shrugged. 'Some get a little merrier than others, I guess,' she said, slipping the change into her pocket. 'Thank you,' she said, turning to go. 'It's very generous of you.'

'Merry Christmas,' he called out, as she walked off. She nodded to herself as she pushed her way back to the bar. *Yeah, Merry Christmas to you too, pretty college boy.*

42

'So, where d'you lot want to go tonight?' Daniel Heinrich Bermann, heir to the ScanCorp fortune amassed by his German-born father, Günter Heinrich Bermann, looked at the three young men lying sprawled out on the couch opposite him and barely stifled a yawn. What was he doing here? He hated hanging around watching them get drunk, stoned and spaced, in that order. He rolled his eyes. Yet another reason to hate Chicago. In London, he would be hanging out with *real* friends, not the spaced-out sons of his father's business associates whom his parents were desperate for him to like. And why *should* he like them? Because, his mother patiently explained to him, 'They're your sort of people, darling.' He'd looked at her in semi-disgust. *Your sort of people.* What on earth did *that* mean? That was the problem with his parents. They had no idea what sort of person he was. He'd been sent to an English boarding school at the age of six by his English mother, anxious for him to have the right sort of accent and antiquated education that she'd had. Only problem was, in the thirty-odd years that had passed since she left England for America to marry the billion-aire Bermann – Günter to his friends and family – England had changed. She just hadn't realised it.

He'd emerged from Eton with three A-levels, just as his mother had wanted, except that instead of joining the family firm as they'd all planned, he'd surprised them by begging to be allowed to go to university – which his father thought a complete waste of time – and to be allowed to study history. His father had looked at him in a mixture of disbelief and disgust. History? Whatever for? A complete waste of time. *Vaste of time.* And money … *his* money. *Never mind, let the boy go. His heart's set on it. My father went to university, you know.* Surprisingly, his mother had come to the rescue.

He looked round the spacious, elegant town house he now owned. His father had bought it for him on his twenty-fifth birthday, a way of luring him back to Chicago. A beautiful four-bedroom town house in Lincoln Park with underground parking for the Porsche 911 he'd thrown in as well. Günter simply wasn't used to *not* having things his way. Daniel would have stayed in London and done a PhD if he'd been capable of it but his mother had seen through his little ruse.

'You'd better come back,' she'd said to him down the phone from their penthouse apartment on Lake Shore Drive. 'He's hopping mad.'

'But Mum … I don't *want* to come back. I want to stay here.'

'You can't.'

And that was that. Twenty years after he'd been put on a plane by his English governess, he was back. Not on holiday, the way he'd been back and forth in his twenty-year exile, but properly back. A job at ScanCorp with an office at ScanCorp's headquarters right next to the Hancock Tower from which he could see out over Lake Michigan and all the way to Indiana, if the air was clean. The town house; the Porsche. He was the third generation of Bermanns to have done well. His grandfather had made money in the Ruhr before the war and his youngest son Günter had had the good sense to emigrate to America afterwards rather than see the fortune he'd amassed wiped out. Günter, when it was his turn, made more millions. The line to which Daniel belonged stretched back to the beginning of time, or so it often felt.

However, having an apartment, a job and a car didn't necessarily mean he actually had anything to *do*. In fact, he had almost nothing to do. His father's grip on all aspects of his business from the newspapers and magazines to the movie theatres he owned was so total and so complete there was no way Daniel himself could have taken a decision on *any*thing. Which made him feel about as useful in his new role as scion and heir as … fuck, even the *security* guard at the front door to his building had more responsibilities.

It was certainly a great pity, he thought to himself just a touch sarcastically as he fished around for a packet of cigarettes, that he didn't like doing what his three friends seemed to enjoy more than anything in the world. They *liked* doing nothing. They lived for it, in fact. So why didn't he? Was it his English upbringing? The fact that he hadn't grown up with them? He didn't know. He just knew he couldn't stand getting high, hated the lazing around that seemed to accompany dope-smoking in large quantities and couldn't ever – *ever* – imagine bending over a table using a rolled-up dollar bill to inhale coke up his nose. Dean and Tag took the piss out of him whenever they could but it didn't bother him. He was twenty-seven years old with a degree in history, a head full of ideas, and nothing to do. *That* bothered him. Enormously. But short of cutting himself off from his parents and moving to Africa, he couldn't see what else he could do. Not that he wanted to move to Africa, of course. It was just a manner of speech.

'So ... c'mon. What d'you want to do?' he asked the three comatose figures tetchily again.

'Who cares, man? We just wanna get high.' Twenty-six-year-old Jon McKinnley, heir to the McKinnley timber fortune, was having difficulty pronouncing his words. Next to him, eyes glazed over, was Tag Weldon – the twenty-eight-year-old heir to Weldon House, the giant publishing conglomerate. And slumped against the arm rest, already asleep, was Fitzroy Brewer, twenty-seven years old and a multi-millionaire, thanks to his mother's fifth marriage. Young, handsome, rich ... and spaced out. Daniel looked at them in disgust. He groped around for the remote control and switched the TV off. Fitzroy had brought over a soft-porn movie that none of them were watching anyway.

'How about dinner?' Daniel tried again. No response. He rolled his eyes and got up.

'Hey ...' Tag had woken up and was stumbling towards him. 'Let's go clubbing, man,' he mumbled.

'OK. But where?'

'How about Liquid, over on Milwaukee? The girls are fuck-ing gorgeous.'

'OK. Let's go. I've been in the flat all day,' Daniel said, relieved to have something to do.

'It's an *apartment*, Bermann, not a "flat". Actually, it's a town house. What the *fuck*? Anyone'd think you were a fucking Limey,' Tag grumbled as he unzipped his fly and headed for the toilet.

'I am,' Daniel said mildly to his disappearing back.

Three hours later, having been turfed out of three nightclubs in a row, the four of them stood huddled around Daniel's car, angrily debating what to do.

'What the fuck?' Tag kept muttering, drawing on his cigarette as if it were his last.

'Well you're not supposed to buy drugs in the toilet,' Daniel said, lighting his own cigarette.

'Shut the fuck up, Bermann,' Jon snapped. 'Just 'cos *you* don't.'

'I'm just saying.'

'Well, don't.'

'Guys … are we gonna stand here all night arguing?' Fitzroy broke in. 'Come on. Bermann, get in the car. Let's go to that place on Southside … The Blue Room or whatever. Where you picked up that cute Mexican chick? Remember? Just before Christmas? It's open till pretty late.' He prodded Jon in the ribs.

Jon grinned. 'Oh, yeah … I remember. OK … let's go.' They climbed into the car and Daniel started the engine. With any luck he'd be in bed by dawn.

Daniel followed them into the club, wishing he'd had the sense to drop them off and go home. It was late – he peered at his watch in the darkness of the club's interior: already past midnight. Fitzroy and Jon headed for the toilets immediately. Daniel followed Tag up the stairs. The club was packed but the balcony seating area was thankfully calmer. They found a circle of seats and Daniel sank down gratefully.

'Hi, what can I get you gentlemen to drink?' He looked up.

It was the waitress who'd kneed someone in the groin the last time they'd been in the club.

'Hey, it's you,' he said, breaking into a smile. She looked at him, coolly polite. 'From last month ... before Christmas. Remember? Some guy was harassing you ... you were going to hit him. Wait, don't remind me ... "You touch me again asshole and I'll crack your fucking skull open." Or something like that,' he added lamely. The girl was staring down at him as though he'd lost his mind. Across from him, Tag was trying desperately to keep a straight face.

'Yeah, whatever.'

'No, really. Don't you remember talking to me afterwards? I was so impressed. I thought you were so cool.' Tag's leg shot out and kicked him, hard.

'Well, thanks,' she muttered, obviously uncomfortable. 'So ... can I get you something to drink?'

'Just a mineral water for me,' he said. 'And a whisky for him.'

'Be with you in a moment,' she said and disappeared.

'You are such a fucking *goon*, Bermann.' Tag roared with laughter as soon as she turned away.

'Shut the fuck up,' Daniel said, embarrassed. He'd just made a complete arse of himself, he was well aware of the fact. But he'd been so pleased to see her. She was beautiful. Her skin was like velvet – a deep, rich colour that made him want to reach out and touch her. Stroke her. He stopped, embarrassed. Beside him, Tag continued to chuckle.

'No, seriously, man ... you are too *much*. If you want to screw a chick like that, why waste your *breath*, man? Just take her down to the toilets and fuck her. Simple. You don't have to *talk* to her. Man, you kill me, Daniel, you know that? Just grab her fuckin' ass and take her downstairs.'

'I believe you remember the line,' the girl broke in on them suddenly, her voice dripping with sarcasm. She put the drinks down carefully and turned to Daniel. 'How does it go? "Touch me again and I'll break your fucking skull?"' She stared at them both, her dark eyes flashing. 'That'll be $10.50, sir. And no, thanks, I don't want the change.'

Daniel closed his eyes briefly. He had never been so embarrassed in his life. When he opened them, she was gone. 'You asshole,' he muttered to an open-mouthed Tag. 'You are *such* an asshole.'

Laure walked away, her cheeks burning with anger. Little prick. It wasn't often a customer upset her to the point of wanting to slap him but she'd had to fight hard to resist the urge to reach across and wipe the smug little grin off his face. Stupid rich jerks – who did they think they were? She certainly wasn't going back to their table. Someone else could listen to their crap tonight. She had to stifle a sudden smile though ... the guy who'd spoken to her ... the look on his face ... he'd almost dropped his cigarette when she came back. She shook her head. Rich college kids. They had no fucking idea. She lifted her tray above her head and wriggled her way through the crowd to the bar. It was a busy night and busy nights meant one thing – busy tips. Time to get on with it.

A few hours later, her shift was over. She collected her coat and bag from the locker and gratefully peeled off her apron. She waved a quick goodbye to Jerome, the piano player, and pushed open the back door. The night air was freezing but fresh after the smoky stuffiness inside.

'Miss?' Someone moved out of the shadows. She looked up. It was him. The one with the funny accent. 'Look,' he began, running a hand through his hair. 'I just wanted to apologise. On behalf of my friend. He ... he was drunk. He didn't mean it.' He looked uncomfortable.

'It's fine,' Laure said briskly, doing up the buttons on her coat.

'No, it's not. He was out of line and ... I'm just sorry you had to hear it.'

Laure looked at him. He sounded like one of those English characters she'd seen on television, wearing a top hat and tails.

A gentler, more rounded voice. 'It's OK,' she repeated, a little softer. 'Really.'

'I ... I just wanted to apologise,' he said, digging his hands into his pockets, 'and I didn't see you upstairs.'

'No. I didn't feel like serving you again, if you want to know the truth,' Laure said. 'Anyway ... it's fine. Thanks for waiting around.' She looked around for her cab.

'Well, I felt I had to.' He seemed to want to say more. 'Can I give you a lift somewhere?' he asked, following her eyes.

'Oh, no ... no, thank you. I have a cab waiting,' Laure said quickly. She indicated the yellow cab at the corner.

'Well, at least let me walk you over,' he said quickly. 'I'm Daniel, by the way.' He held out a hand.

Laure hesitated, then shook it. 'I'm Laure,' she said slowly. She wished he would go away.

'What a lovely name. Look, do ... do you live far away?' he asked as they fell into step walking across the parking lot.

Laure sighed. She stopped and turned to him. 'Daniel, thank you for waiting to apologise on behalf of your friend. And thank you for walking me across the parking lot. But, if you don't mind, I'm really tired and I'd rather just be left alone. You don't have to make conversation with me. You've said you're sorry and I've accepted it. Now, please just leave me alone.' And with that, she turned on her heel and walked off.

As she got into the taxi and it turned round to head towards the freeway, she caught sight of him standing exactly where she'd left him, hands in his pockets, looking strangely lonely and dejected. She turned her head. It was none of her business.

43

Somewhat predictably, Steve didn't seem to share Melanie's enthusiasm for her new friend. Fucking joined at the hip, they were, he snapped at her one day. Like twins. Kim told her just to ignore him. He'd get over it, get used to it. Especially as Melanie, under Kim's own expert tutelage, she pointed out, was becoming more and more *goddamn beautiful* every day. 'It's true!' she cried. 'Just look at you!' Kim had decided to take Melanie 'in hand' as she put it and inject some serious style into her wardrobe. One afternoon she came round and threw out almost everything Melanie owned, admonishing her for her *goddamn Englishness* – no more pastels, flowers, lace, A-line skirts and shirts with puffy sleeves. Kim didn't give a damn what the girls on the King's Road wore – *where the hell is King's Road anyway?* She persuaded Melanie to cut her waist-length hair. When Scott finally allowed her to look in the mirror, the three of them gasped; Melanie with shock. Gone were the two long, straight planes that had been hers since the age of ten. In their place was a shoulder-length, severe bob, cut straight across the eyes, just below her eyebrows. It made her instantly older and even slimmer ... and about ten times more sophisticated. Kim bent down to hug her and Melanie caught sight of the two of them, Kim's beautiful, golden face and short, blonde hair contrasting sharply against Melanie's classical, pale beauty. Scott declared that they would just have to have a picture of the two of them – it made the best advert for the hair salon any of them had ever seen. *Stunning, babe, stunning.* Melanie couldn't drag her eyes away from the mirror. She'd never pictured herself that way.

She started going to the gym three times a week – she who had never seen the inside of one – *and no cheating*, Kim admonished. She was six years older than Melanie and had been a gym-goer for most of her teenage life. Within a month, Melanie's face had completely lost its last remnants of puppy fat and her body was gradually becoming longer and leaner ... just like Kim's. She was, as Kim fondly said only ten times a day, almost LA-ready. Almost. Nearly there, she kept saying, encouragingly. Nearly where? Melanie wasn't sure what she meant.

★

At Christmas, she flew to New York to meet her mother. She hadn't seen Stella in nearly a year and a half. Stella couldn't quite believe her eyes. She walked straight past her – twice! – and it was only when Melanie yelled out her name that she turned in the lobby of the Four Seasons and nearly dropped her bag.

'You look so grown-up, Mel,' her mother kept saying over tea, her hands nervously straying to her own face.

'I *am* grown-up,' Melanie said, slightly irritated. Honestly, what did her mother think? That she would stay fifteen for ever?

'I know, darling. But ... your *hair*? Why did you cut it? I *liked* your old hairstyle. It was ... well, it was *you*.'

'Well, this is the new me,' Melanie said tartly. She looked around the hotel lobby. 'It's not a bit like LA,' she said, biting into a scone. Her mother looked even unhappier.

'Oh, Mel, you've changed so much. Even your voice. You didn't sound so American on the phone ... What's happened to you?'

'Mum ... will you stop? I'm exactly the same, just a bit older, that's all.'

'But ...' Her mother stopped, seemingly unsure of what to say. They continued drinking tea in uneasy silence. After so long spent away from home, it came as a surprise to Melanie to find just how quickly her mother got on her nerves. They were supposed to spend ten days together in New York – what on earth were they going to talk about? Or do? Thankfully her father was due to join them on New Year's Day. Now, *that* she couldn't wait for. She couldn't wait to show off her new, sophisticated look. She was sure he would approve.

He didn't come, of course. Rang on the morning of the day he was supposed to arrive and said he'd stop by LA some other time. *Some other time.*

Melanie flew back to LA in a rage of predictable disappointment. Luckily Kim was on hand to cheer her up. There were parties nearly every night. Steve, unusually, had had to go to

Mexico 'on business'. He was in a foul mood as he left – he hated being away from LA. He didn't like the feeling of not being one hundred per cent in control. And he was *especially* unhappy about leaving Melanie alone with Kim. Melanie couldn't work it out. What did he have against Kim? Kim was an 'it' girl, the kind of girl everyone wanted to be seen with; the kind who got invited to every party and whose presence *made* every party. Melanie was a bona fide celebrity; she'd spent most of her life trying to avoid the limelight, not court it. She hated the press and she hated photographers even more. Whenever a flash bulb went off in her face it usually meant a horrible story the following morning in the tabloids – the headline after she'd flunked her English A-level still rankled. 'A Chip off the Old Block', something ghastly like that. Mike had left school without a single O-level but the *Daily News* didn't bother to report that she'd got both her other A-levels and that she'd *walked* out of the exam, not failed it. There was a difference, not that anyone, least of all Mike, cared. Kim had never heard of A-levels and was bemused by Melanie's anguish. What the hell was she upset about? Who *cared* whether she scored a perfect mark in some dumb exam? Kim *loved* photographers. She was at her happiest when the paparazzi were around.

A few weeks later, she persuaded the driver to let her take Steve's convertible BMW to Kim's new Malibu apartment by herself. It was late January yet warm enough to leave the top down. Melanie was enjoying the winter sun on her face as she drove. She pulled up outside the block of condos that overlooked the beach. It was breathtaking. Kim had only just moved in – an admirer was paying the rent, she told Melanie, grinning. *The only way to do it. Get someone else to pay.* Melanie just shook her head. Kim was almost entirely without scruples. She had one man paying for her car; another for her home, yet another for her clothes … everything was taken care of. What was the point of working? Melanie asked her. Who says I work? Kim giggled. Melanie had to laugh.

★

Kim was lying on one of her new white leather couches, painting her toenails. Melanie winced as she came in — one false dab and the entire couch would be ruined. Kim was in a buoyant mood. 'Look!' She waved a thick, white envelope in Melanie's face. 'Look at this! We've just been invited to this *major* party in Malibu — some Hollywood director!' She put the nail polish bottle down on the fluffy white carpet, ignoring Melanie's pained expression. 'I heard from Lori Weinberg that he asked for the *hottest* girls in town — guess who he meant? You and me! Did you see that picture of us in *EW*?' Melanie shook her head. 'We looked soooo *hot*. I was in that white dress, remember?' Melanie shook her head again. 'The Dior one — the one with the gold belt?'

'Oh, *that* one.' Melanie dumped her bag on the chair. She needed the bathroom.

'Yeah, *that* one. So ... what're we gonna wear to this party?'

'Dunno. Can I use the loo? I'm dying — I just drank a whole bottle of water.'

''Course you can, darlin'. I just love the way you say that.'

'What?'

'Loo. Looooo,' Kim giggled. Melanie shook her head and walked into the bathroom. Like everything else in Kim's new apartment it was pure, brilliant white. Just like Steve's. It was obviously an LA 'look'. She admired the organisation — all products decanted into identical white plastic bottles and stowed carefully behind the huge mirrored doors above the sink; soft white floor mats, fluffy white towels. Nothing out of place. She unbuckled her trousers and sat down on the toilet. Something suddenly caught her eye. It was a gold cufflink, lying just between the base of the toilet and the wall. She frowned. It was oddly familiar — Steve had one just like it. She bent down and picked it up. A small, flat gold surface with a black bull's eye. She felt her insides suddenly go cold. No ... it wasn't possible ...? She stared at it. No, there had to be hundreds of cufflinks just like it. It probably belonged to one of Kim's many boyfriends — or her drug dealer — anyone. Of course it wasn't

Steve's. He didn't like Kim; he said so half a dozen times a day. She was being silly. Paranoid … Kim wouldn't do that to her. Of course she wouldn't. She picked up the cufflink and laid it on the sink. She stood up and flushed the toilet.

'You OK?' Kim said as she came out of the toilet. She could still feel the heat in her cheeks.

'Yeah … yeah, I'm fine.' Melanie flashed her a quick smile. No, she really was being silly. There was real concern on Kim's face. 'So. We going shopping, or what?'

'That's my girl,' Kim whooped, almost upsetting the nail polish. 'I just need to let these dry …' she said, wriggling her toes. 'And then let's *hit* Rodeo!'

Melanie drove home from Rodeo later that day, several thousand dollars lighter. There were so many bags in the back of the convertible that she had to put the top up for fear of them flying away. She pulled into the drive, grabbed as many as she could and walked into the kitchen. Steve wasn't home, thank God. She finished unloading the car, tossed the keys back to Carlos with a promise 'not to tell', and went for a swim. Then she took a nap, exhausted from all the shopping. She and Steve were supposed to go out to dinner later that evening and the last thing she wanted was to look tired.

She woke in darkness, a few hours later, disorientated by the silence in the apartment. She sat up, squinting at her watch. It was almost nine-thirty. Steve *still* wasn't back. She frowned. Hadn't he said nine? She swung her legs out of bed and padded over to the phone. She dialled his beeper number and waited. He usually rang straight back. She waited another five minutes and then dialled it again. There was still no answering call. She sighed. Where the hell was he? It wasn't like him to be late. She'd even bought something special to wear that evening, and something even more special to wear underneath it. She walked to the bathroom. By the time she'd showered, he'd either have rung, or shown up. Either way, she ought to get ready.

She had just finished drying her hair when she heard his car pull into the driveway. At last! She slithered into the cream silk dress she'd bought and quickly did up the zip, turning to look at herself in the mirror. The material clung to her in all the right places, just as the salesgirl had said. It was an extraordinarily beautiful dress; long, shimmering, with delicate ruffles at the neck and hemline. Simple, but stunning – Kim had really worked hard on her dress sense.

'Hi,' Steve said as he burst into the room. He could never enter a room quietly. 'We're late.'

'We're late? *You're* late,' Melanie said, smoothing down her hair. 'Where were you? I paged you, twice.'

'In a meeting,' he said, shrugging off his jacket and flinging it, together with his shirt, on to the bed. 'Gimme five minutes. You look good.' He slid a hand under her hair and pulled her towards him. His mouth tasted of wine. A meeting? She immediately fought down the suspicion that rose in her. She hated the way her insecurities leapt out, given half the chance. Maybe they'd had a bottle of wine at the meeting? It was possible, wasn't it?

44

It was hot in the upstairs bar; sweat was pouring down Laure's back as she raced up and down between stairs, balancing her tray of shot glasses above her head. Winter had finally come to an end and spring was in the air. She liked Thursdays; it was her night to do the Kamikaze shots – a blend of rum, triple sec and amaretto – and she always managed to sell at least six bottles a night. That alone was a two-hundred-dollar profit – all hers, too. Don worked out a pretty fair rotation with the girls but for almost three months now, Thursday nights were hers.

'Only one, sir?' Laure asked, smiling. The two men sitting in the booth looked at her, then at each other and gave each other a high five.

'What the heck, pretty lady ... give us another one!'

Laure set two more glasses down and waited for them to take a third, probably a fourth, maybe even a fifth. She'd been doing it for so long the lines tripped automatically off her tongue. *What? Only one shot? One shot's no fun, sir ... have another one. This one's on the house.* The man in question would wind up buying five, paying for four and leaving her at least a ten-dollar tip – which, considering the cost of a shot to her was less than a buck, was a pretty good margin.

Sure enough, ten minutes later she walked away with a twenty-dollar tip, leaving behind two rather befuddled middle-aged men. She was smiling as she made her way upstairs to the bar.

There was the muffled sound of an argument going on downstairs. She peered over the balcony – an altercation between two men, no doubt, probably over a woman. She looked around for Don. He'd probably spotted it already and was on his way to find one of the bouncers. Don kept a pretty sharp eye on the crowd. The last thing he wanted was trouble of any kind. She pushed her way through the ring of people who'd gathered to watch and headed for the bar. Whatever the argument was, it was loud – she could hear someone shouting over the music. 'What's going on?' she asked Dave, the good-looking young bartender.

He shrugged, lifting a stack of glasses. 'I don't know. Some guy came in half an hour ago, lookin' for someone. Miguel told me he might be trouble. I guess he found him.'

'A bit loud, aren't they?' Laure said, looking round as the shouting intensified. She was just turning back when she heard a sound like a huge, enormous gasp, then a woman screaming ... and then all hell broke loose. There was a single '*crack!*', the sound of a gun going off, and then everyone starting scream-ing and yelling. The music cut suddenly, the whole air was electrified – Laure saw people in front of her start scrambling for the exit doors. The noise was deafening, the sound of five hundred people stampeding towards a single point. She turned back to Dave, her eyes wide with fright. There was a second shot, and another ... more screams. There was the sound of glass falling – a thundering roar as the enormous mirrored wall behind the DJ's booth splintered into a thousand tiny pieces ... more screaming, people falling, trampling on bottles of beer and wine glasses left on tables. She could hear her own heartbeat, a sudden heavy thud as she began to panic. The stairs were completely blocked with people struggling to get out. She looked around her wildly ... Dave had sprinted over the bar and was shoving his way through the crowd, desperate to get to the front door. She could smell smoke; out of the corner of her eye she saw a sudden flame – *whoosh!* One of the faux-leather seats had caught fire; a cigarette had probably been left burning somewhere as everyone scrambled for cover. It was at that point she really began to panic. Only a few weeks before she'd seen a nightclub go up in flames somewhere on Southside. Most of the people inside had died as a result of smoke inhalation, she remembered the newscaster saying. A cold feeling of fear started to creep its way up her body. She ran to the stairs along with everyone else amidst the screaming and crying and tried ineffectually to push her way through. Bodies started to close in on her as people lost their heads. She could feel herself slowly being squeezed, not by anyone in particular but by the sheer weight of the mass straining to get downstairs. She began to labour for breath; her chest was being slowly crushed. Within seconds, she started to fight for air. The smoke pouring out of the corner of the room had nearly reached the centre, she could see it rushing towards them, thick and white. She could hear herself panting, a horrible, animal-like sound as she struggled to breathe.

Suddenly she felt someone grab her arm. She tugged at it, terrified she was going to faint but whoever it was held on to her and started dragging her in the opposite direction, towards the smoke. She was too weak to resist. She looked up, her head spinning. It was Don. 'Put a hand over your nose!' he was shouting to her as he dragged her bodily through the smoke. She thought she was going to black out. 'Here, put this over your mouth,' he yelled, and thrust something at her – a handkerchief. 'There's a boarded-up ...' he started to shout, then stopped, overcome by the fumes.

'Wh ... where ... wh ...?' Laure gasped as they ran together through the thick cloud. She thought she would pass out. Smoke was in her eyes, her hair, her lungs. Still he pulled her along. Just when she thought she couldn't stand it for a second longer, there was a huge crack; the sound of something being broken ... and the rush of sweet, clean air. She was barely conscious as he hauled her through the plywood partition that had been a door only seconds before, and pulled her up beside him on the shaky metal fire escape. She just had time to look up at the night sky before the grille of the staircase came rushing up to meet her and she slumped to the ground.

She came to lying on the sidewalk with a paramedic bending over her while he took her pulse. She tried to get up, but her legs just wouldn't obey her.

'Take it easy, miss,' the paramedic in the orange overalls said. 'Just lie back for a minute.'

'Wh ... what ... happened?' she struggled to speak.

'You just keep still, miss. I'll be back in a second.' He got up and ran back towards the blazing building. She could see the red fire engines parked at the side of the road and figures running towards the blaze. There were police and ambulances everywhere, their yellow and blue sirens flashing continuously in the inky night. She was lying on something ... a stretcher. She could feel the metal rails at her sides. She drew in a breath, wincing. It hurt even to breathe.

Don appeared at her side. He knelt down, taking her hand. 'Listen, Laure, the paramedic says you're OK to go home, so long as someone goes with you. Is there anyone I can call?'

Laure lifted her head but a wave of tiredness and emotion washed over her. 'I'm ... it's not ...' she began weakly.

'I'll take her home.' Someone had suddenly appeared. Laure looked up. Through lashes magnified by tears she saw someone she vaguely recognised ... the young man who'd come in the week before ... she tried to remember his name ... Donald? David?

'Laure? Is that OK?' Don was talking to her. 'Is that OK with you? Is this guy a friend?'

'I ... I ... yes ... from the ...' Her voice trailed off. She felt sick.

'You sure?' Don leaned over her. 'Otherwise you'll have to go to hospital. Do you have insurance?'

Laure shook her head. No. No insurance. 'Yes, I know him,' she whispered, putting a hand on Don's arm.

'OK, baby. Look.' He turned to the man who was kneeling beside her. 'Can you take her home? The paramedic said there's nothing wrong with her that a good night's sleep and some aspirin won't cure. Her bag'll be in the locker but she wears her key around her neck.' Laure could feel him gently pull her collar aside. 'Yeah, that's her apartment key. She lives over on Greenview, just off Division, I think.'

'Yes ... Greenview. 1307 North Gree ...' Laure tried to sit up.

'Don't even think about it,' the young man said, crouching down beside her. He slid an arm under her back. Before she could protest further, she felt herself being lifted. He was carrying her. She must have passed out again because the next thing she remembered was the scratchy feel of his sweater against her face as he lowered her into the passenger seat and reached across to fix her belt.

45

She was heavier than she looked, Daniel thought to himself as he lifted Laure's inert body through the doorway, balancing her against his shoulder while he tried to open her door. She kept slipping in and out of sleep, which, although worrying, was to be expected, as the paramedic had explained at the scene. He still couldn't quite believe what had happened. He'd been driving down Hyde Park Boulevard, just after midnight after having bailed out of a club on Milwaukee where Tag and Jon were holed up in the bathrooms chasing lines. He'd picked up his jacket, slung it on to the back seat of the car and instead of going north, as he normally did, he'd swung round and gone south on Lake Shore Drive, not really knowing why. He was restless, as usual, and there was something magical about driving through Chicago late at night when all the lights in the skyscrapers were still on and the lake was absolutely still. He turned right on State and was just about to head back when he heard the fire engines' siren. He pulled over, as he was supposed to, and watched them race past on Lake Shore Drive, heading towards the university. It was an impulse – he just swung the car back on to the road and followed them. It was only when they reached the corner of Martin Luther King, Jr Boulevard and went screaming across the intersection that he saw where they were headed. A rush of adrenalin surged through him. It was the Blue Room, the club where he'd met the waitress, Laure, whom he'd been unable to stop thinking about for over a week. The entire building was on fire. He swung across the road blindly, not even thinking about what he was doing and screeched to a halt. He didn't even bother to lock his car. There was already a police line across the sidewalk but the place was in pandemonium. Screaming, hysterical people were being led out of the building by firemen, paramedics, police officers. Someone shouted to him to keep away, but he ducked under the yellow tape and started running towards the building. He still didn't know how he saw her – he was looking around desperately when he saw a paramedic leaning over someone on the sidewalk nearest to the road. Then he saw someone else run up – it was the manager, he'd seen him talking to Laure the night he'd made such a fool of himself … he began to run towards them. He could hear the guy saying something to her as he bent down – *Laure? Can you hear me?* – and he experienced such a surge of ridiculous relief that his legs almost buckled under him. He ran over and heard the manager ask if she had anyone who could take her home ... he'd stepped right in without even thinking.

'Laure?' he said as he kicked the front door shut with his foot. 'I'm just going to put you down,' he said, staggering with her to the couch. She slumped forward, almost hitting the small coffee table as she crumpled. He managed to catch her and prop her against the cushions. He was sweating. She was beginning to come round, mumbling something. He patted her hand awkwardly, not really sure what to do next. He looked around the tiny apartment. It was sparse but scrupulously clean. She mumbled something again ... he couldn't understand her. Her eyes opened for a moment, struggled to focus on him, then closed. Small, even breaths told him she had slipped back into sleep. He'd better get her to the bedroom. He got up and half-carried, half-pulled her through the door.

There was hardly any space to move in the bedroom. She flopped immediately on to the bed, rolled over on to her stomach and slept on. He paused, then bent down and pulled off her shoes. He thought about taking off her tights, but stopped himself. It would have been too ... intrusive, somehow. He went into the bathroom, took the face cloth that was hanging neatly on the edge of the sink, rinsed it and went back to her. Very gently he tried to wipe the worst of the soot and dirt from her face. She didn't wake up. He pulled the sheet around her, switched on the small bedside lamp – the one object of any aesthetic value in the place – and walked out, pulling the door almost shut behind him.

He looked around again. He'd never seen a person live with less. A TV; a few books lined up neatly against the wall; no pictures, no posters ... nothing. A couch, the glass coffee table ... that was it. It was practically empty. He walked over to the fridge and pulled it open. A pint of milk, six eggs in their tray; a loaf of brown bread and a punnet of strawberries, still wrapped in cling film. He shut the door gently. Every surface in the kitchen was wiped clean; not even a fingerprint on the glossy worktop. He opened a cupboard door. A box of cereal, the edges neatly pressed inwards, as per the instructions, a packet of sugar and a large bag of rice. He was aware of a sharp, unidentifiable pain in his chest, somewhere just above his ribs. He thought of his own flat – of the giant TV screen and the video and sound decks surrounding it; of the Bose speakers cleverly hidden in the ceiling; of the kitchen with the thousand and one devices and bits of equipment he'd never opened, let alone used. Of his bedroom with the king-size bed and the TV suspended from the ceiling. The pain in his chest intensified. There was a sparse dignity to the contents of this girl's flat that he admired so much it hurt. He pulled open a drawer. A single knife, fork and spoon on a neatly folded paper towel. He shut the drawer quickly, alarmed by the sudden lump in his throat. He walked over to the couch, kicked off his shoes, put the single cushion under his head and lay down. The last thing he remembered before he dropped off to sleep was the soft, heavy feel of her hair in his hands as he'd pushed it up into a clumsy knot before letting her drift back to sleep.

Laure woke the next morning with a splitting headache, forgetting for a moment what had happened the night before. She lay in bed, wondering why she still had her clothes on ... and then she remembered. She groaned, closing her eyes. The club. The gunshots. The fire. The Blue Room – the last thing she remembered was seeing the place go up in smoke. She felt sick to the stomach. Then she sat bolt upright in bed, the pain in her head causing her to wince. The young man! He'd brought her home ... Where was he? She looked around the room. He'd obviously carried her in; her shoes were lined up neatly beside the bed ... her hand went up to her neck. Her key, which she carried on a chain around her neck while she worked wasn't there – he must have used it to open the door. Her purse – her raincoat ... still in the lockers at work. She winced. Ignoring the thudding pain in her temples, she got out of bed. Her legs still felt shaky. She staggered to the bathroom, gasping as she turned on the light. Her face was streaked with tears and dirt but someone had obviously tried to wash her face. There were streak marks down the side of her cheeks and neck. Her hair had been pulled back into some sort of loose bunch. As she prised her curls loose, the smell of acrid smoke filled the little bathroom. She felt her stomach turn. She rinsed her mouth with mouthwash and switched off the light.

She pushed open the living-room door and stopped. There he was, fast asleep on her couch. She blinked. The sight of the young man stretched out on her sofa was unnerving. She stood there for a few minutes, unsure as to what to do. Should she wake him up? But how? He looked incredibly peaceful lying there, one hand flung across her single cushion, long jeans-clad legs sprawled over the arm of the chair. She hesitated. In the club she'd thought of him as nothing more than one of those rich, silly college boys who often came into the club – the waitresses even had a word for them ... she frowned – they were 'slumming it'. She'd laughed the first time she heard it and someone explained it to her. That was what she'd thought of him and his stupid friends. They were slumming it. But he'd spoken to her nicely, she remembered ... and then last night he'd been so kind and so helpful. He'd even washed her face – she couldn't remember the last time someone had done that for her. And then he stirred, mumbled something and slowly opened his eyes.

'Hi,' he said warily, wishing he'd thought to cover himself with his jacket before falling asleep. He was painfully aware of his early morning hard-on – nothing to do with her, just automatic, on waking – and of the fact that his mouth tasted like shit.

'Hi,' she said, her arms wrapped around her, her voice guarded.

'I ... I didn't want to leave you alone,' he said, trying to roll over as unobtrusively as possible.

'I ... uh, th ... thank you for bringing me home,' she said warily, arms still tightly wrapped around her. 'I ... I don't remember much ... of what happened.'

Probably a good thing,' he said, looking oddly embarrassed. 'Er, can I use your bathroom for a sec?'

'Yes, of course. It's through there. Although you probably know where it is already,' she added almost bitterly.

'Yes, I do. Thanks.' He got up and bolted through the door.

As soon as he'd disappeared into the bathroom, Laure rushed over to the kitchen and opened the cupboard door. She took out a packet of aspirin and swallowed two tablets with a glass of water and then stood back, frowning. What could she offer him? Coffee ... maybe even some toast ...? She opened the fridge. There wasn't much in it but she could make some scrambled eggs and toast, perhaps? She couldn't just turf him out, not after he'd been so kind and brought her home. She could hear the toilet being flushed and the sound of the tap being turned on. Seconds later, he came through the door.

'I've decided,' he said, running a hand through his hair, 'to take you to breakfast. If you're feeling up to it, of course.'

Laure looked at him in surprise. 'No ... no, you don't have to ...' she said automatically.

'But I'd *like* to.' His voice was firm.

'But ... I ...' She looked down at herself. 'I need to have a shower and wash my hair and ...'

'No rush. I've got plenty of time. Unless you have to be somewhere?'

She shook her head slowly. 'No ... I only work during the week. Although – I don't know – I guess I'll have to go over later. To the club.'

'I could drive you over?' he said immediately. 'Or maybe we could phone?'

'I don't have a phone.'

'Oh.' He seemed surprised.

'I ... it just didn't seem worth it,' Laure offered, feeling the blush rise in her cheeks. She swallowed. 'Well, I guess I'll just have a shower,' she said, moving towards the bedroom.

'Of course. I'll wait here, shall I?' He sat down again on the couch. She nodded and fled. She closed the bathroom door behind her and leaned against it. Breakfast? He wanted to take her to breakfast? What was she going to wear? She blew out her cheeks. Grateful as she had been for someone to bring her home, she wished it hadn't been him. She didn't want to have to feel indebted to him – to anyone. She didn't want to have to wash her hair, put on clean clothes and step outside her apartment just to make conversation with someone who, despite his very obvious wealth, looked almost as lonely as she was. And most of all, she didn't like the damned butterflies that started up in her stomach every time he spoke.

'Here ... try this.' Daniel speared a piece of pancake, dripping with maple syrup and passed it across the table to Laure. She hesitated, then took it, feeling rather self-conscious as she put the fork in her mouth and then had to put a hand to her lips to stop the trickle of syrup running down her chin. She wished he would stop staring at her. 'Awfully good, isn't it?' he said cheerfully.

She nodded reluctantly, quickly scooping the trail of syrup from her chin with her forefinger. She could feel his eyes on her face, following the progress of her finger in minute detail. It made her even more self-conscious.

'You've never been here before?' he asked, tucking into his plate of pancakes. Laure shook her head cautiously. His cheerful, friendly manner was unsettling. *I'm just a cocktail waitress*, she wanted to shout at him. *You didn't have to buy me breakfast and you certainly don't have to be friendly.* 'It's a bit out of the way,' he continued, spearing a strawberry and popping it into his mouth in a way that made the heat rise in her cheeks.

'Out of the way for you, perhaps,' Laure said, a little more sharply than she intended. 'I live round here.' It was his damned cheeriness and the way he kept smiling at her, his dark brown eyes never leaving her face. She was grateful to him for bringing her home; she'd said so, more than once – why couldn't he just leave it at that *and leave her alone*? She didn't need his friendship and she certainly didn't need his pity.

'Touché,' he said, conceding her point. It unnerved her even further. There was a short, rather prickly silence. 'So ... how long've you been working there?' he asked, signalling to the waitress for two more coffees at the same time. Laure opened her mouth to say she didn't want another coffee, *thank you very much*, but he was already on to his next question. 'You're French, aren't you?' he asked, his chin on his hand as he stirred sugar into his cup. 'I can tell from your accent – and your name, of course. Laure St Lazâre. I ... I saw it on one of the bills at your place. It's a pretty name. Very distinguished.'

Laure was silent. It wasn't even lunchtime and already the day felt unreal. The night before she'd been saved from a burning building; a stranger had driven her home, put her to bed, washed her face. Now here she was, sitting in a café talking to some rich college boy whom, under normal circumstances, she would never meet ... and now he was telling *her* that *she* had a distinguished name? She shook her head, as if to clear it. It was all threatening to overwhelm her.

He was sensitive, she saw. He immediately noticed her change of mood and was quick to drop the forced cheeriness which he'd obviously thought appropriate. Instead he asked her a few questions about working at the Blue Room, drawing her skilfully out of the momentary lapse into despair ... fifteen minutes later, he actually managed to coax a smile from her.

It was with the tiniest twinge of regret that she got up half an hour later and told him she really had to leave. She watched as he signalled discreetly for the bill, saw the flash of a gold credit card and the soft appreciative 'thank you' from their waitress that indicated a large tip. Yes, he was nice to talk to and generous and good-looking and funny and all of that. Under normal circumstances, perhaps, but – and it was a huge 'but' – her circumstances *weren't* normal. She was a waitress with nothing behind her, a few hundred dollars in savings in a drawer in an apartment in which she didn't even have a phone; she had only the foggiest idea what the future might bring and, probably more importantly, she understood that it was up to her to bring it about. The young man opposite her had it all mapped out for him. From the little he'd said she could just about picture his life. Wealth, security, options, possibilities ... all laid out for him. All *he* had to do was choose. It was different for her. And yet there was something about him that she liked. *Really* liked. Daniel. She didn't even know his last name.

Two people died at the Blue Room on the night of the fire, one of them shot by the man who had started the panic. Laure stood with Don, Shelley and a couple of the other waitresses in the doorway, surveying the ruins. Don put a hand on her shoulder, shaking his head.

'Six months,' he said heavily. 'That's what the insurers say. I'm real sorry about it, girls. It ain't gonna happen any faster. I can give you each a little something to help you through till the end of the month but I can't do more, I'm afraid. That's the way it goes. Casual staff, that's the problem. I guess you'll have to find other jobs. Man, I'm sorry.'

'It'll be fine,' Laure heard herself saying, although she didn't believe it. 'We'll find something else. I'll drop by at the end of the month, see how it's coming on. As soon as you're ready again, let us know.' She was bitterly disappointed. She liked Don and she liked working at the Blue Room. In the few months she'd been there, a real team spirit had developed among them. The thought of looking for another job was almost too depressing to contemplate. But it was true; they were all either illegal or working for cash under the table. For them there was no such thing as compensation or severance pay.

Thanks, sweetheart,' Don said, his voice suddenly thick with emotion. 'It's good of you. You know I'll take care of you.' He gave Laure's shoulder another squeeze.

A few days later, she was walking up Greenview to her apartment carrying a bag of groceries under each arm, wondering how to find another job, when someone in a black sports car across the road blew a horn at her. She looked around, bewildered. Had she done something wrong? It took her a few minutes to work out that the young man sitting inside the car was actually waving at her. She peered a little more closely, and then the butterflies in her stomach gave one gigantic lurch. It was Daniel.

'Hi!' He opened the door and jumped out. 'I was about to give up and go home!'

'Hi,' Laure stammered. 'Wh ... what are you doing here?'

'I came to visit you, of course. I don't know anyone else on this street. How are you?'

'Fine. I ... I just went shopping.'

'So I see. Here, let me help you.' He took the bags from her, ignoring her protests. 'Lunch?' He took a quick look at the contents. 'And here I was, hoping I could take you.'

'To ... to lunch?'

'Yeah. We've done breakfast. Lunch is next, isn't it? And then ... well, assuming you'd want to, of course, there's ... well, perhaps you'd ...' he stumbled over the words as if he weren't sure how to proceed. Laure's eyes widened. 'You know ... there's dinner. After lunch, I mean. Look, would you like to go to lunch with me?' he managed finally, running an agitated hand through his hair.

Laure looked at him in surprise. His nervousness was down-right disconcerting. Was he really asking her out? 'I'd ... really like that,' she said softly, watching a relieved smile break out across his face. 'But ... in this?' she gestured at her jeans and plain blue jumper.

'You look great,' Daniel assured her hastily. 'You'd look good in sackcloth and ashes.'

'Eh ...?'

'It's an expression. I don't know how to say it in French. No, hang on a minute ... of course I do. *Vous êtes belle. Très belle.*'

Laure felt the heat rise in her cheeks. 'You're teasing me,' she stammered finally.

'I assure you, I'm not.' Daniel's voice was surprisingly grave. She glanced up at him. His eyes were on her. She looked away, a smile tugging at the corners of her lips. She liked him. Oh, yes. She really liked him.

46

By the end of April, Laure's savings had dwindled to almost nothing – and she had only herself to blame. She just couldn't help it. She hadn't found herself a new job, mostly because she'd been preoccupied with something else. Some*one* else. Somehow, Daniel had charmed his way into her life and she was slowly but surely falling for him. It meant that she worried about what she wore; the way she fixed her hair; the number of times he took her out *and* paid for it. There was no way she could appear downstairs in front of her apartment in the same jeans and sweater he'd seen her in that first day and there were only so many ways to dress up a plain white T-shirt. She went to the cheapest stores she knew and it took all of her imagination to make each outfit appear special, and new. He simply wouldn't hear of her paying for dinner – it wasn't even his money, he said, laughing, it was his father's. It didn't help. She was so used to taking care of herself that it felt strange and sometimes even wrong to be driven around in that little sports car of his; to have the door opened for her and for the bill to be whisked away by the waiter before she'd even had a chance to look.

He took her out almost every evening. They went to dinner, to the movies, to a bowling alley once where she surprised both of them by beating him hands down. He took her to the theatre and held her hand and once to the opera where she cried through the second half. He drove her around Chicago at night with the top down and pointed out the buildings in the city that called itself the architectural capital of the world. He would have liked to study architecture, he told her once as they were parked outside her apartment. It was nearly midnight but he seemed reluctant to leave.

'Why didn't you?' Laure asked, surprised. Daniel could be anything he wanted.

'My father didn't think it a practical application of his

money,' he said. She looked at him in the dim light of the car's interior. His mouth was set in a way she hadn't seen before. He sounded angry.

'Does it matter what he thinks?' she asked after a while.

He sighed, fiddling with the ignition key. 'Unfortunately, yes, it does.' He turned towards her with a rueful smile. 'I come from a complicated family, Laure. Sometimes – I'm ashamed to admit it – I hate my father.'

Laure was quiet. 'I never knew my father,' she said eventually. 'He disappeared before I was born.'

Daniel looked at her. 'That's about the most you've ever told me about your life,' he said slowly. 'You never say anything. I keep wanting to ask you … but … I don't know … I don't want to pry.'

Laure looked at her hands. She didn't know what to say. 'There's not much to tell,' she said finally, drawing a deep breath.

'But you must have, I don't know, a mother somewhere? Brothers and sisters? What was your life like before you came here? You never say a thing.'

She swallowed. His questions had brought her alarmingly close to tears. She turned to him. 'I … think I'd better go,' she whispered, opening the door.

'Laure! Did I say something …?' Daniel opened his own door. She turned away from him, the tears flowing thick and fast. She shook her head, unable to speak clearly.

'No … please. I'm just … I need to go.' She practically ran up the staps. She thrust the key in the lock and pushed open the door. As she closed it, she caught sight of his bewildered face. She hurried up the stairs. She put her hands over her mouth as she sank on to the floor in front of the couch, afraid of the sounds that were coming from her throat. She'd allowed Daniel to get under her skin and now she was paying the price.

A knock on the door woke her. She jerked awake, disorientated. She was lying on the floor, her hair sticking to her tear-stained cheeks. How long had she been lying there? She looked at her watch – it was almost two in the morning. She stumbled to her feet, her heart thudding. The room was in pitch darkness. A second knock. 'Laure?' She stood still, rooted to the spot. It was Daniel. Had he been standing there all this time? She swallowed. 'Laure? Let me in. Please.' She pushed her hair away from her face, ran a hand over her cheeks and slid the bolts back.

He stood there in the doorway, his face so full of tender concern that she could find nothing to say. In the harsh overhead light of the corridor, she looked at him. Properly. Thick, short dark brown hair, curling away from the crown, slightly longer at the top, soft dark brown eyes, already creased at the corners in a fine web of criss-cross slivers. A long nose with delicate scrolls around the nostrils and a blunt, tip; the mouth ... a thin upper lip that almost disappeared when he smiled, the lower lip surprisingly full; his teeth were regular and white; the angular jawline with its under-the-surface shadow of hair, darker now ... he looked as though he hadn't slept. She realised she had never really looked at him before. Perhaps she'd been afraid to? Afraid to look at something for fear of losing it? She took a step backwards.

'I'm sorry,' he said, spreading his hands helplessly in front of him. 'I couldn't leave. I've been waiting outside for hours. I just ... I had to come up.' He leaned against the door frame. 'I woke you up, didn't I?' he asked, looking more miserable than ever.

'It doesn't matter,' Laure said softly, beckoning him in. She turned to lead the way to the couch but he put out a hand, touching her on the shoulder. She drew in a deep breath, and very slowly turned around. His face was only inches from her; she could feel the gentle rise and fall of his breath on her cheeks. As if in slow motion, the next moves fell gently into place. The step forwards, the feel of a hand against her shoulder blade, the gentle but insistent pull towards him. She felt her own hands reach up and touch the back of his neck. The hair at the nape was so soft, like silk ... her fingers slid into it and pulled, towards her. Lips ... a tentative brushing; pulling away, coming closer, as if seeking something ... then the wet, warm surprise of his mouth and tongue. She felt his own hands slide up her back, fumbling with the knot of her hair and the unexpected pleasure of hearing him groan as he buried his face in it, holding great clouds of curls in his hands as if he couldn't possibly, ever, have enough.

There was no awkwardness as she turned and pulled him with her into the bedroom. The slow burning sensation in her stomach and groin seemed all the guidance she needed. She sank with him into the softness of the mattress and gasped aloud as his hand pulled at the fabric of her T-shirt, quickly finding its way across the heat of her stomach ... up, up, up. His fingers were a question mark ... here? Here? There? His hand went round the swell of her breasts – first one, then the other and her own hands sliding down the flat, hard, trembling plane of his stomach answered him. Yes. There. She arched against him, feeling with relief the familiar but long-forgotten rush of sweetness as he shuddered with the force of his own climax and buried his face in the heat of her shoulder. 'Laure.' She heard him whisper her name. 'Laure.' It was neither a question, nor an answer. His lips moved against her skin. Laure. His arm lay across her stomach as if *he* were dead, as if it would be moved from her only by force.

In a sly reversal of roles, it was Daniel who lay awake long after Laure's regular breathing told him she was asleep. He longed for a cigarette but couldn't bear the thought of moving away and separating his body from the heat of the woman sleeping next to him. Her hands were cool, he noticed, turning over a palm in his hand, but everything else about her – breasts, stomach, face – burned. He slid his length carefully against her, content to just lie there inhaling the scent of her hair and skin that was already identifiable to him as hers. Laure. He had never felt this way about anyone in his life. Never. He couldn't even say what it was he felt. Love? Compassion? Admiration? He'd never met anyone like her.

He moved away from her and slid out of bed. A cigarette. He

desperately needed a cigarette. He fished around on the floor for his jeans. He found them and carried them out, closing the bedroom door behind him. His shirt was lying on the ground outside; his cigarettes were inside the pocket. He drew one out, found his lighter and opened the doors that led on to her porch. The night air was cool. It was the end of April but there was still a faint chill in the air. He shut the door behind him and looked out across the narrow yard. It was almost five a.m. The city was beginning to stir. There was a gap in the alleyway from which he could see the elevated strip of the freeway. Cars whooshed past silently, trailing ribbons of white and red light. In the distance he could just see the light-studded skyscrapers of downtown. He was seized with a sudden impatience, an urge to get out, to go somewhere where Laure could feel the wind in her hair, away from the grind of her daily routine. New York? He could take her to New York. New York in springtime. The nightclub where she worked wouldn't be open for at least another few months – there was his father's apartment on the Upper East Side, completely empty. She would love it. *Just as he loved her.* He paused for a second, his fingers touching the door handle. *He was in love.* The realisation came to him quite suddenly.

47

Améline neatly reversed the car into the slot the examiner had indicated and switched off the engine. She waited beside him, her hands folded in her lap, not daring to look at the little score-card on which he made his notes. After a few minutes, he turned to her with a small, satisfied smile. 'Well, Mrs Blake. I think that's it. You've passed.'

Améline stared at him, almost speechless. 'Really?' she said breathlessly.

'Yes.' He was English and not prone to enthusiastic out-bursts.

'You mean I can drive on my own?'

'Yes, Mrs Blake. You may.'

'Oh, *thank* you. Thank you *so* much.' Améline was almost in tears. She'd passed her driving test! She could drive a car! It had been a good month. She'd passed her final English test and was now practically fluent. She could follow the news on TV, listen to the radio, hold a decent conversation with Viv ... she even spoke English to Iain once in a while, just for the pleasure of hearing herself speak. And now she'd passed her driving test. She could scarcely believe the change in her life. She'd been taught back in Haiti by Madame and then a succes-sion of tutors who'd been hired to teach Laure after school; she loved reading and listening to the tutors speak, but in truth, she hadn't really had much opportunity to learn. She'd never been in a classroom, never competed with other children, had never had the satisfaction of putting up her hand in class and getting the answer right. All of that had come as a pleasant surprise to her at the College of Further Education in Worcester where she'd taken her English classes. Now that she could drive, well, there were lots of other courses at the same college that she'd seen and liked. Catering. Hotel management. Typing. Even dressmaking. Iain had promised her a little car if she passed her test. She could suddenly see a whole world opening up for her – and much to her surprise, it was Viv who gave her the greatest encouragement, not Iain.

That, she reflected on as she caught the bus back up the hill after returning the car to the driving school, had come as something of a shock to her. It was Viv, really, who'd brought it about. She hadn't liked her at first, she recalled. But in the year and a half that she'd been in the small town in the west of England, it was Viv who had slowly sought out her friend-ship – although to begin with, Améline had no idea why. She was like an older, wiser sister – nothing like the relationship she'd had with Laure, but welcome nonetheless. There were certain things Améline would never tell her – she said very little about her life before meeting Iain, though it was nice to talk to someone about Laure. It helped ease the ache that nearly two years apart had done nothing to dull. And she certainly never said anything to her about *that*. Of *that* she'd spoken to no one. But it was Viv, in her brusque, abrupt way that Améline later came to realise was just her way of *not* showing her true emotions, who sorted out the little practicalities in Améline's life that made things a bit easier. She pushed Iain into giving her driving lessons; into giving her her own bank account … even taking Améline along to her doctor to fit her out with something that would make sure she didn't get pregnant unless she wanted to, much to Améline's embarrassment.

She got off the bus and walked the few hundred yards to the house. She looked at the garden with pride as she pushed open the little gate. It was a far cry from the weed-choked, neglected mess she'd arrived to find. Now the tiny lawn was trimmed (albeit slightly before time), the pretty flowers she'd planted along the sides were in bloom. She had roses, azaleas, geraniums, even sunflowers. Anything to brighten up the dullest of English days. She longed for the sun in a way she'd never even imagined one could. February and March were the worst months, she'd come to realise. After the bitter, damp cold of Christmas, New Year and the entire month of January when it seemed as though the sun had abandoned the world, there were still two more grey, drizzling months to be endured before the first real signs of spring. She'd never thought it possible to *ache* for the feel of heat on her face. Iain wanted to spend their holidays that year in the south of France – he wanted to rent an old villa from a school friend somewhere near Avignon and spend the whole of June and July down there, writing. Or at least he would write. Améline could do whatever she liked; there was a pool – did she know how to swim? She shook her head shyly. The thought of two months in a place where the sun shone was like a drug to her. It was May. Only another three weeks to go.

She unlocked the front door. The smell of a good, rich casserole wafted through from the kitchen. Cooking was another passion she'd discovered, now that it was no longer her job.

244

She watched Iain's waistband slowly start to expand. She loved to bake, too. Light, air-filled sponge cakes with jam oozing from the middle; dark, rich chocolate cakes from Germany; wafer-thin biscuits; dense, thick shortbread. Slowly the kitchen was filling up with cookery books and equipment the likes of which she'd never known existed.

She quickly checked the oven, made sure everything was simmering at exactly the right temperature and shut the door. She glanced at the clock. It was eleven-thirty a.m. In approximately half an hour, Viv would push open the gate and come through to the kitchen at the back of the house. Améline would make them both a coffee, open the tin of biscuits she'd made the previous day or lay out a slice or two of cake, and the two of them would sit together in the conservatory that Iain had built at the back of the kitchen, talking and laughing. Neither ate lunch; Viv was always watching her weight – or at least she claimed to be watching it – and Améline was rarely hungry during the day. She hadn't gained so much as an ounce since she'd arrived; she knew because the few clothes she'd brought with her still fitted her perfectly.

'Hullo, gosh … that smells wonderful!' Viv had come through the door, interrupting her thoughts. 'God, what a day … and it's only just *begun!*' She flopped down on to her favourite chair. Améline smiled. The routine of the day had just reasserted itself. She switched on the kettle and quickly laid out a tray.

'Have you ever thought about doing this for a living?' Viv asked her a few days later, picking up a third scone and pretending to examine it critically before breaking it in half and popping it in her mouth. She closed her eyes in mock bliss. 'Without *question*, these are the *best* scones I've *ever* tasted.'

Améline smiled, used to Viv's rather excitable way of describing things. But, to her surprise, everyone nodded enthusiastically, helping themselves not only to the scones but to the lemon drizzle cake, the Swiss roll filled with rose-petal jam and – Améline's favourites – the raspberry macaroons.

'I couldn't agree more,' Susan Whittaker, who lived opposite and was now another firm friend, said, eyeing the pretty china plate of strawberry towers – miniature stacks of light-as-air sponge cake, interspersed with whipped cream, sliced strawberries and a fresh mint leaf. 'You really ought to think about opening up a tea room or a little café. These are simply scrumptious.'

'Oh, you're very kind ...' Améline murmured, feeling ridiculously pleased. Although Iain ate everything she put on the plate in front of him, he didn't seem to think she had any special talent for cooking ... or anything else, come to think of it.

'No, no ... really. I mean it. There's only that crappy tea shop on the high street and it's full of school kids. Can you imagine a *proper* tea room in Malvern with cakes like these?'

'You really should think about it,' Susan said. '*I'd* help you. I'm bored out of my mind sitting at home all day. Anything to get out of the house.' She winked at Viv.

Améline looked shyly from one to the other. 'Well, maybe. One day.'

'That's what I always used to say,' Viv said warningly. 'But one day never comes.' The two woman laughed and soon the conversation turned to the rather more predictable topics of husbands and children – Susan had a teenage son with a long list of emotional problems that Améline simply couldn't follow. Adolescence? Haitian children didn't go through anything as traumatic as Susan described. She listened with half an ear; the conversation had touched something in her though she couldn't quite say what. For the first time since she'd arrived in England, something of the spirit that had propelled her to walk three and half miles to get a job began to surface. Cooking ... *have you ever thought about doing this for a living*? Viv's seemingly innocent question hung in the air.

48

Jon leaned back against the leather sofa and stared at Daniel. 'You're kidding, right? Tell me you're fucking kidding.'

'No, I'm not. I ... I really like her.'

'Dude ... she's a *waitress*.'

'So what?'

'So ... *every*thing. She's poor. She's an immigrant. Man, she's probably even illegal.' He started to laugh. 'Look, even *I've* had a black girl before. It's no big deal. Pretty much the same as anyone else, if you ask me. Which you didn't, I have to remind you. However,' he leaned forward, warming to his theme. 'The point here, my friend, is that you are no ordinary guy.'

'What are you talking about?' Daniel was beyond irritation. He sorely wished he'd kept his mouth shut.

'What am I *talking* about? I'm talking about your money, man. Moolah. What do you call it? Dosh? Yeah, *that's* what I'm talking about. People like us have to be careful, Daniel. That's just a fact of life.'

'Your life, perhaps,' Daniel said stiffly, getting up and walking over to the window. 'Not mine. I don't care about money. You, of all people, should know that.'

'Ah, but we're not just talking about *you*, Daniel. Look. These are the facts. She's poor, she's black, she's probably got a kid somewhere in ... in ... well, wherever it is these people live. She meets you, you seem like a nice guy, you take her out a couple of times, you fuck ... what*ever* ... next thing you know, dude, she'll be asking you for money. Rent, her phone bill, money for her kid ...'

'I don't have to stand here and listen to this shit,' Daniel broke in angrily. 'I thought you were my friend, Jon. I thought I could talk to you about ...'

'I *am* talking to you. Just because you don't like what I'm saying doesn't make it *my* fault,' Jon said, his temper also beginning to rise.

'Just shut the fuck up.' Daniel's voice was low and angry.

'No, *you* shut the fuck up. Look, go ahead and marry the bitch for all I care. Support her and her whole fucking tribe. Pay her mom's rehab bills and bail her stepdaddy out of jail. Do whatever you like. But don't say *I* didn't warn you.' Jon got up off the couch. 'And anyway,' he said as he grabbed his jacket and headed for the door. 'I'd like to see *you* stand there and tell your father you're going out with some wetback waitress. See what *he* says. Won't be any different to what *I'm* telling you.' He yanked open the front door and slammed it shut.

Daniel stood by the window, fists clenched unconsciously, seething. What a fucking jerk! He couldn't believe what he'd just heard. What the hell was wrong with him? He should have known better. What the fuck made him go and open his big mouth? He drew in a deep breath, letting the air out of his lungs slowly. He needed a cigarette. Christ. Couldn't Jon see Laure was different? She didn't care about his money. Anyone could see that. Maybe he ought to show her off to his friends? Five minutes with Laure and they would surely come round. Ever since they'd started dating, he'd kept her firmly out of his world. Not because he was ashamed of her, but because he was ashamed of *them*. Maybe that had been a mistake?

A week later, he stood behind her, looking at her in the mirror. She looked beautiful. He, on the other hand, was nervous as hell – and it showed. He'd invited her to join him at a dinner party that Jon was holding. He desperately hoped it would go well. She noticed his gaze and gave him a quick, rather tremulous smile. 'Are you sure this is a good idea?' she asked, reading his mind.

'It'll be fine,' he said, sliding his arms down her sides and giving her a quick squeeze. 'We'll have a nice time and then we'll come back to my place. You'll see. You'll enjoy yourself.' He said it almost to reassure himself.

'Then why are you so nervous?'

'Me? I'm not. I just … I don't really like Jon. Any more.'

'Then why are we going?'

'Well, I just think ... you know ... it's important.'

'Why?'

'Well, because. You're my girlfriend. He's my friend. Well, he used to be.'

'So why don't you like him any more?' Laure had a way of getting straight to the point that he found disconcerting at times. He moved away from her and ran a hand through his hair.

'We just sort of ... outgrew each other,' he said, after a minute. It seemed the kindest way to put it.

'If that were true, Daniel, we wouldn't be going tonight and you wouldn't be so nervous about it.'

'Look, we're going to have a good time. There'll be loads of other people there ... you'll enjoy it. You'll see.' He picked up his keys. 'Come on. Let's go and get blind drunk. That way we won't remember whether we had fun or not!'

Laure rolled her eyes at him and followed him out the door.

An hour and two glasses of wine later, he wondered why he'd been so nervous. Laure was on sparkling form. She was seated opposite him, sandwiched between Jon and his on/off girlfriend, Sophie, the spoilt daughter of a movie producer. She and Jon had been at high school together. Daniel sometimes wondered if Jon knew anyone who *hadn't* been to the exclusive Lincoln Grove High School. Fitzroy, Tag, Justin, Sophie, Carmela, Betthany ... the list went on and on and on. The tight little social circle that had seemed so appealing to him when he'd first come back was now downright claustrophobic. Sophie had once been Tag's girlfriend, then he'd passed her on to Fitzroy who had swapped her for Betthany ... Dean had been out with them both; he'd tried to palm Carmela off on to Daniel one holiday. It hadn't really worked. Carmela had complained all the time that she couldn't understand Daniel's accent – not, Daniel thought privately, that it would have made much difference. They barely talked. Fucked, mostly.

He looked across at Laure. God, she was different. She was

so different. She was his passport out of his narrow little world. No, *he* was different. He'd *chosen* Laure – that, in itself, was proof enough. He looked at her proudly, listening to the rise and fall of her voice; to the husky, hard-to-place accent and the infectious quality of her laugh. She was telling them about her first, pathetic attempts to speak English when she arrived in the States. The men were staring at her as though they might swallow her up, there and then. She had a way of talking about herself that appealed to the self-deprecating Brit in him; to the Americans present, she was just charmingly mysterious. He began to relax. Laure, it seemed, could handle herself.

Justin leaned over and winked at him. *She's hot*, he mouthed across the table. Daniel nodded. *He* knew that about her; he'd known it all along. Now others were beginning to see it. Perhaps bringing her into the narrow circle of his world wasn't going to be quite as bad as he'd feared? He looked at her. She was talking with her hands as much as her voice about the Blue Room, an amusing little story about some of the customers. Set against the painfully stiff, rigidly inert bodies of the women around her she was all movement and light. And then it started to go wrong.

'Really?' he heard Sophie's high, nasal voice rising an octave or two as she stared at Laure. 'You're a *cocktail waitress*? You're *kidding*, right?' Her comment cut right through the conversation and laughter and brought it to a halt. Sophie was looking at her as though she'd swallowed something unpleasant.

'Didn't you know?' Dean's voice rang out. 'That's where he met her.'

'Ohmigod. You *work* there?' Sophie's voice rose even further.

Laure looked at her coolly. 'No, I just happen to stand around four evenings a week. Of course I work there,' she said curtly.

'Look,' Daniel broke in suddenly, breathing fast. 'There's absolutely nothing wrong with working for a living. You should try it,' he looked at Sophie. 'Instead of watching TV all day, you might like to ...'

'Oh, shut the fuck up, Daniel. Like *you* work for a living.' Sophie's voice carried all the sarcasm she could muster. 'Besides,' she continued, turning to Laure. 'I did work once.' She smiled across the table at Daniel. His heart sank even further. He could almost tell what was coming. 'D'you remember?' she gave a quick, high giggle. She was obviously quite drunk. 'That summer you came over from England? You gave me ten dollars for a blow job.' She turned to the rest of the table. 'He'd never had one and he was sick of being teased about it,' she smiled cattily at Laure. 'I guess it's not *that* far from what you do in that horrible little club. A blow job's *kinda* like work, isn't it? Least it was with *you*, Daniel.' There was a sudden intake of breath, then everyone around the table started laughing.

He looked at Laure. She was sitting quite still, holding her wine glass by the stem, twirling it slowly round. She raised it. 'Ten bucks?' she murmured, looking straight at Sophie. 'That's not very much, is it? Pretty cheap, I'd say. Actually, looking at you now ...? Yeah ... ten bucks sounds about right.' She lifted the glass to her lips and finished off her wine. Then she pushed back her chair and stood up. 'Ready, darling?' she asked Daniel, ignoring the speechless faces of the girls around her. Daniel got up. His face was on fire, but with pride, not with shame. Even Jon looked at her admiringly. Tag's face was simply one of lust.

'Absolutely.' He touched her elbow lightly and in complete silence, they left the room.

Laure took the pins out of her wild mane of hair as they waited for the elevator and shook it free. Daniel was speechless.

'Cheap little whore,' Laure said, tartly taking his arm. 'She's lucky I didn't take off my shoe and slap her. That's what I'd do if I were at home, you know.' Some of the St Lazâre spirit had returned to her.

'Laure,' Daniel said, turning to her. He took her face between his hands. 'That was the coolest thing I've ever seen,' he whispered, looking down into her eyes. She smiled faintly. 'No, I mean it. You have such poise ... and they are such *arseholes*. I can't believe I spend so much time with them.'

'Well, why do you?' Laure asked mildly.

He looked down at her. 'I don't know,' he said finally, shaking his head. 'I don't know why I even bother with them.'

'Then don't.'

He nodded, still holding her head. He bent to kiss her, passionately, like a man drowning. 'I won't. I love you,' he whispered between kisses. 'I love you.'

49

Melanie drummed her fingers on the dashboard impatiently. What the hell was Steve doing? She squinted up at the apartment block he'd disappeared into. Gone to collect something, he'd said. Gimme five minutes. She looked at her watch again. He'd been gone *twenty* minutes, not five. Where the hell was he? She opened the door and got out of the car. He'd taken the car keys with him, however, and she didn't dare leave his precious convertible unlocked. Especially not in *this* neighbourhood. She looked around her. She didn't even know where they were – somewhere between Steve's place in the Hollywood Hills and Redondo Beach, which was an awfully long stretch of the city. They'd been invited to a summer barbecue at some film producer's house – another one of Steve's odd contacts and they were already over an hour late. She looked up at the building again. He'd been gone almost half an hour. The thought suddenly struck her. What if ... what if something had happened to him? He hadn't said who he was going to see but by now she knew enough about him to know that the restaurant was certainly not his only means of income – quite the opposite, in fact. The restaurant cleaned up the proceeds from all the other things he did. The Pink Palm made everything legal. Legit. Which was why occasionally Melanie found herself waiting for him outside venues she would normally never enter, such as the apartment block in front of her. It was a nondescript three-storey building with an internal garden that she could just see through the surrounding railings – just another of the faceless blocks of accommodation that had sprung up like weeds all over the city. How many apartments were in it? she wondered. Ten? Twelve? If he wasn't back in five minutes, she'd find a way in and look for him herself.

Five minutes later he still wasn't back. Melanie was starting to get really worried. He'd been gone for almost forty minutes. She could see someone coming down the garden path towards the entrance door. It wasn't Steve. She quickly shut the car door and walked up the sidewalk. The man held the door open for her, giving her a quick, appraising glance as she slipped past. The gate clacked shut behind him and she was alone in the courtyard. She looked around her. Everything was quiet. She was right – there were perhaps ten apartments in all. She couldn't see a list of occupants, not that it would have told her anything. She had no idea who he'd come to see. She walked along the footpath and peered into a couple of the apartments on the ground floor but everything was quiet. She climbed up the stairs to the second floor. There were four doors on her right. She walked past quickly, listening for the sound of voices, anything.

She had almost reached the last door when she heard something – a stifled sound, like a suppressed cry. A man's voice. She stopped. Seconds later, she heard it again. A muffled sound, as though someone were holding a hand over his mouth. It came from the apartment she'd just passed. Number 4. She turned round, her heart beginning to beat faster. The door was shut but she could hear the sound of voices inside. A woman's voice, a low, animal moan. The skin on the back of her neck prickled uncomfortably. Her heart was thudding. She pressed her head to the door, not caring if anyone saw her. She could hear Steve's voice ... yes, that was his voice. He was groaning, as if in pain. She didn't stop to think. She yanked the handle and the door opened immediately.

It took her a few seconds to properly register what she was

looking at. Steve's back, yes. That was his back. His shirt had been pulled out of his trousers, which were lying in an untidy heap at his ankles. One shirt-tail hung down, just covering his buttocks. The other was held tightly in someone's hand. Long, dark red fingernails clutched his back. A pair of tanned, toned legs were wrapped around his. He was fucking her standing up. The woman's face was partially obscured but as Melanie stood there in the doorway, her insides slowly turning to jelly, she moved her head, opened her eyes languidly and stared at her over his shoulder. Melanie felt her mouth open, as if to scream. Kim looked at her but said nothing. Steve was too busy concentrating on his own pleasure to notice she'd stopped moving against him. Slowly, exquisitely slowly, she slid one perfect leg down his to rest on the ground, the other perfect leg still held by his arm. Melanie could see the muscles in Steve's back shuddering as he came. There was an awful, heart-stopping silence as Melanie saw Steve's head turn to see what Kim was staring at.

'Shit.' That was it. That was all he said. Melanie turned on her heel and ran. She had no idea where she was going as she clattered down the stairs in her high-heeled sandals. She wasn't even thinking about where to go. All she wanted to do was run from the horrible, screaming, roaring noise that had erupted inside her head. She could hear Steve running after her. She pushed open the gate, blinded by tears. It was the same thing, over and over again. No one ever wanted her for long. Mike, Norbert, Rudy, Steve ... They all drew her in and then, when they'd had their fill, they tossed her aside. Found someone else. Someone new. Now it was her turn to moan like an animal in pain.

50

Laure hummed to herself as she moved around the apartment, cleaning. It was August and the summer heat was almost unbearable. Her place was air-conditioned but she didn't like sleeping with it on. The dry air left her with a headache each morning and she switched it off on the nights Daniel wasn't around. She didn't much like going over to his place. She felt uncomfortable there, surrounded by a thousand and one gadgets that she had no idea how to work. And she really didn't want to meet one of those assholes he called his friends. But after the dinner party a few months earlier, he hadn't spoken to a single one from the group he used to call his friends. Not one. At first Laure couldn't believe it. She occasionally overheard a message on his answering phone – 'How come you don't call us any more? Sorry about what happened and all that but call, will you? Don't be mad at us. Call.' He never did. Laure looked at him in awe. Just like that – he'd cut them out of his life. He shrugged whenever she brought it up; they were assholes. They'd treated her badly and for that he would never forgive them. She knew him well enough by now to know that the slight muscle movement at the back of his jaw meant he was angry – and every time he spoke about them that little muscle jumped around all over the place. No, they were gone, vanished, banished. In a heartbeat he'd discarded them and there was clearly no going back. Laure was the only person he cared about now. So they spent most of their time at her place, despite the heat and the lack of comforts.

She pulled the sheets off the bed. It was a Monday morning when the rest of the tenants in the building were at work. The Blue Room was just about to reopen and she was taking the last opportunity of her self-enforced vacation to clean her apartment. She had the laundry room downstairs to herself. She had the whole day to sweep, dust, polish ... she enjoyed it. Cleaning her surroundings made her feel *clean*. Nice. She

bundled the sheets together and picked up the pillows. She
didn't see it at first – the slim white envelope. It was only as
she started tugging the pillowcases off that her eyes fell on it.
She frowned, let the pillow drop and picked it up. It wasn't
sealed – she opened the flap. Inside was a cheque for a thousand
dollars. Made out to her. From Daniel. It was a colossal slap in
the face.

Daniel had to hold the phone away from his ear to properly
understand what Laure was screaming at him. He jumped up
from his desk, closed the blinds in his office and tried to calm
her down. She was crying so hard she could barely speak. His
heart was hammering. Jesus Christ! What had he gone and
done?

'You ... you *bastard*!' Laure sobbed down the phone. 'I
have never, *ever* ...' Daniel put the phone down, panicking.
He grabbed his car keys, flung open the office door and was
running down the corridor before his secretary could even look
up to see what was going on.

He made it from Lake Shore Drive to Division in less than
twenty minutes. He parked the car illegally at the side of the
road, not giving a damn about what might happen to it and
ran across the road, praying she was still at home. And that
she would let him in. Luckily someone was coming out of
the building at the same time. He ran up the steps and straight
through the doors. He bounded up the steps, three at a time.
He stopped outside her door, gasping for breath. 'Laure?' he
banged on the door. 'Laure? It's me ... Laure? Are you there?'

The door was flung open. Laure was standing there in a
pair of his boxer shorts, tears streaming down her face. He had
never seen her so angry. In her fist she held the crumpled ball
of what had been his cheque. He put up his hands. 'I'm sorry,'
he began, his voice cracking. 'It was stupid of me. I'm sorry,
Laure ... I shouldn't have—'

'Have I ever asked you for a thing? Have I ever asked you
for a penny?' Her voice was shaking with rage.

'No ... no ... I just wanted ... I just thought—'

'This is what you do to *prostitutes*, Daniel. You leave an envelope under the pillow. Is that what you think of me?'

For the first time in his life, Daniel felt fear. He stared at her, too scared to speak. She looked as though he'd hit her; all the fire was gone out of her eyes. He'd shamed her, yes ... that was what he'd done. He put his hand up to his face, knowing it was already wet. 'Please, Laure, don't leave me.' It came out as a whimper but he couldn't stop himself. 'I'm so, so sorry ... I just didn't think. I didn't mean ... What you just said ... I would never ... Laure, *please* don't leave me.'

'Daniel, you're crying,' Laure's voice was strained. 'You're crying.'

'Of course I'm fucking crying,' he sobbed, wiping his cheeks furiously with the back of his hand. '*Please* don't ...'. His breath came in huge, uneven gulps. He hadn't cried like this since ... since childhood. He sank to the floor. A wave of shame burned over him as she bent down and put both hands on his shoulders, forcing him to look at her.

'Shh,' she whispered, tracing the line of his tears with her finger. 'It's OK.' He closed his eyes. The humiliation was almost unbearable. What must she think of him now? He felt her lips against his cheek, softly brushing away his tears. Her hands were curled around his neck; he moved uncomfortably ... she was too close, his nose was full of the scent of her hair; he could feel himself starting to get aroused. He squirmed. That would be too fucking much. A cry-baby with a hard-on for her. But Laure kept him there, her mouth moving under his; hands going under his shirt, pulling at his belt. He responded – of *course* he responded to her. He wanted her so badly it hurt. She balanced on his knees, wriggling herself out of his boxer shorts and then she was back on top of him and then there was nothing but the warm, wet feel of her, his hands digging into her thighs, her hips ... clutching at her hair. He exploded almost immediately, his cry of release swallowed by her mouth with him shuddering and gasping for air. She was utterly still. She bent her head until their foreheads were touching, her soft warm breath on his face.

'Marry me.' The words were out before he could even think. They hung, like drops of water, in the silence between them.

Marry me. Laure lay awake long after Daniel had fallen asleep. The rage that had blown up inside her as soon as she'd seen the cheque was almost spent. It was Belle – that was the reason she'd seen red. She'd been unable to stop herself. She couldn't bear the thought of being in any way like Belle. That was what men did to Belle – they put twenty dollars under the ashtray in the living room when they left in the early hours of the morning. Or a ten-dollar note pinned carelessly to the cork-board in the kitchen. But Daniel wasn't like that and she wasn't Belle. She still couldn't quite believe it. He'd asked her to marry him. How was that possible? Daniel had everything – *every*thing. He had a future that she couldn't even imagine – wealth, security, opportunities … *choices*. He didn't have to work four nights a week running up and down stairs with a tray balanced over his head. Much as she liked Don and the girls at the Blue Room, there was no denying it wasn't what she pictured herself doing for the rest of her life. She did it because she had to. But he didn't. Daniel could do whatever he wanted, when he wanted. He had the whole world at his feet. And with all that in front of him, he'd chosen *her*? Did she love him? She had so much to thank him for. But where was the line between love and gratitude? He was only the third man she'd ever been with and the first hadn't exactly gone down on his knees for her. She'd grown up her whole life hearing only about how hard it would be to find a husband; how nature and Belle's disastrous choices had conspired to make a good marriage practically impossible. She'd responded by claiming she didn't *want* to get married; she never would. So *what* if she had come out too dark and was the daughter of a whore? Who cared? Certainly not her.

But now Daniel was offering her *his* future too. His choices would become hers. The flood of gratitude that swept over her as he asked her to marry him was overwhelming and it had taken her a few seconds to be able to speak. 'Without you, I'm nothing,' he said, meaning it. But there was a shadow hanging over his words that only she could see. There were so many things about her that Daniel didn't know. She would sooner have cut off her tongue than admit to some of the choices *she'd* made; and to the one thing she wished more than anything else she'd never done. She closed her eyes as she thought about her son. If he knew *that* about her he would never have asked her to marry him. How could he? How would he ever understand what she'd done? Daniel was offering her a future – but did she dare accept?

'Yes,' she said suddenly, surprising herself. 'Yes, I'll marry you.'

And that, she realised a few days later with a sinking heart, was the easy bit. They had their first argument. Daniel wanted them to get married before they told his parents. Laure was aghast. 'It's the only way to do it, Laure. I promise you,' Daniel said stubbornly. 'If I tell them beforehand, there'll be all sorts of ... well, there'll be all kinds of paperwork and lawyers and all of that crap. I just don't want to deal with it. I don't want *you* to have to deal with it.'

'But, Daniel, it just seems so ... so *wrong*. It's a marriage, not a funeral. It's supposed to be a happy occasion. Running off to Las Vegas ... it feels as though we're doing something wrong. As if we're ashamed of getting married.'

'Laure, you have no idea. You don't know my parents. My father ...' Daniel got up from the couch, suddenly agitated. 'He'll do whatever it takes to ... to stop me. To stop *us*. And I'm not going to take that chance.'

'But what can he do?' Laure asked, knitting her brow. 'What's the worst he can do?'

Daniel gave a short, unhappy laugh. 'There's an awful lot of money at stake, Laure. I know you hate talking about it but the truth is, I'm *absolutely stinking rich*. Oh, it's not *my* money – you know me, I couldn't give a shit about it. But I'm the only son and there's billions in the bank.' Laure was silent. She was suddenly very worried. She shivered. 'That's why we need to do it first,' Daniel said, trying to reassure her. It wasn't working.

'Once we're married, there'll be nothing he or my mother can do about it, short of rewriting his will. And besides, I don't give a fuck. I don't need his money!'

'Oh, Daniel ... be practical. You've never even worked before ...' Laure stopped suddenly. There was a hurt look on his face. 'I mean, apart from working for your father,' she added hastily.

'I can easily get another job,' he said angrily. 'That's the least of my worries. I just don't understand why you're being so timid. It's almost as though you're scared of him. You're the bravest person I know! You're not afraid of *anything*. You have *no* idea how much I admire you ... how I wish I was more like you. But I don't understand why you're afraid of someone you've never even met! What are you so afraid of?'

'I'm not *afraid*,' Laure stammered, taken aback. 'I ... I just think it's better to tell them beforehand, that's all. It'll be such a shock to them. They don't even know I exist. I just think it's a better idea to prepare them for it.'

'Trust me, darling. It's not.'

They were married in a tiny chapel in Las Vegas, three weeks after he proposed. It was unbelievably easy. When the city clerk asked for her documents, she handed over her passport with her heart in her mouth. At the very worst she could say she hadn't noticed her visa had run out ... the licensing official simply glanced at it and handed it back. He was much more interested in the fee. There was a five-minute wait inside the lobby, a five-minute ceremony with the couple behind them as witnesses – and then it was done. She signed the register with a shaking hand. Her knees felt weak as they walked back down the tiny aisle. She stepped out into the blinding sunlight, shielding her eyes against the sun. They were married. Her name was Laure Bermann. She was an American now. Everything had changed.

And then came the bit she'd been dreading. Daniel had told her a thousand times what to expect from his parents but their reaction still came as a shock. They went to the Bermann's country home in the Indiana dunes. His sports car ate up the miles along the freeway and then they turned off on to country roads that revealed an unexpected wilderness close to the lake's edge. It was September, the prettiest time of the year in the Midwest. The prairie flowers were in the last few days of bloom; the wind was warm and balmy and the skies were clear and blue. Laure barely registered the details. Her stomach was tied in knots of tension and she was dreading what lay ahead.

They swept up the long driveway to the house, nestled in a clump of gently waving trees. Daniel took her hand as they walked up the steps to the verandah that ran the entire length of the house and looked out over the still, blue surface of the lake.

'Anyone home?' he called out, pushing open the sliding doors.

'Daniel!' From somewhere inside the house came the answering shout – it held a note of pleasure.

'Mum? Where are you?' Daniel tugged a reluctant Laure forward. 'There's someone I want you to meet. Where's Dad?'

A woman came through the open doors at one end of the long, luxurious room. Laure had just enough time to take in the elegant cream and pale green décor, the deep-pile rugs and expensive-looking paintings hanging on the wall before Daniel propelled her forwards to face a woman who looked as if she'd just found something unpleasant sticking to the sole of her shoe.

'Mum, I think you'd better sit down.' Daniel's voice carried the faintest tremor.

'Oh my God, Daniel. *No.*' Octavia Bermann's reaction was followed swiftly by her husband's. He came into the room, took one look around and promptly lost the cigar from his mouth. There followed a fast and furious conversation in German between Günter Bermann and his son. Laure was thankful she couldn't understand a word. Understanding its tone was bad enough. When it was over there was absolute silence in the room. They sat there, all four of them frozen players in a tableau that none of them seemed to know how – or wished – to break. Then his mother rose from her chair and turned to the two of them. 'No one must know,' she said, her voice icily calm. 'No one. Is that clear? There will be a *proper* wedding here in Chicago in due course. We will ignore what you did in Las Vegas.'

'Mother,' Daniel began, a note of exasperation in his voice.

The impossibly thin, impossibly elegant woman turned to him, her eyes cold. 'I have nothing further to say,' she said, ignoring Laure altogether. 'I wish to lie down.' And with that, she swept from the room. There was a further exchange between Daniel and his father, and then Bermann, Sr, too swept out of the room.

Daniel and Laure were left to stare at one another. Daniel sighed. He'd warned her. It would take them a while. Laure shook her head. Her eyes filled with tears. She had news for him. It wasn't going to take them a while. It wasn't going to take them any length of time at all. *You want to know why? Because they are never going to accept it, Daniel. Never.*

He pulled her towards him, cradling her head in his hands. *Shh. They will. You'll see.*

The 'proper' wedding was planned for December, three months away. Octavia Bermann complained that it wasn't nearly enough time to get everything done. A wedding planner was hired; a cheerful young blonde woman named Mindy whom Laure could quite happily have strangled. Within minutes of meeting her, it was quite clear that this was Mindy and Octavia Bermanns' wedding, not hers. The two of them held endless meetings at the Bermanns' lakeside penthouse apartment, meetings to which Laure was not invited. Occasionally Octavia Bermann would relay a message through Mindy or Daniel; 'they' had decided on pale grey for the winter wedding; 'they' had chosen the flowers; 'they' had hired a set designer to redecorate their Indiana holiday home. A priest had been chosen who'd been carefully briefed – no one was to know the two were already married. It was to be a very small wedding – only the closest family and a few friends. If the media got wind of it, their little secret would soon be out in the open. No one asked Laure whom she intended to bring.

About six weeks before the big day, Octavia Bermann summoned Laure to the Bermanns' Lake Shore Drive residence. Laure took a taxi, assuring Daniel that she would manage on her own. It was a blustery November day; the sun was out but a brisk, chilly wind blew in off the lake. Laure stepped out of the cab at the corner of Pearson and Dewitt, just round the corner from the Bermanns' penthouse apartment. She needed a few minutes to compose herself. She walked down Pearson, turned left on Lake Shore Drive and looked up at the towering skyscraper; a sheer, vertical wall of black steel and glass. Daniel had told her it had been designed by a famous architect – she couldn't remember his name – but the building seemed stark and soulless, a rectangular box of money and power. Lake Shore Drive. Delroy's words came back to her, suddenly. *A long, beautiful street by the lake. Lots of skyscrapers, real nice.* She swallowed, a lump suddenly appearing in her throat. She was able to say his name, now ... touching it lightly. *Delroy.* But she never allowed herself to go any further, deeper. She couldn't afford to. No one knew the effort it took *not* to think about it. About *him*. Somewhere in the city was her son. Somewhere. Especially not now, not when she was about to meet the cold, frosty woman who was her mother-in-law. She shook her head, both to rid herself of the accidental memory and the image of Octavia Bermann's disapproving face.

Half an hour later, Laure stood in her underwear, inwardly seething with indignation, as the three women – Octavia and the two dress designers she'd chosen – prodded and pinched and pulled, almost in complete silence. The dress itself was a nightmare, a fantastical concoction of lace, silk and yards of tulle. In a million years it wasn't something she would ever have worn. She was told to stand up, turn, sit down, pirouette – and all the while they stood there, discussing her as though she were a cut of meat.

'I might as well not have been there!' she told Daniel angrily later that night. 'They never ask me what I think. They just expect me to stand there like a dummy ... and they poke and pull and talk among themselves. As if I don't exist!'

'It'll be over soon, darling, I promise. It's just my mother – this means so much to her. The whole ordeal'll be over before you know it. We're going to Paris the day afterwards ... and then we've got the rest of our lives!'

'But it's not an ordeal, Daniel, it's a wedding! It's not like going to the dentist, for God's sake. *That's* an ordeal.'

'You don't know the people I come from,' Daniel said dryly. 'Believe me, it's an ordeal. Why d'you think I was so keen for us to go off and do it alone?'

'I know.' Laure suddenly felt exhausted. She pulled back the bedsheets and flung herself down on the bed. Daniel reached across for her hand.

'You asked me once what I wanted to do for the rest of my life. Well, I know now. I want to make you happy. That's it. That's all I need. I just want to make you happy. Darling, why are you crying?'

51

'You have no family?' Octavia Bermann's impeccably polished and shaped nail worked its way down the guest list. 'And who are these? Your friends?'

Laure's eyes narrowed. 'Yes, they're my friends. And no, I don't have any family,' she said shortly.

'I find that hard to believe. No one? Not a single family member?'

Laure fought to keep her voice under control. 'No, there's no one here. In the States, I mean.'

'I see. Well, if he will insist on marrying a foreigner,' Octavia murmured to herself but loud enough for Laure to hear. 'Most odd. I don't know how I'm going to pull this whole terrible affair off.'

Laure had to bite her tongue to stop herself from flinging a rude expletive at Octavia as she swept out of the room in a cloud of expensive perfume. She had the art of patronising humiliation down to perfection. Laure's whole body burned with indignation. She pulled the list towards her and looked at it miserably. Of the eighty-odd guests coming to the wedding, two were hers. Don and Shelley. Who else could she invite? She was too embarrassed to go back to Irazú after she'd quit working there and there was absolutely no question of inviting Belle. Daniel's father would have to give her away. She longed for Améline. Even Grandmère. She couldn't help thinking that she would have approved – she would probably have enjoyed it. After all, even though Grandmère had none of the wealth that was at the Bermanns' disposal, the Bermanns' world wasn't a million miles away from what Grandmère knew and approved of. *If* the circumstances in Haiti had been different, *if* Belle hadn't run off with a stable hand ... If, if, if. Imagine, it would have been Grandmère presiding over a wedding every bit as grand in its own context, as this. She felt the prick of tears behind her eyes and quickly left the room.

'Daniel,' she said, a few days later, coming up behind him and sliding her arms under his jacket. He leaned his head against hers; he loved her holding him. She could feel the nerves in her own voice. 'This is crazy, isn't it?'

'What is?'

'This. The wedding. Everything. It must be costing a *fortune*. I haven't paid for a *thing*.'

'Neither have I. Don't worry about it.'

'But you're bringing so much to this. I'm bringing nothing. No, I'll tell you exactly how much I'm bringing into this marriage ...' She withdrew her arms and turned to face him. '$3,133.76. *That's* how much I have. Down to the last cent.'

'Good thing I'm marrying you for your body and not your

money, then,' he said. 'Isn't it?' He bent his head and kissed her until the breath almost left her body.

There were other issues to deal with. Their wedding posed legal difficulties, as Daniel's father angrily pointed out to him. There was no point in getting Laure to sign a prenuptial agreement *since they were already bloody married*! Daniel sat through the tirade, relieved that he'd had the guts to go ahead and do it as he'd planned. If not, they'd have been sitting in front of lawyers and accountants for the next ten years. Günter Bermann was faced with the unenviable task of explaining to his lawyer that no, he'd decided *not* to make his son and his fiancée go through the unnecessary turmoil of a prenuptial agreement but he'd decided to limit his son's inheritance instead. Steve Kleinhoff, the Bermanns' family lawyer, looked at Daniel and promptly shut his mouth. Obviously Daniel had done something silly like run off to Las Vegas and marry the girl beforehand. He would never say it, of course, but in Daniel's shoes, he'd have probably done the same himself.

On the eve of the wedding, at Octavia's insistence, Laure spent the night at the Bermanns' lakeside apartment. 'It's a custom, Laure,' Octavia informed her. 'I don't expect you follow the tradition in … well, wherever it is you're from,' she said haughtily, 'but we do here. It's an important part of the ritual of marriage.' Neither met the other's eyes. Laure was shown a large, spacious guest room in one wing of the apartment. She unpacked her overnight bag and laid out her clothes. Her wedding gown and all the accessories that went with it were already hanging in the wardrobe. Her suitcases for their honeymoon were packed. She sat on the edge of the bed, pressing her knees together. They were leaving the following morning for Paris. Two weeks in Paris and a week in London. She'd never been to either. If Régine could see her now what would she think? And Améline … what wouldn't Ameline give to see America, or Paris, or London? She closed her eyes, picturing Améline's little, curious face. Two years had done nothing to dull the ache in her heart whenever she pictured Améline's face. Perhaps now she could begin to think about going back to Haiti? To find her?

She got up off the bed and walked over to the windows. It was almost midnight. Daniel had dropped her off after dinner. She wouldn't see him until his father – in the absence of hers – would place her hand on his in the church the following morning. It seemed an awfully long time to wait. She opened the window, ignoring the icy blast of night air on her face. The catch slid open silently. The shimmering surface of the lake glinted in the moonlight; the faint sound of the streets far below drifting up the walls. There was a balcony running around the apartment. She stepped outside, and walked along, hardly daring to look down the thirty-odd storeys to the ground. On either side, the buildings were lit up, providing a thousand simultaneous openings into each other's lives. Across from her she could see a woman walking across the living room of an equally spacious apartment; she paused at the window, just as Laure was doing, but didn't see her. She caught a glimpse of a man moving between rooms on the floor above. She looked away. She walked to the edge of the balcony that flanked the west wing of the apartment and was just about to return when she heard Octavia's voice. She paused. They were in the living room; one window was open and the sound of the conversation floated over to her. She was just about to walk off when she heard Octavia sob, quite distinctly.

'*Ach, nein*,' she heard his father say. 'Too late for that, my dear. We have to go through with it. No other way.'

'But what have we *done*, Günter? What didn't we do?' His mother's voice was almost hysterical. 'I'm sorry, I can't stand the sight of her.' Laure felt something cold creep over her skin and it wasn't the chilly night air.

'Don't worry, don't worry, leave it to me. They're married, yes ... we have to live with it. But they won't stay married for ever.'

'Dear God. A *divorce*? Can you imagine the shame of it?'

'Octavia, *mein Gott* ... You behave as if we were living in the Middle Ages. Yes, people get married but people also get divorced. Come on, *schatz*, half this town is divorced. It doesn't matter.'

'I'm *Catholic*, Günter, or had you forgotten?'

'Look, what do want? You want to have coloured grandchildren? Is that what you want, *hein*? A litter of half-breeds?'

'No, no ... of course not! But Daniel's changed, darling. He's become, I don't know, he's almost *stubborn* these days. Sometimes,' Octavia gave a half-laugh, half-sob, 'no ... don't laugh at me ... sometimes I don't wonder if she hasn't *bewitched* him or something. Don't they practise black magic down there? What do they call it ... voodoo? Oh, this is just too *appalling* for words.'

'My dear, didn't I tell you to stop worrying? I'll take care of it. Just give me a little time. I'll get her, the cheap, little gold-digging whore. She's hiding something, I can see it in her eyes. I'll get her in the end. Come, have some more wine.'

Laure almost passed out. She crept back to the guest room on tiptoe, shaking from head to foot. She slid into the room and closed the door, her heart thudding. She closed the window, sliding the bolt into place and stood there, wringing her hands together in agitation. She stuffed a hand in her mouth; how could they hate her so? How could they hate someone they barely knew? She sat down on the bed and put her head in her hands, gulping huge breaths of air. What had his father said? *I'll get her. She's hiding something.* She felt physically sick.

52

There was almost total silence in the little room adjacent to the hall in which they were to be married. Octavia stood stiffly to one side as Mindy made the last-minute adjustments to Laure's dress. She could hear the low murmur of the guests as they took their seats in the flower-filled hall. Günter Bermann was going to give her away. She felt sick at the thought of walking down the aisle with him, her arm placed on his. His words echoing around her head: *I'll get her in the end.* It felt as though the end had already come.

The door opened and Günter Bermann entered the room. He nodded brusquely at her and adjusted his tie. No one spoke. The opening chords of the wedding march were sounded; the murmur in the hall died down to an almost deathly silence. Slowly the doors creaked open; Laure turned to stand next to her father-in-law as Octavia fixed a smile on her face and walked out in front of them. At the far end she could see Daniel waiting for her, his own face tight and anxious. Then there was the thundering sound of the organ as the slow processional melody was struck. She placed her hand on Günter Bermann's arm as she'd been instructed to do and she was led slowly away from the room towards Daniel. She looked neither right nor left, afraid that she might burst into tears. She could hear the murmuring wave of comments as she passed each row but kept her eyes firmly fixed ahead. Somewhere, hidden among the Bermanns' guests, were Don and Shelley. She couldn't even look for them; she wasn't sure she could trust herself not to burst into tears.

As soon as he was able, Daniel took her from his father's arm and gripped her hand tightly. As if from a great distance, she heard the voice of the priest. 'Dearly beloved.' Her mind spun away from the proceedings taking place all around her, slipping back in space and time to two young girls, sitting on a patchwork quilt on the bed, discussing who and what they would marry when they grew up. Rich. Handsome. Fair. They would live in Pétionville, right at the top of the hill and visit each other every single day. Régine wanted three children; Laure wanted four. And Améline would live with her, of course. They would go shopping together in Miami and take their holidays in Martinique. 'Do you, Laure Estelle St Lazâre, take this man to be your lawfully wedded husband, to have and to hold ...'

'I do.' She felt Daniel's grip on her hand tighten.

'And do you ...' Laure closed her eyes. Seconds later, she heard the priest instruct Daniel. 'You may kiss the bride.' There was a second's delay and then a muted cheer from the assembled guests. She felt the cool, firm pressure of his lips and his hand at her elbow, turning her around to face their guests. A few claps, a cheer or two ... someone shouted 'hip, hip, hooray', as she'd seen them do in English films ... and then she really couldn't make out anything as she and Daniel walked back along the aisle to shake hands and smile at those who offered their hands. No one knew her well enough to see that the smile she affected didn't quite reach the corners of her eyes and that the hand holding onto Daniel's gripped it in fear.

53

They arrived in Paris just after dawn on a misty December morning. The countryside around Charles de Gaulle was blanketed in fog. With her face pressed against the glass Laure could just make out hazy dark green fields, a church steeple; a row of poplar trees swaying in the early morning breeze. She had slept most of the way, her hand held loosely in Daniel's, in the soft reclining leather seats. First class. 'What a way to travel,' she'd whispered to him as the lights were dimmed and he'd shown her how to slide the seat out.

'Darling, it's the *only* way to travel, don't you know?' he whispered back. She'd snorted in mock disgust.

They were among the first passengers off the plane and were cleared through customs in minutes. A porter was waiting with their bags and as they came through into the arrivals hall, someone else was waiting to take their bags to the car. Laure slid into the back seat of the waiting Mercedes, too excited to speak. As a schoolchild, she'd seen pictures of the city Haitians considered the most beautiful in the world – outside Port-au-Prince, of course – and now she was actually here. The car slid away from the kerb; again, she pressed her face to the glass to watch the city unfold. The Arc de Triomphe, the Eiffel Tower, the Seine … Semi-familiar landmarks swam in and out of view. The car finally glided across Place Vendôme and pulled up in front of the Ritz. The Imperial Suite was theirs for a fortnight Daniel told her. Christmas and New Year in Paris. All theirs.

'Is this real?' she kept asking as she wandered around the suite. 'Really real?' She picked up a gold-edged teacup. 'And this?' A miniature silver clock.

'Laure, will you stop casing the joint and get into bed?' Daniel's muffled voice came through the doors.

'What does that mean? Casing the joint?'

'Never mind. Come here.'

'I'm coming.' She pushed open the doors to the bathroom. *Wow*. There were bathrobes hanging on the back of the door. She pushed her face into the downy softness. *Wow again*. She opened the little cabinet doors and peeked at the toiletries laid out in neat rows. *Ohhh*. By the time she finally walked back into the room which held the enormous, satin and silk-covered bed, Daniel was almost asleep. She reluctantly took off the robe and slid into bed beside him. She didn't give a damn what anybody thought about her, she thought to herself, before turning and pushing herself into the sleeping form of her husband. *This* was the sort of luxury people died for. The sort of luxury that, once experienced, gave you such a boost that you could accomplish anything you set your mind to. Anything. Anything at all. She felt her earlier optimism returning. Her father-in-law hated her? So what? He was out to get her? Let him try. His mother couldn't stand the sight of her? Well, neither could she. She felt Daniel slowly come to life, his hands already pulling at the strings and bows of the silk nightdress someone had given her as a wedding gift. She felt one of the straps tear as he struggled impatiently to get rid of it. Oh, well. What was it someone had said to her about the slow decline of passion once they were married? It wouldn't happen. Not to them.

★

Two days later, she stood, semi-clothed, in front of a mirror while two women fussed around her with their tape measures, lifting her arms up and down, measuring her across the shoulders, chest, waist, hips … Was there anywhere they wouldn't go? Madame Hélène Garrel sat across the room, sizing Laure up with a critical and professional eye. Octavia's wedding present. A complete wardrobe makeover for her daughter-in-law. Only Laure knew how much it would have killed her to say those words.

'You have a very good figure, Madame Bermann,' she pronounced at last. Laure breathed a sigh of relief. Thank God for that, as Daniel would say. '*Très classique*. Full, yes, but not too much. Good height. You studied ballet, *non*?' Laure nodded cautiously. '*Oui, ça se voit.*' She jotted something down in her leather-bound notebook. 'No children yet, hmm? You will have to be careful when you do. We Europeans, we are slim, like boys – no breast, no hips, straight down. But you … your women are very feminine. You will have to watch what you eat.'

Laure winced. *No children?* If only she knew. Thinking about him produced the same, sharp pain, just below the ribs; a pain that time had done nothing to dull.

'Shoe size?' Madame Garrel asked imperiously.

'Er, thirty-eight.'

'*Bon*. A good size.' She closed the notebook with a snap. '*Alors.* You will come back to me here, at this place, tomorrow afternoon. I will have a few outfits ready for you to try on. According to your *belle-mère*,' she glanced down her pince-nez at the list Octavia had sent over, 'you require the following – three evening gowns, four cocktail dresses, four suits and a range of leisure clothes for the races, the yacht, garden parties and so on.' She frowned at Laure. 'Something is wrong, Madame Bermann?'

'Er, no … I was just wondering, do I have to have all of them?'

'All of them? What do you mean?'

'Can't I just have one?'

'Madame Bermann,' Madame Garrel drew herself up to her full height. 'I think perhaps you do not understand. Your *belle-mère* is making you a very generous gift. Imagine. For someone like yourself. I would accept it, Madame Bermann. With gratitude.' She swept out of the room. There was a sudden silence. The two assistants had stopped working and were kneeling, staring open-mouthed at the door. Laure looked down at them. Then she slowly turned round and flipped her middle finger at the door. One of the girls, the younger of the two, giggled. The other looked horrified and quickly excused herself from the room.

Laure looked at the girl and shrugged. 'I'm Laure Bermann,' she said, holding out a hand. The girl scrambled to her feet.

'I'm Nicole,' she said, shaking Laure's hand vigorously. She turned to gather up her things. 'Madame Bermann,' she said suddenly, turning around again. She was blushing. 'If you like ... I mean, I don't know ... but if you would like me to show you some other places, here in Paris, I could help you.'

Laure looked at her. 'Help me?'

'Yes, with shopping, perhaps. I couldn't help ... I'm sorry, I was in the room yesterday when Madame Bermann rang from America. If you want, I know other boutiques ...' She stopped, obviously unsure if she'd overstepped the mark.

Laure was touched. 'No, no. Thank you, I'd like that very much. I suppose you heard – I'm rather new to all this,' she said, looking around her.

'You can call me, tomorrow morning, on this number,' Nicole said, quickly scribbling a phone number on a piece of paper. 'But please don't say anything. We're not supposed to ...'

'Don't worry, I won't. I don't think *I'm* supposed to, either,' Laure said, smiling ruefully. 'I'll ring you tomorrow morning.'

Laure held the fabric in her hands, enjoying the feel of silk against her skin. Next to her Nicole looked on admiringly as Laure laid the shirt against the linen trousers she'd picked out. The linen was a dark, almost bottle-green; the silk was a very pale grey-lilac. Each piece on its own was unremarkable; brought together by the rich colour of Laure's skin, they looked fantastic.

'*Parfait,*' Nicole whispered, wishing she'd been the one to pick them out. Laure Bermann's taste was exquisite. Everyone was wearing black and white that summer; safe, monochromatic choices that could hardly go wrong. Within the space of two hours, Laure had chosen colours that Nicole had barely heard of – butter-brown; chalk-white; iridescent green; Jamaican ginger ... As she picked out a skirt from this store, dashing back three shops to team it with a scarf she'd seen earlier and a pair of shoes she'd spotted from across the road, Nicole shook her head. *This* was the penniless ingrate Madame Bermann had been wailing about? The way she and Madame Garrel had talked about her, Nicole had been half-expecting a wild creature, dressed in a grass skirt.

'Oh, Madame Bermann, *merde* ... it's nearly two. We're supposed to be back at the *atelier* in half an hour. The couture dresses ...'

Laure nodded reluctantly. She couldn't remember the last time she'd enjoyed herself as much. The morning had simply flown by. She'd been a little hesitant at first, not just about spending Daniel's money, but about her own judgement. She'd never really shopped for clothes before. Oh, a skirt or a dress here and there, on the odd occasion she'd had something to spend. But *this* – trailing around one gorgeous boutique after another, encouraged by Nicole who was no slouch herself in the fashion department – this was bliss. She found she remembered more than she thought she knew about fine fabrics and a good cut. A bittersweet memory of dressing up with Améline in Grandmère's room, pulling one exquisite outfit after another out of the enormous trunks that lay hidden at the back of her attic floated through her mind.

Half an hour later, as instructed, she pressed the doorbell at Madame Garrel's. She was led upstairs, as before, and shown into the *atelier*. This time there were several tailor's dummies dotted around the room and two different assistants were busy pinning her mother-in-law's choices for Laure to see. Her heart sank. Baby-blue chiffon, lavender silk and pink tulle – not the teals, fuchsias or dusky pinks that would have looked good on her but the washed-out, bland-looking pink that very nearly matched the colour of Madame Garrel's skin. Behind her, she heard Nicole let out a barely audible gasp of disappointment. Each dress, Nicole had told her, was more than ten times the equivalent of what they had spent that morning. Laure looked at each one, wondering how on earth she would summon up the necessary enthusiasm to try them on.

The afternoon dragged on. Each dress had to be fitted right down to the last millimetre. *Breathe in, breathe out; arms in, arms out; head up; turn around* . . . She pirouetted around endlessly. Finally, at almost five o'clock, Madame Garrel pronounced herself satisfied with the first round and Laure was free to go. It was only the thought of the stacks of bags waiting for her at the hotel that had kept her going all afternoon. She brightened as soon as she left the suite. *I'll call you later,* she mouthed to Nicole and practically ran down the stairs. As usual, a sleek black car was waiting for her outside and she climbed in, marvelling at the discreet but highly efficient organisation that wrapped itself around Daniel's life – and now hers. She never had to ask for anything. It was all there, waiting for her, before she even knew she needed it.

'Do you like it?' she asked Daniel excitedly, standing before him in a long, floaty dress with an asymmetrical hem and tiny spaghetti straps. Daniel peered over the edge of his newspaper.

'Um . . . yes. You look lovely. You always look lovely.'

'Daniel,' Laure pulled a face at him. 'What about this one?' She held up another, almost identical dress but in a different, unidentifiable colour. He nodded again.

'Yeah. That too.'

'You're not paying attention,' Laure cried, unfastening the straps and slipping out of it.

'Now I am,' he said, lowering the paper. He caught a glimpse of white lace panties before Laure grabbed a handful of clothes and stomped off to the bathroom, glaring at him. He sighed. What else was he supposed to say? She always looked great. Even better without any clothes on.

He heard the shower begin to run. He looked across at the mound of bags and piles of shoes lying in one corner of the room. Making her happy brought him an unexpected happiness. He could have cared less about the clothes themselves – women's clothes were a complete mystery to him – but it thrilled him to see her so excited. Come to think of it, he suddenly realised, he'd probably never seen Laure behave the way she had today – carefree, sunny and spontaneous. It was a quality in her he'd only ever seen glimpses of, before. He pushed the paper to one side and stretched out, thinking about her. At times the strength of his passion for her surprised him. Disturbed him, even. The cool, rational, *English* side of him was wary of excess, in any shape or form. There were times when just the thought of her could floor him, render him practically speechless, with lust, admiration ... love? He didn't know. He rolled over onto his stomach, breathing in her scent on the pillows and listening with half an ear to the water still going strong in the bathroom. Her life was a blank, closed canvas to him. She occasionally let something out – a small anecdote, a name from the past – but most of the time it was locked up inside her, fiercely and possessively guarded. He longed to ask her more, to know her in the way he thought she knew him. He kept nothing from her – that was his nature, to be open, generous, inviting. Laure was the opposite, but it was a forced opposition, not a natural one – *that* was what drove him crazy. The woman he loved was really two women overlaid so tightly on top of each other you could be fooled into thinking there was only one. But *he* knew the fit wasn't perfect – what he couldn't work out, not yet at any rate, was whether Laure knew it too.

The shower stopped. He could hear her picking up a bottle; the soft sound of something being squirted. Then, seconds later, the door opened in a cloud of steam. He was still lying on his stomach, peeking at her from underneath his arm. She was wearing some sort of loose, shiny dressing gown. It was new – the burnt orange colour suited her. It shimmered as she moved towards him, caught on the twin peaks of her breasts. He felt himself stirring, already and instantly full of desire for her. She walked towards the bed, unpinning the thick river of curls that she'd tied on top of her head. There was nothing, Daniel reflected, as he surreptitiously watched her slip off her robe and slide into bed beside him, quite so sexy as a woman who was unaware of herself being watched. Nothing in the world.

Laure stepped out of the limousine, nervously adjusting her skin-tight silk dress and her fur wrap and felt for Daniel's hand as they walked up the red carpet towards the front door. To her left there was a sudden movement then a flurry of flash bulbs went off in her face, almost blinding her.

'Come on,' Daniel said in her ear, 'just keep going. They're here for the politicians and the society ladies, not for us.' She gripped his hand and followed him. They were attending the opening night of the new Opéra de la Bastille, an enormous white and steel box that resembled more closely a giant pharmacy than an opera house, she whispered in an aside to Daniel as they walked up the carpet and away from the annoying photographers. He smiled. The foyer was crowded with women in full evening gowns, men in black ties and formal suits. Laure, still clutching Daniel's arm, was secretly pleased she'd decided not to wear the powder blue taffeta nightmare that had been delivered to the hotel with great pomp and circumstance that afternoon. She knew exactly how much it had cost – five thousand dollars – but after trying it on once and observing how it deadened her skin colour, sucking all the vibrancy and richness out of it so that she wound up grey and dull, she quickly unzipped and unfastened it and hung it carefully at the back of the wardrobe. She had no idea what she would tell her mother-in-law if she asked, but what the hell, the woman was six thousand miles away; she'd probably never know. She'd pulled a gorgeous shantung-style black silk dress out of the closet and laid it carefully on the bed. A pair of black velvet high-heeled sandals; a pale grey and silver silk scarf of an intricate paisley pattern … a thick bangle of Ethiopian silver that covered almost half of her forearm and a pair of ornate silver and amber earrings. She contemplated the outfit for a few minutes. Unusual, perhaps, but striking. She had no idea what kind of women would be attending the opera that evening but she was damned if she was going to appear in a dress that had so obviously been intended for someone else. *Someone blonde and blue-eyed, perfect for their son.* She zipped up the black silk and turned to study the effect in the mirror. Nicole was right – the dress fitted her as if it had been made for her. Laure smiled to herself as she recalled the price – just over four hundred dollars. Compare that with the five thousand dollars the insipid, puffy blue number had cost; it was *madness* what these women spent on clothes. She began to unpin her hair from the large rollers she'd put in a couple of hours earlier. Her hair now hung in thick, shimmering waves rather than tight, spiral curls. The effect was softer, sleeker. Longer, too. The waves curled their way down her back, stopping just before the swell of her buttocks.

It took her ten minutes to apply her make-up and then the door opened and Daniel walked in. He stopped in his tracks when he saw her.

'Bloody hell,' he said, his voice full of admiration. 'My mother chose *that*?'

'Er, no … no. They did send the dress over but it didn't quite fit … just a little baggy around the waist. I figured she'd want it to look perfect. I'll send it back and wear it to the next outing,' Laure said quickly.

'Darling, you're so thoughtful,' Daniel said, shrugging off his jacket and coming towards her. 'Of course she'll want it to look its best. She told me how much it cost … unbelievable. You could buy a car for that money,' he said.

Laure snorted. 'You could buy a *house*,' she said, tilting her head to one side as she fastened an earring.

'But you look incredible. Just don't tell me how much *this* whole outfit cost,' he said, beginning to unbutton his trousers. He saw her watching him. 'No, don't worry, I'm not going to rip it off you – much as I'd like to,' he laughed. 'We're due at the opera at eight. Just taking a shower,' he said and disappeared into the bathroom. Laure smile to herself. Eight hundred bucks for the whole outfit. Four thousand, two hundred dollars less than his mother had spent on one dress. She applied her lipstick with a steady, confident hand.

And now here she was, sitting next to a woman whose dress, if anything, cost *more* than her mother-in-law's gift – but she was too excited to care. She'd only been to the opera a couple of times before; once in Haiti, but she'd been so young she'd fallen asleep halfway through, bored and exhausted with the struggle of following a language she couldn't understand. But tonight was different. The clothes, the jewels, the drinks, the conversation – Daniel seemed to know so many people. *Bonsoir, let me present my wife . . . hello, have you met Laure? May I present . . .?* She was kissed, grasped, hugged . . . the men looked her up and down appreciatively, the women narrowed their eyes. Laure was oblivious. She followed Daniel into the box that had been reserved for them and a few friends of his mother's. The theatre's interior, in stark contrast to its bleak, rather clinical exterior, was plush and opulent. Thick, burgundy carpeting, exquisitely polished and crafted wood, seats the size of sofas. Laure sank back, accepted a glass of champagne and tried not to stare.

The opera, *Les Troyens*, was the story of the sacking of the city of Troy, the sending into exile the Greek and Trojan princes and the epic journey of Aeneas, arriving in Rome by divine command after his notorious love affair with Dido, the north African Queen of Carthage. Laure sat, hour after hour, in the epic, mammoth performance, utterly spellbound. The story held special resonance for her, but it wasn't just the tale of the ill-fated lovers that gripped her – it was *everything*. The music, the orchestra playing below her in the pit; the way the conductor held them, and the audience, in the palm of his hand

– one flick of the wrist, a tiny gesture, a signal somewhere for someone to start or stop ... She drank it all in, wishing desperately that the evening would last all night. Afterwards, when it was over and she walked through the doors into the cool evening air, there were so many flash bulbs going off at once she couldn't tell whether one had been aimed at her. Her mind and heart whirling from the high emotions the performance had triggered, she held Daniel's hand, unaware that her gloriously flushed, excited expression singled her out among others on whose faces the habitual look of bored, sated indifference was frozen. The clicking and the whirring continued beside and around her as she and Daniel slipped into the chauffeur-driven car and sped off into the night. The following morning they woke up early. Daniel was leaving for Frankfurt to meet his father who was flying back from the Far East. 'Only for a day.' He smiled at her downcast face. 'I'll be back before you notice I'm gone.'

'Not unless I plan to be asleep for the next twenty-four hours,' Laure said tartly, getting up and tying her dressing gown. She padded across the floor in his slippers to pick up the papers that the bellhop left for them each morning. She loosened the tie that held them together as she walked back to the bed. *France-Soir, Le Figaro, Le Monde*, the *International Herald Tribune*, as well as a few assorted daily and weekly magazines that presumably the staff thought would interest her – *Paris Tempo*. She pulled *Paris Tempo* out of the stack with her free hand and almost dropped it in fright. There, in glorious colour, splashed across the front page, was *her*! Her face. Coming out of the Opéra de la Bastille the night before. She squealed.

'What is it? What?' Daniel opened his eyes. He'd been dozing for a second. 'What's the matter?'

Wordlessly, she turned the magazine round to show him. Her eyes were wide with shock. 'This! I ... just picked up the papers ...'

'So? It's a great picture of you,' Daniel laughed, taking the magazine from her. 'Madame Laure Bermann at the opening night of the Opera Bastille.' He grinned. 'Madame Laure

Bermann, the Haitian-born, aristocratic young wife of Daniel Bermann, son of millionaire Günter Bermann and heir to the ScanCorp fortune, made an impressive début at the Bastille's opening night. Dressed in black silk, the stunning Laure Bermann, who attended the same school in Haiti as Michèle Bennett Duvalier, the glamorous wife of Haitian ex-President Jean-Claude Duvalier, turned her back on tradition with a daring outfit ...' He put the magazine down. 'What're you worried about – they *loved* you!'

'I never went to school with Michèle Bennett,' Laure wailed, wringing her hands in agitation. 'I'm not from the aristocracy. What are they *talking* about?'

'Oh, you know reporters. They'll make anything up,' Daniel said, putting the magazine aside and reaching for a paper – a proper paper. 'Don't worry about it. So long as it's nothing negative ... besides, they know better. ScanCorp casts a pretty long shadow.'

'But ...' Laure began worriedly. 'What ... what if ...' She stopped. Daniel was already buried in the day's stories. She swallowed hard on the little knot of fear that was trying to force its way up her throat. What if someone saw it? Someone she knew. Someone who knew *her* from before? Someone who might have seen her ... *it*? She threw Daniel a worried glance then forced herself to walk calmly to the bathroom. She closed the door and leaned against it, her heart beating hard and fast. The dress had been a mistake. She'd *invited* the attention; she should have just worn the blue silk and that would have been it. It was stupid, just *asking* for trouble. Well, she certainly wouldn't do it again. She turned on the shower and stood under the blast, her mind still whirling.

54

Améline walked around the room, her eyes darting around her. A broken window sash, a pane missing in the French door leading on to the tiny courtyard garden; a broken downpipe. Mrs Evans, the owner, stood nervously in the doorway with her son, a surly-looking young man with terrible acne.

'I'd want to change the tables and chairs,' Améline said, looking again at the condition of the furniture. Most of the pieces were old and run-down, adding to the rather melancholy air of the place.

Mrs Evans nodded cautiously. 'But you won't be asking me for ...'

'No, no. I'll bring in my own furniture. But I *would* like to discuss some sort of discount in the rent, of course.' Améline walked towards the door. Mrs Evans and her son hesitated. It was clear they had never dealt with anyone like Améline before.

'Would you ... would you be wanting to take a look at the kitchen, miss ... er Mrs Blake?' her son stammered. He didn't quite know how to address her.

'I've already had a look, thank you,' Améline said briskly. She turned to Susan. 'I think that's it, don't you?'

'Er, yes.' It was clear Susan had never seen this side to Améline either.

'Great. Well, Mrs Evans, I think a twenty-five per cent reduction's more or less fair. In light of the furniture and the state of the kitchen, of course. I'd have to redo it from scratch. Shall I leave you to discuss it with your husband? And your son, of course.'

'Twenty-five per cent?' Mrs Evans spluttered.

'Mmm. I'll leave you to think about it, shall I?' Améline shouldered her bag, smiled at Susan and led the way out of the door.

'Gosh,' Susan said, as soon as they were safely out of earshot, 'that was awfully clever of you. You sounded *ever* so professional.'

'Horrible little woman.' Améline grinned. 'Imagine charging that amount of money for that horrible little place.'

'It's in a very good location, though,' Susan countered.

'That's why I didn't press for fifty per cent.'

'Hard as nails, you are,' Susan said admiringly. 'D'you think you'll get it?'

'Twenty-five per cent? I should think so. The place has been empty for over a year. There's hardly a queue.'

'Shall we have a drink to celebrate?' Susan said gaily. 'The bar at the Great Malvern's open.'

'Well, I haven't quite got there yet,' Améline said, a smile tugging at the corners of her mouth.

'But you will. I'm sure of it. Come on, let's have a G and T. A gin and tonic,' she added, seeing Améline's puzzled expression. 'You must have had one of those before.'

Améline shook her head. 'But it sounds lovely. Come on, it'll be my treat.'

'Absolutely not.'

'What'll you call the place?' Susan said when they'd taken their seats by the lovely bay window overlooking the gardens.

'Lulu's,' Améline said without hesitation. She looked at Susan and smiled.

'What a lovely name. Someone you know?'

Améline was quiet for a moment. Laure's name no longer produced the same sharp stab of pain – it was more like a dull, intense ache. She'd grown used to the loss; not that it made it any better, it had just changed its shape. 'She was like a sister to me,' Améline said slowly. 'At home ... before I came here.'

'I must say,' Susan said, leaning towards Améline. Two G and Ts had made her expansive. 'You're not a bit like I expected, you know.'

'Oh? What did you expect?' Améline said, sipping her own drink.

'Oh, you know, when I heard ... from Viv. About Iain. She wasn't over the moon about it in the beginning.'

'So I heard,' Améline said dryly.

'Well, you can imagine. What it looked like.'

'Not really. *I* was terrified, you know.'

'Were you? Of what?'

'Of course I was. I'd barely been outside my neighbourhood before. It was the first time I'd ever been in an aeroplane. And I couldn't speak a word of English.'

'Gosh. I'd never really thought about it.'

'I suppose that's the hardest bit, isn't it?' Améline said, taking another sip. 'It's almost impossible to know what it's like for others. When I first saw you,' she continued, beginning to laugh, 'I couldn't imagine we would ever be friends. Like when I saw Viv for the first time. She looked as though she wanted to kill me!'

'Well, you can hardly blame her. Oh, I know it was all over between her and Iain, but they're like brother and sister, really. I think she was afraid he was making a fool of himself. You know, older, white tourist meets young native girl on a tropical beach. That sort of thing.'

'That's exactly what I thought when I saw him the first time. I used to work in a hotel – you saw it all the time. But Iain wasn't like that. He really helped me and he never seemed to want anything back.'

'Are you happy, Améline? Here? With him? With us?'

Améline was quiet for a moment. 'I'm not *un*happy,' she began carefully. She had opened her heart to Viv but it didn't mean she was quite ready to open it to anyone else. 'I have a good life here,' she said. 'Iain is very ... kind to me. He's a good man. And there's this, now ...' She waved a hand in the direction of the town. 'If I manage to do this, it'll be the first time in my life I'll have something of my own ... just for me. *That* will make me very happy.' Susan nodded hesitantly. Her own life, Améline saw, was very different. A loving husband, a healthy teenage son, despite his adolescent behaviour, her parents still alive and together and living not far away; an ordinary, stable

English life. Améline liked her. Like Viv, she had a softer side to her rather brusque character that, once found, was never far away. She had been absolutely steadfast in her encouragement, even offering to go into business together but Améline was desperate to do something for herself, *by* herself. She'd reluctantly turned down her offer of financial assistance and instead they'd agreed that if it did indeed get off the ground, Susan would simply work *for* Améline; an arrangement that suited them both. In the meantime, she would act as Améline's sounding board and adviser. After all, she'd been the one to give her the necessary push when Iain's tolerance for the 'crazy' idea of running a tea shop ran dry.

Remembering her last conversation with Iain, Améline smiled. At first he'd been resolute – there was no way he'd brought her into the country to act as a glorified servant to others ... serving tea indeed! What did she think he was? A fool? He sulked for days.

But Améline was no fool, either. She'd watched Viv and listened to the stories she told of their marriage, and simply bit her tongue. There were more ways than one to make a man give in – and besides, she disliked arguing. In the end – it took two months – she got her way. He put up the cash for the initial investment and even went so far as to make a few useful comments on how she might market herself.

Viv, typically, was full of admiration. 'How d'you do it?' she asked Améline several times. 'He'd never have done that for *me*.' Améline smiled but said nothing. She had the feeling Haitian women could teach their English counterparts a thing or two about getting what they wanted.

'And anyway,' she said, lifting her glass, 'that old life is finished. I couldn't go back now even if I wanted to. There's no one left. Everyone's gone.'

'That's a shame,' Susan said, speaking from the shallows of her own experience. 'My parents still live in the house I grew up in. We're there almost every week. I can't imagine what it's like for you, never to be able to go back.'

'And I can't imagine your life, just hopping in the car and going home,' Améline said, draining her glass.

'It's not all it's cracked up to be,' Susan said, laughing. She looked at her watch. 'Speaking of which ... I've got to pick Tim up. Shall I give you a lift?'

'No, thanks. I think I'll walk up the hill. The sun's out – that's another thing I miss – the sun.'

'Yes, don't see much of it round here. Well, here's to Lulu's. I can't wait!'

It took much longer than she thought. There were so many things to think about. It was the first time in her life she'd supervised a team of builders and, by the end of five long months, she swore it would be the last. The little shop was stripped back to its bare bones; floors were ripped up, the kitchen was dismantled and ripped out; even the ceiling was taken down. Améline had a clear idea of what she wanted; rich, warm colours, but no clear idea of how to actually get there. Fortunately, Susan and Viv had – six or seven house extensions between them and there wasn't a builder in Worcestershire they couldn't handle. They stood, hands on hips, as the men hacked their way through a couple of decades of neglect and then followed them as they proceeded to build the place back up. Améline had never known there was so much stuff behind the smooth surface of a plastered wall. Pipes, conduits, wires, cement ... The list of things to do and put into place seemed endless. They made a funny trio – two smart, middle-aged women in their posh clothes and heels and the little dark-skinned girl from up the hill. By the time the signboard went over the front door, there wasn't anyone in Malvern who didn't know Améline and 'the two witches', as the builders not-so-privately called Susan and Viv. But it was all good for business, Susan said, smiling. By the time Lulu's finally opened, there wouldn't be anyone left standing within a twenty-mile radius who hadn't heard all about it.

'Can't wait, dearie!' an elderly, half-deaf woman shouted at Améline as she polished the outside windows for the last time. 'Brought a bit of colour to the place, you have!' Améline smiled at her nervously, not quite sure what she meant or how to respond.

Finally, unbelievably, it was all done. A week before Christmas; it was the best present she could have given herself. Améline stood in the doorway between the gleaming kitchen and the tea room, an apron tied around her middle and a makeshift scarf over her head, and let out a sigh of pure contentment. It wasn't fancy in any way; few items had cost more than £20. She and Viv had run up the tablecloths on Viv's ancient Singer; a pretty yellow and white gingham check pattern – Viv had found the material in John Lewis's in Worcester. They'd found most of the chairs and tables in second-hand shops and had had them sanded and painted. The mix 'n' match aspect of the room only seemed to add to its charm. The walls were a lovely deep yellow, the colour of the sunflowers in the front garden in Pétionville. A few colourful, cheap framed prints of flowers and tropical gardens and white, lace-edged curtains; it was exactly the kind of place you'd want to stop in at on your way back from the shops or for a quick coffee with friends in the morning after dropping the kids at school. Just what Améline had wanted.

She straightened a tablecloth for the last time, made sure there was a little vase with a single white carnation on every table and switched off the lights. It was almost midnight. Iain was still in the kitchen, fiddling around with the boiler and doing other, more *manly* tasks, as he liked to call them. He'd slowly come round to the idea of her owning a business and doing more with her time than looking after him. Still, Améline knew she would have to tread carefully in the coming months. Yes, it was her initiative that had made Lulu's happen but it was his that had brought her here in the first place. It was something she would do well not to forget. She turned the key in the lock and stood in the doorway for a second. Laure. What wouldn't she give to see her again?

PART FIVE

55

Beirut, Lebanon 1991

Something woke him up. He lay in the dark for a second, his heart thumping as he struggled to recognise what he already knew. There was a second's lull, the sudden, eerie quiet and then the dull, aching 'whump' as the sky fragmented in a hailstorm of explosions. He was out of his bed before the wailing and screaming began a few seconds later. He slept in his clothes, now. Plucking a jacket from the back of a chair, he ran out of the room and was downstairs and on to the street in seconds. His beeper started to buzz furiously; it would be Doménico or Lara, the two medics who lived closer to the camps. He sprinted up the street towards the main road, scanning the horizon for signs of a taxi and was lucky. 'Sabra,' he instructed the driver. 'Hurry!'

The driver turned to look at him in surprise. 'Sabra? Are you crazy? Don't you know what's happening there?'

'I'm a doctor,' Marc said curtly. The driver nodded slowly, a sad, almost wistful comprehension breaking out over his face. They drove in silence through the empty streets as the violent dawn came up.

The driver wouldn't go all the way to the camp. He dropped him off a few streets away, close to the plastic sheeting and corrugated tin roofs that marked the beginnings of the refugee camp. Marc thrust a bundle of notes at him and ran down the narrow streets. He could hear women wailing in the near distance. Gunfire rattled all around him. He turned the corner and sprinted towards the clinic. 'Marc!' Lara shouted, running towards him, a small, bleeding child in her arms. 'Doménico's at the mosque ... there's a group of women, they're hysterical,' she yelled. 'Will you go in and see what you can do?' He nodded and ran in the direction she pointed. A rocket attack. It was hard to tell who or where it had come from. Doménico and the two other Croatian doctors would already be there, tending to the wounded but it fell to Marc to establish some kind of order in which the doctors could work. Speaking Arabic was one thing; having the kind of presence that immediately brought calm and the smallest measure of relief to hysterical, frightened people, usually women and children, was quite another. It was for the latter than Marc Abadi was known. It was the reason why everyone wanted him on their team.

Half an hour later, the sobbing, incoherent crowd of thirty-odd women and children were quiet. The seriously injured had all been taken away in ambulances or been treated on the spot. An exhausted-looking Doménico leaned against a wall for a second, passing his forearm across his face in a gesture of ... compassion? Pity? Frustration? Marc couldn't tell. Doménico was both fearless and tireless but seven weeks of working in conditions that could only be described as hellish was beginning to take its toll on everyone. For over a year, all sides in the conflict had been wreaking destruction on Beirut, the city that had been home to Marc for the first seventeen years of his life. He could not recognise it now. Torn apart, fractured, disfigured ... He'd been back once in the seven weeks he'd been in Beirut to visit their old apartment on Afishreyeh Street, where he'd lived with his grandmother before her death, and his aunts, of course, only to find the building reduced to rubble. His aunts had long since fled; one to Paris and the other to Toronto. There was nothing left of the elegant, spacious apartment in which he'd learned to play the piano and his grandmother and her friends played bridge on Thursday afternoons on the balcony overlooking the seafront. Now he lived in an older, run-down building with the six other members of the medical team in the Muslim quarter of the city, an area he'd barely known existed. But that was before. Now Beirut was different. He was different.

He walked up to Doménico. 'You OK?' he asked quietly, as Doménico fished in his pockets for a cigarette. The familiar bearded face crumpled for a second, then Doménico quickly pulled himself together.

'Yeah. Bad day, yesterday. We were just about to leave when it hit. Fucking *bastards*, whoever it was.' He and Lara had obviously been there all night.

'Get some rest,' Marc said, lighting his own cigarette. 'You won't be able to operate like this.'

'I know. But ... I get home and I can't. Close my eyes but sleep just doesn't come.'

Marc nodded. As always, he was aware of treading a very fine, faint line between professional and personal concern. He liked Doménico; in another context, far away from the screaming missiles and bombs falling around them, they might have been friends. Hung out together; played a quick and furious game of football. As it was, they were plunged, headlong, into a world of such extraordinary despair that it didn't seem possible, somehow, to believe in the existence of another place or time in which they might have done just that – hung out together. Talked. Laughed. He hadn't heard laughter in almost two months. Sometimes, in the early hours of the morning and on the rare occasion the three of them were home at the same time, he heard, coming faintly though the walls, the sound of Doménico and Lara making love. He understood their relationship to be one of desperation; they hadn't known each other before they'd arrived in Beirut and it wasn't likely they would continue after they'd left, but still, he understood it very well. Something, someone, anything ... Any tiny little thing to remind each other of a life beyond the 'crack' and 'whumpf' that signalled only death. And more death.

He stubbed out his cigarette and gave Doménico's arm an ineffectual squeeze. His job, as his director had reminded him in the beginning, was to distinguish between those he could help, and those he shouldn't. It was ironic, really. Part of what he did on a day-to-day basis, when rockets weren't falling and the medical emergencies came before everything else, was to listen. Allowing the refugees and those they treated to voice their despair and fear was as necessary as replacing a torn-off limb. *Médecins du Monde* were different from most other emergency relief operations in that their personnel did not land *after* the trauma of war; they worked alongside the refugees as the conflicts occurred, providing medical and psychological care to help strengthen their defences and keep their communities, however fragile, together. Marc Abadi was one of the first emergency psychologists the organisation had ever trained. He was aware, all the time, of breaking old rules and making new ones as he went along. He took care of everyone; that was his job. But in the midst of the trauma around them, no one, himself included, ever stopped to wonder who took care of *him*.

56

London, UK 1991

Melanie picked up a blusher brush and listlessly began to powder her cheeks. She stared at her reflection in the mirror. She'd never regained the weight she'd lost since she left LA – almost four years ago, now. Not that she was complaining, mind. She liked the newly hardened look of her face and the lean, slender lines of her body. She'd never been even remotely fat but now she'd completely lost the soft, curvy look of her teenage years. She was twenty-four. No longer a child.

She flicked her hair away from her face impatiently. It needed cutting but despite the fact that she had very little to do these days – no, make that *nothing* to do – she hadn't got around to it. Yet. But soon, she promised herself soundlessly. Any minute now. She'd organise herself; figure out what she wanted to do with herself – maybe even go to college. She had to find a career, make new friends, move out of her mother's house ... The list was long. She looked at herself again and frowned. Standing in front of the mirror with her lipstick in hand suddenly reminded her of LA – all those wasted hours spent at the mirror writing silly messages to herself that no one ever saw; not A Good Thing, as Dr Hislop suggested to her in their twice-weekly sessions. Definitely not A Good Thing. The trick, or so he insisted, was to look *forwards*, not backwards. Focus on the *future*, not the past. 'Positive thinking' was his current mantra. He was her mother's 'adviser' although privately Melanie didn't think the term sufficiently described everything that Dr Hislop did. A short, balding 'non-medical practitioner, specialising in practical, forward-looking ways for you to gain clarity on what you don't like about your life, showing you powerful ways in which you can do something about it', was how he described himself, both in speech and in print. Melanie wasn't convinced. What exactly was a 'non-medical practitioner', anyway? After six months of listening to him prattle on about how to 'unleash her potential' and 'closing the gap between where you are and where you want to be', she'd recently decided she'd had enough. Dr Hislop was busy 'unleashing the potential' of half a dozen of Stella's friends and relieving them of spectacularly large sums of money in the process. It was all very dubious and not in the least bit helpful. Mike, of course, was unsympathetic. 'Get a job,' he said, before jumping into his latest sports car and roaring off up the King's Road. 'Like everyone else.'

But that was part of the problem. She didn't know anyone else. Polly, her old schoolfriend no longer lived three doors down – she'd moved to Australia 'to marry a farmer', Stella told her in tones that left Melanie unsure whether to laugh or cry. There were a couple of other girls she'd been at Weldon with, but they too had moved on; the truth was, there were very few twenty-four-year-olds who still lived at home or were still undecided about what to do with their lives. Even if few of them had careers or jobs to write home about, most of them at least had a 'significant other' in their lives who gave it the sort of direction and focus Melanie felt she *ought* to have, but didn't.

After the spectacular fashion in which she'd been let down – yet again – by a man, Melanie wasn't sure if she could bring herself to trust anyone else – least of all another man. The few times she'd roused herself to meet other friends, she'd sat in the corner of the bar, pub, restaurant, wherever, bored to tears by the talk of weddings, holidays, babies, moving to Chiswick … Was that all anyone ever talked about? Her LA life appeared to her to be other-worldly, as theirs did to her. They had nothing in common any more and, what was worse, they didn't seem to care. They wrinkled their pert little noses when she tried to describe what living in LA was like, or what it had been like to be Steve di Marco's girlfriend (she left out the bit about what he'd done to her). They turned their blue eyes towards one another, 'imagine!' or 'really?' in that perfectly polite, perfectly English way she'd forgotten that signalled utter disbelief – and that, pretty much, was that.

She was lonely. Again. Of course, the fact that she didn't *need* to get a job meant that she could afford to sit in her room or mope about the house, but that didn't make her feel any better. In fact, her lack of ambition was beginning to annoy even *her*. It was time to stop indulging herself and do something about it. But what?

She sighed and turned away from the mirror. Downstairs she could hear her mother ordering the caterers over the phone. She sighed again. Dr Hislop had clearly assisted Stella in carving out a new role for herself – she was now the Leading Lady of Charities, on the board of Oxfam, ActionAid, ChildrenFirst and half a dozen other organisations Melanie had never heard of – but Melanie just didn't understand it. Why? What for? 'It's about giving something back,' her mother had said primly when Melanie asked her.

'Giving what back?' Melanie was puzzled. As far as she could see Stella Miller was only doing what she'd always done – hosting cocktail parties and elaborate dinners. She still spent her mornings shopping and afternoons in the gym … what had changed? Fine, so she'd turned vegetarian, had recently stopped dying her hair that awful platinum colour and had even gone to church a few times, but *charities*? Her mother didn't have a charitable bone in her body.

'I don't expect you to understand it,' Stella said tartly, plucking a wilting yellow rose from the vase in the hallway and chucking it straight in the bin, 'but when you get a bit older, Melanie ... you'll see. Sometimes one needs *fulfilment.*'

'But you've always *hated* animals ...' Melanie started to say, staring at the card her mother had just received from the RSPCA thanking her for hosting such a wonderful charity dinner at the Ritz. 'Have you forgotten? What about that time I brought that stray cat home and you wouldn't even let me bring it up the driveway?'

'That was *different.* God only knew *where* it had been. And anyway, it was a long time ago. They're very *clean* at the animal shelters now, you know.' Stella looked unperturbed.

Melanie now finished applying her lipstick, resisted the temptation to scrawl something on the mirror and slipped on her shoes. She stuffed a grey silk scarf in her handbag in case it turned chilly and shut her bedroom door. 'What's tonight's dinner in aid of? Remind me ...' she asked her mother as she came down into the kitchen.

'It's this new organisation,' Stella said eagerly. '*Médecins ... médecins ...* something or other,' she said, struggling with the words. 'I only became an official patron about a month ago. Molly Graves set it up. She's on the board as well. You remember Molly, don't you?' Melanie shook her head. 'Well, anyway, Molly organised this wonderful supper for them last year at the Penrys Gallery, you know ... the one on Bond Street?' Melanie shook her head again, bewildered. 'Oh, Melanie, you've forgotten *everything.* Well, it was an absolutely *delightful* evening, *everyone* came, just *every*one. And tonight, there's this young doctor ... I think he's a psychologist, or something ... Molly showed me his picture. He's getting an award. *I'd* give him an award,' she murmured, dropping her voice.

'Ugh, Mum. Don't. Please. But why were they holding the awards in a gallery?' Melanie was genuinely puzzled.

'Because. That's the way it's done. It's to raise *money*, darling.

You have these *events*, you see, and then people pay for a table, or a ticket, or whatever; you organise everything and get all your friends to come and then the charity gets the money. It's really very simple. I don't know why you're frowning.'

'I'm not.'

'*And* I've managed to get the Bermanns on board. Patty Leatherbarrow introduced me.'

'Who're they?'

'Oh, *Melanie*.' Her mother gave one of her theatrical sighs. 'Honestly, I don't know *where* you've been for the past couple of years! Laure Bermann! She's married to Daniel Bermann — you know, the media people. She's absolutely divine. And, of course, they're loaded.'

'Ah.'

'Anyway, you'd better get ready. The car'll be here any minute.'

'I *am* ready,' Melanie said looking down at her dress, slightly confused. Wasn't it obvious?

'Is that what you're wearing?'

'What's wrong with it?' She'd chosen a simple black wrap-around dress with a thin gold belt; bare legs and a pair of high-heeled peep-toe shoes that she'd been unable to resist buying the previous week. There was something almost Fifties about them which she very much liked.

'Nothing,' Stella said reluctantly. 'Only it's a little ... well, *plain*, darling. A bit severe.'

'It's simple, Mum, not plain,' Melanie said tartly, looking scornfully at Stella's ridiculously complicated outfit with pleats and tucks and swags in half a dozen places, none of them particularly flattering. 'Classic, if you prefer.'

'Boring,' Stella corrected her. 'It's important to make an *effort* at these things,' she said earnestly. 'It helps with the fund-raising and—'

'Can we just *go*, please?' Melanie interrupted her. The last thing she wanted was a lecture on her looks. Or anything thing else for that matter.

'Oh, darling, why are you always so *negative*?'

'Negative? Me?'

'Mmm. Terribly negative, darling. Oh, goody ... the driver's here.'

There was nothing to distinguish the overdressed socialites walking through the doors at Café Royale from their equally overdressed counterparts on their way to the theatre or dinner. Melanie looked around her and tried not to giggle. She'd never been around so many platinum blondes in her life – and she'd spent three years in LA! Most of the attendees were glamorous women like Stella. It was obvious that, in the time she'd been away, charity had suddenly become an industry. She straightened her shoulders, fixed a smile on her face and tried to ignore the flash bulbs as she and Stella climbed the stairs. Not that anyone was pointing a camera in her direction specifically. Not even the tabloids were interested in her any more. Now there were hundreds of other pretty, young, rock-star daughters in town with much higher hemlines and the sorts of fast-living crises that made front page news. No one was curious about twenty-something-year-old Melanie Miller in her simple, classic outfits and general, all-round lack of direction. Who'd want to read about *that*?

'Stella, how *wonderful* to see you ...'

'Darling, you look positively *edible*.'

'Oh, I love your dress!'

'Gosh, haven't seen you in simply *ages*, darling, where've you been?'

Melanie rolled her eyes. The circus had begun.

Marc looked out across the sea of carefully styled hairdos, watched the cigarette smoke curling upwards in the air mingling with the heavy scent of expensive perfume and ran a finger under his collar. He wasn't used to wearing a tie. He sighed. Show time. He understood well enough the advantages of evenings like this but he still couldn't get over the surprise of leaving Beirut in one breath and arriving at – he glanced down at the programme in his hand to check – the Café Royale the next. His ears were still attuned to the sounds of gunfire and the steady thump of exploding bombs, not the tinkle of wine glasses and the murmur of small talk. It was surreal. He looked around for Doménico and Lara. They were sitting at the table closest to the stage. They too wore the bemused expressions of people in a state of heightened unreality. He glanced at Lara again; it was the first time he'd seen her in anything other than combat fatigues and grubby T-shirts. She fidgeted nervously with the straps of her evening dress.

'Marc ...' Someone spoke behind him. He turned. It was Dr Villela, the outgoing director of the organisation he worked for. 'Glad you could make it,' she said. 'Thought we'd never manage to drag you away.' She beamed at him. 'Congratulations on the award, by the way.' Marc nodded his thanks. It still seemed too far away from his daily reality to take it in. He wasn't sure he could even remember what he'd been awarded. 'I hope you've got your speech ready,' she murmured, noticing his expression. 'That's what they'll all be waiting to hear.' She gestured at the crowd.

'Something'll come to me.' He smiled faintly. 'I'm still getting used to wearing clean clothes.'

'I'm sure it will. Look, you're on the second table on the right. You'll be sitting with Stella Miller and her daughter. Lord Carruthers is also on the table; be as nice as you can, won't you? We're desperately in need of new funding streams.'

'Always,' Marc said, straightening his shoulders. He stood back as she walked into the room. He could see his aunt about to take her seat, positively glowing with pride. She'd flown in from Paris that morning. He smiled again. The evening meant a lot to her. If not to him.

Twenty minutes later, the little ceremony was over. Marc stepped away from the podium that had been erected in the middle of the room, his fingers still tingling from the pressure of shaking half a dozen hands. He couldn't remember what he'd said, only that he'd resisted the temptation to lecture the hundred-odd guests dotted around the room who probably wouldn't be able to point to Lebanon on a world map. He'd understood as soon as he looked out over their eager, expectant faces that that wasn't why they'd each paid over two hundred pounds to attend the evening's dinner. A small fortune, especially when he thought of what it could buy elsewhere. But that wasn't the point, he reminded himself as he threaded his way to the table Dr Villela had pointed out. Unfortunately, his aunt was seated elsewhere. She obviously couldn't provide the sorts of contacts that Lord Carruthers could.

'Dr Abadi,' a blonde, fussily-dressed woman gushed as he approached. She half rose from her chair as he took his. 'That was *too* wonderful for words. You're an absolute *inspiration* to us all.' She beamed at him expectantly. Marc wondered what on earth he was supposed to say. Someone giggled softly, somewhere. He glanced at the young woman sitting on the blonde's right. She'd quickly covered her mouth with a hand but her eyes sparkled mischievously. 'I'm Stella Miller,' the blonde said, claiming his attention again. 'May I introduce you ... Lord Carruthers ...'

'Good evening,' Lord Carruthers said, swallowing a mouthful of wine before extending his hand.

'And this is my daughter, Melanie.' The young woman who'd giggled held out a hand. He shook it, aware as he did so of the sudden and unexpected rush of blood to his face. She was beautiful; he registered the details almost automatically. Long, glossy dark hair, startling blue eyes, pale alabaster skin, and at the base of her neck a single diamond nestled in the small hollow between her collarbones. He sat down. Perhaps the evening wouldn't be quite as tedious as he'd feared?

'This must be ghastly for you,' she murmured as he took his seat beside her. Marc turned to look at her in surprise.

'Ghastly? How so?'

'Well, I can't imagine what Beirut's like but I bet it's nothing like this,' she said in a low voice, her eyes sweeping across the room.

Marc looked at her again. She had the kind of voice he'd only ever heard on television – perfectly modulated, slightly husky. No one he knew spoke like that. 'Er, no ... it's a little different.'

'I'll say. Look, shall I pour you some wine? Mummy's going to monopolise you for the rest of the evening. Brace yourself.'

He laughed. There was something intriguing about her that had nothing to do with her looks. He would have liked to talk to her but, just as she'd warned, her mother laid a hand on his arm and for the next hour, at least, there was little opportunity. But he remained aware of her. She chatted and laughed in the same low voice with the man who was sitting on her right and Marc found himself inexplicably agitated, listening with half an ear to their conversation, unable to take part. It was only towards the end of the evening when people began to leave their tables and circulate that Stella Miller finally got up and left his side, releasing him. He turned to her but she had pushed back her chair and was already on her feet.

'Leaving?' he asked, looking up at her. She was wearing a black dress of some soft, unidentifiable material that clung to her, skimming lightly over the two just-visible peaks of her hipbones and sweeping up the long, taut plane of her stomach. A thin gold belt caught the light as she moved. He swallowed.

'Only to the loo,' she said, laughing. 'Back in a sec.' He watched her walk away. It had been months since he'd experienced the kind of sharp, dizzying hunger to know more about a woman he'd only just met. Years, even. He picked up his wine glass, twirling the thin stem between his fingers. He felt even more out of place.

Standing in front of the long mirror in the ladies' powder room, Melanie quickly retouched her lipstick, thinking about the man who'd been sitting next to her for over an hour. She'd barely spoken to him but there was something about him that intrigued her. Dr Marc Abadi. Her mother, for once, had been right. As soon as she saw him winding his way carefully through the tables towards theirs, his height and physical manner setting him apart from every other man in the room, she'd done a double take. She'd so thoroughly primed herself for a boring evening spent sitting between some old, balding, smug do-gooder and the pompous Lord Carruthers that when her mother pointed him out to her, walking towards them, she'd thought at first she was joking. He wasn't much older than her! 'Early thirties, tops,' her mother whispered. 'He's just lovely, don't you agree? I can't remember where he's from ... Somewhere in Africa, I think. Although he's not *terribly* dark, is he? Not like some of them. Oh, I don't care *where* he's from, he's just lovely, isn't he?'

'*Mum*,' Melanie hissed at her, watching nervously as he approached. 'Will you stop?' But he was already at the table and her mother was in no mood to stop. In fact, she so thoroughly monopolised the lovely Dr Abadi that Melanie could barely get a word in edgeways. She'd spent most of the evening drinking wine and pretending to talk to the creep sitting on her other side, all the while with a growing awareness of the man with skin the colour of chocolate and dark, aubergine-coloured eyes sitting right there. So close she could reach out and touch him. She stared at her reflection, unnerved. She was drunk, that was it. And her nose was shiny. She quickly dabbed at it with a tissue and closed her purse. Her fingers were trembling slightly. She walked back into the dining hall, aware of the faint but growing knot of excitement in the pit of her stomach.

He was still sitting where she'd left him. She slid into her seat and turned to him, smiling widely. He was interested, she could tell. Something about his slow, almost lazy blink as he looked at her and the subtle shift of his body towards hers. Melanie was good at reading the signs. Someone came up to talk to him. She studied his face for a minute or two as he talked. It wasn't just that he was good-looking. In fact, she realised as she watched him talk, his appeal was as much to do with his manner as with anything else. He was ... she searched for the right word ... still. Yes, still. There was a quiet certainty to his manner that she found herself inexplicably drawn to. She was long accustomed to being surrounded by physically perfect human beings but that sort of beauty had nothing to do with the calm, quiet aura of this man who, it was hard to grasp, was only a few years older than her. There was something so reassuring about his quiet, self-assured grace that answered a restless, unformed yearning deep inside her. The taut edginess that she'd found so attractive in Steve suddenly seemed childish and attention-seeking in the face of this man's cool, watchful gaze. Surprisingly, she didn't feel at all nervous. Without saying a word, he'd managed to bring out a certain playfulness in her own manner; he liked it, she could tell. It made her just that little bit bolder, more like her old self.

'How long are you here for?' she asked, gracefully tucking a strand of her long hair behind her ear.

'I go back tomorrow.'

'Already?'

''Fraid so.'

'Gosh, they don't let you out for long, do they?' she smiled, almost ruefully.

'No, not really. Though,' he turned in his chair slightly, 'I wouldn't want to get too used to this.' He indicated the rest of the room with a slight gesture. 'I still can't quite believe I'm here.'

'Well, where else would you rather be?' He glanced at her, surprised. Melanie swallowed. She saw he'd understood the question exactly as she'd intended, consciously or not.

He looked at her carefully for a moment. They stared at each other. 'What're you offering?' he asked eventually, his voice giving nothing away.

'Whatever you want.' No, it wasn't just the wine. She'd never been this bold before.

She could see her mother's questioning eyes on her as she got up and left the table with Marc Abadi. *I'll be back later*, she mouthed over the heads that separated them. She didn't wait to see her response. Marc bent down to say something to an elderly woman sitting at the table in front of theirs – his mother? – and then suddenly they were standing outside, set down among the crowds still scurrying along Regent Street. She turned to him. 'My place or yours?' she said with a slightly awkward laugh.

'Whichever. I'm staying in a hotel not far from here.'

'Then let's go there. I live in Chelsea – it's miles away.' She gave another laugh. 'And my mother might burst in on us.'

'Embarrassing,' he agreed, laughing. He stepped into the road and flagged down a cab. 'Claridges,' he told the driver as he held open the door.

'Claridges?' Melanie murmured as the cab pulled away from the kerb. 'I thought you were an aid worker?'

'My aunt,' he said with a smile in his voice. 'Her second home.'

'Was that her at the table in front of us?'

'Yes. She came in from Paris this morning.'

'Ah. I thought it might be your mother.'

'No.' His answer was short. Melanie leaned back in her seat. What on earth was she doing with a complete stranger sitting in the back of a black cab on the way to his hotel room? But Marc Abadi didn't feel like a stranger. And when, in the gloomy darkness of the cab's interior, he touched her knee lightly, she turned to him with the whole length of her body and the kiss was slow and long, and only the beginning.

He held her arm as he paid the taxi driver – the distance to the hotel was so short they could have walked faster – and was acutely aware of her scent on his skin and, strangely, in his mouth, as they stepped into the lift. Three floors up with the sweet, heavy feel of her body against his. He followed her into the room, conscious only of the smell of her hair and the taut arch of her back under his hands. She shrugged off her coat and guided his hands along the thin fabric of her dress. At last he was able to trace the path of the necklace he had admired. He trailed the tips of his fingers down her ear lobes, across the hollows of her cheekbones down to the swell of her breasts. She stiffened, her whole body shivering with pleasure. She mumbled something inarticulate and grabbed hold of his hand. She was smiling; he could just make out the flash of teeth in the dark and then suddenly she was on top of him, lifting her arms above her head as she unwrapped her dress in that

305

languid way that only women knew. He was taut with desire. She unbuckled his trousers and with the minimum of fuss and gesture slid on top of him, her hair falling over his chest as she swallowed him, whole. He came almost at once. It was the most exciting thing that had ever happened to him. Melanie. Wine. A hotel room. He closed his eyes.

She woke early, distracted by the unfamiliar sound of someone snoring gently above her left ear. It took her a second to work out where she was and how she'd arrived there. Then her whole body was suffused with a tender, pleasurable blush as she recalled what had passed between her and Marc Abadi, the man who lay sleeping next to her, one arm thrown casually across her stomach, his face buried in the pillow beside her head. He stirred, as if he sensed her gaze, and the hand lying across her turned, catching hold of her arm, just above the elbow. She felt herself being pulled into the hot, tight fold of his arms and the blush that had started in the depth of her stomach began to spread slowly through her as his excitement grew. This time it was different – there was little of the frantic rush of the night before. He took his time, and the pleasure that he wrung from her at the last moment was like nothing she'd ever felt before. She put a hand to her face as he slipped from her; it would have seemed odd, she thought, for him to see her cry. She buried her face in the pillow and pretended to fall asleep. She lay awake in the semi-darkness beside him, listening to the sound of his breathing until she too dozed off.

'Melanie.' She struggled awake again. Marc was standing beside the bed, fully clothed. She struggled upright. 'No, don't get up. Sleep as long as you want.'

'Wh ... where ... where are you going?'

'To the airport. My flight's at ten.'

'What time is it?' she asked, looking around for her watch.

'It's just after seven. Stay as long as you want.'

'No, no ... I'd better get up.' She sat up in bed, holding the sheet to her breasts. She was suddenly gripped by panic.

He was leaving. In a few minutes he would walk out the door and she would probably never see him again. She glanced at him. He was already packed. He was closing his small neat suitcase, which lay across the table at the far end of the room. He was ready to go. 'So ...' she said, trying to make light of the situation. 'That was fun, wasn't it? Not the sort of thing I usually do, mind you. I never know quite what to say in these situations, do you? See you around, I suppose ...'

'Melanie ...' He looked up at her, a strange expression in his eyes. 'I'll call you from Beirut.'

'Oh, don't be silly. You don't have to call. No pressure. It was fun. We should do it again if you're ever in town. I—'

'I'll call,' he cut her off. 'Give me a number.' He jotted it down, walked quickly to the bed and kissed her, hard. 'See you, Melanie Miller.'

And then he was gone. The sound of the door closing gently behind him was the most desolate thing she'd heard in a long, long while. He'd call. Yeah, right. Wasn't that what they all said?

57

Daniel stood at the tall windows in the living room and watched Laure run down the steps, her hair flying behind her. She was meeting Shelley, the girl she'd worked with at the Blue Room and with whom – oddly, it seemed to him – she'd stayed in touch. She'd said something about the two of them going to the Caribbean markets up near Skokie; part of Chicago he'd never been to, never seen. As she hurried across the road to meet her, it occurred to him, not for the first time, that there were parts of Laure herself he'd never seen. She was a strange combination of almost polar opposites; warm, wonderfully affectionate, even playful one minute, closed and sealed off the next. There were times when something crossed her face; a look, a fleeting glance at something and he could physically see it; the shutters coming down, the immediate withdrawal into some private place in herself that he could never, would never, reach. Every time he thought about the first time he'd seen her, standing over that man who was three times her size, all the anger and hurt in the world in her voice, he felt stupidly close to tears. He'd wanted to rush over and hold her, hold fistfuls of those black, tight curls in his hands and take the pain in her away.

Ridiculous, really – he gave an embarrassed laugh. Laure didn't need anyone to take care of her, or wipe away her pain. He'd understood that later, after he'd got to know her a little better. She was one of the strongest people he'd ever met. She said so little about where she was from. He knew the basics; the bare facts of her life that he'd managed over the past four years of their marriage to extract from her. She hated talking about herself, she told him. She'd grown up with her grandmother and someone called Améline, a sort of half-servant, half-family member. From what she'd told him, he gathered she and Améline were close, more like sisters, she'd said. She'd gone to a small private school in Pétionville which he knew was where the rich in Haiti lived. So she was rich. Or at least the family had been, once? He was full of curiosity. She'd shrugged. No, not rich. But yes, educated. They spoke French at home, not Créole. He knew, too, that her mother had run off when she was very small and that she'd come to the US to live with her. It obviously hadn't worked out, he was able to surmise, which was why she'd worked in a *burrito* bar and as a cocktail waitress when he met her. In his mind's eye, a picture of Laure had been formed; of someone who'd had more than her fair share of bad luck and lousy circumstances and whose life, if things had been different, wouldn't have been all that removed from his. She was different and yet she was the same; a peculiar contrast that had kept him spellbound. He suspected it always would. Just when you thought you'd got to the real Laure, another layer peeled off and something else was unexpectedly exposed. But if there had been some awful, ghastly tragedy of the proportions he sometimes, almost fearfully, imagined, surely she'd have said? She didn't. Without ever saying it outright, he understood that she was asking him to trust her. To let her open up to him in her own time and in her own way. Laure – at one level the most straightforwardly accepting and uncomplicated person he'd ever met and at another, the most hidden.

He turned away from the window and walked over to his desk. The step he was about to take would change everything. He hoped Laure would approve. It was something he'd been dreaming about for years, before he even met her. He wanted out. He wanted to leave ScanCorp and Chicago, the cloying, watchful eyes of his parents and his friends. He snorted, brought up short by the word. *Friends?* Arseholes. Every last one. He was *still* angry over the way they'd treated Laure. It was the Bermann in him, as his mother always used to say. Slow to anger, slow to forget. When he was younger, she was forever being called in to the headmaster's study at Eton to try to explain why Daniel wouldn't speak to some unfortunate child who'd once kicked him or who'd copied his notes without asking. 'But he's a bully,' Daniel would protest, looking from one to the other in bewilderment. 'Why should I speak to him?' Or, 'He cheated. I hate cheats!' He'd always had the most ridiculously over-developed sense of justice. That came from her, his mother said proudly. From her side of the family. It certainly wasn't a Bermann trait. She used to tease him about all the stray waifs he brought home for half-term and at Christmas. So-and-so's parents were away, or worse, dead. He'd once brought home twins from Hong Kong whose parents had just been killed in a car crash. They'd stayed at the Bermanns' holiday home in Provence for the *entire* summer. In the end, even he'd been relieved to see them off. Honestly. 'What a funny little boy you are,' she'd said to him, ruffling his hair in a rare gesture of affection. 'You'd adopt the staff, if you could!'

He picked up a picture of himself taken almost twenty years ago. Laure liked it. His first day at prep school. His trusting, open face stared back at him, his curls hidden by the stiff-peaked cap. He put it away from him, embarrassed by the innocence in his eyes. That was before he'd been sent away to boarding school; before he'd realised that whatever else his mother wanted in life, she didn't really want him. It was the *idea* of a son she liked, not the flesh and blood. Especially when he refused to conform to plan. *Her* plan, not his, he reminded himself, lips compressing in a single, tight line.

His plan – the one he'd been working on for almost a year now – was quite simple. He wanted to leave. He and Laure would move away from Chicago, not just from his parents but from the narrow, claustrophobic world of the people he knew and relocate to London. In London, there would be his old university crowd; interesting, thoughtful people who would love Laure. They wouldn't give a damn about the colour of her skin or the fact that she'd worked as a cocktail waitress. In London, they'd be free to start a new, better sort of life. Laure had always talked about going to college, studying art, perhaps; there were hundreds of art schools in London – she would love it. London would love her. And for him – his stomach tightened in pleasurable anticipation at the thought of what he wanted to do. The film distribution company he wanted to set up with three university friends would change the way ScanCorp ran its media empire. Their company would help finance and distribute the sorts of films he wanted to see, not just the sort that made ScanCorp stacks of money. Independent, edgy, avant-garde films. Films that reflected the kind of life he wanted to live, not the kind he'd been born into. Films about politics, people and places that were a million miles away from the Lincoln Park drawing rooms and the cellars stacked with wine. Yes, moving to London would be the best thing for them both. Of that he was quite, quite sure.

But if he'd thought – even for a single, fleeting second – that his father would let him leave ScanCorp without a fight, he saw that he was mistaken. There were scenes in his parents' apart-ment that he thought he would never, ever forget. Günter's face, purple with rage; his mother's swollen with tears. *Didn't he understand that everything they'd worked for was for him? How could he even think of walking away? It was that woman, wasn't it?*

She'd put him up to it, hadn't she? His mother was convinced. She knew something like this would happen. *Just look at the way she threw her gift of clothing back in her face. Did she have any idea the trouble she'd gone to? No breeding. None whatsoever.* The accusations came at him, thick and fast.

But Daniel was adamant. He kept Laure well out of sight until he'd finally – and not without pain – convinced them that a few years of living and working independently of them would suit everyone. It would polish and sharpen him up, hone his skills. In a few years, he promised, he would come back into the fold. He was married now. Time to start a family. London would be a good place to do it. His mother closed her eyes briefly in genuine anguish as he said it.

It took him a while to find the right moment to talk to Laure about the move. Once he'd broken the news to his parents, it occurred to him suddenly that he'd made rather a lot of decisions without even asking her what she thought. With everything in place, he could hardly present it to her as a choice, could he? What if she didn't want to go? He put it off several times for fear of spoiling a particularly nice dinner or a trip to the theatre. Finally, when he couldn't think of another reason *not* to bring it up, he just blurted it out.

'What would you say … how … Look, Laure … would you like to live in London?' he said to her over breakfast one morning, his words betraying his awkwardness. She stared at him, her mouth full of cereal. 'I … I thought about Paris but my French isn't all that great and … and I just thought London would be … a … a good place for what I want to do …' he trailed off.

Laure swallowed quickly. 'For what you want to do …?' she repeated, sounding a little unsure of herself.

'Well, yes … you know the film company I've been talking about. It looks like … I've sort of decided … Look, the thing is …' he stammered, wondering why on earth he hadn't thought to bring it up with her beforehand, properly. It occurred to him that he was behaving in precisely the same way his father did.

Decisions were always presented as a *fait accompli*, no discussion, no input, no right to his own opinion. 'I'm sorry,' he said finally, when he couldn't stand the silence any longer. 'Look, darling, I know I should've talked to you a bit more about it. Look, here's the thing ...' he said nervously, launching into a long and complicated explanation of his motives for moving.

Laure listened to him, her mind racing. She couldn't quite believe he'd sprung the move on her in that way ... just like that. A snap of the fingers and there they were, in a new home, a new country, a new career. It was all so easy for him. She tried to imagine London; from the little she knew of it, it was an enormous, grimy city with none of the charm of Paris, for example, and terrible food. Wasn't that what everyone said about the British? She shivered suddenly. Leaving Chicago would mean leaving everything she'd tried to build for herself in the years she'd been there. A few friends, the places she liked to go: Wicker Park in the spring and Navy Pier in the summer; the sight of the boats, nosing and jostling each other in the marina as soon as the lake had melted and there was warmth in the air. The skyscrapers clustered around downtown ... the towers ... she swallowed. It would mean leaving Belle behind and ... and her child.

'I'm sorry,' Daniel was saying, his face full of concern. 'I'm a pig to spring it on you like this. We won't go if you don't want to, I promise ...' His voice was miserable.

Laure shook her head slowly. 'No, of course we'll go. It ... it's the best thing for you ... for your company. I'm sure I'll ... I'll like it.'

'Of course you'll like it! Why don't we go next weekend, just to have a look. See if you like it.'

Laure stared at him. 'Next week?' she said, stunned yet again by the speed at which things moved in Daniel's world.

'Yes, we could leave on Friday night, spend a week or so there. How does that sound?'

Laure smiled, shaking her head. 'It sounds ... incredible.'

The relief on his face was palpable. He jumped up, full of energy and enthusiasm again. 'Right, I'll get Betty to sort out tickets. Oh, you're going to *love* it, darling, I know you will. Just wait and see.'

Laure nodded slowly. 'I'm sure I will,' she said, touched by his concern. She watched him rush from the room, his mind already full of the details that required his attention. She got up and walked to the window, arms wrapped around herself. Apart from meeting Daniel, Chicago had brought her nothing but pain. She could leave it all behind, make a fresh start. Forget about everything, including ... *him*. The street below suddenly blurred with tears. Could she really do that? Forget about him? Give up the mad, dangerous hope that lay buried at the bottom of her heart of bumping into him one day, somewhere in this vast, anonymous city; give up the chance, however remote, of seeing him for herself, knowing that he was all right, that he was being looked after and cared for in a way that she wouldn't have been able to do herself. Without ever daring to say it out loud, she'd been carrying around the tiniest hope that she might one day see him again. She would sooner have died than admit it, even to herself, but every once in a while, when a child crossed her path or she walked beside a group of schoolchildren of roughly the age he would have been, she stopped, shoving her hands in her pockets to stop them from shaking and searched the faces in front of her, scanning them desperately for some sign of recognition, a cast of the features that would remind her, in whatever small way, of Delroy ... even of herself. But so far, there'd been nothing. Not a single child in whose image she could see anything – anything at all.

And now he wanted to take her away. To London. Where the chances of *that* happening were less than zero. But there was another way to look at it, she thought, wiping her face in the privacy of the bathroom. Without realising it, Daniel was offering her a way out of the painful labyrinths of her own memory. She ought to take it. She *would* take it. She would make the best of the unwitting gift.

The move itself was surprisingly easy, nothing like the moves she'd made before. Aside from the few personal possessions she'd brought with her when she married Daniel and moved into his town house, and the clothes and shoes she'd bought since, Laure had very little to contribute to the teams of removal men who staggered up and down the stairs. She looked on dubiously as they carted away pieces of furniture that Octavia Bermann had obviously chosen for him that would be put into storage for what Daniel called 'the foreseeable future'. She was relieved to think none of it was meant to accompany them; she'd never much cared for Octavia's taste. Daniel was beside himself with excitement and optimism; it was infectious. Laure began to count the weeks until their departure and even when Daniel broke the news to her that he would have to go a couple of weeks ahead of her to organise things, she simply smiled. He was setting up the grandly titled Institute for Contemporary Film with two university friends whom, he swore, were nothing like the friends he'd had in Chicago. Laure hadn't yet met them but it would be one of the first dinner parties they would hold, he promised. He couldn't wait to show her off.

On her last night in Chicago, she finished clearing the bathroom shelves of the few items that hadn't made it into the packers' boxes and emptied the waste-paper basket. She couldn't bear the thought of her mother-in-law poking about in their home and finding anything worth complaining about. She gave the empty shelves one final wipe and closed the door. Her suitcase lay, open-jawed, on the bed. There was only one thing left to pack. She crossed the room to the wardrobes and pushed back the sliding door. A set of underwear and a silk camisole were all that remained of her undergarments; everything else was already on its way to London. She drew the small, tissue-wrapped package from one of the empty shelves and took a deep breath. It was more than four years since she'd bought it and not once had it left her side. She unwrapped the little jumpsuit for the umpteenth time, pressed the soft blue linen to her lips and inhaled. It still smelled new, unworn, but she didn't care. It was the only thing she had ever bought for him, the only physical reminder of the boy she'd never seen. She laid it tenderly back in its tissue sheath and carried it to the suitcase on the bed. It would go with her to London; it would go with her wherever she went.

The following morning, she flew alone to London. Daniel was waiting for her with the largest bunch of roses she'd ever seen and a smile that threatened to split his face in half. It was September in London and the leaves were just beginning to turn. After the humid, white heat of Chicago, the soft grey light was a welcome relief. She loved the roomy black cab that ferried them from the airport to the Bermanns' Chelsea apartment overlooking the Thames. He had a surprise for her, he said, opening the front door to a grand, old-fashioned apartment that, to her, looked pretty much the same as their Chicago home. Rather staid and dull. What was the surprise? He wouldn't say. It was a surprise.

'But where are we going?' she asked him for the umpteenth time the next morning as they climbed into the back of another black cab.

'You'll see,' Daniel said enigmatically. His face was impassive. He gave the driver an address ... Primrose Hill ... where was that? You'll see. She shook her head at him. It was most out of character; normally he couldn't keep a thing to himself.

Half an hour later they pulled up outside a tall, white house sandwiched in the middle of a crescent-shaped terrace with a small garden in front. Laure peered up at the elegant façade. 'Who lives here?' she asked as Daniel paid the driver and pushed open the little gate.

'We do.'

Laure stared at him. 'We? This ... this belongs to you?'

'Us, darling. It's ours. I bought it last week.'

'But ... you didn't say ... you didn't tell me you were look-ing for a house,' Laure said, watching incredulously as he pulled a large bunch of keys from his jacket pocket. 'When ...?'

'I knew you wouldn't want to live in my parents' place – not that I wanted to live there either,' he added hastily, pushing her gently through the front door. 'And then Doug mentioned he'd seen this place for sale. He lives just on the other side of the park. I came by to look at it about a fortnight ago and we've only just completed the sale. D'you like it?' he asked anxiously.

'Like it? I *love* it!' Laure exclaimed, staring up at the gracefully curving staircase above them.

'Oh, thank God for that! Come on, let me show you around.' Daniel pushed open a set of doors to the right of the hallway to reveal a pair of large, elegantly proportioned rooms, separated by a folding door. 'Living room,' he said, opening the folding panel. 'And the dining room.' He walked over to the wooden shutters and opened them. Laure gasped. The dining room overlooked a large garden that sloped away from the house and ran down to the canal. A small wooden pier jutted out into the water; the early autumn light filtered its way through the yellowing leaves of the trees she couldn't name at the foot of the garden.

'The garden? It's ours, too?'

'Every square inch,' Daniel said, unable to keep the smile out of his voice. 'Come on, there's lots to see.'

It took them the better part of an hour to go through the whole house. Three bedrooms on the second floor and a charming little attic apartment on the third; the formal living and dining rooms on the first; and then the kitchen and the large family room in the basement. It was huge, even by Chicago standards. Laure followed him from room to room, almost unable to take it all in. This was *theirs*?

'It needs decorating,' Daniel said as they walked into the empty kitchen. 'I thought ...' He turned to her almost shyly. 'I thought ... maybe you'd like to ...?'

Laure stared at him. 'I ... I've never decorated anything in my life,' she said, a little nervously. 'I wouldn't know ...'

'Oh, we'd get someone to help you,' he said quickly, 'you wouldn't have to do it alone. But I just thought, well, I'm going to be so busy with the Institute and everything ... it might be something to do. Just for a couple of months, until you settle in.'

Laure nodded, her mind already beginning to race ahead. The house was beautiful, there was no doubt about it, but it was old and slightly shabby – new colours, new furniture, new fabrics ... She turned to him, her eyes sparkling. 'I can't think of *anything* else I'd rather do,' she said, the excitement in her voice rising. 'I can't believe you've done this! I'm going to *love* it.'

'I knew you would,' Daniel said, grabbing hold of her and pulling her close to him. He kissed her, hard. 'Do it exactly the way you want it,' he said against her mouth. 'Just the way you like.'

'But you've got to like it too,' she murmured.

'I like what *you* like. As simple as that.'

'But ...'

'But nothing. You've always got a "but" hidden up your sleeve,' he said teasingly. 'I just want you to have fun, darling. I just want you to be happy.' Laure buried her face in his neck. There it was again. *I just want you to be happy.* Didn't he realise how little it took? She slid her hands underneath his shirt and rested the palms against the soft, warm hair on his chest. She could feel his heartbeat against her skin. His generosity was overwhelming. What on earth had she done to deserve it?

58

Lulu's was an instant success, just as Viv and Susan had predicted. From the first morning the doors opened, the place was packed. In the morning, there were the shoppers on their way to Worcester and Cheltenham popping in for a cup of tea and succumbing to the pastries and home-made biscuits laid out on the gingham-covered wooden table in front. At lunchtime she just couldn't keep up with the demand for her open sandwiches and light, fluffy quiches. In the afternoon, droves of school kids came in, having abandoned Serendipity's across the road almost as soon as she opened. By five p.m., when she pulled the curtains shut and locked up the kitchens, Améline had just enough energy to walk to the bus stop. By the time the bus pulled up outside her house, she was fast asleep. Evenings were spent baking and preparing supplies for the following day. After the third week when Iain complained his way through the entire weekend that there was nothing to eat in the house and that he'd barely seen his wife, she realised she needed help. As usual, it was Viv who came to the rescue.

'You need staff, Améline. You need someone to open up in the mornings and someone to help you out at lunchtime ... preferably someone who can cook. I'll ask around. There's bound to be someone around here. There's at least half a dozen catering colleges between here and Worcester, for Christ's sake!' Améline looked at her gratefully. It was hard work. Not that she was afraid of hard work – on the contrary. But Iain's complaints were beginning to wear her down. With the confidence that had come from talking to Viv and the encouragement she and Susan had given her, so too had come the realisation that perhaps she wasn't as hopeless a case as she'd always imagined. Perhaps she wasn't the desperate, orphaned refugee Iain had been kind enough to take in. Perhaps – and it still required a certain amount of nerve to even *think* it – perhaps she was more in control of her own life than she'd always thought?

At the end of her first month in business when she, Susan and Viv sat down at the kitchen table to take stock, she almost wept when she realised just how much money she'd made. Susan showed her how to reconcile the books, what monies to put aside for taxes, wages, overheads ... The list of things to pay for seemed endless. But even then, when everything had been squared away, there was a tidy little sum left over – profit. *Her* profit. She deposited the amount in her bank account with shaking hands. Viv had found and interviewed a young local girl named Claire, who'd just finished her third year at catering school and was hoping to earn enough money to go to Australia one day. She was a bright, cheerful girl with an accent Améline could barely understand but she was a hard worker and she seemed able to handle the lunchtime rush while Améline got on with the cooking. That way, she didn't have to cook at night when she got home and Iain's complaints slowly began to dwindle away.

One morning in late February, when the daffodils had just begun to poke their yellow heads through the hard, frosty ground, a group of workmen came tramping through the door. Améline looked up from the counter; she liked the fact that Lulu's attracted all sorts of people, from the affluent, middle-class mums who parked their Land Rovers across the street and gathered in the mornings to chat to each other, to the local school kids, mouths stuffed with chewing gum that made it even harder to understand the slow, lilting Worcestershire burr; even the builders from the huge shopping centre that was under construction down the road ... She liked the buzz and warmth of the different groups who came through the door.

'Mornin', love,' one of them said, walking towards the counter. She'd seen him before – a young, rather nice-looking man with startlingly blue eyes and a jaw that always looked in need of a proper shave.

'Hello,' Améline smiled back. 'Claire will be with you in just a moment.'

''S all right,' he said, squinting at the cakes she'd laid out on the counter. 'Think I'll 'ave summat different today, like.'

Améline blinked. 'Sorry?'

'A change. I'll 'ave summat else for a change. Been 'aving butties a' week ...' He broke off, laughing. 'I'm only teasing,' he said, his accent suddenly much clearer. 'I heard from one of the other lads you don't follow the way we speak round here.' He grinned at her. 'Not that that's how we speak, mind you ... I'm just havin' you on.'

Améline smiled. 'No, sometimes ... it's a little hard,' she said shyly.

'Not from round here, then, are you?'

'No,' she said, shaking her head. She wondered why he'd

come up to the counter to talk to her. She could see his friends looking across the café at them, grinning.

Well, where're you from, then?'

'From Haiti. It's an island, in the Caribbean ... near Cuba.'

'I know where Haiti is,' he said, laughing. He had a wide, infectious grin, she noticed. 'I remember when ol' Baby Doc scarpered a few years back, wasn't it? Good riddance, too, I expect.'

Améline stared at him in surprise. Few people in Malvern had ever head of Haiti, never mind Baby Doc's departure. It wasn't quite the sort of thing she expected a builder to know about. She stopped, embarrassed by her own assumptions. 'Sorry,' she said. 'It's just ... well, not many people know where it is.'

'Must be a bit hotter there than here, I'd imagine.'

'Yes.' She didn't quite know what to say. Should she say anything else? She looked around, wondering if anyone could see her awkwardness. Fortunately for her, just at that moment, Claire came bustling through the doorway, a plate of freshly baked flapjacks in her hand. His attention was distracted by the flapjacks and, somewhat relieved, she quickly slipped into the kitchen. She was used to chatting to the customers but there was something rather disconcerting about the way the young builder had come up to her, smiling as though the smile was meant for *her*, specifically. She wasn't sure anyone had ever smiled at her that way before. She stayed in the kitchen until she heard them leave again, calling out to Claire as they trooped through the door.

'He's lovely, he is,' Claire said, as soon as she appeared in the doorway.

'Who?' Améline was feeling rather flustered.

'Him. His name's Paul Wates. He's from down the road. Used to go to my school. I remember when his mum died. Got run over by one of them buses.' She nodded at the street outside.

Améline stared at her. 'That's terrible.'

'Yeah. Happened about five or six years ago. He was all set to go to college, he was always clever, like. But then, after the accident, he joined up with his dad. His dad's a builder. He's lovely, he is. Always got a smile on his face. Shame, isn't it?'

Améline didn't answer. She was suddenly full of pity for the nice young man whose kind words had thrown her into such a silly state of confusion.

'Are *you* Lulu, then?'

Améline looked up, feeling the blood rush straight to her face. She hadn't seen him come in. 'No!' she said, louder than she intended. 'No, that's not my name.'

'So what's your name, then?' he asked, raising one eyebrow. He'd shaved, Améline noticed, blushing even harder. Properly.

'Améline.'

'That's lovely. French names always sound much better, don't they?' he said, still grinning at her. Améline looked quickly around the café. It was almost empty. She looked at the clock on the wall. It was eleven.

'I'm a bit early. Or late, depending how you look at it. Got a couple of days off work,' he said chattily. 'Thought I'd just stop in for a bite.'

'Oh.' Améline swallowed. He looked different out of his workmen's overalls and paint-splattered jeans. He was wearing a pale green jumper and black jeans. He looked fresh, and squeaky-clean. She suddenly felt rather weak at the knees.

'What's on the menu, then?' he asked, rubbing his hands.

'We ... we have sandwiches,' Améline said faintly, '... and pie. Chicken and mushroom pie ...'

'Oh, I'll have a pie. That sounds just about right. Coffee, too, please.'

'I'll ... I'll bring it over,' Améline said, and fled from the counter. In the kitchen Claire looked up as she bolted through the door. She ignored her quizzical look and busied herself with preparing his plate. What the hell was wrong with her?

'That looks great,' he said appreciatively as she put the plate down in front of him. Alarmed by the friendly expression on his face, she couldn't find anything to say. She gave him a quick, fleeting smile and then retreated once more into the safety of the kitchen. When he left, whistling as he went out, she pretended to be studying the order sheets.

'He must like your food,' Claire said to her as she stacked the dishwasher. 'He's been here every day this week!' Améline glanced up at her sharply. But Claire was smiling. Nothing wrong with someone liking your food, she seemed to be saying. Améline sighed. She was making a fuss over nothing. Claire was right. Nothing wrong at all with satisfied customers.

Still, she couldn't help thinking to herself as she locked up the café later that evening, despite being flustered that afternoon, there was something undeniably *exciting* about being that, well, excited. It wasn't an emotion she was particularly familiar with. Now, if only Lulu were there, she'd have known what was happening and what to do about it. Lulu knew about things like that. She stopped suddenly. It was the first time she'd ever thought about her without immediately feeling a sharp stab of pain. Lulu would have known what to make of her feelings. The thought was somehow comforting as she walked slowly up the hill.

59

Laure shook hands with the young woman Daniel had hired to help her with the daunting task of renovating the house and breathed a sigh of relief. The meeting had gone well; it was the first time she'd ever met an architect, let alone the architect whose job it was to transform the enormous house she still had difficulty understanding was theirs. Hers and Daniel's. He was so busy with his new project that he'd more or less left everything to her, turning a deaf ear to her protests. To her great relief, Jessie Smith, the architect, was warm, friendly and very funny. Best of all, she'd listened intently to Laure's halting description of what she would do to open up the house, transforming the rather dark basement rooms into the kind of space Laure had been imagining but didn't know how to describe. Best of all, she'd listened intently to Laure describing the sorts of colours and textures she liked and by the end of their two-hour lunch meeting, Laure felt as though they'd reached a perfect under-standing. Jessie sketched while Laure talked, and showed her the drawings she'd done afterwards. Laure was stunned. It was exactly as she'd imagined it. Right down to the colours.

'You mean the colour of sea pebbles,' she said, when Laure described the cool, delicate colours she wanted in the liv-ing room. 'Buff, sand, olive ... I know just what you mean. Nothing too overpowering but with a bit of life.'

'Yes, exactly.'

'What sort of furniture do you have? Modern? Antique?'

'Furniture? Oh ... we haven't got any. Yet. I don't know ... I haven't really thought about it,' Laure stammered. Furniture? She was supposed to buy furniture as well? Oh, Daniel ...

'Gosh, we are going to have fun,' Jessie giggled. 'You're the kind of client most architects only dream of having, d'you know that?'

'Well, it's mostly Daniel. He's paying for it,' Laure said, almost embarrassed.

'Ah, but you're the one coming up with the suggestions,' Jessie said, smiling at her. 'You've got a really good eye. I've never heard of half the colours you describe but I can imagine them. Sounds *fabulous*!'

'I hope so.' Laure's voice was timid.

'Oh, it will be. Trust me. That's what you're paying me to do. To make it happen.' Laure said nothing. She couldn't quite believe the scale and size of the project Daniel had so carelessly left her in charge of. Knocking down walls, ripping out fireplaces, new windows ... it was *enormous*. So much could go wrong.

It took almost seven months. The basement was gutted com-pletely, leaving only a set of small storerooms at the rear of the house. The effect of opening up the front and back walls to light was dramatic. Cold, northern light flooded into the huge space that had been cleared; perfect for the neutral off-whites, stone and grey colours she'd envisaged. She and Jessie spent almost three months looking for just the right kitchen – she found it eventually in one of the fancy German kitchen stores just behind Oxford Street. She could barely pronounce the name – *Poggenpohl* – but with its austere grey cabinets, ice-cool steel appliances and shiny, wooden flooring, it transformed the dingy, dank basement completely. The new space was light, calm and efficient-looking, just the way she'd pictured it. One wall at the far end was painted a beautiful, rich iron red, a colour that reminded her of the reddish soil at home. Jessie looked at it admiringly when it was finally painted and told her how interesting it was that all the shades she'd used were mineral shades, from the red of iron ore to the greys and off-whites of stone. Laure just looked at her blankly. She had no idea what she was talking about. They chose a wonderful reddish-pink marble table slab with black and grey veins tracing a delicate, meandering pattern along the fissures in its smooth, shiny surface. A set of heavy oak chairs with cushions made of a striking grey, black and warm pink African batik finished the room perfectly.

The stairwell leading from the basement to the rest of the house was carpeted in a thick, brown-grey carpet with just the faintest blush of dirty purple. The balustrades were replaced with a light grey-brown oak that complemented the colours of the hallway and slowly drew the eye upwards, towards the skylight that Jessie had suggested at the top of the stairs. Laure loved looking up the sweep of the stairs to the sky-window, as she called it, watching the quicksilver changes in light and the colour of the London sky.

They left the three rooms on the ground floor intact, simply replacing the beautiful but broken wooden shutters at all the windows and stripping the floor back to its original oak planks. The room that she'd seen when she first walked in was kept as a study. Laure loved to stand at the tall windows looking down at the garden and across the rooftops of the single-storey houses in the street next to theirs. Jessie said again and again that she had a very unusual eye for colour, putting a palette together that most people would have shied away from. Somehow, it worked. Pebble, bone, sand … She sought out paler versions of the vibrant tones that reminded her of Haiti but, again according to Jessie, she seemed to instinctively know exactly how to handle them so that nothing in the house was garish or out of place.

Daniel was stunned by the transformation in the house, she could tell. He wandered through the rooms that still contained the builders' debris and pronounced it the most exciting space he'd ever seen. He'd been so busy in the six months that his project was under way that he'd hardly paid attention to what Laure and Jessie were planning. It was amazing what she'd done, wasn't it? Jessie asked him as they showed him around. He grabbed Laure's hand.

'She's got a really unusual eye,' she said as they led him upstairs. 'She's absolutely fearless. But it works, don't you think?'

'Absolutely.' Daniel gave Laure's hand a squeeze. Laure blushed to the roots of her hair. She was so relieved he liked it; hearing Jessie talk so admiringly of her was simply the icing on the cake.

'I keep telling her, if she ever wants a job …' She heard Jessie's voice trail off as she led Daniel into the upstairs bathroom. She turned and left them to it. She wasn't used to compliments. She didn't know how to respond.

She stopped just before the landing to the living rooms and leaned her head against the freshly painted wall. She was indescribably happy; only one thing would have made the picture complete – Améline. Without ever saying it out loud, she'd decorated the little attic space at the top of the stairs entirely for her. Améline had been uppermost in her mind as she selected fabrics, colours, patterns. A wild, silly fantasy perhaps. It had been nearly seven years since she'd seen her, and after the first few letters from Haiti when she'd first arrived in Chicago, she'd heard nothing. She was too afraid to contemplate what the silence might mean but she'd never given up hope of seeing her again. And now that this house was properly hers, she'd made sure there was space for Améline. There would always be space for Améline. Always.

'Darling, you are such a star,' Daniel said, closing the front door after Jessie had gone. He wrapped his arms around her from behind, kissing an ear lobe.

'Shall we have that party?' she asked, thinking how nice it would be to invite people to share something she had made. She could feel Daniel's mouth move against her hair. He nodded vigorously. 'I hardly know anyone here ... apart from Jessie and the builders, and Doug and Katie. I've just been so busy with this but now ... Couldn't we have the party you promised?'

'Sure.'

'But not like the ones back there,' she said in a low voice.

''Course not.'

'Daniel, what are you doing? Stop ... what ... whoa!' He'd picked her up. 'Where are you taking me?'

'We're going to start upstairs, *mon amour*. And then work our way down through every room in the house. It's an old English tradition. It's called christening the rooms. There are quite a few, you know.'

Daniel was eager to show off Laure's work – and Laure herself, of course. She listened rather nervously to his plans, remembering what had happened the last time she'd been introduced to a group of his friends. 'Don't worry,' he insisted. 'This lot are nothing like the others. You'll see. They'll love you. I promise.'

She and Jessie spent the next few days putting the finishing touches to the place, Laure mentally preparing herself to step outside the cosy little world they had inhabited for the past six months. Jessie had become more than simply the architect they'd hired to do the job; she'd become almost a friend. Indeed, she was Laure's only friend; she wrote to Shelley and Don occasionally but the truth was her life had changed beyond recognition since her marriage to Daniel and it bore very little relation to theirs – or what hers had once been like. In Chicago, she'd kept very much to herself; in the first year, at least, just being with Daniel had been enough. At the start of their second year of marriage, much to his amusement, she'd enrolled herself at a local community college not far from their town house and had taken – and passed – her high school diploma, something that had been bothering her since she'd left Haiti. At the time she'd been unable to explain, even to herself, why it meant so much, but as soon as she held the parchment certificate in her hand she knew why she'd done it. Daniel was not the only one with brains and ambition – without a high school diploma, college was out of the question. It was a very small, very tentative start on her part, but it was a start nonetheless. And then, of course, he'd sprung the surprise of moving to London on her ... and then there'd been the house ... and now, six months later, Jessie Smith was the only person she'd really come to know and soon their relationship would be at an end. The party would be their first real social event together and as nervous as she was about it, there was also a part of her that longed for her own circle of friends, people to talk to – people like *her*.

On the evening of the dinner party, she sat at the mirror in the dressing room adjacent to their bedroom, suddenly unsure of herself. She could hear Daniel humming to himself as he shaved. She stared at her reflection, as if seeing herself for the first time. Her hair was scraped back from her forehead, fastened at the nape with an elaborate, black velvet rose. The wild curls, tamed by regular visits to a hairdresser, cascaded across her shoulders and fell in a thousand tight ringlets halfway down her back. Her face was as it had always been. The same dark, almost black eyes; curled, thick eyelashes, touched with mascara, lips, full and red, the way Daniel liked. She examined it, as if searching for something, some sign that would point to everything that had happened in the years that had followed her hurried departure from Haiti. Surely there was something? Some little mark, an expression, the telltale signs of guilt ...? But no, there was nothing. The expressionless, carefully

327

made-up face stared back at her, the same face that looked out from the heavy, silver-framed wedding pictures that Daniel liked to leave on display. A blank, innocent canvas. But she wasn't innocent, was she? She had done ... Daniel's voice interrupted her suddenly.

'Wow! You look good enough to ...' he murmured suggestively, coming to stand behind her. 'Where did you find those?' He pointed to the silver, ornately wrought earrings she'd placed on the dressing table in front of her.

'These? Oh, in some little shop. I went shopping with Jessie the other day.'

'They're pretty. Put them in – let me see what they look like.'

Laure smiled. It was typical of Daniel – he had an eye for things most people wouldn't even notice. She slipped the earrings on, relieved that he'd interrupted her thoughts. Now was not the time to be sad. 'Are they all right?' she asked, looking at him in the mirror.

'Perfect.' He touched her shoulders lightly, almost regretfully, looking at his watch. 'Come on, Mrs Bermann ... half an hour to go. I'll go and open the wine.' He gave her a quick smile and disappeared down the stairs.

Five minutes later, Laure closed the bedroom door behind her and followed suit. As she stood at the top of the curved stairwell, looking down the elegant swoop of the balustrade, her earlier melancholy struck her again. Look at what she now owned, where she now lived. From the spare room at Belle's without even a shelf to call her own ... She had come so far. Had all of this really happened to her? She drew a deep breath and continued down the stairs. She prayed the evening would go well. She didn't want to disappoint Daniel – there was so much to be grateful to him for.

60

Placing the call to Melanie Miller took the better part of a day. The lines in the street were down; he'd had to cross over to West Beirut and go into the lobby at the old de Monfort Hotel, near the beach. Their international lines were also down but the doorman told him he could book a call through the operator and wait a few hours for it to come through. He was sitting outside in the summer air, secretly enjoying the interruption in his day when the doorman summoned him again. Ten minutes for the line to be connected and then another few minutes while it rang, unanswered, somewhere in London. Where had she said she lived? Chelsea?

'Hello?' She picked it up on the eighth ring. She sounded breathless. He was surprised to find himself sweating.

'Melanie. It's Marc Abadi.'

'Marc?' The surprise in her voice was clear.

'Yeah. Sorry it's taken a while to call – it's hard to get through from here.' He paused. It wasn't the only reason it had taken him a month to call. 'How are you?'

'Me? I'm fine.' She sounded breathless.

'Did I catch you at bad time?'

'Oh, no, I ran up the stairs, that's all. I was just on my way out.'

Was she pleased he'd rung? He couldn't tell. He could feel the trickle of sweat slowly making its way down his back. 'Listen, I'm going to be in Paris in a couple of weeks' time ... for about ten days. I was just wondering ...' he paused, took another breath, and continued. 'Would you like to meet, perhaps?'

There was a moment's hesitation. Then that voice, deliciously indifferent; he could almost see her shrug. 'Um ... yeah, all right.'

He waited. Was that it? Was she playing it cool? 'So, is that a "yes"?' he asked, laughing, surprised at how nervous she made him feel.

'Yeah, I s'pose so. Why not?'

He grinned. She really *was* a tough cookie. 'OK. I'll call you when I get to Paris.'

'I'll be waiting.'

He rang off, still smiling. He was surprised at how much he wanted to see her again. It wasn't his usual style.

Melanie put down the phone, sat down abruptly and only just managed to muffle her scream. She had waited four weeks – she looked at her watch – *and eight hours* to pick up the phone and hear that deep, faintly accented voice. A month! She'd almost given up. And then he'd called. *He'd called!* He'd said he would call – and he had. Four weeks late! She buried her face in her pillow, almost in tears. She'd spent the past month since she'd left his hotel room in an utter daze, and no, it wasn't just because it was the best sex she'd had in her entire life. She couldn't get Marc Abadi out of her head. He was like no one she'd ever met. The mere thought of him was enough to make her go weak at the knees and yet she hardly knew him. She rolled over, picked up the phone and, on impulse, rang Polly in Sydney. Hang the expense. She *had* to talk to someone.

If Polly sounded surprised to hear from her, she hid it well. After a few minutes of inconsequential chit-chat, Melanie blurted it out. 'I've met someone,' she declared breathlessly. 'I can't describe him. I just can't. He's gorgeous. I'm meeting him in Paris the week after next. I can't *wait*! He's perfect. Just perfect.'

'Oh, Mel. No one's perfect. Who is he?' Polly sounded sceptical.

'He's a doctor … I think. I met him at some awards thing. He was being given an medal or something. Something to do with refugees.'

'Christ … find out what he does before you leap halfway across the world to marry him.'

'I'm not going halfway across the world. I'm only going to Paris. And I'm not going to marry him. Not yet.'

Polly ignored her last comment. 'Is he French?'

'No, I don't think so. I mean, he speaks French, but he's half-Lebanese or something. He's gorgeous.'

'So you keep saying. Well, it sounds to me as though you've got a lot of finding out to do, Mel. Be careful, won't you?'

'What d'you mean?'

'Oh, you know what you're like; you'll probably wind up in his harem, or something. That'll be the next phone call.' Polly never let Melanie forget the fact that she'd hardly bothered to keep in touch while she was off 'doing her LA thing', as Polly put it.

'Don't be silly. I'm only going for a few days.'

'Yeah, well ... where've I heard *that* before?'

The next few days passed in an excited, feverish blur of shopping and day-dreaming. Melanie made every preparation possible; even going so far as to book an appointment at a salon on the King's Road to do what Kim had suggested the first time they went shopping together. Melanie paused for a second after she'd put the phone down. Kim. She hadn't thought about her in a while. Everything that had happened to her in LA seemed to have happened to someone else. She thought about Steve; what was he doing now? Probably the same as he'd been doing when she was there. He wouldn't change; but she had. And now she was about to change even further. Just thinking about Marc Abadi sent a tremor straight through her. That proved it. She wouldn't have felt that way about just *any*one, would she? He was special. Anyone could see that. Now, when *exactly* did he say he'd call?

61

Iain watched Améline take the roast potatoes out of the oven. It suddenly occurred to him that she hadn't said a word for ...

he glanced quickly at the kitchen clock ... oh, over an hour. At least.

'Am,' he said, frowning. 'Are you all right, love?'

'Who? Me?' She looked at him, so genuinely surprised by the question that he resolved there and then to buy her a bunch of flowers the next morning, or maybe bring her a cup of tea in bed. Had he really been so neglectful?

'Yes, you ... you seem a bit distracted. Lulu's going all right, is it?'

'Oh, yes, fine. Everything's fine.' She gave him a quick smile and went back to the oven. It was Sunday afternoon and she was, as usual, making the Sunday roast he so liked. She'd been up for hours, he noticed. There were bags of freshly baked scones and the new orange peel biscuits she'd been trying out on the side, waiting to be taken down the hill.

'Want me to do anything?' he asked, sticking his head round the paper a few minutes later.

'*Do* anything?'

'Well, yes ... I could ... I don't know ... lay the table or something?'

'Yes, that would be nice.'

He glanced at her warily. Was she being sarcastic? He contemplated the thought for a few minutes but was interrupted by Améline noisily banging plates down on the table.

'Oh, sorry, darling ... was just about to get up.' It occurred to him, if only fleetingly, that offering to help wasn't quite the same as actually helping.

'Lunch is ready.'

She was quiet all the way through lunch, too. Even his loud comments of praise seemed to fall on deaf ears. She washed up afterwards in silence then said she was going for a walk. His old knees and weak heart were no match for her strong, wiry legs – he'd been up on the Malvern Hills with her once when they'd first arrived and he'd sworn never to do it again. He nodded and pulled a mock-serious face. 'Don't get lost, will you? All sorts of bogeymen creeping about on the hills.'

'Bogeymen?'

'Never mind. Will you be back in time for tea?' Her reply was lost as she opened the front door and stepped out. It was drizzling slightly – awful weather in which to go for a walk but there was no accounting for the things women did, Iain had come to realise. He settled himself into the comfortable sofa in the living room with the papers and a pipe. A quick nap, too, if he was lucky. The blank screen of his word processor awaited him in his study; he'd been trying to start on a new book for months now. Nothing seemed to come to him.

Straight up the hill, over the small turnstile and then follow the track to the left of the hills. She knew the path by heart. Soft, light drops of rain fell on her plastic anorak but she didn't mind. She found the weather almost soothing. Within minutes, the last of the houses had fallen away and then there was only the yellowish grass of the hills to her right and the verdant fields falling sharply away down the hill towards the town at the bottom. She climbed higher, hearing her own breathing loud in her ears and lifting her face every now and then out of the protective circle of her anorak, letting the cold, stinging water brush her face. Was she crying? She couldn't tell. For weeks now, she'd been carrying a lump of fear around in her chest that brought on the most dreadful panic attack, mostly of guilt. She hadn't done anything. *She hadn't done anything.* She repeated the phrase so often it ceased to mean anything. *Yes, you have. Thinking about it's the same thing.* Her conscience mocked her. She stopped to catch her breath. The truth was, *she would have liked to do something.* That was the horrible bit.

Up, up, up … She strode up the path that led to the summit. It was raining harder now, and the ground underfoot was squelchy and wet. Paul Wates. She couldn't bring herself to say his name out loud. Thanks to Claire, she knew more about Paul Wates than she knew about her own husband. Well, almost. The thought stabbed her sharply. An unfair comparison. He'd taken to coming into the café at the oddest hours, usually early in the morning before the mothers and the other workmen arrived, and at closing time, when again it was empty and he could walk up the hill with her to the bus stop. He was so easy to talk to. He asked her lots of questions – what Haiti was like, about her family, about coming to England … about Iain.

'I'm married …' she'd blurted out, a few days after he'd started walking with her to the bus stop. She didn't know what else to say.

He'd looked at her, a funny, distant look in his eyes. 'I know.' They'd walked on in silence for a few minutes, Améline's mind racing. Had she offended him? Had she said the wrong thing? 'Does it bother you?' he asked suddenly, just before her stop.

She looked at him warily. Yes, she longed to say, but not for the reasons you'd think. 'No … I … it's nice. Talking to you, I mean.'

'Good.'

And then the bus arrived and there didn't seem to be much else to say. The following morning, he was there at 7.45 a.m. as usual. They didn't speak of it again.

The problem was, she mouthed the words aloud, speaking to herself in the absence of anyone to talk to, was that it *was* a problem. She couldn't stop thinking about him … *in that way*. In the way she wasn't supposed to. In the way she remembered Lulu talking about that boy in her class … what the hell was his name? Philippe. Philippe Delacroix. She smiled at the memory. Every time she thought about Paul Wates, she experienced a giddy, sweet sensation *all over her body* – it made her feel faint. She'd never so much as touched him and yet all she could think about when she was alone was him touching her. It made it even more difficult to lie next to Iain. Thank *God* he'd been too tired in the past few weeks to make any sort of amorous advances towards her. She wasn't sure she'd be able to stand it. And yet lying next to his sleeping form in the middle of the night she was overcome with a physical hunger for Paul that left her drained and shaking, too frightened to move. She dreamt about him in a way she'd never, ever dreamt about a man before – half the time she was too scared to go to sleep just in case she moaned his name out loud.

She sat down on the blackened stump of a tree. What was

wrong with her? She shivered. There was no one she could talk to. This was certainly not something she could ever share with Viv. Iain was like a brother to Viv – this was a betrayal. Of the worst kind. *Oh, Lulu.* She could taste the salt on her cheeks mingling with the cold rain. *Help me.*

62

Laure liked all of Daniel's friends. She said so, repeatedly. She particularly liked Jayne, a tall, striking redhead who owned a clothing store just up the road in Primrose Hill. She also liked Clarissa, a pretty, lively brunette who ran a furniture business she'd inherited from her father. Jessie had also introduced her to two of her friends, Malcolm and Patricia, an architect-fashion designer couple who seemed equally taken with Laure. After their first dinner party she had invitations to several more and to all sorts of interesting, creative events: an up-coming art exhibition; a new play; even a trip to Paris to look at fabrics for Clarissa's spring outdoor furniture collection. She'd sat through dinner at one end of the long, beautifully polished table and listened in pleasure to the conversation around them. Art, politics, fashion, local gossip – she'd only just realised how starved she'd been in the past few years of company like this.

'They're lovely, Daniel,' she said afterwards, putting away her dress and shoes and shaking her hair free.

'I told you, didn't I?' Daniel mumbled from his side of the bed. 'Come on,' he said eagerly. 'Get over here, will you? I've been waiting all bloody night for this.'

'Don't be so impatient,' Laure said primly, shutting the wardrobe door. She liked to make sure everything was neat and tidy before going to bed. It drove Daniel to distraction. We've got maids to do that sort of stuff, he complained. She always ignored him.

'Look, if you'd been me, sitting at one end of that insuffer-ably long table – whose bloody idea was that, anyway? I've been staring at my beautiful wife all fucking evening and— Ouch!'

'You swear too much. *C'est impoli.*'

A few days later, she met Jayne and Clarissa for lunch on the King's Road, near Clarissa's shop. She'd spent the whole morn-ing getting dressed, changing outfits, pulling clothes on and off, tying her hair up, leaving it down – quite unlike her but she was nervous, she had to admit it. Jeans? Too casual, perhaps. A suit? Too formal. Skirt? With or without heels …? She finally decided on a knee-length linen skirt with a crisp, white blouse and a soft, dark green woollen jacket. She tied her hair up with a bolt of green, rust and white African print material and fastened two large, silver hoop earrings. Stylish, but not too fussy.

'I *love* that material,' was the first thing Clarissa said as they met in front of the café. 'Where d'you find it?'

'Um, in a shop … Somewhere in Shepherd's Bush, I think? There's an African market …'

'Listen to you! You've been here less than six months and you already know where to go. It's lovely.'

'Hi,' Jayne came striding up the road towards them. 'Sorry I'm late. Guess who I saw? In the chemist's?'

'Who?' Clarissa leaned forward eagerly. She was an avid gos-sip, Laure remembered from the party. She smiled. They were intelligent, successful women, but they were also a lot of fun.

'Melanie Miller. Remember her? She was standing right next to me!'

'Who's Melanie Miller?' Laure felt emboldened to ask.

'Mike Miller's daughter.' Clarissa turned her green eyes on Laure in surprise. 'The rock star. She used to be in the papers all the time … You can't imagine how thin she is!'

'What does she do?' Laure asked, amused.

'Not a lot,' Jayne said cheerfully. 'One of those silly girls who doesn't really *do* anything.'

'Except look pretty,' Clarissa snorted. 'Very Important. To Look Pretty.' The two women giggled. Laure was silent. It had suddenly occurred to her. Was that what everyone also thought of her? What did *she* do?

'Daniel,' she said to him at breakfast a few days later. 'I've been thinking ...'

''Bout what, darling?' He turned the pages of the newspaper he was reading.

'About finding something to, well, do.'

'Do? You don't have to *do* anything,' he murmured without looking up.

'Well, that's what I mean. It was fine when I was doing the house up, but now ... Well, I'd like to find something to do. With myself.'

'Oh. Right.'

'I was thinking ... maybe ... well, what about if I studied something? You know, took a course in something ...?'

'Darling, you can do whatever you like. I keep telling you. You don't have to ask *me* permission. Just do it.'

Laure paused for a second. 'I was thinking about textile design,' she said hesitantly. 'Or maybe interior design. I really enjoyed doing the house and ...'

'Of course, darling, whatever you fancy,' Daniel interrupted her, looking at his watch. He had an important meeting ahead of him, he'd told her. 'Shall I get Sophie to find things out for you?' Sophie was Daniel's scarily efficient PA. Laure shook her head.

'No, don't bother her. I'll find something myself. Are you sure you don't mind?'

'Mind? Why on earth would I mind?' Daniel looked at her, puzzled.

'Well, it just means I'll be busier than ... normal.'

'If it makes you happy, Lulu— What? Did I say something? What's wrong?' He looked at her suddenly stricken face. 'What is it?'

'Pl ... please don't call me that ...' Laure stammered. It was the first time he'd ever called her Lulu.

'Why? Don't you like it? Was it your nickname? At school?' Daniel's voice was teasing.

'No ... please.' She pushed back her chair and got up, appalled at her own reaction. 'I ... I just ...' She stopped, afraid she was going to burst into tears. She turned and ran from the room. She prayed Daniel wouldn't come after her. Now was not the time for explanations. Luckily, he didn't. She stayed in the bathroom until she heard his car pull away from the kerb.

He'd been right about one thing, however, she discovered. London was indeed full of colleges offering a wide range of courses for women, much like herself, she supposed; young and not-so-young, rich, bored – descriptions she would never have *dreamed* she would one day use about herself. She went along to several 'open days' where a variety of tutors tried to persuade her to part with inordinately large sums of money in return for a 'certificate' or a 'diploma', neither of which seemed worth more than the paper they were printed on. After a week, she reluctantly decided it wasn't quite as easy as it looked. In the end, she turned to Jessie for advice – and by the end of the following week, was enrolled on a bona fide course in Print in Fashion at Central St Martin's, somewhere along a busy road in a part of London she didn't know, but liked from the first. Two days a week, she told Daniel, wide-eyed with enthusiasm. She loved her tutors, she loved the subject, she loved the course ... she loved *him*. She could never, ever thank him enough. For what, he asked, bemused by the sudden outpouring of gratitude. *For giving me this chance.* He buried his face in her hair. Laure sometimes confounded him. The way he saw it, she would have done it for herself, regardless. He often thought privately to himself that she simply didn't know her own strength. She was the strongest person he'd ever met. Why couldn't she see that? She shook her head against his chest in denial, again and again. She was not to be convinced. He gave up. There were other, equally pressing things to do on a rainy Sunday morning in bed.

63

Who was it who'd once sung something about it being 'never as good as the first time'? Whoever it was had obviously never met Melanie. *Every bit as good as. Even better.* It dawned on him after he'd picked her up from Charles de Gaulle and they'd driven into the city, Melanie chattering in her amusing, self-deprecating way beside him, that he was in danger of falling for her. Unusual, for him. In his line of work there hadn't been much opportunity to meet bright, vivacious, sparkly girls who made everything around them seem light and fun. He liked her sense of humour and her quick, sharp wit. He liked her. Full stop. More than that, he was drawn to her. Behind the banter something else lurked, although it was too early to tell what, exactly, and he was wary of turning his professional eye on her. But she intrigued him and that was unsettling enough. His relationships had been few and far between. There had simply never been the time. It wasn't as though he could step into a wine bar after work, or meet someone by chance at a dinner party. In the conditions in which he worked, 'normal' life seemed an impossible luxury. He told himself he didn't need a relationship or want one. And until he met Melanie, he believed it. Now, after only two brief, if highly pleasurable, meetings, he was struggling to get her out of his head. He went over the reasons why it would never work: she was too young; he was unavailable; she wasn't the kind of girl to be satisfied with a hurried ten days every once in a while. He went over the reasons why it shouldn't last longer than the brief leave he'd been granted – and saw, of course, that it made little difference. He liked her. A lot. And he had five days with her now, in Paris.

On the last day, he left the flat early for a meeting somewhere in town. Melanie got up late and went for a walk along the Seine. There was an open-air market on Rue des Rosiers, a few streets away from the flat. She wandered among the stalls, breathing in the peppery scent of celery, the weak perfume of strawberries and raspberries, their plump, bursting skins catching the early morning light; her nostrils contracting as she passed the creamy wheels of Camembert and the thick slabs of crumbling, blue-veined cheeses. Glistening fish, their skins still slippery with seawater; wooden buckets of ice and red, stiff-clawed lobster; the hot, sweet fragrance of bread. People stopped, touched, examined the goods on display, a world away from the supermarkets in London. They chattered continuously around her; there were conversations about price, flavour, the weather ... She moved in a languid, dreamlike state among the shapes, textures, shine and pattern of produce, her body still sweetly alive with the memory of everything that had passed between her and Marc only a few hours earlier. She walked back to the flat with a box of purplish, swollen grapes, some cheese and a stick of French bread. I could live here, she thought to herself as she climbed the stairs. He wasn't back yet; she opened the door to an empty flat.

She put the food in the small fridge and washed her hands. It felt a little strange to be alone in his flat. She looked around her; everything was so neat and tidy. She opened one of the cupboards – a stack of clean plates, cups, glasses. Even the cupboard under the sink was clean. She wandered into the living room. There was a silver-framed photograph above the fireplace. She hadn't noticed it before. She picked it up – three girls; one of them unbelievably beautiful. She put it down, aware that her heart was racing. Who was she? Who were they? They all looked alike, sisters, perhaps, but they looked nothing like Marc. She walked into the bedroom and pushed open the French doors on to the little balcony. She needed a cigarette. She wondered again about the photograph.

He came back not long afterwards, bearing almost exactly what she'd bought – fruit, cheese and bread.

'Shall we eat outside?' he called out to her from the kitchen. 'It's not too hot for you?'

'No, it's lovely.'

'Oh ... by the way,' he popped his head round the door, grinning at her. 'The girls in the picture on the mantelpiece? My half-sisters, in case you were wondering.' Melanie blinked. How had he guessed? 'You mean you *didn't* look at it and wonder who they were?' he said, walking towards her with a tray in his hands.

'Noooo. Well, OK. I *did* sneak a quick look ... but I didn't really think anything ...'

'No?' His voice was teasing.

Melanie blushed. 'OK, OK. I *did* wonder ...' she admitted, raising her hands in an admission of guilt. She'd thought one of them might have been a girlfriend. 'They're your half-sisters?'

'Yeah.' He speared a piece of cheese. Melanie watched him warily. 'From my dad's second wife.'

'Oh. Where are they? Here?'

'No, they live in Accra.'

'Where?'

'Ghana.'

'Where's that?'

'West Africa.'

'You're *African*?' Melanie was surprised.

'Sort of. My mother was Ghanaian.'

'Was? She's ... dead?'

'No. But I was brought up by my grandmother. In Beirut.' Melanie shook her head. 'Fuck. I thought *I* was complicated. I still live in the same house that I've lived in since I was ten.'

'Different circumstances, that's all.' He shrugged.

'That's ... that's *everything*! You've got ... I don't know ... two families, three mothers, four homes ... What a crazy life!'

'Nothing special, Melanie, just circumstances.' His voice was quiet.

'But ...' She stopped. His eyes carried a warning she couldn't quite read. She took the glass of wine he offered and hoped he wouldn't notice her shaking fingers. Five days, and she was already head over heels. She hoped desperately that he felt the same way.

341

64

Laure was dreading Christmas, and with good reason. In the year they'd been in London, Daniel's parents had mercifully stayed away. She'd almost managed to forget they existed. But their presence came crashing through the walls one November evening with a phone call in which they were both summoned – yes, that was the word – to their Indiana holiday home to spend the season with them and assorted members of the Bermann extended clan.

'Do we have to?' Laure asked Daniel, almost pleading.

''Fraid so, darling,' Daniel said, pouring himself a stiff drink. 'Want one?'

She shook her head. 'You ... couldn't you say we've already made plans?' she asked.

It was his turn to shake his head. 'Look, it'll only be for a week. We'll jet in and out – we'll be back here for New Year's. It won't be so awful. They're not *that* bad, are they?'

'I ... I just like it here. I thought ... it would be just the two of us ...' Laure said miserably. How could she tell him? Yes, they *were* that bad. They were worse.

'It'll still be just the two of us,' he said, draining his glass. 'Look, I know you're not overly fond of them but they're still my parents. They've come round, just like I said they would. They're looking forward to seeing you. Honestly.'

'Now *that* I find hard to believe,' Laure said dryly. She still remembered the venom in her father-in-law's voice the night she'd overheard them.

'They have. My mother completely accepts you. I told you she would.'

Laure gave a small sound of exasperation. What planet was Daniel living on? 'The only way your mother is ever going to accept me,' she said crossly, moving away from him towards the door, 'is if I have a skin transplant. And last time I checked, they hadn't got round to doing those yet!' She didn't wait for Daniel's response but slammed the door behind her and walked upstairs. It was the *last* thing on earth she felt like doing. Christmas with the Bermanns. Never mind the fact that she was now also a Bermann.

Daniel was on the phone downstairs; his voice carried faintly up the stairwell. Phoning them, no doubt. She walked into the dressing room and closed the door. She opened one of the wardrobe doors and pulled out a white storage box. Nestled in the familiar white tissue paper was her secret talisman. She touched it lightly, her breathing slowly returning to normal. She found it soothing to look at, despite the ache of sadness it brought on. Sometimes days, weeks, would go by without her thinking about it. But every once in a while, when she was alone, she would step into the dressing room, shut the door and pick the little garment up. She cried sometimes, silent, bitter-tasting tears – for him, for Améline whom she'd left behind. But it helped her, too, in ways she couldn't articulate. The little jumpsuit was there to remind her never to forget. Holding it, remembering him, Améline didn't feel quite so far away, and she felt less alone.

They flew to Chicago just before Christmas, as planned, Laure bracing herself for the twelve days that lay ahead, made bearable only by the thought of seeing Don again. Shelley had moved to the suburbs, 'another planet', as Don said in his last letter. Laure smiled. They would spend a couple of days at their empty town house in Chicago, then drive up the side of Lake Michigan to the Bermanns' country home.

'Tell me again who's going to be there?' Laure asked as they stepped into the back of the limousine sent to pick them up from O'Hare.

'Two distant cousins from Hamburg, my Uncle Stephan – that's my dad's brother – and his wife, Aunt Brunhilde. Then Jules Williams's coming over on Christmas Day – he'll spend a couple of nights with us. I told you about him, remember? He's the guy we're hoping can get us some backers. His parents are friends of ours. And then there's Mother and Papa, you, me … maybe a couple of neighbours … not many.'

'And we're all going to be staying in the same house?'

'Yes, but it's huge. Don't worry, we'll hardly see anyone.'

Laure said nothing. Ten whole days with seven or eight strangers. *Merry Christmas*. 'What d'you think I should get your parents for Christmas?' she asked, racking her brains.

'Dunno. You'll think of something.' Daniel was preoccupied. He rarely talked in detail about the Institute. She'd gathered, from snatches of overheard conversations, that they needed a major funder and he was reluctant to go to his parents. Rightly so, she thought. Günter Bermann already owned too much of their lives. Oh, the accounts were in Daniel's name – and hers, too – but it was quite clear where the money came from. She didn't think she would ever get used to walking up the stairs into the plush foyer at Coutts, the Bermann family's bankers. Someone rushing forward to offer a seat, a coffee, the papers … would she like to make a withdrawal? *Make a withdrawal* – minutes later, the buff-coloured envelope with the pretty gilt edges would appear, crisp, clean notes in whatever denomination she'd asked for. Everything transacted in the hushed, reverential tones the English favoured when speaking of money. *That* was a bank?

Later that afternoon, after they'd arrived and unpacked, she wandered down the Magnificent Mile, her body buried in a long, protective sheepskin coat. It was freezing. Her memories of winter in Chicago weren't pleasant – perpetually cold, wrapped up in thin, cheap winter coats that did little to keep out the wind. This time she walked wrapped in a cocoon of warmth. Christmas in Chicago had always been a depressing time; watching happy families out together on the last day of shopping, buying gifts, drinking hot chocolate in the windows of the cafés. How many times had she pressed her face against the glass of some children's clothing store, numb with pain? She'd never been able to afford much – something small for Don, a pair of cheap earrings for Marilí, a tie for Julio – he'd laughed in astonishment when she presented it … a tie? *Where the hell was he gonna wear a tie?* But he'd hugged her all the same.

Now ... well, as with everything else, this time it was different. A present for Don; something for Shelley, even though it was unlikely they'd see each other. And perhaps something for Léon and Julio ...? Enough time had passed, it would be good to see them again. She chose carefully, enjoying the pleasure of walking through shops, confident in her ability to buy anything she wanted, thanks to the little silver and gold cards tucked neatly in her purse. Anything she wanted. Giving, she decided, was so much better than getting. Nothing too expensive; she was careful not to select gifts that would embarrass anyone. A pretty silk camisole for Shelley; a box of fine cigars for Julio and a bottle of Scotch for Léon; a small, solid silver hip flask for Don. She watched each gift being wrapped; a feeling of real pleasure spreading through her as it was done. Walking through the racks of children's clothing was hard; there wasn't a single item she didn't long to reach out and touch, buy, keep. But she'd made a promise to herself – nothing other than the little jumpsuit. Nothing more until the day she was able to set out and look for him herself. She *had* to stick to it. She would have bought half the store otherwise ... and how would she explain *that* to Daniel?

A couple of hours later, she was almost finished. She had Daniel's presents carefully wrapped – a beautiful cashmere sweater; a new camera; a couple of rare jazz albums from a second-hand dealer on Ontario. She'd even managed to find something for the dreadful parents – an oil painting she'd seen in a gallery close to the lake. Expensive, but she wasn't about to give Octavia the satisfaction of turning up her nose. It would be delivered to the apartment early the next day, the gallery owner told her, obviously delighted. Yes, an expensive purchase. Laure was beginning to appreciate the relationship between price tag and smile.

They drove to Indiana the following morning, the roads already covered in a thin blanket of sleet. The sky was low and threatening and matched her sinking mood. Daniel had tellingly raised an eyebrow when the painting was delivered, sending her into a frenzy of self-doubt. *He* thought it was lovely, he tried to reassure her. It only made her feel worse. Wrong, wrong, wrong – everything about her was wrong. *She* was wrong. Period. Nothing she ever did would change that. It amazed her that Daniel didn't see it.

65

Améline shifted her weight awkwardly. Wasn't she supposed to kneel? Or should she sit, perhaps? There was a little, cloth-covered stool in the confessional – she'd never been inside the small, curtained space before – but it wasn't clear to her how to use it. She'd only ever once been inside such a grand church and that had been the cathedral in front of the Palais National, in Port-au-Prince. Then the Macoutes had been everywhere, shouting at people, ordering them around. It was clear what you were supposed to do. This was a small church tucked away behind the railway station in Malvern. She had no idea how she was supposed to behave. She knelt down, clasped her hands in front of her and bowed her head.

After a few minutes, she heard a rustling from behind the screen. 'Yes, my child?' It was the priest. He had a deep, kindly voice. She wasn't entirely sure what to say next.

'Er, bless me, Father. I ... I have ... can ... could ... I would like to confess something, sir. Father.'

'Yes, my child. How long has it been since your last confession?'

Améline gulped. She'd never confessed anything to anyone before. Père Estimé wasn't exactly the type of priest you told anything to. She stammered. 'A long time, sir. Father.'

She heard the priest sigh. 'What is it you want to confess?' he asked, not unkindly. Améline took a deep breath. And found that once she'd started, she couldn't stop.

Half an hour later, feeling infinitely better, she left the church. She'd been struggling with the dilemma she'd just blurted out for over six months and now, for the first time, she felt as though the burden had been lifted somehow. She didn't mind how many 'Hail Marys' he'd instructed her to say – of far greater importance was the feeling of having told someone and of hearing the priest say she'd done nothing wrong. Not yet, at any rate. The priest had cautioned her. Her marriage vows were sacred. She was to do nothing that would jeopardise or threaten them in any way. She pulled on her gloves and wrapped her scarf around her head. It was bitterly cold. She walked back up the hill, wondering about the afternoon ahead. Claire was more than capable of handling the afternoon teas but with a week to go until Christmas, there was tons to do. It still felt strange to her to walk into the little tea shop that was hers, see the fruits of her labour on display and, strangest of all, see Claire looking to *her* for instruction. It was usually the other way round – she'd always taken orders from others. Well, not any more.

She pushed open the door, relieved to see there was only a couple of elderly ladies sipping tea in the corner. Paul wasn't there. Thank God. She wasn't sure she could handle seeing his face after all she'd just confessed to. She smiled at the two ladies, took off her coat and went through to the kitchen. There was work to be done. She was determined to make it a Christmas at Lulu's that Malvern would never forget. She'd drawn up a list of things to bake and make – everything from delicious sourdough bacon rolls to her own special cinnamon and nutmeg-flavoured fruitcake and those delicious little mince pies the English so loved. She'd bought all the recipe books she could find, had bored Viv half to death with her questions; all that remained was for her to roll up her sleeves and get stuck in.

The bacon rolls were first on her list. She began by kneading the dough until it was smooth and elastic, enjoying the feel of it under her hands. After it was done, she covered the bowl with cling-film as the recipe directed and left it to stand for an hour. In the meantime, she began work on the Christmas cake. It wasn't long before the tangy, pungent scents of nutmeg, ginger and cloves filled the air. She mixed the dried fruit – cherries, sultanas, raisins – added almonds – and began to beat the butter and sugar together by hand. Grandmère had always instructed Cléones to shun electrical mixers, not that Cléones would ever have used one. She was right; there was something satisfying about beating the mixture by hand, watching it blanch in front of your eyes. She added the eggs, taking care not to curdle the mixture until it was as light and fluffy as air. Next she folded in the flour and the mixed fruit, added a dash of rum and the grated ginger ... Claire stuck her head round the door to ask if she could eat the mixture raw. The smells were wafting out from under the door, she said, and driving everyone mad. Then it was back to the bacon rolls, slicing the dough in long strips and then laying a rasher along each length. She pinched the ends, added a sprig of rosemary and popped them in the oven.

By teatime, the entire café was redolent with the aroma of spices and warm bread. The two Christmas cakes were in their boxes, soaking gently in rum. They would stay there until the weekend. She'd made fragrant, dense mince pies; dark chocolate and orange *biscotti*; tiny pistachio and lemon tartlets; loaves of almond bread ... The priest was right. For the three or four hours that she'd been standing over the hot stove, she hadn't had the chance to think about anything else, let alone Paul. It would help with the temptation, he'd told her. It had.

Claire left just before six, after helping Améline to put up a pretty row of Christmas lights above the counter, and a little posy of berries and a single Christmas candle on every table. Améline was busy counting out the tablecloths and napkins when there was a tap at the door. She looked up. It was completely dark outside. She peered through the curtains and then her heart did a somersault. It was Paul. She jumped up and rushed to unlock the door.

'Hi.' She held the door open. He looked very uncomfortable. 'Here, come in ... it's freezing outside.'

'Hi ... I was ... just walking past. I didn't expect ... I

thought you'd be gone by now ...' he stammered, shaking the drops of water off his jacket.

'No, I was ... I came late this afternoon I ... I had to do something,' she said, acutely aware of her flaming cheeks. He wasn't the only one ill at ease. She shut the door. The two of them stood there in the semi-darkness, neither one, it seemed, knowing quite what to say.

He ran a hand through his wet hair. 'I didn't come in today,' he said, trying to sound diffident. 'Well, actually, – I was *going* to come, got all the way down the hill. But then, I thought ... Well, I wasn't sure if ...' His voice trailed off. Améline stared at him. She'd never seen him so unsure of himself.

'Is everything all right?' she asked, concerned. She almost put out a hand to touch him.

'Yeah. No. Yeah. Yeah, everything's fine.'

'Are you sure? You seem a bit ... upset? Did something happen on the site?'

Paul hesitated. He lifted a hand to his hair again, but it somehow landed on her shoulder. She stood there, too stunned to move. She heard him take a breath, felt his hand slide from her shoulder to the nape of her neck and then slowly, as if he had all the time in the world, he slid his hand under her chin, lifted it and kissed her. The keys she'd been holding in one hand fell to the floor. The other, entirely of its own accord, went up around his neck and then she was kissing him back, excited and terrified at the same time, her mouth opening to draw his warm, wet tongue inside her. She felt something slacken in his body as both arms went around her; the cool, delightful shock of his hand on her bare stomach, under her clothes. Her whole body began to melt; she pulled him behind the counter, away from the window, the priest's words receding further with every wave of pleasure.

'Améline,' he gasped, breaking for air. But he couldn't stop; neither did she want him to. They made hasty, trembling love right there on the floor behind the counter. Améline thought she would surely die. This was what Lulu had been talking about. *This* was what she'd seen in films and read about in books and never once – no, not *once*! – imagined would be hers. She held onto his young, strong arms, kept her eyes firmly shut and gave in completely to the surprising torrent of emotion that poured out of her, long after he was spent.

Christmas dinner *chez* Bermann was an elaborate, dressed-up affair. Laure saw as soon as she descended the stairs that she hadn't put quite the right amount of effort into her outfit. She was wearing a simple black jersey dress with a wide leather belt, a large silver buckle and long, silver, drop earrings. Octavia looked as though she were about to head out to the theatre in a ridiculously over-the-top velvet and taffeta evening dress, strands of pearls roped around her scrawny neck. She opened her mouth as soon as she saw Laure coming down the stairs and forgot to shut it. Laure gulped. God, it was going to be a long evening ahead.

They assembled in front of the elaborate Christmas tree in the living room overlooking the lake. 'Presents first,' Günter announced in as near to a jocular tone as Laure had ever heard. The relatives from Germany looked at her in open incredulity. Laure stayed close to Daniel's side as if he might physically protect her from whatever terrors lay ahead. Octavia led the way in opening the gifts. Laure's heart sank.

'How very … *modern*,' Octavia murmured, drawing the painting out of its wrapping. She looked at it once, then put it aside, moving smoothly on to the next present. Laure breathed a sigh of relief. At least she hadn't said she *hated* it.

'I don't think she liked it much,' she said to Daniel, as they finally climbed the stairs to bed. It had been a very long evening indeed.

'Well, *I* like it,' Daniel said loyally.

'You're not *meant* to like it. It's not your present,' Laure retorted.

'Oh, who cares? How many more days to go?' he whispered. Laure looked at him in surprise.

'You're the one who wanted to come,' she said, poking him gently in the ribs.

'I'd forgotten what it's like,' he said dryly. 'You only remember the good bits, I suppose.'

'And which were those?' she teased.

He grabbed her arm, suddenly serious. 'Promise me,' he whispered against her ear. 'That you'll never do this to our children. Promise me that they'll always *want* to come home.' Laure couldn't speak. Her eyes had suddenly blurred over without warning. She struggled to compose herself. 'Promise?' he whispered again. She held herself very still and nodded, as carefully as she could manage.

'I ... I'm just ... I'll just run to the bathroom,' she whispered, turning before he could catch sight of her face. 'Back in a sec.' She turned and fled. When would she be able to control these sharp, unbearable stabs of pain, she asked her reflection in the mirror. When would the tidal wave that sat just below the surface of her heart finally subside? Would it always be like this? For ever? She splashed cold water on her face, careful not to smudge her mascara. It was hard enough trying to keep it safe from her tears – if she wasn't careful, she'd wind up looking like a racoon. *Then* they'd really have something to stare at.

66

'Darling,' Stella looked at Melanie sharply. 'Are you eating properly?'

'Oh, *Mum*,' Melanie sighed crossly.

'Don't you "oh, Mum" me,' Stella retorted. 'Look at you. Nothing but skin and bone!'

'I'm fine, all right? Absolutely fine.'

'Where've you been lately, anyway?' Stella asked. 'I've hardly seen you since the evening of ... Wait a minute, didn't you go off with him after the dinner?'

'Who?' Melanie tried unsuccessfully to feign ignorance.

'Marc Abadi. You didn't, did you? Have you ...?' She looked at Melanie even more closely. 'Have you been seeing one another?' Melanie was silent. 'You have, haven't you? That trip to Paris ... you said you were going with Pippa or someone.' She sighed. 'Oh, *Melanie* ... you *silly* girl.'

'What are you talking about?' Melanie asked, her temper already beginning to rise. 'What's so silly about it?'

'Darling, he's ... he's just not your *type*. He's a very *serious* young man.'

'What the hell's that supposed to mean?'

'You *know* what I mean. He's very dedicated to his work. Yes, he's adorable but I just don't want to see you get hurt, darling. *That's* all.'

'What ... and *I'm* not serious? I'm not a serious person?' The accusation stung, partly because it was true.

'Well ...' Stella hesitated, fidgeting with her rings. 'Of course you are, darling, just ... just in a ... a ... *different* way.'

'Oh, for fuck's sake, Mum. Why don't you just spell it out? You think I'm stupid, don't you? Stupid and lazy!'

'No, of *course* not! You're very bright, Melanie, especially when you put your mind to things, but he lives in ... in ... I don't know, in the middle of *wars* and things. I can't imagine ...'

'That he'd want to go out with someone like me? Why don't you just say it? You think I'm useless, don't you?' Melanie yelled suddenly, shrugging off the hand her mother had tried to place on her wrist. She ran out of the kitchen, slamming the door behind her so hard the panes rattled.

Stella sighed, worried. Melanie could get so *upset* over things, she thought to herself anxiously. She could easily see why Melanie would fall for someone like Marc – Christ, half the women in the room had already fallen by the time he walked up to the podium, herself included – but even she could see he was *way* out of Melanie's league, for all sorts of reasons. Nothing to do with Melanie's beauty, or how bright she was – she was her daughter, for Christ's sake – but she just didn't want to see Melanie get hurt. A man like Marc Abadi simply wouldn't have the patience for someone like Mel. He was married to his work; she'd seen the type before. She'd been *married* to the type, for crying out loud. Oh, Mel. She squared her shoulders and went upstairs. From the sounds of noisy sobbing coming out from under Melanie's door, it seemed like the damage was already done. Oh dear.

She had it all wrong, Melanie thought furiously to herself. *Completely* wrong. She didn't even *know* Marc. Just because *her* marriages hadn't worked out. She stopped, a pang of guilt hitting her suddenly, just below the breastbone. She chewed her lip. Why was her mother so set against Marc? Maybe she was – Melanie considered the possibility carefully – maybe she was *jealous*? After all, who wouldn't be? He was perfect. He was everything she'd ever dreamed of; in a weird way, it felt as though she already knew him, was already in love with him before they'd even met. Now, wasn't that strange? He answered her every need without her even realising. They were *meant* to be together. Anyone could see that.

She looked at the phone beside her bed. The physical ache of longing to hear his voice was almost unbearable. It was impossible to phone him – she would just have to wait until he managed to get a line through to her. She curled up, child-like, on her bed, and closed her eyes. She would have given anything to hear the sound of his voice again. It would be six long, hard weeks before she saw him. What the hell kind of a job did he have anyway?

It was almost seven weeks before he did come back. Seven weeks of counting the hours, minutes, *seconds*, even, before she could touch him, trace her fingers along the rough, sandpapery line of his jaw, touch the rock-hard muscles beneath his jacket sleeve. She ran straight through the crowd of anxiously waiting relatives and friends at Heathrow and barrelled into him, almost knocking him over as he walked out, his customary bag slung casually over one arm. She couldn't speak; she was shy with delight. She drove with one eye on the road and the other on him as if she couldn't quite believe he was there.

'Whoa,' he laughed, as she narrowly missed a cyclist on her slightly unsteady route across a roundabout. 'Slow down, what's the hurry?' What was the *hurry*? Was he serious? She'd been thinking, dreaming, breathing, *waiting* for this moment for the past forty-six days, six hours and God knows how many minutes ... and he thought there was no rush? She took her foot off the accelerator suddenly. Did it mean ...? 'Hey, Mel, d'you want me to drive?' he asked, as she narrowly missed a bus. She shook her head, suddenly too scared to speak. Had she ... misunderstood? Was it just possible he didn't feel the same way about her? She drove the rest of the way to the hotel she'd booked for a week with her heart in her mouth.

No, she hadn't misunderstood. He did feel the same way about her. She saw the way he looked at her as she pulled her sweater over her head to reveal the tiny, wispy black lace bra she'd bought the previous day, heard his sharp intake of breath as she wriggled out of her skirt and knelt astride him, catching and holding his hands as he tried to touch her. No, she shook her head, calm again. Not just yet. It was the same, sweet, giddy rush to the head, the realisation of the power she had over men in that erotic, weak moment. He was hers. There wasn't a thing she couldn't – wouldn't – do. She moved on top of him, very slowly, and watched in almost sublime satisfaction as he closed his eyes, drunk with the pleasure she brought. She leaned forward until her breasts were resting against his chest and his face was entangled in the long, glossy sweep of her hair. *Melanie.* She heard him whisper her name. *Melanie.* She could have stayed there with him still inside her, all night.

The week was gone almost before it began. On their way to the airport, they had their first argument. Marc knew it was coming. Since the previous evening, she'd been withdrawn and sulky, as if to punish him for going away.

'But ...' Melanie said tearfully, looking at his profile as he drove on to the Hammersmith flyover. After that first drive back from the airport, she handed her car keys over with a smile. 'Can't you ring and tell them you need another week or something?' Her voice was plaintive.

Marc sighed. 'Look, Melanie, we've been through this already. I just can't. I have a whole team of people out there, waiting for me. I can't just decide not to go.'

'But *I'm* waiting for you. Why doesn't that count?'

'It does, but this is my job. I'll be back in six weeks. You'll come to Paris. We've already discussed this.'

'Six *weeks*. Marc, that's *years* away. How'm I going to last six weeks? What am *I* supposed to do?'

He gave a short laugh. 'Six weeks is hardly any time at all. Come on, Mel. It'll be here before you know it.'

'It won't,' she said sulkily. 'It's ages away.'

Marc felt an earlier irritation begin to surface. She was behaving like a spoilt child. 'Look, I'll try to get a fortnight off next time, all right? We can go somewhere – Spain or Portugal, somewhere by the sea, if you like. Make it a proper holiday. How does that sound?' he said, trying a placatory approach.

'It's still six weeks away. I don't care what we do *then*.'

'Melanie,' his voice was suddenly quiet. 'Don't. Don't do this.' He was aware of having to control his temper. She was spoiling for a fight.

'I'm not doing anything,' she said angrily. 'You're the one who's leaving *me*.'

He pulled the car over abruptly and came to a halt on the hard shoulder. He could see Melanie look at him in trepidation. The speed with which two people could descend from intimacy into the kind of argument that Melanie seemed determined to have never ceased to amaze him. 'Look,' he said, his voice quiet with the effort of controlling his irritation. 'You need to get one thing straight, Melanie. I'm not leaving *you*. I'm going to work. It's what I do. If we're going to go beyond what's been a really great couple of months, then you are just going to have to accept that this is what I do, OK? Like this, we won't even last the next fortnight.' He looked at her. Around them, the cars whooshed past on their way to the M4. Not the best place to have this kind of argument, he thought to himself. But where was?

He could read the instant capitulation in her eyes. She backed off, immediately, instantly contrite. She was upset – she hadn't meant to make such a fuss. Of course she understood. It was just hard for her, that was all.

'I know you're not meant to say it – at least not this soon,' she said, fiddling nervously with her hair. He knew what was coming. He put up a hand as if to ward her off, but it was too late. There were tears in her eyes. 'After all, we've only known each other a couple of months, but I can't help the way I feel. I love you. I do. There, look, I've said it.' There was silence for a few minutes. He could feel her looking anxiously at him. He didn't know what to say. She was right – it *was* too soon. They hardly knew each other. He looked at her. She took a deep breath, then the words came rushing out. 'It's OK. Go ahead and dump me ... That's what happens, isn't it, when a girl—'

'Melanie,' he cut her short, taking one of her hands and holding it tightly. 'I'm not going to dump you, don't be silly. I'm just saying I have a pretty difficult job. You're just going to have to be patient.'

The relief in her eyes was so palpable it almost hurt. She couldn't get the words out fast enough. 'I will be, I promise. I'm sorry, Marc, I'm really sorry ...' She sounded close to tears. Marc shook his head, baffled.

'It's fine. It's all right. People argue ... it happens. OK? Look,' he said, pointing to the clock on the dashboard. 'We'd better get a move on or I'll miss my flight. You all right?' he asked, starting the engine. Melanie nodded tearfully. 'Come on. Six weeks away – why don't you choose somewhere nice for us?'

'OK.' Her voice was small. He felt his heart contract. She was such a funny thing – tough as all hell one minute, soft as butter the next. He swung out into the traffic. He had just over an hour to catch his plane.

★

Later that afternoon, on the flight from London to Larnaca, he went over things in his head again. In some ways – in bed, for example – she was bolder than anyone he'd ever met; a fact he found unbearably exciting. She'd whispered things to him in the intimacy of darkness that made his head swim ... and then the next morning, behaved like a child whose candy had been pinched. He shook his head. He recognised the danger signs – alternately neglected and then over-indulged. He knew a little about her father – a famous actor or singer, something along those lines. He was on his fifth or sixth wife, barely older than Melanie herself. Her mother was on her third or fourth ... Yes, a classic textbook case. And although he'd warned himself about applying what he'd learned in school to his personal life and the people he met, in Melanie's case it was blindingly obvious. She was a bundle of nervous insecurities. And what had Freud said about *those*?

67

There was definitely something about Jules Williams that Laure didn't like. He had snakelike, hooded eyes, for one thing, and they seemed to hover over her in a way that made her skin crawl. For another, he'd obviously known Daniel 'back in the old days', as he put it, which meant he was part of that group of friends of his she so detested – not a good sign.

'He's *creepy*,' she said to Daniel, half jokingly, as they dressed for dinner.

Daniel sighed. He looked at her in the reflection of the dressing table mirror. 'Look, Laure, I *know* this is a bit of an ordeal for you, and I *know* you don't like my parents and I *know* you sometimes don't like the fact that I'm so tied into my family but for Christ's sake – this is who I am!'

Laure was startled. She hadn't meant to upset him. 'Sorry,'

she said, rather taken aback by his outburst. 'I didn't mean ... I just ... look, I'm sorry.'

'These people are my *family*. I've known Jules almost all my life. What the hell do you want me to do about it?' he asked, his cheeks reddening.

'I'm sorry,' she repeated, meaning it. 'It was rude of me. I didn't think.'

'Fine. Now, can we *please* go down to dinner without an *endless* string of snide remarks?'

'Of course. I'm *really* sorry. I just didn't think ...'

Daniel straightened his tie. He was angrier than she could ever recall seeing him. 'It's fine. Let's just *go*.' He switched off the lights without waiting for her and walked off down the corridor. Laure sat on the bed in the dark, stunned. She'd never seen him so irritated, least of all with her. Perhaps she *had* been going on a bit. He was right. It wasn't polite. And it wasn't fair. She hurried out of the room after him.

He calmed down quickly enough. He wasn't the type to sulk – at least not with her. In four years of marriage, she'd only ever seen him angry once or twice, and she'd had nothing to do with either occasion. She squeezed his hand under the table and was relieved to feel his answering pressure. 'I'm sorry,' she whispered in his ear during a particularly loud part of the conversation elsewhere. He kissed her hair. She made a greater effort to chat to his cousins, to his Aunt Brunhilde; she swallowed her pride and talked to his Uncle Stephan about Haiti and the sorry mess the country was in. She even managed to summon up a smile for Jules Williams. The dinner went on until midnight, unusual for the Bermanns. Laure saw that she had, in part at least, contributed to the lighter mood at the table; for once, the wine and conversation flowed. Perhaps Daniel was right. She hadn't given them enough of a chance.

They got up from the table around midnight, wishing each other a good night. She shook hands with her father-in-law and there was even a small peck on the cheek from Octavia. She swallowed, unexpectedly touched by the thawing of hostilities, however wine-induced. She was just moving out of the way when Jules Williams stepped forward, holding his arms open as if about to kiss her on both cheeks. She submitted demurely, turning her cheek left ... and then suddenly, he said something that made her blood run cold. She drew back. She looked at him in some confusion – what ...? Maybe she'd misheard him? His hand was still on her arm. He leaned forward again, touching her right cheek. No, she hadn't misheard. He whispered it into her ear. '*Voodoo Princess*. Great film!' And then he walked away, slapping Daniel on the back as he climbed the stairs to his room. Her blood turned to ice.

She had no idea how she made it from the dining room to the bedroom; she had no recollection whatsoever of wishing everyone a good night or picking up her little clutch purse that had fallen to the floor as soon as Jules Williams had whispered in her ear. She left Daniel, walked a little unsteadily to the bathroom, shut the door and leaned against it, her whole body shaking with fear. How had she ever thought she could escape it? *Voodoo Princess*. She'd been stupid enough to think she could forget about the shameful, sordid things she'd done, bury her past so that no one would remember, and start again, all nice and clean, the fashionable wife of a rich, handsome, young man. What had she been thinking? Of *course* it didn't work like that. Of course she would be made to pay. Of course ...

'Laure?' Daniel called out to her from the bed. 'What're you doing in there? Come to bed, darling.'

'C ... coming,' she stammered, her heart sinking. What was going to happen next? Jules had recognised her – surely he wasn't going to leave it at that? She stared at her tortured, frightened face in the mirror. He wanted something from her, she was sure of it. The way he'd looked at her all day ... she knew it! She *knew* there was something menacing about him. Her eyes began to film over. What was she going to do?

'Laure? What are you doing?'

She quickly washed her face, splashing water on to her neck and arms to cool herself down. 'Just a minute,' she called, patting herself dry. 'I'll be out in a sec.'

'Bloody hell,' Daniel grumbled sleepily as she opened the

door. 'You don't half know how to make a man wait,' he said, drawing back the covers for her. He was naked. Laure felt her stomach turn.

'I ... I ... not tonight, Daniel ... I don't feel very well,' she stammered. She wasn't lying. She felt sick.

'Something you ate tonight?' he asked, his voice full of tender concern. 'It was the little tiff, wasn't it? I shouldn't have snapped at you.'

'No ... not that.'

'But you saw, didn't you? They do like you ... all of them. Even Jules.'

Laure thought she might throw up. She turned into her pillow, hugging her stomach. 'I ... I'll be fine in the morning,' she mumbled, hoping he would fall asleep quickly. She had a feeling she wouldn't sleep a wink.

An hour later, she was still tossing and turning, disturbing Daniel who woke every time she moved. She pulled back the covers and slipped out of bed. She was thirsty and the wine at dinner had left her with a dull headache. She pulled on her dressing gown and opened the door. The house was dark and silent. She had some aspirin in her handbag; she would just go down to the kitchen for a glass of milk. She padded softly downstairs in her bare feet, careful not to make any sound. She walked into the kitchen, decided against switching on the lights and walked quickly over to the fridge. She pulled open the enormous steel door, screwing up her eyes against the harsh light from its interior. She had just put her hand on a bottle of Evian when someone spoke.

'Well, hello, there.' She almost dropped the bottle. It was Jules Williams. Of course. She whirled round. He was sitting in the dark at the kitchen table, playing loosely with something in his hand. 'Cigarette,' he said, holding up the lighter he'd been playing with. 'Couldn't sleep, you see. Came down to have a cigarette on the patio outside. Cold, isn't it?' His voice was chatty. It filled her with fear and loathing. 'I guess you can't sleep, either, hmm? I wonder why?'

'What do you want?' Laure said quietly. 'I don't know what

the fuck you're talking about.'

'No? You sure about that?' He flicked the lighter open and held the blue flame in front of his face. 'No idea what I'm talking about, huh?'

'Look, I think you've mistaken me for someone else. I don't know who you are, I don't know where you think you've seen me but …'

'Cut the crap, Laure. We both know *exactly* what I'm talking about.' His voice was suddenly harsh. She felt the cold hand of fear creeping over her. 'I don't know how you managed it, but you've wrangled yourself a pretty cushy number here, don't you think? I mean, from *Voodoo Princess* to Primrose Hill? That's a pretty steep hill you've climbed, wouldn't you say?'

'I'm not listening to this,' Laure said, closing the fridge door.

'Oh, but you should. You see …' He rose from the table and moved towards her. Laure's hand went to her belt. '*My* favourite part in the whole film … do you remember? It's when she gets down on her knees and opens her mouth, wide … like this,' he said, coming closer. He put out a hand to touch her.

'Get your *fucking* hands away from me,' Laure hissed, stepping back. 'If you even *touch* me, I'll scream.'

'Oh, yeah?' He was inches away from her. 'And what would you say? "Oh, Daniel, I was just showing him the part where …" Hey, where the fuck are you going?'

'Stay away from me,' Laure said, her voice hoarse with anger. 'Just stay away from me, d'you hear? Stay the *fuck* away!' She turned and almost ran back down the corridor, not caring who might hear. Anything to get away from the sound of his voice. She failed to see the figure of Günter Bermann, half hidden by the thick drapes that lined the passageway from the kitchen to the stairs. She wouldn't have known he'd been there for quite some time.

She was right. She didn't sleep a wink. She lay beside Daniel's heavy, even breathing until dawn, her mind blank with fear. What would she say? What could she say? *It was only that once*

... I was desperate. Why were you desperate? The lies she'd told; everything would come tumbling out. Delroy, leaving Haiti, Belle ... the baby. And then what? She was literally shaking by the time Daniel finally surfaced, heavy-headed from the night before. She fetched him two aspirins and could hardly hold the glass.

'Are you all right?' he kept asking. 'You look terrible.'

'I think I'll stay in bed for a bit longer,' she mumbled, getting back into bed and pulling the sheets over her head.

'Do that, you look awful, darling. I'll come up and see you a bit later. Jules is going back to Chicago before lunch. Shall I tell him goodbye from you?' She nodded, not trusting herself to speak. 'Get some rest,' he said, kissing the top of her head. She heard him go into the bathroom and then the tears came. Unstoppable. This time, there would be no waiting for the storm to pass.

But nothing happened. She stayed in their room most of the day, dozing fitfully, jerking awake whenever Daniel entered the room, expecting to see the darkened signs of anger, hurt, pain on his face ... but there was nothing. He came in around six p.m., his face cold from the freezing air outside. He'd been for a walk with the cousins ... wouldn't she come down for dinner? The neighbours had left ... it would just be the family. She reluctantly got up, showered and dressed, following him downstairs with a heart so heavy she felt it would surely fall to the floor. Octavia was even solicitous towards her, which only made her feel worse. Günter didn't speak to her at all during the meal, but that was hardly unusual – he barely spoke to anyone. It was a relief to escape back upstairs, to lose herself in the cool, linen sheets and to close her eyes against the fear that was gnawing its way through her skull.

Two days later, she and Daniel were sitting side by side, on their way back to London. Nothing had happened. Every time the phone rang, her heart almost stopped. She searched his face anxiously as soon as he entered the room for some sign that he'd been told ... that Jules Williams had done exactly as he threatened. But there was nothing. If anything, he was gentler with her. He appreciated the effort she'd made, he said, nuzzling her ear. And she'd seen, hadn't she? His mother was starting to come round. She'd been so worried on that last day, when Laure had been in bed. 'She even asked me if you might be "expecting", that's exactly what she said. She came over all embarrassed – can you imagine?' He grinned delightedly. 'I told her there was always a possibility but I didn't think so. She went bright red, I promise.' He laughed. 'You're not "expect-ing", are you, darling?'

'No,' Laure whispered. 'Nothing like that.'

'*I* wouldn't mind,' Daniel said mildly. 'In fact, I'd—'

'Daniel ... please. I ... I'd rather not talk about it. Not just now,' Laure said miserably. 'Can we talk about it some other time?'

'Of course,' Daniel looked at her in surprise. 'Still not feel-ing well?'

She shook her head. He drew her hand into his, his fingers running lightly over the platinum and diamond engagement ring as if to remind himself – and her. She was his. She kept her eyes closed most of the way to London.

68

'Her name's Laure Estelle St Lazâre. I want you to find out everything there is to know about the little bitch. *Every*thing. I don't care how much it costs or how long it takes. I don't care where you have to go. You bring me everything, you understand me?'

'Sure thing, Mr Bermann. When d'you want me to start?' Saul Lopez, PI, had worked for Bermann before. The man had deep pockets, he knew, and the well of his patience was even deeper. Bermann could wait a very long time to get what he wanted.

'Now. Right now. That's the name of the film. *Voodoo Princess*. Some kind of porn film, I don't know when it was made. But I want this done discreetly, do we understand one another?' He pushed the file across the table and got up heavily. 'Absolutely no publicity, do I make myself clear?'

'Sure, Mr Bermann,' Lopez repeated. That, too, he could do. He waited until Bermann had left the room. He opened the file and whistled. He looked at the photocopy of the marriage certificate between Daniel Günter Bermann and one Laure Estelle St Lazâre. He raised his eyebrows. She was married to his son? No wonder the old man wanted it kept quiet. He picked up his keys and left.

69

Guilt, Améline discovered, was a terrible, unruly thing, like toothache – dull, nagging, persistent, never far from attention. Just when you got used to its rumbling, ruminating presence, it would lash out, strike you down, stop you dead in your tracks. The worst thing was, it was entirely unpredictable. She was living on a roller coaster. One minute she was sitting next to Iain, wishing he would stop droning on and on about some petty little incident at his publishers, or some stupid little row he'd had with the train conductor, or some silly little conversation with some insignificant person he'd spoken to at the newsagents, and then the next minute, she was struck with remorse when he looked at her, sensing her inattention. Most days it was all she could do to keep herself focused on her business, remembering what to order, what they were running short of, whether Claire had said she would bake the scones the following morning or not. In spite of the guilt, her head was filled with the taste and touch and smell of him. *Paul.* Just thinking about him brought on a rush of emotion so intense it left her weak, sometimes shaking. It was as if she'd been walking around half deaf, or half blind – immune to the beauty and colour and joy in the world. He was in her head, all day, every day. She was slowly going mad.

'Where d'you want to go on holiday this year?' Iain asked her a few days later as she began to load the car with food. He had stopped going into London quite as frequently and it was beginning to wear on Améline's nerves.

'Holiday?' she repeated, suddenly panicking. It was the last thing she wanted to do.

'Yes. We've been to France almost three years in a row. Just thought you might fancy somewhere different, that's all. Don't sound so surprised.'

Ouch. There it was again. The sharp, ever-ready stab of guilt. 'I ... I haven't really thought about it,' Améline said, closing the boot. 'I've just been, you know, the café ... Maybe we could go later in the year?' she asked hopefully. Anything to put it off. She just couldn't think about a fortnight alone with Iain.

'Of course. Just have a think about it. We don't need to decide now.'

'I will. Are ... are you going into London this week?' she asked. Bang. Another stab.

'Actually, I've got to go up this afternoon. I'm meeting Bernie. I'll probably be back tomorrow – late afternoon-ish. I've got a meeting with my bank tomorrow morning. Will you be all right?'

She looked at him in surprise. He normally spent a few days a week in London. 'Of course I'll be all right.'

'It's just, well, you've been looking awfully tired lately,' he said, smiling back at her. 'Thought you might be coming down with something. Flu or something.'

Ouch. Another sharp stab, deeper this time. 'I'm fine,' she said, as naturally as she could.

'You all right?' Iain asked again. 'You do look rather peaky. Should I postpone Bernie?'

'No! No ... no, of course not. I'm perfectly fine. You go, don't worry about me. I'll pick you up tomorrow evening, shall I? You'll be on the five forty-five?'

'Probably. Unless he persuades me otherwise! I'll ring you from the station.'

She watched him leave, his briefcase in hand and his coat slung over his shoulder. He gave her a quick wave from the gate, then he was gone, on his way down the hill to the station. Améline stood where she was, steeling herself against the awful temptation to pick up the phone. Since that night, almost a week ago, she had seen Paul only once and Claire's presence had thankfully steered the situation in the right, proper direction. It couldn't happen again. She'd avoided his eyes and spent most of the half an hour he was in the café hiding in the back. And yet, as she'd locked up the café each subsequent night, she'd lingered outside for a few minutes, half hoping, half fearing he would step out of the shadows ... but no. He'd had the good sense to stay away. She closed the lid of the boot and walked back inside the house. She had twenty minutes before she had to leave; time enough for a cup of tea. She'd just put the kettle on when she heard Viv's footsteps. That, she said, steeling herself, was possibly the hardest part of it all. She *longed* to tell her what had happened. But she couldn't. It only increased her guilt.

The day went smoothly enough; the café was busy, though there was no sign of Paul, or his mates. She found herself oscillating wildly between elation and despair. What if he'd decided never to come back? What if, after the last time he'd been in and she'd refused to meet his eyes, she'd offended him? What if she never saw him again? The memory of what they'd done – the way he'd made her feel – brought tears to her eyes at the thought of never experiencing it again. Claire stuck her head round the door and she'd had to feign a sneezing fit. It sounded awkward, even to her own ears.

At five-thirty, she locked up, slipped the keys in her pocket and made her way to the car. And there he was. Standing under the street light, his hands in his pockets, looking, if it were possible, more miserable than she. Her heart lifted; there was no stopping the rush of pleasure and relief that flowed through her as soon as their eyes met.

'Am,' he said, spreading his hands in front of him helplessly. 'I'm sorry. I tried to stay away … I just can't.'

Améline stood still, the sound of her own heartbeat unnaturally loud in her ears. The feelings of guilt she'd been struggling with for the past week disappeared as soon as she saw his hurt, uncertain face, heard the desolation in his voice. She could no more have stopped herself from walking up to him and taking hold of his hands than she could have stopped herself breathing. In a daze of sweet, trembling anticipation, she followed his directions to a small terraced house in a part of the village she'd never been to, held on to his hand as he took her into a narrow, dark hallway and then, right there, with the scratchy feel of the carpet underneath her bare skin, he did it to her again, and again.

It was almost dawn before she drove her little car up the hill, parked across the road and switched off the engine. Both her house and Viv's were shrouded in darkness, to her relief. She crept out, ran across the road and slid the key into the lock. She ran a bath and lay in the cooling water until the light began to filter in through the blinds. The words of the priest came back to her, mocking her. 'What you have done once, you will do again. You should not give in to the temptation, my child.' Well, she had. Not once, but twice. She was damned. There was no going back, now. Not now.

70

Back in London, the days began to rapidly slip past. Laure went to college twice a week; Daniel went to work – and still nothing happened. There was a card from Octavia, addressed to them both. The painting was in the hallway at their Lake Shore Drive penthouse and several friends had admired it ... perhaps Laure would like to know? Daniel stuck the card triumphantly on the refrigerator door.

They went to Geneva for a few days at the end of January and still nothing happened. Slowly, very slowly, Laure began to relax. Perhaps she'd done the right thing by standing up to him? Perhaps she'd scared him off? Perhaps ... perhaps nothing would come of it. After all, if he'd been planning on telling Daniel, surely he would have by now? What would be the point of waiting? Relief began to seep through her; for the first time since it had happened, she was able to sleep through the night. She would never lie to him again. Never, ever. One morning after he had gone to work, she pulled the little parcel from the back of the drawer and held it in her hands as she swore she would never hide anything from him again. She was not religious, at least not in the conventional sense of the word, and making that sort of pledge with her hand on a Bible – even if she could have found one – seemed false, somehow. Her talisman seemed more appropriate.

She lay back, holding it against her stomach, thinking about what she had just narrowly managed to escape. If, at any point in the past four years, she had ever doubted the strength of her love for Daniel, she no longer did. In the beginning, she'd worried about the fine line between love and gratitude – made all the more hazy by Daniel's generous nature. When he'd asked her to marry him, she had genuinely agonised over her response – how could she separate what he offered from what he was? Money, wealth, choices ... Those were as much a part of Daniel's character as his easy-going laugh, the way he couldn't pass a beggar on the street without dropping a coin, his passion for black-and-white westerns that she couldn't bring herself to share; *those* were Daniel, just as the house in which they lived was part of what he brought. What had she brought to the marriage? she often wondered. A few thousand precious dollars in hard-earned savings? No, that wasn't all. There was more; he just didn't know it. A whole, hidden, secret life in which she'd had a child, sold him and made a film which she couldn't even think about without drawing her knees up to her chest in shame. Her fear at the thought of losing it all over something she'd done in absolute desperation was real enough. No, she had no doubts about her feelings for Daniel. He had given her everything, including the one thing she'd never expected to find again – her self-respect. How was it possible that someone had come to take it all away again?

She sat up, aware suddenly that her mouth was full of her own tears. She folded the little jumpsuit and slid it back into her drawer. She supposed she ought to be grateful, in a funny, roundabout way, to that horrible Jules Williams. Without intending to, of course, he'd made her see things more clearly. For that, she supposed, she ought to be grateful. Sometimes you needed a crisis to help you find your way.

The start of the new term at Central St Martin's brought a new tutor to the college. Jill Teague was a handsome, striking woman in her late forties whom the students instantly adored. She took them out of the stuffy, overheated classrooms and dull, badly lit lecture halls and introduced them to the vast collection of textiles at the V&A, to the small but beautifully preserved Geffrye Museum on the Kingsland Road, in the East End, where she also ran her studio. Laure fell in love with the large, messy space, full of cuttings, postcards, samples and snapshots. She spent as long as she dared wandering around in Jill's workshop, examining her sketchbooks, picking up objects, looking at her photographs. There was nothing, it seemed to her, that Jill discarded; all of life's experiences, from a line of a poem to the colour of the washing-up liquid on her kitchen sink, were rich sources of inspiration. She ran a very small company, JT Designs, that specialised in upholstery fabrics – Laure longed to do the same one day. From Jill she learned about scale, texture, composition, pattern ... She read about the Chinese silk trade, about the rise of the Byzantine Empire and the maritime cities of Italy like Venice and Florence, who traded textiles with the East. She pored over descriptions of 'toile de Jouy', from nineteenth-century France, and researched the wool mills of England and the tartans of the Scots. Jill encouraged them to look further afield: at the intricate embroidery of India and Pakistan; the woven cloths of the Ashanti from West Africa, the geometry of Islamic art. By the end of the term, Laure's head was spinning. The study, which she'd envisioned as a quiet, calm space of reading and reflection, had slowly turned into a messier, more chaotic version of Jill's workshop. Daniel complained that he would have to extract his precious business studies books from the room for fear of finding them paint-splattered or ink-stained or worse. The day he came upon her carefully tearing strips off old copies of *The Economist* to create a collage was the day he'd had enough. Why didn't she get a studio of her own? He would buy her one, if that was what she wanted. How about a small place next to that tutor of hers, what was her name? Someone had told him there were properties going for almost nothing in the East End. Madness, really. Who the hell would want to live there?

By the end of the week, Sophie had come back with a list of small workshops for sale. Dirt cheap: they cost less than the kitchen they'd put in at home.

71

Günter Bermann watched the tape all the way to the end. His face was a mottled, puce colour by the time Laure's mouth faded from view. He sat in his enormous leather chair for a few seconds, drumming his fingers on the silky-smooth surface of his vast desk. Spread around him were several documents, the evidence of Lopez's two months of hard work. He arranged them neatly, in chronological order, and then extracted the tape from the VCR. He slid everything into a large, padded envelope, then placed it in his safe. The moment to strike had to be right. He'd suspected the little gold-digging slut from the start. Oh, it was easy to see how his son had been taken in. The bitch was beautiful, no question. What a body. As much as it disgusted him, the film had been undeniably erotic. If he'd been a few years younger ... He stood up, agitated. There was only one place for a girl like that. On her knees, just as she had been in the film. She'd found her natural place – all he had to do was get her back there. Before she completely trapped his son. He adjusted himself uncomfortably. The little bitch. She'd even managed to excite *him*.

72

Surely it would get easier? Melanie stared at the walls of her bedroom and thought she would go mad. It *had* to get easier. By now, she ought to have been used to the rhythm of their visits. Two weeks of heaven followed by six or eight weeks of hell. Like a record, playing endlessly. Two weeks, six weeks; two weeks, eight weeks. Without, as he kept saying, the possibility of parole. *That* was his job; that was him. She *had* to get used to it, no other way. But it had been nearly a year now and she was still finding it difficult. If anything, it was worse. Each time he left, a little piece of her died and it took her six weeks to recover – by which time he was already preparing to come back and repeat the whole thing all over again. It was killing her. There *had* to be a way out of it. Marc had to be made to see sense. It was all very well for him – he was the one jetting off to Beirut, Ramallah, Gaza City, Kabul … to places she'd never heard of. After they'd been together about eight months, he told her he was being transferred. Even further away. Uganda, Burundi … She'd had to buy an atlas, tracing spidery lines across the African continent to find out where he was. At least she had some idea of what Beirut looked like; she'd seen enough bulletins on the news. This latest place he said he was going – Goma, Boma? – fuck, she'd never even *heard* of the country. She couldn't picture him. When, on the extremely rare occasion he managed to put in a satellite call to her, she couldn't imagine where he was, what his surroundings looked like. There was only the faint, disembodied voice on the other end of a line that broke frequently. She was going insane. There had to be a way out of their horrible, horrible situation. There just *had* to be.

'Oh, Mel,' her mother said, walking into her room one morning. 'I wish you wouldn't just lie around all day when Marc's not here. It's not healthy, darling. You need to do something else. You can't just lie there.'

'What else is there to do?' Melanie snapped, aggrieved. Why couldn't her mother just leave her alone?

'I don't know … Go out, make some new friends … do something. Anything!'

'What, like you? Where do *you* go? The gym? Church?'

Her mother sighed and quickly shut the door again. Melanie lay back on her bed, exhausted. She didn't know how to explain it – the feeling of cold dread that came over her every time Marc prepared to leave. The panic usually started two or three days before his actual departure. It was always the same. He'd grow ever so slightly distant, his mind already elsewhere. She remembered the first time it had happened; on his third or fourth visit. They'd gone to a restaurant, somewhere in Paris. She'd been chattering away, about silly, amusing stuff, when she'd realised suddenly that his attention wasn't on her. He was listening, pausing between mouthfuls of food to nod and murmur – *mmm? Yes? Really?* His eyes were on her but the real conversation was going on elsewhere, not with her; he addressed an audience she couldn't see. A cold, glittery panic took hold of her. She was thirteen again, watching her father withdraw; she was fifteen, looking at the face of a stepfather who was looking straight through her. *I'm here*, she wanted to scream across the white linen tablecloth and the beautiful goblets of wine. *Don't do this to me.* But when his attention came back to her, she grasped it as if she were drowning. Since then, she'd learned to recognise the signs and put out her own signals to deflect it. A sore throat, a sudden crying spell; she'd even managed once, with supreme effort, to claim she didn't want to make love on his last night. But she was running out of tactics and Marc was a clever man. She'd caught him looking at her once or twice, as if trying to figure something out. No, she couldn't go on like this. She had to do *something*.

He moved through the tangled undergrowth on his way back to his bungalow, his whole body alive to the smells and sounds around him. The pungent smell of the earth, recently released by the rains, hit the back of his throat, tasting of iron. New shrubs, leaves and grasses danced in a miasma of green, dissolving light; it was the season of growth in Africa. Including – his hand went to the letter nestled in his back pocket – a child. His child. He'd received the letter from Melanie that morning. His first, immediate reaction had been one of trepidation. *I'm not ready for this.* But he'd sat there, alone for once in the makeshift office and read and reread the letter until it had finally sunk in. It was vintage Melanie. First the little stuff, amusing bits of gossip about London and the life that now, sitting somewhere in the bush in the middle of the continent, seemed as though it could never have existed. She wrote beautiful letters; opening them and reading the first lines was like diving headlong into cool, fresh water. She had the knack of bringing him back to that other life, far from the camps where he worked and where they were assaulted almost daily by storms, natural and otherwise. Then the practical stuff: the boiler had packed up;

her mother was distraught. She'd gone into the cellar to take a look. It amused him to think of her crouched down among the pipes and inexplicable wiring of the house, a spanner in hand. And then the big news. 'I've been to see Dr Mallinder. I know it's not the right time and I know it will come as a bit of a shock – I'm pregnant. There, I've said it. I'm still too nervous to say it out loud! Tell me you're pleased!'

He touched the letter again. It was five in the afternoon but the air still held the midday heat; underneath his shirt, his chest and back were bathed in a thin film of sweat. He reached the little bungalow, unlocked the door and switched on the fan. In the distance, he could hear the steady hum of the generator which was now as familiar to him as the sound of the traffic racing alongside the Seine. He stripped off his damp clothes and headed for the shower.

Half an hour later, bathed and shaved and feeling almost light-headed with the news, he made his way back along the path that led to the canteen where the staff ate together every night. Night fell quickly, as it does in the tropics, going from light to dark in just under thirty minutes. The sky closed in, a thick, tangible blackness, like water. They were in the middle of nowhere. Khartoum lay almost a thousand kilometres to the north. Here, almost at the border with Niger where the Sahara petered out into savannah, the UN had set up a camp for the thousands of refugees displaced by the civil war raging to the north. Marc had flown out to meet the regular camp staff in April; it was now October and his fourth month-long visit. They were a good crowd; dedicated and naïve in almost equal measure. He liked the operations manager, the improbably named Felicity Feinberg – *don't ask* – from England. In the way he'd noticed the English often did, everyone called her Fid. Her initials, she explained. *Felicity Isobelle Darla. I told you not to ask!* She was a big, cheerful girl who had worked 'all over the place' as she put it. Ethiopia, Sumatra, Albania. She'd left London in the wake of some unhappy relationship, he found out and, in the way he'd come to recognise of most of the people he met 'in the field', casually took up with another aid worker or a visiting official when the mood or circumstances allowed. She was tough as nails, too. Nothing frightened her. Snakes, scorpions, soldiers, sunstroke … she'd seen it all before. She rallied the group of twenty-odd staff around her and somehow, Marc saw, impressed, she kept the disparate group together.

He pushed open the door to the bungalow that served as canteen, living room and occasional spare bedroom and found Fid sitting in front of the radio, twiddling dials.

'Hi,' he said, flopping into the nearest chair.

She looked up. 'Hi. Have you heard? There's been a breach in the ceasefire. I heard it on CNN about fifteen minutes ago but I can't get the BBC. The transmitter must've gone down.'

Marc sat up. A breach in the precarious balance between the two groups slugging it out over the future of the country meant only one thing: yet more refugees pouring into the already overstretched camps. It was always the same. In the capital or wherever such decisions were taken, politicians and soldiers made and then broke the rules. And, sure as night follows day, it was the civilian population who paid the price. He sighed. He'd lived here for almost three weeks; what wouldn't he give for a decent shower and a good bottle of wine?

'Bastards,' Fid said, reading his thoughts. She stood up, looking for her cigarettes.

'Melanie's pregnant.' The words slipped out of his mouth before he'd had a chance to think.

'Oh? Was that the letter this morning? I saw it in the post.'

'Yeah.' Marc nodded, suddenly self-conscious. He saw that Fid was a little taken aback. It wasn't like him to divulge such personal information, particularly to strangers. But that was the thing – living as they did in such close physical proximity, the people around him had gone from being strangers to being like family in less than a week. He had an inkling of why Fid's amorous attachments never lasted.

'You *are* pleased, though, aren't you?' Fid asked curiously.

Marc nodded slowly. 'I think so. Yes, I am pleased.'

'I expect it'll take a while to get used to. It'll change a lot of things for you.'

'What d'you mean?'

'Well, – this sort of stuff.' She waved a hand in the general direction of the camp. 'It'll all seem a bit, I don't know, other-worldly, I should imagine once the baby arrives. I can't imagine your wife'll be all that keen for you to disappear every other week.'

'She's not my wife.' Again, the words were out before he could stop them.

Fid looked at him and smiled. 'She soon will be,' she remarked tartly, and turned back to the radio. Marc remained where he was, smoking cigarette after cigarette, lost in thought.

His last week went by agonisingly slowly. He tried several times to place a call to London but the lines were always down. He found it hard to believe that less than three thousand kilo-metres away, a woman would be waiting for him in a sunny Parisian flat with a child growing inside her. He found himself filled with an impatient tenderness for her; even for her faults. He lay in bed at night, smoking, thinking. He recalled the spider's web of veins on the delicate skin on the inside of her right knee; the tiny criss-cross of stretch marks on her buttocks that she hated and on which she spent God knows how many thousands of francs on creams that were *guaranteed* to make them disappear. The way she always bit the nail on her left pinkie when she was puzzled or afraid. He was entranced by her, all over again.

Finally, just when he thought he couldn't stand it another second longer, his last day arrived. He packed his bags, said his last, agonisingly painful goodbyes to the children whose care he had supervised, and got into the passenger seat of the white UN 4x4 that would drive him six hours south to Niamey. From there it was a four-hour flight across West Africa to Bamako, and from there another six hours to Paris.

In Paris, nervously waiting for him to arrive, Melanie paced the floor of his apartment. He wouldn't hear of her coming to the airport. They'd spoken briefly the day before. He was happy, he promised her. There was no question about keeping the child. They'd talk when he got home. She folded her hands across her stomach and tried to quell her nerves. She looked down at her stomach. She'd told him two weeks ago that she was seven weeks pregnant – she'd been careful to work it out properly – but did that mean she should already be showing? She hadn't a clue. Fuck. She heard a car turn the corner and rushed to the window. There he was, his head emerging from the back seat, raincoat over his shoulder. Her heart began to beat faster. She watched him pay the driver, look up quickly at the first floor windows and then watched his tall, broad frame disappear through the doorway.

Two seconds later, she heard his key in the lock. He must have run up the stairs. Her heart hammering, she rushed to the door.

'Mel.' His arms went around her and she clung to him, overcome by the feel and smell of him. There was a tenderness in his embrace that brought tears to her eyes. Flustered, she bent down to pick up his case but he pulled her back. 'No lifting,' he said, his voice warm. 'When did you get in?'

'Yesterday,' she whispered, trying not to cry.

'What's this?' he said gently, his hand going under her chin. 'Why the tears?'

'I ... I didn't know ...' she said, beginning to cry in earnest. 'I wasn't sure ...'

He held her for a moment, then laced his fingers through hers. 'Of course I'm happy. You do want the child, don't you?' She nodded, not trusting herself to speak. 'Then that's settled. We'll get married, we'll do it properly.'

Melanie stopped crying. She felt weak at the knees. She looked up into Marc's face – was he joking? 'Are you serious?' she finally croaked out.

'Of course I'm serious.'

'But ...' Melanie swallowed painfully. 'It's not just because of the baby, is it?' she asked in a whisper.

He pulled her close to him again, burying his face in her hair. 'No. I would have asked you anyway. This just brings it closer. We're going to have a child, Mel ... I want to do it properly. The right way.'

Melanie closed her eyes. It was all the reassurance she needed. All she'd done was hurry things along a little; he would have asked her anyway. He'd said it himself. He loved her. He wanted to marry her, with or without a child on the way.

'Have you told your mother?'

'You've only just asked me!' Melanie protested weakly, her hand going up to the nape of his neck.

'No, about the baby?'

'Oh. No, no … it's supposed to be bad luck. You're supposed to wait …'

'I'll have to tell Tante Layla. She'll be over the moon,' he said, kissing her. It wasn't strictly true. Tante Layla hadn't taken to Melanie in quite the way he'd hoped. Still, a child would change all of that.

'No! You can't!' Melanie took a step backwards in genuine fright. 'What if … what if something happens?'

'Nothing's going to happen,' Marc said, pulling her towards him again. 'Don't be silly. I'll have a word with Dr Villela and see what we can do about my next trip. Maybe I can wrangle things to stay for a bit, at least towards the end.'

Melanie couldn't think of anything to say. It was what she wanted more than anything else in the world. And yet, now that she'd got it, all sorts of doubts were beginning to creep in. What if Marc could somehow tell she wasn't pregnant when he touched her? Or when they made love? He was a doctor, wasn't he? She closed her eyes. She actually did feel sick.

Later that evening, sitting curled up next to him on the sofa, as he talked to someone on the phone in Arabic, something began to take shape in her mind. What if … what if she really *did* get pregnant? He'd asked her to marry him; he seemed certain he wanted to spend the rest of his life with her, just as she did with him. He was so pleased about the baby – never mind that there *was* no baby, as yet – it would just be a matter of weeks, surely? She could always say Dr Mallinder had got the date wrong. She leaned into him, breathing deeply with excitement. All of a sudden, it seemed the most logical thing to do. She could be pregnant in a couple of days; possibly even that night! Why, she hadn't actually *lied* at all. She'd just anticipated the truth. All she'd done was bring the inevitable forwards a little, that was all. No one could blame her for trying to do that, surely. It was what Marc wanted. It was what *she* wanted. It wasn't wrong at all. She'd just done what she had to, that was all. Nothing wrong with that.

73

'What you have done once, you will do again.' Not once, not twice but whenever the opportunity presented itself. She hated herself for it, but couldn't stop and Iain, reticent and increasingly forgetful, made it even easier. Améline couldn't actually remember the last time she and Iain had slept together. Six months ago? Eight? She wasn't sure. All she knew now was that it would be physically impossible for her to go back. Paul had shown her something else and she knew there was no going back. The guilt, on the other hand, was killing her. Viv knew there was something wrong. Améline was just thankful she wasn't the prying kind; two or three more questions and she was sure she'd blurt it out. It would hurt Viv dreadfully. She was so fond of Iain and there was no way around it – it was just plain wrong. Wicked. Sinful. She closed her eyes against the images of fire and pain that the word *hell* conjured up. Wherever it was, she would burn in it.

The phone rang, interrupting her thoughts. It was Iain. He wouldn't be back on the afternoon train that day; he and Bernie were going out to dinner in London. He'd be back the following day. No, not to worry, he'd catch the 11.05 and be back in Malvern in the early afternoon. He'd take a taxi from the station.

Améline replaced the receiver, her heart thudding. Could

she ...? Would she dare? It would be easy ... Paul could slip in unnoticed after ten. Viv always went to bed around nine-thirty; she would no more think of opening her curtains to peer outside in the darkness than Améline would – and Améline hated the dark. Her hands felt clammy with excitement. A whole night together ... She would at least have the delicacy to suggest they slept in the spare bedroom. It was a pretty room; she'd made the yellow, sunny curtains herself and the bed was deep and wide with a plump down duvet. It would be so much more comfortable than his bare little flat with its single bed and the naked bulb swinging above it. She bit her lip. She was damned anyway. The opportunity was too tempting to resist.

'It's amazing,' Paul said, propping himself up on one elbow, feeling the texture and soft, cloudy springiness of her hair. Améline's face was on fire. He'd insisted on keeping the light on, watching her face underneath his as he moved inside her, pinning her wrists above her head and waiting patiently for her pleasure, as well as his.

'No, it's not,' Améline said, trying to wriggle away.

'No, don't move. It's so soft. It's like cotton wool. Why don't you wear it loose? You always keep it tied up.'

'It's just easier,' Améline said, squirming pleasurably. When was the last time anyone had said anything nice about anything other than her cooking? 'But you should see Laure's hair. My sister.' She stopped, shocked. It had just slipped out.

'I didn't know you had a sister,' he said, his voice very close to her ear. He slid a hand down the length of her back, resting it against the curve of her hip. Améline thought she would faint. 'Where is she? In Haiti?'

'I ... well, she's not really my sister. We have this ... thing,' she said, turning her body inwards, the better to fit against his. 'I was the *reste-avec* in the house. It's like someone who grows up with you.'

'*Reste-avec*,' Paul murmured. 'Doesn't that mean "stay-with" or something?'

'Yes!' Améline smiled, enjoying the sound of her language in his mouth. 'Exactly.'

'What's her hair like?' he murmured, still touching hers.

'Oh, it's very long, very curly, not like mine. Hers is soft, you can run your fingers through it.'

'Hmm. It'd be pretty hard to get my fingers through this. How'd you get a comb through it?'

'I don't.' They both giggled softly.

'So where is she? Your sister-who's-not-a-sister?'

Améline was quiet for a moment. 'I don't know,' she said finally. 'She left Haiti when I did – eight years ago. She went to America. I never heard from her again.'

'Blimey. That must be hard. Not knowing what's happened to her, I mean.'

'Yes. Yes, it *is* hard. Sometimes I think it would be better if she were dead. I mean, at least then I'd *know*,' she said. 'Like this … I just wonder all the time. Where she is, what she's doing, what could have happened to her.' Améline was stunned. She had never even told Iain about Laure and here she was, lying in the spare room in her husband's house, her legs wrapped around a man who was half his age, opening her heart.

'When my mum died,' Paul said, after a moment. 'I thought the world had ended. She'd always been there, you know. After school and that. She stayed at home and my dad went out to work. Like most people around here, I suppose. I had friends in Worcester, though … their mums worked. I remember one of them, Timmy Gallister, he had a key on a chain round his neck. His mum was never home. She was a cleaner, or something … cleaned offices at night. I thought it was the funniest thing – a key round your neck.'

'Claire told me she was killed by a bus?' Améline's voice was hesitant.

'Yeah. Just happened one afternoon. She was crossing the road and the driver didn't see her. Just like that.'

'Wh … when did it happen?'

'Six years ago. Six years and two months. I was all set to go to college, had my place and everything. Cardiff. Engineering.'

'What happened?'

'Oh, I couldn't leave me dad. He was all broken up … all over the place. We all were. And my little brother was only ten. I couldn't have left the two of them alone.'

Améline thought her heart might burst. She did the only thing she knew how; she pulled his head down, and began to kiss him, softly, hoping to soothe something of his pain.

When the door opened, it took her a few seconds to work out where she was – it was still pitch dark and whoever was standing there was fumbling for the light. Something clutched at her insides; next to her, Paul breathed deeply, evenly. She heard Iain swear softly, as he hit his hand against the switch and then the whole room was flooded in the warm, yellow light of the shade she'd chosen: silk, with a single, long tassel hanging down towards the bed. The bed in which she lay, naked, with her lover, not her husband. The confusion on Iain's face as he took in the details – Améline's clothes, leading in an untidy trail to the coverlet which lay on the floor; a pair of jeans, workmen's boots, a jacket slumped over the arm of the easy chair. And then Paul's voice, thick with sleep: 'Am? What's going on? Oh, fuck. Oh, fuck.' And then everything seemed to slow right down. One minute Iain was standing there, the confusion and pain written all over his face; the next his face had slowly darkened, his hand slipped from the light switch and he was going down, down, down.

'Iain!' she leapt out of bed, grabbing the sheet to cover herself as she tried to catch him. He was a big man; a terrible sound came from him, a half-groan and then he caught his breath, as if struggling for air. 'Paul!' she screamed. 'Help me! He's falling!'

Paul was beside her in a second, grabbing on to Iain's jacket as his face hit the floor, shattering his glasses. Améline whimpered helplessly as she struggled to lift him, terrified that the broken glass would cut him but he was far too heavy and there was something terrible about the angle at which he lay. 'Améline,' Paul said, his own voice breaking in fear, 'call an ambulance. You've got to call an ambulance! Right now! Go on ... I'll hold him. Get the phone!'

She struggled upright, terror written all over her face. 'Wh ... what shall I say?'

'He's had a heart attack. Améline ... Oh, *Jesus*, Améline. I think he's dead.'

PART SIX

74

'Oh, Daniel,' Sophie, his PA, looked up just as he was on his way to lunch. 'This just came for you. I think it's from your father,' she said, holding out a parcel. 'There's a note. He asked if you could ring him this afternoon when you've had a chance to look it through.' He took the parcel from her, wondering what his father had sent him. To his surprise, his father had more or less left him alone with ICF – unusually, there'd been very little interference.

'Thanks,' he said, tucking it under his arm. 'I won't be long – I'm meeting Jim McRae at the Ivy. You did book us a table, didn't you?'

'Yes ... for one.'

'Thanks.' He walked to the lift. It was June and for once, it wasn't raining. April showers were obviously late that year. He walked the short distance to the Ivy and arrived about fifteen minutes early. His table was ready and he sat down, taking the package and placing it on the table. He opened it; there were several buff manila envelopes and – he drew it out, brow furrowed – a video tape. He turned it over; there was no label, no indication of what it was about. He shrugged and slit open one of the envelopes. It took him a while to understand what he was looking at. A birth certificate. A report on some woman named Belle St Lazâre. A photograph of a peeling, rather rundown house, somewhere in the tropics. A small boy, four or five years old ... Laure's eyes. He swallowed. He pulled out another envelope. Laure, in a variety of poses; scantily clad, semi-naked, sucking suggestively on a lollipop. He swallowed again. He looked up. No one was watching him. He stuffed the

387

papers and the photographs back into the large envelope and stood up. He felt dizzy. He picked up his coat, mumbled some excuse to the *maitre d'* about not feeling well and fled from the restaurant.

Sophie saw him come through the doors, his face white with shock. 'Are you ... is something wrong?' she asked, concerned, as he brushed past and hurried towards his office.

'Call McRae's office,' he said, his whole body shaking. 'Apologise for me. Tell him I'm not feeling well. I'll reschedule lunch.'

'Are you all right?' she asked.

He didn't answer. He shut the door and locked it. For a second, he thought he was going to be sick. He walked over to the sideboard, poured himself a large brandy and opened the package again. He slid the tape into the small VCR on the console, took a large gulp of brandy and then sat for forty minutes watching his wife service two unknown men. And then he vomited.

75

Hue, value, shade, tint, chroma. Primary colours, secondary colours, tertiary colours. Complementary, subtractive, vibrating. Laure's pen flew over the sheets as Jill spoke. *The ability to mix colours and create dynamic or harmonious colour relationships is achieved through practise and observation.* She sighed. Everything Jill said was interesting. She thought of the colours of home, the bright, bold yellows, reds, greens ... Primary colours, as she was learning to call them. Haiti was an island of primary colours. England was more muted, almost achromatic. *Achromatic.* She loved the sound of the word. Something else to tell Daniel that evening.

He liked it when she talked about what she'd learned. His days were filled with more mundane practicalities; a lot of number-crunching and statistics; marketing, advertising. There wasn't much room left over for the really creative stuff which was what he often longed to do – nowadays, he said rather ruefully, he had to settle for hearing about it from her.

She glanced at her watch. It was almost five. She and Daniel were going to dinner at Jayne's that evening and she'd promised to be back by seven. It would take her almost an hour to get to Primrose Hill from Holborn and despite his protestations, she always took the Tube. She couldn't imagine arriving at college in his chauffeur-driven Mercedes. No way.

Jill wrapped up the class. A few more pointers on the week's homework and then it was over. Laure put away her notes, turned down the offers to go across the road to the pub, and left the building. It was a shame, she often thought to herself, that she had such a busy social life outside the course. She'd been across the road to the Fox and Hounds, or whatever it was called, several times, even with Jill. She liked the mixed crowd of fellow students: Mary, the retired art teacher who wore such wild, bold clothes; Jorge, from Spain, who wanted to be a fashion designer but whose parents thought he was studying medicine; Christopher, the straight-faced accountant who was following a childhood passion ... Everyone had an unusual story to tell, though not many of them appeared every now and again in the pages of fashion and tabloid magazines. She still smiled when she thought about the first time Chun Yee, the diminutive student from Hong Kong, had seen her in *Hello!*. She'd brought the copy into class, almost beside herself with glee. The others had all crowded around, open-mouthed in disbelief. *Was that really her?* Laure shrugged, embarrassed. She hardly ever paid any of the magazines any attention. Like Daniel, she'd learned to smile vacantly whenever a photographer turned up, which wasn't *that* often; just when she and Daniel got invited to some film premiere or the opening of a new gallery ... that sort of thing. The photos usually came with some small headline about her striking fashion sense. She couldn't see what was so striking about it – any one of the others on her course were far bolder than she was.

She surfaced at Camden Town, pushing her way past the weary market shoppers, students, ticket touts and drug dealers and walked quickly up Parkway. Halfway up the road, the buildings began to change subtly; fresh coat of paint, new windows, a smart car or two ... by the time she reached St Mark's Crescent, the shabby, faded glamour of Camden had been completely spruced up. She pushed open the small, white gate to number 13 and fished in her purse for her key. She glanced up. The curtains were drawn, all the way to the top of the house. She frowned – Daniel must have closed them – but why? The key was suddenly stiff, refusing to turn in its usual double pattern. She pushed it in, exasperated. It was almost six and she still had to take a shower and wash her hair. No, the key wouldn't budge. Was it damaged? She pushed against the door; it was firmly locked. Blast. She rang the doorbell, half laughing, and waited. Nothing. There wasn't a sound from inside. She frowned, went to the gate and peered down the road. Yes, there was Daniel's car, parked across the street. She walked back, lifted the heavy brass knocker and rapped loudly. Perhaps he was in the shower? She waited for another five minutes but still there was no answer.

She looked around. Perhaps ... She quickly walked round to their neighbour's door and knocked.

'Hi,' she said, as the door opened. 'Sorry to trouble you. My key's not working and I just wondered if you'd seen my husband come in? It doesn't look like there's anyone home.'

The neighbour, an elderly busybody whom Laure had never particularly liked, was only too delighted to tell her. 'Yes, I saw him come home, oh, about three or so? Yes, about three. And then someone came round to change the locks. I saw them working on the front door. Did you have a break-in?'

'No,' Laure said slowly. 'I don't think so. So ... he hasn't gone out again? He's still at home?' She was puzzled.

'Yes, he's definitely home. I heard music, about half an hour ago. It was awfully loud, I have to say.'

'Thanks,' Laure said, turning to go. She was aware of a cold, shaky feeling beginning to make its way up her body. 'He's probably got the headphones on,' she said, swallowing. 'Thanks again.'

'Not at all.' The door closed but Laure knew she'd be peering at her through the peephole. She walked across to her own door and tried the bell again. Her eye was caught by a movement just above her. She looked up. The curtains in the front guest bedroom that overlooked the street moved. She saw Daniel's head, quite clearly, behind the gauzy net curtain. She froze. He stood there for a few seconds, his expression hidden. But he made no move to open the door. Laure was too afraid to stir. Then the curtain slid back silently and he stepped away. Laure closed her eyes. There was no mistaking what he'd done.

She walked a little unsteadily to the pub at the corner of the road. She went inside, not hearing the bar girl's friendly greeting; she and Daniel often came to have Sunday breakfast in the little patio garden at the back. She sat down at one of the tables, conscious of keeping her back very straight. She was shaking like a leaf. She pulled out her wallet with trembling fingers. Twenty-odd pounds and a few pence. Enough to buy a drink, at least.

'You look like you've just seen a ghost,' one of the familiar waitresses said to her as she sat there, too stunned to move.

'Huh?'

'You all right?' The girl looked more closely at her. Laure held herself very still. She was afraid she might burst into tears.

'No ... yes, fine. Could I ... could I get a drink? A ... a rum and Coke?'

''Course. You sure you're all right? You don't look very well.'

'I'm fine. Thanks.'

'No prob. Won't be a minute.' She disappeared. Laure sat there, shoulders hunched, as the enormity of what had just happened began to sink in.

'There you are, love. On your own tonight?' she asked cheerfully. Laure just looked at her. Then, to her horror, she felt a fat, warm tear slide down her cheek. The girl's eyes widened. She was suddenly embarrassed. 'Sorry, I'll ... I'll leave you alone, shall I?' she stammered, her face going red. Laure nodded, blinking desperately. The girl quickly put a pile of napkins in front of her and then beat a hasty retreat. Fortunately, the pub was almost empty. She sat very still, breathing deeply as she tried to regain her composure. She took a sip of her drink but could hardly swallow. It was nearly seven o'clock. On a Tuesday night. Where was she going to go? A hotel? Were there any hotels nearby? But where else could she go?

'Is there a payphone in here?' she asked the bar girl, getting to her feet.

'Yeah, just down the hall, by the toilets.'

She walked to the phone, took a deep breath and dialled. On the third ring, Jessie picked up the phone. She listened to Laure's halting story of having lost her keys and Daniel not being in town; could she possibly stay at Jessie's for the night?

'Of course. Come straight over.' The relief was so great Laure thought she would burst into tears again but she managed to hold herself together until she reached Jessie's Kentish Town flat half an hour later. She'd walked all the way.

She rang the doorbell, tucked back her hair and tried to put as normal a face on as possible. Jessie came to the door, a worried look on her face. 'Come in,' she said, holding the door open.

'Thanks,' Laure said, trying to smile. 'It's so stupid of me – I must have left them at college and Daniel's in Paris ... He'll be back tomorrow so it's just for the night.'

'Laure. Daniel's at Jayne's. It's her dinner party tonight, remember? I just rang – I got in late from work so I decided to give it a miss. Have you ... have you had a quarrel or something?' Jessie interrupted her gently. Laure looked at her aghast. Of course. She'd forgotten – they all knew one another. One big, happy family. They were probably talking about her at that very moment. 'Come into the kitchen. D'you want a cup of tea?' Jessie asked. Laure realised how awkward it must be – she'd been Jessie's employer, after all. Although they were friendly, she was conscious of the fact that Jessie had gone on to win jobs after having done their house – she was indebted to Daniel, just as she was.

She followed her into the little kitchen and sat down heavily. She didn't know what to say.

'Milk?' Jessie asked, putting on the kettle.

'No, thanks,' Laure croaked. Her throat felt dry and her head ached. 'I'm sorry,' she said haltingly. 'I shouldn't have come ... I shouldn't have asked you ...'

'Nonsense,' Jessie said quickly. 'It's perfectly all right. I don't expect you know many people in London, do you?' Laure shook her head, fresh tears beginning to form behind her eyes. 'Look, I'm sure it'll blow over, whatever sort of argument you've had. Daniel's a very sweet guy. Just let him cool off.'

Laure closed her eyes. It was true. Daniel had always been kind to *her*. But she remembered now how he'd cut those awful friends of his – what were their names? Tag? Dean? – straight out of his life. At the time, she'd been amazed. One day they were there, next day they were not. And as far as she knew, he'd never spoken to either of them again. Ever. She opened her eyes, tears spilling over and running down her cheeks. 'You don't know,' she gasped eventually, unable to keep a handle on her fear, 'what I've done.'

The noise of the dinner party came to him as if from a great distance; the chink and tinkle of glasses, the soft pop of a bottle being opened and the falling sound of liquid being poured. He was conscious of turning his head towards Jayne, who was seated to his left, of answering questions from the others about Laure – *Where was she? Was she all right? Not feeling well?* He answered them patiently, aware all the while of the sound of his blood coursing through his veins, of his heartbeat in his ears, a dull, thudding sound that almost, but not quite, drowned out the memory of his own shouting as he paced around the bedroom, the evidence of his wife's past lying scattered across the floor. Every so often a shudder ran through him, causing his hands to shake.

He left their flat early but instead of taking a cab back to Primrose Hill, he instructed the driver to take him to Chelsea, to his parents' flat. Once inside, he poured himself a large glass of whisky, picked up the phone and dialled his father's private line. He heard Günter's calm, slow voice on the other end and grasped it as though it were a lifeline. 'Dad,' he said, his voice breaking suddenly, 'tell me what to do.'

76

Melanie looked warily at Marc. 'Move to Ghana?' she repeated, frowning. 'You mean ... where you grew up? In Africa?'

'Yes. We'd be there for four years.'

'Four *years*? Wh ... when would we leave?'

'When I get back from Sudan – in about two months' time. Look, Melanie, it's what you want, isn't it? You can't stand me travelling all the time; you want us to be in one place, together. OK, it's not New York or Berlin or whatever, but there aren't a huge number of refugee camps in any of those cities. This is about as good as it gets, I'm afraid. And I've got family there. You won't be on your own.'

Melanie swallowed. 'You'll be there as well, won't you?' she asked tremulously. The thought of being left alone in Ghana with his family appalled her. He *never* spoke about his family; she had no idea what they were like.

'Of course I'll be there. I'll be the regional director. There'll be a little bit of travel, nothing like what I've been doing but, look, if this is what you want, Mel, then let's do it.'

She swallowed again. Something had changed in Marc after her supposed miscarriage. Nothing she could put her finger on. Outwardly, he was the same as he'd always been but there was *something* ... The way she caught him looking at her every once in a while, as if he didn't quite believe her; a certain irritability in his manner towards her. She'd discovered that he, too, could keep secrets. It bothered her enormously. When she told him she'd miscarried, he'd come all the way from Uganda or wherever it was he'd been but even then she could tell he didn't quite believe her. He didn't say anything – not a word – just listened to her excuses about medical reports having been sent to the wrong address, she'd get a copy if he wanted to look at it ... but he just shook his head and didn't say anything. She'd been too afraid to continue. He didn't say anything further but that afternoon he went out and wouldn't say where he'd been. Melanie tried everything, every trick in the book, to get him to say where he'd gone. But all he would say was 'out'. It drove her mad. But he was as obstinate as she was persistent and in the end, he'd won. He was cleverer than she was.

'So ... shall we do it?' he asked, getting up from the couch. He fished in his pocket for a cigarette. Melanie looked at him. It was kind of him to say 'we' – the truth was, it was her decision. She swallowed again. And then nodded. 'Good,' he said slowly. 'It won't be as bad as you think.'

'Marc?' she asked suddenly, looking up at him. 'Are you ...' she drew a deep breath, 'are you still angry at me?'

He looked at her with the maddeningly unreadable expression she'd grown to dread. 'Why would I be angry at you?' he said evenly.

'I don't know, you just seem ... a bit distant these days, that's all.'

'No, I'm not.' And then he picked up his coat. 'I'm going to nip out and get the papers,' he said, stubbing out his cigarette. 'Want anything?' She shook her head numbly. In the early days of their relationship, before the 'miscarriage', he would have held her, said something at least marginally more reassuring than 'No, I'm not.' She listened to his footsteps in the hallway and the soft click of the front door. Ghana. It wasn't quite the future she'd pictured for the two of them. She'd imagined something more ... well, more like London. Or Paris. Maybe even New York. But *Ghana*? Was that the name of the city, as well?

It wasn't. It was 'Accra'. A week later Melanie had most of the information she needed and she didn't like the sound of it, not one little bit. Hot, humid, hopeless. That pretty much summed it up, according to the young man who answered the phone at the Home Office. Ruled by a young, charismatic former army officer, it had gone from being one of the richest countries in Africa to the poorest. Melanie's heart sank. There was a curfew at seven o'clock every night, he went on to tell her gleefully, a few international hotels, a British Officer's Club, and not much else. Melanie put down the phone, biting her lip. What on earth was she going to do there? Marc was packing to leave for Burundi. He'd be gone for a month, during which time, he told Melanie, she could organise the move. He would fly directly from Bujumbura to Accra, probably via Harare, and join her there. Melanie listened to his travel plans, bewildered. But what did that mean? she asked him helplessly. 'What'm I supposed to organise?'

'We'll stay with my father for a couple of weeks until I find us a place. Don't worry, it's perfectly civilised,' he'd said, noticing the expression on her face. 'It'll be better than any of the hotels, at any rate.'

'Wh ... what shall I pack?'

'You'd better take everything; as much as you can.'

'But ... like what?'

'Melanie,' he'd said, lifting his shoulders, 'I don't know, whatever you need. Clothes, shoes, kitchen stuff ... everything.'

'*Kitchen* stuff?' she'd squeaked. 'What sort of *kitchen* stuff?'

In the end Tante Layla came to the rescue. She flew over from Paris and invited Melanie and Stella to tea at her Claridges suite. She had a long list of 'survival tips' as she called them, including practical advice on how to find a house, what to look for, where to go. Marc would help her look for a house, of course, 'and as soon as you've found one, I suggest you come back, buy everything you need and have it shipped out there. It'll take a couple of months but that way you'll have everything you need. I'll give you the name of a good shipping agent.'

'Africa,' Stella said dreamily. 'Can you imagine?' The three of them were sitting in the tea room at Claridges.

'Now, now,' Tante Layla said, a warning note in her voice. 'It won't be at all what you expect, you know. It's not Kenya, I can assure you.'

'But she'll have servants and things, won't she?' Stella asked anxiously. 'I mean, it's still British, isn't it?'

'Depends what you mean by "British",' Tante Layla said cryptically. 'Do they speak English? Well, yes. In a way.'

'Oh.'

'Don't worry, you'll manage. Who knows, it may even bring the two of you closer. It'll help you understand him better. See where he comes from.'

Melanie stared at her. What did she mean? They understood one another perfectly well already, didn't they?

'They've got hospitals and things, haven't they?' Stella asked, a note of alarm in her voice. 'And swimming pools?'

'Oh, yes. Plenty of those. There's even a pool in Guillaume's garden. Small, mind you, but perfectly adequate.'

'Oh, goody. Well, that sounds all right, doesn't it, Mel?'

Melanie could only nod. With every fresh revelation, her heart sank even further.

She flew from Gatwick on a muggy August morning after a hideously tearful farewell in the departures lounge. Her return ticket was booked for early September. Surely a month would be enough time to look around, find a house and get settled? Then she would come back to London, make all the necessary purchases and Tante Layla would help her organise the shipping. It sounded simple enough. Melanie knocked back one G and T after the other on the flight, hoping it wouldn't be as bad as she feared. And Marc would be there at the airport to meet her. Her heart lifted at the thought.

And then they landed and she walked out of the aircraft into a heat so dense and thick she thought she would die.

The heat. The heat. The heat. Like a drumbeat. Impossible to even *think* about anything else. Melanie lay in the shuttered darkness of the house to which he'd brought her and struggled to breathe. She was simply not suited to living in a sauna, she gasped to Randa, his impossibly beautiful stepmother. She could not, would not, survive. Randa simply shook her lovely head and smiled. 'You'll get used to it,' she said in her low, charmingly accented voice. 'We all did.'

How? Melanie longed to ask but even speaking required an effort which she was simply incapable of mustering. She could barely summon the energy to lift her arm and call for yet another glass of water. She watched Randa and the pretty teenager, Wajiha, Marc's half-sister. The two other girls – the beautiful girls she'd seen in the photograph in Paris – were both married and had long ago left the country. That was the other strange thing: at the dinner table in his father's house, it was all they ever talked about – leaving the country. Why had she and Marc come if everyone was in such a hurry to leave? She couldn't quite work it out.

Marc had promised her he would take her along to look for a house but he was so busy getting to grips with the new job and sorting out the new office that she barely saw him. They'd been in Accra a total of two weeks and she could count on the fingers of one hand the number of times they'd been alone together. Randa had put them in a guest room next to the enormous room she shared with Marc's father. He was a taciturn, heavy-set man with a face uncannily like his son's ... and there the resemblance ended.

It was strange to be among his family. The fragmented, piecemeal life she and Marc had lived before coming to Accra had really only featured the two of them. He lived in far-flung places she would never visit, among people she would never meet; they came together every so often and the nature of his visits meant that there was never enough time left over to socialise or include others. Now, living together in this vast, silent house, she was suddenly conscious of the gaps in their understanding of each other's lives.

His relationship with his family was a source of constant bewilderment to her. No one ever spoke about his mother. Who was she? Was she dead? Marc simply refused to say. There was a permanent, uneasy truce between him and his father. Randa hovered between them, a calming hand on her husband's arm, a furrowed brow to Marc; nothing was said and yet everything was. Melanie, never having had to interpret such subtlety, was lost. Their conversations were conducted in a confusing mixture of English, French and Arabic, sometimes all at once in the same sentence. She looked from one to the other, a look of permanent confusion on her face. And over and above the confusion, there was the heat. It was too hot to even think of making love – not that Marc would have agreed to it *in his father's house*. She remembered the first time he'd shown her his childhood room at the far end of the corridor, five or six doors down from where they now slept.

'It's huge,' Melanie said, looking round. It was. It was practically empty. A single bed in the corner by the window; a small desk, a couple of posters that had not been taken down. Neat, compact, rather like his Parisian flat. 'How long did you live here again?'

'Just over a year. I came when my grandmother died.'

Melanie peered outside. The light bouncing off the surface of the swimming pool almost blinded her. She wondered why she'd bothered taking off her sunglasses; even indoors the light was too bright. She walked towards him, a smile playing around the corners of her lips. 'So ...' she murmured, slipping an arm round his waist. 'This was your room. Did you ... you know, bring your girlfriends back here? To this little bed?'

'Mel, cut it out,' he gave a short, embarrassed laugh.

'No, come on, tell me,' she whispered, putting a hand up to draw his head down to hers. He caught hold of her hand and held it tightly.

'Don't,' he said softly, the same, unreadable expression in his eyes that she just didn't get. 'Come on. Let's go.' He propelled her gently out of the door. It wasn't the first time he'd made her feel foolish.

Marc watched Melanie pull herself out of the water and wring the dark, thick rope of her hair before tossing it over her shoulder and bending gracefully to pick up a towel. She was beautiful, even when she was angry and confused and afraid. Had he made a mistake in bringing her to Accra? They couldn't have continued as they had been; even he could see that. All he wanted was to find some sort of compromise that would make it possible for them to go on. He took a deep breath and loosened his tie. It was four o'clock in the afternoon, the heat of the day was finally beginning to wane, and he had good news. He'd found a house. Finally. After nearly four months of living with his parents; Melanie would be over the moon. He was surprised she'd lasted this long, to be honest. He watched her wrap the flimsy sarong around her waist, slip her feet into the plastic flip-flops everyone wore and walk towards the patio. His father wouldn't be home until six or so – just as well. He'd have a fit if he saw her wandering, half-naked, around the compound. Yes, it was a good thing he'd found a house – and it had a pool. He wasn't sure Melanie would have stayed without one.

'Hi,' he said, pushing open the sliding doors as she came up, her flip-flops slapping wetly against the concrete. 'How was your swim?'

'Fine,' she said, squeezing the last drops from her hair. She paused, sensing he had something to tell her. 'You're early,' she said, looking up at him.

'Mmm. How fast can you get changed?'

She looked at him, a smile of such pure, clear pleasure breaking out over her face he felt his heart contract. Being with Melanie was like being with three or four different people, none of whom seemed to bear any relation to each other. 'Have you ...?' she asked excitedly.

He nodded. 'I think so. I want you to see it first, though. The owners gave me the keys. Come on, before it gets dark.'

She kicked off her wet flip-flops and ran barefoot up the stairs like an excited child, two at a time, leaving damp footprints on the glossy tiles. He smiled. Her excitement was infectious. It was one of the things he most liked about her. He complained that she was over-dramatic but in truth, he liked her best when she was animated, passionate. It was the very quality in her that had attracted him first.

'D'you like it?' he asked, half an hour later as they stood in the doorway of the large, high-ceilinged room of an old, colonial bungalow in Cantonments, not far from his father's house.

'I *love* it!' Melanie's high, clear voice echoed in the empty space. 'When can we move in? Tomorrow?'

'Hang on,' he laughed, catching hold of her arm. 'There's nothing here. No furniture, no air-conditioners, it needs painting ... there's nothing ...'

'I don't care! I'll sleep on the floor,' Melanie said, hugging him. 'Oh, Marc, can't we move in tomorrow? I'll find us a mattress, whatever we need ... fuck, I'll even the paint the walls! Please?' She was almost feverish with excitement.

'Is it that bad where we are?' he asked, feeling genuinely guilty.

'Noooo,' she said slowly, 'but it's not ... home. It doesn't feel like home. And you're different when you're there. I ... I just want us to be *alone*.' Marc was surprised to see her bottom lip quiver.

'Hey,' he said, pulling her towards him. He knew from past experience how quickly she could move from smiles to tears. 'There's no need to be upset. If you like it, I'll sign the lease tomorrow.' He could feel her nod against his chest. 'We'll have to get the place cleaned up, I don't think there's been anyone here for a while. It'll take a few weeks, Mel ... this is Ghana. Nothing happens quickly, you know that already. D'you want to go back to London and wait while it's done?'

'I just want to be with you,' she whispered into his shirt. 'I hate us being apart all the time.'

He sighed. 'Well, if you're sure you can handle it,' he

said slowly, stroking her hair. 'And I promise, it won't be for much longer.' She nodded, her hands suddenly burrowing under his shirt to touch his bare skin. Her hair was still damp from the swim; it smelled faintly of chlorine and sunscreen. She opened the first two buttons on his shirt and spread her palms against his chest. 'Hey,' he said, laughing. 'What're you doing?'

She mumbled something indistinct against his skin, her fingers busy at his belt. He looked around; they were quite alone. Darkness had fallen in the time they'd been talking. He was surprised at how quickly it happened; one minute they were looking out over the garden, the next they were making love, standing up against the wall, just like that. He could feel her nails raking his back. He lost himself in her in seconds. 'Melanie,' he groaned. What could he do? She was the most maddeningly difficult, dangerous person he'd ever met.

It took almost two months for the house to be ready. Melanie left halfway through the process and returned, six weeks later in the middle of January, with an entire household in a container somewhere in the mid-Atlantic behind her. She brought something else with her, too. She was pregnant. This time, he saw, it was true. But again, like the last time, he wasn't sure quite how he felt. Melanie was over the moon.

77

After the funeral, a quiet, sombre affair during which Viv cried incessantly and Améline was unable to shed a tear, Bernie, Iain's long-time friend and agent, drew her to one side.

'My dear,' he began gently, holding out a large manila envelope. 'I understand this may not be quite the right time ... perhaps there never is? But I happen to know this was something Iain was working on, just before ... I thought you might like to read it.'

Améline took the envelope from him with shaking hands. 'Wh ... what is it?' she asked, her throat constricting painfully.

'It's a novel. Unfinished, of course, just the notes, but the gist of it's there. I thought ... well, you might find it helpful.'

'Thank you,' Améline said, holding it against her chest. 'Will ... will you come to the house? There's tea and ...'

'No,' Bernie shook his head. 'It's very kind of you. If you don't mind, I'd rather get along. You've looked after me splendidly, my dear. I shan't forget it. If there's anything I can do ...' He grasped her hand. There were tears in his eyes. He'd been at the house for almost a week, helping her and Viv with the funeral arrangements, comforting them whenever he could.

'Thank you,' she whispered, holding his hand tightly. 'For everything.'

He nodded and walked away. A light rain began to fall; the guests turned from the graveside and started walking back to their cars. In an hour or so it would all be over. Everyone would be fed, they would all receive a hug and a whisper of thanks, the front door would close and she would be alone. Viv and Susan would offer to stay, of course, and Iain's sister, Della, whom she'd met for the very first time – ironic, wasn't it? But Améline needed to be alone, properly alone. She could see the hovering, hesitant figure of Paul, who'd come along with Claire to pay their respects but she couldn't face him. Not yet. She'd pushed him out of the house that night as soon as she'd dialled for the ambulance and she'd been unable to speak to him since. Oh, it wasn't that she blamed him – the opposite, in fact. She blamed no one but herself.

Viv and Susan walked up to her, each offering an arm. She leaned into their comforting presence and together they walked the short distance to Viv's car, Bernie's envelope still pressed against her chest.

It was almost two in the morning when she finished reading the notes Bernie had left her. It was still raining, a light, steady drumbeat against the kitchen window that sent quavering streaks of reflected light into pools of collected water on the sill. She put the pile of typewritten sheets to one side and walked to the window, staring out into the blackness. Her head was swimming. Some of Iain's carefully constructed prose was lost on her; no matter how well she spoke the language, English still remained a chore to read. But the rest was clear. He'd called it a novel but it was not fiction he had written. It was a story of their lives together – hers, as well as his – and in it, there were answers to questions she'd never even known to ask.

She turned from the window and switched off the light. She walked upstairs to the little room Iain had used as his study, pulled open the drawer in which he kept his documents and leafed through them until she came to the folder she sought. Pale yellow, not large. '*Améline*' written across it in Iain's lovely, neat handwriting. She took a deep breath and opened it. It took her a few minutes to leaf through the sheets until the last one and then she simply stood and stared at the information he'd come across, just as he'd said in his novel, that would provide her with the courage she needed to get on with the rest of her life.

78

Laure stared at the little advice slip that the young man handed her and swallowed. £2,176.54. He coughed discreetly. Laure looked up. 'Would you care for the monies in cash?' he asked. 'Or a cheque?'

'A cheque?' She was momentarily confused.

'Er, yes. The account ... well, the account has been closed, Mrs Bermann. On ... on your husband's instructions. We are instructed to ... ahem, *allow* this withdrawal, and then the facility is closed.'

'Facility?'

'Madam, you are no longer a Coutts account holder. How would you like the cash?'

Laure looked at the slip again. £2,176.54. It suddenly dawned on her. It was roughly three thousand dollars, the amount she'd come into the marriage with. She swallowed again. 'Cash, please,' she whispered. 'Cash would be fine.'

'Certainly, madam. If you'd like to wait here a moment. Fifty-pound notes? Or twenties?'

'It doesn't matter,' she said wearily. 'Anything.'

Five minutes later she walked out of the bank, her cheeks flaming. She'd had to hand over her credit cards, one by one, her chequebook and cheque guarantee cards and watch as the sanctimonious little creep of a bank manager cut them neatly in half, right there in front of her. She had never felt so humiliated in her entire life. The young trainee cashier in the corner had looked up, caught her eye and then looked away again, but not before Laure had seen the sniggering, faintly triumphant expression on her face. *Rich bitch. Now look at you.* Word had obviously gone round. Laure had turned and walked out without a word.

She caught the bus at the corner and made her way upstairs. The bus trundled through the City of London, past the fine old buildings she'd come to love. She looked at the grimy, white dome of St Paul's; caught a glimpse of the river as they turned up Fleet Street. She leaned her head against the glass – it had been over a week since Daniel had locked her out and in that time, not a word. Not a single word. She'd phoned and left messages at the house, called the office, left endless messages with Sophie until Sophie's voice the previous Friday had made it clear there was no point calling again. She had even – her cheeks burned at the memory – tried to get into his office. Surely, once he saw her … but the two security guards on the front desk, Adé and Ayo from Nigeria – she liked them; they liked her – but they had their orders. No, they were terribly sorry, Mrs Bermann. No, she wasn't allowed up. Very sorry. She'd gathered what little dignity she had left and walked out, tears streaming down her face. She'd borrowed a hundred from Jessie when she'd been unable to get money out of the cash machines and finally, today's little episode at the bank had rammed the message home in a way that couldn't be misread. Things couldn't possibly get any worse, could they?

She put the key in the lock and opened the door. The flat was quiet. Jessie was probably still at work. She closed the door gently behind her and took a deep breath. £2,176.54. No, make that £2,076.54 – she owed Jessie a hundred pounds. What was she supposed to do next? The cold knot of fear that had been sitting at the bottom of her stomach all morning gripped her even more tightly. Where would she go? She was just about to push open the door to the kitchen when she heard Jessie's voice. She was on the telephone.

'I don't know what to do,' she heard Jessie say quietly. 'I mean, I can't just throw her out. I don't know what the hell happened between them, but Daniel made it really clear to Geoff this morning. If I let her stay here, we can forget about the ICF building. God, I just don't know what to do. I really like her, you know I do ... but ...' her voice trailed off. Laure stood rooted to the spot. Her whole body was on fire; she was shaking from head to toe. She heard Jessie's voice again but she couldn't bear to hear any more. She turned and walked as quietly as she could back towards the front door. She opened and closed it silently behind her and walked off down the street.

The Crown B&B. Two Stars. Five minutes from Camden Town. *Vacancies.* She pushed open the glass-panelled door and rang the bell. Yes, single room, was it? Lucky her, last one free. A small, wizened woman in a garish purple and gold sari showed her up the stairs. 'Toilet's on the landing, dear. Bath, too. *Twopoundforhotwater.*' It came out in a single breath. Laure handed over forty-two pounds.

'Where's the bathroom?' she asked in a voice she hoped wasn't trembling.

'Yes. Downstairs. *Turnrightindiningroomphoneonleft.*' The woman turned to leave. *'Breakfastatseventhirty.'*

'Thank you,' Laure whispered and shut the door. The room was tiny, barely the size of the pantry at home. She stopped suddenly. Home? What did that mean? Could she really go on thinking about the beautiful house at number 13, St Mark's Crescent as home? The panic that rose in her at the thought of never seeing it again was almost tangible. She sat down heavily on the edge of the narrow bed and held her head in her hands, struggling to breathe. She had to believe Daniel would calm down; that he would reconsider, that he would take her back. If she didn't ... well, what then? What would become of her then?

Half an hour later, having washed her face and hands, she went downstairs and walked out into the street. She stopped at the newsagent's on the corner of Camden High Street and bought a small bunch of daffodils and a card. She scribbled a short 'thank you' to Jessie on the counter and then walked up the Kentish Town Road to deliver it. She couldn't impose on Jessie's kindness any longer; and as painful as it had been to overhear the conversation that morning, she was grateful to her for having given her somewhere to live in the first place. Even though she still had the keys, she rang the doorbell first. She could hear footsteps and then the door opened. Jessie's face went red.

'Laure ... hi,' she stammered. 'Look, I'm really sorry about this morning – I heard the door close behind you and I realised you—'

'Don't worry, please,' Laure said, feeling equally embarrassed. 'It was time for me to move on, honestly. I've found somewhere temporary, just until ...' she swallowed. 'Look, here's your key,' she said, holding it out, 'and just a small "thank you" card and some flowers. I ... I know it wasn't the easiest thing ...'

'Oh, you shouldn't have ...'

'No, really. I'm really grateful. And here's the hundred pounds I borrowed. I ... managed to get some money out of my account so ... Well, here. Thanks again.'

'Laure,' Jessie said slowly. 'Look, there's something else.

Daniel asked me to give it to you. I'm sorry, I really hate to be in the middle like this. He … he asked if you could … well, sign for it …'

'What is it?' Laure's heart suddenly lifted. Had he …?

'I'm not sure. Look, hang on a minute, I'll just get it.' She left the door ajar and ran down the corridor. She was back a minute later, with two envelopes. 'He … er, he asked if you would open this one and sign for it,' Jessie stammered, obviously embarrassed. Laure looked at both. One was an elegant, cream-coloured envelope with the gold, scrolled lettering of the law firm his father used. Kleinhoff, Slavin, Slater. The other was a plain manila envelope. She swallowed. For the first time since the previous Tuesday, she felt the stirrings of something other than fear. She looked at it and then handed the embossed envelope back. Jessie looked at her, a worried expression on her face.

'Tell Daniel,' she said, her voice suddenly shaking with anger, 'that if he's *that* desperate to get rid of me, he ought to have the guts to do it himself.' And then she turned on her heel and walked quickly away.

As soon as she slid her finger under the flap, she saw it. Ten dollars. A green, crisp note. She knew exactly what it was. Her mind flashed back to the first time Daniel told her he loved her. It was after the dinner party back in Chicago when she'd snubbed his friend. The words came back to her as clear as day. *Ten bucks? That sounds about right.* She let the envelope flutter to the floor. She knew. Oh, God, she *knew*. She knew what the papers were – and why he'd been so insistent on having them signed. It was the way she'd seen it done on television. Divorce – someone always had to sign. She couldn't believe it. Was it only ten days ago that they'd sat together at the kitchen table, discussing the purchase of a studio space for her to work in? It was almost too painful to remember. He'd spread out the photographs the estate agent had brought over. She'd protested, of course, it was ridiculous, no one else on the course had a studio. All she needed was a room to work in, why the expense? Daniel had kissed the top of her head and shrugged. What was wrong with it? He knew she was going to be one of the best designers the textile world had ever seen. What was wrong with wanting the best for her? She was his wife – couldn't he do something nice for her once in a while?

She lay back on the bed, too drained of emotion to even cry. Was it the same man? Was it possible for him to have changed, *snap*! Just like that – overnight? And her course? That would have to end. At the thought of it, she groaned out loud. With just over two thousand pounds to her name, how could she possibly go on? What in God's name was she going to do?

Something – or someone – was hammering on the door. Laure surfaced momentarily, groggy with sleep and then buried her head under the thin pillow, hoping it would go away. There was a minute's respite, then the banging started again. She lay still for a few seconds, her eyes adjusting painfully to the thin sliver of bright daylight shining through a strip in the curtain, then she reluctantly swung her legs out of bed. She was fully clothed in the same jeans and shirt she'd been wearing for almost two weeks. She'd washed the shirt a couple of times and hung it to dry on the back of the sink and, in desperation, had bought a packet of cheap, cotton underwear from a stall in Camden market, but she hadn't been out of the hotel since … when? She struggled to remember. The banging started up again, louder this time. 'I'm coming,' she croaked, wiping her mouth. She yanked the door open. It was the proprietor, standing in front of her door, scowling.

'*Whatdoyouthink? Youonlypaidforoneweekit'stwodaysnow*?' she screeched. Laure blinked. '*Youpaytodayoryouleavingtheplace.*'

'What?' Laure suddenly yelled back at her. 'I don't understand you!'

'You only pay for one week,' the woman said, slightly taken aback. 'If you want stay more, you pay.'

'Fine! I'll come downstairs and pay for another week, all right?' Laure glared at her.

'OK.' The woman seemed suddenly mollified. 'You just tell me, OK?'

'OK.' Laure dropped her voice.

The woman looked at her. 'I no see you since Friday. Today Monday. I don't know if you OK,' she said, looking at her with some concern.

'I'm fine.' Laure swallowed. 'Thank you. I'll ... I'll be down soon.'

'OK.' The woman turned round reluctantly and headed back down the stairs.

Laure shut the door with shaking hands. Monday? She looked around her. Where was her watch? She fumbled on the tiny dressing table. There ... she peered at the date. 25th May. She made a quick calculation ... and sat down on the edge of the rumpled bed. Was it possible? She'd been in that tiny little room for two days? She remembered going out to buy food on Friday evening – a sandwich, a carton of orange juice, and the half-eaten sandwich was still lying on the bedside table. She picked up the orange juice. It was empty. She must have drunk it all. She began to cry. Quietly, at first, then in huge, loud sobs, her chest heaving. She'd been in that room since Friday night and she couldn't remember a thing? She was losing her mind. What if that woman hadn't thought to check on her? Would she have lain down in that narrow, little bed and just ... died? She sat up, stunned by that sobering thought. She lay there in the morning light, listening to the sounds of traffic whooshing past and to the creak of the chambermaid's trolley as it trundled past on her floor. She thought about Améline – in that last letter, the very last thing she'd heard from her, she too had been pushing a trolley up and down corridors, much like this one, pausing to tap on doors, just like hers, behind which people slept, hid, made love – or simply got on with the messy business of living.

Outside on the street, a car horn blew; a woman shouted at her child. Laure's mind wandered, coming back to the same point, time and again. She could hide, just as she was doing, or she could get up and go on. She'd done it before. She could do it again.

She sold her engagement ring and the Rolex Daniel had given her on her last birthday. The wedding ring she kept. She found a studio flat just off Shoreditch High Street, up a flight of rickety stairs next to a shop that sold Turkish sweets and in whose hallway the cloying smell of honey clung to the walls. A single room with a shower and toilet at the back. 'No sink, I'm afraid,' said the landlord, 'you'll have to clean your teeth over there by the cooker.'

'It's fine,' Laure said briskly. It was cheap. A month in advance, no references, no credit check, no employment papers; compared to Chicago, this was easy. She bought a mattress, bedding, fashioned a pole across one corner of the room and hung the few clothes she'd bought. There was a rickety little cooker of the kind she'd never seen before; cast iron, too heavy to move, with two burning hotplates and a tiny oven. It worked. The area was full of second-hand and junk shops; if only Daniel knew how little it took to furnish oneself and survive. She bought rolls of the cheap, African fabric Jayne and Clarissa had so admired and made curtains for herself, blocking out the harsh neon light. She couldn't afford paint so she covered the walls and found a huge, curved standard lamp for next to nothing on the Hackney Road.

The East End was nothing like the rest of London, she saw quickly. There was a gritty toughness that overlaid a warmth that took her completely by surprise. All of the world was here – tough-talking Cockneys whose accents she found impossible to follow; dreadlocked, garrulous West Indians who reminded her of home; smooth-talking, suave West Africans, driving taxis and pretending to be lawyers. Further east, along the Commercial Road, there were women the likes of whom she'd never seen – diminutive, cloaked from head to toe, the occasional flash of a ruby nose-ring or the jangle of an earring showing slyly from within. Somalis, Pakistanis, Kurds, Arabs ... she slowly began to distinguish between the various accents and garb. The Italian family who ran the bakery on the corner were the only Europeans that she met, other than the artists who worked in the spaces around Hoxton Square but who didn't seem to live in the East End. It was possible in that place to drop far beneath the radar of her earlier life; there was nothing to suggest the young woman in jeans and a plain white T-shirt was the same Laure St Lazâre who had once been snapped coming out of the Tate, head-to-toe Versace, fingers loosely linked to her husband's. To the Armenians who ran the taxi rank on the corner, she was just the pretty girl who lived across the road, who occasionally smiled at their compliments but walked quickly away. To the owner of the second-hand shop a few hundred yards away, she was the girl who sometimes came in and always, always spotted the good stuff among the junk. And to the young man who ran the flower stall on Columbia Road, she was the girl who looked at the sunflowers with something like hunger in her face. When he presented her with one, one Sunday morning – 'No, really, this one's for you. Go on, just take it' – her face lit up with a smile the likes of which he'd never seen. It made his heart beat just that bit faster every time she walked by.

She found a job at a Spanish tapas bar at the end of Columbia Road, barely ten minutes from her flat. Same as before, cash in hand, under the table, five nights a week. When she got home late at night, she washed the smoke from her hair and brushed her teeth under the shower. The only thing she missed with a pang that was like a knife in her chest when she dared think about it, was the little package hidden behind the piles of lacy, glamorous underwear – none of which she missed. Of everything she'd been forced to leave behind, it was the only thing she'd have given anything to see again.

79

It took Améline almost six months to sort out Iain's affairs, close the tea shop and pack everything up. She sold the house, knowing she would never come back to Malvern again. On the morning the papers were signed, she and Viv sat alone in the kitchen and drank their last cup of tea together. Neither Viv nor Susan had the energy or desire to take Lulu's over. It had been Améline's idea and Améline's flair that had begun and sustained it; now that she was leaving, it seemed almost inappropriate to keep it on.

'When's your flight?' Viv kept saying, as if she couldn't make the information stick.

'Tomorrow morning, at eleven,' Améline answered, smiling a little. It was Viv's way of saying she would be missed.

'Right. Keep forgetting. You all packed, then?'

'Yes, almost. D'you want the breadmaker, I keep meaning to ask you.'

'Mmm. Lovely. Won't be the same, though,' Viv said suddenly. 'Won't be able to get the crust the way you do it. Susan'll be disappointed.'

'No, she won't,' Améline said gently, laying a hand on Viv's arm. They sat in silence for a few minutes. Viv was her closest friend. She thought back to the day she'd arrived in Malvern. 'D'you remember your face?' she asked, smiling a little.

'What? When?'

'The day he brought me here. D'you remember? Your *face*!'

Viv groaned. 'God, do I remember? I'm ashamed to admit it.'

Améline nodded. 'Well, *now* I can see what it must have looked like,' she said, taking a sip of tea. 'But back then I couldn't understand a word anyone said. It was probably better that way,' she said ruefully.

Viv sighed. 'Took us all by surprise, you did.'

Améline looked at her. 'Me? Iain, you mean.'

'No, it was easy to see why *he'd* done it. No, you were the real surprise.' There was a catch in her voice. 'I never expected to *like* you so much. I don't think any of us did.'

'Oh, Viv. Don't.' Améline put down her cup. 'I've done enough crying in the past six months to last me for the rest of my life.'

'I don't care,' Viv said, sniffing and laughing at the same time. She wiped her eyes with her sleeve. 'I was saying to Susan, just this morning, I don't know what I'm going to do without you, Am. You ... you were like the daughter I never had. I will *miss* you so.'

Améline opened her mouth but found she couldn't speak. It was the singular, most touching thing anyone had ever said to her. Viv, of all people. Iain's first, touchy, tough-as-nails, marvellous wife. In more ways than one, it was Viv for whom she grieved.

She waved Viv off and was just about to close the door when she caught sight of someone standing a little further down the street. Her heart missed a beat. It was Paul. He waited until Viv had disappeared and then he walked up the garden path towards her. 'Don't,' he called out softly, seeing that she might close the door. 'We've got to talk, Améline,' he said, putting out a hand to catch hold of the door. 'You can't keep shutting me out like this.'

Améline closed her eyes. In the six months since Iain had died, she'd tried to put Paul out of her mind. The guilt of having been the cause of Iain's death was too much to bear. She couldn't even bring herself to think about the events of that night. 'I ... I can't,' she said, gripping the door as though she might fall.

'You have to. *We* have to. Look, Am, I can't tell you how sorry I am that it ... it happened. But it's not your fault. It's not my fault – it's nobody's fault. He had a weak heart; you told me that yourself. Jesus, Am, you can't blame yourself. You mustn't.'

'Paul,' Améline said weakly, closing her eyes. She couldn't bring herself to look at his face, full of tender pain and concern for her – she saw that immediately. Even the sound of his voice was threatening to undo her. 'I'm sorry,' she said a few minutes later, opening her eyes again. She shook her head. 'I'm sorry for everything that happened. I can't tell you how sorry I am. And I know it wasn't your fault, believe me. But I just can't live with it ...' she swallowed painfully. 'Knowing that it was because ... because I allowed it to happen and I shouldn't have. I was *married*, Paul. I shouldn't have done what I did. Iain saved me – you have no idea what he did for me. And look at how I repaid him.' She put up a hand to wipe away her tears. 'So I'm asking you, please, leave me alone. Just forget about me. Forget anything ever happened between us. *Please.*'

Paul's expression was hard to read. He stood in the doorway, his hand still on the door, almost touching hers. They stared at each other for a moment and then he took hold of her hand, very gently, as if afraid it might break. He looked at her and shook his head, very, very slowly. 'No,' he said softly, almost to himself. 'I can't, Am ... and I won't.'

'But I'm leaving tomorrow, Paul,' Améline cried, her hand burning where he'd touched her. 'I've already got my flight.'

'Then I'm coming with you. You're not going to stop me.'

The blazing surf of burning fields was the last Améline had seen of Haiti when she left and the blackened sweep of empty, barren hills was the first she saw of it coming into land, seven years later. She and Paul flew in on a small charter plane, her face pressed against the window as they dropped, buffeted by the winds coming straight in off the sea. Much had changed in the time she'd been away. A military junta headed by someone named Cedras was now in residence at the palace from which Baby Doc had been chased. There were soldiers everywhere, she noticed as they landed and made their way through the chaotic bureaucracy of the airport. But in other ways, nothing had changed. Paul's hand held hers tightly as they negotiated their way through the chaos surrounding the airport. As the taxi pulled away from the kerb, Améline felt as though she'd never been away. Seven years since she'd opened her mouth to speak her mother tongue; now it came flooding back to her, water over sand, the sound and taste of it sweet in her ears. Protocol, the driver who'd singled them out in the crowd of arrivals, shouted to her as they roared their way along La Grand Rue towards the highway that would take them south to Pétionville. 'Miami? New York? No? Where? Mal-vern. Where's that?'

'Angleterre,' Améline said, half smiling to herself.

'Ah. England. Speak English good, *moi*. Love America, *moi*.'

'Yes, so I see.' She rested her head against Paul's, her stomach churning at the thought of what lay ahead.

Just outside the city they began to climb into the hills. Tête de l'Eau, Morne Calvaire, Bois Moquette; Améline mouthed the signs to herself, her heart lifting with each one passed. Into Pétionville itself, then left into Rue Pinchinat, right by Plâce St Pierre and then down Rue Lamarre until they reached Rue Rigaud. She tapped Protocol on the shoulder – '*C'elle là*. That one. On the right.' He pulled up to the kerb and switched off the engine.

'You mus' be rich, lady,' he murmured, opening the door for her. She didn't reply. She didn't wait for Paul but stood there in the middle of the street, staring up at the house which had been home for the first twenty-odd years of her life. Older now, the paint peeled almost completely from the walls, the windows closed and shuttered against the sun. After seven years in the wet, cool dampness of Worcestershire, the heat was hard to take. She took a step towards it. She had no idea if Madame was still there, if she was still alive. In seven years, not a single letter, not a single phone call – only silence from the sleepy-eyed façade.

'Blimey,' Paul said, just above her ear. 'It could use a coat of paint.' He gave her hand a squeeze. 'Lovely, though.'

'Will you wait a minute?' Améline turned and asked Protocol. 'I just need to see if there's anyone in.'

'Sure thing. Your money, lady,' Protocol shrugged. He didn't care. He was in no hurry. He lit a cigarette.

Améline crossed the road clutching Paul's hand, her heart beating so fast she was almost dizzy. She pushed open the little gate and walked up the front steps. When she'd lived here, she'd only ever used the back gate. The front was for guests and for Laure and Madame. She and Cléones used the servants' entrance, on Rue Clerveau. Well, she wasn't a servant any longer. With the money she'd made from Lulu's and the sale of Iain's house, she'd come back infinitely better off than she'd been when she left. But more importantly, she'd left England with a document that, provided it were true, would give her something whose value far outstripped the money now lying in her account. It was Iain's last, best gift to her. A birth certificate. It had brought her a step closer to finding something out – who she really was.

She lifted her hand and knocked loudly, with growing confidence, on the door. Please let her still be alive.

As soon as the door was opened, the scent of the cool interior swept out, flooding her senses so that it took her a few seconds to realise who was standing there, back bent painfully over, wrinkled, gnarled fingers clutching at the handle.

'Cléones!' The name was wrung from her in a gasp. The old woman stared at her with a milky, rheumy gaze. Then the lips split in what Améline realised was the first time she could recall ever seeing her smile.

'Am … Améline? *C'est toi?* Améline?'

A second later she felt the old woman's head move against her stomach. Cléones had shrunk to almost half her size. She hesitated for a moment – she couldn't recall ever having touched Cléones in her entire life – and then she too put her arms around her, hugging her with all her might.

Five minutes later, their faces wiped of tears, halting explanations over, Cléones led her and Paul upstairs. Améline introduced him as her husband; it seemed easier all round. There was a sharp pang of guilt as she said it, remembering poor Iain's face, but Paul's touch on her arm meant that the guilt at least was shared. She followed Cléones, marvelling at how little everything had changed. The same creak on the fourth stair, the same crooked watercolour of Notre Dame on the landing. The scent of camphor and Cléones' cooking still hung, lightly suspended, in the air – it was as if time had stood still. 'She may not be awake,' Cléones panted, walking ahead of her. 'These days she mostly sleeps, you understand? Doctor said it won't be long now …' Her voice trailed off as she knocked lightly on the door. The painfully twisted hands fumbled, then pushed downwards to let the door swing open. Améline told Paul to wait outside for a moment, as she and Cléones went in.

The room was in shadow; it was just after eleven in the morning and the sun was almost overhead. The shutters Améline remembered so well were partially closed and the fine lace curtains were drawn; even more threadbare than when she'd had to carefully wash and iron them, they hung flat and motionless in the still, silent room. Her heartbeat thudded in her ears.

'Madame?' Cléones whispered, shuffling towards the bed. 'Madame?' There was a faint stirring under the thin cotton sheet. Améline's eyes widened as a tiny, slender body moved. 'Someone's here to see you, Madame … you'll never guess …?'

'Laure?' The old woman's whispered question came straight from the heart.

Améline's eyes pricked. Down on her came the silence and pain of the past seven years, the longing and fear, fear of the unknown. She shook her head through her tears. 'No, Madame, not Laure,' she whispered. 'It's me, Améline.'

'Améline?' The figure moved. Cléones struggled to help her upright. 'Améline? Come … closer.'

Améline moved towards the bed. Like Cléones, Madame had shrunk to a sliver of her former self. Améline could just make out the high, smooth forehead and cheekbones of the once-imposing, handsome woman. Cléones had warned her – cancer, spreading fast – but nothing could have prepared her for the sight of the tiny, shrunken body. The hair was almost gone; the long, almost straight, silvery-white hair of which

Madame had been so proud; and the eyes, those fine, blue eyes pointing to an ancestry that distinguished her, in those same eyes, from ninety-five per cent of her fellow Haitians, they, too, were almost gone, hidden by the loose folds of skin that hung where her eyelids had once been. Even her skin had darkened, the pigmentation the result of the drugs she'd been given, Cléones had said. Everything gone, sullied, distorted. As if that which she'd been so careful to protect against all her life had suddenly arrived to claim her, at the end.

Améline swallowed her tears. There was no way on earth she could confront this dying, emaciated old woman with the truth she'd been stunned to receive. How could she? It was clear the woman of whom she'd been so terribly afraid all her life was close to the end of hers. What difference would it make now? Who cared about the past? Laure was gone; she would probably never return. It would make no difference to anyone if the secret Madame had been guarding for the past thirty years was out.

There was a sudden movement from the bed. Améline looked down. The old woman's hand was moving agitatedly towards her own. She stared at it. In the twenty-four years that she'd lived in the house, she couldn't once remember being touched by Madame in any capacity other than a slap. The trembling fingers sought her own. She clutched at Améline's hand, pulling her closer, closer to her face. Cléones looked on, astounded, as Améline's head almost touched the pillow.

'*Merci, ma fille*,' Madame whispered, so only she could hear. 'You came back. You came back to me.'

Améline's eyes filled with easy tears. She knew. Between them, the truth was finally out. '*Oui, Maman*,' Améline whispered, her voice breaking, 'I'm here.'

80

Notwithstanding her excitement at the arrival of the container, being pregnant in a climate where the temperature never dropped *below* 30°C was no joke. In spite of her pleasure at seeing all the lovely items she'd bought in London unfold on the lawn in front of her, Melanie could barely summon the energy to smile. She'd blown up like a small hippopotamus, or so Stella said when she arrived. She was furious with Marc. How could he have done this to her? She ought to be at home, in London, where she could *cope*. What was he *thinking*? Any minute now, she'd *explode*.

'Mum,' Melanie groaned from the couch where she'd been lying for almost the past fortnight. 'Stop fussing. I'm fine. We'll be home in a couple of weeks.' It had been decided that she would give birth in London and that Stella would come out to Accra to accompany her home. Stella had only been in Accra for a week and already Melanie found herself wishing she'd never come.

'Like hell you are. Look at you! You're only six months gone and you look as though you'll deliver it tomorrow.'

'For God's sake. Will you ask Gifty to bring me some water?'

'Of course, darling. *Gifty!*' Stella bellowed at the top of her lungs.

Melanie rolled her eyes. '*I* could yell too,' she said pointedly. The irony was lost on her. Gifty appeared at a running trot.

'Madam?'

'Some water, please,' Melanie croaked.

'Chop-chop,' Stella instructed, *sotto voce*.

'Jesus, Mum. Where did you pick *that* up from?'

'What d'you mean?'

'Chop-chop?'

'Oh. Well, I can't understand a thing she says and, anyway,

she's so bloody *slow*. It takes her an hour to get from the kitchen to here. What do they *feed* them? Valium?'

'Mum, you're making me ill. Why don't you let Festus drive you to the beach?'

'Oh, I'm not going there on my own. Anything could happen.'

You should be so lucky, Melanie muttered under her breath. 'Nothing's going to happen to you, don't be silly. What about the Club, then?' The (mostly) British club had been pronounced 'all right' by Stella after the High Commissioner's wife had recognised her from some outdated copy of *Tatler* that had been kicking around the residence for a while. Stella was thrilled – it had been a while since she'd been featured in anything. In fact, it was a while since any of the Millers had been photographed, anywhere. Apart from Melanie's wedding, when Mike had turned up, half an hour late, drunk and with a girl in tow who really *was* younger than Melanie, it had been ages since she'd come out of a shop or a restaurant to find a flash bulb in her face. Going to Africa, she'd discovered, was a bit like going to the moon. The real world, her world, seemed awfully far away.

'Oh, all right,' her mother said, getting to her feet. 'Darling, will you organise the driver for me? I'm afraid I just can't understand what he says.'

'Just get ready, will you, Mum?' Melanie said wearily. Dear God. Another fortnight of this ... could she cope? She'd known all along that it would be a bad idea. As soon as her mother arrived at the airport to find it not the way she'd imagined – all servants in crisp white uniforms with red cummerbunds, bowing at the waist and waving palm branches as she walked by – she'd all but collapsed. The heat. That pungent, tropical smell. 'Dreadful,' she said, at least a dozen times on the journey to the house, a handkerchief pressed firmly against her nose. 'Simply dreadful. Too dreadful for words.' Even the sight of her *adorable* Marc failed to revive her. Melanie sat beside him, her ears burning in shame. He said nothing. These days, Marc was very good at saying nothing.

Once inside the house, her spirits revived a little, aided by the soft purr of the air-conditioner. Melanie didn't have the heart to tell her not to get too used to it; power cuts were a daily occurrence. She was just grateful the supply was still on when they arrived.

'Not bad,' was Stella's comment as they sat in the cool, spacious living room, an ice-cold G and T for Stella, brought by a servant – not in a white uniform with a red sash but a servant nonetheless – who smiled and bobbed and showed a row of the most startlingly white teeth Stella had ever seen. She stared at him as he backed out of the room. 'Extraordinary,' she murmured, taking a large gulp.

'D'you like it?' Melanie said, relieved that something seemed to have met with approval.

Stella looked around at the large, beautifully furnished room. Melanie had indeed done a lovely job: huge, slip-covered sofas; wicker chairs from India; enormous, lacquered chests from Bali and China; gauzy curtains from Liberty's … Shopping for everything had been such fun. But – and it was a big 'but' – nothing could have prepared her for the heat and the dreariness of the place. She'd been expecting a ranch, or an old colonial farm at the very least, with a long, elegant driveway, palm trees and the odd roar of a wild beast – in the distance, of course. *This*, she looked out into the garden and was annoyed to see the neighbour's roof peering above the hedge, this was a bit like one of the more dreadful parts of London; Peckham, perhaps, only hotter. With terrible roads. 'It's lovely, dear,' she murmured in a voice that indicated it was anything but. She saw Marc and Melanie exchange a quick glance, then Marc got up. Sorry he couldn't stay … had to be in the office. He would see them both at dinner.

'*Mum*,' Melanie hissed as soon as he left the room.

'Well, I'm sorry,' Stella said huffily, draining her glass. 'I mean, honestly. I'm so cross with him. What was he thinking, bringing you here? Really. I'm *so* cross.'

★

And th... her mothe... arrived. A fo... London. Marc... her stomach. 'Bo... other day as she wa... any supervision; Gifty w... ever be, or cared to be.

'I don't know,' Melanie sa...

'Oh ... I hope you get a b... bringing you money.'

Melanie smiled faintly. She didn... only thing that mattered was that it was... Here, at long last, was the proof she nee... ing for, or so it seemed, all her life. A child... together in the way she longed for. A child wa...

And then, suddenly, it was time for them to leave... difficulty convincing the BA staff that she was only six... gone. No, she wasn't just about to give birth. It was the... she was all swollen up. She wept nearly all the way to Londo... – three whole months without Marc – how the hell would she... cope?

But she did. She had to. And almost three months later to the day, she gave birth to a healthy, dark-haired little girl. Not so little, she reminded everyone who came to look. A whopping 8lb 2oz, just look at her! Marc was in love, all over again. She left the private room at the Wellington that Stella had booked and moved back home with the baby and Marc. He was impatient to return to Accra with the child; Stella was outraged. Melanie needed to rest, recuperate, gather her strength. And never mind Melanie, how could he deprive her of her only grandchild, just days after she'd arrived in the world? He shook his head; what could he do? He stayed with them for a fortnight and flew back alone. Melanie, too exhausted by the sudden demands of a child she now realised she simply hadn't

81

Améline stared at the little card Cléones had given her. They were in the kitchen, Cléones practically hopping up and down with excitement. She read the inscription. Saul Lopez, Private Investigator. An American telephone number. 'Who is he?' she asked.

'He was … a … a … in … in … something …' Cléones couldn't pronounce the word. Neither could she read. He'd come one day, out of the blue, she said, just the way Améline had. About a year ago.

'But who sent him?' Améline asked, puzzled. She showed the card to Paul.

'I don't know, he didn't say. But Madame, she was too sick to see him, and anyway, he wanted to talk to *me*,' Cléones said proudly. 'He asked all about Laure, 'bout the *bébé* ... He was nice. Real nice. He didn't speak Créole, though. We had to call 'Ti Jean's son from the city.'

'He asked about Laure?' Améline said, turning the card over in her fingers.

'Yeah, he wanted to know what she was like, what Belle was like, where she went ... you know. He knew a lot about her.'

Améline stared at her. Who on earth would have sent a private investigator to Haiti to find out about Laure? Could something – she could hardly bring herself to think about it – could something have happened to her? She turned, agitated, desperate to find a telephone. The line in the house hadn't been working almost since she'd left Haiti.

She grabbed her bag, leaving a surprised Cléones and Paul standing in the kitchen, and ran all the way to the small general store a few blocks away. With shaking fingers, she dialled the number and waited, the sound of her heartbeat pounding in her ears. Please God, let her be all right. On the third or fourth ring, a man answered. He was, as Cléones said, perfectly nice, but he would not divulge a single thing about his trip to Haiti or the reasons for it. Améline's heart sank. 'Could ... could I ask ... is she ... alive?' She could barely bring herself to utter the word.

'Oh, very much so,' he chuckled, sensing her distress. It was a small measure of relief.

She walked slowly back to the house, her sense of frustration deepening. Now that she was back in Laure's house, among Laure's childhood possessions, the longing to see her again had only intensified. What had happened to her?

Madame died on a Saturday morning, a few weeks later. Ameline was in the garden, watching Paul pull the weeds from the sunflower beds that 'Ti Jean had long since given up managing, when she heard Cléones' voice, exactly as it had been when she was a young girl – 'Améline! Oh, Améline!' She ran across the lawn as fast as her legs would carry her but it was too late. The conversation Améline had shied away from would now never take place.

She died peacefully, the doctor said, emerging from her room half an hour later. He'd also arrived a few minutes too late. He was surprised she'd lasted so long, he added. When the disease was first diagnosed, he wouldn't have given her more than a month. Surprising, wasn't it, what the mind could do. Shame that the granddaughter – Laure, wasn't it? – hadn't been found. He knew, in the last years of Madame's life, that she would have liked to have seen her. Did Améline perhaps know of her whereabouts? Améline shook her head, her eyes full of tears. About a year before she'd arrived back in Haiti, she told him wistfully, there'd been a visitor, someone asking after her – but it had come to nothing. Belle, Madame's daughter, was no longer at the Chicago address from which Améline had received the first few precious letters. None of Laure's old classmates had heard from her. Régine de Menières (unmarried, Cléones pointed out triumphantly) still looked down her nose at Améline, though she was more than a little taken aback at her manner and dress and the sight of the good-looking, friendly white man sitting in the kitchen chatting to Cléones in his limited French. 'You were in Europe? You're married? To an Englishman? Really? Well, well, well.' Her comments were not lost on Améline.

There were further surprises. About a fortnight after Madame's death, her old lawyer and friend, M. Lavallois, drove up and parked his ancient black American car across the road. He had been to the house once or twice since Améline's return and she greeted him warmly. She invited him into the parlour and sat stiffly opposite him in the room that had once only been hers to clean. He made a great show of pulling papers from his ancient black leather suitcase and arranging them on the green baize-covered table on which Madame and her guests once played bridge. Améline stared at the typewritten sheets, wondering why he'd asked to see her. She'd wondered what provision Madame would have made for Cléones and 'Ti Jean. She had given them both a generous sum when she first arrived but she was aware there were questions over their continued stay in Pétionville now that Madame was no longer with them.

'Ahem,' M. Lavallois said, clearing his throat. He pushed his fingers together and placed them carefully under his chin. 'Some surprises ahead, Améline,' he said gently. 'It's taken a while to get her papers in order. But,' he said, pulling a sheaf towards him, fingering the pages and coughing to cover his obvious embarrassment, 'there's something I've known about for ... well, for *quite* some time, I feel bound to confess. It seems,' he coughed again, 'that you ... er, you were *related*, as it were, to Madame St Lazâre. Not,' he added hastily, 'in the capacity to which you had no doubt *believed* yourself to be. That is to say,' he stumbled on, 'that ... you ...'

'That I was her daughter, M. Lavallois,' Améline broke in gently. 'Yes, I knew. I found out some time ago.'

'Oh, I see!' M. Lavallois exclaimed, obviously relieved. 'Oh, well ... yes. Rather *unexpected* news, I should imagine. Yes, I spoke with Madame St Lazâre a week or so before her ... *untimely* death and we decided, Madame and I, that her existing will should be changed – she wished, no doubt, to make ... *amends*, as it were ... I do believe ...'

'M. Lavallois, what are you saying?' Améline said faintly.

'I'm saying that, well, she left it all to you.'

'To me?' Améline echoed, still not fully understanding. 'Left what to me?'

'The house, my dear. Her possessions; everything. She left everything in your name.'

Améline stared at him. There was silence for a few seconds. In the background, she could hear the slow, unhurried tick of the grandfather clock. They both broke it at once. 'Why would—?'

'She was trying—' He stopped, graciously giving way.

'Why would she have left it to me?' Améline said haltingly. 'Laure ... Laure was her granddaughter. She should have it – the house, money, whatever Madame left.'

M. Lavallois looked closely at her. 'But you were the daughter, *n'est-ce pas*?'

Améline shook her head. 'By birth, perhaps. But no, not really. I was the *reste-avec*. We never spoke of it.' She hesitated for a moment. 'My birth certificate ...' she stammered. 'The ... My father is listed as unknown ... I just wondered ... if I might be so bold as to ask ... if she ever ... said?'

'Unfortunately, no,' M. Lavallois said, getting to his feet. Améline sensed he was out of his depth. 'It wasn't something we ever discussed. But the fact of the matter is, my client assigned her worldly possessions to you, M'lle St Lazâre. Not to her granddaughter. Now, if you don't mind, I have rather an important meeting to attend; I really must be on my way. There'll be some forms to fill out, of course, which I'll send to you in due course. All very tedious, I'm sure.' Still muttering, he allowed Améline to show him to the door. Her head was spinning. It was the first time she'd ever been addressed by – well, by her *real* name. Améline St Lazâre. She had spent the majority of her life as plain 'Améline', and, apart from the seven years she'd spent as 'Améline Blake', she'd never really paid much attention to the fact that she didn't know her own surname. It had been an enormous shock to realise she'd been Améline St Lazâre all along. Who, she wondered, almost fearfully, had her father been? Ever since she'd found her birth certificate in Iain's file with the name 'Olésia St Lazâre' filed as 'mother' and 'inconnnu', next to the space indicated for 'father', the question had nagged at her. Who was her father? He was obviously not Belle's father – the legendary Gustave St Lazâre whom she'd heard about but never seen. No, she wasn't Gustave's child – she was far too dark for that. Was it possible – the thought teased at her – could Madame have done what her daughter did? Could she have had a child with a stable hand? Or a gardener? Someone dark enough to have produced a child of Améline's complexion? She swallowed.

She closed the door behind M. Lavallois and leaned against it, overwhelmed. Her life, once so simple, had turned into a series of mirrors, each more distorted than the last. The joke that had so often been said about her and Laure – *that they were more like sisters than anything else* – was no longer quite so funny. They *were* related. Laure was her … niece. Améline and Belle were half-sisters. She frowned. She could no more think of Laure as her niece than she could Belle her half-sister. Was this what it was like, she wondered, her eyes half-closed, to be a St Lazâre? Nothing was ever as it seemed. Was this the real price of admission to the family she had once so admired?

It wasn't long before the news of Améline's sudden inheritance reached the ears of Cléones and 'Ti Jean, along, Améline supposed, with half the servants in the neighbourhood. Quite how it had leaked out was a mystery. But then again, servants, she recalled, had ways of finding things out. Cléones, predictably, was not in the least bit surprised, either at the news that Madame St Lazâre had left everything to Améline, nor at the news that Améline was, in fact, Madame's daughter. She had known all along, it seemed. In a rare show of delicacy, she would not be drawn on the subject of Améline's father. If she'd survived for so long without knowing, Cléones said tartly, she could continue that way. It wasn't for her to say.

Both she and 'Ti Jean were happy to retire – Cléones to her family in Jacmel, some two hundred miles to the south, and 'Ti Jean to his home in the north of the country. Both had spent their lives working for Madame St Lazâre; now, her life had ended and they were happy to return to theirs. It took surprisingly little time for both to pack their belongings, including various pieces of furniture and items that Améline thought might be useful in their retirement.

Cléones left the following Saturday morning in a chartered taxi, her belongings and the green baize-covered table from the parlour strapped rather incongruously to the roof. Améline and Paul stood and waved until the car disappeared below the horizon. 'Ti Jean had left the previous day; she and Paul were all alone in the large house. They wandered into the garden. The jacaranda outside Laure's room was in full bloom; it shook its purplish, heavy flowers at them as they strolled. Améline still couldn't get over it. She had wound up a woman of property, of some substance, a far cry from her earlier position and that, she understood, was to be the real price of her success. With the money Iain had left her and the savings she'd taken with her from Lulu's, she was in a position to do almost anything she wanted. But what did she want? She and Paul had been in Haiti almost six weeks. Paul would soon have to leave to go back to England. They hadn't really spoken about the future; Paul, out of the same respect and intuition that had first surprised her when she met him, seemed to understand that, more than anything, Améline needed time to get used to the change in her circumstances. It was no small thing, he whispered to her as they lay in the narrow bed in Laure's old room that night, to go from being a servant to the owner of the house in which she'd worked, just as it was no small thing to go from being married to a widow overnight. It would take time for her to sort out her own feelings and decide what to do. In the meantime, he was there for her, just as he'd always been. Améline couldn't put into words just how grateful she was.

82

Through the French doors that led to the cool, shady verandah, Melanie watched Ama, the girl who'd been hired to take care of Susu, lift her up, almost throwing her up in the air, and heard Susu's ecstatic shrieks as she caught her again, and swung her round her legs. Susu never squealed like that when *she* carried her, she thought to herself morosely. She put down her glass and walked over to the window. The pool shimmered turquoise in the late morning heat; the bamboo trees quivered in the wind; the lawn was watered and cut – all was as it should be. The maid was busy with her child, her husband was busy in his office. Everything was taken care of, there was nothing for her to worry about. There was also nothing for her to do. They'd been in Accra for almost two years and Melanie was no closer to finding something to do than she had been the night she arrived. Getting used to the heat had taken up most of the first few months; then she'd gone back to the UK to have Susu … It was hard to believe she'd been back almost a year. Susu was six months old; in another six there'd be the excitement of her first birthday party – and then what?

She yawned widely, bringing tears to her eyes. She glanced at the watch on her slim, permanently tanned wrist. It was eleven o'clock in the morning. What was there to do? Gym, a quick swim, lunch at her favourite café, and then the slow hours of the late afternoon until Marc came home from work. Although … she furrowed her brow. Was it tonight he'd said he would be late? Something about a meeting at one of the ministries? She sighed. You'd think it would be easy enough to keep track of things, given that hardly anything ever happened, but no, she could barely recall what Marc said to her these days. He used to talk to her about his job and about the things he saw when he went on those infernal trips to God-knows-where, but lately he seemed to have lost interest … or was it the other way round? If she were really honest – really, *really* honest – she had to admit it bored her, just a little bit. After all, it was just so damned difficult keeping up with all those bloody conflicts that seemed to spring up out of nowhere – one minute he was off to Rwanda, the next minute it was Burundi … or was it Burkina? She just couldn't keep all those damned names straight. Besides, they were forever changing their names. Côte d'Ivoire one month, Ivory Coast the next; the Democratic Republic of Congo couldn't seem to make up its mind – Zaire? Congo? DR Congo? French Congo? Belgian Congo? Oh, it was all too bloody much.

She watched Johnson, the new garden boy, hauling the heavy pink hosepipe across the lawn. What an odd colour, she thought to herself as he struggled to connect it to the sprinkler she'd brought over from the UK. She watched him for a few moments, noticing almost absent-mindedly the way the muscles in his bare back flexed and moved under the effort of picking it up. He was really rather good-looking – a compact, muscular body; dark, velvety skin; a strong smile, showing the brilliant white teeth most Ghanaians seemed to possess. Yes, he *was* nice-looking. And hardly a boy. She turned quickly from the window, suddenly flustered by her thoughts. She picked up the little silver bell on the table beside her and gave it a sharp jangle. A few seconds later, she heard the soft shuffle of bare feet on the terrazzo floor.

'Madam?'

'Another G and T, please, Gifty. Lots of ice.'

Just as it had been, before, with her stepfather, it started out as a silly game. The first time she spoke to him after noticing him through the windows, she experienced a flutter in her stomach – something she hadn't felt for several months, she realised, as soon as she walked away. The fact that he was seemingly so appreciative of every word she said didn't help, either. He just stood there, smiling with those perfect teeth, his entire face lit up with delight when he realised she was addressing him ... damn! It had been ages since *anyone* – never mind Marc – had been so thoroughly pleased to see her. She rather liked the soft, quiet way he said 'Madam?' every time she approached. She quickly found a whole host of reasons to speak to him. The pool needed cleaning; the lawn needed raking; the hedge needed clipping.

She began to take an uncommon interest in the garden. Marc was pleased; it was good to see her doing something other than going to the gym, or to lunch with the gaggle of women she called her friends, he said, on one of his trips back home. Melanie's pang of guilt was quickly replaced with a frown. She just couldn't understand why he was so disapproving of her friends – what else was there to do? They were perfectly nice people, she insisted. Marc shrugged. But who else was she to befriend? The few women *he* introduced her to were either too withdrawn and quiet to be able to get much out of them or they were the opposite: so full of their own accomplishments that when they found out she did nothing – literally – they looked down their noses at her and quickly turned away. One (admittedly beautiful), haughty doctor whom he'd introduced her to had actually had the nerve to murmur, 'You're very different, aren't you?' Then, seeing Melanie's blank stare, continued, 'You and Marc, I mean. An odd couple.' And walked off, leaving Melanie almost breathless with rage. After that little encounter, she preferred the gentler, less demanding company of the expatriate crowd. By the end of her first year, she was best friends with Petra Tynagel, the blonde, innocuous-looking wife of the head of a Danish aid agency and Barbara – 'Oh, do call me Barb!' – Donaldson, the wife of the head of one of the many mining companies. Barb was from Newcastle, a fact she was usually at pains to hide, but she was lively and quite witty and played a devastating forehand – and she'd been a huge Mike Miller fan as a teenager. She seemed to consider it quite a coup that she was now best friends with his daughter. Melanie found her amusing.

Both Barb and Petra were exceedingly proud of their friendship with Melanie – not only was she beautiful and obviously wealthy, she'd also managed to bag the devastatingly handsome Marc Abadi whom all the expatriate women *adored*. Sadly, the adoration wasn't mutual. No matter how hard they tried, Marc Abadi remained as aloof and elusive as ever. When he and Melanie first appeared on the tiny (it had to be said) expatriate social scene, everyone fell over themselves to invite them to dinner, lunch, weekend beach parties, cocktail parties … anything. Marc put in the odd appearance or two in the beginning but quickly withdrew. It was obvious he preferred the company of his own kind, though no one could say quite who that was. His wife, on the other hand, was much more promising – she quickly became a fixture on the burgeoning art scene and whenever she disappeared back to Europe for a few weeks, her absence was keenly felt. She brought a touch of class and life to the cocktail parties and the little openings celebrating this new-found artist or that. The fact that she occasionally bought a painting or an oversized sculpture which then sat, covered, in her garage for the next few months, only added to the drama and glamour of the events. Unlike most of the women present, she didn't have to consult her husband or boyfriend every time she opened her wallet. She did as she pleased, when she pleased. She was a player in her own right, which made her just that little bit more special.

Melanie turned sideways in the mirror, scrutinising her image. It was all good; breasts still high and surprisingly full, even after breast-feeding (a month, which was all she could manage) – no one had told her Susu would clamp on to her for *hours* on end!). Stomach flat, bottom pert, thighs long and lean. She faced herself again. Narrow, boyish hips, legs tapering elegantly at the knee and ankle … little had changed. If anything, she looked better than ever. The olive-green bikini she'd selected after half an hour's indecision suited her dark hair and lightly tanned skin. She liked the way the halter top pushed her breasts together, giving her a nice, rounded cleavage. She pulled her hair on top of her head, fastened it with a clip and put on her sunglasses. Time for a little poolside relaxation. It was eight-thirty – she could lie out until about ten, until the heat became too intense and she would surely burn.

Susu and Ama were busy in the kitchen; she could hear Susu's gurgles as Ama walked around, Susu wedged firmly into the side of her hip. Melanie wondered how on earth she managed to walk around all day with the child permanently attached to her like that – she could barely manage ten minutes – she certainly didn't have enough of a hip to provide a seat for a child. Marc just laughed. That was the way they carried children here, he said. Either that or tied to their backs with a piece of cloth. Melanie was horrified. Tied with a piece of *cloth*? Petra told her that was the reason half the kids on the streets had such bandy legs – their legs had been wrapped around their mother's backs for too long. Marc rolled his eyes when she pointed it out. She quickly put a stop to *that* nasty little habit. She didn't want *her* daughter to wind up with bandy legs.

She walked through the living room, a white sarong tied loosely around her waist, and pushed open the doors that led on to the verandah. It was nice and cool. Marc said, almost grudgingly, she recalled, that the English certainly knew a thing or two about building in the tropics. The shady strip that ran around the entire house prevented any direct sunlight from coming in and provided a cool buffer zone between the house and the generally scorching garden. She walked across the freshly cut lawn, the heels of her mules sinking into the soft earth. Johnson must have watered the garden that morning; there were still sparkling drops of water clinging to the blades of grass. The air was still and slightly damp. She kicked off her shoes and sat down on one of the loungers. She looked around cautiously. There was no sign of Johnson. She lay back, arranged herself as prettily as she could and tipped the brim of her wide straw hat down over her eyes. It was the one thing Stella had insisted upon; keep your face shaded, she'd said, over and over again. Through the brim's patterned lattice, she could see the flamboyant purple and cerise bougainvillea at the far end of the garden, the waving, fan-shaped traveller's palm that stood on the other side of the pool; the dark green and white jasmine bush that crept up the side of the wooden pergola. Then, finally, she heard Johnson's low, soulful whistle coming up the path from the boys' quarters, behind the house. She stretched out one leg, the other bent slightly at the knee, and closed her eyes. She heard him come around the corner, still humming. He caught sight of her and stopped. There was an exquisitely held moment of tension as he took in her sleeping form, all sleek, pale curves and she saw him, through the furry fringe of her lashes, looking at her in undisguised appreciation; then he backed away softly, not wishing to disturb. He liked what he saw, she knew. All at once she was sixteen again and had just succeeded in getting someone to notice her. She lay there for a few moments longer, basking in the warmth of her own power.

If Marc noticed Melanie's sudden animation, he said nothing. He was busier now than ever – running six camps in four countries took up every second of his working day and beyond. He was rarely at home before nine, and was out of the house before dawn. But he missed being in the 'field', out in the camps. Not just the feeling of being out in the open in places he would, in all likelihood, never visit again once his contract was over, but the camaraderie of co-workers, the sense of accomplishment when they managed to get the simplest things done; even the misery in which they often moved. He felt alive out there in the bush in a way that he simply didn't stuck in his air-conditioned offices three floors above the ring road, watching the traffic crawl past. When he allowed himself to think about it, which wasn't often, he realised that taking the desk job had been a mistake. In trying to appease Melanie, he'd only made things worse. He'd been at the regional headquarters for almost two years. The thought of staying a further two made him feel slightly nauseous.

'Why doesn't she ever come to visit us?' his stepmother asked him the following Sunday. He had taken Susu to see her grandparents; Melanie was at the beach with her friends. She'd never really enjoyed the family get-togethers that Marc had forced upon her in the beginning. After a while, he'd started going by himself, or with Susu, of whom Randa simply couldn't get enough.

'She's busy,' Marc said, hoping it wasn't going to turn into an hour-long discussion about Melanie's rejection of everything Randa had to offer.

'Busy with what? She doesn't work – what does *she* have to be busy about?' Randa's voice carried the irritation she felt whenever she talked about Melanie.

'I don't know. Look, she's found a few friends, she's happy doing whatever it is they do, let's just leave it at that, shall we?'

'Ai, Marc,' Randa said, shaking her head. 'I'm telling you,

it's not a good sign. She should be here with you, with Susu. The child can barely speak English. The house-girl only speaks to her in Twi, you know. Thank God *we're* here to teach her Arabic. Otherwise ...'

'Randa,' Marc said quietly. 'Drop it.'

'Well, don't say I didn't warn you,' Randa said darkly.

'I won't.'

A few hours later, Marc extracted his sobbing daughter from Randa's arms and bundled her into the back of the car. As he pulled out of the driveway, he narrowly missed the black Mercedes belonging to the old retired judge who lived next door. He waved his apology, catching a glimpse of the stony-faced elderly man sitting in the back before the electronic gates shut silently behind them.

Melanie's car was in the driveway, he saw with some relief as he pulled up. He carried the sleeping Susu into the house and handed her over to Ama. 'Where's Madam?' he asked, looking quickly in the living room.

'Please, Master ... she's ... asleep.'

He looked sharply at her. There was something in her voice. The slightest hesitation over the way she said 'asleep'. No, he was imagining it. He walked out of the kitchen, still frowning.

Melanie was indeed asleep. He pushed open the bedroom door and saw her lying with her back to him, the graceful curve of her hip visible under the linen sheet. He smiled. She always looked so peaceful when she slept; the tiny frown that had taken permanent root between her brows relaxed and the slight downward tilt to her mouth that had become more pronounced as their time in Accra lengthened, reversed itself so that she appeared to be almost smiling. He walked around the bed and sat down, watching as she slowly surfaced out of sleep. He smiled at her. 'When did you get back?'

'Mmm ...?' she murmured, struggling to focus. It was almost five – the room was bathed in the last of the afternoon light. Soon it would be dark.

'From the beach?'

'Oh, I ... I didn't go,' she said, yawning. 'Petra cancelled at the last minute.'

'You could've come with us,' he said mildly, bringing his hand to rest on the slope of her hip. He began to caress her slowly. She shifted and then suddenly got up, pushing her hair away from her face with both hands. She slid out of bed and before he could say or do anything further, she walked into the bathroom and shut the door. He frowned, slightly taken aback. It wasn't like her to reject an advance, however tired or sleepy she might be. He heard the sound of running water. She was drawing a bath. He got up. There was something about the afternoon that disturbed him, though he couldn't say what.

83

It was winter again in London; grey, leaden skies and rain, no snow. It was hard to believe it had been over two years since she'd moved to the East End, Laure thought to herself as she walked along Columbia Road, avoiding the puddles, her hands shoved deep in her pockets. But in a strange way, it felt more like home than Primrose Hill ever had. She knew most of the shopkeepers along the road; she'd begun to manage the other waitresses at ¡Viva!, where she'd been working for almost eighteen months. She had a couple of friends; no one particularly close but someone to spend a Saturday night with if she wasn't working, and a few telephone numbers to call. It was a lesson she'd learned well – she saw now just how lonely she'd been when Daniel appeared in her life and she was determined not to make the same mistake twice. Of the old crowd, she saw no one. It was better that way. Her life was so different now – what would she have spoken to Jessie or any of the others about? She was still angry with Daniel for the way in which he'd ended it. She'd been tried, condemned and discarded without ever having been allowed to speak. And sometimes, in the dead of night, when she lay awake and thought about what she'd lost, little things came back to her: the sound of his voice, the way his hair turned up, just above the nape; the fresh, sunburned smell of his skin when they'd been on holiday together ... Odd things, fragmented, disjointed. There was pain mixed in with the anger. And hurt. She hadn't so much as looked at another man since then. It was as if that part of her had suddenly died. She couldn't imagine ever trusting a man enough to allow him in. She was slowly beginning to learn that everyone she touched was either taken from her, or left of their own accord. Améline, the baby, Belle, Daniel. Far better to keep the world at a safe distance; she might never have what she *thought* she'd had with Daniel, but better that than risk losing it again. It was best that way.

'All right, Laure? How's it going?' It was Pete, the flower man who'd given her a sunflower the very first week she'd moved in.

'All right,' Laure said, smiling. She liked the way people round here greeted one another. *All right?* All right. It had taken her a while to understand it. She bent down to look at a bunch of the huge, blood-red calla lilies he had in a bucket. There had been flowers like that in the garden in Pétionville.

'Nice, ain't they? No flowers today?' he said, rubbing his hands together to keep them warm.

'Not today. I'll pop by on my way to work tomorrow. Cheaper then,' she grinned.

'Gotcha.'

She straightened up and turned, accidentally bumping into someone as she moved, almost knocking her off balance. 'Oh, I'm sorry,' she said, putting out a hand to steady herself. The paper bag the woman had been carrying slipped from her grasp.

'Oh, shit! The eggs!' the woman cried just as the bag hit the ground. There was a horrible cracking sound as half a dozen eggs split open, instantly splattering the ground.

'Oh, *no*! Oh, God ... I'm so sorry,' Laure said, bending

down, mortified. She picked up the loaf of bread and the carton of orange juice that had tumbled out, but the bag was soaked. She looked up.

'Laure?' There was a look of incredulous recognition on the woman's face.

'Jill?'

'Laure ... I don't *believe* it! I just don't believe it! What on earth happened to you? You just stopped coming.' Her old tutor looked at her as if she couldn't quite believe her eyes. The broken eggs lay, untouched, on the ground.

Laure stared at her, hoping desperately that her face wouldn't crumple. Her cheeks were on fire as she struggled to find the right, nonchalant note with which to answer. She held out her hands – Jill's loaf of bread in one, orange juice in the other – what could she say? 'I ... it just ... I just couldn't continue,' she said finally, lamely.

'But you were my *best* student,' Jill practically wailed. 'I couldn't believe you'd stopped. Is everything ... are you all right?'

'Yes, no ... well, yes. I ... it's a long story,' Laure stammered finally. She didn't quite know what to say. A wave of fierce longing for the course and the classmates she'd never said goodbye to came over her suddenly.

'What're you doing down this end of town?' Jill asked, finally bending to retrieve the sopping paper bag.

'I live here; just on the other side of the high street.'

'Really? I thought you lived in Primrose Hill?'

'Um, yes. Well, I ... I ... moved out.'

'Oh. Oh, I'm sorry, just me being dense as usual. I didn't realise ...'

'No, it's fine. It's ... well, it happened a while ago.' Laure looked at the ground. Jill was silent.

'Look, are you free?' Jill said suddenly. 'Would you like to have a coffee? You've been to my studio before, haven't you? Why don't we go there?'

'Oh, no ... I ...' Laure hesitated. She looked at Jill's patient, kind-but-not-prying expression and smiled suddenly. 'Well, if you're sure you're not busy,' she said hesitantly. 'I'd really like that.'

'Fantastic. Come on, let me find a bin ...' she said, gesturing at the bag.

'Give it here,' Pete said, stepping forward and taking the sodden mess from her. 'Enjoy your coffee, ladies,' he said with a wink at Laure. 'See you tomorrow. I'm keeping them red ones for you.'

Laure laughed. It had started out a typical dull, winter's day – it suddenly felt as though the sun had come out.

Jill's studio was exactly as she remembered it; the smell of paint and glue, the low buzz of the computer and the occasional click and shriek of the fax machine hit her as soon as she entered. Oh, she'd missed this. How she'd missed it!

'Here, take your coat off,' Jill said, switching on the fan heater. 'What'll you have? Tea? Coffee?'

'Coffee would be great,' Laure called, stealing a sidelong glance at the enormous table in the centre of the room. Jill was obviously working on a new range of fabrics; there were little colour swatches, torn-out scraps of patterns, a pot of paint-brushes and wooden spoons dotted around, as well as several paint-splattered aprons and mopping-up rags. A long length of off-white fabric stretched taut over a metal frame lay along the table with a large tub of something brown and liquid standing by. Several flat, rubber boards lay to one side ... she wondered what they were.

'Squeegees,' Jill said, walking back into the centre and noticing her glance. 'I don't think we'd covered silk-screen printing by the time you left. That's the mesh we use on the table,' she said, 'and this ...' she pointed at the tub of paste, 'is Manutex. I'll show you how it's done in a minute, if you like.'

'I'd love to see it,' Laure said, taking her cup of coffee. 'I'm not in the way, am I?'

'Course not. I'm bang in the middle of a new set of designs. Liberty's are interested ... we'll see. It'll be fun for you to watch. Have you been doing any art work since you left?'

Laure shook her head. She could feel the butterflies of

excitement begin to dance in her stomach; something she hadn't felt in two years. She gulped her coffee down.

She stayed until six-thirty, almost six hours straight of doing nothing but watching, listening, drinking the information in. She hadn't felt so alive in ... well, in two years. It came to her again and again that afternoon just how much she'd missed using her brain. When she did look at her watch and saw that she was at least half an hour late for her shift, she almost cried – not because she was late, but because the afternoon was over.

'Thank you *so* much,' she said to Jill, hurriedly putting on her coat. 'This was fantastic. I can't tell you how much I've missed ... this. I'd better run, but thanks again, it's been fantastic. I loved it.'

'Laure,' Jill turned to her, suddenly serious. 'Why don't you come back? To the course?'

'I ... I can't, I'm afraid,' Laure said, her face falling instantly. There was nothing she would have liked more but it was out of the question. 'I wouldn't be able to afford it,' she said truthfully. 'Not now, anyway.'

'Look, I know you've got to run but if there was a way to work it out ... I don't know, maybe we could get you a bursary or something? Why don't you come by the college on Thursday? Thursday morning? Could you do that?'

Laure's heart began to race. 'In the morning? Yes, I could. I usually work evenings.'

'Good. You remember my office, don't you? On the third floor? I'm not promising anything but there's got to be a way. You're so talented ... it's a complete waste.' She stopped. 'Look, you've got to run, I know. I'll see you on Thursday, all right?'

Laure nodded, her eyes shining. 'Thank you,' she said softly, picking up her bag. 'For ... everything.'

Jill smiled at her. *We'll work something out*, she seemed to be saying. And then Laure really did have to turn and run – all the way back to Columbia Road. She didn't even have time to go home and change.

On Thursday morning, her stomach churning as if it were her first day at school, she knocked on the door of Jill's office. 'Come in,' she heard Jill call out. 'Oh, hi, Laure, come in, sorry about the mess. It's bedlam in here, I know. Here, grab a seat. Yes, that one ... can you manage?'

Laure stepped over piles of books, papers, reports, newspaper cuttings and fabric samples and sat, rather awkwardly, in the chair Jill had pointed to. 'No, it's fine ... I'm fine,' she assured her. Her heart was hammering. Had she ...?

'Well, good news and bad news,' Jill said, getting straight to the point. 'Bad news first. We don't actually have any bursaries or grants available for this year, I'm afraid. We're already half-way through the year so applying for funding for this year's out, which is a pity.'

'Oh.' Laure's heart plummeted all the way to the soles of her feet.

'But, the good news is – and it's a stroke of luck, really – you actually paid for the whole year, when you, or whoever it was, paid the fees so I got Lucy to rummage around in the records and it seems there's a term's credit due to you.' Jill looked at her triumphantly.

'Wh ... what does that mean?' Laure asked.

'Well, it means that you've already paid for a term which you didn't attend when you enrolled – you can use that credit to enrol *now*. Finish up the first year. There'll be a small ad-ministrative charge, I expect, but it means you could get the diploma that we offer at the end of the first year. It's not a degree, as such, but it's something. The other thing I was going to ask – forgive me if I'm being a little pushy here,' she said, looking at Laure quickly, 'was whether you'd like to do a spot of part-time work for me. During the day, of course. I think you said you work in the evenings? I can't pay very much, but I need a good pair of hands to help with this next collection and ...' She leaned back in her chair, palms upturned.

Laure hesitated. She looked at the ground. 'I don't know how to say this,' she said finally, in a low voice, 'but ... but what would you say if I said no to the first part, and yes to the second?' She swallowed.

'What d'you mean?'

'I can't take his money,' she said quietly. 'My husband. He paid the fees. I ... I just can't. If I do come back to college, I've got to pay for it myself. Not him. We're not together any more.' She twisted her fingers agitatedly. She was too embarrassed to look up.

Jill said nothing for a moment. Then Laure heard the squeak of her chair as she tilted forwards. She looked up cautiously. There was something ... a strange expression in Jill's eyes. 'I understand,' Jill said, her tone suddenly serious. 'Absolutely.' She stood up. The meeting seemed to be over. Laure scrambled to her feet. 'So. About the job. When can you start?' Jill asked, holding out a hand. Laure took it, surprised. Jill's shake was firm.

'Uh ... anytime ... any day ... it doesn't matter which ...'

'How about Mondays and Thursdays, to start with?'

'That,' Laure said fervently, 'sounds great.'

'See you Monday, then.'

'Yes. Monday.' In a daze, Laure stumbled across the books and papers and opened the door. She looked back quickly. Jill was watching her with that same odd expression. Laure gave her a fleeting, nervous smile and closed the door. She walked down the corridor, still dazed. In her wildest dreams, she'd never dared to hope for anything like this.

She walked out of the building, stunned. It suddenly came to her as she hurried down the street to the Tube – the expression on Jill's face? Respect. She had looked at Laure with respect. She felt the sharp prick of tears behind her eyes. It had been so long since anyone had looked at her that way.

By the end of her first week, Laure felt as though her head would burst. There was still so much to learn and do. Jill ran a tight ship and Laure had to struggle just to keep up. There were several commissions that had come in during the past month; Jill selected one that she thought Laure would enjoy and pretty much left her to it. It was from Osborne & Little, who were looking for a new range of fabrics, entitled 'boudoir', and for which they'd produced a list of key words: *silks, lingerie, delicate, fragile, cut-work, embroidery, fine drawing, skin tones, make-up colours*. Laure threw herself into the project, collecting fabric samples, making small, tentative sketches, producing the sorts of colours she imagined they would like. She was so grateful for the chance to have something else to think about other than whether table ten had paid or not, or whom she could call on a Sunday morning to replace a missing waiter. She spent every waking minute of the next week producing the sketchbook of ideas and samples that Jill could take and begin to develop further, and it was with a real sense of pride – not to mention trepidation – that she handed it over, almost a week after she'd begun, and stood back, nervously waiting to hear what she thought.

Jill studied the pages carefully, then looked up. The disappointment in her eyes was all too plain. Laure's heart sank. 'These are … nice, Laure,' Jill said, the disappointment in her voice equally clear. 'But they're not you.' She closed the book with a snap. 'They're perfectly functional; the colours are nice, the patterns are nice, but you can do much better – I know, I've seen your work. Look, why don't you take a break? You've been in here practically every hour since I gave you the brief – go out, take a walk, go somewhere inspirational … anywhere. Come back later this afternoon and we'll talk.'

There was little Laure could say – Jill was absolutely right. She pulled on her coat and stepped out into the road, her eyes burning with unshed tears. Go somewhere inspirational? Jill obviously didn't understand the level to which her daily existence had sunk. Inspiration? She barely knew the meaning of the word. She walked down Kingsland Road, her heart heavy with frustration and disappointment, but just before she reached Shoreditch High Street, her eye was caught by a piece of brilliantly coloured sari fabric, draped rather loosely over a headless model in one of the nondescript shop windows along the road. She stopped. The sheer, gossamer fuchsia jumped out at her amidst the monochromatic greys and dull browns of its surroundings. Suddenly, it came to her. 'Boudoir' needn't mean delicate or floral or pale – whose skin tones were they talking about, anyway? She stared at the chocolate-coloured skin of her own arm – she loved bold, strong colours; sensual, rich textures and fabrics, not the light, airy, tentative patterns she'd spent the past week struggling to make. She almost ran across the road to the bus stop at the corner. Shepherd's Bush market – *that* was where she would find her inspiration, among the saris and African prints, not in the fabric section at Liberty's! She boarded the bus impatiently. It was as if a light bulb had suddenly gone on in her head. She would show Jill her trust hadn't been misplaced. Another lesson learned the hard way; it was time to stop being what everyone wanted or expected her to be – and start being herself.

Three days later, Jill's reaction was exactly what she'd hoped. She took one look at the pages in front of her and whistled; a long, low sound full of excitement and real pleasure. Laure smiled, exhausted, but relieved. She'd fashioned her own colour wheel using bold, deep colours and from it, produced rich, obscure mixtures against which she'd scribbled names of her own making – cinnabar, oxblood, silk, quarry, ruby. She'd created a palette that drew on her memories of home – of the beautiful fabrics and unusual textures she and Améline had come upon that day in the attic when they'd opened Belle's trunks. She'd found pieces of antique black lace and teamed them with rich, bold velvets; there were photographs of a fringed mantilla, the gold embroidery on the hem of a burgundy sari, silver and turquoise stitching and the stunning colours of peacock feathers; whorls and streams of tropical, bold colours and rich, sensuous textures ... sequins and the fiery flash of sapphires, emeralds and rubies; strong, African-inspired graphics and not an animal print in sight. It was a bold, sexy 'boudoir', not the chaste, girlish examples that she'd started out with. Jill's quick, professional eye moved smoothly over the pages and when she was finished, her smile told Laure everything she needed to know. She'd done it. By God, she'd done it.

It took her and Jill almost a month to produce the first round of mood and sample-boards for their meeting with Lydia Gray, the head buyer at Osborne's. Jill made up the large, card mood board, using photocopies of Laure's sketchbook and small, square samples of the first few prints they'd made. She showed Laure how to iron the fabric samples and overlock them on the machine, to stop the edges from fraying. There were ten samples in all, each attached to the card with a white strip of linen with the letters JTD – Jill Teague Designs – printed in simple, black lettering across the middle. It looked so professional; Laure couldn't stop staring at it. She cut the card straight down the middle, as Jill showed her, taking care not to cut all the way through, so that the sample board could be folded, like a book. She watched as Jill slid the board into her beautiful, large black leather portfolio and got ready for the meeting. She went to work that evening, her mind barely on her duties. All she could think about was Lydia Gray's reaction to her work and whether or not she would like it. Jill had promised to ring her first thing in the morning and let her know – how was she going to get through the night?

'She *loved* it!' Jill cried down the phone. Laure hugged the receiver to her chest and let out a silent whoop. She was too pleased to speak. 'She was completely bowled over!' Jill said, laughing. 'When are you next in? We've got loads to talk about.'

'Did she really like it?' Laure asked, almost shyly.

'I'm telling you, she *loved* it.'

The success of Laure's 'boudoir' range resulted in two further, large commissions for JTD. Lydia Gray wanted a range of wallpapers to complement the lingerie fabrics and a range of fabrics for outdoor garden furniture. Laure was busy for the next month, producing the sketches and mood boards that she and Jill would take and develop, and at the end of the month, when everything was finally completed and the orders confirmed, Jill asked her if she would consider coming into the studio on a full-time basis. For Laure, it was almost too good to be true. Within the short space of a couple of months, her life had again turned full circle. The salary Jill offered was less than she took home from her restaurant job but she would have done it for almost nothing. The sense of accomplishment that came over her every time she finished a sheet or a print was sweeter than anything she'd ever felt.

PART SEVEN

84

Tickets, passport, wallet. Laure quickly ran through the list in her head. Yes, everything was in hand. There was a short hoot from outside signalling the arrival of the minicab driver. She looked around the flat one last time, picked up her suitcase and opened the front door. It was raining, of course but for once she didn't care. She was off to West Africa for two months! She locked the front door and handed her bags to the driver.

'Heathrow, miss?' he enquired, getting back in and starting the engine. Laure nodded, almost too excited to speak. 'Where you off to? Anywhere nice?'

'Yes, I hope so. I'm going to Ghana.'

'Oh. Where's that, then?'

Laure smiled. 'Africa.'

'Oh, yeah? Well, I expect it's better weather out there than here,' the driver said, pulling out into the traffic along Graham Road. ''Ope it's not like this all bloody summer. You got family out there, have you?'

'No,' Laure said, shaking her head. 'It's a business trip.'

'Oh, right.' He didn't seem to know quite what to say after that and, to her relief, they drove towards Heathrow in silence. She hugged her small portfolio to her chest. Two whole months in Ghana doing nothing but collecting inspiration and ideas for their up-coming season. It was Jill's idea. An old university friend of hers, Kofi Quarshie, had suggested it one night, after seeing some of Laure's work in a portfolio that Jill had taken home. He'd been struck by the similarity of some of her designs to the woven textiles of his own country; his sister was often in Accra – she would be delighted to meet Laure and show her around if she came ... why not?

Jill put the idea to Laure the following morning. Laure, predictably, was thrilled. In the two and a half years that she'd been working for Jill, the little studio had more than tripled its output and quadrupled its profits. Jill had finally stopped asking whether or not she intended to finish the course and had offered her a partnership instead. JTD was now Teague St Lazâre. In beautiful, chocolate-brown and pink lettering. Yes, TSL could certainly afford it. Why not? she echoed Kofi.

'There we go,' the driver said, interrupting her thoughts. He helped lift the suitcase on to a trolley. 'Thanks very much,' he added, looking at the generous tip she'd left. 'Have a lovely time out there.'

'Thanks.' She pushed the trolley across the road and walked into the building.

It took her almost an hour to check in – Ghanaians, she noticed immediately, were a lot like Haitians. There was the same struggle to sneak giant suitcases through the check-in counters; the same vociferous, pointless protests over the baggage allowance; the same chaotic rush for the next available counter. She smiled to herself as she left the crowded counters behind and walked through to the departure lounge. She found a seat near the window and settled down to wait until the flight was called. She looked out at the planes lined up in front of the giant windows. She thought about Haiti again and about going back to visit. Grandmère would be in her seventies now ... did she ever talk about her to anyone? She'd seen what had happened to Belle. Would the same thing have happened to her? Améline wouldn't forget her but Grandmère ...? She shook her head briskly. Now was not the time for such thoughts. She was on her way to West Africa to find the inspiration she needed for the coming year. It was a good time; she was in a good place. God knew it had been hard enough getting there.

Suddenly there was a great commotion and the beginnings of a stampede around her. She looked up. The flight to Accra had just been called. She picked up her bag, slung her portfolio over her arm and took her place at the end of the heaving, jostling queue.

The soft, warm air that rushed at them as soon as the aircraft doors were opened almost brought tears to her eyes. Despite her resolve not to think about Haiti, it took her straight back to Pétionville and to the heat of the streets along which she and Régine walked each afternoon. Even the rhythm and cadence of the languages unfolding around her seemed familiar.

There were a few red and sweaty-faced Europeans among the crowd that tumbled down the steps, the women fanning themselves desperately as they sank further and further into the sticky, humid cloud. Laure breathed in deeply; she hadn't even set foot on Ghanaian soil and already she loved it. She followed the crowd into the customs hall and with remarkable efficiency, despite the shouting and apparent confusion around her, collected her bags, located the entrance *and* the minivan that Kofi had assured would be there to meet her. 'Brightest Spot Guest House', in lurid, Day-Glo colours along the side of an old jeep. It was hard to miss.

The driver rushed forwards to greet her enthusiastically. His name, he declared proudly, was Bright. Bright of the Brightest Spot. Laure suppressed a giggle. 'Pleased to meet you, Bright,' she said, clambering into the back. Was she the only guest to be picked up?

'Yes, please, madam,' Bright called out above the noise of the spluttering engine.

'How far is it? To the guest house?' she asked, as they wove through the narrow exit lanes amidst passengers and porters.

'Not far, madam,' was his reassuring answer. Bright's 'not far' turned out to be five minutes away, just across the main road. Laure peered out in the darkness at what appeared to be a residential area – so close to the airport? 'Oh, yes, madam. Airport Residential Area,' he called. '*Ve*-ry nice, madam. Top class.'

Twenty minutes later, she was shown to her room. Bright,

she'd soon discovered, was not only the driver of the Brightest Spot Guest House, he was also the cook, porter and night receptionist. The guest house was a pleasant, if slightly run-down series of small bungalows dotted about a large garden. As they walked down the path towards Bungalow No. 3, she caught a glimpse of a small pool and a covered patio where several couples sat, listening to the hi-life music playing softly in the background. The room itself was large and cool; Bright switched on the noisy air-conditioner as soon as they entered. Bathroom, cupboards, tiny kitchenette … She nodded, relieved to see it was clean, just as Kofi had promised. His sister Beatrice was unfortunately away on holiday in the UK for a few weeks; for the first month she'd be on her own, he'd told her in London, anxiously wondering if she'd be able to cope. Laure laughed. Didn't he know where she was from? Cope? Of course she'd cope! In fact, she rather liked the idea of being on her own for the first few weeks – that way, she'd get to see what Ghana was *really* like, instead of being shown what others thought she ought to see. She thanked Bright for the third or fourth time that evening, pulled off a couple of notes from the pile she'd been given at the airport and closed the door gently on his declarations of gratitude. She was tired and the heat, despite feeling so at home, was making her drowsy. She switched off the rattling air-conditioner and opened the shutters, breathing in deeply the night air. The long-forgotten but still familiar sound of crickets and cicadas came at her so that she closed her eyes momentarily against the rush of nostalgia that swept over her. She stood there for quite a while, thinking, thinking.

At breakfast the following morning she lingered over the small buffet table – ripe, moist papaws, sharp, lemon-yellow pineapples, green oranges, giant, bruised mangoes … the fruits of home. She helped herself eagerly. Although the service was rather shaky, the waiter's apologetic smiles seemed so heartfelt and genuine, she hadn't the heart to return the fried eggs he'd suddenly put down on her plate without being asked, or request some hot water for her empty teacup. A group of Americans in the far corner of the dining room were doing enough complaining for the rest of them. She took the bottle of cold water that the waiter had given her by mistake, and escaped back to her room. The night before she'd asked Bright if it were possible to organise a taxi and a driver for the entire day and by the looks of things, he'd found one. There was a young man standing, nervously expectant, outside her door as she approached. Yes, he was the taxi driver. He was Bright's brother. His name? Adonis, pronounced *Ah*-donis. Laure smiled to herself. Even the names sounded familiar.

Twenty minutes later, armed with her camera and sketch-book, Laure and Adonis trundled out of the hotel parking lot and joined the steady stream of traffic heading towards the centre of town. As they drove out of the residential area and into the city proper, the landscape changed. It was a flat, low city, she noticed; to the right-hand side of the freeway were thousands and thousands of little rusted tin shacks, not much different from those she'd seen occasionally in Cité Soleil. Goats, bicycles, bandy-legged children ran good-naturedly alongside the traffic; miraculously, no one seemed to get in the way of anyone else. Even the goats appeared to know when to stop or which way to turn. There were little makeshift kiosks strung all along what would have been the pavement – selling everything from lottery tickets to live chickens. The traffic crawled along; the vendors of little plastic sachets of water weaving their way dangerously in and around the cars. '*I-i-i-ice water! I-i-i-i-ce water!*' Adonis cursed, Laure smiled. Inch by inch, they moved forward.

White, colonially graceful mansions; stark, dirty concrete office blocks; rickety street-side markets ... all passed before her eyes. There were people everywhere; getting on and off the small vans with their brightly coloured slogans – 'God Dey'; 'Still A Man'; 'Weep for Me, O Jesus' – which halted and then swung out at random points along the road; a clutch of hand-some, red-roofed buildings that Adonis said were the law courts and then suddenly, glimpsed through the tangled undergrowth on one side of the road, the sea, a flash of dark, brilliant blue, rippling unsteadily towards the horizon. A policeman in a start-lingly white uniform and white gloves orchestrated the traffic; his hand gestures as delicate as any conductor's – *left, right, go on, stop*.

They swung left after the law courts and then, suddenly, without warning, they were inside the market. The taxi crawled to a halt as the vendors grew in thickness and number, until all Laure could see in front of her was the graceful, swaying backside of a woman balancing the most enormous tray of ... Laure peered out of the window ... *snails* on her head.

'Madam, I will park over there, please,' Adonis shouted to her above the din of buying and selling going on around them. 'Kindly alight.'

'Here?'

'Yes, please, madam.'

'Is this the textile market?' she asked, rummaging in her bag for Kofi's instructions.

'Yes, please.'

'Oh. Erm ... how ... how will I find you again?'

'Madam, I will find *you*,' Adonis declared confidently. 'Don't worry, just keep going to your left. You will see the cloth market.'

Laure got out of the taxi, nervously pressing her bag to her chest and was almost immediately swallowed up by the crowd. She had little option but to allow herself to be swept along, wedged between brightly coloured shirts, wraparound skirts and the yellow-and-brown uniforms of what she supposed were schoolchildren. The sensation of losing herself in the heaving mass of bodies brought Haiti and the bars to which Delroy had taken her immediately to mind; like Alice plunging after the White Rabbit, she disappeared into the crowd until she was no longer sure who followed whom, carried along by the bodies on either side of her. The entire street was one big sales pitch; at the sides of the road were carefully constructed towering piles of whatever was on hand to sell: books; second-hand shoes; shoelaces; giant, oversized ladies' underwear and the kinds of enormous, engineered bras she'd seen in American magazines as a child flapped in the wind; shiny aluminium pots and beautiful, locally made ceramic bowls stacked in precarious pyramids; pink china cups, glasses, saucers, bulky washing machines, silver standing fans ... There was nothing, it seemed, that couldn't be found along the streets of Makola. She spotted a woman carrying bolts of fabric on her head and began to follow her, hoping she would lead her towards the section which sold cloth. As the household goods stalls began to give way to second-hand clothing and sewing equipment, the crowd too began to thin out. The street was once again open to buses and vans and the stalls seemed to disappear into 'proper' shops on either side of the road.

She stopped to ask the way and an enormous, grinning woman took her by the hand and threaded her way delicately through the sidewalk stalls. 'In there,' she pointed, through an archway that led, as far as Laure could tell, into darkness.

'Are you sure?' Laure asked nervously. She couldn't see beyond the archway.

'Yes!' the woman laughed, sensing her hesitation. 'It's quicker. Just go there, turn left ... you will see. One, two minutes. If you go by the road ...' She turned and shrugged, calling out something to the women who sat on low stools, legs spread, with basins full of green leaves in front of them. They laughed, but there was nothing malicious in their voices. 'Yes, you can go!' they called, one after the other, clucking and shaking their heads. *Silly tourist.* Laure smiled ruefully, held on to her bag and marched forwards. She ducked through the doorway, stepped over an open gutter and suddenly she was inside an enormous, covered hall. It took a few seconds for her eyes to adjust to the gloom and then she gasped. It was indeed the cloth market and it was like nothing she'd ever seen.

The hall had been divided into rows of cage-like stalls, each with a small viewing platform where the owner sat, surrounded by hundreds of neatly folded bales of material stretching upwards into the gloom. On one side was the display rack, where selected bolts had been opened and draped, side by side, to display the full length of a single print. Laure moved among the first few stalls, her mouth open. Colours, the likes of which she had never seen, rose above her in dizzying, dazzling streams. Even in the poor light, the effect was mesmerising. Sharp, clean blues, smoky turquoises, dirty browns and muddy oranges; flashes of yellow-gold, deep, rich blacks ... She stopped, she had never known black could hold so much variation in tone and depth.

'This one is morning cloth,' one of the women told her, deftly opening up a bolt and spreading it out.

'You wear it in the morning?' Laure said, stroking its smooth, waxy surface. It was black, interspersed with a dull, burgundy red. A sombre, earthy cloth ... She smiled suddenly. 'Oh, you mean *mourning* cloth?'

'Ye-es, morning cloth. For funeral.' The women around her nodded and smiled, pleased with her obvious appreciation. 'You like to buy it?'

'It's beautiful,' she breathed. 'But no, I'm just looking around.'

'Come, come ...' one of them called to her. 'Ve-ry nice cloth. Come and see.'

For the next hour, she was led from one little stall to the next, each revealing rows of wax printed cloth, their dazzling patterns taken from the daily rituals and shapes she could see around her. There were the irregularly rounded gourds and calabash bowls she'd seen coming into the market, the tiny guinea fowl, the elaborate hairdos of the young women who walked like models, gliding, rather than stepping over the ground. Everything was here – sun, moon, stars, raindrops, plants, leaves, animals ... The stall-owners, delighted with her delight, allowed her to take photographs and as many six-yard bolts as she could carry. She staggered out of the hallway under the weight of her purchases to the cheerful sounds of their goodbye cries and ran straight into Adonis.

'Adonis!' she cried, wondering how on earth he'd found her. She gratefully surrendered most of her cloth. 'How did you know?'

'Oh, madam, you didn't believe me,' he said mournfully.

'Didn't I say I can find you?' He winked at her. 'Come, please. The car is over here.'

By the end of her first week, Laure had enough material to begin the sketches for the new season. She had quickly turned her room at the Brightest Spot into a temporary studio; there were bolts of fabric spread across the bed, the walls, the furniture, her suitcases – every surface was covered in materials she'd either bought or found along the way. Under Bright and Adonis's careful guidance, she'd even found a roadside seamstress who had quickly run up a number of simple shift dresses out of her favourite prints. She took one out now, holding it against her and opening the wardrobe door to look at herself in the mirror. It was Friday night, exactly a week after she'd arrived and, after meeting a Dutch journalist in a café the previous day, she'd somehow found herself invited to a dinner party at the house of the Spanish ambassador. She chose a dress with a circular dark olive-green and vibrant orange pattern, overlaid with tiny, black dots. It was certainly striking. Perhaps tying her hair back wasn't such a bad idea after all – with a full head of curly hair *and* the psychedelic print dress, the whole outfit might have been a *little* over the top. She chose a pair of flat, simple black sandals, picked up her bag and walked out into the hot night air to wait for Silke, the journalist who had promised to pick her up. Despite her misgivings, it felt good to be going somewhere rather special for once. Her social life in London was almost non-existent. In fact, she'd practically forgotten how to have one.

85

'Will you stop *fussing*!' Melanie snapped irritably at Agnes, the hairdresser, who was desperately trying to interject a few curls into Melanie's straight, sleek locks. 'I *like* it straight. That's why I use *this*,' she stabbed the bottle marked 'straightener' with a red-tipped forefinger.

'Yes, madam.'

Agnes's calm, unflappable response only irritated her further. It was all anybody here ever said. *Yes, madam; no, madam; three bags full, madam.* She was sick of hearing the word 'madam'. She was in an especially foul mood for two, very good reasons. One, Marc had refused point blank to accompany her to the Spanish ambassador's dinner party and two, of much graver consequence, was the news he'd delivered the previous night that he was extending his contract by another year. It was *not* the news she'd been waiting for. He'd already extended it once, by a year, which meant that they'd been in Ghana for four, long, drawn-out years; the news that he wished to stay for another one was enough to make her scream. 'How could you accept it without talking to me first?' she'd shrieked.

'I *haven't* accepted anything,' he'd protested, his face darkening in anger. 'I'm discussing it with you *now*, for God's sake!'

'You're *not!*' Melanie screamed, almost hysterical with rage. 'You say you are but I *know* you! You've already decided, you don't *care* what I think, or what I want,' she cried, her voice breaking. 'You just go ahead and do exactly as you please, just as you—'

'Melanie!' Marc yelled back at her. 'Stop it! It's my *job*! What the hell else d'you expect me to do?'

'Why can't you be like everyone else,' Melanie sobbed. 'Why can't you just have a *normal* job? Why can't we live somewhere civilised, like London, or Paris, like we used to? I hate it here, Marc ... I *hate* it!'

Marc just looked at her in the way she'd come to dread. 'Pull yourself together,' he said coldly, shaking his head. 'And stop screaming. You'll wake the kids up.'

'*Fuck* the kids!' Melanie screamed wildly as he walked out the door. '*Fuck you and the kids!*' She'd thrown back the sheet and stormed out of the room at four a.m., stubbing her big toe on the dresser on the way out. Now the toe was swollen to twice its usual size which meant that the delicate high heels she'd been planning to wear to the party simply wouldn't work – and all this because Marc had decided, without consulting her first, to accept the offer and *stay another year*. In hindsight, perhaps attacking him as soon as he walked in the door wasn't the best way to have gone about it. But it was too late. As usual, the damage had already been done.

Oh, well, she thought to herself, taking one last look in the mirror at Agnes's efforts before fumbling in her purse for a cigarette. Damage done. She lit it with shaking hands. She'd really gone and done it this time. Fuck the *kids*? Even *she* winced. He thought her a terrible mother, she knew. She didn't know how to explain it to him – that sometimes they didn't even feel like her children. They spent more time with the servants than they did with her. Half the time Melanie had no idea what she was supposed to do with them. As far as she could remember, Stella hadn't done much with *her*; she'd been shipped off to boarding school almost as soon as she could walk and she could count on the fingers of one hand the number of times Mike had been around. No, the happy family gatherings that Marc seemed to expect were simply beyond the grasp of her imagination. Plus, both Susu and Guy spoke English as their third or fourth language; at four, Susu sounded like a childish version of Efua, Ama's replacement – it made Melanie's ears burn – and most of the time, Guy refused to speak anything other than Twi and Arabic, much to Randa's delight. And that was another thing – she positively hated her mother-in-law. Or her *step*-mother-in-law – was there such a thing?

How was it possible, Melanie thought miserably to herself as she paid for her quick wash and blow-dry, that she felt so alienated from her own children? She looked at Susu sometimes, searching for some resemblance in the chubby brown cheeks and curly brown hair for a sign, *any* sign, that the child actually *belonged* to her. Both were the spitting image of Marc, born two years apart. Two perfect little beings, in his image alone. Of *course* she loved them; the day Guy had fallen in the swimming

461

pool while Ama was looking the other way was still the worst day of her life. She'd been sitting on the patio, idly thumbing through a magazine that Barb had dropped off when something made her look up. She had no idea what, but seconds later she was running across the lawn in her bare feet, her heart thudding in her mouth as she jumped, fully clothed, into the pool and dragged his lifeless body out, too frightened to even scream. From deep inside her memory, her school lifesaving drill had come to her; kneeling beside him, she'd opened his little mouth, placed both hands on his chest and pumped, breathing into him with deep, regular breaths until the water erupted from his lungs, along with the remains of his breakfast, and he started to wail. She'd slapped Ama as hard as she could in front of Susu's shocked and terrified face and then had walked into the house, her entire body freezing despite the midday heat, and collapsed. Marc was in Liberia that time. It had taken her two days to get a message to him and by then she'd fired Ama, taken Guy to the most expensive hospital in town for a battery of pointless (it later turned out) tests and hired a small boy whose name she couldn't pronounce and whose job it was to sit by the pool from dawn to dusk.

No, she loved her children. It was just that, well, sometimes they didn't seem to want to *be* her children. They belonged elsewhere. They belonged, like Marc, to this godforsaken country to which she would never – *ever* – acclimatise, much less belong; and there didn't seem to be a damned thing she could do about it.

'*Ahlan*, Melanie,' someone said. She turned round. '*Marhaba?*'

She frowned. It was Fatima, the Lebanese owner of the salon. *Why, oh why*, she thought to herself as she smiled a wan greeting, *did they insist on speaking Arabic to her? Didn't they get it? She would never speak the damned language. Never. She didn't care if Marc did; she wanted nothing to do with it.* 'Fine, fine ...' she said quickly.

'She did a good job?' Fatima indicated Melanie's hair.

'Yes, yes ... must run, thanks ...' Melanie said and hurriedly

462

exited the salon. Irritating woman. Couldn't she *see* Agnes had done a good job? She got into her car and drove off. It was almost three p.m. She'd have a quick nap and then begin getting ready for the party. Damn Marc. She hated having to go alone.

'Ambassador,' Melanie took his limp hand, smiling graciously. 'Thank you for the invitation. It's *so* nice to see you again.'

'Madam Abadi,' the ambassador gave a short bow, peering at her above his pince-nez. 'And Mr Abadi? He did not accompany you?'

'No, unfortunately not,' Melanie gave a little laugh. 'Working, I'm afraid ... You know how it is, I'm sure.'

'Indeed. Please ...' He indicated the way to the formal sitting room beyond.

'Melanie, darling!' It was Victoria, the ambassador's New Zealand-born wife. 'You look divine, as always. Come ... I want to introduce you to someone. And then I want you to tell me *all* about your trip to London. Did you see any good shows? You *must* tell me.' Melanie smiled. It was the unlikeliest of marriages – Victoria was a former dancer at Sadler's Wells and, at sixty, still retained her slim, boyish figure and blonde, ethereal good looks. The ambassador was probably the same age, but looked twenty years older; a tall, stoop-shouldered patrician of the old school of diplomats – rather aloof, faintly disapproving and impossible to gauge. Melanie liked Victoria, unlike Marc – but then Marc didn't like any of the people whom Melanie called friends. It was just one of the many sources of tension between them. 'Now,' Victoria said, tucking her arm chummily into Melanie's and guiding her towards the patio doors, 'do you remember that Dutch journalist who was going round the orphanages? Taking photos, I mean?'

'I think so ... the dark-haired girl?'

'Absolutely. Silke. Well, she's got the most *darling* girl with her from London; she's a textile designer and she's here for a couple of months looking at fabrics, or something. Anyhow, she's simply *stunning* and when I met her earlier, I thought to myself, now, there's somebody Melanie ought to meet. Ah, there they are.' She nosed Melanie in the direction of the pool. Melanie felt a sharp twinge of jealousy at Victoria's words – after all, *she* was used to being the one everyone else ought to meet, not the other way round. She looked to where Victoria pointed, and swallowed. The woman standing next to Silke-the-journalist was indeed stunning. Tall, lithe, dark brown skin, thick black hair pulled back tightly off her face; wearing the most amazing dress, large silver hoops in her ears, a thick silver bracelet and flat, thin-but-not delicate sandals. She turned as Victoria approached and smiled. Melanie's heart sank. She had one of those wide, beautiful smiles that lit up her entire face.

'Laure, darling,' Victoria cooed, claiming her with a hand on her arm. 'I want you to meet a dear, dear friend of mine. I was just telling Melanie, I really have to introduce you two. I think you'll get along like a house on fire,' she said, with a flourish, as though showing off a prized pet. 'Melanie, this is Laure.' Victoria took Silke by the arm and led her away, wanting to show her off to someone else, no doubt. 'Now, Silke, darling, there's someone I want you to meet . . .' Her voice trailed off.

'Nice to meet you,' the woman said, turning back towards Melanie and holding out a hand. Melanie's heart sank even further. A low, husky voice with the sort of placeless, intriguing accent that drew you straight in, made you wonder where she was from. Kim immediately sprang to mind. Melanie's friends were generally less attractive and certainly less beguiling than her. She wasn't about to make *that* mistake again. Even Laure's handshake was nice and firm. 'Are you . . . you're living here?' she asked pleasantly.

''Fraid so,' Melanie said, looking rather glumly around her. 'Look, shall we get a drink? Victoria's boys always make the best punches. Come to think of it, I don't know where they are tonight. They're usually falling all over you.'

'Her sons?'

'No, silly. The servants,' Melanie laughed. 'Come on, let's find one. I'm absolutely *parched*.'

★

By the end of the evening, she'd found out that Laure St Lazâre – perfect name for her – was a textile designer, that she'd just bought a flat in the East End – 'Really?' Gosh, that's brave. I've never even been there!' – and was in Ghana for the next couple of months. She'd also found out that she'd bought the fabric for the stunning dress she was wearing just the day before from that beastly Makola market that Melanie had only ever visited once, *and* had had it sewn up for her by a roadside tailor. Melanie was dumbstruck. The woman was just too cool for words! They arranged to meet on Sunday morning at Laure's guest house for coffee. Melanie left the party early, for once, thrilled to have found someone new and interesting to talk to. Even if she *was* rather too beautiful for Melanie's comfort.

Marc looked up in surprise from the book he was reading. He glanced at his watch. It was only eleven – Melanie usually didn't get home from these things before two.

'You're back early,' he said, his voice guarded.

'*And* I only had two glasses of wine,' Melanie replied, almost flirtatiously. She tossed her handbag on the chair beside him and sank on to the couch. Marc looked at her closely. She was animated, her cheeks lightly flushed, either with the wine or the company she'd been in. He wondered, briefly, which was worse. 'Are you still sulking?' she asked, pulling a quick face.

'Me?'

'Yes, you.' The tone in her voice was decidedly flirtatious.

He sighed and put down his book. Melanie's moods were impossible to predict. 'No, I'm not sulking. Did you have a nice time?'

'Mmm. I met this woman. She's a fashion designer ... no, fabric designer. Her name's Laure. She's *really* nice. You'd like her, honestly.' Marc gave a gentle snort. 'No, I mean it. She's not a bit like, well, like the women you *don't* like. Anyhow, I'm meeting her on Sunday, for coffee. Shall I invite her for dinner next week? Will you promise to behave?' Melanie got up from the couch and came to stand behind his chair. He was aware of the heady scent of her perfume as she leaned over him, her hair falling over his face and spilling out in silky waves across his shirt front. Her chin slid into the space between his shoulder and his cheek; he caught her hand as it slid down his chest. It had been a month or more since he'd made love to her and as he pulled her from behind the chair and buried his face in the folds of her skirt, it came to him again – when she was on form, there was no one quite like her. She pulled him off the chair, almost roughly. 'Kids asleep?' she whispered, before her soft, warm mouth covered his. He could only nod. Her hands were busy on him, guiding him impatiently into her. It was the way she was – nothing for weeks, she shied from his touch. And then, right out of the blue, a night like this one. He never could figure her out.

86

Améline watched the last of the vans pull away from the kerb and then she turned round, walked up the last couple of steps and closed the front door behind her. She looked around. It was suddenly peaceful in the almost-empty hallway. Paul was in the garden, supervising the last of the planting. She and Paul had decided, after nearly two years of deliberating, to turn the house into a bed and breakfast. The timing was right; the economy was slowly gaining strength. The previous year, the politician René Préval had been elected with almost ninety per cent of the popular vote. Unemployment was at last beginning to fall; private companies were beginning to trickle in, as were the tourists. Things were starting to look up. It had been Paul's idea, really. He was the one who thought of it. He loved it in Haiti – here he could *do* things, he kept saying to her. Back in England what was there in Malvern for him – for *them* – other than a slow, back-breaking descent into retirement? Améline laughed at his melodramatic expression, but he was right.

There were opportunities in Haiti, now. Who cared if he'd been a builder and she a *reste-avec*? They'd talked and planned and worked everything out and yes, they could do it. Between them they had the capital *and* the skills ... It would have been silly *not* to.

Would Laure approve of their decision? She wandered through the empty rooms; the parlour, the formal sitting room, the dining room; then down the corridor to the two guest bedrooms on the ground floor, emptied of everything except the beds. The kitchen too had been cleared out to reveal a spacious, pleasant room in which she and two others could easily handle breakfasts and the light snacks she intended to serve all day. She walked upstairs to the first floor. Clearing out Laure's room had been the hardest thing to do. She opened the door and looked in. As with the other bedrooms, only the bed remained; an old-fashioned, brass-knuckled single bed. She'd given the mattress to Cléones – it hadn't been used since Laure's departure. Laure's few possessions and the clothes she'd left behind had all been carefully transported to the attic, to lie alongside Belle's. Ironic, really, that their things should wind up next to each other. Everything stowed away, waiting for the day one of them might come back to claim them. Améline got up, dusted her hands on her apron and gently shut the door.

There were a few advantages to having a builder around, she teased Paul. Just a few. As soon as they'd made up their minds, it was surprising how quickly everything fell into place. Paul would supervise the building and the general refurbishment of the house while she took care of the details of turning it into a going concern. She was very clear about what she wanted; a simple, comfortable guest house, six bedrooms, three bathrooms, a cool, welcoming dining room where guests could eat breakfast, and the shaded verandah at the back of the house for afternoon tea. Nothing fancy; just *comfortable* in the way Iain had taught her life could be. She thought of him sometimes, his voice coming to her in the most unexpected places. *He* would have approved, she thought, of her coming home, finding a use for the large, old house she'd been left. He would have liked to see the changes in Haiti's fortunes, too. The optimism that was slowly beginning to return to the streets of Port-au-Prince would have delighted him.

She and Paul took a long walk one Sunday afternoon in the direction of the hill to which she'd once run. The Palme d'Or was no longer there; its rusty sign hanging by a nail, swinging forlornly in the late afternoon breeze. She asked an old man weeding the garden what had happened to the owner. He'd died, apparently, the old man said, straightening up painfully. Not long after Baby Doc had fled. Terrible times, those, he reminisced, leaning on the handle of his makeshift rake. Things were getting better, though, weren't they? Paul asked. He nodded slowly. '*Oui, oui, peut-être, m'sieur*. But this is Haiti. Anything can happen.' Améline smiled and turned to leave. It was true. Anything *could* happen. A former *reste-avec* could wind up the owner of a house on Rue Rigaud. No, she corrected herself as they began the long descent back down the hill, she was the joint proprietor of a guest house named Blake's. *That* was who she was about to become.

87

Melanie's house was very much like Melanie herself; complex, a little hidden, unexpectedly sensual in places, at times almost cold. The gardens were immaculate; the pool shimmered invitingly in the distance, the bougainvillea were flamboyant and delightfully rich in colour. Cool, dark interiors, expensive furniture and interesting artwork – but little sign of its occupants. She'd told Laure she lived with her husband and children but Laure couldn't see much evidence of either. She followed her dutifully through the living room into the airy, spacious dining room.

'Kids are already asleep,' Melanie said, anticipating her question. 'I'm awfully strict, I'm afraid. Seven o'clock at the very latest.'

'And your husband?' Laure asked, seeing that there were only two places set at the long, highly polished table.

'Oh, he might join us later. He's working late.' Melanie rolled her eyes. 'He's *always* working late.'

'What does he do?' Laure asked, sliding into the seat she'd indicated. A servant entered silently, carrying an already sweating bottle of white wine on a tray.

'I hope that came out of the freezer,' Melanie said to him briskly. He looked blankly at her. 'Fridge or freezer?'

'Fri … freedger, madam,' he stammered, obviously clueless as to what he was being asked.

Melanie rolled her eyes again. 'Oh, just put it down, will you, please.'

'Yes, madam.'

'Hopeless,' Melanie said as the door closed behind him. 'Absolutely bloody hopeless.'

'It looks cold enough,' Laure said mildly. 'Here, shall I pour you a glass?'

'Oh, yes, please. I've been *dying* for one all day.'

'What do you do during the day?' Laure asked delicately.

'Me? Oh, I … well, I … play tennis, go to the gym … meet people. I don't know really. I just never seem to have enough hours in the day,' Melanie said brightly, and, Laure noticed, a touch defensively. 'Marc's always telling me to get a job, or do something *useful*, as he puts it, but I *am* useful. At least I think I am. I bring people together. I throw *really* good parties …'

'And you have two young children,' Laure said. 'That's a job in itself, surely?'

'Yes, of course it is. You're right.' Melanie suddenly brightened.

The kitchen door opened and the same servant crept out, an enormous bowl of salad in one hand and a grilled fish on a beautiful ceramic platter in the other. Melanie dismissed him and served them both; chatting almost non-stop about her friends, their friends, the beach parties she organised, the fund-raising events for this charity or that; as they ate, Laure was surprised to realise just how well she understood Melanie. In an odd, unexpected way, she reminded Laure of herself – her married self. For the first few months of her life with Daniel, Laure too had found herself at a loose end without a clear plan of what she was going to do with her life. As it had been for her, money was obviously not a problem for Melanie; whatever it was that her husband did, there seemed to be plenty to spare from her side of the family. With a mother now on her fourth husband; a father who had never really been around … As the evening wore on, she found herself unexpectedly touched by the picture she was forming. There was something essentially *likeable* about Melanie, despite her poor-little-rich-girl performance and her air of bored insouciance. Laure suspected that there was more to Melanie than met the eye and, as Melanie opened the second bottle of wine, she caught glimpses of a much more interesting past. By ten p.m., and a bottle of wine later, Laure learned she'd gone to LA after some horrible incident with her stepfather; she'd lived with a drug dealer for a while, who, it turned out, had been sleeping with her best friend … it was all beginning to sound like one of those deliciously naughty American novels she and Régine had pored over as teenagers. Sex, drugs and rock 'n' roll.

And then the front door opened and Melanie instantly sobered up.

'Oh, *shit*. It's *Marc*,' she whispered urgently, quickly swapping Laure's empty glass for her own. Laure looked on in surprise as Melanie tucked her hair behind her ears and tried to look as demure as possible. 'Quick, put that bottle under the table!'

'You've only had a few glasses. It's not as though you're driving anywhere, are you?' Laure whispered back.

'Doesn't matter … it's … oh, hu*llo*. You're late, darling,' Melanie said, pouting. Laure glanced at the door. A tall, powerfully built man with skin the colour of hers stood in the doorway, looking at them. She blinked in surprise. She hadn't realised Melanie's husband was *dark*. She'd always assumed he was white, like Melanie. 'Come and join us,' Melanie cried. 'This is Laure, darling, remember I told you about her?'

He shrugged and nodded curtly at Laure. 'I'm off to bed,' he said shortly. 'I'm working tomorrow.' There was a slight but distinctly noticeable emphasis on the word 'working'. Laure felt the heat in her face begin to rise.

'Oh, you're such a *bore*, Marc,' Melanie said, wagging a finger at him. He glanced at her, almost contemptuously, and then disappeared without even saying goodbye. Laure stared at the doorway in disbelief. She'd never met anyone quite as rude in her life! He hadn't even said 'hello'!

'Is he angry about something?' she asked Melanie, eyes widening in sympathy as Melanie's crumpled. She'd obviously had far too much to drink.

'Oh, he's *always* cross with me. I drink too much, I don't spend enough time with the kids, I don't work … Honestly, there's a list as long as his bloody arm. Well, I don't care. If *he* doesn't like it …'

'Melanie,' Laure interrupted gently. 'I think I'd better get going. Can you call me a cab?'

'Call a cab?' Melanie started to laugh. 'How? How did you get here?'

'With a taxi,' Laure said, puzzled.

'Didn't you tell him to wait?'

'The whole evening? I've been here since seven,' Laure said, shaking her head.

'It doesn't matter. *They* don't mind waiting.'

'Maybe, but still … Well, I'll just catch one on the corner, then, shall I?'

'You must be crazy. No, I'll get Marc to drop you home,' Melanie said, getting unsteadily to her feet. 'You only live a couple of miles away. But it's late, it's not safe.'

Laure put out a hand to stop her. She would rather have walked the three miles than let Melanie's husband take her home. But Melanie had already disappeared through the doorway. Laure closed her eyes in genuine annoyance. It was the *last* thing she wanted. It was probably the last thing *he* wanted to do as well.

A few minutes later, Marc appeared in the doorway again and his expression hadn't improved. 'Next time either get the driver to wait, or, if you're offended by that, get him to come back for you.' Again, there was the faint emphasis on 'offended'. Laure positively bristled. He probably thought she was one of his wife's society friends, Laure thought as she followed him as calmly as she could from the dining room.

'I'm sorry,' she said stiffly. 'I didn't think of it. I thought it would be easy enough to call a cab.'

'It's not London.'

'I'm aware of that,' she snapped, unable to stop herself. He said nothing. In fact, he said nothing all the way to the Brightest Spot. Three miles in complete silence. Laure's face was on fire by the time he pulled up in front of the gates. He blew the horn sharply but Laure opened the door before the night watchman came running. 'Don't bother driving in,' she said, getting out of the car. 'Thanks for the lift. And, by the way,' she said, just before she turned to go. 'I'm also *working* tomorrow.' She let the door slam shut and without looking back, walked quickly up the slope and pushed open the side gate. She heard his tyres squeal as he pulled away from the driveway in a hurry. Arrogant jerk!

She didn't see Melanie for the rest of the week. She was busy sorting out a trip to Bonwire, just outside Kumasi, which Kofi had told her really was the centre of the *kenté* cloth weaving industry. It was too far a journey for Bright's little taxi, he told her ruefully. Better to hire a 4x4 and a driver. Ve-ry expensive. His face fell at the thought of someone else garnering the job.

'Isn't there any other way to get there?'

'You can take STC, madam. State Transport Corporation. Is a bit slow.'

'Slow's fine. Where can I catch the bus?' Laure was excited at the thought of a long, slow journey up the country. It would give her a chance to see something of the countryside. Accra, she'd rapidly discovered, wasn't terribly picturesque.

Bright arranged to pick her up the following morning just before dawn and take her to the central bus terminal. She would spend the night in Kumasi, take a taxi to Bonwire and take the bus back to Accra the following day. It sounded simple enough.

The bus that roared and swayed out of the station was modern, air-conditioned and packed to the rafters. Several cockerels were also on board. It was dawn; they crowed incessantly. The driver doubled up as a lay preacher, exhorting passengers to work hard, save money and respect their elders. By the time they reached the stretch of open road that led to Kumasi, some forty minutes out of Accra, Laure felt as though her head would burst open. Hymns were sung, a small argument broke out at the back, her neighbour unwrapped a newspaper stuffed with roasted plantains and hot, flaking groundnuts and seemed mortally offended when she politely declined. 'American?' he asked jovially. Laure shook her head. 'British?' She shook her head again, smiling politely. All she wanted to do was sleep. 'French? American? Swedish?'

'Haitian,' she said, before he began on a long list of unlikely candidates.

'Haiti?' he said, frowning.

'The Caribbean.'

'Ah, Jamaica.'

'Er, yes.'

'Me, I *like* Jamaicans,' he said happily, splitting open a steaming yellow plantain. 'When I was in London, I met *so* many Jamaicans.' He munched his plantain contemplatively. 'But, in fact, the one thing I did not like about Jamaicans is you like drugs *toooo* much.'

'Er, not *all* Jamaicans,' Laure said, a trifle wearily.

He appeared not to have heard her. 'In fact,' he went on, warming to his theme, 'our Lord Jesus Christ says that ...'

Laure closed her eyes. Her companion seemed content

to preach to her slumbering form; he kept up a one-sided dialogue almost all the way to the first rest-stop, about an hour later. She was contemplating begging one of the other passengers to swap seats with her but found, to her immense relief as they reboarded the bus, that he'd beaten her to it. He'd moved further up the bus to preach to a group of young girls who did exactly as Laure had done and closed their eyes.

She found herself next to a young woman named Belinda, a student at the university in Kumasi. The rest of the journey passed quietly enough. Laure and Belinda chatted away for most of it; Belinda was studying accountancy and hoped one day to go to America. Nothing Laure said could dissuade her. America, Belinda confessed shyly, was the promised land.

They reached Kumasi just after ten. Laure found a taxi to take her to City Hotel on the prettily named Rain Tree Road. The hotel was clean and airy; after a cool shower and a quick discussion with one of the receptionists at the front desk, she arranged for a driver and taxi to pick her up after lunch. Remembering Marc Abadi's advice, she also arranged for him to wait for her while she toured the small weaving village. She took a quick nap and at one, just as she'd arranged, she was called downstairs to meet the driver.

Jonas was a cheerful, talkative young man who drove without once touching the brakes, or so it seemed. He knew all about Bonwire; by the time they actually arrived at the rather nondescript cluster of buildings that signalled the beginning of the village, Laure had learned practically everything there was to know. She looked around curiously. It certainly didn't look like the centre of the weaving universe: rows of the same, depressingly incomplete, cement-block houses; the ubiquitous chickens and goats running around, narrowly escaping death-by-car-tyre; and children pushing old, wobbly bicycle tyres round and round with thin, spindly sticks. Jonas pulled the car up under an enormous shady tree and motioned to her to follow him. He pushed open a door that led into a large, workshop-like space. Laure bent her head to enter and when she straightened up, her mouth dropped open. It stayed open for most of the next hour.

There were twenty or thirty men in the room, each working his loom furiously; the clacking and open-and-close motion of the looms created a loud, squeaking noise, like children jumping up and down on springy mattresses. They were bare-chested; in the dim, almost golden light, sweat ran down their bodies in glinting streams. The looms were incredible – seemingly makeshift, as everything in Ghana seemed to be, fashioned from irregularly shaped beams and posts, held together by pieces of string. The long, taut yarns in every colour imaginable spun round the workshop like a giant, gaudy web: back and forth, back and forth; *click-clack, click-clack*. The men's hands flew over the loom in a blur ... in the space of a few seconds, the resulting patterned cloth began to emerge at the other end. *May I take a photo?* she motioned with her camera to the older man who strode around the space. 'He's Mr Gyasi, the master-weaver,' Jonas whispered to her. Mr Gyasi nodded graciously. Three rolls of film later, she wished she'd brought more.

Mr Gyasi explained the significance of one of the cloths. '*Adwena'asa apremoo*,' he called it. 'That means, in our language, that "my skill is exhausted". We call it like that because the design is ve-ry, ve-ry difficult. You can be ve-ry tired.'

Laure laughed, running her finger gently over the intricate surface. 'What are these?' she asked, pointing to the oval-shaped patterns in the centre of the cloth.

'This place, we call it *ntomatire*. That means, the "edge of the cloth". We call the middle of the cloth *ntoma finfini*. The middle of the cloth shows many *apremoo*, that means "canons". Now,' he went on, warming to his theme, 'you can see that the *ntomatire* has a shield, *akye*. So the edge of the cloth is protecting the middle of the cloth. We also call this cloth *Fa Hia Kotwere Agyeman*. That means, "the chief will protect you from poverty".'

'Wow.' She looked again at the beautiful yellow, burgundy and gold design. 'So, each of these cloths tells a story,' she said, pointing to a neighbouring loom. 'They all mean something.'

'Ye-es. You can see this one.' He got up and walked over to one of the other weavers. 'This one, we call it *Asam Takra*. The *ntomatire* is called *nkyinkyim*. That means, something like a ziggy-zaggy.' He made a quick gesture with his fingers. '*Asam takra* is the name of the feathers for the guinea fowl. You see the way they are running? Ziggy-zaggy.'

'Zig-zag,' Laure laughed, delightedly. 'Yes, I see,' she pointed to the warp and weft weave pattern. 'That's it exactly!'

She spent a further hour with Mr Gyasi as he patiently explained the meanings and proverbs behind each pattern and design. She bought several large cloths and smaller strips and explained that she was a textile designer (without a fraction of the skill of his men, she hastily added) and had come to Ghana to learn about the rich, vibrant history of Africa's most famous textiles.

'Where are your children?' he asked her unexpectedly as they were preparing to leave.

'My children?' Laure asked, wondering if she'd heard him correctly.

'Ye-es. Your family. Are they in America?'

'No ... no, I ... don't have any children,' she stammered self-consciously.

'Oh. That is very sad. And your husband?'

'I ... I'm not married,' she said slowly. 'I ... I live alone.'

'Oh.' Mr Gyasi looked genuinely stricken. 'Sorry, oh.'

Laure swallowed. His question had taken her completely by surprise. 'Well, I'd better be going, Mr Gyasi. Thank you again, it's been wonderful. I ... I've learned so much.'

'Wait,' Mr Gyasi said, calling out something to one of his apprentices. A minute later, the man appeared, carrying a small piece of beautifully patterned yellow, black and pale green cloth. 'I would like to dash you this piece. Do you know what we call it?' Laure shook her head slowly. '*Aberewabene*. That means "brave woman". That is what I feel for you.'

Laure was speechless. Her eyes suddenly smarted with tears. Fortunately Jonas was on hand to stow away her purchases and offer profuse thanks on her behalf, and in a hail of goodbyes from the weavers in the workshop, they drove off in a cloud of dust, twenty children with bicycle tyres and sticks following them in hot pursuit. She was able to blink back her tears and pick up the threads of Jonas's conversation without too much effort. If he noticed, he said nothing. Ghanaians, she was only just beginning to discover, were quite possibly the most delicately discreet people she'd ever met.

The trip to Bonwire unleashed a storm of creative energy. After developing the photos, she spent the following week almost exclusively in her room, drawing, sketching, making collages and endless pattern repeats. She had used up her entire stock of paper and almost covered the pages of her sketchbook by the time there was a knock on her door and Melanie's head appeared. Laure looked up in surprise.

'Oh, hello,' Melanie said, as if she'd just popped round by accident. 'I've been phoning you for *ages*.'

'Oh. Oh … I haven't really been out much, I …'

'I know. The lady at the front desk said she hadn't seen you since Sunday. I thought I'd better come and check you were still alive!'

'I'm fine. I've just been working, you know what that's like …'

'Actually, I don't,' Melanie said good-naturedly, coming into the room. 'What've you been doing? Gosh, are these yours?' she asked, pointing to the large sheets of paper that Laure had stuck on the wall.

'Er, yes. Those are a few pieces I did after coming back from Bonwire.'

'They're beautiful,' Melanie breathed, examining them closely. 'I didn't realise … you're an artist. You could *frame* these!'

'Oh, they're just ideas,' Laure said modestly. 'We'll work them up properly when I get back home.'

'No, *seriously*. Look, I've just had an idea – why don't you do a small exhibition? We could even do it at my place. Just invite a few people – you could show the work you've done and maybe give a little talk. It would be *such* an inspiration. You don't know how *starving* we all are for a bit of culture.'

'But the place is *full* of culture,' Laure protested. 'Everywhere you look.'

'Well, you're obviously wearing better spectacles than I am, darling, because *I* can't see it. Nothing but funerals and rubbishy tourist carvings. *Do* say you'll do it. Please? It'll be *such* fun!'

Melanie's enthusiasm was hard to resist. Laure wavered; Melanie pounced. She *had* to agree.

'But don't make it a big thing,' Laure begged, as Melanie got ready to leave. 'Just a few people. I hate talking about my work. I'll be hopeless.'

'Of course you won't. Don't worry, it'll just be a few of my friends ... no more than a dozen.'

'Promise?'

'On my honour.' Melanie waved at her. 'Nothing grand; I'll help you frame them and we can put them up in the living room. I'll organise the wine and the food ... It'll be lovely! I'll pick you up tomorrow at nine,' she called out as she disappeared through the door. Laure nodded, still bemused. Not only had she been roped into an exhibition, she'd also agreed to go to the beach with Melanie the following day. How had *that* happened? She was supposed to be working; not on holiday. But it was true – Melanie really *was* hard to resist.

88

Marc pulled into the driveway and was disconcerted to find his parking space taken up by a host of large, expensive-looking 4x4s, some of them complete with a slumbering driver. Several of the cars had diplomatic plates. He frowned. What was going on? Was Melanie having one of her interminable bridge parties?

He parked his car where he could and got out. It was nine o'clock on a Wednesday evening; he was due to fly to Côte d'Ivoire the following morning and being sociable was the last thing on his mind. It was a sore point. He was already feeling rather guilty over the way he'd treated her latest friend, Laure whatever-her-name-was. She'd taken him by surprise. Melanie's friends were usually either inappropriately flirtatious or downright rude. Several of them, including that dreadful Petra Tynagel, made no secret of the fact that they thought Melanie had made a spectacularly bad choice. He couldn't be bothered to dig further into the roots of their hostility but he had a pretty good idea. He'd overheard Petra saying one afternoon, as she and Melanie sat smoking on the patio, 'Well, darling, what d'you expect? I mean, to be perfectly frank, African's bad enough, but Lebanese *as well*? You really *have* bitten off more than you can chew, poor darling.' After that, it was open warfare between them. He barely acknowledged her presence which, he imagined, only made things worse. He couldn't have cared less.

He pushed open the kitchen door and greeted James who was busy cutting up red and green pepper wheels and arranging them on a plate. He popped one into his mouth and walked through to the hallway. He could hear the sound of laughter, then Laure's low, calm voice. He stopped. He peered through the doorway. The lights were off; she was showing slides. In the flickering bluish light he saw that there were perhaps ten or fifteen of Melanie's friends sitting around listening to her. Where on earth had Melanie found a slide projector? he wondered. The whole set-up was so different from the usual social evenings she held that he found himself standing in the doorway, straining to hear Laure's voice.

Suddenly, there was a movement behind him and he turned, knocking his hand against the glass door. It was James with the plate of peppers and a small bowl of some unidentifiable dip. Melanie jumped up, Laure stopped speaking and he, of course, was caught in the act of eavesdropping.

'Darling,' Melanie called out in that voice he had learned

to dread, 'don't just stand there, come *in*. Laure's telling us all about her work, it's *fascinating*.'

'No, no, I was just passing by. Evening, everyone,' he said, nodding quickly at the heads turned towards him. He caught a glimpse of Laure's profile as she turned – extraordinarily beautiful – and then he fled.

He shut the door to his study and leaned against it for a moment, exasperated. He hadn't felt so foolish in years. He shook his head, unsure whether to be annoyed or amused at himself. He walked over to his desk and sat down. He wondered briefly what Laure had been talking about. He'd seen a couple of the slides, strikingly beautiful images of the *kenté* cloth that everyone seemed to love ... well, she was a fashion designer, wasn't she? It was her job to run around looking for pretty things. But, he had to admit, as he began organising the documents he needed for his trip the following morning, that it wasn't just the slides that had caught his eye. There was something oddly disconcerting about her as well. It wasn't simply that she was beautiful, which she undoubtedly was. No, it was something else, something in her manner, her gaze. She looked at him as if she *knew* him. He had no idea why.

'You really should have come in,' Melanie said crossly an hour later as they both prepared for bed. The last of her guests had departed; he'd seen Laure get into Petra Tynagel's enormous Land Cruiser from the bedroom windows. He'd grimaced. He wouldn't have wished Petra's company on anyone. 'You're so *rude* to my friends.'

He sighed. Something about the evening had unsettled him; he simply wasn't used to feeling out of his depth and that was exactly what the blasted woman did to him. It irritated him. 'I doubt they even noticed,' he said dryly, pulling his T-shirt over his head. 'You were all so busy receiving her little pearls of wisdom—'

'Oh, fuck you,' Melanie snapped, turning her back on him. 'Just because we don't sit around talking about fucking *refugee* camps doesn't mean we're not intelligent people.'

'I never said that,' Marc said, slightly taken aback.

'You don't have to. She's a really interesting woman, if you'd just give her half a chance.'

'Melanie, she's *your* friend. She's leaving in a couple of weeks. Who *cares* what I think about her? Or any of your other friends?'

'*I* do,' Melanie said, suddenly almost tearful. 'I just hate the way you judge everybody before you even know them.'

Marc said nothing. He continued undressing in silence. Deep down, he knew she was right. He *did* make blanket judgements. The problem was, most of the time he was right. Ten years of working in development circles with Westerners had produced a brittle, protective mask behind which he hid his true feelings. He didn't know how to explain it to her. He didn't know how to explain it to anyone. Just another one of those issues on which he kept his mouth firmly shut. He had learned the hard way that it was safer, by far, to say nothing. Just before he fell asleep, he wondered, disconcertingly, what Laure would have made of *that*.

89

Three weeks later, he was still wondering about her. The heat hammered at the walls of the abandoned mission house that was now the office of the Larabanga camp. He walked among the children and young adults whose temporary flight from fighting in the north of the country had turned into a fully fledged exile, and he couldn't get her out of his mind. He worked until dawn, preparing the reports and the mindless administrative tasks that might someday, somewhere, result in the release of desperately needed funding to the forgotten corners of the globe in which he worked. The mission house was without curtains; at the same time every day, a bar of sunlight came to

481

rest on the stripped wooden desk where he typed and smoked. He was filled with a strange, restless impatience. It puzzled him. He was not a man who enjoyed puzzles.

'It's incredible,' Laure said to Jill, her own voice echoing down the fuzzy international line. 'I *love* it here. I can't describe it. You'll see from the pictures I bring back.'

'It sounds wonderful. When are you coming back?'

'In a fortnight. Beatrice is back; she's lovely. Just like Kofi. She's trying to find someone to take me to the Volta Region, which is the only major weaving place I haven't seen. You really have to come, Jill, you'd love it here.'

'I'm sure. Well, this call's costing me a fortune – I'll tell Kofi you're having a good time – he'll be so relieved. Will you ring me just before you leave? Just let me know that you're on the flight and I'll meet you at Heathrow. Oh, by the way, we've just had another big order in ... I'll tell you about it when you get here. Hurry up and get back, won't you? There's tons to do!' She rang off, laughing.

Laure replaced the receiver slowly. There it was again. That strange flutter in her stomach whenever she thought about home. London suddenly seemed unreal to her. She found it impossible to picture the flat she'd recently bought on Wilton Way and that she still couldn't quite believe was hers; the way the afternoon light filtered through the rice-paper screens; the sound of the council collecting the rubbish early on Thursday mornings and the occasional soft whirr of a bicycle going past. Did she really live there? Was that what she was about to return to? In the damp, soft heat of an Accra evening, sitting in her room with its paper patchwork of sketches and photographs, the enormous, lushly rich *adwena'asa* cloth spread across the bed, it was difficult to picture her flat with its cool grey walls and sparse furniture. She got up, strangely agitated. Perhaps a swim would help?

Later that evening, she stood in front of the mirror again. Beatrice had invited her to dinner with some of her friends. She was looking forward to it; despite finding Melanie Miller fun to be with, there was an air of strained unreality about Melanie's life and the people she called her friends that Laure sensed came from their positions as relatively wealthy, bored Europeans living in a country they could never call home. Melanie didn't seem to know very many Ghanaians. Plus, there seemed to be some mystery or tension around her husband's background. From what Melanie said, it seemed he was half-Ghanaian, half-Lebanese, but had been brought up in Beirut by his father's mother; at the age of three months, his Ghanaian mother had dumped him unceremoniously on his father's doorstep. Laure felt a sharp pang of both sadness and guilt when she heard the story. There was obviously more to Marc Abadi than rude behaviour.

She picked a full-length skirt of a bold, graphic design – another one of the prints she'd turned into clothing as soon as she arrived – and teamed it with a sea-green halter top and wedge-heeled sandals. She pulled her hair up, but let it out at the back instead of scraping it into its habitual tidy bun. She fastened a pair of the intricately carved jade earrings she'd found in a second-hand shop on Portobello Road and placed a thick tortoiseshell necklace around her neck. Her skin had acquired the same deep, dark tones of her childhood after two or three days in the sun and on the beach. She'd forgotten just how dark she could be – she enjoyed catching sight of herself in the mirror, surprised by her own reflection.

At eight on the dot, Beatrice arrived. 'Don't look so surprised,' she laughed as she stuck her head round the door. 'Occasionally, we Ghanaians can be on time!'

'I wasn't ... I'm not,' Laure protested, laughing. 'Well, only a *little* surprised ...' she said, as they walked out of the room together.

'I'm taking you to Pimiento,' Beatrice said, opening the car door for her. 'It's our best restaurant. French, very nice food and the service is great.'

'I'm honoured,' Laure smiled. 'But I'm dying to eat some

real Ghanaian food – everywhere I go they seem to serve the same thing.'

'Chicken and rice?' Beatrice asked dryly. Laure nodded. 'I think they think that's what most foreigners will eat. Come to my house on Sunday. I'll cook you a *proper* Ghanaian meal.'

'Oh, I didn't mean . . .'

'Of course not. But Sunday lunch is a big tradition in my house. Mummy will be there; she'd love to meet you, I'm sure. She's also into fabrics. And my brother Kojo will also be there. You guys will really get on, I'm sure.'

'How many brothers d'you have? I only know of Kofi.'

'There's thirteen of us,' Beatrice said with a smile. 'Seven boys, six girls.'

'Thirteen?' Laure couldn't keep the surprise from her voice. 'How many are you?'

'Just one.'

'Only you? That must have been lonely.'

Laure was silent for a moment. There was something warm and comforting about Beatrice; if she were staying longer, she was someone she could imagine being friends with in a way she hadn't experienced for a long time. 'No, there was Améline. She's more like a sister,' she said, and quickly explained the *reste-avec* system in Haiti.

'We have something similar,' Beatrice said, nodding. 'I can't count the number of kids Mummy took in; when people ask me how many are in the family, I never know quite what to say!'

Laure laughed. 'I suppose with thirteen, one or two more won't make much difference.'

'None whatsoever,' Beatrice agreed. 'Well, here we are.' Laure looked up. They'd only driven a few streets. They were in front of a bright yellow house, surrounded by expensive-looking cars. 'It's always packed,' Beatrice said, greeting the security guard who'd rushed forward. 'Like I said, it's probably the best food in town. I hope you like steaks.'

The entrance door swung silently open as they approached. 'Good evening, madam,' a voice said as they walked through.

The waiters bowed deeply. The interior was a lovely warm, apricot colour, with large paintings and elegant wooden sculptures adorning the walls. To their left was a small bar, the bottles and glasses stacked high and reflecting prettily in the mirrored wall. It was a long, L-shaped restaurant with perhaps twenty or so white-covered tables, each with a small, tropical flower in the centre. The restaurant was indeed packed; there were men in suits and impeccably well-dressed women standing at the bar, chatting and smoking. The owner came forward and kissed Beatrice warmly on both cheeks. They spoke in French; he chastised her for her long absence from the restaurant. The others had already arrived, he said, he'd shown them to the table.

There were six or seven people seated at the table, which looked as though it was meant for ten. She was introduced to Danny, a jazz musician who looked to be in his early forties; Diane, his partner, who was a lawyer; Francis, a banker, and to his left, Della, a marvellously voluptuous woman with an exceptionally sweet, pretty face. Laure shook hands with each one, noticing at once how different this gathering was to the one at Melanie's house. There were obviously a number of vastly different social circles in town.

'Who else is coming, Bea?' Della asked, lifting her glass of wine.

'There's Chloé and Winston – they're the furniture designers I told you about, Laure. She's Dutch, he's Ghanaian, and ... oh, and Marc, of course. I don't think his wife is coming, but he's always late. A *real* Ghanaian,' she added with a wink.

'Marc?' Laure asked, her stomach giving an odd lurch.

'Marc Abadi. I heard you met his wife at Victoria's party.'

'Oh.' Accra, like Pétionville, was obviously a very small town. At least in some ways.

'Have you met him?' Beatrice asked, obviously noticing the look on Laure's face.

'Er, yes ... once or twice.'

'Was he rude to you?' Della laughed. 'Don't mind him – he's always rude.'

'Who's always rude?' came Marc Abadi's voice behind her. Laure swallowed nervously. The evening wasn't turning out quite the way she'd expected.

'*You* are!' Della lifted her generous arms and beckoned him over. 'Me first. You know the rules. *I* get the first kiss.' Marc grinned and bent his head obligingly. Laure felt the heat rise immediately in her cheeks. 'Now you can greet the others,' Della laughed, releasing him.

'You never told me you'd already met her,' Beatrice said, presenting Laure. 'And I hear you were rude to her.'

'No ... no, I didn't say that ... I just ...' Laure protested immediately. Beatrice was laughing.

'No, no ... you're right. I was. I do apologise,' Marc said, taking her hand. Was he teasing her? Aware that her cheeks were still on fire, she lowered her gaze. He slid into the seat opposite her and from the animated conversation that flew back and forth across the table, it was clear that he hadn't been seen in a while. Fortunately, the arrival of the last few guests created further waves of distraction and she was able to compose herself so that when he finally turned his attention back to her and asked, in a voice that bore no traces of the impatience she'd previously associated with him, what she was doing in Ghana, she was able to answer quite calmly, and clearly – and to her immense surprise, he seemed genuinely interested.

The food was good; the company even better. Laure warmed to every single person at the table, even Marc Abadi. His aloofness hid a quick, dry sense of humour and an obvious intelligence – he understood immediately what she was trying to do in terms of using traditional African patterns and techniques and even offered a few suggestions of his own. 'Look at the reverse side of some of the *kenté* cloths,' he told her. 'You'll be amazed. They usually leave the threads hanging – it looks like a furry carpet, and it's often just as beautiful as the front.' Laure could only nod and gulp her wine. She asked him a little about his background but realised he was extremely skilled at deflecting the conversation away from himself whenever a question came too close for comfort. Chloé, the Dutch designer who was seated next to her, appeared to have been at school with him and the two of them kept up a steady, amusing banter all evening.

It was with a real sense of regret that she got up when Beatrice did and said her goodbyes. Several of the people there asked when she would be coming back. She was touched. 'I don't know. I leave next Friday. It's been an amazing trip, honestly. I've really enjoyed it.'

'Oh, you'll be back,' Chloé laughed, waving a hand at her. 'I can feel it. We haven't seen the last of you, Laure St Lazâre! Come by the shop next week if you can.'

Laure smiled. 'I'd love to,' she said, meaning it. She turned to Marc, who was also standing. 'Well, I … I really enjoyed talking to you,' she said, suddenly self-conscious. 'It's a shame Melanie missed it. I … I don't know if … Well, in case I don't see you before I go … goodbye,' she said suddenly, the words tumbling out rather awkwardly. She held out a hand, hoping for something, some indication that he'd enjoyed talking to her? It wasn't to be. His mood had changed, she noticed immediately. The shutters had come down. It was like a slap in the face.

'Goodbye,' he said, giving her hand a quick shake. And that was it. He sat down again, turning back to Chloé. Laure was effectively dismissed. She blinked, then turned, moving away before any of the others could see her face. Luckily it was dim in the restaurant and Beatrice was already busy saying goodbye to the owner. She pushed her way through the crowd still standing around the bar and walked out into the warm night air, breathing deeply. Her head was ringing, not just with the wine and the stimulating conversation, but, more ominously, with the sound of Marc Abadi's voice, dismissive as it had been, ringing in her ears.

Her last week was spent in a whirlwind of activity – rushing to take her last photographs; spending an afternoon with Beatrice; one last coffee with Melanie; going to see Chloé and Winston's magnificent shop and spending the last of her dollars on presents for almost everyone she could think of. And then, suddenly, it was Friday evening again, she'd been in Ghana two months and she felt as though she never wanted to leave. She'd turned down offers from Beatrice, Melanie and Chloé to take her to the airport – Bright had brought her in, Bright would drop her off. In truth, she didn't relish the idea of crying all the way back to London. She had never felt such an immediate affinity with a group of strangers in her entire life. Even Melanie, with whom she had the least in common, was open and warm and seemed to want nothing more than her company. She hoped Chloé was right – that she would soon be back – although she couldn't quite see how. Perhaps she could persuade Jill to let her go for another two months the following year. She'd rung Jill that afternoon from the front desk just to confirm she was on her way back. Jill was animated; orders were flooding in; she was thinking of hiring a couple of assistants; the weather was truly awful – 'Hurry up and get back here!' She felt the tug and pull of London and was surprised to find herself resisting it.

She hadn't seen Marc Abadi again, which, if she were completely honest, was probably a good thing. After a few days, the sound of his voice in her ear died down and she was able to concentrate on other, more important things. He was the most maddeningly enigmatic person she'd ever met which was why she'd had such difficulty extracting him from her head. He'd made it clear that he hadn't been particularly interested in talking to her and he probably hadn't revised his first opinion, which was that she was just another one of his wife's airhead friends. It was probably just as well, she told herself sternly.

She flew out of Accra on BA081 at 11.35 p.m. on an August night that was as hot as the day that preceded it, with sixty kilos of overweight luggage. Luckily Bright had a 'connection' somewhere inside the British Airways check-in office ... Was there anywhere he *didn't* have a 'connection'? She left with a head full of ideas and a heart that stubbornly refused to lift, even as the aircraft did, circling out over the dark, silent Atlantic Ocean. All she could think about as they ploughed their way northwards over the great bulk of the continent was the expression in Marc Abadi's eyes as she'd described what she'd seen in Bonwire. It wasn't just that he was attentive, he seemed to be reading something in her that she wasn't even aware she possessed. Marc Abadi had *seen* her in a way no one else ever had. But he belonged to someone else.

90

Melanie was having an affair. That was a fact. He'd suspected something of the sort about a year earlier – one of those horrible clichés that, in the end, turn out to be true. She'd sacked the garden boy not long afterwards and deep down, he'd known. Of course he'd known. He just hadn't wanted to admit it. The second time, a few months later, she'd given herself away almost before she could help herself. The oldest giveaway in the book. She'd done something in bed she'd never done before. A dead giveaway. Then, too, he'd closed his mind to it. He was good at doing that. He was trained to do it.

This time, however, his training had deserted him and he found himself sitting on the edge of the bed, his hands trembling. Beside him, lying just where he'd thrown it, was the evidence. A plane ticket and hotel itinerary. To Copenhagen, when she should have been in London, and the bill for a hotel in the name of Mr Christian Tynagel. Chris Tynagel. Petra's husband. Melanie's best friend. She was doing to Petra what had once been done to her. It was such a fucking cliché it would have been funny if it weren't true. He wasn't sure what part of it disgusted him the most – the fact that she was having the affair, or the fact that she was deceiving her best friend. It was one thing to have a one-night stand or a quick fling with someone – God knew *he'd* been tempted once or twice in their seven-year marriage – but *this* required forethought. Planning.

It involved his children. His stomach tightened at the thought. She'd left Susu and Guy alone in London with her mother while she'd flown off to Copenhagen for … he bent down and picked up the hotel bill … *five* days. Five, whole fucking days. *She'd left his children alone for five days.* He closed his eyes. What was he supposed to do? At first Melanie's lack of maternal instinct had alarmed him, frightened him, actually. She seemed to view the children simply as an extension of their relationship; the proof she'd been seeking all along that it would work, would last. She loved them; he didn't doubt that. It was just that Melanie's definition of love was different from most other people's. For her it was all about the *measurement* of love. How *much* do you love me? This much? *More* than this? More than her? There was nothing he could do to persuade her that it had nothing to do with anyone else. Nothing to do with the imaginary 'her' who had crept into their marriage almost from the beginning and continued to define it, regardless of what he said or did. She seemed to be *waiting* for him to walk out – nothing he said could convince her otherwise. Everyone else had. Why not him?

He heard a car pull up outside. It was probably Melanie. He looked at the ticket in his hand. What, he asked himself again, was he supposed to do? Somehow the textbooks he'd devoured as a student hadn't said anything about this. He'd read plenty about love and family and marriage in the abstract, of course, but he'd somehow never grasped that one day, some day in the not-too-distant future, *he* might be the subject of his own reading. *He* was the one who needed help. The front door slammed; his stomach tightened. Help. He wasn't the kind of man who easily asked for it.

As soon as she walked through the bedroom door, she knew. While she was adept enough at hiding her feelings behind the various masks she wore, Marc never could. He looked up at her with the most naked expression of hurt she'd ever seen and her heart simply fell to the floor. For a second, they stared at each other, then she dropped her eyes.

'You haven't seen Susu's tennis racquet, have you?' she asked in as steady a voice as she could manage.

There was again that moment of carefully held tension, then it was Marc's turn to drop his eyes. 'No.'

Melanie drew a deep breath. Whatever confrontation might yet be coming, it wasn't going to happen now. She swallowed. She could see the ticket and hotel bill lying on the bed next to him. Of course he knew. She made a great pretence of looking in the wardrobe and over at the dresser – as if a racquet could possibly be lying there! – and left the room as quickly as she could. Outside in the corridor, she leaned against the wall, aware of the sweat trickling between her breasts. He'd found out. And he'd said nothing. She didn't know which fact made her feel worse.

She drove Susu and Guy to their tennis lessons at the Labadi Beach Hotel, a horrible, cold feeling in the pit of her stomach. Petra was there with her own two children; as she walked towards the terrace where she sat, her spirits sank even further. It was as if the guilt of the past few months had suddenly caught up with her. The strangest thing of all was that she didn't even particularly *like* Chris Tynagel. He was dull, boring, not particularly attractive *and* pompous to boot. The first time he'd grabbed her, in the kitchen of his own home at a dinner party he and Petra were giving, she'd almost laughed out loud. There was something so pathetically silly about his shiny, red face, sweaty with the heat and the drunken, irrational lust that had come over him. He was crazy about her, he whispered, his Danish accent becoming more pronounced. *Cray-sie*. He couldn't sleep, he couldn't eat, he couldn't concentrate on a damned thing; he was going out of his mind. And then the house-girl had come back into the room and he'd sprung apart from her as though he'd been shot. But – and it was an awful thing to admit to – she was *flattered*. Dr Christian Tynagel, head of one of the most powerful aid agencies in Africa, couldn't eat, sleep or work for thinking about her. He found her beautiful and wild and fascinating, all the things that, deep down, she was beginning to understand really weren't her. It was like one of those French films she liked, full of sidelong glances and repressed, understated emotions, in which she played the starring, ingénue role. Oh, she was flattered! It had been so long since she'd exerted that sort of power over anyone. Marc simply knew her too well. Sex with Marc was only ever explosive when she was honest and she was finding *that* harder and harder to achieve.

She climbed the steps to the terrace wondering how she would get through the morning.

'Gosh, don't you look *awful*!' Petra said gaily as she approached. Years of expatriate postings had produced a strange, hybrid Home Counties-Danish accent with the sort of vocabulary Melanie remembered from Enid Blyton novels.

'Thanks,' Melanie said dryly, grateful for the wave of irritation that rolled over her. Irritation, she realised, was better than guilt.

'Did you go out last night? You *naughty* thing – you should've called me. I was *all* alone last night – Chris went somewhere. Some dreadful office function or something.'

Melanie swallowed. 'No, I just had a couple of bottles of wine …'

'What? All on your own? Good *gracious*, no wonder you look wrecked,' Petra said, turning to wave at Helle, her six-year-old daughter who'd just managed to hit the ball across the net. 'Well done, darling!' she called out across the terrace. 'That was *super*.'

Melanie rolled her eyes surreptitiously. She could have kicked herself – she and *Chris* had drunk two bottles of wine. In some horrible little hotel suite in Adabraka.

'Oh, I forgot to *tell* you …' Petra said suddenly, bending down to retrieve a magazine from the large, woven basket she always carried around with her. She flopped it down on the table in front of them with a flourish. 'You dark horse,' she said, dropping her voice admiringly. 'You never said a word. Does that make you a … how d'you call it … a duchess, or something?'

'What're you talking about?' Melanie asked irritably. She

looked at the magazine. *Celebrity You*. It had been years since she'd appeared in any of its pages. What was Petra blathering on about?

'Here ... look!' Petra picked it up. It fell open at its centre page; an enormous, double-paged spread featuring Sir Michael and Lady Miller. Melanie stared at her father's features suddenly made sombre and respectable by the grey top hat and morning suit he wore. At his side, wearing the most ridiculous hat, was his wife. Cosima Sutton-Miller. *Lady* Cosima Sutton-Miller. She hardly looked a day over sixteen. The youngest daughter of some City financier. Melanie swallowed. Mike Miller, along with a few other ageing rock stars, had been knighted. Their wives, pictured together in one, indistinguishable blonde bubble, were naturally delighted. Melanie shoved the magazine back across the table. She hadn't even known he was *married*.

'I just didn't want to ... *upset* you, darling,' her mother said placatingly over the phone. 'You seemed to have enough on your plate with the kids and the ... er, *garden* and everything.'

Melanie flushed. Her mother's last visit to Accra had co-incided with the beginning of her first indiscretion. In fact, without her mother on hand to occupy the children and supervise the staff, she probably wouldn't have had the time to ... pursue the matter, as it were. 'But, Jesus Christ, Mum, she's half *my* age!'

'I know, I know. But what can you do? And now *she's* Lady Miller. It makes my blood boil.'

'Where are they now? Don't tell me he's decided to move to some pile in the countryside and start paying taxes like the rest of us.'

'Actually,' Stella said glumly, 'they have. He's buying Clive Brompton's old house in Wiltshire, Ashdeane. Lord and Lady of the Manor. Can you *believe* it?'

'No. No, I can't.'

'Well, it's his life. That's what I've always said,' Stella said briskly and untruthfully. 'How are *you*, darling? When are you coming over?'

'Mum ... I might ... I might come soon. Like this weekend, if I can get a flight.'

'Ooh, super. Is ... is everything ... all right?' Stella asked cautiously.

'Fine, fine. I just need a break, really.'

'Of course you do, darling. Will you bring the kids?'

'No, it's the middle of term. Susu's just started in a new nursery group – she'd have a *fit* if I took her out just now.'

'Well, just let me know when you've got your flight. I'll have Dawes pick you up at the airport. And darling ...'

'What?'

'Don't let this silly business with your father upset you. He does love you, you know. I know he doesn't always—'

'Mum, I have to go,' Melanie croaked, her eyes suddenly filling with tears. 'I'll call you when I've got my ticket.' She put down the receiver with trembling hands. She needed more than a break – she needed to get away from the mess that she'd made of things, and it was only just beginning to dawn on her that things were a lot worse than she'd allowed herself to believe.

'How long?' Marc looked at her, the expression in his eyes unreadable, as always.

'Um ... maybe a fortnight?' Melanie said, trying her best to sound bright and cheerful. 'Just to help Mum out with the whole knighthood thing,' she said weakly.

'Why? Did she get one as well?' Marc asked sarcastically.

'No, of course not. But ... you know ... the media and stuff.'

'No, Melanie, I don't know. But if you want to go what am *I* going to say? You lead a pretty hectic life, yeah ... you need a holiday every once in a while, I suppose.'

'Stop it, Marc,' Melanie whispered, unable to look him in the face.

'I think that's what I should be saying to you, Melanie. Stop it. Just stop it.' He picked up his car keys and walked out of the room.

It's over, she longed to scream at his departing back. It was over almost before it began. *He means nothing to me, nothing!* But saying it was over would mean admitting to the affair in the first place – and Melanie was nothing if not a coward. She heard the front door slam and the crunch of tyres as his car slid down the driveway. She sat down, suddenly exhausted. She stayed there, not moving, until the children were brought home.

91

Laure picked up the phone on the third ring. It was a Sunday morning, the one day in the entire week when she allowed herself to sleep as long as she liked or needed with no alarm clock to interrupt her dreams. She fumbled with the receiver, struggling to focus. 'Hello?' she said, squinting at the clock beside her bed. It was 8.33 a.m. Who the hell would ring her at 8.33 a.m. on a Sunday?

'Laure? It's Melanie!'

'Who?'

'Melanie … from Accra. I'm here, in London! Are you free?'

'I'm hardly awake,' Laure groaned. 'Where … when did you arrive?'

'A couple of hours ago. Sorry, did I wake you up?' she asked contritely. Then, without waiting for an answer, she somehow managed to invite herself round immediately which was why, at eight-fifty, after the quickest shower ever, Laure was rushing around her flat, tidying her work away and wondering if she had time to nip to the shop for a pint of milk.

'Melanie,' Laure said, opening the door, still slightly bemused by the urgency of her visit. It had been three months since she'd seen Melanie in Accra and in that time, she hadn't received so much as a postcard. Not that she'd sent one; she'd been too busy at work. But still, what on earth could be so important that Melanie had come directly from the airport to visit *her*? Surely she had other, better friends to see? 'Come in, you must be exhausted.'

'Oh, no, first class, darling. You just lie down and go to sleep.' Melanie's voice was light and playful. She could probably sense Laure's confusion.

'Oh. Right.'

'What a *lovely* flat,' Melanie said, shrugging off her beautiful black coat with its glamorous fur collar and tossing her leather gloves on the couch. 'It's *exactly* how I imagined it.'

'Would you like a cup of coffee?' Laure asked faintly. Melanie's enthusiasm, while touching, was a little overwhelming at that hour of the morning.

'*Love* one. Milk, no sugar, darling.'

'Of course.' Laure had to smile.

Two hours later she'd almost got to the bottom of why Melanie had chosen to come and visit her – it was clear that things weren't going well in the Miller–Abadi household. Laure was a good listener, or so Jill always said. She reckoned it was the fact that Laure appeared to have seen more in the first third of her life than most people did in their entire lives, and *that*, she assured Laure hastily, had more to do with her own intuition than anything Laure – or anyone else – had told her. Despite the fact that they were close friends as well as business partners and worked together six days out of seven, Laure had always been careful not to give too much away. She sensed, even in the beginning, that certain confidences were better left unshared. Theirs was primarily a business relationship and it was healthier for both of them if it stayed that way.

Melanie, on the other hand, was a different story. 'But,' Laure said gently, as Melanie finished speaking, 'surely things aren't *that* bad. Marc's ... well, I hardly know him ... but he's easy to talk to, isn't he?'

'Oh, he talks to strangers, all right. And his patients. But he doesn't ...' Melanie paused. 'The thing is,' she said carefully,

'Marc doesn't *trust* me. He never has. Not even in the begin-ning.'

'No, you can't mean that, surely? I mean ... why would he have married you if he didn't trust you?' Laure hoped her voice was steady. Talking about Marc Abadi in this most intimate of ways was having an alarming effect on her. How, she wondered, had she and Melanie gone from being mere ac-quaintances who'd met a couple of months ago to best friends, sitting opposite each other at her dining table, talking about the state of Melanie's marriage? Melanie didn't seem to find it odd. She kept repeating how it was such a relief to be able to *talk* to someone; *really* talk. There was no one in Ghana she could talk to. Everyone was just waiting for her to fall flat on her face; she could tell. They all hated her; even Petra. She seemed about to say something more, but stopped herself just in time.

'*I* was the one who wanted to get married, not Marc. I ... I sort of made it happen,' Melanie said, turning her lovely blue eyes on Laure. 'I just thought he was the most *perfect* man I'd ever met. He was so *good* at everything. Everyone just *adored* him.' She looked at Laure for confirmation. Laure could feel her cheeks going hot.

'He's very ... nice,' she said lamely, at last. 'I ... just never really got the chance to talk to him ...'

'Really? He said he'd met you at some dinner – one of those awful dinners that Beatrice Quarshie's always arranging. They *never* invite me; Beatrice can't stand me.'

'I'm sure that's not true,' Laure said automatically, her pulse racing. What had Marc said about her? She was dying to know. 'Yes, I sat opposite him but there were so many other people there.'

'Oh, he just said something about having misjudged you. He said you weren't a bit like all the other airheads who I call my friends. You see ... that's *exactly* what I mean. He's got absolutely *no* respect for anything I do or say. He thinks *I'm* just like my friends.'

'Well, if you agree,' Laure said delicately, 'that they're not the sort of people you *really* want to be friends with, why don't you find new ones? It sounds as if you could use a *real* friend or two.'

'But that's why I was so pleased to meet *you*,' Melanie cried, suddenly getting up from the table. She seemed agitated. 'You don't know what it's like out there! I hate all those women; they're so *fake*. Fucking Barb with her stupid gin parties and her *fucking* dogs. That's all she ever talks about ... *those fucking dogs*. I'm *sick* of them! And as for Petra and that fucking stupid husband of hers ... *God*, every time I see his pathetic naked ...' she stopped immediately, her face suddenly flushed scarlet. She put a hand to her mouth. 'I didn't mean that,' she said slowly, looking anxiously at Laure.

Laure shook her head faintly. She spread her hands. 'Don't feel you have to tell me everything,' she said slowly. 'After all, you hardly know me.'

'But that's the whole point,' Melanie said, wiping a tear from her cheek. 'I *don't* know you all that well, but it doesn't *matter*. Weird, isn't it? You've been a better friend in the past hour than those bitches have been in the past five years. I can tell *you* anything – I can't even tell that lot that I burnt the chips,' she said, beginning to laugh. 'Not that *I* ever cook any, but you know what I mean.'

'Actually,' Laure said, nodding slowly. 'I do.' The memory of standing in the hallway, listening to Jessie Smith explaining why she was afraid to have anything more to do with her surfaced suddenly. How the mighty were fallen. In the aftermath of the break-up with Daniel, no one had said a word to her. None of them, in the few days after it had happened that she'd stayed at Jessie's – not even Jessie herself – had said anything. No '*sorry to hear what happened*', or '*if you need anything*', or even '*how are you?*'. No, they all pretended it was none of their business, except *she* knew – oh, of course she knew! – that they'd chewed over the story again and again until there was nothing left but her humiliation, and who wanted to go on talking about *that*?

'It's just that living with someone so ... so bloody perfect ...

it just makes you want to go off the rails a bit, that's all. They don't mean anything to me … of course not.'

'Why don't you try talking to Marc?' Laure suggested, the heat still pulsing in her face.

'Oh, he'd go mad,' Melanie said, blowing her nose. 'So I keep it a secret. But sometimes … it just … just eats at me, d'you know?' she asked rhetorically. She sighed. 'Oh, I don't suppose you would know,' she said dispiritedly. 'I can't imagine you keeping secrets. You're far too honest.'

Laure blinked. The urge to say something had come upon her suddenly, without warning. Perhaps it was the way Melanie had looked at her, or the faint emphasis on 'you' – *I can't imagine you doing anything like this*. Some memory of sitting on her bed at home in Pétionville with Régine, giggling girlishly over their childish secrets and hopes. She opened her mouth and the words just came tumbling out. 'Actually, I do know what you're going through. I did something once … I've never told anyone else. I sometimes can't believe I did it.'

'What did you do?' Melanie had stopped crying.

Laure took a deep breath. She'd spent so long keeping her emotions in check, keeping a lid on everything, never daring to trust anyone, that Melanie's simple question threw her off guard. The longing to tell someone suddenly overwhelmed her. Melanie had brought out a long-buried side to her that she'd assumed she'd hidden for ever. She was Régine and Martine and yes, even Sandra, rolled into one. There was something unbelievably infectious about her laugh and the light, easy way she carried herself … somehow Melanie had forced her guard down without her even noticing. She looked at her for a second, then opened her mouth. The words seemed to come out of their own accord. 'I had a child,' she said slowly, 'when I was seventeen. I never saw him. I gave him up for adoption as soon as he was born. That was why I had to leave Haiti. I … I gave my child away.'

'Gosh,' Melanie said after a moment, her voice gentle. 'That must have been hard.'

Laure nodded, shocked at how good it felt finally to be able to tell someone. Her face was hot; she put up a hand to her cheek. 'Not a day goes by when I don't think of him,' she said slowly, tracing the pattern on a cushion.

'Gosh,' was all Melanie could find to say for the second time. There wasn't much else that could be said. She leaned across the couch and squeezed Laure's arm. 'Don't think about it,' she said ineffectually. 'It'll only make you sad. And I don't like seeing you sad. It doesn't suit you.'

Laure gave a shaky laugh. It was a typical Melanie remark and somehow, in its banal absurdity, it served its purpose. She plucked a tissue out of the box and blew her nose. 'I don't know why I told you that,' she said, her voice still quavering slightly. 'I've never told anyone else.'

'That's because we're *friends*,' Melanie said earnestly. 'I *told* you. We can tell each other anything. That's what friends are for. Now, I'd better get going,' she said, rising to her feet. 'I've got to be at the hairdressers' in half an hour. I've *got* to get my hair sorted out,' she said, flicking a glossy lock over her shoulder.

'What's wrong with it?' Laure asked, relieved to be able to change the subject.

Melanie rolled her eyes. '*Everything*,' she said dramatically. 'I'm just going to sit back and let Nicky take care of it. I'll see you tomorrow night, all right? We'll go out for dinner. I know this great little place just off Regent Street. I'll call you. Bye, darling.'

It had been so long since Laure had experienced the kind of giddy, excited friendship that Melanie offered and she found herself, not for the first time, unexpectedly drawn to it. Although she was nothing like Améline, in either looks or character, there was a warmth to Melanie that brought Améline to her mind – a certain shyness in the way she looked at her, both seeking approval and wanting to please, all at the same time. But there was also something childish about Melanie that irritated her, made her want to shake her. In *that* respect she was nothing like Améline – the memory of Améline's gritty toughness and sheer determination was what helped Laure when she was down; she somehow couldn't see Melanie inspiring the same. Melanie needed help; she certainly didn't give it.

92

'*It's funny to think of you, sitting somewhere where the temperature's 105 and the sea is blue. It's spring here in Malvern, finally. The leaves in the park are starting to bud; it's beautiful. Not long to go now! Only a couple of months! I can't wait!*' Améline swallowed. She still hadn't told Viv about Paul. But before she could dwell on it further, there was a sudden crash from upstairs. It felt as though someone might fall through the ceiling. Améline put down the letter with a frown. Clouds of dust fell around her; the light bulb jangled precariously. What the hell was going on? She sighed. At the time, it had seemed like a good idea. Paul had estimated it would take them four to six months to get it done. It had crossed her mind fleetingly when he said it that a four-month building schedule in the UK might not be *quite* the same in Haiti but she'd accepted it without comment. Now she was beginning to understand the depths of her mistake. Eight months later they still weren't finished. Not an evening went by without Paul telling her incredulously what had happened during the day. He couldn't understand how *anything* got done in Haiti. While the workmen were the nicest, most affable bunch of builders he'd ever met, he told her, their sense of time was practically non-existent. They'd need another six months, he reckoned. And that was being optimistic. Améline listened with a worried frown on her face. She didn't have six more months to wait. Viv was arriving for a two-week visit at the beginning of July. Less than three months away.

She opened the parlour door and peered up into the dark abyss upstairs. 'What happened?' she called.

'*Pardon, madame,*' the foreman's apologetic voice floated

down to her. She could hear Paul cursing. Améline shook her head. They were only retiling the bathrooms and painting the walls – what would've happened if she'd asked them to *build* anything?

'Anyone hurt?'

'*Non, madame.*'

She rolled her eyes. The last time Fanfan, the hapless plumber, had taken one of the sinks off the wall, the entire bathroom had been flooded in a matter of seconds. It unfortunately hadn't occurred to him to switch off the mains tap, the foreman apologised. Yes, *most* unfortunate. The foreman, whose name she could never remember, was always apologising.

She walked back into the parlour and picked up the letter again. '*Mrs Dickens – you remember her? She used to run the post office at the top of the road, just after the school – she passed away last Saturday. Susan came with me; it was funny, just being the two of us. Susan misses you almost as much as I do!*' There was another almighty crash. Améline put down the letter again. It was at moments like this that she most missed Malvern. In Pétionville, there was nowhere to go if the noise in your house became unbearable. In Malvern, there were always the Malvern Hills to escape to. She closed her eyes for a moment, picturing the heavy, towering hills that rose directly behind the house. She liked to remember them in autumn, when the gorse had turned to burnt amber and the leaves were just beginning to fall. The grass was still green then, brilliant and glistening underfoot. Her favourite walk was from St Anne's Well, straight up to the summit of the lower of the four hills that made up the chain. From there she could see across three counties, as Iain had told her when he first took her there. Worcestershire, Herefordshire, Gloucestershire. She'd stared at the words. How …? Then she'd thought it unimaginable that she would ever get used to the cold and damp, to the rain-sodden weeks and the smell of rotting leaves in the air. She'd hated the way her breath scrolled out before her on winter mornings, or the way one sunny day rarely preceded the next.

But it had happened; she'd slowly, almost imperceptibly,

grown used to it; and then learned to love it, as Iain had. Now she would have given almost anything to leave the heat and dust and cries of the men working upstairs and disappear amongst the yellow-gold leaves of the wide, generous trees.

93

'She's certainly gregarious,' Jill said, smiling, as the door shut behind Melanie. 'And if what she says about her father's new wife is true ...'

'I wouldn't bet on it,' Laure said dryly. 'Melanie's always got lots of bright ideas. As far as I can work out, she's never even met the woman.'

'Oh, well. Would've been a great plug,' Jill said, pulling a face. 'I'd give *anything* to get our stuff in one of those makeover magazines. Then we'd really have it made.'

'Help! *I'm* the one who's got to keep coming up with new ideas,' Laure cried. 'We can't take on any more orders. I've only been back a couple of months and I'm already running out of stream!'

'Why don't you get yourself a little studio out there?' Jill said, turning to her. 'You know, nothing big or fancy, just a small place that you can go to a few times a year. Maybe not for two months, but if you had somewhere of your own ...' she mused, tapping a pencil against her teeth. 'It's not very expensive, or so Kofi says. And I'd like to come out and visit. Anything that gets you producing this kind of stuff,' she pointed to the screen print drying on the middle table, 'is worth it.'

Laure stared at her. Was she serious? 'You're joking,' she said finally.

'No. Not at all. I mean, I do all the administration, which I *like* doing, don't get me wrong. But if we play our cards really carefully – that's why I got so excited over what your friend said – well, we could be producing three or four times what we currently sell. I'd much rather sell a smaller range to a few different places than get ourselves tied up in one enormous commission for a single store.'

'I agree,' Laure said hesitantly, her mind whirling. 'But it's awfully far away?'

'Ghana? It's only a six-hour flight. It'd take you the same amount of time to get to the south of France. And it's a *lot* warmer.'

'I'd never even considered it,' Laure said, hoping that the excitement building up in the pit of her stomach wasn't yet showing on her face. Some hope.

'I'm sure you hadn't,' Jill laughed. 'But seriously … It seems to have been a real source of inspiration and I still think your best work is yet to come – that's the teacher in me, sorry.' Jill laughed. 'Why don't you look into it? I'm sure your friend Melanie would be only *too* pleased to help.'

She was. In fact, Melanie was over the moon. She would start looking for a place *as soon as she got back. The very minute!* 'Hang on,' Laure laughed over the phone, 'I'm still not sure it's a good idea. It depends on how much it costs, how difficult it is … I've got to work out a whole lot of stuff before anything happens.'

'I know, I know. Oh, by the way, I *did* phone my dad. And my stepmother – gosh, it sounds so weird saying that – wants to have a look at some of your stuff tomorrow. Have you got anything you can show her?'

Laure almost dropped the receiver. 'Er, yes,' she said, as calmly as she could. 'Yes … we've got the portfolio we did for Osbourne & Little. And the one we did for Designer's Guild. And there are some samples I can take her …'

'Perfect. D'you want to come down with me and show her? I'll get Mum's driver to take us. It's only a couple of hours and it's really pretty down there, much as I *hate* to admit it.'

'Are you serious?' Laure couldn't quite believe her ears.

'Of course I'm serious. I'll pick you up tomorrow at ten.'

Laure put the receiver down and stared at Jill.

'What?' Jill said, noticing her odd expression.

'That was Melanie. Her dad's new wife wants to see our work. Tomorrow.'

'You're kidding.'

'I'm not.'

Melanie couldn't really explain what had come over her when she picked up the phone and dialled her father's number. She hadn't even planned it; it just happened. Ever since she'd had that long, early morning conversation with Laure, it was as if something had slowly and silently fallen into place. It wasn't anything Laure had said – in fact, she'd said very little. It was more ... she was surprised at how peaceful she felt *after* she'd finished speaking. As if something had been lifted from her shoulders and it was only once it was gone that she realised how heavy it had been all along. What was the point of being angry with Mike? What was the point of clamouring for his attention? Being good hadn't helped; neither had being bad. She might as well just give up ... and just *be*. Be her. Just as she was. Faults and all. She'd never really been herself around Mike; not that he'd given her much chance. But now, well, she was nearly thirty years old, for Christ's sake. How much longer was it going to take?

Dawes pulled into Penn Street and crawled along slowly, looking for Teague St Lazâre Studios. Melanie wrinkled her nose. What an *odd* place to have a studio, she thought to herself, looking at the woefully dilapidated buildings on either side. Most odd. Were they even in the right place? Suddenly she saw Laure stick her head out of the studio door and look down the street. It was funny, she thought to herself as she waved her over. Laure was right; they hardly knew one another but, in an odd way, she felt as though they'd always been friends. Laure was like the wiser, calmer older sister she'd never had. She felt that bit more in control and in charge of herself when Laure was around. It was fantastic that she was thinking about making

Ghana a permanent place to work. She couldn't forget the feeling of pride that had crept over her when Marc – finally! – said he approved of her. He hated her friends; he would never know just how much it meant to her to hear him praise her for a choice *she'd* made. *She* was the one who'd brought Laure to the house. She was Melanie's find, no one else's. It felt good. Better than good. In fact, so many things were suddenly starting to make sense. She'd spent most of her life worrying about Mike's approval when it was Marc's she really desired. She'd been so wrapped up in herself that she just hadn't paid their relationship the right kind of attention. Nor the kids. She'd been selfish; that was what the whole, pathetic thing with Chris and that blasted gardener – what the hell was his name? – was about. Her own selfish needs. Not Marc. Not her children. Well, things were going to change. She'd finally seen the light. Marc wouldn't know what hit him when he returned. A sweet blast of tenderness for him stole over her so that when Laure finally located the car and opened the door, Melanie's face was unaccountably flushed.

'Hi,' Laure said, sliding gracefully into the seat beside her. She was wearing a long, grey coat-dress with a pair of wide-legged black trousers and flat, black riding boots. She looked, as always, gorgeous. Her skin still held some of the sunny colour she'd acquired in Ghana and with her wonderfully wild, curly hair loose about her shoulders and back, she looked more like a model on her way to a fashion shoot than someone about to make a sales pitch. 'You all right?' she asked, noticing Melanie's reddened cheeks.

'Yes, just hot in here,' Melanie said, rolling down the window. 'Wiltshire, please, Dawes,' she said, leaning forward. 'My dad's new place.'

'Right-o.' Dawes swung the heavy car around in the narrow, cobbled street and joined the traffic heading west out of the city.

Ashdeane House, once owned by an eccentric English artist, was everything Laure had ever imagined an English country house should be. To begin with, the weather, as they drew closer to Wiltshire, suddenly changed, rain clouds parting to reveal blue, wispy skies and white, cotton-puff clouds. It was early winter; the trees were almost stripped of their leaves and the landscape was beautifully stark. Finally, Dawes pulled up in front of a set of heavy, wrought iron gates and a man appeared, looking every inch the country estate gamekeeper. The gates slid open silently and he even tipped his hat. Laure had to stifle a giggle. The whole thing was so far from her experience of England as to be laughable.

But there was nothing remotely laughable about the house. They drove along a gravelled driveway, surrounded on both sides by the greenest, neatest lawn Laure had ever seen – even the trees looked manicured. Nothing was out of place. Then they took a sharp left by a clump of stately, imposing oaks and began a gentle descent towards the house. A handsome, rather austere building of red brick, it sat nestled in its own private valley, the thickly wooded hills rising on all three sides around it. To say it was huge was an understatement; it spread itself outwards, away from its starkly beautiful façade, in a collection of smaller houses and buildings, each of which was probably a hundred times the size of her Hackney flat. Her eyes widened as she turned to Melanie.

'I know, I know. Unbelievable. You wait till you see *her*.'

'*Her*' turned out to be an impossibly tall, impossibly thin, impossibly blonde young girl who couldn't have been more than twenty. She carried a pair of dogs which, she informed them in a little girl voice that made Laure wince, were called Snowy and Blackie. Not terribly original as the dogs were, predictably, black and white. Melanie's father popped his head round the door to greet them laconically. Despite the presence of his wife and daughter, he ran his eyes over Laure in the way of a seasoned ladies man – she found herself shaking her head as he left to 'get away from all the bloody noise', as he put it. Suddenly a number of things about Melanie were beginning to make sense.

The house was enormous and in dire need of decoration. Laure's imagination began to run wild. Decorating the house in Primrose Hill was nothing compared to this. She began to visualise colours, textures, fabrics, furniture, even artwork. God, what must it be like to own a home like this? She trailed after them, stopping every now and then to gaze out of the perfectly placed, perfectly proportioned windows that looked on to the estate.

An hour later, a ten-minute conversation with Jill and a two-second conversation with Mike Miller and it had all been decided. She and Melanie drove away from the stately home, Melanie with a satisfied smile on her face and Laure with a £1m budget, a fifteen per cent commission and the niggling certainty that it was all about to go wrong.

94

At the mention of Laure St Lazâre's name, Marc stiffened. He'd barely listened to anything Melanie had said – since her return from London the previous month, she'd talked almost non-stop about how things were about to change; how life was about to get better; how good the coming New Year would be. She said nothing about her own culpability, he noted, rather everything was swept under the carpet as if it had never been. It was all about the future, she said imploringly. No point in talking about the past. He was too tired to argue. But what was that she'd said about Laure?

'She's going to get a little studio here,' she said excitedly. 'I promised to find one for her. I was thinking ... maybe something in Kokomlemle, you know, behind the Swiss School?'

'Are you out of your mind?' Marc said, glaring at her. 'In Kokomlemle? It's not safe, don't be ridiculous.'

'God, all *right*,' Melanie snapped at him. 'There's no need to bite my head off. I was just *thinking*. Loads of artists live there, that's all.'

'Sorry,' he mumbled, rather taken aback himself. The idea of Laure living in some one-bedroom little shack in Kokomlemle had alarmed him. 'I . . . it's just not a particularly safe area, that's all. Why don't you try somewhere more central . . . Osu, or something?'

'Isn't it a bit noisy?'

'At least it's safe. You'd be beside yourself if anything happened to her while she was here.'

'Yeah, you're right. You're *always* right. OK. I'll do some scouting around in Osu. At least it's near *your* office; it'll be good to have you nearby.'

Marc couldn't answer. His words were suddenly stuck in his throat. He busied himself with stuffing an envelope until he could speak. 'When did you say she was coming?' he asked, as off-handedly as he could. 'Only I hope it's not soon . . . I've got those conferences coming up and I'll bet she'll want help moving her stuff and all that.'

'I thought you *liked* her,' Melanie wailed, rolling her eyes at him. 'What does it matter? I'll get Mensah or someone to help her. She wouldn't *dream* of asking you, don't worry.'

'Right.' He cleared his throat. 'I've forgotten something at . . . at the office,' he said quickly. 'I'd better run along and get it.' He desperately needed to get out of the house.

'At this time?' Melanie looked at her watch. 'It's almost ten. Can't it wait till tomorrow?'

'No, I've got a meeting first thing. I won't be long. Don't wait up.'

He was gone before she could respond.

The next few weeks were among the hardest he could recall. For the first time in his life, he was unable to control his own thoughts. He was waiting for something – but what? On the surface, not much had changed, despite Melanie's predictions of a better, brighter future. He still went to work every day; she still lay by the pool or took the kids half-heartedly to their various after-nursery activities. He came home in the early evening after the traffic had died down and she lay on the couch, seemingly exhausted by the efforts of putting the children to bed. An hour or so later, the kitchen door would squeak and Efua or Nana would walk quietly out – *they'd* been the ones to sit beside the kids, not Melanie. He grew weary of it.

Christmas came and went, followed by a rather quiet New Year. In late January, Marc went to Liberia for a fortnight and his leave-taking was filled with a strange disquiet. What if Laure came while he was away? Melanie hadn't said anything but such things were always arranged rather quickly, weren't they? The camp was hot, tedious and tense and only added to his own sense of rising frustration. In calmer, more rational moments, he recognised his own behaviour as ridiculous. She probably had a boyfriend – he was pretty sure she was unmarried. *He* was married, for Christ's sake. He was bored, lonely, seeking a diversion. He wished to be her friend, nothing more. He'd recognised something in her that perhaps he himself sought. Friendship, nothing more. He reduced himself to the condition of a fictional patient in order, he thought, to get to the bottom of his dangerous discontent.

When he came back and found she was thinking of coming in a month's time, his relief was so palpable and overwhelming as to make a mockery of his resolve.

95

Melanie waited for Laure's arrival impatiently. She was feeling good about herself. She'd come through for Laure on more than one occasion, and that, as everyone who knew her would agree, was no mean achievement. She'd found the small house with the large garage that could be converted into a work-ing studio; she'd introduced Laure to Cosima; and now she'd come up with the brilliant suggestion that Laure give a two-day workshop at Susu's nursery school for which the headmistress would be so profoundly grateful that there would be absolutely no *question* that Susu would eventually get a place in the much-coveted junior section of the prestigious International School. In fact, Laure wouldn't even have to actually *give* the workshop to ensure Susu's place. The mere fact that Melanie had approached them with the idea would be enough to cement Susu's name in their minds during the highly competitive decision-making process. Yes, it was all falling into place nicely.

The only fly in the ointment, of course, was Marc. He wasn't quite as thrilled with her plan-making as everyone else. He seemed to have revised his opinion of Laure – now he seemed irritated whenever Melanie brought the subject up. Oh, he was just so difficult with his ridiculously high expectations of everyone. In the whole business of coming to Ghana on a more regular basis, Laure seemed to have upset some previous opinion he'd formed of her, but Melanie was tired of trying to figure out what. Perhaps he thought she shouldn't have taken on the job from Cosima? He'd accused Melanie more than once of overwhelming people, trying too hard to insert herself into their lives – her cheeks burned angrily as the thought came to her. She *wasn't* trying to insert herself into Laure's life! They were friends, that was all. Contrary to Marc's opinion, friends *did* help each other when and where they could. She'd had a lifetime of friends doing exactly the opposite; it was such a *relief* to find Laure, who seemed to want nothing of hers, liked her as she was and was interesting, beautiful and fun to be with into the bargain. What could possibly be wrong with that?

Laure finally arrived a week later. She thought the house and garage Melanie had found for her fantastic and perfect and exactly what she would have chosen if she'd gone hunting herself. Melanie positively glowed. Laure could only stay a fortnight this time, and most of that time would be spent getting the studio organised but she had plans to return in April and work for a month. Her work in London was all going brilliantly thanks to Melanie's help. A TV company had been in touch about doing a documentary on the refurbishment of Ashdeane and several newspapers and magazines had already run articles, one of which had somehow found its way to Ghana. Melanie was beside herself with excitement.

A couple of days after Laure's arrival, someone stopped Melanie in the supermarket. It was a woman she recognised vaguely, though she couldn't remember her name. She asked her if the beautiful young woman she'd just seen in last week's *Sunday Times* magazine was that friend of hers? A friend had brought the magazine over from the UK. She pulled the magazine out of her bag. She'd seen the two of them, just the other day, sitting together at Ivy Café. The article had mentioned Ghana. She'd put two and two together ... it *was* her, wasn't it? Melanie nodded impatiently. She looked quickly at the pictures. There were several of Cosima, two very good ones of Laure and a few of the house itself. Her eye was suddenly caught by a line, '*Laure St Lazâre, one half of the designers Teague St Lazâre, is also the estranged wife of film and media executive Daniel Bermann, the director of ICF. The couple separated in 1998 ...*' Melanie almost dropped the magazine.

'Can I borrow it?' she'd begged the woman, closing the magazine. 'I'll give it back, I promise!' There was nowhere to buy a copy in Accra. The woman agreed reluctantly and scribbled an address for the driver. Melanie rushed out of the shop, looking for Mensah.

At home, she read the article from cover to cover then immediately phoned her mother. The name 'Daniel Bermann' rang a bell, dimly. Half an hour later, she put down the phone, grinning with pride. She'd got it. At the charity dinner where she'd met Marc almost seven years earlier, Laure and Daniel Bermann had been the prize guests who hadn't showed. Even Stella was impressed. She sat there in the living room, open-mouthed, until Marc suddenly came in through the door.

'I'm going over to ... What's the matter?' he asked, staring at her.

Melanie held out the magazine. 'I had no idea . . .' she began, almost speechless with surprise.

'About what?'

'About Laure. D'you know who she's *married* to?'

The word sliced through him, causing him to wince. 'I thought . . . didn't you say . . . isn't she single?' he managed eventually.

'They're separated – it looks like they've been separated for quite a long time – but she was married to *Daniel Bermann*!' Marc looked blank. He was struggling to digest the information. 'His father's Günter Bermann, you know, he's like Rupert Murdoch. They're absolutely *loaded*. I never knew. She never said a *thing*.'

Relief coursed through him, wild and sweet. 'Well, if they're separated . . .' he said faintly.

'Oooh, I'm going to *clobber* her with this,' Melanie said, waving the rolled-up magazine. She was smiling.

'Don't.' The word was out before he could stop it.

'What d'you mean?'

'Sometimes,' his voice unconsciously adopted a professional tone, 'it's better to let someone come forward—'

'I'm not one of your bloody patients, Marc,' Melanie said crossly, getting up. 'Laure's *my* friend, not yours. I think I can just about manage on my own, thanks.' She walked out of the kitchen, the rolled-up magazine still clutched in her hand.

He sighed. Bravo, he thought to himself ruefully. You handled *that* really well.

Two days later, having been roped into attending a cocktail party for the new UNICEF director in Ghana, he stood in the middle of the room at the Golden Tulip Hotel, sipping a rather poor whisky and listening with half an ear to Melanie and Barb chatting to two men whose faces bore the faintly bemused air of men who'd been staring down a woman's cleavage for too long. In this case, Melanie's. He swallowed another mouthful of weak, watery whisky and glanced around. And then, suddenly, he saw her. She walked down the wide, double-sided entrance stairs entirely unselfconsciously, her skirt opening at the side to reveal a perfectly shaped calf and the soft swell of her thigh as she descended, her heels tapping lightly on the polished terrazzo floor. He swallowed an ice cube whole. His carefully constructed, constricted soliloquies about wanting to be her friend simply flew out of the window. He wanted *her*. End of story. Simple as that. And impossible. That, too, was simple enough.

He danced with her once that evening. To have avoided her would have been silly, and obvious. He had done nothing wrong and yet every second of the ten-minute song was laced with the most tortuous, exquisite guilt. Once he'd admitted to the truth, he couldn't turn the clock back and pretend that it wasn't so. That every time he looked at her, he *didn't* feel his stomach turn; that every time she put up a hand to lift the heavy mass of curls resting on her shoulders he *wasn't* overcome with the sharpest desire he'd ever known to put a hand there, trace the dark, soft skin with the tips of his fingers, feel the weight and texture of the tightly curled, whorled ringlets of hair. When she spoke, her voice was low and hesitant, a voice for his ears alone.

He left the party early, pleading a headache brought on by the terrible whisky. The driver dropped him off and promised to return for Madam Melanie and Madam Laure later. He stripped off his clothes, stood under the ubiquitous cold shower for as long as he could bear, then fell into a guilt-laced, tortured dream from which, he knew, even as his eyes flew open at five-thirty from the shrill sound of the alarm, there was no awakening.

With her working and living spaces set up – two rooms, one with a bed and a tiny kitchen and bathroom – Laure flew back to London without running into Marc Abadi again. It was just as well. At the party, when Melanie had insisted that he ask her to dance, the expression on his face was so pained it was almost comical – if it hadn't hurt quite as much. He'd danced with her because he'd been forced to. In front of Melanie and her friends it would have been unbearably rude to have refused. But, as his every expression and move indicated, he'd rather have danced with a piece of furniture than her. She'd tried, once or twice, to make conversation, to say something – anything – that would lighten the angry tension emanating from his tall, broad frame, but he just looked away. Or looked through her. Whatever the cause, she was fed up. Moody, unpredictable, surly and *rude* – Marc Abadi could go to hell.

96

From his new penthouse office on Hopton Street, overlooking the vast, teeming construction site that was to be the new Tate Modern, Daniel could see across the flat, murky surface of the Thames to the City. They'd only been in their new premises for a few months but he never tired of the view. The river was mercurial ... grey, silver, blue ... its silky surface picking up changes in the sky overhead.

He flicked quickly through the newspapers as he did every morning, glancing quickly at the main headlines, tossing the sports section in the bin and then concentrating on the culture and business sections which were infinitely more interesting to read. The *Telegraph* mentioned the renovation of Ashdeane House in a small byline on the cover. He raised an eyebrow – someone had mentioned the sale of Ashdeane at a dinner party the other day. Mike Miller, that ageing rock star, had apparently married someone almost forty years younger than he was and they were busy trying to pass themselves off as landed gentry. He flicked through the pages looking for the article. Seven years of being back in Britain had done nothing to diminish the faint exasperation he felt with its ridiculously old-fashioned snobbery. So what if he'd married someone younger than his daughter? So what if they wanted to live in a draughty old pile in the middle of the country? Perhaps America had had more of an impact on him than he cared to admit. He flicked through the pages and then suddenly stopped. It took him a second to realise he was looking at Laure's face. He felt the blood drain out of his own.

It took him a month to make the call. Twenty-six days of agonising over it, picking up the phone and dropping it before it rang; sitting in his office and staring unseeing out of the window, remembering the things he'd sworn to forget, including those that made him physically ill all over again. He told no one. Sarah, his girlfriend, gave up asking him if there was something wrong; she was busy with her friends and her horses – she wasn't one to pry. There was a pressing need to talk to Laure, he reasoned silently with himself – in order to get the divorce papers signed. That was all. A formality. Maybe he wouldn't even have to see her – someone could take the papers round to her address, she could sign them and that would be the end of it. Why did he have to call? Why couldn't he just send someone round? His imaginary questions and answers almost sent him round the bend. In the end, twenty-six days after seeing her face, he picked up the phone and dialled.

'Hello, Teague St Lazâre. How can I help you?' A very professional-sounding voice. A young woman. Secretary, perhaps? Receptionist? An art student, maybe, sitting at a large, glass table? 'Hello? Can I help you?' she asked again patiently.

'Oh. Yes … er, could I speak to Laure Ber … er, Laure St Lazâre, sorry. Please.' Daniel's mind wandered. He gripped the receiver, aware of the sweat slowly beginning to trickle down his left temple. He felt nauseous.

'Laure's not in the country at the moment, I'm afraid. She's in Ghana. She'll be back on the fourteenth. Can I take a message?' the young woman said brightly.

The disappointment was like a blow. He opened his mouth to speak, and couldn't. He put the receiver down. Ghana? Where the fuck was Ghana? And what was she doing there?

He wiped his forehead with his handkerchief and looked at the calendar on his desk. The fourteenth was ... about three weeks away. In three days' time, however, he was leaving for the US, for almost the entire summer. He felt faint.

97

'*We can see, therefore, why restoring people to a state of mental equilibrium where they are able to exercise choice, freedom and the ability to act on their worlds are as essential as feeding them, keeping them warm and nursing them. This paper suggests that by connecting and co-ordinating ...*'

Marc stifled a yawn. Connecting and co-ordinating; possibly two of the words he feared most in his line of work. Valuable time taken away from the field work, the *real* work, to be spent on reports that no one ever saw, ever read or ever acted upon. He looked around the conference hall at the hundreds of rapt, naïve young researchers and new professionals busy scribbling down every word and the 'old' hacks like himself, trying not to yawn or to catch one another's eyes. Ridiculous, really. Why didn't they simply walk out? Leave those who still believed in such things to their wide-eyed, wholesome dreams of 'freedom' and 'choice'. A fleeting image of the queue for the water tap at the Larabanga refugee camp flashed before his eyes. Freedom? These people were insane.

Suddenly, almost without thinking about it, he stood up. He climbed over the knees of those sitting nearest to him and walked up the auditorium steps. He caught a glimpse of someone looking rather admiringly at him as he let the doors swing shut behind him and then, all of a sudden, he was out of it. Away from the stale, air-conditioned atmosphere and the droning voices whose timbre and pitch positively vibrated with defeat.

He walked down the steps and through the revolving doors on to the wide, impressive plaza in front of the building. It was early June in Geneva and the city was at its loveliest. He looked down Avenue de la Paix towards the impressive UN Building, the flags of dozens of nations fluttering in the wind along its approach. Everything here was ordered, still, calm. He walked down the enormous steps towards the road without any clear idea where he was going, or why. He'd last been in Geneva over ten years ago, for his first interview with *Médecins du Monde*. Although there hadn't been a conference on at the time, he himself had been one of the young, fresh-from-college enthusiasts, hanging on to every word that was said, desperately and simultaneously trying to recall everything he'd ever learned in his chosen profession to work out whether, from the body language of those interviewing him, he had the job or not. It seemed like another life. Another person, not him.

He crossed the road and jumped on a tram, heading for the city centre. The sober, measured scale of the city was seductive after the disorganised frenzy of Accra. The grand, sombre buildings reminded him of Beirut, where he'd spent the first seventeen years of his life and which he occasionally thought of as home. But his return, nine years later, had thrown his nostalgia into perpetual confusion from which he sometimes felt he'd never quite recovered. It was ironic, he thought to himself as the tram rumbled towards the main square, the lake coming into view on his left, he lectured, treated and attempted to treat people on the importance of 'home' as the source of all healing – and he himself had none. The Beirut he had left behind after his grandmother's death, all elegance, charm and pristine countryside, only just beginning its slide towards destruction, had completed it by the time he returned. He'd come back to a landscape he no longer recognised. The bullet-ridden, bombed-out buildings he stumbled across bore no relation to the formal, beautifully imposing hotels and businesses of his childhood. Concrete monstrosities, illegally built structures and the cheapest, quickest fast-food outlets had invaded the Corniche, once one of the most beautiful and unspoiled seafronts in the world. It had taken him a while to get to grips with this new, altered reality. In a way, though, that was what made it possible for him to carry on, moving from one place to another, Goma to Gaza and everywhere in between. Home was simply where he found himself. Others in the teams he worked in found it difficult to adjust; every trip home was a struggle in terms of the effort it required to adapt. Not him. He walked in and out, able to sleep, work, rest anywhere.

But not any more. Something had happened to him in the past few months that had suddenly upset his equilibrium. He had a pretty good idea what it was – who she was – but he was damned if he knew what to do about it and why it had struck him so hard. On the surface of things, he had it all. He enjoyed his work, he had two children who clearly adored him and a wife who … loved him. Yes, Melanie loved him. She didn't understand him, perhaps, but she loved him. What more did he want? He couldn't believe he was thinking of cheating on her. No, he corrected himself suddenly, fiercely. He had *already* cheated on her. Infidelity, as he well knew, had nothing to do with sex.

98

As surprising as it seemed, Laure was slowly becoming accustomed to the dramatic change in her lifestyle. She was even getting used to the two major commutes in her life; one, to Wiltshire, the other, to Africa. Absurd as it sounded, the switch and sheer magnitude of the difference between the two places suited her. She wasn't sure how to explain it but leaving the cool, ordered world at Heathrow behind only to emerge, six hours later into the warm, damp chaos at Kotoka got her mind going in ways she couldn't fathom. Accra was a complex mixture of strange and familiar; it was half home, half foreign. She loved the smell, taste and feel of the city; even the languages she couldn't understand were familiar enough to make her oblivious to their sound. The gestures and exclamations of people on the streets had their identical counterparts in Port-au-Prince, if not Pétionville. It was like home, and yet it was not. Then, just when she'd settled into the noise and the sound of the crickets outside her bedroom window, it was time to leave. Back to the world of work, of meetings, interviews with the journalists who were driving down the sandy track to Ashdeane with increasing enthusiasm. The project was going well under Jessie Smith's supervision. She was glad she'd had the nerve to call Jessie. She'd walked into her office with a new pair of shoes and one of the skirts she'd made for herself in Ghana and had been gratified – yes, she had to admit it: *extremely* gratified! – to see the look of surprise, followed quickly by respect, on Jessie's face. A survivor, she read in Jessie's eyes, and one who'd come out on top. Under her own steam. It was more satisfying than anything she could have imagined.

She spread out the photographs she'd taken on her last trip in April and began pinning them to the wall. She was looking for a colour palette for the formal dining and entertaining rooms at Ashdeane – eight of them in total – and, as usual, was looking for a starting point that was neutral but not boring or dull, against which she could play with stronger, bolder colours. She finished tacking them up and stepped back, her eye going swiftly and critically over the finished effect. She'd grouped the images into bands of colours; greens, blues, yellows, reds – they were photographs of simple things – plants, the leaves, the sky at different times ... She frowned. Speaking of the sky, why had it suddenly gone so dark inside? She walked over to the garage door, pushed it open and looked out. She gasped. There was a thick, dense black line across the horizon, so straight as to appear unnatural. The palm trees at the bottom of the garden were swaying stiffly and a gust of cool air suddenly swept across the lawn. It was the beginning of the rainy season and she'd never seen anything like it. She switched on the lights and went back to the window.

Across the road, she could see and hear the *kenkey* sellers scrambling to pack up their makeshift stalls, clucking dismally over the mounds of unsold, soured dough balls that Laure hadn't quite yet managed to develop a taste for. Eating a ball of *kenkey* was like eating cement, she'd heard Melanie say. A bit softer, perhaps, but the taste was the same. She smiled. Melanie had a way with words. The neighbour's chickens were running helter-skelter across the yard, wings flapping in agitation at the approaching wind and rain. Suddenly, the lights flickered wildly, then the entire studio was plunged into darkness. Blackout. Melanie had warned her it happened rather more frequently in the rains. She'd forgotten to buy candles, another tip she'd been given.

She peered anxiously at the approaching black line of cloud. There was a little kiosk just up the road, just before the petrol station – he sold candles. It would take her about five minutes to run up the road ... did she have enough time before the heavens opened? She peered out again. Only one way to find out. It could be hours before the lights came on. She shut the garage door, pushing against it with some difficulty as the winds picked up, and ran across the lawn. Everyone was animated by the approaching weather; dogs barked in unison, children ran here, there and everywhere; it was like a carnival. She was laughing by the time she reached the kiosk.

'Pretty mama,' the stall owner greeted her as he always did.

'Box of candles, please,' Laure said, out of breath.

'Oh, madam ... sorry, oh. Candle finish. Because of rain and light off.'

'Shit.'

'Please, madam, if you go to my brother, over there ... at Nando's back. You can find some over there.'

Laure peered down the crowded road. 'How far?'

'Not far.'

She pulled a face. It was the standard Ghanaian response.

Everything was 'not far'. Even London. 'All right. But you're sure he's got some?'

'Yes, please.' She smiled. Another standard response, which often bore little relation to the truth. She decided to risk it anyway. She wound her way through the traffic and had almost reached the other side of the road when there was a deafening '*crack!*', a flash of brilliant, white lightning and the skies exploded in rain. Within seconds, she was absolutely drenched. She was almost at the shop; might as well buy the damned candles and run back.

Two minutes later, she stood by the side of the road clutching a box of sodden candles, trying to work out which moment might be the safest to sprint across the streaming road when a vehicle suddenly pulled up beside her, its hazard lights flashing in the rain. She made a small sound of annoyance and tried to move around it but someone leaned across and opened the passenger door, right in her path.

'Laure!' A man's voice called out to her from the interior. She lifted the sopping mass of wet hair away from her eyes and peered in. It was Marc! 'Come on, get in. I'll give you a lift. Where're you going?'

'Oh, no ... I'm soaking ... honestly, I ...'

'Just get in,' he said impatiently. 'You're letting the rain in.'

It was on the tip of her tongue to remind him that he'd been the one to stop, she hadn't asked for a damned lift but then there was another enormous thunderclap and the rain started coming down even harder. She hauled herself in, closing the door behind her. 'I'm sorry,' she gasped, as water sluiced off her on to the seat and floor. She was utterly drenched. She tried to hold the thin, white T-shirt away from her body, aware that every single curve, band, piece of lace, not to mention her nipples, were on full display.

He glanced at her briefly. 'I saw you run across the road,' he said, putting the wipers on to their fastest mode and peering out of the side window. He swerved into the road suddenly. 'Sorry, it's difficult to see. Where're you going?'

'Oh, just to my studio. It's just down the road. There was a blackout and I realised I didn't have any candles ...'

'A power cut?'

'Yes, Melanie said they happen all the time, especially in the rainy season.'

'That's odd. My office is just around the corner and there wasn't a blackout when I left. It's down here, isn't it?'

'Yes, the second building on the right. The pink one.'

'But your neighbours have lights,' he said, peering through the rain. 'Look, the street lights are on.'

'Oh. Maybe it came back?' Laure said hopefully. He pulled into her driveway. 'No, look ... I left the lights on in the garage. That's where I usually work.'

'It's probably a fuse. Have you got anyone who can change it for you?'

'I think I can change a fuse myself,' Laure said, smiling. Her feet sloshed around in her sandals as she opened the door.

'Wait, I'll come with you. Some of these old houses have really dangerous wiring,' Marc said, unbuckling his seat belt. He pulled up the handbrake, opened the door and together they ran up the muddy path to the verandah.

'I've never seen anything like this,' Laure shouted to him above the din and roar of the rain. 'It's incredible.'

'Oh, it'll be over in an hour. It rarely lasts long.'

'The noise ...' Laure gestured towards the roof.

He smiled. 'Good old corrugated sheeting. You haven't had any leaks yet, have you?'

'I don't know, it's the first time it's rained since I started coming here.'

'Well, we'll take a quick look. Now, where's the fuse box? Have you got a torch?'

'No. But I've got these?' Laure held out the dripping packet of candles. They both laughed.

'Why don't I take a look. I imagine it's probably in the garage. You'd better change out of these clothes, too. You'll catch a cold.'

'In this heat?'

'Nothing to do with the heat,' Marc said, turning to go. 'You don't want your body temperature to keep going up and down, that's all.' He turned and gave her a quick smile. 'Doctor's orders.'

Laure felt herself go weak at the knees. Yes, he was the most maddeningly arrogant man in the world, but ... that smile. And those eyes. *And wake up, girl, that's Melanie's husband. Stop.* She turned, not without difficulty, and pushed open the door.

Five minutes later, her hair towelled dry and tied back in a ponytail, she walked back into the living room. He was still in the garage and the house was still in darkness. She lit one of the candles and put it on the table. She was suddenly conscious of the shabby, spare interior. It was a small, two-roomed house; the bedroom was a little more cheerful. She'd painted the walls and hung pieces of her favourite cloth around the room but the 'front room', which ought to have been a living room, only contained an old wooden table that Melanie had found somewhere and three mismatched chairs. She peered out of the window again. Through the mosquito screens she could just make out Marc's head moving around in the garage. A few minutes later, she heard the doors close and he came running up the steps on to the verandah. He was soaking; she quickly opened a cupboard and handed him a towel as he came through the door.

'I can't find it,' he said, taking the towel from her and rubbing his head vigorously. 'I don't where they could have put it. It doesn't look like it's in here ...' he said, glancing around.

Laure shook her head. 'It's not in the other room, I looked. Maybe the kitchen? D'you want some coffee, by the way? I've ... I brought some proper stuff with me.'

'Yeah, thanks. I'll just take a quick look in the kitchen and maybe send one of the electricians from the office if we can't get to the bottom of it. I'm sure it's not a major problem.'

She opened the door to the tiny kitchen. 'Not many places it could be,' she said, picking up the little Italian stove-top coffee pot.

'No ...' He opened one of the cupboards. 'Ah. Thought

so. Here it is. And … yes, a fuse has blown. Can you pass me a candle?'

Laure lit one from the stove and moved a little closer. He made room for her, motioning to her to lift the candle higher. She glanced at him; his face was drawn in concentration as he prised apart the plastic casing of the fuse box. His shirt was soaked and clung to his body; she took in the bulge of his biceps outlined beneath the wet sleeve and his forearm showing strong and beautifully etched where the muscles slid over one another, tapering at the wrist. He had nice hands, she noticed, almost distractedly. Strong, capable, the tendons marked clearly against the mocha-coloured skin … The glint of his wedding ring as he extracted the fuse brought her sharply back to her senses. He was Melanie's husband. What on earth was she doing?

She took a step backwards and in that instant, he looked up. Their eyes met and for a few moments, neither spoke. He still held the fuse box in his hands, she noticed. He set it down carefully, his eyes never leaving her face. The light began to dance wildly and it took her a few seconds to work out that her hand was shaking; the hand that held the candle. He reached out and took it from her, setting it down beside the blown fuse. Her heart was beating so fast it was almost painful. They stared at each other, neither moving. And then someone did move – Laure couldn't have said whom. She was conscious of the edge of the kitchen counter pressing against her, cutting into the small of her back and then the feel of his arms around her. He was warm and solid; his skin was damp and smelled faintly of rain and aftershave. *I have been waiting my whole life for this.* The thought slid into her mind as soon as they touched. She felt his hands slide down her back, pulling her towards him. She lifted her arms and touched the fine, short hair at the nape of his neck. He hesitated for a fraction of a second and then it happened. He kissed her. Hard. Then slowly, passionately. The stubble of his jaw scraped against her cheek as she pulled away to bury her face in the heat of his neck. Speech was out of the question. Stopping, too, was out of the question. It was impossible to protest, to draw back. Not even for a second. The kiss was long and hard and it was she who slid her hands underneath the shirt he wore, almost tearing at the buttons as she pulled it away. She was shocked at her own boldness. His bare skin underneath her fingers was a kind of intoxication; she spread her palms against the hard, flat stomach and across the rounded, muscular contours of his back. He met her demands, touch for touch. This was not the gentle fumbling she remembered with Daniel or even the childish sense of wonder she'd felt with Delroy. This was like nothing she'd ever experienced.

She had no recollection of how they moved from the doorway to her bed but when she felt the weight of his body she sank into it, drawing him urgently to her. He lay on top of her, his body covering her completely. The rain had stopped and a single shaft of sunlight came in through the shutters, falling on his face; she caught sight of it, beautiful in its expression of intense, inward concentration, all feeling in her body gathered in that moment when his hand slid up her thigh and touched her, *there* . . . like drowning, dissolving, disappearing. He moved into her slowly and it was nothing short of perfect. *I have waited all my life for this.*

99

Améline looked anxiously at Viv. 'So you're sure you don't mind?' she asked, for the hundredth time.

Viv shook her head firmly. 'Améline, you *deserve* a little happiness,' she said, reaching across the table and squeezing her arm. 'After what you've been through these past few years. And I don't mind telling you, I think he's lovely. If I were a few years younger myself . . .' she smiled, winking at her. 'I always knew he fancied you,' she said, looking at her fondly. 'After the first few times I saw him in Lulu's – nobody could drink *that* many cups of tea. Not even a builder!'

Améline's face was on fire. From upstairs came the sound of banging. They'd at least managed to get Viv's room finished; the former spare bedroom at the end of the corridor from Laure's room, in which she and Paul now slept. 'I ... I just thought ... maybe it was too soon ...?' Améline whispered. 'You know ... after Iain.'

Viv looked at her. 'Am, Iain loved you. I know that. But, forgive me for saying this, he was more of a ... a protective figure, wasn't he? He'd already had a wife and a whole life before you met. You were such a little slip of a thing, d'you remember? Could barely speak a word of English! But if you've found someone to do all the things with that ... well, that married people should do – have kids, start a family – make a *life* for yourself. Iain – he already *had* one. Don't forget that. And I really mean it.'

Améline's eyes were bright as she looked at Viv. She opened her mouth to speak when another ear-splitting crash sounded from upstairs. She laughed shakily. 'It's like this every day,' she said, dabbing her eyes quickly with her handkerchief.

'Well, you're in good hands,' Viv said, chuckling. 'With the building work, I mean,' she added with a wink. She jumped up suddenly, rushing to her bag. 'Oooh! God, I nearly forgot!' She pulled a crumpled magazine out of her flight bag. 'Look at this! I picked it up at Gatwick,' she said, smoothing out the pages. 'There's an article on page thirty, I think ... here,' she quickly turned the pages. 'Look – is that ... d'you think that could be ...?'

Améline gasped. She felt as though someone had poured ice-cold water over her head. She grabbed the magazine with both hands. She pointed to the picture of Laure, her mouth open. 'That's her! That's Laure!'

'I didn't even dare hope. I read it in the departure lounge and I noticed her name,' Viv shouted, as excited as Améline. 'She's a designer, she's the one who's ...'

'Viv ... how can I reach her?' Améline's black eyes were enormous with tears.

'Well, it says right there ... Teague St Lazâre. That's her

company. We must be able to find them in the phone book, or through the operator or something. You're sure it's her?'

'It's her! That's Laure,' Améline whispered, holding the magazine to her chest. She couldn't believe it. There were no words to describe the rush of tenderness and longing that had swept over her as soon as she'd set eyes on Laure's face. Older, harder, perhaps, but still Laure. 'What does it say about her?'

'Read it, you daft thing,' Viv said, her own eyes bright with tears. 'Bloody hell, Am, I've not been here more than five minutes and I'm already in tears. Thought you said this was going to be a holiday,' she said, laughing shakily.

'It is. It will be. This is the most … the best thing you've ever given me, Viv,' Améline said, her own voice shaky. 'Read it with me … here,' she spread the article out on the table. She was a slower reader than Viv but by the time she'd got to the end of it, her heart felt as though it would burst. Laure was a success. She'd made something of herself. She hadn't wound up like Belle, or worse. She put her head in her crossed arms and wept.

It took almost a whole day to find the telephone number. In the end, Viv phoned Susan in Malvern from the shop on the corner and found the number for her. 'Why you don't have a phone or the internet is beyond me,' Viv complained as they walked back from the store together. 'It's too bloody hot to walk about in the middle of the day.'

'They keep promising they're coming to install the line,' Améline said, suppressing a smile. Viv just wasn't used to the Third World. Things took time. A *long* time.

'Well, you've got the number, at least. What time is it? Ten o'clock? What time's that in London? Four? If we ring first thing tomorrow morning, we ought to catch her.'

Améline didn't sleep a wink. At six on the dot she got up, her heart thudding. She slipped out of the house without waking Paul or Viv. She had to be alone for this most important of phone calls. She ran all the way to the corner shop in the cool dawn air. With trembling fingers, she dialled the numbers.

Laure wasn't there. 'No,' the receptionist said kindly. 'She won't be back until the fourteenth, I'm afraid. Would you like to leave a message?' she asked pleasantly.

'Yes, please,' Améline almost shouted down the crackling international line. 'Améline. A-M-E-L-I-N-E. From Haiti. She can call this number. Someone will take a message.'

'Lovely. I'll let her know. Bye.' The line went dead. Améline's shoulders slumped. The build-up to the receptionist picking up the phone had almost killed her. Now all she had to do was wait. Easier said than done.

To take their minds off the two weeks until Laure was due back, she and Viv decided to spend a weekend at a beach resort, south of Port-au-Prince, next to the pretty town of Jacmel while Paul finished things up at the house. It was only the second time Améline had been to the sea. There was some confusion over their rooms. 'No, of *course* she's not the bloody maid!' Viv was heard to say indignantly. 'We booked yesterday. Two rooms. What's the matter with you?' Améline shook her head warningly at her. It was a common enough mistake. There were few people at Hotel Les Cayes with skin as dark as hers. Among the guests, that was. Plenty more of her kind behind the bar. 'It's just the way it's always been here,' she said to Viv as they followed one of the staff to their beachside rooms. 'It'll take a while for things to change.'

'If they ever do. The *cheek* of it!' Viv was still reeling from the affront. She simply couldn't understand why Améline wasn't outraged.

'That's just how it is.'

She watched from the safety of the little parasol as Viv bravely walked into the waist-deep water. It looked calm enough, but Améline knew there were all kinds of dangers lurking just beneath the turquoise surface. She had never learned to swim, of course, and as a child had even harboured reservations about taking a bath – until she moved to Malvern and found there was simply no alternative. But Viv seemed to enjoy it; she kept catching sight of her, red-tinted hair plastered down on her head like the pip of an old mango. The tourists were slowly coming back to Haiti; all around them at the beachside restaurant she could see them; pale, hesitant bodies shyly shucking off their clothes. The women who had been there a few days or more were like bold, boiled lobsters, comparing flesh and notes on the groups of raucous young men who hung around on the resort's edges, jeering at the foreigners in their own language. Some of them made a living out of it; occasionally Améline would see a middle-aged white woman, standing out among the gaggle of dark, light-fingered youths, and once or twice a bolder one, in open defiance of the management, would invite one of those youths to sit with her, pay for a meal ... and whatever else. Was that how she and Iain had appeared? It was ridiculous, she thought to herself, drawing a circle in the sand with her toe, the importance attached to such things. Who cared what a person looked like? Look at Viv: in Haiti, it was automatically assumed that Viv was rich, privileged, spoilt, even – nothing could have been further from the truth. Améline was by far the wealthier of the two and whatever else might be said about Viv, she certainly wasn't spoilt. There were no other couples like her and Viv; friendship between an older white woman and a younger, dark-skinned Haitian was about as unlikely as a peaceful Haitian election, if the previous year's shambles were anything to go by. Oh, well, perhaps she would just have to go about changing people's perception here, as well as over there.

'What're you looking so serious about?' Viv said as she staggered over to her sun-lounger. She was still in the initial throes of sun-worship and her pale, delicate skin was beginning to blush.

'Oh, I was just thinking ... d'you remember that little old lady who lived at the bottom of the hill, just before the turning on the left?'

'Mrs Holmes? With the blue hair?'

'Yes,' Améline said, starting to laugh. 'D'you know what she said to me once?'

'I dread to think. Bigoted cow.'

'No, it was funny,' Améline laughed. 'I was coming up the road with the shopping one day ... oh, it must've been six, seven months after I'd come to Malvern. Anyway, she saw me going up the hill and she came out of the house, you know how those houses have that tiny little garden in front, just a patch of grass, really. Well, she came out and said, "Oi, you. Darky ... I must tell you, I never used to think much of you lot, but you're a real little worker, you are. Seen you going up and down. I 'ope he treats you right. Live in, then, do you?" I just stood there – I didn't understand a word. I mean, I understood what she said, but I didn't understand what it meant. I went home and asked Iain where "darky" was. Was it a country?'

The two of them howled with laughter. 'Oh, Am,' Viv said, wiping her eyes, 'you get it everywhere, don't you? I don't know how you stay so calm about it. That man, just now; I could've *hit* him.'

'D'you know how you can tell a Haitian?' Améline asked mischievously. Viv shook her head. 'When a Haitian gets really mad at someone, he takes off his shoe and slaps him with it. It's true. Iain taught me that. He said the difference between us and the English was that when an Englishman gets mad, he purses his lips. At least that's what *he* did.'

'Well, all I can say is that I'd be carrying around a shoe in my right hand all day long if I had to put up with as much as you do. I don't know how you do it.'

'I'm learning to purse my lips.' Améline smiled. 'Although I do think it's easier for you,' she giggled, pointing to her own, generously full lips.

'Thin and mean?' Viv laughed. 'You may be right there. Talking about mouths, what time is it? I'm *starving*.'

'You're always starving.' Améline laughed. 'Come on, let's see if the restaurant's open. I don't fancy eating chips in the sand.'

'Chips? You? I don't think I've ever seen you eat a chip, Am. And *that's* why you're slim and I'm not.'

'Slim? Me?' Améline looked at her in surprise. 'You mean *skinny*. I've always been skinny.'

'No. You've got a lovely figure. I don't know why you cover it up like that – you've got the most appalling dress sense, I have to tell you,' she said, laughing.

'I know,' Améline said glumly. 'That was another thing Iain said about Haitians.'

'What, that you've all got terrible dress sense? Not true, look around you.'

'He used to say that when the temperature drops below twenty-five degrees, we lose all sense of control,' Améline giggled, remembering. 'I think he said it after I put on two woollen hats and tied a scarf round my waist. I couldn't quite work out what went where . . .'

'Mmm. He might be right. Look at you! It's not below twenty-five degrees now and just look at yourself. You've got a pair of cycling shorts on *underneath* your swimsuit. Whatever for?'

Améline looked down at her legs. Perhaps Viv was right, she did look a little odd. But it would have felt odder still to walk around with her legs showing *all the way up to her bum*, like everyone else did, Viv included. Why *anyone* would want to expose the backs of their thighs to the world was beyond her. Another one of the thousand and one things she would have to ask Laure about. At the thought of Laure, her heart swelled. She calculated quickly – another ten days. In ten days' time, she would finally, *finally* speak to her. The list of things they had to talk about was growing every day.

100

He couldn't stay away. He understood that as soon as he drove off. Nothing in the world would have kept him away from her. Not Melanie, not his children, his family – nothing. The hunger she stirred in him was the strongest he'd ever known. She was leaving in a week. Not enough time to do anything other than think. He knew exactly what others would have done. He could almost *hear* his friends telling him to have an affair, set the girl up in a hotel or something ... get her out of your system. After all, it was the way things were done in Accra, wasn't it? No one risked their marriage or their social position over a woman who'd suddenly walked in from the cold. Divorce was out of the question. Besides, you could hardly start thinking about divorce on the basis of one quick screw, no matter how good it was.

But it wasn't a quick screw and Laure wasn't someone to put up in a hotel. This was different. More than anything he needed time to think. This, he knew, was something that was about to change his life.

Melanie wasn't in when he got home, he saw with relief. He pulled into the driveway, the tension seeping from his body like sweat. He showered quickly, feeling the imprint of Laure's touch all over his body. Laure. He'd watched as he entered her slowly, heard the sharp gasp of delight and seen her beautiful face transformed by the tender rush of her own pleasure. When it was done, and he'd moved away from her to lie with the strangely familiar feel of her curls spread across his chest, he understood that this was only the beginning. That was what had drawn him to her, right from the start – the sense that whatever was said or done between them, there was more to come. In the satiated clarity that sometimes follows love-making, he understood that there were possibilities in Laure that could only be glimpsed at; the exquisite pleasure of being with her, in her, was only a fraction of what she could make him feel. He swallowed. To have experienced it was one thing. Giving it up was another.

He lay down on the bed and slowly smoked one cigarette after another.

A kind of madness permeated her last week in Accra. Marc came to her almost every evening, sometimes only for half an hour, sometimes longer. It wasn't only about sleeping together;

far from it. She'd never experienced such easy, early intimacy with anyone in her life. Marc was like no one she'd ever met. From the very beginning it was as if they'd recognised immediately that everything could be said between them – almost everything. Sitting at the tiny table in the kitchen, she made coffee for him the way they both liked it – on the stove-top – and drank it out of bowls, French-style. He talked; not the hesitant mumblings of a spoilt daddy's boy or the practised, slippery patter of a young marine, but the easy, adult fluency of someone who had seen things, *done* things that most people would never see or do and yet had somehow managed to remain profoundly respectful of everything life had to offer. He spoke to her of his work in the camps; his childhood split between Ghana and Lebanon; university in France; even Melanie. He held nothing back. What was more, he seemed to understand without anything being said that she could not offer the same, not now, not just yet. He was extraordinarily perceptive. She had to remind herself that it was his job to be perceptive.

On her last night in Accra, he came to her late in the evening, just after ten. They made trembling, hasty love on the rug in the sitting room, not even bothering to fully undress. 'How long can you stay?' she whispered.

'Not long.' He exhaled slowly. 'Melanie thinks I'm at the office. She's at a party at the Tulip.'

She looked at him in the dark, tracing the outline of his lips with a confidence that surprised her. Delroy had been the first to awaken the fiery sensuality that he had seen beneath the schoolgirl demeanour, and he'd been the first to extinguish it. It had taken Daniel a long, long time to find it again and then he, too, had snuffed it out, leaving her with the cool, cautious exterior that had become her habitual mask against the world. It had taken Marc Abadi a single kiss. He lay next to her, his breathing slowly coming to its resting state, matched by her own. Eventually he got up. She watched him as he shrugged himself back into his clothes; the thighs with their dark covering of hair; the taut, concave curve of the stomach as he buttoned his jeans; the broad, muscular expanse of chest with the tapering crucifix of hair that disappeared beneath his waistband – she had to suppress the wild desire that rose almost immediately to reach up and pull his head back down again, pull his body back into hers. He finished dressing and with her heart in her mouth, she waited for his next words.

'Will you be all right?' he asked, crouching beside her so that his face was level with hers. Not 'I'll call you', or 'that was great' or 'let's do it again'. She nodded, not trusting herself to speak. As he'd done before, he touched the side of her face lightly and disappeared quietly through the door.

Melanie stopped by the following morning. It was her last day. Laure was busy rolling up her prints and putting them into cardboard tubes when she saw the midnight-blue 4x4 pull up. She took a deep breath and went to the door.

'Hul-*lo*,' came Melanie's familiar, warm greeting as she walked up the path. Laure breathed out. Guilt and relief, equally intense, swept over her. 'Where were you last night? We missed you ... Regis had an exhibition on at the Tulip.'

Laure looked at her blankly. 'Regis?'

'You know, the painter I introduced you to last time. The Brazilian guy ... Oh, it doesn't matter. There weren't that many people there. Gosh, I can't believe you're leaving again,' Melanie said, looking at her suitcases in the corner of the room and pulling a face. 'It seems like you just get here and you're off again.'

'I ... yes, it's gone pretty quickly,' Laure stammered, hoping her voice was steady and the ache in her heart didn't show in her eyes. How could she do this to Melanie?

'I'm coming to London at the beginning of September ... you'll be there, won't you? Marc might even join us. I'm taking the kids, can you believe it? Cosima says the guest wing at Ashdeane'll be ready by then. It'll be so much fun! You must come and stay.'

'I ... I ... yes.' Laure couldn't think of anything to say. Fortunately Melanie, never the most perceptive of people at the best of times, didn't notice.

'Look, I'll let you get on. I've got a tennis lesson in a minute, anyway,' Melanie said, picking up her straw bag. 'You sure you don't want me to drive you to the airport? I can always get Marc to do it. He'll probably be working late and he's only round the corner. It'll be no trouble at all.'

Melanie's words went through her like a knife. 'No, no … that's … I'll manage perfectly well. Don't bother yourself or …' she swallowed '… or Marc, either.'

'You're as stubborn as he is!' Melanie chucked. 'All right, well … let's talk over the phone. Give my *love* to Cos, will you?' She giggled. 'Only joking. See you in September. I'm expecting you now … don't let me down.'

'I … I won't.' Laure returned Melanie's hug and stepped back, feeling slightly nauseous. She watched Melanie swing her basket as she walked towards the car like a small child. Laure sat down at the table and put her hands to her temples, pushing her hair away from her face. Of all the shameful things she'd done in her life, this was close to being the worst. Only one thing ranked lower and that fact brought her no comfort at all.

IOI

He'd said nothing about when or if they would meet again. During that whole week of summer madness, it seemed impossible that they would not. But as the plane began its slow descent towards Heathrow at six-thirty in the morning and she looked out at the swirling, neat pattern of the city laid out before her, it suddenly seemed impossible that they would. Had she dreamed the whole thing? In the cool, crisp light of early summer in London, the week they'd spent together took on an even stranger, more implausible aspect.

She took a taxi home from the airport. She'd promised Jill she would come straight into work. It was now – she calculated rapidly – just over twenty-four hours since he'd closed the door behind him; with each passing hour, the fact of their togetherness grew ever more unreal. When she thought about it – about him – the memory of it sent a shiver of sensual delight running through her, merging with the half-threat of fear that came to her now, in daylight. How could she go on with everything – her life, her work, her friends – as if it hadn't happened? And what assurance did she have that it would ever happen again?

'Oh, Laure …' Kirsty, the receptionist, turned to her as she walked into the studio a couple of hours later. 'Did you get your messages? There were quite a few … I left them on your desk. Did you get the one from Améline?'

Laure stopped. A cold shudder washed over her. She turned to Kirsty. 'What did you just say? Who called?'

'Améline. I think that's how she pronounced it. From Haiti … the number's on your desk. Someone else rang, but he didn't leave his …' she stopped. 'Oh, *shit* …' she half shouted as Laure suddenly pitched forward, hitting her head against the table before slumping straight to the floor.

When she came to, she could just make out Jill's white, anxious face hovering above hers. A pair of hands were at her temples, smoothing back her hair. She blinked, slowly. The noises of the studio – the whirr of the copier, the soft hissing sound of the boiler – all came to her slowly and at a great distance, as if through a tunnel. She tried to move.

'Don't,' Jill said softly. 'You hit your head as you were going down. Can you hear me?' she asked nervously. Laure nodded very slowly. 'You just lie right there. Kirsty's gone to get some brandy. You poor thing. What happened?'

'I … I don't know,' Laure whispered. 'I … everything just went blank. I … I don't think I've eaten anything …' she said slowly.

'Oh, Laure. Look, let's get you sitting up. Can you move your head? You've got a bit of a bump.'

Laure nodded. She did feel rather light-headed and it had only just dawned on her that she hadn't eaten anything for quite a while. Kirsty rushed back in with the brandy and after a few cautious sips, she was able to stand up. Jill immediately dispatched Kirsty to buy something to eat and she helped Laure on to the sofa in the back office. 'Did she ... did she really say "Améline"?' Laure asked, wondering again if she'd dreamed it all.

'I think so. Shall I get the message?' Jill hurried over to her desk. 'Yes, here it is. It's an overseas number.'

Laure took it from her with trembling fingers. She looked at the clock. It was ten-thirty a.m. Four-thirty a.m. in Haiti. *She doesn't have a number yet, but you can call this number and leave a message for her.* She read Kirsty's neat handwriting. She would have to wait at least another two hours before waking up whoever Améline was staying with. By six-thirty, wherever it was, the household would be awake. Marc Abadi had all but vanished from her mind.

'Améline?'

'Lulu?'

The silence of almost thirteen years rolled out before them, coiling itself around the tight spirals of the telephone cord. Neither spoke for a few seconds; there was only the fuzzy static of the line and then suddenly, neither could get her words out fast enough. A sentence in English and then the wonderful, warm, slippery sensation of Créole on her tongue. She carried the phone to the back of the studio, trailing wires behind her as she went.

The phone call lasted over an hour. Every now and then Jill and Kirsty heard a sound that was halfway between a shriek and a laugh. Both raised their eyebrows – neither had ever seen Laure so animated. There was a long silence when she finally put the phone down; they could hear her controlling her sobs, and then she emerged, looking dazed with that ridiculous bump on her head, and announced her immediate departure for Haiti.

Jill just stared at her. 'When will you be back?' she called helplessly.

'I don't know ... I'll call you!' came Laure's voice as she picked up her bag and flew out of the door.

'Unbelievable,' Jill murmured. And then caught sight of Kirsty's open-mouthed stare of admiration. 'Oh no, you don't,' Jill said quickly, grinning inwardly. 'It's only because she's so damned talented. *Other*wise ...' She let the sentence drop. Kirsty was one of her second-year students. She didn't want *her* getting any ideas.

It took a little longer than half an hour to organise a flight to Haiti. There was the small issue of her out-of-date Haitian passport ('*pay a fine when you get there, ma'am*'), and the fact that Air France only flew twice a week ('*I can get you on Saturday's flight, ma'am*') but within the hour, it was done. In two days' time she would be on her way. Then she went home, unplugged the phone and slept for almost twelve hours straight.

102

'*Bienvenue, Mesdames et Messieurs, à l'aéroport international de Port-au-Prince.*' The engines began their slow, screaming wind-down to silence. There was a small struggle to open the door but at last it gave way, swinging outwards and the Air France crew began preparations to let the passengers disembark. It was the height of summer and the tourist season; they mingled easily with the returning Haitians, some of whom bent down to kiss the ground as they set foot on it, the first time, for some, in many years. Laure had no desire to follow suit; her whole body was filled with a restless impatience to get through customs and out the other side. All she wanted was to see Améline again. The hollow in the pit of her stomach was nerves, pure nerves. The fact that again, as before, she'd been unable to swallow food, was incidental.

She pushed her way through the chaos of the arrivals hall, charmed her way through customs without paying the hundred-dollar fine, but with a promise to purchase a mobile phone for the hapless customs official who declared, over and over again, that she was the prettiest thing to come through Port-au-Prince all day. Seeing as it was only seven o'clock in the morning, Laure wasn't overly impressed. She collected her luggage and steered the trolley with the broken wheel diagonally across the floor, her heart thudding in her ears. She could hear her own breathing, harsh and insistent as the automatic doors opened and she walked out into the gaze of a hundred nervously expectant faces, anxiously scouring those who emerged from the secret place within; a place most of those waiting would never see. *Ah? C'est lui? Is that ... no, no ... it's not him. There ... is that ...?* She heard the agitated murmurs rising and falling around her as she moved past, the trundling squeak of the broken wheel loud on the concrete floor.

Suddenly, she slowed the trolley to a halt. There, standing not more than a dozen yards away was a woman of roughly the same age as herself. Still slim, even wiry, dressed in a rose-patterned cotton frock, of the sort she'd worn herself a decade earlier, a pair of pink rubber sandals on her feet. She wore a scarf over her head but the unmistakable imprint of four pleats, each sticking up slightly beyond the pins and clasps she'd employed to hold it down, gave it a lumpy, uneven look. Under her arm she carried an incongruously expensive-looking handbag. Améline.

'Lulu?'

She forgot about the trolley and her suitcase and ran towards the metal barriers, dropping her handbag and her camera as she went. A shout went up from those standing closest to her; people started to murmur – *Silly girl ... look what she's done. Doesn't she know there are thieves about? ... Somebody go pick them up for her ... Oh, look. Look. Aww ... sweet, isn't it? Sisters, d'you think?*

The first touch in thirteen years. They hugged until Laure felt the breath leave her body. Améline's scarf came off, their foreheads bumped as they both bent to retrieve it. There were cries of thanks and teasing admonishments as Laure's things were handed back to her, one by one. People beamed at them and stood back to let the two girls pass. There was someone with her, Améline said, he would be waiting for them at the house. The Créole voices rose and fell around her, as if she'd never left. She stepped into the traffic after Améline, a clutch of small, jeering boys bringing her luggage behind them. It was almost exactly as it had been when she left.

Améline broke the news of Grandmère's death in the taxi on the way up to Pétionville. Hearing it, Laure felt a sharp, painful contraction just below her heart. She was still angry, she realised. And now there would never be an opportunity to ask Grandmère the things she'd puzzled over half her life.

'She never wrote back,' Laure said bitterly, turning to look out at the fields. 'Not once. I must have written ten, fifteen times … nothing. I was too afraid to call.'

'She died peacefully,' Améline said after a moment. 'That's how you should remember her. That's how I've tried to re-member. She … there were things … she was a very unhappy woman,' she said slowly. 'Unhappier, I think, than any of us realised.'

Laure was silent. 'Why did she hate you so?' she asked finally, turning to look at Améline.

It took Améline a while to answer. 'I don't know,' she said quietly. 'But she tried to make amends before she died.'

'How?' Laure asked, a touch of scorn in her voice.

'She left me the house,' Améline said hesitantly. 'She didn't … we didn't know where you were or how to find you … so … she left it all to me. I … I didn't want to accept it, at first, it's yours, Laure, all of this. Not mine. By rights, all of it …'

'Not another word,' Laure interrupted her suddenly. 'It's yours, Améline. You deserve it more than I can ever say. Not another bloody word. Or I'll cry.'

Blake's Guest House. A dark grey signboard with elegant, white lettering hung from a simple steel post anchored into the ground, just behind the freshly painted white fence. The house was completely transformed. The faded, light green façade that she remembered from the length of her childhood – never painted, never cleaned, not once – had been stripped back and peeled off. The intricate, wrought-iron balconies and wooden fretwork above and below the gables had been restored, repaired and painted. The house now wore a shy, pretty look, gazing out coyly at the street through brand-new wooden shutters and brickwork that framed the windows like eyelashes. The overgrown, tangled garden had been cut back, uprooted and pruned so that the small hill sloping away from the downstairs verandah was like a smooth green skin, bordered at the edges with rows of bulging, purple hydrangeas and the wispy, delicate bushes of jasmine that opened in scent in the night.

Laure turned to look at Améline and Paul, the good-looking, pleasant-faced young man she'd introduced as her 'partner'. Laure felt a surge of happiness as she bent forward to kiss him on both cheeks. Améline, at last, had found peace. And someone to share it with. She couldn't have been happier for her. 'What happened to it? It's so ... *beautiful*,' she exclaimed, staring up at the house.

'D'you like it?' Améline said shyly, her hand sneaking towards Paul's. 'We've only just finished it. Paul'll tell you ... it's been a *nightmare*!'

'Oh, it's not been *that* bad,' Paul laughed. He had a deep, warm voice. Watching the two of them in their easy, uncomplicated intimacy brought Marc sharply and painfully to mind. Laure was silent. There were so many things about Améline that astonished her. Was it possible that this self-assured, *modern* young woman, despite her rather odd clothes, was the same timid scrap of a girl she'd left behind? *My partner*. Like her, Améline spoke a mixture of Créole and French, but she kept slipping into English and the effect was startling. Améline had barely been able to say 'how are you?' when she'd left – now just listen to her! She made whatever modest success Laure had enjoyed seem paltry by comparison ... what *hadn't* Améline endured to get to this point? She squeezed her arm suddenly.

'It's absolutely beautiful,' she said, opening the door. 'I can't wait to see the rest.'

'Régine de Menières will be thrilled to see you,' Améline said to Laure, much later that night as they sat in the kitchen talking. Apart from a short nap that afternoon, they'd pretty much stayed in the same spot, filling in the gaps of the past thirteen years. Paul, wisely, had given them a wide berth. They had an awful lot of catching up to do, he said, leaving them to it.

'Who gives a shit about Régine de Menières?' Laure said indignantly. 'Not *one* letter. Not *one* fucking letter!'

'Oh, well,' Améline laughed, secretly pleased. 'She probably didn't have much to write about. She's still unmarried, or so I hear.'

'Funny, isn't it ...' Laure mused, looking into her glass of wine. 'I always thought she had everything. Nice house, nice mother, a nice boyfriend ...' she chuckled. 'Not that *I* have those now either, mind you.'

'What happened to ... to your husband? I saw in the article ...' Améline said hesitantly. 'It said you were separated.'

Laure was quiet for a moment. 'Yes. After three years. I ... there were things I did, back then, Améline. In Chicago ... I couldn't tell him, you know?' She looked up at Améline almost pleadingly. Améline nodded slowly. 'Things I did. I ... I wasn't proud of them but ...' She stopped.

'We've all done things we'd rather forget,' Améline said gently. 'It was different for people like us.'

'I guess so,' Laure said unsteadily. 'I ... I just wish I'd been able to tell him. Before. So that he didn't have to find out from someone else.'

'What did he do? When he found out?'

'He ... he ...' Laure hesitated. 'I left,' she said finally. It seemed too petty to say he'd thrown her out.

'Where did you go?'

'I stayed in London. It seemed like the easiest thing to do. I didn't really have any money to go anywhere else. I worked in a bar, did a bit of cleaning ... I managed. And then I started working for this woman – Jill Teague. She was my tutor at college. Before. Before Daniel and I split up. I worked for her for three years and then she asked me to join her. And the rest, as they say, is history.'

'You've done so well,' Améline said admiringly. 'I couldn't believe it when I saw the article that Viv brought. I always knew ...'

'No. No one knew what would happen to either of us. Grandmère thought I would wind up like Belle. I could see it in her eyes. It was you I used to think of, walking up the hill to the Palme d'Or. You remember that letter you wrote me, just after you left? *That's* what I thought of whenever things got bad. I just used to think of you and how bloody *brave* you were ... no, don't cry ... it's true.'

Améline paused, the hand holding the pan trembled slightly. She swallowed. Laure's question had caught her off guard. 'Wh ... what would *I* do?' she asked, as if she couldn't quite understand the question.

'Yes,' Laure said, stirring her coffee slowly. 'If you were me. If he were married, what would you do?'

Améline set the pan back on the stove and turned to face her. 'I did something like that,' she began slowly. 'With Iain. I ... I ... cheated on him. With Paul,' she said simply. 'I never loved Iain. Not in that way, not the way I should have. And he always knew it. I don't think it made him unhappy, though. By the time Iain married me, I think he'd given up trying to find *that* sort of happiness. He'd been married before, you see, and I think there'd been lots of women, but with me, it was ... different. He was a father to me, not a husband, but I don't think he minded. I think at that point in his life, it was what *he* wanted. I had nowhere else to go – Iain saved me. He'd given me a whole new life. And when I met Paul I just couldn't stop myself.' Améline took a deep breath. 'Iain had a heart attack when he found us. He died right in front of us. We were lying in bed. In the spare room.'

'Oh, Améline.' Laure's face was stricken.

Améline shook her head. 'For a while I thought I would die of guilt. I thought God would reach out and strike me down. But even though the guilt never goes away, I don't regret it. I *can't*. Paul was the best thing that ever happened to me. If I hadn't met him, I would never have known that this ... this *other* kind of love was possible. I would've stayed with Iain for the rest of my life and I would never have known what *loving* someone could be like. I cheated on him but I can't regret it. I can't. Otherwise I'd regret being alive. And I can't do that.'

Laure looked at Améline wonderingly. They were not so different, she and Améline. It stunned Laure to think Améline had both the courage and the insight to say what she had. Not for the first time in her life her admiration for this plucky little misfit soared. How was it that Améline, who'd been given one-*tenth* the opportunities and advantages she'd had, always managed to say exactly, precisely what should be said?

Astonishingly, there was no sadness in leaving Améline this time. Exactly a week after she'd arrived, she zipped up her suitcase and opened the door. Protocol, Améline's oddly reliable driver, was waiting outside. Améline and Laure wandered through the rooms one last time, arms loosely around each other. Each night they had talked until the early hours of the morning; spent the days in the garden, Améline eager to share her ideas for the just-about-to-open guesthouse. They'd helped each other in ways they couldn't possibly have foreseen and the best thing of all, as Améline shyly pointed out on Laure's last night, was that they had all the time left in the world to continue. This wouldn't be Laure's last visit; and coming to England later in the year wouldn't be Améline's, either. There were a dozen new ways for the two of them to stay close and in touch; this wasn't a final goodbye. It was simply a new beginning.

Laure stood at the doorway of Blake's as Protocol loaded the car. They were both in tears, but not of the desperate, hopeless kind. One final hug, a gentle squeeze of the arm and a kiss, and then the taxi coughed its way into life. She waved until she couldn't see the two of them, Améline and Paul, standing in the doorway of the home that they'd rebuilt.

103

The weeks that followed Laure's departure from Accra were among the worst of his life. Everything had been thrown off balance. He'd sat alone on a rooftop terrace bar in Osu the night she left, watching the planes take off, circling gracefully out over the Atlantic before turning and heading north, towards Europe. There were days when he was unable to concentrate on a single thing aside from the fact that he had to see her again. He went over the situation day after day, hour after hour. There were a million other things to think about but he couldn't stop himself. Laure. A kind of gentle madness possessed him and he could think of little else. That last night he'd gone round to see her, he'd been planning to say something very different. He knew that Melanie would take the swiftest and keenest revenge if she found out. She wasn't the type *not* to. He would never see his children again, of that he was absolutely certain. Melanie knew, correctly, that if Marc ever strayed, it wouldn't be because he was momentarily unhappy or unsatisfied, it would mean the end of their marriage. That, she'd pointed out to him in one of their many arguments, was the difference between them. Her affairs meant nothing to her; his, if it ever happened, would be different. He'd gone round to tell Laure that he didn't think he could do it – give up his children. That he couldn't risk losing them, in spite of what he felt. And of course as soon as she'd opened the door, the words just stuck in his throat. He couldn't live without her. That, too, was certain. Of all the questions running through his mind, two things had to be settled first. One was that he had to see Laure again, no matter what it cost him, and the other was that he had to tell Melanie himself. He would never forgive himself if she had to find it out or, God forbid, if she heard it from someone else.

He got out of the car and walked up to the front door. He pushed it open cautiously. The house was in darkness; Melanie was probably asleep. He walked quietly along the corridor, pausing for a second outside Susu and Guy's room. He could hear the soft whish of the fan and, a few seconds later, the grunt of a child moving in sleep. He closed his eyes. She would make him pay for this. Oh, how he would pay.

'What's the matter with you?' Melanie asked him the following morning as he walked into the kitchen. 'You look like shit.'

'Thanks,' he said dryly, opening the refrigerator door.

'No ... really. Are you coming down with something? Malaria?'

She sounded genuinely concerned. Marc felt even worse. 'I doubt it. Just tired. Has Mensah taken the kids to school?'

'Yep. They left about an hour ago. Aren't you late for work?'

He glanced at the clock. It was almost nine. He couldn't remember the last time he'd been in the house at nine in the morning. He'd hardly slept a wink all night. 'Yeah ... I just ... I worked late last night ...'

'I think I heard you come in ... 'bout midnight? You're working too hard, darling. You need a rest, honestly. You'll wear yourself out if—'

'Mel, I'm fine,' Marc said, unscrewing the cap off a bottle of water. He lifted it to his lips, ignoring her irritated glance.

'I do wish you'd get a glass,' she said crossly, glaring at him. 'How'm I supposed to stop Susu and Guy from doing it if you—'

'Can we argue about this later? I'm late for work.'

'Fine. I'll put it in the diary. Argument tonight. Or tomorrow night, whichever you prefer.'

He had to smile. Melanie could be very funny at times. 'Sorry, I'm ... tired, that's all.'

'Listen, darling,' Melanie said, immediately contrite. 'I've been thinking. You know I'm going back to London in September, don't you? Well, I was thinking about the house that Laure's doing for Dad and Cosima. It'll be nearly done by then and we could all go down, have a holiday. With Laure, too, of course. Dad and Cos'll be there some of the time … it's enormous, remember I told you? There's a pool and there are horses … it'll be so good for us. We can drink lots of wine and if the weather's good …'

'I've got to go, Mel.' Marc interrupted her, his voice sounding loud and unnaturally stiff, even to his own ears. 'I'll see you this evening. I might be late. I'll call.' He picked up his briefcase and walked out. He couldn't listen to another word. *Guilt, desire, fear. Fear, desire, guilt.* A kaleidoscope of shifting colours in which the patterns remained the same.

Melanie blinked in surprise as Marc grabbed his bag and rushed from the kitchen. What on earth had got into him? He'd been so moody lately … he was working too hard. She tried to remember what he'd told her about the projects they were currently running. There was a big camp somewhere in the north, wasn't there? And another one in Côte d'Ivoire … or was it Liberia? She shook her head. She could still barely remember where the bloody countries *were*, never mind whether there was a refugee camp in this one or that, or which one her husband had recently visited. No, his last trip had been to Europe, to Geneva. She smiled, pleased with herself. He always complained she never listened – see? Of course she listened.

She got up from the table and walked down the corridor to their bedroom. Perhaps when they came back from Europe, they should think about moving into a bigger house. She needed a change – perhaps they *all* needed a change. They'd been in this one since they'd arrived and while it was nice enough, there was something about watching what Laure and Cosima were doing that had inspired her. Perhaps *she* needed a new project, a new direction in life? It would be the most enormous fun to do up a new house. She'd loved going round the shops in London with her mother when they'd done this one. Yes, perhaps that was what she needed – a new house. Something to *do* with her time. She picked up her basket of tennis things and walked out to the car, feeling immeasurably better. They would have a lovely time together; Marc would leave her and the kids behind and come back to Accra to find a list of suitable properties ... She continued her daydream until she pulled up in front of the reception at the Labadi Beach Hotel. She was looking forward to a fast game of tennis before the heat became too intense. She hadn't seen Petra for a while. She'd disappeared to Copenhagen a couple of months earlier and this was their first tennis game together since her return. She walked across the parking lot to the courts, her mind still pleasurably occupied with plans for the coming few months.

An hour later, having been thoroughly beaten by Petra who displayed an almost maniacal desire to win, they walked towards the pool together to cool off.

'Bloody hell, Petra,' Melanie grumbled as they negotiated the narrow path. 'You've been practising in secret, haven't you?'

'No,' Petra said grimly. 'I just kept imagining it was Chris's head I was whacking every time I hit the ball.'

Melanie stopped, her blood suddenly running cold. 'Oh? Er, why?'

'Let's get a drink and I'll tell you.'

Ten minutes later – the longest ten minutes Melanie had ever spent – she turned to her and said. 'He's been having an affair. Can you *believe* it?'

'Who?'

'Chris. Who else?'

'Do ... d'you know ... who with?' Melanie asked cautiously. She felt like a bitch. She hadn't expected to feel *this* bad.

'No, that's the worst thing. I've had him tested for every disease going, I can tell you. He's not coming near me until I get the all-clear from the doctor. The *Danish* doctor. I'll bet it's one of those disgusting prostitutes from that club ... what do they call it? Macumba?'

Melanie gaped at her. 'He goes *there*?'

'Course he does. They *all* do. I found a pair of knickers in my drawer. *My* drawer. The fucking maid must've put them there. God knows where she found them. I tell you, Melanie, they're all dogs. Nothing but fucking *dogs*.' Petra almost downed her G and T in a single gulp.

'But how ... er, what did they look like?' Melanie asked cautiously.

'What?'

'The ... er, underwear. I mean, they might not belong to a ... a prostitute ...' she said, her voice trailing off. She was suddenly sweating again.

'Hah! They were pink, nothing but two strings with – get this – "Daddy's Girl" written in rhinestones on the crotch. Disgusting! Ooh, I don't know how I'm going to bear it, Melanie, I tell you. If it weren't for the kids ...' Petra's weak blue eyes filled with water.

Melanie felt faint. 'I ... I think I ... I'd better run, Petra,' she said suddenly, jumping up. 'I forgot ... I've got to pick Susu up.'

'But it's only eleven,' Petra protested, surprised. 'They don't get out until noon.'

'I know, but she's ... she's got a doctor's appointment. I *totally* forgot. I'll ... I'll see you later. Sorry about, you know, about Chris.'

'Oh, well, what can I do?' Petra said, sniffing. 'The kids ...'

'I'll call you later!' Melanie shouted, breaking into a run.

She put her foot down on the accelerator as she tore out of the hotel parking lot and didn't ease up until she pulled up in front of Dr Asare's clinic. 'I need to be tested,' she told the surprised nurse who was filing her nails when Melanie burst in. 'Now. Right now. For *everything*.' Even though the affair had ended ages ago, if Chris Tynagel was sleeping with prostitutes now, then in all likelihood, he'd have been doing it *then*. Oh, God ... she felt faint.

It took almost a month for the results to come through. Dr Asare tested her for every sexually transmitted disease they could think of. In that time, Melanie was convinced she was already dead. She wouldn't go near Marc, nor did she kiss or hug the kids. Not that they even noticed, she thought bitterly, watching them through teary eyes. Marc seemed only too relieved to flop into his side of the bed each night. As for Susu and Guy, they hardly even registered her presence these days, they were both so busy with their friends and their after-school activities. *If* she got better, *if* the test results weren't as bad as she feared, *if* there was no reason to think she'd soon be dead ... Well, she was just going to have to change a few things around the house, she thought to herself, sitting wrapped up in a pashmina shawl on the verandah, despite the heat. She couldn't even light a cigarette. Why, the way the three of them were behaving, they'd scarcely *miss* her if she died. Would they even *notice*? A fresh wave of tears slid down her cheeks. If she'd only *known*! If she'd had even the *slightest* inkling that he was fucking anyone else, never mind one of those disease-ridden whores who stood by the side of the road ... oh, God! Please, please, *please* ... *please let me be all right. I will be such a good mother; I will be such a good wife. I will never, ever complain about anything again. I will never cheat on my husband, I've learned my lesson. Please, God. Just give me another chance.*

The results came back. All clear. Nothing to worry about. *See, didn't I tell you. You're perfectly fine. Blood sugar's a little high, that's all. Otherwise you're in great shape.*

It was like being reborn. She waltzed around the house, singing, startling the kids, the servants, the dogs and especially Marc. He didn't understand it, he said irritably. One minute she was moping around the house, weeping like a widow, the next she was warbling at the top of her lungs. What the hell was going on? The three of them were due to leave the following week; Marc would follow them in a month's time.

She made love to Marc the night before they left with such intensity, crying with relief, that it wasn't until they were on the plane heading towards London that it came to her ... she'd made love to *him*. There had been something oddly passive about him; oh, he'd done the job, but she'd had the feeling he wasn't there, his mind was elsewhere. It was the first time she'd ever sensed such complete distraction. What was he thinking about? He was probably fed up with her changing moods ... that was it, wasn't it? He'd said so himself. He found her confusing. But he'd always found her confusing, hadn't he? Wasn't that what he said? She sat stiffly upright in her first-class seat while the children snored beside her. She tried to rationalise what she felt and by morning, as they began their descent, she'd *almost* succeeded. But it kept coming back to her, that cold, sinking feeling as she recalled the look on his face. Resigned, a little impatient ... and that faraway look in his eyes. She'd never had a man look at her that way, least of all Marc. She was good in bed. Always had been. It was the one thing she knew how to do. So how was it, without saying anything, that he'd made her feel as if she couldn't even do *that*? In that single, brief glance, he looked as though he'd rather be a million miles away. But where? Where else did he want to be?

104

There was so much to do when Laure arrived back in London. With everything that had happened, she'd been away for almost a month continuously and now she was paying for it. She and Jessie commuted almost daily from Ashdeane House to their respective offices; most of the main house was now, gloriously, complete but the guest houses were still under construction and they'd wanted everything completed by the middle of the month. 'Not a chance,' the contractor said, sounding pleased. 'You're lookin' at August. Mebbe even September.' Laure left Jessie to battle it out with him and wandered round the main house alone. The transformation of the draughty, stuffy and rather grubby country home into a spacious, light-filled modern mansion was almost complete. Jessie had cleverly stripped back all the heavy wooden panelling and replastered the walls, leaving Laure a sumptuously smooth, clean canvas on which to work her magic. Using a neutral, natural palette of cane, pebble, misty white and the palest, warmest greys she could find, she brought together the entire ground floor of reception and family rooms in the same broad, wide sweep. There was sisal carpeting throughout, but with a nice, generous weave to make it comfortable even in bare feet; the enormously tall, elegant shutters had all been repaired or replaced and painted a single shade darker than the wall colours in each room, lending an air of sparse, stately grace to the windows, unadorned by fussy curtains or swags. She'd found a firm that made modern, awe-inspiring chandeliers and three of their fantastical, magical creations hung from the five-metre-high ceilings, sending dazzling shards of light and colour across the minimally furnished rooms.

In the dining room, wanting to bring a little warmth to the pale, serene backdrop, she'd turned to the earthy primary colours of the early Minoans and Mayans – a deep, rich Etruscan red and a warm, aquamarine blue with a hint of sage. A pair of Teague St Lazâre custom-made Roman blinds hung from the windows, using the same colours but in a lighter, paler tone. It worked, she thought, standing back from the windows and judging the effect. With the pale blonde Scandinavian wood furniture and the bold, abstract art they'd chosen, the effect was grown-up, sophisticated and yet somehow still playful. She breathed a sigh of relief. It was always a gamble and the results, no matter how carefully you planned it, were always a surprise. She continued her inspection of their handiwork for the next hour or so, wondering, with a trembling hollowed-out feeling in the pit of her stomach, what Marc would make of it all.

That evening, Melanie phoned to say they'd just arrived; she would be staying with her mother for the next couple of weeks

... she wanted to meet up straight away. How about a drink that evening?

'Why don't we meet at Ashdeane on Saturday?' Laure parried, unable to face the thought of meeting Melanie just yet. 'I've just got so much on at the moment – meetings all day today, and I've got a ... a business dinner tonight.'

'Oh, but that's *ages* away,' Melanie said, sighing. 'It's only Tuesday today. I'm going to be stuck here with the kids until then. Marc's gone off to New York for some bloody conference. I really wanted to go too ... can you imagine the *shopping*?' she said, her voice rising an octave or two in excitement.

'Wh ... why didn't you go?' Laure said, Melanie's words slicing through her like a knife. He was in *New York*?

'Oh, you know what he's like ... who's going to look after the kids, it's all been arranged, he won't have any time, blah, blah, blah. Honestly, if I didn't know him better,' she said, her voice suddenly dropping, 'I'd be half tempted to say he was *hiding* something from me, I can't imagine what.' She gave an odd little laugh. Laure swallowed. She had no idea how to respond. Was it possible ... was Melanie hinting at something? 'But I don't think so,' Melanie said, brightening, a few seconds later. 'That's the thing about Marc ... he's so bloody transparent. He thinks he isn't, but he is. If there really *was* anything, I'd know. Straight away. I'm lucky like that, I suppose.'

'I ... I guess so,' Laure said faintly. She wanted nothing more than to get off the phone. Her entire body was washed in shame.

'So, I can't persuade you to come out tomorrow night either, then?' Melanie asked.

'No, I'm snowed under at the moment,' Laure said, relieved the conversation was at an end. Her mind was spinning. *New York?* She hadn't heard from him since ... that night. It hurt like hell just to hear his name, no matter what Améline had said. 'I ... I'd better go. I'll ... I'll see you on Saturday.'

'Can't *wait*. I've got tons to tell you!'

Laure put down the phone, her heart thumping and her palms clammy with sweat. She felt as though she were slowly being torn in two – Melanie was her *friend*; Melanie's husband was her lover – what, then, did that make *her*? She wrapped her arms around herself protectively. She couldn't bring herself to think about it – not yet. She couldn't bring herself to think about anything other than when and if she would see him again.

The illuminated numerals on the bedside clock glowed red in the dark. 4:15 a.m. Marc rolled from one side of the enormous bed to the other, exhausted but unable to sleep. His mind was in freefall, jumping from one desperate idea to the next, every solution he thought of undermined by the dreadful uncertainty – did she feel the same way about him? When it came down to it, he realised, he knew very little about her. She hadn't said much – brought up by a grandmother for reasons that were still unclear; she'd gone to the US when still quite young and yes, she'd been married before but they'd been separated for quite a while. She didn't elaborate and at the time, lying next to her, conscious only of the gentle rise and fall of her beautiful breasts and the fact that he would have to leave in a minute, he hadn't pressed her for details. Now, as he lay tossing and turning in an anonymous hotel room somewhere in Manhattan, he realised there was still so much to know. When would he see her? And how?

4:35 a.m. He glanced at the clock as he turned over yet again. Three more days of a conference in which he'd lost all interest … it would be as it always was. They would congregate, take notes and write policies to which no one would ever pay any attention and then in another six months' time, they would congregate again, take further notes and devise new policies which would correct the mistakes of the previous ones … and in a further six months, and so on and so on. Pointless, meaningless. And in the meantime, his wife and children were on their way to the UK, he lay tossing and turning, and somewhere, in the heart of London, was Laure. He closed his eyes as he recalled the precise scent and weight of her hair.

★

The following afternoon he sat in the conference hall listening to those around him speak. Then he gathered his papers, whispered something to the colleague sitting next to him on the podium and got up, ignoring the surprised looks around him. He left the building, aware of the great knot of tension inside his stomach slowly beginning to dissolve. The conference proceedings were not the only futile endeavour that morning; this, too, was futile, he thought to himself as he walked quickly down Washington looking for a travel agent. He had to see her again.

Twenty minutes later, he signed the credit card slip with fingers that shook just a little. He'd just managed to get a seat on the eleven-thirty flight that night out of JFK. He would be with her the following morning. He practically ran back to the hotel, his mind blank of everything other than the fact that in less than fourteen hours, he would see her again.

It was a misty, cool morning of the sort that brought Paris sharply back to mind, the fresh, early morning crispness that was not to be found anywhere in Africa. He caught the train from Heathrow, and then took a taxi from Paddington, breathing in the moist summer scent of the streets as they negotiated their way across the city in the full blare of the morning rush hour. He sat in the back with the windows open, looking out at the city where his relationship with Melanie had begun, aware all the while that it wasn't yet over. He was on his way to meet someone else, somewhere else. He glanced at the scrap of paper on which he'd written her address. Teague St Lazâre. Penn Street. He had no idea where it was.

An hour later, the taxi pulled up outside a warehouse in the middle of what looked like a grim housing estate of the kind he'd known on the outskirts of Paris. He looked around dubiously. The taxi driver nodded firmly. 'Yeah, this is it, sir. Artists, are they?' He quickly drove off.

Marc peered at the name plate screwed to the wall. Yes, there it was. 'Teague St Lazâre. Ground Floor.' He was just about to press the buzzer when the door opened suddenly and

a pretty blonde girl walked out. He stepped back. 'I'm sorry ...
I was just about to ring the bell. Is ... Is Laure St Lazâre in?' he
asked, the inside of his mouth suddenly dry.

'Yeah, she's in the back. The last office. Just go in,' she said,
holding the door open.

'Thanks.'

He walked in. He was inside what looked like an enormous
hall with high, beamed ceilings running overhead with a door to
the right that seemed to lead to several box-like offices. A row
of basins ran down one length of the hall and the central space
was dominated by three or four enormous, paint-splattered
tables. An empty receptionist's desk sat incongruously in the
middle of the space.

He looked around; the place seemed empty. He walked
towards the door that appeared to lead to the offices and
knocked.

'Who is it?' Laure's distinctive voice floated above the low
wall separating the offices from the workspace. He said nothing. It seemed like an eternity before he heard the scrape of a
chair and then the sound of footsteps coming towards him. She
opened the door. He swallowed. Jeans, a white shirt, sleeves
pushed up to the elbow; her hair was twisted around a pencil
that stuck up behind her head; glasses, thick, black-framed,
pushed off her forehead. He registered the details mechanically.
She stood in the doorway, a hand at her throat. 'Marc?'

'Hi,' he said, as casually as he could. 'I ... I was just passing.
I was in New York and ...' He spread his hands by way of
explanation. 'I thought I'd just drop in.' He moved towards
her and then suddenly she was in his arms. The doubts and
uncertainties that had plagued him ever since he'd set eyes on
her simply fell away. 'Can we,' he mumbled against the warm,
scented clouds of hair, 'get out of here?' Her felt her whole
body tremble.

'Yes,' she whispered. 'Yes.'

There was a feather, escaped from the stuffing of one of her
pillows; it rose and fell with her breath, quivering and settling

as she did. Marc was asleep, hands still loosely clasped across her stomach. Outside, it was not yet lunchtime. It was the summer holidays and children played noisily in the street. Every now and then a shout would float up through the partially open window. *It's my turn! You've had your turn!* Laure shifted her body slightly. She lay encircled by his arms, the crumpled bed sheet binding them tightly together.

'You awake?' His voice was a low, soft rumble against her ear. She nodded. 'What time is it?'

She lifted her arm and peered at her watch in the curtained gloom. 'Almost twelve. Are you hungry?'

'Starving,' he chuckled. 'I couldn't eat on the flight.'

'I'll get you something,' she said, wriggling out of his embrace. 'Stay here and don't move. I'll be right back.'

She threw on a dressing gown and went through to the kitchen. Eggs, coffee, toast, orange juice. She took the tray back into the bedroom. He was sitting upright, leaning against the wall, his eyes going over the collection of books and newspapers she kept on the bedside table. She drew in a sharp breath. In the half-light that came in through the curtained windows, he was even more beautiful than she remembered. She'd never had a man in her bed in this flat before; the sight of his smooth, muscular body lying against her white sheets was more than she could take. She wanted him again.

'Breakfast,' she said lightly, putting the tray down carefully on the bed. 'It comes included.'

'Does it now?' he said, immediately picking the tray up and moving it aside. He took a bite of toast and patted the space beside him. 'Come,' he murmured, 'and put that dressing gown right back where you found it. I don't think I've paid for the room yet.' She turned and began to kiss him, unable to stop herself. It seemed inconceivable that there was a world outside, beyond the room in which they were making love, in which *his* wife and children were waiting for the next moves in a drama which could only, surely, explode?

★

Melanie looked out across the parched lawn of her mother's house, saw Susu's billowing black cloud of hair as she ran on short, stubby legs after someone whom she couldn't see. There were six or seven children playing in the garden; God knew where they'd sprung from. She sank into one of the large, comfortable sofas and drew her legs up under her. She was being silly; there was nothing going on. And certainly nothing between Laure and Marc. She shook her head at her own idiocy. He didn't even *like* her. He was in New York ... it was absurd to think that he ... that she ... she shook her head again. She was being silly. *More* than silly – she was being absurd. She leaned back against the pillows. It was all Kim's fault; her face still burned with anger when she thought about that afternoon all those years ago in LA. When the penny had finally dropped and she'd understood what was going on between her and Steve, the shock was so overwhelming that it brought memories to the surface of events she'd forgotten. Her mother neglecting to pick her up from school, of waiting in the corridor outside the staff room, until someone noticed her crouching behind the radiators, took pity on her and called Stella; of dressing up on a Saturday afternoon, choosing one outfit after the other until she'd settled on something she was sure her father would like and then sitting downstairs in the empty house for hours and hours, waiting for him ... her mother would have gone out with her friends or her latest boyfriend – 'But he *said* he was coming to pick you up, darling. I would've come back if I'd known!' Sometimes it seemed as though her whole life had been one long wait for those she loved to notice her – and as soon as they did, they disappeared. Or were taken. Same thing, wasn't it? Whatever the manner of their leaving, they were gone.

But, she hugged her knees to her chest, Marc hadn't left her. He wasn't like the others, though God knew she'd pushed him at times. She wasn't sure why she did it – the affairs, the silly, meaningless lies, even the big lie, the one about the baby-that-never-was. No, she did know why she'd lied that time. She'd been terrified he would leave her; she just wanted to make *sure* he loved her and at the time it seemed such a tiny, inconsequential little slip. Within a year of telling it she was pregnant any~way ... what difference did it make? The thing was, though, it did make a difference. If she could steel herself to think about it, which wasn't often, he'd said something to her in a fight they'd had, not long afterwards. *You only have to break trust once.* She'd accused him of all sorts of things – of punishing her, putting words and actions into her mouth, even bullying her. The truth of the matter was, however, that he was right. She'd got away with it that first time and so she'd done it again. And again. He'd allowed her to get away with it. It was partly his fault, wasn't it?

She looked across the garden again. As usual, Guy had fallen over or something – he staggered towards Susu, holding out his arm, wailing. She could hear the sound through the glass. Susu came running towards him; Melanie could see her anxious little face. And then it came to her. Her son went to his sister when he was hurt. It was Susu who bent over him, her hand going out round his shoulders, examining the damage together. It was she who held him and pressed a kiss against his cheek. The realisation settled over her skin uncomfortably. Her son was two years old. He already knew who to turn to. And it wasn't her.

105

The following afternoon Melanie put down the phone, the cold hand of dread beginning to clutch at her insides. Something *was* going on. Marc had sounded so distant. Politely distant. He'd rung from the hotel where he and Jefferson Owusu, his deputy, were staying to say he'd be back in Accra the following day. The conference was boring. They were with colleagues at the moment but he'd ring as soon as he got back home. Kids all right? She'd answered cheerfully but she just couldn't shake off the feeling that there was something wrong, something wasn't quite adding up. She bit her thumbnail in agitation. She picked up the phone again and quickly dialled his mobile. It was switched off. Her heart was beginning to beat faster. She rang his office in Accra. It took her almost half an hour to get the name and telephone number of the hotel they were staying at. The organisation secretary confirmed that Marc and Jefferson were staying at the Park Plaza in Manhattan. They were scheduled back in Accra the following night. Melanie put down the phone, her hands shaking. It was all as he'd said. And yet there was *some*thing. She picked up the phone again. There was a sinking feeling in the pit of her stomach as the familiar single, long beep of an American phone began to ring. It was nine-thirty a.m. in New York.

'Good morning, Park Plaza. How may I direct your call?'

'Marc Abadi, please. I don't know his room number, I'm afraid,' Melanie heard herself say. 'I just spoke to him.' She waited, almost forgetting to breathe.

'I'm sorry, ma'am,' the receptionist's bright, bubble-gum voice came back at her. 'But Mr Abadi checked out on Tuesday morning. However, I notice that his colleague, Mr Owusu, is still with us. Would you like to be put through?'

Melanie let the phone slide from her grasp. She felt as though she couldn't breathe. Something sharp had lodged itself under her ribs, stabbing her every time she took a breath. She picked up the phone, her hands shaking, and dialled Laure's mobile. She had to talk to someone. It was switched off. She rang the office, hearing in her ears the sound of her own, ugly, ragged breathing. 'Is Laure there?' she managed to gasp.

'No, she's at home. She's not feeling well,' Kirsty said. 'She hasn't been in since Wednesday. She's got a cold, or something. Have you got her number?'

'Yes ... I've got it. Thanks.' She put the phone down with trembling fingers. She was being ridiculous. Maybe he'd just switched hotels. He was always complaining about the sorts of places *Médecins* booked them into – that was it, wasn't it? He'd just moved to a better hotel, that was all. Surely? She picked up her bag and the car keys her mother had left on the sideboard. She called out to the housekeeper as she left. She'd be back later; could she keep an eye on the children? She had to talk to Laure before she went completely crazy, and speaking to her over the phone just wouldn't be enough. She had to *see* someone. The fears were beginning to pile up inside her head and she didn't know what to do.

It took her well over an hour to drive from Chelsea to Hackney. She drove with the radio on but she couldn't hear a thing. Everything was drowned out by the growing panic and the certainty that something was terribly wrong. She'd only been to Laure's flat once before but at last she found the turning off the Queensbridge Road and drove along slowly until she recognised the pale blue door. Number 14, Wilton Way. She parked the car across the road and switched off the engine. She opened the door and got out. It was a warm day but she shivered as she crossed the road. She was shaking by the time she rang the doorbell. *Please God*, she prayed as she waited for Laure to appear, *let me be wrong*.

'Who is it?' The sound of Laure's voice sent a wave of relief running straight through her. She thought she might burst into tears.

'It's me, Melanie. I just dropped by ... open the door, please. Quickly!'

There was a moment's hesitation. 'I'm ... not feeling very well, Melanie,' Laure said slowly. Her voice was muffled.

Melanie frowned. 'Oh, for God's sake, open the door. I've just driven all the way from Chelsea!'

There was another moment's hesitation then she heard the bolt being pulled back. The door opened and Laure's face appeared. They stared at each other for a second, then Laure dropped her eyes, sending another shudder of fear through Melanie. She was wearing a dressing gown, Melanie noticed as soon as she stepped into the living room. Her hair was dishevelled – perhaps she really was sick?

'Are you all right?' Melanie asked slowly. 'I called the studio. Kirsty said ...' She stopped suddenly. Someone had moved across the floorboards upstairs. She looked at Laure questioningly and then suddenly turned her head. Everything slowed to a halt. There, in the corner of the room, stacked against the wall ... was Marc's suitcase. She swallowed. There was the creak of someone's footsteps down the corridor and she saw Laure's stricken face turning from the suitcase towards her. She opened her mouth to wail but terror blocked the sound in her throat. She backed away, knocking over the African statue that sat on the console beside the door. The sound as it crashed to the ground was loud and horrible in the space. And then his head appeared in the doorway and everything suddenly went quiet. They stared at each other.

'Wh ... what are you doing here?' she whispered, the awful question an answer in itself.

'Melanie—' Laure turned to her, putting out a hand.

'Don't touch me,' Melanie grunted, her breath coming faster and faster. 'Marc? Get in the car. I'll take your case and I'll—'

'Melanie.' Marc's voice was quiet. She shivered. 'Don't,' he said, walking towards her. She stared at him. He was wearing the shirt she'd given him last Christmas. It was blue, with small navy buttons. He *liked* blue. She knew that about him. He was standing in front of her, wearing the shirt she'd given him in her friend's living room. Why was he here? Why wasn't he at home with her? The children. At the thought of the children, the wave of nauseous fear rose in her throat again.

'Marc,' she said, swallowing with some difficulty. 'Come home. This ... this is silly. It's not ... it's not *you*,' she said, struggling to get the words out right. She couldn't look at Laure.

'Mel, go back to your mother's. I'll come by this afternoon.'

Melanie stared at him. What did he mean? Come by? What did that mean? 'No, I don't want you to "come by". I want you *to come home*.' She was aware that her voice was beginning to rise. 'The ... the kids are at home. They'll be wondering—'

'The kids will be fine, Melanie. Leave them out of it.' Marc's voice was dangerously quiet. 'Just go back to your mother's. We need to talk.'

'No, Marc ... please. We don't need to *talk,* we just need to go home and to—'

'Melanie?' It was Laure. She took a step towards Melanie. She was wearing a champagne-coloured silk dressing gown, Melanie noticed, with the hem of a white silk slip showing. She'd only just pulled her clothes on, she could see. It was almost five o'clock. They'd just got out of bed. Who knew how long they'd been there? A day? Two days? The thought of it made her sick. She put up a hand to ward Laure off.

'Stay away from me,' she said, her voice shaking with anger. 'Just stay away from me.' She began to run through the betrayals in her mind. She'd *helped* Laure; without Melanie's help and encouragement, she would never have returned to Ghana; there would be no little studio in Osu, no driver to take her around on all those little 'research trips' as she called them, no introduction to Cosima, no Ashdeane House. God, she'd been so *blind.* Laure had *used* her – and then when she'd taken everything she could, she turned on the last thing Melanie had to offer. Marc.

Her head was spinning. If she stayed in the room with the two of them any longer she would be physically sick. She stared at Laure, her fists clenched as she struggled to bring her voice under control. 'It wasn't enough, was it?' she said, her voice ragged with pain. 'Nothing's ever enough for you. I *helped* you, Laure. Without *me* ... Just wait till my father hears about this. You can forget about Ashdeane, you can forget about—'

'Melanie,' Laure broke in suddenly, a catch in her voice. 'This was never about you. I never meant for this to happen ... neither did Marc. Believe me, we—'

'*Believe* you?' Melanie's bitter laugh filled the room. She turned to look pleadingly at Marc. He met her gaze coolly. And then it hit her. He wasn't coming home. He would never come home. In Laure he'd found another, better, one and no amount of pleading would alter that fact. She felt the knife beneath her ribs twist again, sending shockwaves of pain up her body. There was absolute silence in the room. She lifted her head and looked at Laure. The words were out before she could even think. 'It wasn't enough that you gave away your own child, was it?' she screamed, noticing with a dull, sharp thrill that her words had hit the mark. 'You're going to make him give up his. Well, I hope it's worth it. I hope the two of you can live with it because you will *never see those children again!*' Marc looked at her, one eye narrowed in pain. No one moved, no one spoke. And then she turned and groped for the door handle, everything in front of her dissolving in tears.

The door slammed shut behind her. Laure stood where she was. Melanie's last words to her echoing loudly in her ears. She could feel Marc's eyes on her but she couldn't bring herself to meet his gaze. It had happened again before she'd had a chance to explain things. Another man who'd had to hear about her past from someone else. The sense of defeat was overwhelming. But who could blame Melanie? Her world had suddenly been turned upside down – who could blame her for wanting to make Laure pay? Worst of all, she would extract the same price from Marc. She lifted her head. He was watching her intently.

'I can't do this, Marc,' she heard herself say. 'I can't. What Melanie said. It's true. I had a child ... a long time ago. I ... I gave him away. I can't let it happen to you as well.' He reached for her but she shook her head. 'There isn't a day goes by when I don't think about him,' she said, her voice breaking. 'I couldn't live with myself if I did that to you. It wouldn't be fair. I can't do that to you, don't you see?'

'You haven't done anything, Laure, that's not how it works,' Marc said, reaching for her again. 'Stop fighting it. If you're telling me you don't want to be with me because you don't love me, that's one thing. I can handle that. But if you're saying you don't want to be with me because of something that happened ten or fifteen years ago, *whatever* it was, that's weak, Laure. How do you *know* I won't be able to handle it when you won't even trust me enough to tell me?' He held on to her forearm, his grip firm against her skin.

Laure stared at him. What was he saying? She shook her head. 'No, you don't know what I've done,' she said, her eyes smarting with the effort of holding back her tears.

'What *have* you done?' Marc suddenly sounded angry. 'You had a child. You were married once before. What, in God's name, is so *terrible* about that?'

'I ... I *sold* him, Marc,' Laure burst out, unable to hold it back any longer. 'I sold my *child*. I gave birth to him and then *I gave him away for money!*' The words simply erupted out of her. She wrenched her arms out of his grip and pressed both hands to the side of her face, too afraid to look at him. Her chest began to heave. 'I sold him! Someone offered me *money*, Marc ... *money for my child!*' She heard the last as a scream that didn't seem to come from her. The whole room was spinning. Any moment now he would step backwards, mumble a few comforting words and then he would leave. He would go back to Melanie and the children he'd realised he couldn't lose and ...

'Laure. Look at me.' He grabbed her by the arm. His grip didn't slacken. She felt his other hand close around her other wrist, prising her hands away from her face. 'Look at me. How old were you? Twenty?'

'Se ... seventeen.' Her voice shook.

'Oh, Laure. You were still a *child*. You've been carrying this *guilt* around inside you for all these years?' He pulled her into his arms, one hand going around her neck, pressing her close to him. His voice was a low, vibrating murmur above her head. 'It was a mistake, Laure, a tragic mistake. You can't go on paying for it for the rest of your life.'

A tragic mistake. There was no stopping the storm that blew up in her on hearing those words. It was the first time anyone had ever suggested that she might not be entirely to blame. Clumsy with emotion, she tried to wrench her hands out of his but he held her fast. He was much stronger than she. It eventually came to her that he simply wouldn't let go – not of her hands, or her arms, or even her body, which he held pressed tightly against his. He wouldn't let go of *her*. Melanie had thrown the one thing at him that ought to have forced his hand, *forced* him to abandon the temporary happiness he'd found with Laure. It didn't. His arms tightened around her as

566

the realisation slowly began to dawn on her. He wasn't going to let go. Whatever she'd done in the past, he thought she was worth fighting for – right to the end. Whatever it took. He thought she was worth it. No one had ever thought that about her, not even herself. She felt herself go slack. *I have been waiting my whole life for this*. This time the words came from him, not her.

PART EIGHT

106

She knew at once who it was. It was the third or fourth time that week she'd seen the black car parked across the road from the studio. She couldn't remember exactly when she'd seen it for the first time – a week or two after Marc had flown back to Accra. Melanie and the children were staying in Chelsea, but she'd been unable to make good on her threat. Marc had gone round to see her and the children the following day. It would take a while to sort things out, she knew, but at least they were talking. Her own friendship with Melanie was over, of course, but as Marc said, it wasn't down to her to shoulder *all* the blame. Just some of it.

She unlocked the studio door and looked quickly behind her before entering. Yes, the car was still there. She wondered how long it would take him to follow her in. She knew from Jessie that he'd been to see her a couple of times. Despite her anger which was as fresh now as it had been the day she'd told Jessie to send the papers straight back, there was still a part of her that wanted to explain, to put things right. She and Marc had done little but talk in the few days before he'd left; she'd never talked to another human being the way she talked to him. There was nothing that couldn't be said. She discovered, to her great surprise, that she was not the only one who carried secrets and that, sometimes, the simple act of sharing something was enough to lighten the load. Trust me, Marc said to her, time and again. It came to her suddenly that perhaps she'd been looking for the wrong emotion. It was love she'd sought – from Grandmère, Delroy, Belle, even Daniel – when all along, what was missing was trust. And in asking her to trust him, Marc had asked the hardest question of all. Could she trust herself?

A few days later, Daniel watched her shut the door behind her and look across the street directly at his car. He was aware of his stomach tightening itself into one giant knot as she began to walk down the street towards him. Fuck it, he'd been sitting here day after day, watching her come in and go out, too scared of his own feelings to open the car door and get out, speak to her, sort things out. How long could he go on? Almost without thinking, he fumbled for the handle and opened the door. There was no traffic about. He stepped out on to the cobblestone surface of the street. She turned her head. It was as if the six years since he'd last seen her simply didn't exist.

'Laure,' he said, hoping his voice was steady. She stopped. Her hands were thrust into the pockets of her raincoat. She said nothing. 'Laure,' he said again, walking towards her. 'I ... I've been watching you ... across the road. For a while.'

'I know.' She said it simply, without rancour.

He felt the great knot of tension inside him begin to ease. How long had it been there? Long before he'd seen the article a few months ago, long before that. He'd been carrying it around inside him for years. 'Can we talk?' he said suddenly, looking around at the deserted street. It was after six-thirty in the evening.

She hesitated for a second, then shrugged. 'Why not?' She pointed to a bar at the end of the road. 'It's usually quiet at this time.'

Ten minutes later, as impossible as it was to believe, they were sitting opposite each other, two glasses of wine on the table between them. His heart was thumping in his chest. Laure lifted her glass and took a sip. 'So,' she said carefully, 'here we are. What did you want to talk about?'

Daniel felt as though he'd been slapped. How could she remain so calm? 'Well, I'd have thought it was pretty obvi-ous,' he said, aggrieved. 'I mean, Christ, Laure, you ... you just disappeared ...'

'Daniel. You threw *me* out, remember?'

'Yes, but ... you were the one who *lied* to me, Laure. What else was I supposed to do? You—'

'No. I didn't lie to you. I didn't tell you certain things, which I will always regret, but I didn't lie,' she interrupted him calmly.

'How can you say that?' Daniel stared at her, anger rising in his face. 'You sat there with my parents, my friends, you sat there and pretended that everything was good and ... and clean and *normal* ... and the whole time you were ... you knew what you'd done, Laure. I just don't understand how you could have just sat there, not saying a word ...'

'No, Daniel,' Laure sighed, putting down her glass. 'I don't suppose you could.'

'Is that *it*? Is that all you have to say for yourself?'

'What do you want me to say? That I'm sorry? I *am*. I'm sorry I couldn't bring myself to admit to my own mistakes. I'm sorry that I didn't have the courage to say to you – look, this is who I am. This is what I've done. Yes, I made mistakes. I did things *you* wouldn't have done but the truth of the matter is, Daniel – you never had to. I'm not saying you didn't have your own problems or that your life was always easy. But the bottom line, Daniel, is that you had everything you needed to make sure you never *had* to make the kind of mistakes I did. And I can't be sorry for that. I did what I had to because I thought that's what it took to survive. And whatever else you've had to go through in your life, you've never had to worry about *that*. So before you pass judgement, just think about all the things you've never had to do, the choices you've never had to make.'

He stared at her. It was not the apology he'd hoped to extract from her. If anything, it was defiance he heard in her voice. 'So that's it?'

'Actually, yes. That's it. I've got nothing else to say. No, there *is* one thing I do regret,' she said slowly, draining her glass.

'Wh ... what?' He felt as though he were on one of those

573

merry-go-rounds he'd hated as a child. His stomach contracted painfully.

'I should have signed those papers six years ago, Daniel. We could both be free right now instead of sitting here trying to force each other to accept the blame.'

'Accept *blame*?' Daniel almost spluttered. 'What the fuck did I do? I gave you everything, Laure – money, a home, a life … a *good* life. You had *nothing* when I met you, absolutely *nothing*. If it wasn't for me, you—'

'You're right,' Laure broke in again. 'Absolutely right.' She got to her feet. It was uncomfortable staring up at her but somehow his legs just wouldn't obey his instructions to get up. 'But you've mixed things up a bit. It wasn't the fact that I had no *money* when I met you that meant it would never work out. Money wasn't the problem. That wasn't what I lacked.'

'Well, what the hell was it?'

'Self-respect.' She picked up her coat and slipped it on. 'D'you remember,' she asked as she tied the belt, 'when you first thought about leaving ScanCorp and setting up on your own?'

He nodded stiffly. 'Yeah?'

'D'you remember what I said to you?' She looked down at him with something close to pity in her eyes. He flushed angrily. Who was she to pity him?

'No, I don't,' he said shortly. 'What are you getting at?'

'That sometimes it's not the things we *can* do that make us who we are,' she said softly. 'It's the things we can't.' She picked up her bag. 'That's all. Bye, Daniel. You know where I am. You can send those papers over any time you like. This time, I promise, I'll sign.' She walked away, swivelling her hips past the tables that were slowly filling up. He watched her go, an unfamiliar sting behind his eyes. It had been six years since he'd last set eyes on her and, if anything, the pain was just as intense. Laure. He had the feeling he would go on saying it for the rest of his life.

Epilogue

The game was slowly coming to an end. She leaned against the wire fence, her hands shoved deep into her pockets, and watched them play. They were conscious of her in the way a group of young men are always conscious of a pretty woman, regardless of her age. Steve, the tall, well-built blond one had noticed her watching and summoned her over. At first she'd shook her head, embarrassed. But he and the other one, not Darrell, had come over, holding up the game.

'I'm just waiting for a friend,' she stammered, aware of the heat in her face. 'I'm a little early ... she's not home yet.'

'So come on in,' Steve smiled easily. 'You can keep score. There's only another ten minutes to the game.'

'Yeah, watch out for this guy,' someone shouted, slapping Darrell on the back. She put a hand to her throat.

'What's your name?' Steve asked, holding open the wire gate for her.

'Laure,' she said, feeling even more awkward.

'Hi, Laure, I'm Steve. This here's Glynn.' They shook hands. One by one the young men came up and shook hands. *Bryant. Philip. Doughboy. Darrell.* 'Doughboy's not my real name,' a pudgy, still adolescent-looking kid explained sheepishly. The others laughed. They were at that odd stage where some of them looked older than they were, already men, and others were the opposite, still boys. She hardly dared bring herself to look at the one they called Darrell. She shook his hand, palm sliding against palm briefly. The first and only touch in thirteen years. She withdrew her hand, her heart racing.

'Keep score, will ya, Laure?' Steve shouted. He was showing

off a little, proud to have been the one to bring her into the game. They played with exaggerated energy, stealing shy, quick glances back at her to see if she was really watching. Someone explained the rules to her; she smiled and shook her head. 'Just tell me when to call time!'

'Five more minutes,' Doughboy shouted.

She watched him play. He was tall, thin with a lanky, adolescent awkwardness that she recognised immediately. He had his father's high cheekbones and his light, almost feline eyes. Her mouth, there was no doubt about it. He was about her complexion, even though Delroy had been lighter than her, and had her wavy, thick hair, cut short as it was. His face was open and easy, there was none of her tightness or fear in his eyes. He looked ... nice. A nice kid. Someday he would become a nice young man. She felt something ease inside herself, letting her go.

'Time's up, guys,' she called, straightening up. Someone lobbed a throw from way behind. It bounced off the board and careened across the court. She smiled at them. 'Thanks,' she said, shoving her hands in her pockets. 'That was fun. I think my friend is probably home now, so I'm going to push off.'

'Where you from?' Steve called out, intrigued by her accent, no doubt.

'Oh, here and there,' she replied, winking at him. She looked for and sought out Darrell's eyes. 'You played really well. You were a pleasure to watch.'

And then she turned and walked away, back in the direction from which she'd come. Now was not the right time, she said to herself as she walked back to the hotel, oblivious to the cold wind whipping her hair around her face. In time, when they were ready, perhaps Howard and Geraldine would tell him about her. He might even make the connection himself. She would send them a letter, explaining her decision. Perhaps even a photograph. He would know then that the woman who'd walked in on a basketball game had said something meant for his ears alone. *You were a pleasure to watch.* She meant it; he was. But it would be his decision to seek her out, not hers. She

576

would make sure he knew where to find her, that was all. In the meantime, she thought, smiling to herself as she turned up Halsted, there was Marc. And the two children Melanie had finally agreed were equally his. They were *her* children now, just as Darrell was her son. Perhaps not quite in the way she'd assumed it would be, but that, as Marc was fond of telling her, was just the way it was. It was a fact she'd learned to live with, and to love.